THE FABER BOOK OF TREACHERY

Nigel West is a historian specializing in security issues and is the European Editor of *Intelligence Quarterly*. In addition to *The Faber Book of Espionage* and *The Faber Book of Treachery*, he has written several controversial histories of Britain's secret organisations, including *A Matter of Trust: MI5 1945–72* (the subject of an injunction by the Attorney General), *Molehunt* ('Urbane, reasonable, convincing' *The Economist*) and *The Friends* ('West has got his hands on some pretty radioactive material' *Evening Standard*).

The Faber Book of
TREACHERY

edited by
NIGEL WEST

faber and faber
LONDON · BOSTON

If I had the choice between betraying my friend and betraying my country, I hope to God I would have the guts to betray my country. E. M. Forster

Never was a patriot yet, but was a fool. Dryden

Patriotism is the last refuge of a scoundrel. Samuel Johnson

First published in 1995
by Faber and Faber Limited
3 Queen Square London WCIN 3AU
This paperback edition published in 1997

Photoset by Wilmaset Ltd, Wirral
Printed in England by Clays Ltd, St Ives plc

All rights reserved

© Nigel West, 1995

Nigel West is hereby identified as author of this
work in accordance with Section 77 of the Copyright,
Designs and Patents Act 1988

A CIP record for this book
is available from the British Library

ISBN 0−571−17333−0

2 4 6 8 10 9 7 5 3 1

Contents

Introduction

Who among us has not committed treason to something
or someone more important than a country?
Graham Greene, Foreword to My Silent War *by Kim Philby*

What is it that compels individuals to betray their country? The violation of an allegiance to one's country is regarded, almost universally, as the most heinous of crimes, and although capital punishment was formally abolished in Britain in 1964, the death penalty remains applicable for the offence of treason under the Treason Act 1814, along with the offences of piracy with violence, and mutiny under the Service Discipline Acts.

But what constitutes treachery? Were the Soviet defectors who fled to the West during the Cold War any more guilty than the anti-Nazis who switched sides during the Second World War? And if the answer is essentially political, can such behaviour ever be justified in a democracy? Who better to consult than those authors who themselves have had first-hand experience of treachery, or at least of the accusation?

E. M. Forster suggested that it was preferable, though not necessarily easier, to betray one's country than one's friends, a proposition that Graham Greene accepted when he considered the conduct of his friend Kim Philby, the Briton who embraced the Stalinist cause to such a degree that his surname has become synonymous with duplicity, except in Moscow where he was welcomed in 1963 and where, even today, he is regarded by many as a hero. Certainly Philby and his fellow conspirators Guy Burgess, Donald Maclean and Anthony Blunt, who deliberately wormed their way into the establishment to inflict maximum damage in the Soviet cause, gave Britain an unsavoury reputation for harbouring dedicated and colourful traitors. Their offences were by no means limited to the casual leakage of esoteric political information; together, the scale of their deceit was unprecedented, appeared to recognize no bounds, and served to taint an entire generation of Cambridge graduates, particularly

I

those who had been members of the Conversazione Society, the university club better known to outsiders as the Apostles.

Philby not only duped his three wives and wrecked the life of at least one of his three sons, but compromised his own sister, Helena, whom he had himself recommended as a suitable recruit for the Secret Intelligence Service. Indeed, his final act of mendacity in January 1963 was to denounce his oldest friend, Tim Milne, whom he had known at school and university before they both had joined SIS, as a Soviet spy. Milne, of course, was entirely innocent, but the charge, contained in a typed document that purported to be Philby's confession, made in return for a formal immunity from prosecution, was taken seriously and investigated. Similarly, Guy Burgess ruined his younger brother Nigel's career in the Security Service, and Alan Maclean left the diplomatic service when his elder brother defected. As for Professor Sir Anthony Blunt, his betrayal, which included the manipulation of his elder brother Christopher (who served in military intelligence during the war) to help him obtain a commission in 1939, was all the more comprehensive and wretched because of his official court position close to his sovereign as Keeper of the Queen's Pictures. Even when he had accomplished his objective of entering MI5 in 1940, on the mistaken recommendation of his old friend Victor Rothschild, whom he had taught French at Cambridge, he had wangled his way into the division of the Security Service which handled the most sensitive secrets, for the sole purpose of betraying them.

The British attitude to treachery is not easy to fathom for Blunt was able to continue his life of privilege and academic honour for more than a decade and a half *after* he had admitted his treason in April 1964. Indeed, the view that nearly prevailed in November 1979, as the new Prime Minister Margaret Thatcher wrestled with the implications of Blunt's imminent public exposure, was MI5's declared opinion that the country's interests would be best served by protecting and preserving the art historian's reputation, even at the cost of tolerating his perjury in the libel courts if the anticipated litigation proceeded.

Blunt himself has not written about what had motivated him to embrace Stalinism and, as he readily conceded, to have given every secret that ever passed over his desk to his NKVD contacts. After his death in March 1983 his autobiography, extending to just 30,000 words, was bequeathed to his friend, John Gaskin, with whom he lived. However, as it was valued for probate at £120,000, which the family considered excessive, the manuscript was presented to the British Library, embargoed at Gaskin's request for thirty years. His other brother Wilfred, one of the very few to have read it, says that he 'found little meat in it' and apparently the document contains no reference to the traitor's covert commitment to communism. Of the others, neither Burgess nor Maclean is known to have given an account of his experiences, and Kim Philby's notorious memoirs, *My Silent War*, are regarded as deeply suspect and self-serving, the key phrase in the book being the author's revealing assertion that 'one does not look twice at an offer of enrolment in an elite force', thereby suggesting that perhaps some warped intellectual snobbery rather than a misguided political commitment had inspired him to become a spy.

The fact that some of Britain's best-known traitors have not offered a public explanation for their behaviour does not mean that others have not seized the opportunity to recount their version of events. Ignatius Lincoln, the Hungarian-born Liberal Member of Parliament for Darlington, fled to New York in January 1915 where he released his candid memoirs, *Revelations of an International Spy*, in which he admitted having offered his services to the enemy. When deported to London the following year Lincoln faced charges of forgery only, his involvement in espionage apparently being too opaque to discern. An intriguer on a grand scale, Lincoln ended his days as a Bhuddist monk in China, a conclusion arguably more bizarre than the fate of the Cambridge traitors who had languished for so long in Brezhnev's dreary Moscow. Unlike Philby, who published only a single volume of memoirs, Lincoln released a sequel, *The Autobiography of an Adventurer*, in 1932. What he did have in common with Philby was the tragedy of their children. Philby's illegitimate son has served several prison sentences for dishonesty, and Lincoln's was executed for murder.

Whereas Lincoln's tale, published in America, was held to be too unreliable upon which to base a prosecution, it was another document of a rather different type that was to seal the fate of Sir Roger Casement, one of the very few Britons to be executed for treason in the twentieth century. An ardent Irish nationalist, Casement had supported the German cause during the First World War and had been arrested in April 1916 soon after he had been landed in Tralee Bay, County Kerry, from the U–boat which had brought him and a pair of supporters from Wilhelmshaven. Although charged with treason, Casement was recognized as a politically motivated Irish patriot and after his conviction forty distinguished personages petitioned Prime Minister Asquith for his reprieve. Pressure for his death sentence to be commuted also rose in the United States, and it was only when compromising extracts from his diaries were circulated that the campaign collapsed. The candid documents revealed Casement to be an extremely active homosexual who had committed some of his most depraved thoughts to paper, and the distribution of the most explicit passages to selected influential figures ensured his condemnation not just as a traitor, but as a reviled pervert too.

In the period between the wars, only one person was charged with offences that might be deemed to constitute treason. Lieutenant Norman Baillie-Stewart, a Seaforth Highlander, was held in the Tower of London after his arrest in March 1933, and charged with having supplied military secrets to a German contact. Baillie-Stewart was convicted by a court-martial and sentenced to five years' imprisonment, but after his release he travelled to Berlin where he remained for most of the war. In May 1945 he was arrested for a second time and he received a further prison sentence for having aided the enemy. After his release, in May 1949, he moved to Dublin where he adopted a new identity and wrote a highly personal account of his experiences, *The Officer in the Tower*.

Like Casement, who had toured prisoner of war camps in Germany in November 1914 to recruit volunteers for an Irish Brigade to start a rebellion in Ireland, Baillie-Stewart had been one of a small band of renegades who had supported the Nazis and either had contributed to anti-British propaganda or had persuaded British detainees to join the Legion of St George, the *Britische Freikorps* branch of the SS. Its ragtag membership was rounded up after the German surrender and its leading recruiters, William Joyce and John Amery, were hanged at Wandsworth. Another suspected turncoat, who narrowly escaped criminal charges, was Ronald Seth, a saboteur trained by Special Operations Executive who was parachuted into Estonia in October 1942, only to be captured within hours of his landing. His subsequent adventures while in German custody, described in his war memoirs *A Spy Has No Friends*, included an explanation for his appearance in Paris during the Nazi occupation with official Luftwaffe documentation. Denounced by several British ex-prisoners of war as a Gestapo collaborator who had worked for their captors as a stool-pigeon, Seth was warned that he was likely to be prosecuted, but evidently he managed to persuade his interrogators of his innocence. Not only did he win his freedom, but he also recovered his back-pay from SOE for the period he had spent on what he claimed had been active service on the Continent.

Like Seth, who avoided arrest despite serious allegations, P. G. Wodehouse was also cross-examined by MI5 about what were considered to have been his dubious activities under the occupation. Having been interned in May 1940 at his French seaside home in Le Touquet,

Wodehouse had subsequently agreed to make a series of radio broadcasts for the Nazis from Berlin. His heavily criticized contributions to the enemy's propaganda aroused much hostility in his native country and, although cleared of having been anything other than naïve by the principal MI5 investigator, (Sir) Edward Cussen, he never returned to England and for many years was denied the honours his literary success should have brought him. Doubtless relieved at not having had to face formal charges, Wodehouse referred only briefly to his period as a German internee in his 1957 autobiography *After Seventy*.

For the rest of his life Wodehouse remained contrite for his ill-judged radio talks, and went to live in New York where he maintained his prolific output. Another Briton who made the same move across the Atlantic was Cedric Belfrage, whose treachery, in contrast, went completely unpunished. A lifelong adherent to communism, as well as a journalist of note, Belfrage had taken up residence in America before the war and in 1941 had been recruited into the New York branch of British Intelligence, known as British Security Coordination, as an expert on propaganda. It was this position of trust, with access to highly classified material, that he had abused to keep his Soviet contacts supplied with British secrets. His duplicity was discovered only some time after the war, and he could not be arrested in the United States on a charge of espionage as he had not committed any offence under American law. He was subpoenaed in May 1953 to give evidence before the House Un-American Activities Committee but, when he refused to answer questions he found awkward, he was arrested and deported to Mexico where he continued to write for Leftist journals. He persisted in his activism and was prominent in the campaign to free the Rosenbergs, the two Soviet spies who had run a network that had penetrated the Allied atomic weapons programme. In his book *The Frightened Giant* Belfrage confirmed his belief in the innocence of the Rosenbergs, whom even Philby was later to recognize as fellow agents of the KGB.

If Belfrage had committed his crimes in England he would probably have suffered the same fate as Harry Houghton and John Vassall, both of whom also served the Soviet interest and betrayed classified material. Whereas Belfrage was always intensely political, and was probably ideologically motivated to help the NKVD, Houghton had worked for their KGB successors for financial gain or, if his autobiography *Operation Portland* is to be believed, under the threat of the exposure of his illicit black-marketeering in Poland while he had been attached to the British embassy in Warsaw. Whichever the explanation, the then Attorney-

General, Sir Reginald Manningham-Buller MP, described his offence to the Old Bailey jury as being 'akin to treason', in a memorable reference to the 1848 Treason Felony Act. Vassall was also coerced into helping the KGB, having succumbed to blackmail over a brief homosexual relationship he had enjoyed with a Russian youth in Moscow. Whereas Houghton never expressed regret for his crimes, in *Vassall: The Autobiography of a Spy* the author, who is now a devout Catholic, acknowledges with candour the gravity of his espionage in the Admiralty on behalf of the Soviets.

Although well versed in the techniques of extracting the co-operation of reluctant agents, the KGB was by no means omnipotent, and the treachery of both Houghton and Vassall was revealed to MI5, not as a consequence of painstakingly efficient counter-intelligence work, but from tips offered by disaffected KGB officers seeking a new life in the West. Despite a plausible smokescreen suggesting the contrary, virtually every case of postwar espionage was uncovered by means of information sold by well-placed defectors who traded their inside knowledge for lifelong protection and a new identity. Not surprisingly, the relevant security agencies preferred to play down the role of defectors and promote the wholly fallacious idea that they could identify traitors without external help. In reality, almost no Cold War spy was caught without that most valuable of commodities, defector information.

When Anatoli Golitsyn defected in Helsinki in December 1961 he arrived equipped with sufficient clues for the clerk John Vassall to be flagged as the source of information that had been haemorrhaging from the Admiralty since the spy's return to London in June 1956. Golitsyn, who makes only the briefest of references to Vassall in his book *New Lies for Old*, is but one of more than two dozen Soviet intelligence professionals who, during the period of communist totalitarianism, which perhaps can be judged to have ended in 1989, opted for a pension in the West and then to write about their experiences. It was these individuals who did so much to ensure the Cold War was won by the West but, by the same token, they were regarded by their own country as having committed the greatest of treasons.

Taken chronologically, the trend can be seen to have started before the war, as far back as 1929, with Georges S. Agabekov, who arrived in Constantinople in October 1929, masquerading as a merchant importing bicycles, whereas he was actually the local OGPU representative, and had previously served in Tehran. Agabekov fell in love with a young Englishwoman whom he had engaged to teach him the language. She was enchanted by him and together they moved to Paris where he wrote *OGPU: The Russian Terror*, in which he condemned Stalin and Beria, and made many damaging disclosures about the OGPU, a highly secretive organization about which very little was known at that time. A marked man, Agabekov was to disappear in July 1937, shortly before the defection of Samuel Ginsberg of the GRU in October of the same year. He had also adopted a commercial cover, the role of an antiquarian bookseller in Holland, and having taken the name Walter Krivitsky, Ginsberg had surrendered himself to the Sûreté in Paris and then had moved to Canada and later, to the United States, where in 1939 he published *In Stalin's Secret Service* (published in England in 1940 as *I Was Stalin's Agent*). He was followed to Canada in July 1938 by Leiba Feldbin, alias Alexander Orlov, who emerged from hiding in America to publish *The Secret History of Stalin's Crimes* only in 1953 when his funds had been exhausted. Both Krivitsky and Orlov had been prompted to disappear because they knew they had been selected for liquidation by Stalin's death squads. Neither had harboured any doubt about the Kremlin's determination to eliminate them, for their friend and colleague Ignace Reiss had been murdered in Switzerland, a tragedy that provoked his widow, herself a communist and illegal agent of long standing, to flee to America and publish *Our Own People*. Another pre-war Soviet defector to move to America was Alexander Barmine, a senior diplomat based at the Soviet embassy in Athens who fell in love with a Greek woman and defected in June 1937. In 1945, having served in the US army during the Second World War with the rank of private, he wrote *One Who Survived*, in which he described his experiences, including his service as a general officer in the Red Army after the First World War.

Neither Barmine, who was a diplomat, nor Victor Kravchenko, who resigned from his post with the Soviet Purchasing Commission in Washington DC in April 1944, was a full-time NKVD official, but as trusted members of the Party they had been in constant contact with the Soviet intelligence apparatus, and had much to say on the subject to their American debriefers. Barmine, a member of the Ministry of Foreign Trade, devoted the remainder of his life to fighting communism by broadcasting American propaganda, whereas Kravchenko took his struggle to the courts in Paris, won an important libel case over his book *I Chose Freedom* but, a decade or so later, was found shot dead at his home in New York.

During the war itself the GRU experienced only one defector, Ismael Akhmedov who, like Orlov, had preferred to remain incommunicado until necessity required him six years later, in 1948, to declare himself and make himself available to the CIA and SIS for a belated interrogation. His story, *In and Out of Stalin's GRU*, was not published until 1984, but in the meantime two significant GRU colleagues had followed his example and remained in the West. Igor Gouzenko, a GRU cipher clerk based in Ottawa, took his wife and daughter into Canadian protection in September 1945 and later wrote *This Was My Choice*, and Grigori Tokaev abandoned his post in Berlin in 1948 and took up an academic position in London, where six years later he produced *Betrayal of an Ideal*, the first of his two autobiographies. A technician employed by the GRU to study German rocket technology, Tokaev was followed to the British in August 1948 by the microbiologist Nikolai Borodin, who published *One Man in His Time* in 1955 but did not make a significant impact. Although the defections of Tokaev and Borodin caused Moscow some minor discomfort, neither inflicted political damage on the scale caused by Yuri Rastvorov, the Japanese-speaking KGB lieutenant-colonel who volunteered to help the CIA in Tokyo in January 1954, and was responsible for the arrest of an entire Soviet spy-ring inside the Japanese Foreign Ministry. Unfortunately Rastvorov has not yet written a book, but he did publish under his name three lengthy articles for *Life* in November 1954 and, like Gouzenko, inflicted tremendous damage on the Soviet intelligence system by the arrest of its most secret assets. The loss of a case officer of Rastvorov's rank not only undermined the confidence of his colleagues, but deterred other fellow travellers from co-operating with the KGB, thereby handicapping its operations.

A rather more junior officer, Anatoli Granovsky, was the first postwar NKVD defector, and he jumped his ship in Stockholm in July 1946 and later obtained political asylum in the United States, where he wrote *I Was an NKVD Agent*. His colleague Boris Bakhlanov switched sides in Vienna a year later and, using the pseudonym A. I. Romanov, recalled his experiences in *Nights are Longest There*.

Although most of these defectors claimed to have been motivated by ideological or economic reasons, the flurry of defections which occurred immediately after the death of Lavrenti Beria was most probably precipitated by a fear of what lay in store for the NKVD personnel who had served the hated intelligence chief so well. In Vienna Piotr Deriabin, later to co-author *The Secret World*, gave himself up to the CIA in February 1954, and a few days later Nikolai Khokhlov did the same in Frankfurt, describing his criminal activities and his eventual escape in his book, *In the Name of Conscience*. Vladimir and Evdokia Petrov, who followed in Australia a couple of months later, subsequently collaborated on their denunciation of the Soviet system, *Empire of Fear*. What made their defection so significant was their relative seniority. Vladimir Petrov had been the *rezident* in Canberra since his appointment, a year after his arrival in February 1951, and as such he possessed a comprehensive knowledge of Soviet clandestine activity in Australia. His wife, also an experienced intelligence officer, had acted as his cipher clerk and was also able to disclose valuable secrets to their Australian hosts. To the more cynical and hard-bitten among the West's mole-hunters, these escapes, made so soon after Beria's demise, were no coincidence, and were more a manifestation of self-preservation than made from any more noble motive. Many of Beria's most loyal lieutenants were purged after his arrest in June 1953 and his execution six months later on charges of treason, having been convicted on trumped-up charges of spying for the British, must have been a potent warning to his surviving supporters who could find refuge in the West.

Although not intelligence professionals like the Petrovs, Aleksandr Kaznacheev had been co-opted to help the Soviet security apparatus operating from the embassy in Rangoon, and after he had been flown out of Burma in June 1959 he explained the overlap of duty between the KGB officials and the regular diplomatic staff, in his memoirs, *Inside a Soviet Embassy*. Kaznacheev was a determined and authentic defector, but the same could not be said of Yuri Krotkov, a Soviet journalist whose decision to stay in London during an official visit in September 1963 proved to be part of a complex counter-intelligence game executed by the KGB. A noted playwright, and an active homosexual with an unpalatable history of ensnaring unwary foreign diplomats and visitors in Moscow honeytraps for the KGB, Krotkov later wrote *The Angry Exile* without ever admitting to having played a dual role.

In April 1969 the KGB's star illegal Rupert Sigl established contact with the CIA, and although he was willing to describe many of his exploits in *In the Claws of the KGB* he drew a discreet veil over the circumstances of his recruitment by the Americans. Similarly, Vladimir Sakharov, who defected while serving as a diplomat in Kuwait in July 1971, understandably preferred caution when referring to his recruitment and his illicit meetings with his CIA handlers in Moscow in his autobiography *High Treason*. Both men inflicted significant operational damage on the KGB's First Chief Directorate.

During the 1970s the flow of defectors from East to West continued, and the release of individual memoirs proved an effective way of subsidizing the new arrivals. Thus Aleksei Myagkov, the young KGB officer from the Third Chief Directorate who crossed over into the British sector of Berlin in February 1974, wrote *Inside the KGB*. He had little to offer in the way of details of Soviet agents operating in the West, but his value lay in his insider's view of the KGB's security apparatus in East Germany in which he had worked for the preceding five years. Similarly, Vladimir Rezun, the GRU officer working under United Nations cover who contacted the British SIS in Geneva in July 1977 and defected eleven months later, used the pen-name Viktor Suvorov to publish *Aquarium* in a series of titles about Soviet military intelligence. His special accomplishment was to shed light on his organization which, in recent years, had suffered relatively few defections. While the modern GRU had seemed largely immune from the phenomenon of defection the KGB suffered grievously at the hands of those taking a 'meal-ticket' to the West. Stanislav Levchenko, a senior KGB officer based in Tokyo who walked into the CIA's local station a year or so later, relived his experiences in *On the Wrong Side*. He made his mark by naming a Japanese major-general as his key source, thus ensuring the spy a prison sentence of twenty years. Levchenko's colleague in the First Chief Directorate, Ilya Dzhirkvelov, opted for the British in Geneva in March 1980, discarding his journalistic cover and later producing *Secret Servant*, about his life in the KGB, from the safety of a new identity in London.

In rather a different category is Arkadi Shevchenko, the respected senior diplomat at the United Nations in New York, who believed his work for the CIA had been discovered when he received an unexpected recall to Moscow in April 1978. Never an intelligence professional, he had approached the CIA a little more than a year earlier and had operated as a highly successful spy before moving into a safe-house near Washington DC, and preparing his autobiography, *Breaking with Moscow*. Quite apart from the information he was able to supply to the CIA while he was still in place, his importance lay in his seniority, for he had held ambassadorial rank and that made him the most high-ranking Soviet ever to defect.

More recently, three other KGB defectors have released books. They are Viktor Sheymov, who says he was simply driven in a car across the Soviet frontier with his wife and child to the West by the CIA in 1980, but he waited until 1993 before producing *Tower of Secrets*; Vladimir Kuzichkin, who collaborated with the British in Tehran before his exfiltration to Turkey in June 1982, and wrote *Inside the KGB*; and Oleg Gordievsky, who was smuggled out of Moscow in dramatic circumstances in August 1985 and subsequently co-authored *KGB: The Inside Story*. Together these three officers, from quite different, compartmented departments of the KGB's Eighth and First Chief Directorates, rendered useless many of the organization's most sensitive operations. From their respective positions, supervising secure cipher systems, building an illegal network in Iran, and running the *rezidentura* in London, they struck a blow to the heart of the Soviet system. When considered with the contribution made by other, less publicized KGB defectors during the same period, one can see how the very foundation of the Kremlin's power was compromised.

Virtually all those listed here were regarded as traitors by the Soviet regime, and most were tried *in absentia* by the Military Collegium of the Supreme Court and sentenced to death. Although Walter Krivitsky and Victor Kravchenko were found dead in America in mysterious circumstances, ostensibly having committed suicide, only Colonel Oleg Penkovsky has had an account of his espionage published posthumously. His controversial memoirs, *The Penkovsky Papers*, which allegedly were compiled from information he gave to his Western contacts before his arrest, were released two years after his execution in Moscow. Like nearly a hundred other titles perceived to be unhelpful to the Kremlin, this book was the subject of a confidential agreement between the CIA and the publisher in which a huge print run was justified by the Agency's undertaking to purchase all unsold copies. Authors that could not attract mainstream publishers often had their memoirs printed and distributed either by specialist firms that received discreet subsidies, or by front companies which were actually secret CIA 'proprietaries'.

The defections undertaken by these authors gave Western intelligence services a series of vivid and accurate glimpses into their opponent's clandestine activities, but it was by no means a complete picture. The Soviet intelligence structure was efficiently compartmented to minimize damage from hostile penetration. Thus a Third Chief Directorate officer like Aleksei Myagkov could say little about First Chief Directorate operations, and a senior KGB case officer such as Stanislav Levchenko knew little about the GRU. Similarly, Igor Gouzenko had much to say about his observations of the GRU from his relatively subordinate position as a cipher clerk, but his knowledge of the NKVD, who had been based in the same building in Ottawa, proved minimal.

The KGB also relied upon other Warsaw Pact services to act as surrogates, and in some relationships, as in those between the KGB and the Czechs and the Bulgarians, the link appeared entirely seamless even to insiders. These agencies were also susceptible to betrayal from within, as was demonstrated by Vladimir Kostov who defected in Paris in June 1977 and later wrote *The Bulgarian Umbrella*. Kostov's interrogation at the hands of Western security and intelligence agencies amounted to a damning exposé of the dreaded Drzaven Sigurnost, and so enraged his former employers that they were provoked into having him attacked in August 1978 by an assassin armed with a pellet gun concealed inside an apparently innocuous umbrella. A tiny quantity of ricin, a deadly toxin, was injected into Kostov, but he survived. However, an almost identical murder bid by the DS, on another Bulgarian dissident, Georgi Markov, carried out ten days later in London in September 1978, proved fatal. After his death Markov's widow Annabel published his memoirs, *The Truth that Killed*, and is still campaigning for her husband's murderers to be brought to justice.

Equally closely allied to the KGB was the Czech Statni tajna Bezpec-nost, the organization from which Ladislav Bittman decamped in protest at the Soviet invasion of August 1968. Bittman then wrote *The Deception Game*, and he was followed by two colleagues, Josef Frolik, who had headed the StB's British section, and Frantisek August. The former's autobiography, *The Frolik Defection*, gave a detailed account of his undercover activities in London, where he had served two years from April 1964 under labour attaché cover, and inflicted great damage on his former employers. Together with August, who subsequently wrote *Red Star Over Prague*, Frolik gave evidence against three StB spies in Britain, two of whom were arrested. Another Czech, albeit of a different generation, to renounce communism was Joseph Heissler, a former Soviet-trained agent and Czech diplomat who had been based at the embassy in London during the communist takeover in February 1948. Heissler had undergone an ideological conversion and remained in London, writing a series of books, including *The Traitor Trade*, under the name J. Bernard Hutton, in which he claimed to expose KGB-inspired plots. Heissler's credibility has always been in doubt, but there could not have been a more authoritative source than General Jan Sejna, the high-ranking military officer whose *We Will Bury You*, written in 1982 some years after his escape from Prague, provided incontrovertible evidence of the Kremlin's commitment to world domination, and of the Czech government's willing acquiescence in the plan.

A few other Soviet Bloc defectors have written their stories, but Orlando Hidalgo is the only Cuban to have rejected his career in Castro's feared Direccion General de Inteligencia. In March 1970 he chose in

favour of a new life in America, which has been supported in part by
royalties from *A Spy for Fidel*. Ion Pacepa, the Romanian lieutenant-
general who had headed Nicolae Ceauçescu's Departmentul de Informatii
Externe, unexpectedly marched into the American embassy in Bonn in
July 1978 to seek political asylum, thus becoming the most senior Eastern
Bloc intelligence defector. His memoirs, *Red Horizons*, seriously undermined Ceauçescu's despotic regime, and gave the first authoritative inside
look at the DIE, an essential but largely unknown organ of the dictator's
power.

In terms of rank, the most senior Soviet Bloc defectors were the two
Polish ambassadors, Zdzislaw Rurarz, who abandoned his embassy in
Tokyo, and Romuald Spasowski, the envoy in Washington DC, who both
defected in December 1981, prompted by the imposition of martial law in
Warsaw. Spasowski's autobiography, *The Liberation of One*, contained
few surprises, but in *An Ambassador Speaks* Rurarz revealed that apart
from his diplomatic duties, he had maintained a relationship with the
Urzad Bezpieczenstwa for more than twenty-five years. An earlier UB
defector, Janusz Kochanski, switched sides in Copenhagen in February
1967, as he described in *Double Eagle*, using the pseudonym Mr X.

The only East German intelligence defector to have written about the
ubiquitous Hauptverwaltung für Aufklarung is Werner Stiller, who
waited until the Berlin Wall had been demolished before he described his
dual role for the West German BND in *Beyond the Wall*. Few HVA
officers have followed his example, no doubt preferring anonymity in
their newly unified country. For years the HVA, under the inspired
leadership of Markus Wolf, avoided defector damage and the organization remained an enigma to its Federal counterpart, unlike the Hungarian
Allam Vedelmi Hatosag, which was exposed first by George Mikes, who
wrote *A Study in Infamy* in 1959, based on documents seized during the
October 1956 uprising in Budapest. His charges were later confirmed by
Laszlo Szabo, who has the distinction of being the only AVH defector to
have given evidence before the US Congress, an event that took place in
March 1966. His fellow Hungarian, Janos Radvanyi, did his best to
undermine the communists by defecting from his post in the embassy in
Washington DC in May 1967 and revealing in *Delusion and Reality* his
Foreign Minister's duplicity in the Vietnam War peace negotiations.

In contrast to the Soviet experience, the Americans have suffered the
loss of relatively few defectors to Moscow, and only a mere handful from
the intelligence community. None, apart from a cipher clerk named John
D. Smith, who said in an interview with *Izvestia* in November 1967 that

he had defected from the US embassy in New Delhi, has ever written about his or her motivation. Bernon F. Mitchell and William H. Martin disappeared together to Cuba in June 1960 and their colleague in the National Security Agency, Victor N. Hamilton, fled to Moscow in July 1963, but little has been heard of them since. Captain C. J. Gessner defected in 1962 and Glenn M. Souther, the US navy photographer, defected in June 1986 and committed suicide in Moscow three years later. Nevertheless, there is a sizeable group of dissenters who, in the eyes of many Americans, betrayed their country. Certainly the Central Intelligence Agency regarded Philip Agee, who wrote *Inside the Company: CIA Diary* after his resignation from the CIA's station in Mexico City, as a turncoat who had probably succumbed to recruitment by the Cuban DGI. The same accusation was never levelled against Frank Snepp, the former intelligence analyst whose critique of the CIA in Vietnam, *Decent Interval*, brought him much hostility, not so much for what he said but for the breach of his employment contract in which he had undertaken to submit any disclosure he intended to make to the Agency first. Similarly, John Stockwell, whose disaffection with the CIA's operations in Angola were articulated in his book *In Search of Enemies*, encountered lengthy litigation with his former employers. Perhaps the most epic legal battle was that fought by Victor Marchetti, whose controversial recollections, *The CIA and the Cult of Intelligence*, were released with large parts of the text deleted. Marchetti's example was followed by Melvin Beck with *Secret Contenders*, which was published with numerous deletions, and Ralph McGehee with *Deadly Deceits*. Both were career CIA officers with a combined forty-two years of experience to transform them into among the Agency's most bitter critics.

Agee, supported by a small band of radicals, has achieved considerable notoriety as an American who has set out deliberately to harm American interests, and he can never expect under any administration to be hailed as a misunderstood hero – perhaps someone deserving of that ultimate accolade, a burial plot in the Arlington National Cemetery, an honour reserved for only the most respected of US citizens. Yet, curiously, there is one occupant there who merits mention in these pages. Herbert O. Yardley is revered by many as one of the world's greatest cryptographers, but within a small circle of the cognoscenti he is known as a genius who in 1930, when short of cash, sold his method of breaking the Japanese diplomatic code to the Japanese for $7,000. Criticized, but not prosecuted, for his indiscretion in writing *The American Black Chamber*, Yardley never used the excuse that his book, which was presumed to have alerted Tokyo to the vulnerability of Japanese ciphers, had not done any harm because the author had already sold the relevant information.

More easily identifiable as Americans with first-hand knowledge of treachery are the Soviet sympathizers like Alger Hiss and Agnes Smedley who embraced communism and worked for the cause. Hiss, of course, denied his involvement in espionage in court and in his first autobiography, *In the Court of Public Opinion*, but Agnes Smedley was rather more candid about her sympathies in her book *Battle Hymn of China*, apparently overlooked by some of her most ardent supporters. She admitted having engaged in espionage on behalf of the Germans during the First World War, and acknowledged her commitment to Marxism during the Second.

Both Smedley and Hiss were identified as Soviet agents by some of their fellow conspirators who later underwent a political conversion. Most memorably, Whittaker Chambers challenged Hiss during a defamation action, and his *Witness* is an account of how his testimony ensured Hiss was convicted of perjury and sentenced to a term of imprisonment. Others to follow the same route were Elizabeth Bentley, who had been at the heart of the link between Soviet espionage and the Communist Party of the United States of America, as she described in *Out of Bondage*. Hede Massing was also to give the FBI important information, as she encapsulated in *This Deception*, and both she and the Hollywood movie producer Boris Morros actually penetrated the KGB's networks in the United States to obtain criminal convictions against its members, as he also recounted, in *My Ten Years as a Counterspy*. Similarly, Michael Straight, who had been recruited into an underground communist cell while an undergraduate at Cambridge University, volunteered a statement to the FBI that was to implicate others, most notably his old friend Anthony Blunt. As Straight explained in *After Long Silence*, the only memoir written by a member of Guy Burgess's *galère*, it was his belated confirmation in 1963 of Blunt's role as a KGB talent-spotter that had prompted the art historian's dramatic confession to MI5 in April the following year.

While the Americans always found it hard to come to terms with communist subversion, the French have regarded political intrigue as a way of life. The gulf between the Left and Right has never been deeper than in France where the communists traditionally have exercised considerable influence, with the Right being tainted by French acquiescence in, and collaboration with, the Nazi occupation. It was this conflict which led the novelist Pierre Boulle to serve two and a half years in various prisons in Indo-China, having been convicted of treason by a court-martial in Hanoi.

His offence had been to back the Free French and join Special Operations Executive with the objective of undermining the Vichy authorities in the Far East, as he recounted in *The Source of the River Kwai*.

Immediately after the liberation those accused of having been in the enemy's service were either subjected to instant rough justice or put on trial. One of the very few to emerge from the experience and write a book was the notorious Mathilde Carré, the woman who was charged with having betrayed an entire intelligence *réseau* in 1941, and who, in a supreme insult to her country, took her German interrogator as her lover. In *I Was the Cat* she gave her side of her extraordinary story, a tale that she wrote in prison while serving a life sentence from which she was granted an early release. Another member of the wartime resistance, but on the other side, was Philippe Thyraud de Vosjoli who, as a young man, had smuggled evaders across the demarcation line near his home between Vichy and the occupied zone. After the war de Vosjoli had joined the Service de Documentation Extérieure et de Contre-Espionnage (SDECE), and had been appointed that organization's representative in Washington DC during the Cuban missile crisis, in which he played a key role. De Vosjoli's close relationship with the CIA was to engender considerable distrust of him in Paris, particularly when he debriefed a KGB defector who gave him graphic proof of Soviet access to SDECE's secrets. His reports of high-level Soviet penetration of SDECE were ignored and, convinced that he might become a target for assassination, he refused to be recalled and instead went on the run in America and Mexico, ending up in exile in Florida where he wrote *Lamia*.

De Vosjoli was denounced as a turncoat by his SDECE colleagues, but they made no effort to prevent the publication of his memoirs, perhaps realizing that the American Constitution guarantees the right to freedom of speech. Certainly the First Amendment was not entirely appreciated by the Israeli authorities who made a futile attempt in September 1990 to injunct *By Way of Deception*, the book written by Victor Ostrovsky in Canada. Ostrovsky had served in Mossad for two years, between 1984 and 1986, and he was the first of its personnel to defy its ban on the unauthorized disclosure of information about the obsessively secretive agency. However, the legal action initiated in Toronto and then followed in New York's Supreme Court proved entirely counterproductive and consequently Ostrovsky's story became a bestseller on the basis that its authenticity inadvertently had been certified by lawyers acting for the Israeli government. The author accomplished his objective, but he now has to live in hiding for fear of retribution.

Ostrovsky's betrayal of Mossad is remarkable, not just because of his unique status as the only Mossad officer to break ranks, but also because of the very real threat to him posed by the organization that has assiduously cultivated a reputation for ruthless efficiency. The author's motivation was supposedly political in nature, a stated wish to expose the misdeeds of an intelligence apparatus he considered to be out of control, but that is not how he is likely to be remembered, particularly by his Mossad contemporaries. Ostrovsky, who was born in Canada, possesses dual nationality and if not for this safeguard it is highly likely that he would have suffered the same fate as Mordechai Vanunu, the nuclear technician who sold details of Israel's arsenal of atomic weapons to the *Sunday Times* in London, and was subsequently abducted by Mossad. Whereas Ostrovsky was obliged to leave his suburban home in Ottawa and go into hiding, Vanunu was shipped to Tel Aviv in October 1986 and sentenced in March 1988 to eighteen years' imprisonment for espionage and treason.

Political motives often lie at the foundation of an act that is regarded as treacherous, but even when individuals have taken a stand against an obviously evil regime, such as the totalitarian state created by Adolf Hitler, their behaviour is not automatically forgiven. Of the three Germans who switched sides during the Second World War, and subsequently wrote about their defections, only Wolfgang zu Putlitz received substantial reward and recognition upon his return. Ironically, he resettled in East Berlin in January 1952, where he wrote *The Putlitz Dossier*, but it was as a committed communist that he was welcomed by the Democratic Republic. The aristocrat had sought refuge with the British in September 1940 when his undercover activities as a valued SIS source in the German Foreign Ministry were about to be exposed by the Gestapo and thereafter he spent much of the war preparing propaganda programmes to be broadcast by the Allies against his own country. So did Otto John, the Lufthansa lawyer who was obliged to flee to neutral Lisbon and thence to London when his involvement in a plot to assassinate Hitler in July 1944 became known to the Gestapo. As he recalled in his memoirs, *Twice Through the Lines*, his inclusion in the postwar administration, in November 1950, as head of the West German internal security agency, brought him nothing but hostility from those who could not forgive his defection from the Third Reich. Similarly, Hans Bernd Gisevius, another conspirator who had participated in the attempts to kill Hitler, and later wrote *To the Bitter End*, was condemned by many Germans for having betrayed his country. Whereas Gisevius, John and zu Putlitz fled abroad, Fabian von Schlabrendorff was one of the handful of plotters who survived torture and a death sentence, and he wrote about the resistance in *The Secret War against Hitler*. The fact that Gisevius, von Schlabrendorff, John and zu Putlitz all gave their help to the prosecution at the Nuremberg trials did nothing to help their standing in postwar Germany. For the Austrian Fritz Molden, the young anti-Nazi who deserted from the Wehrmacht, the moral issues centring on his betrayal of his head of state had been eased because, by an oversight, he had never been required to take the customary oath of allegiance to Adolf Hitler. Instead he disappeared from his unit in Italy and made contact with Gisevius in Switzerland, as he recounted in *Exploding Star*. Thereafter he undertook several extremely hazardous journeys to Vienna to build an Austrian resistance organization.

The Baron zu Putlitz, another determined anti-Hitler conspirator who also deserted his overseas post, eventually took up permanent residence in the Soviet zone of Berlin, and for a period Otto John also seemed to have embraced communism, and moved to East Berlin in mysterious circumstances, apparently the victim of an abduction, in July 1954. Zu Putlitz is now dead, and John resides in Austria, but still living in a grim suburb of the new capital of a unified Germany is Ursula Kuczynski, a devoted and unrepentant Marxist who operated as a GRU agent successively in Shanghai, Geneva and then Oxford. As a fervent anti-Nazi she plotted against Hitler's regime; as a key Soviet organizer she supervised a GRU network in Switzerland; as a naturalized British subject she acted as a handler for the atomic spy Klaus Fuchs. In her book, *Sonya's Report*, she makes no apology for having conspired against not just her own country of origin but even her adopted country. Although she concedes that the socialist experiment has failed, perhaps only briefly, she maintains her belief in the cause and is unwilling to elaborate on the most fascinating periods of her operational life for fear of compromising other comrades.

The issue of breaking silence when others are conforming raises the spectre of the whistle-blower, as personified by Gordon Winter, the Briton recruited by the South African Bureau of State Security. His account, *Inside BOSS*, was released in 1981 soon after he had abandoned his cover as a Johannesburg-based newspaper correspondent with strong anti-apartheid sympathies. In reality Winter had worked for BOSS and its predecessor, the Security Police, continuously since his recruitment in 1961, and his book was intended as an exposé of his illicit activities.

Some of the authors mentioned in the pages that follow have been inspired to take what others see as a path of treachery because of a sense of injustice and a desire to set the record straight. Others have written more in the form of an apologia, an explanation of the conduct that has brought them such opprobrium. To that extent their books are but extensions of the act, and not the objects of criticism themselves. That description certainly would not be true of two recent authors, Brian Crozier and Desmond Bristow, who both risked prosecution in England for the offence of having gone into print about their covert careers. Thus there was nothing in the course of their clandestine activities that caused them any disquiet, it was merely the fact of having sought to disclose them in a public forum, in the face of opposition from the Secret Intelligence Service, that made certain they would be accused of disloyalty. Neither *Free Agent* nor *A Game of Moles* can be categorized as anything more harmless than fascinating memoirs of men with exceptional records of service to their country, albeit in a covert organization, but that does nothing to minimize the scale of their offence as perceived in Whitehall. Certainly the British authorities have inherited an almost pathological fear of any disclosure, even in the form of fiction, that might in any way compromise or embarrass the government. This might seem a harsh indictment, but the 1989 Official Secrets Act extends even to novelists whose previous careers in the security or intelligence services might lead the public to believe their work contained an element of verisimilitude. Nor is this a recent manifestation of paranoia. In 1950 the first Viscount Norwich was threatened with prosecution if he persisted with his plan to write a novel, *Operation Heartbreak*, based upon a genuine deception scheme, the details of which he had learned in April 1943 while a member of Churchill's war cabinet. The former MP, then British Ambassador in Paris, chose to ignore the warnings and successfully called the government's bluff. While he escaped with nothing worse than a single poor review, other authors have not been so lucky.

Treachery and betrayal are older than the thirty pieces of silver paid to Judas, but at the end of the twentieth century they are concepts that appear increasingly subjective. Are whistle-blowers to be discouraged as selfish monomaniacs, or are they to be celebrated as protectors of valuable rights? Are defectors nothing more than selfish careerists, or are they brave martyrs defying oppression to stand on principles? In an era which has seen the political pendulum in Europe swing from totalitarianism, to democracy, and then back again to democratic socialism, and during a period when the individual can be seen to have triumphed over the state, the choices are less clear cut. So what was it that compelled the minority to try to change history?

Author's Note

This anthology is intended to be a comprehensive study of those who are perceived to have committed treachery against their own country, and written about their experiences in the English language. An additional criterion is the requirement for the author cited to have made disclosures that can be seen to have adversely affected the regime which he or she rejected. However, there are a few titles, invariably claiming a connection with the KGB, which do not appear to qualify for inclusion. Examples include Maurice Shainberg's *Breaking from the KGB* (Shapolsky Books, 1986) and Alexander A. Ushakov's *In the Gunsight of the KGB* (Alfred A. Knopf, 1989).

Abbreviations

ASIO	Australian Security Intelligence Organization
AVH	Hungarian Intelligence Service
AVO	Hungarian Secret Police
BCRA	Gaullist French Intelligence Service
BfV	West German Security Service
BND	West German Intelligence Service
BOSS	South African Bureau of State Security
BSC	British Security Coordination
CIA	American Central Intelligence Agency
CPGB	Communist Party of Great Britain
CPUSA	Communist Party of the United States of America
DGER	French Intelligence Service
DGI	Cuban Intelligence Service
DIE	Romanian Intelligence Service
DINA	Chilean Intelligence Service
DS	Bulgarian Intelligence Service
DST	French Security Service
FBI	American Federal Bureau of Investigation
FBIS	Czech Intelligence Service
FCD	First Chief Directorate of the KGB
GRU	Soviet Military Intelligence Service
HUAC	House Un-American Activities Committee
HVA	East German Intelligence Service
KDP	German Communist Party
KGB	Soviet Intelligence Service
KOS	Yugoslav Intelligence Service
MfS	East German Ministry of State Security
MI5	British Security Service
MI6	British Secret Intelligence Service
Mossad	Israeli Intelligence Service
NID	British Naval Intelligence Division
NKVD	Soviet Intelligence Service
OGPU	Soviet Intelligence Service

ABBREVIATIONS

OSS	American Office of Strategic Services
PIDE	Portuguese Security Service
PLO	Palestine Liberation Organization
PWE	Political Warfare Executive
SB	Polish Intelligence Service
SD	Nazi Security Service
SDECE	French Intelligence Service
SED	East German Socialist Workers Party
SHAPE	Supreme Headquarters, Allied Powers Europe
SIS	British Secret Intelligence Service
SOE	Special Operations Executive
SRI	Romanian Intelligence Service
StB	Czech Intelligence Service
SVR	Russian Federation Intelligence Service
UB	Polish Intelligence Service

CHAPTER I

The Britons

This was a case of political conscience against
loyalty to country: I chose conscience.
Anthony Blunt, 20 November 1979

Often treason and treachery have been confused in England, but in legal terms there is a distinction. High treason, of course, has always been well understood to cover the crime of seeking to overthrow the monarch, or perhaps his or her government, by unlawful means. Less known is the offence of petty treason, which covers counterfeiting the King's Privy Seal, or slaying one of the King's Justices of Assize. The terms of the Treason Act of 1351, which dates back to the reign of Edward III, refer to seven provisions, including 'violating the King's companion, or his eldest unmarried daughter, or the wife of his eldest son' and the rather vaguer offence of adhering to the King's enemies. Conviction meant a lingering death involving being dragged along the ground to the place of execution on a hurdle, hanged, drawn from the gallows, having one's entrails torn out and being burned, before the victim was finally beheaded and cut into quarters. In 1814 the law was changed to allow the traitor to die *before* he was quartered, and it was not until 1870 that this final indignity was eliminated. Women convicted of treason had a rather easier time. Until 1790 they were simply burned at the stake, but thereafter they died, like ordinary murderers, on the scaffold.

When Sir Roger Casement returned to Ireland to inspire a rebellion against the Crown, few could doubt his guilt on a charge of treason, not least because in September 1914 he had written a letter to the correspondence columns of the *Irish Independent* from New York, urging his fellow Irishmen to fight the English, not the Germans. Certainly driven by political motives, he had combined with the King's enemy (actually his cousin, the Kaiser) to drive the British from Eire. Fortunately for Casement, the King declined to exercise his ancient right to substitute as punishment decapitation for hanging. The law of treason remains full of splendid anachronisms, including in Scotland the right of the Lord Lyon King of Arms to try appropriate cases, such as misuse of the Royal Arms, for which the death penalty still applies.

The Treachery Act, rushed through both Houses of Parliament in a single evening in May 1940, identified a new offence, which was intended to plug a gap in the law that the authorities feared might be exploited by German spies. The Official Secrets Act, which protected the nation's secrets during peace and war, did not include a capital offence, and it was considered there might be cases in which it would be difficult to demonstrate to a jury's satisfaction that any secrets had been acquired by the accused, thereby allowing those guilty of espionage to avoid execution. Similarly, the Defence of the Realm Act boasted a maximum penalty of life imprisonment, so there was a danger that a civilian suspect, who could not be tried under military law by a court-martial, might deploy a defence which would enable him to elude justice, particularly if, as a foreign national, he fell outside the scope of the ancient Treason Act of the fourteenth century. During the debate in the Commons, which lasted just over three hours for the entire passage of the Bill, the Home Secretary, Sir John Anderson, justified the fact that the new offence of treachery allowed only one penalty, death:

> I regard an act of treachery against one's own country as perhaps one of the most abominable crimes any man can commit – as an enormity. It is such an odious thing to do, that for my part I am prepared to set aside principle on the general question of capital punishment and see imposed the extreme form of penalty for such a crime as this. I do so more readily because, like so many others, I have an appreciation of the fairness of British justice and the manner in which our courts deal with offenders.

The new Act's objective was to provide a death penalty for enemy aliens, a classification of people that hitherto, even after eight months of war, had been overlooked. Indeed, even after the Treachery Act had been entered in the statute book, three enemy agents, who had waded ashore on the Kent coast near Dymchurch in September, were tried at the Old Bailey. To the embarrassment of the prosecution, only two were sentenced to hang; their companion, a twenty-eight-year-old Dutch refugee named Sjoerd Pons, was acquitted, and was interned as an enemy alien for the duration.

Pons's acquittal was the only one of its kind during the Second World War, and there was only a single case of a spy, that of Josef Jakobs, being tried by court-martial and shot by firing squad. Of the total of sixteen German spies who were executed in England, only three were British subjects. The first to hang was George Armstrong, a thirty-nine-year-old communist seaman from Newcastle who had welcomed the Molotov–Ribbentrop Pact and had accepted his party's official view that the war should be opposed, and accordingly had volunteered his services to the Abwehr while in America. He was arrested in Boston in October 1940 and deported from the United States to face trial in London, and was hanged in July 1941, by which time the Soviet Union had been attacked by Nazi Germany, and the CPGB had been forced to make an embarrassing reversal in its policy towards the conflict. Overnight the so-called capitalists' war, which had been denounced as irrelevant to the interests of the workers' struggle, had been hailed as an essential part of the proletariat's determination for justice. The irony had not been lost on Douglas Hyde, the editor of the *Daily Worker*, who saw the somersault as final proof that the CPGB was not an independent political party, but really nothing more than an adjunct of a foreign power's intelligence agency. His gradual conversion, as he later recalled, brought him to realize that, like so many other Britons, he had been duped into assisting Moscow exercise totalitarian control over communist parties across the globe. 'As a communist I had had a vested interest in disorder, in economic crisis, social injustice and chaos, military defeat. My hopes had been pinned on world unrest and national instability.'

Always an active communist, Hyde had joined the Party before he was eighteen, when he was still a student of theology, and for the next twenty years he worked assiduously as a strike organizer and Party activist. He was assigned to the *Daily Worker*, for which he became the news editor, and ran a campaign against the Roman Catholic church. He was sued for libel by the Catholic *Weekly Review* when he accused it of having links with the Fascists, and in preparing his defence he found his own belief in socialism was undermined.

His doubts about the Party grew after its position on the Molotov–Ribbentrop Pact reversed overnight when Hitler attacked the Soviet Union. In 1948 he renounced Communism and converted to Catholicism, joining the *Catholic Herald* as a journalist.

As a former leading member of the Party, he was never forgiven for his conversion, but he continued to campaign against what he came to recognise as subversion in *The Peaceful Assault: The Pattern of Subversion, Dedication and Leadership: Learning from the Communists, The Roots of Guerrilla Warfare* and, in 1972, *Communism Today*. His booklet *United We Fall*, released in 1966, is regarded as the most comprehensive study of communist front organizations ever published.

In 1950 Hyde wrote *I Believed*, a bitter denunciation of the CPGB's total reliance upon Moscow which led his former comrades to denounce him as a traitor. He survived their opprobrium and now lives in Wimbledon, still defiant of those who felt betrayed by his political conversion.

Another communist, a seaman who suffered the same fate as George Armstrong, was Duncan Scott-Ford, who was arrested in Salford in August 1942 and charged with having agreed while on a visit to Lisbon to work for the Germans. Then aged twenty-one, Scott-Ford was hanged in Wandsworth in November 1942. The third British traitor was the rather more elderly Oswald Job. Resident in Paris, where before the outbreak of hostilities he had manufactured glass eyes, he had been interned for three years by the occupation forces at St Denis and then recruited as an agent. He had arrived in London, via Madrid and Lisbon, in November 1943 but MI5 had already been alerted to his duplicity through a tip from a double agent code-named Dragonfly. Job was arrested later in the same month and hanged at Pentonville in March the following year.

After the German surrender the Security Service had the distasteful task of having to sort through the motley band of renegades who had collaborated with the enemy. Some, like 'Lord Haw-Haw', had achieved notoriety either by broadcasting propaganda from Berlin or by touring prison camps to find volunteers willing to join a British battalion of the SS, known as the Legion of St George, to fight the Soviets on the Eastern Front. William Joyce and John Amery were hanged for their treason, but Norman Baillie-Stewart, who had played a less prominent role, escaped with a prison sentence. Ronald Seth, who was also suspected of having worked for the Nazis, underwent an uncomfortable interrogation after he had turned up unexpectedly in Switzerland, two years after he had been parachuted into enemy occupied territory. He was accused of having collaborated with the Gestapo, but he was freed without charges. He later wrote more than two dozen books, but none except his autobiography mentions the awkward situation he had found himself in in 1944 which nearly led to his appearance in the dock at the Old Bailey.

The humorist P. G. Wodehouse was also in Paris in August 1944 as the victorious Allies swept into the French capital. He too was questioned by MI5 concerning the five notorious radio talks he had given in Germany, and despite considerable public pressure for him to be prosecuted, it was decided that he had not committed any crime. Nevertheless, he was strongly advised not to return to England, where several others were facing capital charges for not entirely dissimilar acts. John Amery, for example, was hanged on 19 December 1945 at Wandsworth, and William Joyce, the Irish American who had been found guilty on one charge of high treason in September, suffered the same fate soon afterwards, on 3 January 1946. Nor were this pair isolated cases. After Joyce was hanged a further 125 Britons, including 57 servicemen, were arrested because they were suspected of having aided the enemy. Indeed, a total of forty-two individuals owing allegiance to the Crown had broadcast propaganda from Berlin, but those who were convicted invariably had their death sentences commuted to life imprisonment. That was the fate of Walter Purdy, a naval engineer captured at Narvik, and Thomas Cooper, who volunteered to join the Waffen SS.

Although William Joyce is often stated to be the last person to be executed in England for treason, that dubious honour is actually shared with Private Theodore Schurch, who was hanged for treachery at Pentonville the day after Joyce. Born in London of Swiss parents, Schurch had joined the British Union of Fascists and had deserted from his regiment, the Royal Army Service Corps, when the Germans captured Tobruk in June 1942. He crossed into the British lines at Alamein, returning to the Italian side successfully soon afterwards, and later he extracted information from British prisoners of war in Italy while masquerading as a British officer. At his court-martial he was convicted on nine separate charges of treachery, and one of desertion with intent to join the enemy.

Since the end of the Second World War very few Britons have been charged with offences that amount to treachery, and even fewer have written of their experiences. With the sole exception of George Blake, who escaped from Wormwood Scrubs in 1967, most have served their sentences and disappeared into obscurity. Only Harry Houghton and John Vassall, who were convicted of having spied for the KGB, have upon their release from prison published their autobiographies. Nevertheless, the Security Service has taken the modern threat of treachery very seriously, and has issued two booklets, *Their Trade Is Treachery* and a sequel, *Treachery Is Still Their Trade*, to warn British businessmen working abroad of the perils of entrapment by ill-intentioned foreign agents. Both documents consist of a selection of sanitized case histories of Britons caught up in espionage and they warn of the dire consequences of mishandling classified information. What makes them remarkable is that, apart from the 1955 White Paper on the defections of Burgess and

Maclean, and the 1993 document *The Security Service*, they are the only MI5 publications ever intended for an external readership. Although in these unusual circumstances one might expect them to reflect a degree of professionalism, they are all marked by rather obvious spelling mistakes and errors of verifiable fact. Details of such famous cases as Donald Maclean and Allan Nunn May are wrong, and there are other grievous blunders. Rather ridiculously, in a couple of instances, the Security Service took the credit for events that were undoubtedly not of its own making. For example, in an abbreviated account of the arrest of William M. Marshall in 1952, the narrative strongly suggests that a known Soviet intelligence officer was kept under surveillance even after he had taken the standard KGB precautionary measures to shake off MI5's famed watchers. In reality Pavel S. Kuznetsov had been spotted entirely by accident meeting his agent, who was later imprisoned, by an off-duty MI5 officer who happened to recognize the KGB man and who took the initiative himself to keep him under discreet observation.

These two publications were distributed 'for official use only' by the Central Office of Information and are the only documents of their kind, prepared by the Security Service for outside consumption. Another title written almost entirely by an MI5 officer, although his role was unacknowledged, was *Handbook for Spies*, ostensibly the autobiography of Allan ('Alexander') Foote, but actually ghosted in its entirety by Courtney Young. This too contained some inexplicable inaccuracies which the Security Service chose to overlook, much to the exasperation of the CIA, even when a second edition was proposed.

Since the conviction in the 1960s of the more famous British spies, including Frank Bossard, Percy Allen and Douglas Britten, it has become clear that a host of Soviet agents have escaped prosecution altogether. After the exposure of Anthony Blunt, others were identified as having served the Soviet cause in much the same capacity, either by having betrayed classified information or, more passively, by having maintained their silence about the networks. Leo Long, once Director of Security in the Control Commission for Germany's Intelligence Division, made a public confession in 1981 of his membership of a KGB ring to which he had been recruited at Cambridge, and both Alister Watson and John Cairncross were subsequently revealed as having played a similar role. Watson made only a partially incriminating statement to MI5 and could not be charged, while Cairncross earned a measure of freedom by collaborating with MI5 in an ill-fated attempt to 'turn' his Soviet recruiter, James Klugmann. Dick Ellis, a senior SIS officer, also admitted after his retirement that he had sold British secrets to the Abwehr before the war, but no action was taken against him, and a dozen others denounced during the molehunts of the period evaded punishment. Another key spy to avoid the dock in the famous Number One Court of the Old Bailey was the journalist and wartime intelligence officer Cedric Belfrage, who had taken the precaution of living in Mexico after he had been named as a Soviet spy by the former communist, Elizabeth Bentley, in 1945. None of these miscreants, of course, were even threatened with prosecution for treason or treachery, and it seems likely that the last public pronouncement of that kind came from Prime Minister Harold Wilson when he warned Ian Smith's government in Southern Rhodesia, during a controversial broadcast, that a declaration of unilateral independence amounted to treason. Considering Smith's loyal and gallant service as a fighter pilot with the Royal Air Force during the Second World War, he made an improbable traitor, even in November 1965 when he made the announcement, much to Wilson's fury.

The first of the Britons to be considered here, who has written at length about his extraordinary experiences, is the former Liberal MP for Darlington, Ignatius Lincoln, whose capacity for deception and treachery against his adopted country knew no bounds, although this was but one aspect of his remarkable career.

Ignatius Trebitsch Lincoln

Diplomatic espionage is much more difficult than either naval or military espionage. It requires more shrewdness, resourcefulness, tact, and cleverness.

The son of a Hungarian rabbi named Trebitsch, Lincoln was born in 1879 in the small town of Paks on the Danube near Budapest. By the age of thirty he had been the Church of England curate of Appledore in Kent, a naturalized British subject, the Liberal MP for Darlington, a friend of David Lloyd George, and a trusted adviser of Seebohm Rowntree, the cocoa magnate. Within a further two years he was a bankrupt, having lost a fortune in speculating in a Galician oilfield, and had started a new career, somewhere in the Balkans, as a spy. Exactly who he was working for while he was in Romania is still unclear but in August 1914 he was back in London, working in the Hungarian and Romanian correspondence section of the Post Office's Censorship Bureau.

In December 1914 Lincoln proposed a complex deception scheme to his contacts at MI5 with the declared intention of deceiving the Germans, but when his suggestion was rejected he travelled to Rotterdam and was enrolled as an agent by the German Consul, a man named Gneist. Upon his return to London in January 1915, with the credentials of an enemy spy, he surrendered Gneist's instructions, which included three codes and some cover addresses on the Continent, but was threatened with arrest. He promptly decamped to New York where in May he published a lurid account of his 'work for the British Secret Service' in the *World*. This was followed by the release of his book, *Revelations of an International Spy*.

Lincoln's claims infuriated the government and in London he was charged with forgery, based upon an affidavit sworn by one of his business associates who had advanced him a loan against a guarantee signed by Seebohm Rowntree, who had denied the signature was his. Thus Lincoln, following his arrest and subsequent escape from custody in Brooklyn, was extradited from the United States to be tried in England on three counts of forgery, for which he was sentenced to three years' imprisonment. Upon his release, in September 1919, he had denaturalized and was deported to Berlin where he was received by the Crown Prince at Wieringen, and participated in the unsuccessful Kapp putsch. When that failed he fled to Hungary, and later moved to China as an adviser to Wu Pei Fu. In China he converted to Buddhism and became a monk in Ceylon under the name Dr Leo Tandler. In 1926 he learned that his son, John Lincoln, had been sentenced to death for shooting a brewer's representative in Trowbridge. He returned to Europe, too late to see his son before his execution, and was later arrested in Belgium. In 1932 he published his second book, *The Autobiography of an Adventurer*. Three years later he was arrested in Liverpool, styling himself Abbot Chao Kung, and deported to China. During the Sino-Japanese War he broadcast Axis propaganda from Tibet, and was reported to have died in Shanghai in October 1943 after an intestinal operation.

Revelations of an International Spy

The aim of the Counter-Espionage is to thwart the schemes and plots of Secret Service agents. It is a most elaborate system and absorbs quite as much money as the espionage itself. How effective the whole system is may be judged by an interview I had with Mr McKenna, then First Lord of the Admiralty, in January 1910.

After my election to the House of Commons in January 1910, I paid a visit to my native country and was quite royally received in Budapest. While there I came into possession of a very valuable secret process which I thought would greatly aid the British navy. The man in possession of the secret only gave me sufficient details to be able to form a judgment on its merits. I immediately wrote to McKenna and told him that the man was willing to accompany me to London and place all the facts before him.

The price he asked was $5,000,000 (£1,000,000). Mr McKenna wired me to bring the man along.

In the afternoon at 3 p.m. of our arrival in London, I saw Mr McKenna by appointment. The man I brought with me from Budapest had to wait in the waiting-room, which had three bare walls, the window being on the fourth wall opposite the door and looking down on St James's Park. It is important to bear this in mind to appreciate the full significance of what will follow later. Being shown to Mr McKenna's private room, I, in reply to a query of his, explained to him the nature of the secret and added:

'The man wants £1,000,000, but for this amount the British Admiralty shall be the sole possessor of the secret.'

Mr McKenna smilingly replied:

'We never give any large amount of money for secrets, for I know within a fortnight of any secret, invention, or process of any navy in the world, and I must necessarily assume this to be the case with your secret.'

This statement reveals the astonishing character of Secret Service plotting and counter plotting.

Towards the close of our conversation a gentleman came in, drew Mr McKenna into a far corner of his very spacious room, and whispered something into his ears – and then left.

When bidding good-by to Mr McKenna, he thus addressed me:

'Will you please ask the man in the waiting-room to return all the Admiralty note-paper he filled his pockets with?'

I rushed into the waiting-room and remonstrated with the man for having thus abused my chaperonage of him. He turned as white as snow and stammered out a few incoherent remarks.

'I can't understand . . . I . . . there was nobody in the room . . . I thought there was no harm . . . seeing it is placed here in the waiting-room . . . eh.'

Those of the readers who have ever had occasion to call at any of the government offices in London were certainly astonished at the long waiting in a waiting-room and at the presence of an abundant supply of note-paper with the royal arms impressed on it.

Now they understand!

Sir Roger Casement

*A man who in the newspapers is said to be just
another Irish traitor, may be a gentleman.*

Born in Dublin of Ulster parents, Casement joined the British Consular Service and in August 1902, after five years in West Africa, was dispatched to the Congo to investigate reports of atrocious conditions there. Casement found that slavery, mutilation and torture were daily events in the landlocked Belgian colony and in January 1906 he presented the Foreign Secretary, Lord Lansdowne, with a comprehensive dossier of institutionalized abuse of the 20 million native inhabitants tolerated by the Belgian authorities. The eye-witness report caused a political furore in Europe and Casement took some well-earned leave and was then appointed British Consul in the Brazilian port of Para.

While based in Para Casement was sent on a second mission, this time to the Putumayo district of the Amazon basin where, according to allegations made in Barbados, British subjects recruited to work on the rubber plantations had been ill-treated. According to Casement's report, which he submitted to Lord Lansdowne's successor, Sir Edward Grey, the claims made about conditions in Putumayo were entirely accurate, and in June 1911 the author was rewarded with a knighthood.

The following year Casement retired in poor health to Ireland and became active in the nationalist cause, encouraging the Irish Volunteers and distributing anti-British propaganda in America, where he was reported to have held meetings with the German ambassador. When war broke out he travelled to Berlin in an attempt to negotiate German help to raise a nationalist army to drive the British from Ireland, and arrangements were made in London for his arrest on a charge of treason.

Casement's efforts to raise an Irish army from the prisoner of war camps in Germany failed so he returned to Ireland with the intention of starting a rebellion himself. However, the movements of the submarine which had carried him across the North Sea from Wilhelmshaven had been monitored by British Naval Intelligence and preparations had been made for his arrival with two companions in County Kerry, in April 1916. Casement was arrested and at his trial the following month he was found guilty of treason and sentenced to hang. There was a considerable outcry against the death penalty, but the protests were silenced by publication of Casement's very explicit diaries which showed him to be an active homosexual. Although some who regarded Casement as a martyr denounced the document as a politically inspired forgery, forensic tests conducted on pages held by the National Library in Dublin and the Home Office in London as recently as 1993 indicate that the five notorious 'Black Diaries' were authentic, a fact never disputed by Casement himself, who was led to the scaffold at Pentonville on 3

August 1916. In April 1994 all the documents were released to the Public Record Office.

The Casement Diaries (1910)

November 23rd. A hot day steaming past Peruvian chacras all day. Some good ones like Manoel Lomas'. Saw mills. River rising. Read Johnston's 'Negro in the New World'. Very good. After dinner spoke to steward Indian Cholo about frejot and he got some for me and then another thing. It was huge and he wanted awfully. He stood for hours till bed time and turned in under table – also small pantry engineer's youth and pilot's apprentice too – all up – till midnight and then at Yaguras and saw two Yaguras Indians in their strange garb. On at 1 a.m. after wood and palms at Yaguras. Three Yaguras Indians on board I think. Steward's Cholo very nice, smiled and fingered and hitched up to show.

November 24th. Due at Iquitos today, will it be peace or war? Gave small boy Victor Tizon 25/P. Very rainy morning. Cleaning brass work. Cholo steward did mine and Captain's and showed it again, huge and stiff and laughed. Smiled lovingly. Got cheques ready for Iquitos. All hands cleaning up. Engineer says we shall be in Iquitos by nightfall. I doubt it greatly. At earliest by p.m. or probably midnight. Slept better last night, but for an attack of gastritis coming on as in Para. Stopped for wood, etc., at Marupa, opposite mouth of the Napo and at 3 on again. Very hot. Nice Indians at Marupa. Many small chacras. Passed mouth of Napo at 3.30 and slowed down and cannot get to Iquitos tonight in time for landing. It is 8 hours steaming from Napo. Will be there in morning. Steward showed enormous exposure after dinner – stiff down left thigh. Then he went below and came up at St Thereza where 'Eliza' launch was and leant on gunwale with huge erection about 8 inches. Guerrido watching. I wanted awfully.

November 25th. Gave engineer's small boy 2$, and steward. Cluma $1. Asked my engineer his name, Ignacio Torres he said, and I asked him to come to Cazes' house. Arr. Iquitos at 7 a.m. On shore to Cazes' and then to barbers with Aredomi and Omarino. Met Sub-Prefect there who gave me warm welcome and told me an 'Auto' had been opened and all was to be investigated! Cazes said the Judge from Lima is a fraud, that all is a sham! Visited Booth's and down to 'Atahualpa'. Dr of her, an Italian, gave me medicine. Saw Reigado and his Cholo sailors – all had been drunk and he put them in the hold, the brute, 'to sweat it out'. Saw Ignacio Torres on the beach looking at me. Visit from Prefect's ADC and also from Pablo Zumaeta, but I was out. Spent pleasant day and was very tired at nightfall. Lots of mosquitoes again I could not sleep well. I talked to Cazes till fairly late. I am very tired of the C's and Iquitos. 'Atahualpa' does not sail until 2nd or 3rd. I hope will catch 'Clement' at Manaos.

November 26th. Called on Prefect with Cazes – long interview from 10.15 to 11.40. Told him much and promised to send Bishop to him on Monday at 10. He says the Commission of Justice will sail next week. A Doctor goes too – and officers and soldiers. In Govt launch. Doubtless 'America' which is being filled already I see. He says they will punish as well as reform. Asked me for help to see that the Comisairio went straight when there. Heavy rain at 6.30. Went to dinner at Booth's and played bridge. Rain all time. On board 'Atahualpa' again and saw young Customs officers from Manaos – great and well indeed – only a boy, almost pure Indian too. Also fair-haired pilot boy, tall and nice, from Para. Took my room No. 1. 'Atahualpa' leaves only on 4 Nov. [*sic*]. Sunday next. Will miss 'Clement' at Manaos. She sails on 7th.

November 27th. Off on 'Manati', picnic to Tamshiako 25–30 miles upriver. Prefect and Lt Bravo and all. Pleasant day. Again told Prefect many things of Putumayo. Saw Indian cook boy on 'Inca' enormous, lying down and pulled often. Huge and thick, lad 17. Also Ignacio Torres told him come 8 a.m. tomorrow. Told Pinteiro come too. Told Bishop get Lewis.

November 28th. Heavy rain all night and this morning, pouring. 9.30: no Bishop – no Ignacio, no Pinteiro and no Lewis! What is up? Ignacio Torres came at 10 clean and nice. Gave him a £1 and a portfolio for Captain Reigado – asked him to return the cover. He has not been to Brazil – many from Iquitos in bare feet. Gets £3 per month. Bishop late sent to Prefect at 10.30 only. He returned at 11.15 had told him everything (in 30 minutes!) and I saw John Brown and S. Lewis and will send them tomorrow. Saw Ignacio Torres below at 2.30 looking for me with my portfolio. J. Clark with him. Door shut so he went on to the office poor boy. I should like to take him too. Saw him later when Cazes and he said he was coming at 8 a.m. tomorrow and then saw him at band. Also saw Viacarra who smiled at me again and again and looked very nice. He was talking to Bishop. Manoel Lomas the pilot stood me a drink of ginger ale and begged me to visit Punchana to see him. Regretted church not here in Iquitos. Played bridge with Cazes and Harrison and walked with latter till 11.30.

Fireworks. Cazes says Judge Valcarel is well spoken of locally as honest.

November 29th. Expect Ignacio this morning – am on the lookout for him. He came at 8.10 with my portfolio and I sent him for cigarettes. He brought wrong kind and I gave him 28/- and patted him on back and said [undeciph.] and he and Lomas today. He left at 8.20. Last time of meeting probably. Will go to Manoel Lomas today. Expect Jermias Gusman this morning to send to Prefect. He came at 10 and I sent him along with Brown and Lewis. Prefect not in. Told by orderlies to come in three hours. They went all three at 1 to 3 and waited but Prefect could not see them and told them to come tomorrow at 10. I walked to Booth's and on to Punchana and to Manoel Lomas' house and then talked to Vatan about things. He said my coming was a blessing to all (not only to Putumayo, but to the whole Department). That the Prefect had acted in a very bad way over this Dutch Expedition and that if it was not for my official position I'd have been shot in the bush; and now they are afraid of me and my evidence and would do something. Walked after dinner to Booth's house and then with Harrison to Square. Walked round it. Many beautiful types Indian and Cholo. Saw Ignacio at merry-go-round and pulled. He smiled and approached. Another Cholo with him. Waited till 10 p.m. and then home to bed.

November 30th. Saw 'Liberal' Cholo sailors going home at 5.30, all smiled. Wrote to Vice-Consul at Manaos to send by 'Clement' the 7 Barbados men who wish to be repatriated – sent for John Brown to go to Prefect and Lewis and Gusman. They all went as far as I know at 10 a.m. but have not seen one of them since. They are lazy swine. Lent J. Clark £3. Saw Vatan again and asked him for Memo on the Dutch Expedition. Went on 'Atahualpa' to lunch. Afterwards back to the house in atrocious heat. Called on Mrs Prefect and told her a good deal of Putumayo. Heavy rain at 6.30 all night. Spoiled all attempt at going to cinematograph at Alhambra. Walked round Square with Mr and Mrs Cazes. Atrocious dinner! Played dummy bridge, a very stupid party. I am as sick of the Cazes as a man can be! and of Iquitos. No sign of Bishop since this morning. I will pay him off tomorrow and finish with him. The 'Rio Mar' left for Manaos with Phillips and J. Clark. I wrote down twice to Manaos about the men there.

December 1st. I fear the 'Atahualpa' will not sail until Monday 5th, certainly not till Sunday 4th. Huge erection Indian boy at C. Hernandez came at 3 to 4, a whole hour. Up at 5.30 and out for coffee. All closed at 7.

Fingered and pulled. Back to tea and out with Booth's at 7.35 again. River risen 7 feet since 'Atahualpa' arr. on 13th. It is now 62 feet, was 48 feet when we were here – a rise of 14 feet since September 6th or 10th. Its highest is about 80 feet, but no-one seems to keep any record. A lazy shiftless lot. Went to Booth's to meet all the Barbados men. Only two came and I sent them to Booth's office to get work. Walked to 'Morona Cocha' with 'Wags'. Very muddy indeed. Letter from Simon Pisango against Captain, in 'Loreto Comercial' of 30th. With Brown in afternoon and he with me to Bella Vista and then Alhambra to cine. Pablo Moronez came in and lots of Indians and peones, splendid chaps, and Cholo soldiers. Back at 11.30 in rain. Brown told me of Lt Bravo's estimate of the Judge Valcarel as a man who could be bribed. Brown says the Indians are all treated badly and tells of the killing of Valdemiro Rodriguez on 'Madre di Dios' by 8 Indians only a month ago. The news came first from the Indians themselves who talked of it on the Plata. No sign of Ignacio Torres since Tuesday night, not a glimpse. Fear he has gone in launch. Saw 'Julio' in white pants and shirt at Alhambra, splendid stern.

December 2nd. Heavy rain in night and all y'day afternoon and it will quite spoil the discharge of 'Atahualpa'. Saw Julio at Pinto Hers., gave cigarettes. He said 'Muchas gracias.' Enormous limbs and it stiff on right side feeling it and holding it down in his pocket. Saw Huge on Malecon. Looked everywhere for Ignacio. No sign anywhere. Very sad. Gusman not got Sub-Prefect. Saw Gusman at 10 a.m. waiting for Prefect with elderly Indian woman. Prefect 'too busy' again, Bishop tells me! At 5 p.m. Gusman was told to come at 3 p.m. This is Friday and he was first sent on Tuesday! To Booth's with Brown, saw 'Julio' again at store and asked him come to Punchana. He said 'Vamos' but did not follow far. He asked when I was going to Manaos. Saw some great big stiff ones today on Cholos. Two huge erections, and then from boys at 5 on seat in front, and then lovely type in pink shirt and blue trousers and green hat, and later in Square with 'Wags' the same who looked and longed and got huge on left. To Alhambra with Cazes at 9.30 seeing many types and 'Julio' in white again in a box. Met outside and asked him come Punchana tomorrow. He said 'Vamos' and asked where to meet, I said at 10 a.m. but he probably did not understand.

Norman Baillie-Stewart

I have heard the view that I was lucky to get off with five
years' imprisonment when my so-called 'fellow-travellers',
William Joyce and John Amery, were both hanged.

The detention of Lieutenant Norman Baillie-Stewart, a Seaforth Highlander, in the Tower of London after his arrest in March 1933 caused a sensation in England and prompted questions in the Commons to the Secretary of State for War, Duff Cooper. Baillie-Stewart was charged with having supplied military secrets to a German contact and upon his conviction by a court-martial he was sentenced to five years' imprisonment. After his release in August 1937 he travelled to Berlin where he took German citizenship and where he remained for most of the war. In May 1945 he was arrested for a second time and he received a further prison sentence for having aided the enemy. After his release, in May 1949, he moved to Dublin where he adopted a new identity, that of Patrick Stewart, and wrote a highly personal account of his experiences, *The Officer in the Tower*. He married a shop assistant in 1950 and had two children. He died in June 1966, only a few weeks after he had completed his book, and according to his ghost-writer, 'he wanted to absolve his children from the stigma that had haunted him for more than thirty years – the stigma of a "traitor" '.

Like Casement, who had toured internment camps in Germany in 1914 to recruit volunteers to start a rebellion in Ireland, Baillie-Stewart had been one of a small band of renegades who had supported the Nazis and either had contributed to anti-British propaganda or had persuaded British detainees to join the Legion of St George, the *Britische Freikorps* branch of the SS. Its ragtag membership was rounded up after the German surrender and its leading recruiters, William Joyce and John Amery, were hanged at Wandsworth. Here he disputes that he was ever guilty of treason, an allegation that apparently few were willing to challenge in the libel courts.

The Officer in the Tower

In passing references to me at least six British writers have stated that I was guilty of treason. It was much against my will that I had to take court actions against them and I won every time without even having to go into court personally. It was inevitable that these actions for libel had to be taken because if I had remained silent my silence would have been interpreted as having no answer to the defamation. Apart from the natural injustice of such a baseless accusation, I was never even charged in court with treason as I shall show later. Those who wrote about me never even took the trouble to look up the court records to find out exactly what happened.

Apart from defending my own character, I have always been most anxious that my children should not have to suffer any public odium for the alleged sins of their father.

That was the background to the hostility of fellow prisoners in Brixton and Wandsworth towards me. It was at times very real and frightening. I remember particularly in Wandsworth being offered cigarettes quite often by a prisoner who, I suspected, was trying to get me into trouble with the 'screws'. I refused his offers. I remember one big, hefty prisoner from the north of Scotland who became friendly with me and confided that two or three of them had been told by a hostile 'screw' to beat me up. It was just after this incident that a principal officer in Wandsworth called me into his office and said, 'I have been keeping a special watch on you because there is a plot to beat you up. Some of my staff are not exactly friendly towards you but while you are under my care you will not be beaten up.' I thanked him and left.

I made a point of associating with the few German prisoners of war in Wandsworth and, as time passed, the hostility towards me died down.

Usually I was exercised around the hospital yard alone, but on occasions, when there was a shortage of warders, another prisoner was exercised with me. When this happened my companion would be one of two Polish murderers, or a man called 'Russian Robert'. On one day it would be one of these murderers and on the next day the other. Since the two murderers entertained a murderous hatred for each other they were never allowed anywhere near each other. Both were subsequently hanged when I was in Wandsworth Prison. The smaller of the two Poles occupied the cell next door to me at Brixton. Sometimes, if I started to whistle a Hungarian tune, the Pole would take it up. He would then whistle his heart out – he could whistle well – until some clod-hopping warder would come along and ask him roughly and facetiously if his canary wanted any bird-seed. If this didn't work he would be told to stop his bloody row. The Pole knew that he was doomed, and whistling seemed to mean a lot to him.

John Amery was in another hospital cell of Brixton Prison when I was there. His cell was actually in another wing, but I had to go to that wing in order to fetch water and to have a bath. Amery's cell was almost opposite to the bathroom recess and his door, unlike mine, was never closed. Instead, the barred iron gate was closed on Amery. He could see through and be seen. And Amery and I were, therefore, able to snatch brief conversations.

Amery was indignant about my treatment. 'They're swinging it on you,' he said. He then described how, when a prisoner of the British in Italy, he had spoken to an MI5 man who had stated: 'We can't get Baillie-Stewart; he has been too clever for us. He is a German citizen.'

I always found Amery surprisingly optimistic and cheerful and I was even able to speak to him on the evening before he went up to the Old Bailey to plead guilty and literally to ask for death. At that time he had already made his decision to plead guilty. He laughed freely and seemed almost exalted. He had indeed made a noble – and perhaps wise – decision, and the reason for this was, as he whispered to me through the prison bars in Brixton, that efforts to provide him with a faked Spanish passport had failed. In the circumstances, John Amery died with immense courage.

Joyce had previously occupied the cell in which Amery was kept. I heard many stories about him from the warders, some of whom hated him and teased him without restraint.

The cell occupied successively by Joyce and Amery was an unlucky one. Three occupants of it were sentenced to death one after the other. The third to be sentenced – a half-German who had served in the Waffen SS – was later reprieved.

I was nearly three months awaiting trial in Brixton Prison, and it was nearly nine months since I was arrested in Austria, before I stepped into the same dock in Room No. 1 of the London Central Criminal Court in which William Joyce had been sentenced to death. Joyce was executed on 3rd January 1946 and I appeared in court exactly a week later. The main reason for the long delay from the time Joyce was sentenced until his hanging was due to his appeals. My trial was accordingly delayed because of the similarity between Joyce's case and my own and I was able to follow the legal arguments in the Joyce trial and the appeals with burning interest because my own life might depend on similar submissions.

As the day of the court appearance drew nearer I got into a panic because of the apparent inaction and failure even to produce the bricks needed to build up the defence. Then, about three weeks before the day fixed for the trial, Mr Kenwright came to see me in Brixton. He had, he said, just seen MI5 and had come from them with a 'proposition' which he wanted to lay before me.

I enquired what the proposition was and was told that the prosecution were prepared to drop the capital and treason charge, on one condition.

'That condition,' Mr Kenwright replied to my question, 'is that you agree to plead guilty to having "aided the enemy" under the Emergency Defence Regulations of 1939.'

I was stunned. 'But this is blackmail; it is putting a pistol to my head,' I protested.

Mr Kenwright shrugged his shoulders. 'Those are the terms,' he said. 'I would advise you to accept. If you fight the treason charges you will go down, and you know what that means – the hangman's rope. Any British jury would be prejudiced against you, and you wouldn't stand a chance.'

'And what if I accept?' I asked.

'You will get five years,' was the simple answer.

I was utterly stunned; first of all the threat under penalty of death and then the price demanded.

I renewed my protest but Mr Kenwright cut me short by informing me that I had been given forty-eight hours in which to come to a decision in the matter. I was to let him have an answer in a guarded, but unmistakable, form of letter. I was also warned by Mr Kenwright that I was to be most careful not to speak to anybody on the subject. If it got out to the Press, he stressed, there would be a lot of trouble and everything might be spoiled.

Mr Kenwright put the proposition to me in such a way that I was led to believe that the prosecution were doing me a great and unusual favour. He urged me to accept, stressing the alternative – hanging if convicted.

Utterly crushed at this new turn in the affair, I told Mr Kenwright that I had no choice but to accept – death being the only foreseeable alternative. He added that he would confirm acceptance in writing, as directed.

Immediately I returned to my cell I rang the bell and asked that the Chaplain should be informed that I wished to see him as soon as possible. The matter was urgent, I told the warder who answered the bell.

Mr Kenwright had warned me not to speak to anybody about the proposition that had been made, but I did not regard a Catholic priest as 'anybody'. I had no one to whom I could turn for advice and had no visitors. The Catholic priest is in most cases a man to whom one can turn at any moment of doubt and trouble in one's life. I decided to turn to him.

Within a short while, Father Vincent Ryan arrived and I wasted no time in telling him of the interview with Mr Kenwright and the proposition that had been made. I also told him of the prearranged sentence of five years which I was to receive on accepting the terms.

Father Ryan was appalled.

'But what am I to do?' I asked. 'I have to accept or refuse the proposition by letter within forty-eight hours.'

Father Ryan shook his head again. 'Choose the lesser evil,' he advised after a moment's thought. 'What other choice have you?'

Subsequent events indicated that some such behind-the-scenes 'arrangement' had been made before I entered the Old Bailey to stand my trial – or rather to hear the sentence.

P. G. Wodehouse

In the desperate circumstances of the time, it was excusable to
be angry at what Wodehouse did, but to go on denouncing him three
or four years later – and more, to let an impression remain that
he acted with conscious treachery – is not excusable.
George Orwell

The outcry that followed P. G. Wodehouse's broadcast on German radio in June 1941 was orchestrated by Duff Cooper MP, then Minister of Information in Churchill's war cabinet. Although very few people heard the original talks, all five written by Wodehouse himself and entitled *How to Be an Internee in Your Spare Time without Previous Training*, the publicity generated by the protestors ensured that his public in America and Britain was outraged.

Wodehouse had been living at his villa in Le Touquet when war broke out, and he and his wife Ethel had attempted to return to London by car when the Germans invaded, but they had broken down. Obligingly, the RAF had offered the bestselling author a single seat on an aircraft, but he had declined because there was no room for his wife or his dogs. Instead Wodehouse spent three months under German occupation, which was not entirely disagreeable. He was obliged to report once a day to the local *Kommandantur*, but this was no inconvenience as Wodehouse enjoyed the walk. However, in July 1940 he was informed that all British citizens were to be interned, and he was placed on a bus and driven to Loos prison.

By international convention enemy aliens aged sixty were eligible for repatriation but Wodehouse, being a few months short of fifty-nine, was interned at an ancient fortress near the Belgian town of Huy. Eventually he was transferred to Poland, to a commandeered lunatic asylum in Tost, Upper Silesia, where he remained for nine months until June 1941 when, without explanation, he was moved to the Adlon Hotel in Berlin. This luxurious establishment was reserved for the use of guests of the German Foreign Ministry, and Wodehouse's release from Tost, where he was reunited with Ethel who had remained in France, was odd for there was still a further four months before his sixtieth birthday. Equally difficult to explain was his decision, within a few days of taking up residence in the Adlon, to give a series of talks on the radio.

The talks were intended to be entertaining and humorous, and so they were, narrated in typical Wodehousian style, but this very act of collaboration, rather

41

than the content, caused the novelist to be denounced as a traitor. William Connor, who wrote the Cassandra column in the *Daily Mirror*, railed against Wodehouse on the BBC, and indignant letters were published by *The Times* from A. A. Milne, among many others. He was expelled by his London club, the Beefsteak, Oxford University was petitioned to rescind his honorary degree, and his beloved old school, Dulwich College, removed his name from its roll of honour.

Wodehouse himself could not understand what offence he had caused, and assured his friends that his loyalty to Britain was never in doubt. Late in 1943 Wodehouse and his wife were moved to Paris where they were installed in the Hotel Bristol, and he was living there when he was visited by Malcolm Muggeridge on behalf of the British authorities.

The task of dealing with Wodehouse and what he himself would subsequently refer to as his 'indiscretion' had been assigned to Colonel A. G. Trevor Wilson, a senior SIS officer who before the war had been a bank manager in France. Trevor Wilson delegated the matter to his subordinate, Malcolm Muggeridge, who was a great admirer of Wodehouse, and was not unsympathetic to his cause. He spent hours with the author, dissecting every detail of his period in German hands, and concluded that Wodehouse had been foolish, but not a traitor. He established that Wodehouse's release from Tost had come about as a result of pleas from influential American friends in Berlin, and not some discreditable pact in which a degree of freedom was granted in return for the broadcasts. Another allegation, without foundation, was the charge that a bargain had been made to allow his wife to join him in Berlin after the last broadcast. Muggeridge's verdict was later endorsed by the distinguished barrister (Sir) Edward Cussen who, on behalf of MI5, interrogated Wodehouse at length, completed a detailed report and advised the author not to return to England. He was, however, taken into custody briefly by the French police in November, and after four days moved to a maternity hospital, but was released without charge after Muggeridge intervened. Early the following year the Foreign Secretary, Sir Anthony Eden, announced in London in response to questions tabled by Quintin Hogg MP that Wodehouse would not face charges, and George Orwell published an essay, 'In Defence of P. G. Wodehouse', having been introduced to the creator of Wooster, Jeeves and Barmy Fotheringay-Phipps, in Paris by Muggeridge. Wodehouse moved to St-Germain-en-Laye, and in 1947 took up residence in New York, later moving to Long Island.

Wodehouse's genius was eventually to receive official recognition in the New Year's honours list of January 1975 when, aged ninety-four, he was awarded a knighthood. Barely six weeks later, he was dead. This passage from his third radio broadcast gives an idea of the offence he committed that denied him so much for so long.

The Berlin Broadcasts

THIRD BROADCAST

In the first of these talks on How To Be An Internee In Your Spare Time Without Previous Training, I mentioned that one drawback to starting on a journey from an internee's viewpoint is that when he moves from spot to spot he never knows where he is going. Another is that when he has to do it in company with a large mob of his fellows, he cannot hope for anything resembling travel *de luxe*. We had started from Paris Plage a little band of thirteen. Forty-four of us left Loos Prison. By the time the train finally got under way we numbered about eight hundred, for all though the day vans had been rolling up, bringing fresh additions to the chain gang.

Our destination, we discovered when we got there, was Liège, where we were to be put up in the barracks, and we made the nineteen-hour trip in those '*Quarante Hommes, Huit Chevaux*' things . . . in other words, cattle trucks.

I had sometimes seen these on sidings in times of peace and had wondered what it would be like to be one of the Quarante Hommes. I now found out, and the answer, as I had rather suspected, is that it is not so good. Eight horses, if they had stunted their growth by cigarette smoking as foals, might manage to make themselves fairly comfortable in one of these cross-country loose boxes, but forty men are cramped, especially if they are fifty men, as we were. I suppose a merciful oblivion comes over a sardine before it is wedged into the tin, but if it could feel, I know now just how it would feel.

Every time I stretched my legs during the night, I kicked some poor human waif. This would not have mattered so much, but every time the human waifs stretched their legs, they kicked me. Looking back on the trip, it is a constant mystery to me how we all got through without mishap. The floors of the trucks were full of holes, through which icy draughts whistled up and curled about our legs, and other icy draughts whistled down from the roof and played about our heads, and we were all men in the middle and late fifties. Yet nobody seemed to get pneumonia or even develop lumbago. I suppose there is a special Providence that watches over internees.

All through the next morning and well into the afternoon we lurched and heaved through Belgium until, agreeably surprised to find that we really had arrived somewhere, we reached Liège. Conducted by SS men, we tramped for miles up what must be one of the steepest hills in Europe and came at last to the fort on the summit where the barracks are.

There we found an atmosphere of unpreparedness. It was as if one had got to a party too early. Everything was in confusion, particularly the arrangements for feeding us.

These had been entrusted to one of those sketchy thinkers, the sort of man who goes about looking surprised when errors and omissions are pointed out to him, and saying 'I never thought of that.' A dreamy, absent-minded chap, probably a poet, he had overlooked the fact that internees eat.

He must have had a bad moment when we all streamed into the barrack square and lined up, licking our lips. Here, it must suddenly have struck him like a blow, were eight hundred men who were going to live mostly on soup, and while he rather thought he knew where to lay his hands on a little soup, if he hunted around a bit, he had completely forgotten that you have to have something to put the stuff in.

'Golly, yes,' he said, when this was drawn to his attention. 'I see what you mean. One ought to have bowls or something, oughtn't one? I suppose they couldn't just go to the cauldrons and lap?'

No, we couldn't just go to the cauldrons and lap. For one thing, we would burn our tongues, and for another the quick swallowers would get more than their fair share. It was due to our own resourcefulness that the problem was finally solved. At the back of the barrack yard there was an enormous rubbish heap into which Belgian soldiers through the ages had been dumping old mess tins, cups, with bits chipped off them, bottles, kettles, and containers for motor oil. We dug these out, gave them a wash and brush up, and there we were.

I had the good fortune to secure one of the motor-oil containers. It added to the taste of the soup just that little something which the others hadn't got.

Liège bore the same resemblance to a regular Ilag, like the one we were eventually to settle down in at Tost, which a rough scenario does to a finished novel. There was a sort of rudimentary organisation. We were divided into dormitories, each with a Room Warden, but that was as far as it got.

The first thing we had to cope with on our arrival was the dirt, and that took some doing. There were alluvial deposits everywhere, and, of course, nothing was issued to us which would help us to tidy up. We just had to scrounge around for old pails and rags and brushes, those who had not managed to find any borrowing or stealing from those who had. Armed with these, we tackled the dormitories, then the corridors, and finally the *bonne bouche* – the latrines. And that, believe me, was something.

Materially, Liège was an improvement on Loos. We had beds and could get out into the fresh air, and the food was better. For breakfast we got two ladlefuls of imitation coffee and a slab of black bread. At eleven-thirty we had two ladlefuls of soup, with rice or potatoes in it. Supper at seven was the same as breakfast.

Parades took place at eight in the morning and eight in the evening, and as far as they were concerned I did not object to having to stand for fifty minutes or so, for they provided solid entertainment for the thoughtful mind.

You might think that fifty minutes was rather a long time for eight hundred men to get themselves counted; but you would have understood if you had seen us in action. I don't know why it was, but we could never get the knack of parading. We meant well, but we just didn't seem able to click. It was the same at Huy and in the early days at Tost, though there we never managed to reach quite the same heights of pure delirium. To catch us at our best you would have had to catch us at Liège.

The proceedings would begin with the Sergeant telling us to form fives, whereupon some of us would form fours, some sixes, and others eights. I think our idea was that the great thing was to form something promptly and zealously, without bothering about trivial technicalities. You could see that we were zealous by the way those who had formed sixes, when rebuked, immediately formed fours, while those who had formed fours instantly formed sixes. Nobody could accuse us of not trying to enter into the spirit of the thing.

At long last, we would manage to get into fives, and a very pretty picture we made, too. But was this the end? Far from it. It was not an end but a beginning. What happened was that old Bill in Row 20 would catch sight of old George in Row 42 and disorganise our whole formation by shuffling across to ask him if he had heard the one about the travelling salesman.

Time marches on. Presently Old Bill, having had a good laugh with Old George, decides to shuffle back, only to find that his place has been filled up like a hole by the rising tide. This puzzles him for a moment, but a solution soon presents itself. He forms up as the seventh man of a row, just behind Old Perce, who has been over chatting with Old Fred, and has just come back and lined up as number six. The Corporal would then begin to count.

He generally counted us about five times before he saw what was getting his figures wrong. When he did, he cut Bill and Perce out of the flock and chivvied them around for awhile, and after a good deal of shouting, order and symmetry were restored.

But was this the end? Again, no. The Corporal, assisted now by a French interpreter, walks the length of the ranks, counting. Then he walks back, still counting. Then he gets behind us and counts again. ('If I have enough money after this war is over,' said Internee Sandy Youl to me on one of these occasions – we were numbers seven and eight of our row of five – 'I am going to buy a German soldier and keep him in the garden and count him six times a day.')

Something seems to be wrong. There is a long stage wait. The Corporal and the interpreter have stepped aside and are talking to the Sergeant. The word goes round that we are one short, and people begin to ask 'Where's Old Joe?' It seems that nobody has seen him since breakfast, and we discuss the matter with animation. Can it be that Old Joe has escaped? Perhaps the gaoler's daughter smuggled him in a file in a meat pie?

No, here comes Old Joe, who has been having a quiet smoke at the other end of the yard. He comes strolling along with a cigarette hanging from his lower lip, and eyes us in an indulgent sort of way, as who should say 'Hullo, boys, playing soldiers? May I join in?' He is thoroughly cursed, in German by the Sergeant and Corporal, in French by the interpreter, and in English by us, and takes his place in the ranks.

The mathematicians among us now feel pretty hopeful. They figure it out that if we were one short before Old Joe's arrival, now that we are plus Old Joe we should come out exactly right. It looks as if at the most one more count from right to left, one more count from left to right and one more count from behind ought to do the trick.

Picture our chagrin and disappointment, accordingly, when we discover, after all this has happened, that we are now *six* short. That is to say, so far from gaining by Old Joe very decently consenting to join the parade, we have received a most serious set-back.

The Sergeant calls for another conference, a sort of General Meeting this time, for the Room Wardens are invited to attend it, and they all stand to one side with their heads together. We cannot hear what they are saying, but we can see the Sergeant's wide gesticulations, and we know that what he is telling the Board is that this looks like funny business to *him*.

'Don't tell me,' he says, 'that six internees can just vanish into thin air.'

'Seven,' says the Corporal with a deferential cough.

The Sergeant dashes back with popping eyes and skims along the ranks. 'You'll think me cuckoo,' he says, coming back, 'but I believe it's eight.'

'Or, rather, nine,' says the Corporal, who, too, has not been idle. 'May I make a suggestion?'

'Do, Heinrich. One welcomes the fresh mind.'

'Let's count 'em,' says the Corporal.

So we are counted again and the official score is issued. Eight short is the figure.

'Did you ever see the Indian rope trick?' asked the Corporal, making conversation to bridge over an awkward pause. But the Sergeant is not listening. He is trying to think what to do, what to do. If we are going to melt away at this rate, he is saying to himself, it will not be long before he is down to his last internee. Eventually, he announces that we are to return to our dormitories, where the Room Wardens will check us up.

My dormitory is so anxious to please that it gets a large sheet of cardboard and writes on it in chalk the words:

ZWANZIG MÄNNER, STIMMT

which our linguist assures us means 'Twenty men, all present and correct,' and when the whistle blows for the renewal of the parade we exhibit this.

It doesn't get a smile out of Teacher, which is disappointing, for we feel that short of giving him a red apple we couldn't have done much more for him. After a lot more counting, just when the situation seems to be at a deadlock, with no hope of finding a formula, the interpreter, who has his inspired moments, says, 'How about the men in hospital?'

These prove to be eight in number, and we are dismissed. We have spent a pleasant and instructive fifty minutes and learned much about the Human Comedy.

It must have been a dream about these parades that made me wake the dormitory up in the small hours one night by laughing heartily in my sleep, for there was really nothing much else to laugh at in Liège barracks. It was a dull, depressing life. We had not yet begun to settle down, and the days seemed to stretch out endlessly. Nobody appeared to be taking any interest in us, and the feeling of being Orphans of the Storm began to weigh upon our spirits. We had the impression that the Germans didn't really want us, but couldn't quite bring themselves to throw us away.

Our chief solace was looking forward to meals. But even these were spoiled by the dreary preliminaries. They were served from large cauldrons outside the cookhouse at the far end of the barrack square, and we got them by lining up in a queue, the whole eight hundred of us, which meant the reverse of quick service for those at the tail end of the procession. It generally took about an hour for them to reach the trough, and one wondered what it would be like on a rainy day.

Fortunately, the rainy day never came. The weather was still fine when, a week after our arrival, we were once more put aboard vans and driven to the station, our destination being the Citadel of Huy, about twenty miles away. The journey took us six and a half hours, travelling as before in cattle trucks.

If somebody were to ask me whose quarters I would prefer to take over, those of French convicts or Belgian soldiers, I would find it hard to say. Belgian soldiers, though purer in their moral outlook and not so prone to draw improper pictures on the walls, make lots of work for their successors. It took us days to get Liège barracks spotless. And without wishing to be indelicate, I may say that until you have helped to clean out a Belgian soldiers' latrine, you ain't seen *nuttin'*.

If someone comes to me a few years from now and asks me what I did in the great war, I shall say 'I helped to clean out the latrine at Liège barracks.' And it is extremely probable that my interlocutor's reply will be: 'I thought as much,' for even now you can still get an occasional whiff, if the wind is in the right direction.

As the fellow said, You may break, you may shatter the vase if you will, but the scent of the roses will cling to it still.

Ronald Seth

In appearing to give my interrogators as much 'information' as they believed I could give, I have to be careful not to betray any important details about the organisation or its personalities.

A Cambridge graduate, and having worked as a lecturer before the war in the University of Tallinn, Ronald Seth was regarded, wrongly in his view, as an expert on Eastern Europe. Accordingly, in 1941 he was transferred from the Royal Air Force to Special Operations Executive and trained in parachute and sabotage techniques. His mission was to be dropped into Estonia in October 1942, but he was captured within hours of his landing and sentenced to death as a spy. His subsequent adventures, while in German custody, are described in his war memoirs *A Spy Has No Friends*, which he compiled after his release from German custody in April 1945.

Exactly what happened after his arrest is unknown, and the only record is Seth's own version. In his book he gives a reasonably plausible explanation for his appearance in Paris in November 1943 with official Luftwaffe identification papers and for the accusations made by several British ex-prisoners of war who denounced Seth as a Gestapo collaborator who had worked for their captors as a stool-pigeon. According to him he was imprisoned in Riga, and then Frankfurt, by the Gestapo, and then handed over to the Abwehr, which intended to send him back to England as a German spy. This plan apparently was vetoed by the Sicherheitsdienst in August 1944 and he was transferred to a transit camp, Stalag XIIA near Limburg, to report on the political opinions of the inmates. After just ten days he was transferred to a permanent camp, Oflag 79 at Brunswick, where he remained until January 1945 when Seth aroused the suspicions of the British officers who discovered a leakage of information to the guards. Diagnosed as a schizophrenic, Seth was withdrawn in March and escorted to Berlin to meet Heinrich Himmler and Walter Schellenberg, who suggested that he travel to Switzerland with a peace proposal for the Allies.

On the night of 11/12 April Seth crossed the Swiss frontier near Bludenz and the following day reported to the British military attaché in Berne. His extraordinary story was accepted and he was later flown to London for debriefing. After the war Seth was warned that he was likely to be prosecuted, but evidently he managed to persuade his interrogators of his innocence. Not only did he win his freedom, but he also recovered his back-pay from SOE for the period he had spent on what he had claimed was active service on the Continent.

Seth went on to write more than sixty books and, under the name Dr Roger Chartham, produced an advice column in a men's magazine and marketed a sex aid. He died in February 1985, aged seventy-three, having returned to Wiltshire from his retirement home in Malta. In this extract Seth recalls the moment he was told his execution was imminent.

A Spy Has No Friends

On December 21st I was taken down to the prison offices, where two German soldiers, a sergeant and a corporal were waiting for me. The sergeant spoke English with an accent he must have picked up within the sound of Bow bells. His friendliness was embarrassing as he took my fingerprints and measured and weighed me. I weighed eight stone thirteen pounds, which was a loss of three and a half stone in the two months since I had left England. I wondered what was the point of it all, unless I were being used as an experiment. I could see no harm in asking, but before he replied there was a pause. Then he said: 'They've told you, have they?'

'They've told me nothing,' I said.

The corporal asked in German what I wanted, and then if the sergeant intended to tell me.

'They didn't say not to,' the sergeant answered.

'Then tell him. It's kinder,' urged the other.

The sergeant suddenly became very busy with his papers.

'On Wednesday you are to be hanged,' he said at length. There was no feeling in me of weakness nor any recoil or fear, only a welling-up of anger.

'I'm to be hanged!' I exclaimed, my voice loud with rage. 'But I haven't had a trial!'

I knew that when a prisoner has been condemned the light is left burning in his cell throughout the night, so that the warders may be sure he does not cheat the gallows under cover of darkness. My light had never been out since long before Matsve Konjovalev had joined me, so I ought to have realised long ago that I was a condemned man; but the thought had never occurred to me because I had had no trial or any chance to speak in my own defence.

'I'm sorry, Captain,' the sergeant said, putting his hand on my shoulder. 'I never thought I should string up an Englishman. But if I refused they'd find someone else and string me up alongside you. But I'll see it's over quickly. That I can do. Don't hold it against me.'

'I understand,' I said.

Back in my cell my rage subsided, and I told myself that what was happening was really what I had been expecting. A trial would have done me no good. I had been taken in civilian clothes, so there was no defence. Now that I knew what was to happen, and what was more important, when it was to happen, a kind of serenity came upon me. I had before me forty hours of life: forty hours in which to make peace with God and myself.

As the time passed I found that I had no doubts at all about God's understanding of man's sins and weaknesses, and with this realisation my feelings of fear disappeared. I had no inclination to lobby my Maker, and most of my thoughts during these hours were not centred on God but on my family. Nor was my sleep disturbed. The routine of the prison ticked by. The so-called meals came round; inspection and roll-call took their usual turns; and when night came I slept until the bread-ration for our wing was delivered in the hour before reveille.

After I had woken it seemed hours before they came for me. I was still physically weak and walked a little unsteadily down the corridors and into the prison yard, where an escort of soldiers in steel helmets and greatcoats trailing almost on the ground was waiting for me. We paused at the desk, where one of the soldiers signed for my body, then he led me to the middle of the escort. An order was shouted and my last march to the Baltijaamplats began.

Dirty, frozen snow crunched underfoot. Tallinn looked more disconsolate and unhappy than ever and the people more cowed. Yet I noticed that the few men we met raised their hats as we passed and two women with shawls over their heads fell on their knees and crossed themselves. Their gestures of respect were gestures of defiance to their conquerors. One or two German soldiers whom we met looked away.

Where the Suur Patarei meets the Saadama tänav we were held up by a road-block. An ill-shod horse drawing a heavy cart had slipped and fallen between the shafts. While we stood waiting for the road to be cleared, a little lean and hungry dog came sniffing round my legs. The odour from my body had grown worse during the last weeks, and having taken one sniff, he sprang off, his tail between his legs, and sat down on the edge of the pavement, baying at Death.

We now quickened our pace to make up for the time we had lost, and the hands of the station clock stood at three minutes to ten as we came into the square; a perfect example of German timing. The clock struck ten, and it quickly became obvious that the schedule had been upset. A train ran into the station, and presently people began to emerge into the square. Again I noticed the men lifting their hats and one or two German officers saluted; but they did not stop.

Slowly the seconds dragged by. I began to shiver with cold – cold that brought with it the beginning of fear, which began to lick with little flames at my heart.

I glanced round, stamping my feet in a pitiful attempt to stop my shivering, and for the first time noticed the scaffold, a platform raised on trestles with uprights at each end supporting a cross-bar; from the middle of this bar dangled a rope at the end of which was a noose. I calculated that the platform was about three and a half feet above the ground and about five feet wide. From beneath the platform, on the right-hand side, protruded a metal bar.

My glance went back to the clock. We had been waiting six minutes, for the hands now stood at three minutes past ten. Never has time passed more slowly for me. I began to wish that it could all be got over quickly. Unless something happened soon I might make an exhibition of myself not at all in the best traditions of the English martyrs.

Presently a car hooted impatiently, and a few seconds later drove rapidly into the square and drew up. From it emerged in great haste a Wehrmacht captain and my two acquaintances, the executioner and his assistant. The whole scene sprang to life, and incongruously the RAF aphorism, 'Wait and then hustle', passed through my mind. I remember feeling cheered by the knowledge that in the super-organised German Army the same thing applied.

The captain and the others rapped out orders in quick succession. I was lifted onto the platform and the sergeant pinioned my arms, while the corporal strapped my feet.

'I don't like this, captain,' said the sergeant, who kept up a sort of running commentary. 'Sorry I've got to do it. But it won't hurt. It'll be over before . . .'

He held a bandage to my eyes.

I shook my head. 'Is that necessary?'

'Rather see where you're going, eh? OK.'

Down in the snow a voice was reciting in badly spoken Estonian. I saw that a little crowd had gathered a few yards beyond the ring of soldiers round the scaffold, as though compelled by curiosity to stand and watch. The sergeant had some difficulty in fixing the noose over my head because I had not had a haircut since the beginning of October. Then he jumped down from the platform.

I watched him march smartly up to the captain and salute, then heard him shout at the full expansion of his lungs: '*Alles in Ordnung!*'

Even now I don't think I had any real belief that in a very few seconds I should be dead. I was still perfectly well aware of what was going on. Another order was shouted. The escort and guards clicked their heels loudly and made a noise with their rifles. I could feel the rope chafing the skin of my throat as my pinioned body swayed. The captain turned about and faced me squarely. His face was grim and his bearing correct and soldierly as he saluted me. Simultaneously with his hand touching his cap, I heard a clatter of metal. The trap on which I was standing suddenly gave beneath my feet, fell a few inches and then stuck.

I heard shouts, and saw blurred figures running hither and thither. Then I fell forward. The rope tightened behind my ears, and my eyes were filled with bright lights and then darkness.

It was early in the afternoon when I came to and found myself back in Cell 13. My neck was stiff and bruised. I eased myself off the bed and with my legs trembling violently, I staggered to the door and knocked. The warder lowered the hatch and peered through.

'What's happening?' I asked.

'I know nothing,' he answered. 'But don't worry.'

I tried to draw him out, but could get nothing more from him.

Someone had been thoughtful enough to fill my bowl with soup, and it now stood on the cupboard top, cold and uninviting, a thin watery liquid with a leaf or two of sour cabbage floating in it. Nevertheless, I drank it and began to feel slightly refreshed.

I lay down on the bed again, believing that I was sufficiently an object of curiosity to flout the rules. It occurred to me that my position must be unique, for I must surely be the only German victim who had cheated the gallows at the very last second. The warder seemed to agree with me, for though he was continually lowering the hatch and peering in, he made no attempt to move me from the bed.

It was cold in the cell, and I began to shake all over, partly from the shock and partly because of the temperature. So I rolled myself up like a dog in my stinking blanket, and when I had got over my trembling I fell asleep.

When I awoke the light was on. So soundly had I slept that I had not even heard them come in to fix the blackout. On the table were four small frost-blackened potatoes and a mug of water that had a layer of ice on it.

I was now less shaky when I stood up, and as I perched on the stool and peeled the potatoes, the hatch was lowered and I saw the face of the young night warder regarding me.

'You all right?' he whispered.

'Yes, thanks,' I said. 'Come in.'

He unlocked the door quietly and came in, pulling it to behind him. Except for the warder on the floor above, who would most probably be dozing, there was little chance of our being disturbed, for the noise of the door leading into the other wing would give sufficient warning.

'Have you heard what happened?' I asked.

'Only rumours. Still, there must be some truth in them. They put the scaffold up yesterday afternoon and left a guard on it, but they drank some vodka during the night, to warm themselves up, and didn't keep a proper watch. Some of our people screwed a couple of slats underneath the trap, so when it was supposed to fall it just stuck. When the crowd saw there was something gone wrong this morning they began jeering and the officer thought it was going to be a demonstration and they might try to rescue you, so he brought you back to prison. You were to be a warning to us not to trust in the Third Possibility – what we're not supposed to talk about. You were to be left hanging over the holidays.'

'And what's to happen now?' I asked.

'One of our old men says they won't try again till the New Year holiday.'

Alexander Foote

The loyalty of a Party member lies primarily
with the Party and secondarily with his country.

Born in Kirkdale, Liverpool in 1905, Allan Foote (he called himself Alexander) was discharged from the Royal Air Force because of his failure to declare his membership of the Communist Party of Great Britain. He chose to fight in Spain and in December 1936 he joined the British battalion of the International Brigade. Upon his return to London in September 1938 he was recruited as a courier by an experienced GRU agent, Brigitte Kuczynski, who was then living in St John's Wood. His first assignment was to travel to Geneva and make contact with a woman in the main post office, whom he subsequently learned was Ursula Kuczynski, his recruiter's sister. She sent him on a mission to Munich where he fell in love with a beautiful KDP activist who was brutally beaten by the Gestapo and later died in a concentration camp.

When Foote returned to Switzerland he was trained as a wireless operator and, until his arrest by the Bundespolizei in November 1943, he managed the radio communications for an extensive GRU network based in Lausanne but with contacts in Italy, France and Germany. Foote was released from gaol by the Swiss in September 1944 and he reported to the Soviet military mission in Paris which arranged for him to be flown to Moscow. Here he underwent a lengthy period of debriefing and training in preparation for a new appointment as a Soviet illegal in the United States. He was intended to travel to America via Germany and Argentina but when he arrived in Berlin in March 1947 he surrendered to the British authorities. His subsequent interrogation by MI5 formed the basis of his 1949 autobiography, *Handbook for Spies*, which was written largely by his inquisitor, Courtney Young.

On the basis of Foote's evidence the Security Service embarked upon a long investigation of Soviet spy-rings in Britain but although Ursula Kuczynski, who had moved from Switzerland to Oxfordshire, was interviewed, no one was arrested or charged with offences. Nevertheless, Foote was regarded as a traitor by his former comrades and he provided MI5 with a wealth of detail about Soviet espionage.

When Foote had outlived his usefulness as a source on the GRU he found a job in the Ministry of Agriculture and Fisheries, and lived in a small residential hotel in north London until his death in August 1956. In this extract from his memoirs

Foote describes how he felt after his final transformation, from an experienced illegal agent entrusted with a clandestine assignment in America to that of an obscure civil servant in London.

Handbook for Spies

Now that it is all over and I am once again a private citizen in England it is possible to look back and sum up those ten years of my life. I joined the International Brigade and fought in Spain partly because of a love of adventure and partly because I felt that the cause was right. I worked for the Red Army Intelligence partly from a love of adventure and partly because I was working against Fascism and the enemies of democracy. I left the service of the Russians because I realised that to continue working would be to work against freedom and for dictatorship.

I can look back on these ten years with no regrets. The fight in Spain failed because the enemies of the Republic were too strong and their friends too weak or too unwilling to realise that this was yet another step in the Nazi programme for world domination. The war against Fascism was successful because all the enemies of Fascism combined together in an all-out effort, and my efforts with the Soviet spy ring in Switzerland contributed in some degree to the ultimate defeat of the Third Reich. With the war over and Fascism defeated and in ruins, it was obvious to me that a new danger to democracy had taken its place in the shape of Soviet Russia. The danger had been there all along, but with the defeat of Germany and Japan, Soviet Russia remained alone as the greatest threat to the peace of the world. As long as the Western democracies and Russia were fighting a common enemy, so long would Russia co-operate with the democracies, and so long was it possible to justify working for Russia against the common enemy. As soon as that frail bond of a common purpose was shattered, then the Russian desire for 'security', which bears a startling resemblance to what was called before the war 'Nazi aggression', came to the fore, and its sequel in Eastern Europe is now history. To have continued after the war to act as a spy for Soviet Russia would have been to be a traitor to those principles for which I and many others fought, and many died, in Spain. When I went to Spain and during the war when I saw the magnificent way in which the Russians fought to save their fatherland it was possible still to believe in the ideas and ideals of Communism. After a period in Russia, and leisure to think back on the actions of Soviet diplomacy and politics in the past, it might have been possible to remain a theoretical Communist, but I found it quite impossible to believe in Communism as practised in Russia today.

The Nazis have been described, quite rightly so, and equally rightly held up to the execration of the world, as ruthless exponents of 'Realpolitik' and 'Machtpolitik'. Russia has nothing to learn from Nazi Germany in this respect. The tactical methods of the Kremlin change with bewildering frequency and speed, the political sails trimmed to suit the prevailing breeze. The strategic aim remains steadily and unwaveringly the same. That aim has been as clearly described by Stalin as was the aim of National Socialism in *Mein Kampf*. The Comintern may be officially dead, but the ghost clothes itself, as soon as peace comes, in the flesh of the Cominform. The ultimate aim is still to spread Communism throughout the world. Such a spread means in effect, if successful, the spread of the power and control of Soviet Russia. It is only necessary to pick up a newspaper to see what that means – suppression of freedom of thought and speech, the power of the political police, purges, arrests, and oppression. The picture is tragically familiar.

I remember during the course of my political instruction in Moscow hearing the Nazis being described as sentimentalists and thus totally unfitted to carry out their desire for world domination. As an example of this sentimentality I was told that, in order to liquidate a few thousand Jews in Salonika they had to be transported halfway across Europe to Auschwitz, as the Wehrmacht refused to carry out executions on the spot. My instructor was interesting on the subject of the Jews, and showed to the full his Russian realism. He explained that the report of the Duke of Wellington on the defeat of Napoleon in Russia could be equally applied to Hitler. The Duke had pointed out that the failure of Napoleon to use the Jews as agents and go-betweens between his armies and the Russians had led to his failure to exploit the Russian territory that he had overrun. It was only the Russian Jew that was able to understand and manage the Russian peasant. Hitler had made a similar mistake in liquidating rather than using the Jewish population in the conquered Eastern territories. No horror was expressed at the ruthless extermination policy of the Nazis and the attendant horrors of the concentration camps and the gas chambers. It was merely coldly expressed as a statement of fact and as a proof of German stupidity.

It is not for me to speculate as to the future of relations between the West and Russia. I am neither a politician nor a crystal-gazer. It is also unnecessary for me to discourse at length on the merits or demerits of Communism in theory and in Russian practice. It is perhaps pertinent to point out, however, that I started in my civil war days believing that

Communism might well provide a solution to the ills of the world and ended by severing all connection with the Party and with Russia and retiring to the 'decadent democracy' of England. I could have remained in Russian service and might now be well established as an important agent in their network working against the West; that I did not and preferred the uncertainty of life in England is proof enough of my present feelings.

Cedric Belfrage

Now we have become accustomed to a person's loyalty being called into question if he proclaims that all men are brothers and acts on that principle.

Although Cedric Belfrage never concealed his Leftist sympathies, or his pre-war membership of the Communist Party of Great Britain, the suggestion that he had spied for the NKVD while working for British Intelligence was made only in August 1945 when Elizabeth Bentley described him to the FBI as having supplied secrets to a Soviet contact. As a former *Daily Express* journalist, his specialist field was propaganda, disseminated on behalf of the Political Warfare Executive, and at the end of hostilities he transferred to the British Control Commission for Germany as a press officer. However, while he was there MI5 learned that there had been a leak in BSC and, through the testimony of a defector, some details emerged of the source. He was described as having had access to classified information, and someone who had given a lecture on British surveillance techniques to a clandestine communist cell. According to a decrypted Soviet telegram, the spy's first name was either Cecil or Cedric, and he was a committed communist. Then a further clue emerged in some decrypted Soviet signals traffic which referred to his wife having recently published a cookbook. This matched Belfrage, and his service in BSC showed that he had once attended a lecture given by a Special Branch detective on keeping suspects under covert observation.

Bentley's confession to the FBI, encapsulated in her book *Out of Bondage*, covered her recruitment as a Soviet agent by an NKVD illegal, Jacob Golos, who became her lover. Golos had died of a heart attack in November 1943 and consequently Bentley had been asked by her Soviet handler to take over the network. The knowledge that she acquired proved enormously important and for the next decade she gave sworn testimony regarding her contacts, one of whom was Belfrage:

> In the summer of 1943 Yasha wanted to turn over to me a young Englishman who was then working for the British Intelligence Service. Cedric Belfrage had been a Party member in Britain and after coming to this country got in touch with V. J. Jerome, who in turn put Belfrage in touch with Yasha. For some

time Cedric had been turning over to us extremely valuable information from the files of the BIS, most of which I saw before it was relayed on to the Russians.

Bentley's 'Yasha' was actually Jacob Golos, who was convicted of being a Soviet agent, and V. J. Jerome was a leading member of the CPUSA. From the moment in 1950 when Belfrage was informed officially he was to be investigated by the FBI, to his eventual deportation five years later, Belfrage conducted a legal battle to remain in the United States. Despite Bentley's incriminating testimony, Belfrage was never charged because the offences he had committed against British interests had occurred in America. In 1948 he founded the Leftist *National Guardian*, the journal whose history he recounted in *Something to Guard*, and later wrote his autobiography, *They All Hold Swords*. Among his other books are *The Frightened Giant*, in which he described his departure from the United States, and *Seeds of Destruction*, a critique of the American postwar occupation of Germany.

In 1953 Belfrage was called to give evidence to the House Un-American Activities Committee and was identified by several witnesses as a leading communist and the organizer of an underground cell but he opted to move to Mexico, where he continued his journalism, and where he died in June 1991.

In this passage Belfrage rails against the FBI and the US Department of Justice, but carefully evades the charges made against him with such precision by Elizabeth Bentley.

The Frightened Giant

When Representative Velde and Senator McCarthy summoned me before their inquisitions, they began the job – on which tens of thousands of your and my dollars have now been spent – of tearing off my life veils that were never there. They made as if my life were mysterious and important. It is neither. I have lived politically in a goldfish bowl. How I came to my faith in socialism as the goal for every country today is on record, as the development of my love for America despite its faults is on record; and as my warm friendliness for the Soviet Union and all countries charting the socialist road – despite their faults – is on record.

Yet this menagerie of elected legislators and hired officials insists I have all sorts of cumbersome objects up my sleeve. First it seemed that I was 'charged' with being a member of an unpopular organization known as the Communist Party, credited by FBI chief J. Edgar Hoover with 25,000 members out of a 150 million population. Second, with trying to 'communize' the German press in 1945, when I recommended two or three frankly designated communist types – and dozens of socialists, Catholics and mild conservatives – for editorial licences under my army orders to find anti-nazi journalists. Third, it seemed I was on a list of 80 people listed by one Elizabeth Bentley as Russian 'spies' and 'couriers' (I was down as a 'courier'). Just for the record, I wrote as follows in the British Liberal daily *News Chronicle* after my session with Velde where I declined to discuss these matters:

'The correct answers would have been: (1) I am not, but have a perfect right to be if I choose; (2) I worked in Germany under precise directives from Gen. Eisenhower, whose lower US brass gave all the orders; (3) A federal grand jury questioned me for two days in 1948 (as Velde must have known, but did not mention) on these same Bentley statements; I answered every question put to me and that was that.'

Looking back over almost a decade of 'cold war', we can see that Washington's drive to turn the American course 180 degrees from peace to war and from tolerance to active bigotry has met with a frustrating blend of success and failure. To sum up briefly, it has brought the American horse close to the dark water of war and fascism but still can't get the horse to drink.

It has been effective in muddying the American melting-pot tradition of live and let live by the many-pronged onslaught upon 'communists' and 'communism'. These are words which not one American in 100 could define intelligently in the confusion deliberately created by the inquisitions, abetted by every organ of public information. The campaign to distort words has been the cold warriors' outstanding success.

The people show signs of wearying of the inquisitions; they do not get as excited as they are supposed to get when more 'communists' are 'revealed'; but they are still in a fog as to the real nature of the inquisitions with respect to American tradition and law, and they still subscribe by and large to the McCarthy concept of 'fifth-amendment communists'. Everywhere the question is still asked, wonderingly or angrily: 'Well, if he's innocent, why doesn't he say so? The fifth amendment to the Constitution protects a man against having to be a witness against himself. Why hide behind it if he isn't guilty of anything?'

The first answer is that in the American tradition there is nothing to be guilty or innocent of, as far as adhering to any political group or set of ideas is concerned. Nor can this be altered by any theory or charge that a given group 'advocates overthrow by force and violence'. The American tradition, plainly set forth by Jefferson and Lincoln and many more, is that among the people's rights is to overthrow a tyrannical government. Presumably, if the government is tyrannical it will take some bloodshed to overthrow it, as the American revolutionists found out. If the vast majority of the people do not think it tyrannical, as is now the case, it will not be possible to overthrow it. To suggest that the present government with its tremendous array of power can be overthrown by 25,000 communists with all the allies they can possibly muster, even supposing that is what they would like to do, is to enter the realm of fantasy.

But progressives are charged with more serious things before the inquisitions – for example, espionage or other activity for a foreign power – and they still invoke the Constitution in refusing to answer in their own defence. It is easy to lend superficial plausibility to such charges in the present state of the world, with one half of humanity moving on the tide of socialism and the other half resisting the tide. The formula is simple: You believe that if our society were more planned, it would be more just ('totalitarianism'), and that planned societies should be left in peace to demonstrate this if they can; Russia is 'totalitarian' and wants to be left in peace; therefore you are an agent of Russia. The picture of an 'agent' or 'spy' is filled in with the inquisitors' verbal propaganda tricks: X, who knows or has met Y, is described as 'contacting' or 'linked with' Y in a circle of acquaintance that becomes a 'cell' or 'apparatus'.

Why is it a lie to accuse the inquisitors' silent victims of 'hiding behind the Constitution'? The answer is another question: What is the Constitution? It did not happen casually, any more than the 40-hour work week happened casually. Men and women who suffered under old tyrannies fought and died for these precious things. The Constitution reflects the burning desire of men set on freedom to write a basic and unassailable code to end the abuses of religious and political inquisitions. The new American inquisitions of today – actually trials under the name of 'investigations' and 'hearings' in which due process of law is simply ignored – are an attempt to make Americans accept once more what their ancestors rejected and sought to make forevermore impossible.

The Constitution is the bill of goods which brought millions of people, including myself, here from other countries. To invoke its protection is to defend it not only for oneself but for everyone in America. If the courts will not always defend it, then the duty of the citizen – and still more of the foreign-born who consciously adopted it when they adopted the US – to do so is that much greater.

In his play of 17th-century Salem, 'The Crucible', Arthur Miller dramatized how completely an innocent person was – and would still be – at the inquisitors' mercy without these constitutional safeguards. If he denied consorting with the devil, he was hanged because he could not disprove the sworn testimony of another; if he admitted it, he was hanged anyway unless he denounced others – it didn't matter whom – who were also 'seen' in Beelzebub's company; and so the hangings and denunciations went on.

Today the punishment for denial has changed to a jail term for perjury; for admission without naming others, to a jail term for 'contempt'. For remaining silent the Salem punishment of being pressed to death beneath heavy stones has changed to consignment to an economic ghetto or, if you are an 'alien', deportation. The dilemmas remain the same. As to yourself, it is no more possible now to prove you are or were *not* a 'communist' or a 'spy' than it was then to prove you were *not* a 'witch'. As to others whose names will inevitably be brought in, you are not permitted to remain silent about them unless you remain silent about yourself.

The danger of citation for 'contempt', if you answer even one question in a given 'area' of enquiry and baulk at any other question in that 'area', leads to such fantastic situations as my own before the Velde committee: I could not tell the simple truth about my accuser Elizabeth Bentley, that I had never seen the woman in my life. Still more fantastic, I could not admit to being editor of the *Guardian*. Velde had prejudiced the issue in advance by calling the paper 'a propaganda arm of the Kremlin'. And had I replied, I would have opened the door to questions I could not legally refuse to answer, and hence to 'contempt' citation if I did refuse. He could have questioned me about conversations with the staff, demanded the subscriber lists and the names of those who help pay our printing deficits, and I could have been put on trial for withholding them. Of course contempt is a mild word for what one feels toward these committees; but offering oneself for a period of enforced impotence behind bars is not necessarily the best way of showing it.

In my own 'case', I had like many thousands of progressives then – and far too many still today – been insufficiently aware of the dangers, and my constitutional rights to protect my innocence, when the FBI came to pester me in my home back in 1947. I answered all the agents' questions on the naïve assumption that they only wanted the truth, rather than to fish for 'leads' which distorted Justice Dept. minds might distil into poison for use against myself and others. I bitterly regret that I did not send the political policemen politely about their business as any responsible person they visit ought to do. But better to defend the Constitution late than never.

Harry Houghton

*What I did was done with my eyes open, and I'm
not complaining unduly about the consequences.*

Harry Houghton had left the Royal Navy in 1945 with an honourable discharge
and a small pension after twenty-four years' service, and having achieved the non-
commissioned rank of master-at-arms, he was found a civilian post in the naval
dockyards at Gosport. For a period of fifteen months between July 1951 and
October 1952, he was attached to the British embassy in Warsaw as a clerk. Before
the war he had married a widow in his home town of Lincoln, but their childless
marriage ended in divorce in 1958 after twenty-three years. He lived in a small,
four-roomed cottage at Broadwey near Weymouth and, since his return from
Poland, had worked as a clerk in what was then the Underwater Detection
Establishment at Portland in Dorset. In January 1957 Houghton was transferred
to the Port Auxiliary Repair Unit at the same base, which had been renamed the
Admiralty Underwater Weapons Establishment.

According to his confidential personnel file Houghton had been denounced as a
spy by his embittered wife Peggy at about the time of their divorce but neither this,
nor the later suggestion that his free-spending habits had drawn attention to his
espionage, had been responsible for tipping off MI5. The vital information had
come from the CIA, and at that stage even the Agency had little idea as to its own
informant's true identity, whom MI5 referred to gratefully as Lavinia. He had
been supplying them with high-grade material anonymously, using the codename
Stutzstaffel ('sniper' in German) to conceal his true identity. He was finally to
reveal himself late in December 1960 as a senior Polish intelligence officer in the
SB (and part-time KGB informant) named Michal Goleniewski, and to request
political asylum for himself and his German girlfriend.

Once the fifty-six-year-old Houghton had been confirmed as the most likely
candidate for the spy with a name like 'Horton' he had been placed under
surveillance. MI5 watchers moved close to Houghton's home, but no attempt was
made to isolate him from classified papers at the Portland base as, theoretically, his
job in the repair unit gave him no access to secrets. Nevertheless, when he travelled
to London by train on a Saturday morning in July 1960 he had been observed to
exchange envelopes with a stocky, middle-aged man carrying a shopping bag.
While some of the watchers had stuck to Houghton, and trailed him back to
Dorset, another group had peeled off and kept their contact under observation as
he made his way to his hotel in Bayswater.

Discreet inquiries at the hotel revealed Houghton's link to be a Canadian guest,
a bachelor named Gordon A. Lonsdale who had only recently moved in. Further
surveillance and an overheard conversation produced a pattern of meetings
between Houghton and Lonsdale, usually on the first Saturday of the month, as

happened early the following August when he was seen accompanied by Ethel Gee, a colleague from Portland with whom he spent the weekend at the Cumberland Hotel, Marble Arch. Both had driven up to London in Houghton's new car and later attended a performance of the Bolshoi Ballet at the Royal Albert Hall with tickets supplied by Lonsdale. Whereas Houghton's job did not give him access to secrets, Gee's position in an adjoining building which housed the Drawing Office records section most certainly did. She had worked at the base since October 1950, and had moved from the stores department in 1955, two years before she had been accepted as an established civil servant. Although she spent much of her spare time with Houghton, Gee, who was known as Bunty, lived with her elderly mother, uncle and disabled aunt in a small terraced house in Portland.

Houghton, Gee and Lonsdale were arrested in January 1961 and three months later appeared at the Old Bailey where the two Britons were sentenced to fifteen years' imprisonment. Houghton claimed that he had been coerced into helping the Soviets after his black-market activities in Warsaw had been discovered. He also insisted that he had believed Lonsdale to be an American intelligence officer. The prosecution challenged his version by pointing out the large amount of cash he had accumulated that had been found in a search of his home. Upon his release from Maidstone Prison Houghton married Bunty Gee and wrote his autobiography. After their return to Portland they moved to the Isle of Wight, where they still live.

As can be seen here, Houghton attempted in *Operation Portland* to minimize the impact of his betrayal, suggesting the data he passed to his Soviet contacts was relatively insignificant, whereas actually he was responsible for haemorrhaging the details of classified submarine detection systems.

Operation Portland

One of my first contacts was a Russian always referred to as Nikki. He was not the most inconspicuous person I have ever met. He favoured the Russian fashion of a long overcoat with padded shoulders, and invariably wore wide trousers and a broad-brimmed trilby. In fact with his flat face and big ears he was the cartoonist's dream of a Soviet spy. Later he was to be superseded by Gordon Lonsdale.

For the work I was expected to do on the Base I was given a Minox camera which fitted snugly into my pocket. It was about $3\frac{1}{2}''$ long, $1\frac{1}{8}''$ wide, and about $\frac{5}{8}''$ thick, and would easily pass as a cigarette lighter at a glance. It was in fact so unobtrusive that it was never discovered when I was arrested. Anything which couldn't be removed from the Establishment could be photographed with this – by which I mean objects, but not documents, which didn't come out so well. For finer work I had an Exacta camera, which took good pictures of anything I could carry off home with me in the evening.

I was summoned to meetings in various ways, usually by advertising matter in the post. A card from the Scotch House wool shop in Knightsbridge had a certain meaning, as did a brochure about Hoover products. If I received an envelope containing advertising matter about the Sun Life Assurance Company, this meant I was to go to a certain lay-by on the road to Salisbury at exactly 8 p.m. the night after I received it. The GPO was a lot more reliable then: under present conditions I can't imagine how we'd have operated! If the contact wasn't made, I was to return at the same time on subsequent evenings.

On one occasion I arrived and was asked by my contact, this time the man I came to know as Roman, if there was any means of knowing when HM ships were due to arrive at Portland and when they would depart. This was an easy one. Every day there is issued what's called the Daily State, giving berths of ships and dates of expected arrivals and departures. Roman was disappointed that only 'a.m.' and 'p.m.' was given, and not the approximate times. Nevertheless I was instructed to get the Daily State for him regularly, though often by the time I was able to pass it on the details were hopelessly out of date.

Then he wanted to know how much I could tell him about the Army artillery ranges at Lulworth. I had to disappoint him. But when we got down to it, it turned out he merely wished to discover if there was any means of checking when the Army would be firing out to seaward. He was taken aback when I told him that such details always appeared in the local press to warn fishermen and were also published in the local Notices to Mariners, which anyone could buy.

On another occasion I was asked what information was available about areas allocated for HM ships to exercise in and the times of such exercises. As with the Daily State, this presented no problems. Each week a programme was issued for the ensuing week specifying ships taking part, together with the place, nature and time of the exercises. Most departments had plenty of copies knocking about, so Roman was placed on the distribution list. If a spare copy couldn't be obtained, I had to make a photographic copy for him.

As parts of this narrative will show, my contacts could never get used to the idea of military information of any kind being available to the general public, or to its being discussed by local inhabitants without fear of immediate imprisonment or banishment to a labour camp.

John Vassall

Having committed a crime I cannot spend the rest
of my life demolishing myself with remorse.

The son of a Church of England clergyman, Vassall served in the Royal Air Force during the latter part of the Second World War and trained as a photographer. In 1954 he applied for a clerk's post in the Admiralty and he was sent to the British embassy in Moscow as secretary to the Naval Attaché.

In Moscow he was befriended by a Pole named Mikhailski who worked at the embassy as an interpreter, and he was responsible for drawing the hapless Vassall into a homosexual honeytrap where he was photographed in bed with a young man. Hopelessly compromised, Vassall succumbed to the KGB's blackmail and, in an attempt to prevent pictures of his indiscretion being circulated, started supplying classified material to his Russian contact. In June 1956 Vassall's tour of duty ended and he was posted back to the Admiralty where he worked in the secretariat to the Naval Staff. His rendezvous with his KGB handlers continued, until the arrest of Harry Houghton in January 1961, when he was told temporarily to discontinue his meetings. Despite being the victim of coercion, Vassall developed a reliance and even friendship with his Soviet contacts, both of whom were later identified as skilled professionals masquerading as diplomats.

Once the public furore about the Portland spy ring had subsided, Vassall was activated again and he held regular meetings with his KGB case officer until his arrest in September 1962. After a lengthy MI5 investigation, which had been initiated the previous April after the CIA had imparted information from a defector, Vassall was charged with offences under the Official Secrets Act and sentenced to eighteen years' imprisonment. He was released from Maidstone, which had also accommodated Harry Houghton, in October 1972 and, after staying in a Catholic monastery, wrote his autobiography. He now lives in north London under an assumed identity and works for a City firm. In his book, *Vassall: The Autobiography of a Spy*, he recalls the trauma of his arrest by Special Branch detectives.

Vassall: The Autobiography of a Spy

My arrest was not entirely unexpected. I had an awful premonition of disaster. That morning when I got up I saw a strange face at the window of a flat I had previously visited for drinks. The man was peering out and down into the courtyard. He looked like a burglar and I left a note telling my housekeeper that I had seen him. In the hall on the ground floor sat a large, burly man who watched me intently as I passed. When I got off the bus in Whitehall at Horse Guards' Parade someone got off behind me. I thought he could certainly not be coming into the Admiralty. But my recollection is that he did, by the Horse Guards' Parade entrance. At the window in the Naval Intelligence division, which I had occupied years previously, was a tall man playing about with a waste paper basket. In fact he was watching me. Why I never connected all these people with myself is beyond my comprehension. I don't remember noticing anyone else until evening. Then I happened to see from my window a strange car right outside the exit to the Admiralty quadrangle. Whenever anyone came out, all those in the car would leap up in their seats, as if waiting for somebody specific. Oddly enough I left by a different exit because of a strange fear that came over me. I went over to the Post Office in Trafalgar Square to draw some money for my holiday in Italy.

In spite of my premonitions, it was a complete surprise when, as I left the north-west door of the Admiralty in The Mall and went to cross the road, two men in mackintoshes came forward *Third Man* style, flashed me a warrant and asked me to accompany them to a car waiting by the statue of Captain Cook. It was as if I had been swept into space; my feet never returned to the ground. I was pushed into the back seat, a woman member of the Special Branch spoke into the car radio, and a few minutes later two superintendents of police arrived and got into the car. One of them was the man who had guarded Khruschev and Bulganin when they had stayed at Claridges. They asked me for my briefcase, and immediately looked through it for any papers that might be of interest. They were disappointed, for there were only private papers. The only thing I said was, 'I suppose this is because I have been in Russia'.

I said nothing as the car sped round Horse Guards' Parade, past the Foreign Office and Ministry of Defence to Parliament Square, and finally to Scotland Yard. I was escorted up several flights of stairs to a large room and told to sit down. One of the superintendents seemed quite breathless with anxiety, but the others were as silent as night. I was told that my flat was to be searched, and I was asked to give them the keys so that the search could take place quietly. I could tell they had been given information that I was the person the intelligence service wanted. (Later I met someone who told me his father had been at New Zealand House in the Haymarket at the time. Apparently the Special Branch had a telephoto lens trained on the Admiralty so that they could watch me enter and leave.) The police were somewhat surprised that I had no secret papers on me and so little money – only a few pounds. But I realized (which was the crux of the matter) that I had rolls of film in my flat which would eventually be found, even in the concealed compartment which the Russians had made for me in a bookcase. There was no point in hiding the fact. I told them at once what was there, including the two cameras.

I realized later that, though involved in espionage, I was not necessarily to be held totally responsible for my actions. The authorities would have had to make out a good case that they were not partly responsible for the events which made this nightmare situation possible. But by telling all and pleading guilty I took the whole responsibility on my own shoulders. I did not involve anyone else by stepping out of line.

Tea and sandwiches were produced to help my explanation along. I was glad, in a way, to be able to unburden myself at last, although I should much rather have done it to the Security Service, who would have had more understanding of the situation. I think my actual interrogator did not know how to handle the situation. To him I was just a plain spy who had highly placed contacts working in an elaborate network. I was in fact a lone individual not connected with anyone. He asked me which department I was working in, and when I said the Military Branch of the Admiralty and one of about ninety personnel, his reply was that there might be eighty-nine others also involved in these activities. For hours I poured out what had been bottled up in my mind for years. I don't know why people ask whether one has remorse; I should have thought it obvious. The Russians are not likely to take volunteers for this work. They much prefer people under stress because they can be controlled. As for the money, it is often assumed that this is the sole criterion. But for anyone who has been coerced into this sort of work, money is the last consideration. Who on earth would do it for money? One would have to have nerves of steel, to be superhuman and insensitive to the realities of the world. All money does is give you a false feeling of security and a certain amount of personal freedom. The whole thing is an illusion, a stay of execution, nothing more.

I suppose I went on talking from about 7 p.m. until 4 a.m., quietly giving the whole story. Later that night a senior official came in, listened in the background, but never said a word. He must have understood my predicament. But by English law no one from the Security Service or other services could speak to me, without permission, until after I had been sentenced. The whole business was like a continuation of the Russian trap in Moscow. It was like Part II, except that it was now happening in London. After I had been thoroughly interrogated by the Russians, the British authorities were doing the same thing from their angle. I must be one of the few people who have been on the receiving end of both Russian and British interrogation systems. I am sure they both found out a great deal of the methods used by both sides in this continuous and yet acceptable game of intelligence work. I felt like a human guinea pig being used by both sides for their greater experience. It was a very unpleasant and dirty game. That night I felt that it was beyond the comprehension of my interrogator; he was somewhat out of his depth, as I told the Security Service later. There was a complete blank as to how I could have got involved; their object, of course, was to get me to make a confession; then it would be all over. Then there would be no need to harangue me. I was only thankful it was now all over. Whatever happened, nothing could have been as terrible as what I had had to endure during the previous years.

The writings of people who describe my experiences very often sound off-key to me. They are written for political expediency or other social reasons. Now and again I have read a more thoughtful account of why these things happened, but I always appear quite unlike my true self. Perhaps no one wanted to know the real John Vassall. Perhaps it was enough, as the Prime Minister, Mr Macmillan, said later, when the Director-General of Security Services went to see him at Admiralty House, that when you have trapped the fox and the hounds have killed it, you don't want the keepers to hang the carcase on the barbed wire so that everyone can smell it. I think the unkindest remark Mr Macmillan made was when he was answering oral questions about me in the House of Commons. In reply to a question about a remark I had made that there were homosexuals in high places, in government and the services, Mr Macmillan wondered if you could believe the words of a convicted spy talking to a fellow prisoner. At that very time I went to see a highly responsible member of our Security Service. I said to him, 'As I sit here talking, the Prime Minister gets up in the House of Commons and puts an entirely different meaning on everything I say or have said to you or anyone else for that matter.'

I was getting more and more distraught by this time. I saw members of the Special Branch bringing back some of my papers from my flat for perusal, which I think they hoped would reveal others who might be involved with me. It must have been a surprise to them to find that I was a lone wolf. When they drafted out a kind of confession in the middle of the night, I did not mind much what was said in it. I was the perfect fall-guy, easy meat for them – as far as I was concerned, they could say what they liked. There would be no need to elaborate. They were doing a job that had to be done and I had no hard feelings towards them. The sooner they got the business over the happier I would be. As dawn approached I signed the document that had been prepared and lay back with my head resting on the large green leather armchair, feeling that I had at last got all this out of my system. My head was spinning with nausea – physical and mental.

Later, when I talked to our security people, I said that presumably they must have some idea of my position and would not prosecute me because I was the victim of circumstances, more to be pitied than hounded by the more vociferous, who are always there to put in the knife for their own interests. I honestly thought that when they viewed the whole situation I would be discreetly moved away from the Admiralty, at least for a couple of years, either to some quiet backwater or abroad to a country like Canada where the Russians could not get hold of me again. My family would be told that I had been given a new job. It would all have fitted in with my career, where I could see no future at that moment. Instead there was an uproar in the press, the Government had to cope with an outcry about yet another spy in the Admiralty, and this time one who had been operating in the Civil Lord's office.

CHAPTER II

The Soviets

Traitors are the scourge of every intelligence service. They are the cause of the majority of failures by agents, cause panic in the Centre, can upset whole governments, and their treachery can serve as grounds for major international scandal.
Oleg Tumanov

Disaffection with a regime or a political system may prove a powerful incentive to move abroad and live in a more congenial climate, but for the vast majority of Soviet subjects, between the Bolshevik Revolution and the eventual collapse of communism nearly three-quarters of a century later, no such choice was available and Articles 64, 65, 70, 72 and 75 of the Soviet Criminal Code laid down dire penalties for any citizen contemplating defection. After the civil war severe restrictions on exit visas, to the extent that for most citizens they were impossible to obtain, and even dangerous to apply for, and a virtual ban on emigration meant that the only means of starting a new life in a more conducive atmosphere was to travel illegally or to fail to return when required to do so at the end of a temporary official posting abroad. Accordingly, the Soviet authorities took great care when selecting personnel for appointments overseas, and ensured they were ideologically suitable. By Soviet standards they were well paid, and where possible they had a dependent family to stay at home in the undeclared role of hostages. As Walter Krivitsky observed, 'No one leaves the Soviet Union unless the NKVD can use him.' Whilst on the one hand this policy determined that only the most reliable supporters of the regime were allowed to take up residence in foreign countries, the corollary was that any Soviet abroad, in however subordinate a position, who was willing to defect, would probably possess useful information. Even a relatively junior Soviet employee, perhaps a lowly chauffeur or an embassy security guard, would be likely to enjoy a knowledge that would prove useful to Western intelligence agencies which often had only a very limited grasp of what was happening inside the closed society. This situation was recognized by the KGB, which kept Soviet personnel attached to trade and diplomatic missions under constant supervision and, wherever possible, required them to live within separate enclaves, isolated from the host community, a practice that extended even to premises in Warsaw Pact countries. The intention was to minimize contamination by foreigners and to provide the KGB's *Sovietskaya Kolonia* security staff with facilities to monitor all employees. Even inside the KGB or GRU *referentura*, there were two categories of officials: those who were limited to the outer area only, and those with access to the cipher room and crypto-equipment who were subject to even more stringent security precautions, and who were never permitted anywhere beyond the embassy's perimeter without an escort, and never allowed outside alone with their spouse, a measure designed to deter joint defections. Within the organization the standard joke was that this meant KGB personnel were permitted to defect only with the wives of other people. The equally subversive rejoinder was that no self-respecting KGB officer would want to defect with his own wife!

Most of the safeguards dated back to September 1945 and the defection of the GRU cipher clerk Igor Gouzenko, the loss of whom Vladimir Rezun termed 'a frightful blow, no less serious, perhaps, than when 190 German divisions were suddenly let loose against the Red Army'. Gouzenko's treachery led to all GRU staff with access to crypto-equipment being heavily restricted while abroad, and obliged to spend their vacations at the GRU's main signals centre at Vatutinki, a small classified establishment fifty kilometres south-west of Moscow. Travel was permitted only with armed escorts under orders to kill their charges in the event of any incident which might leave them vulnerable.

A Soviet citizen's decision to defect was never an easy one, for there was the absolute certainty that any relations left within reach of the state organs would bear the brunt of the inevitable retribution. Thus the few that did switch sides were often those with the least family ties at home, and most made an effort to engineer circumstances in which they could bring their wives and children with them, a trick exceptionally difficult to accomplish, and one with haunting implications for failure. If any close relatives remained in the Soviet Union the KGB invariably traced them and arranged for their harrowing pleas to be relayed to the defector. With the state apparatus exercising complete control over housing, employment, transport, medical care and every other aspect of normal Soviet life, it needed little imagination to recognize the likely consequences for any unfortunate victim of the KGB's repression. An early postwar defector to the British, Colonel J. D. Tasoev, changed his mind in May 1948, almost as soon as he had reached London. Formerly the head of the Soviet Reparations Mission in Bremen, Tasoev's defection was considered by SIS to have been an impressive coup. His loss of nerve and demand to be returned to the Soviet Kommandantura in Berlin was the source of much embarrassment and even questions in the House of Commons.

As late as the 1980s, ostensibly hardened professionals who had opted to defect, such as the counter-intelligence expert Vitali S. Yurchenko in 1985, were persuaded to change their minds and return to the *rodina*, the beloved motherland. Appeals of the same kind, made to Anatoli K. Chebotarev of the GRU in Brussels in October 1971, ensured his return within three weeks. The KGB's Artush S. Hovanesian defected in Turkey in July 1972 and went home in September the following year. Nikolai G. Petrov, of the GRU *rezidentura* in Jakarta, lasted fourteen months in the West. Yevgeni G. Sorokin abandoned the GRU in Vientiane in September 1972 but redefected thirteen months later. The pressure applied to Andrei A. Rekemchuk, who had pleaded to be allowed to stay in Montreal in June 1987, was equally effective: the wretched defector, who had perhaps spent years preparing himself for the move to the West, transformed into a hapless, shell-shocked victim begging his new guardians to be allowed to rejoin his family, regardless of the predictable consequences. Suffice to say that none of those who have redefected has left a written record of his test of the KGB's tolerance or hospitality, although Yurchenko was once produced for the Western media in Moscow in a rather obvious bid to end speculation about his fate. Similarly, Rekemchuk, a thirty-three-year-old interpreter attached to the International Civil Aviation Organization, was widely quoted in the Soviet press in September 1988, three months after he had been reunited in Moscow with his wife Galina and five-year-old son Pavel.

During the Cold War the KGB earned an unrivalled reputation for applying pressure on dissidents both internally, through the notorious Fifth Chief Directorate, and externally via counter-intelligence personnel from the First Chief Directorate. The KGB was also believed to be behind the Rodina Society which campaigned for the return of Russian exiles. Certainly the organization's vice-president, Yuri Izyumov, the head of the international section of the *Literary Gazette*, also held the rank of major-general in the KGB.

There were other hazards too. Assassins had dealt with the White Russian General Aleksandr P. Kutepov in Paris in 1930, and had been sent to eliminate Leon Trotsky in Mexico in 1940, and there have been numerous other examples of state-sponsored murder, which was not a phenomenon limited to the early Bolshevik rivalries of the 1920s. Indeed, two KGB turncoats, Bogdan Stashinsky and Nikolai Khokhlov, gave dramatic proof of the exclusively homicidal objectives of a sinister KGB unit, designated the Thirteenth Department of the First Chief Directorate, which had been responsible for the deaths of several opponents singled out for liquidation. As Khokhlov confessed in February 1954 in testimony that he repeated before the Senate Judiciary Committee, and was to be confirmed by Stashinsky seven years later, their special skill was to make a death appear an accident, adding a further degree of uncertainty to those weighing up, in anticipation of defection, the likely efficiency of any attempt at revenge. Even when, as happened in 1984, Boris Bakhlanov was found drowned in London, and his death was considered to be suicide, some element of doubt persisted, which inevitably acted as a persuasive deterrent. As he knew was likely, if not inevitable, Khokhlov himself was the subject of an assassination attempt in September 1957 in Frankfurt after he had adopted a new identity and had published a series of articles in the *Saturday Evening Post.*

Not all dissidents and Soviet defectors were regarded by the Kremlin as traitors. In the early years of the revolution some disaffected supporters of the Bolshevik regime opted to flee the country and that decision was not in all cases automatically regarded as an act of treachery. Trotsky suffered deportation and Stalin's own daughter, Svetlana Allilueva, moved to the United States where she published *Only One Year*, a damning indictment of Lavrenti Beria and the malign influence he was alleged to have held over her father. Yet she was still allowed to return to Moscow when she tired of life in America. Thousands of others, particularly White Russians who made their homes in Paris after the civil war, have escaped charges of treachery by maintaining a low profile, by avoiding public criticism of the regime and, above all, by not writing books deemed to undermine the Soviet system. Aleksandr Solzhenitsyn was arrested and charged with treason in February 1974 when *The Gulag Archipelago* was published in France and the United States, but after a disagreeable night in Lefortovo Prison he was flown by Aeroflot to Frankfurt for exile in Zurich, and later in Cavendish, southern Vermont. However, this treatment was quite exceptional, and Soviet citizens were discouraged from remaining abroad; to oppose communism was a crime; to betray secrets, however mundane, about the organs of the state was a capital offence.

One accurate guide to the communist attitude to those definitely regarded as having committed treason is the KGB's official arrest list, a

460-page document with 2,000 entries, that was obtained by Ukrainian nationalists in 1985. Issued by General Siomonchuk, deputy chief of the Second Chief Directorate, and dated 14 September 1971, it includes all those wanted during the period between May 1945 and April 1969 and lists a total of 470 *perebezhchiki* (defectors). Accompanying it was an order signed by the deputy Chairman of the KGB, General Viktor Chebrikov, requiring 'active measures' to be taken to apprehend all those on the list.

Almost qualified for inclusion are those who did not write books but compounded their crime in other ways, like Yuri A. Rastvorov who abandoned his KGB post in Tokyo in January 1954, and Colonel Yevgeny E. Runge, who switched sides in Berlin in 1967. Both were deemed to have committed almost as grave an infraction by virtue of their appearances before the US Senate Committee on the Judiciary in 1956 and 1970 respectively. Rastvorov denounced two Soviet sources in the Japanese Foreign Ministry, Hiroshi Shoji and Shigeru Takanore, who were arrested after the lieutenant-colonel had been resettled in the United States. He later married his CIA case officer, and he now lives in California. Certainly his testimony before that select audience and his contribution of three articles to *Life* magazine were regarded in Moscow as equally damaging, in political and diplomatic terms, as anything he could have produced in the form of memoirs.

To abandon socialist principles and live abroad was frowned on and, where possible, prevented by Stalin and his successors. A decree issued by Stalin in November 1929 required anyone who failed to respond within twenty-four hours to an order to return home, to be 'shot on recognition'. The most serious punishment, that of a death sentence passed *in absentia*, was reserved for those considered to be guilty of the most heinous of crimes, treason committed by an intelligence officer. In the KGB's code there was only one punishment for desertion to 'the main adversary'. Imperilling the safety of agents and their networks was considered the most fundamental betrayal and was deterred by what was alleged to be the absolute certainty of terminal retribution. This was accompanied by grim warnings that the KGB had penetrated most Western intelligence agencies and was often in a position to intervene almost as soon as a putative traitor had made even the most tentative approach to the opposition. Stanislav Levchenko recalls how he had been told of Kim Philby's tip in September 1945 that had led to the abduction in Ankara of Konstantin Volkov, the Soviet military attaché who had tried to negotiate terms for his defection, not realizing that the news would be passed by SIS to a mole. Levchenko remembered having been shown photographs of Volkov, drugged and in a straitjacket, being bundled aboard a Soviet aircraft bound for Moscow to face certain execution. He was also told by General Kir G. Lemzenko of a traitor named Konstantinov, who had been buried alive, and assured that the only way out of the GRU was through the chimney of a crematorium. This was a ghoulish reference to an incident that had occurred in 1959. According to several witnesses, new recruits to the GRU were required to watch a film of a traitor, believed to have been Major Piotr Popov, being pitched live into a furnace, thereby reinforcing the message that death was an inevitable consequence of disloyalty. This was the penalty suffered by Walter Krivitsky, formerly the GRU *rezident* in The Hague, who was found dead in a Washington DC hotel room in 1941, and Viktor Kravchenko, who supposedly shot himself in his New York apartment in February 1966. Even though they had fled abroad and had been resettled by the American authorities, there was no protection from the murder squads. As for Georges Agabekov, the Armenian OGPU officer who decamped with his English sweetheart to Paris from Turkey in 1929, the circumstances of his death remain as mysterious as ever. He had previously served the OGPU in Tehran and had arrived in Constantinople under commercial cover, as a merchant importing bicycles, in October 1929. He fell in love with the woman he had hired to teach him English and later published *OGPU: The Russian Terror*, which ensured him a death sentence from his former masters. According to his widow, Isabel Streater, who died in New York in 1971, he disappeared while smuggling Spanish works of art across the Pyrenees in July 1937, but Pavel Sudoplatov, who engineered several 'liquidations' for the NKVD, says he was murdered by a pair of specially commissioned assassins in Paris who lured him to a safe-house and stabbed him to death.

When Ignace Reiss was found shot dead by the side of a road outside Lausanne in September 1937 his widow, Elisabeth Poretsky, had no doubt about the identity of his killers and went into hiding. As she was herself an experienced NKVD officer she was particularly well qualified to elude the assassins dispatched to find her, and to write an authoritative denunciation of Stalin, *Our Own People*, from the safety of America.

Naturally the murders of Reiss and the other victims of Stalin's purges were never publicly acknowledged by the Soviet leadership, just as the existence of Smersh (literally 'death to spies') was not recognized formally, and in subsequent years the silence extended even to the official executions for treason which had been sanctioned by a court. When

Colonel Oleg V. Penkovsky of the GRU faced a firing squad in May 1963, after a show trial in Moscow, both his sentence and the fact that it had been carried out were the subject of an official announcement. However, since then, the policy of discretion relating to this single crime was maintained, perhaps in the belief that any statement would amount to an admission of a structural failure, and an acknowledgement of the existence of dissent. Thus, since 1963, death sentences are known to have been handed down only in the rare cases of V. G. Kalinin in February 1975 and Anatoli Filatov in July 1978. In more recent times A. B. Nilov was executed in March 1980 after he had been convicted of espionage, and in March 1988 a GRU general, Dmitri F. Polyakov, was shot after having been found guilty of twenty years of clandestine collaboration with the CIA. Colonel Vladimir I. Vetrov, who acted as a source inside the FCD's Directorate T for the French DST for two years, was also executed, but only after he had been sentenced in 1982 to twelve years' imprisonment for an unrelated crime, the stabbing of his girlfriend and the murder of another Muscovite whom he had mistakenly believed to have been part of a KGB surveillance team. According to an account supplied by the defector Vitali Yurchenko, who as a counter-intelligence specialist was regarded as a reliable authority on the case, Vetrov had confessed to the more serious crime of espionage within a year of his conviction for homicide. He had volunteered a detailed confession, and had even remarked in this lengthy document that his 'only regret is that I was not able to cause more damage to the Soviet Union and render more service to France'. Allegedly Vetrov's idealism had inspired Yurchenko, although the latter was to spend less than three months in the West before redefecting in November 1985.

Coincidentally, the KGB officer under diplomatic cover chosen to escort Yurchenko back to Moscow, Valeri F. Martinov, was himself an FBI source, and he was arrested soon after his arrival, together with two other assets in the KGB: another third secretary at the Washington embassy, Sergei M. Motorin, who had arrived with Martinov in 1981 and had been recruited by the FBI a couple of years later, and a senior counter-intelligence officer in the Second Chief Directorate, so far identified only by his CIA cryptonym, GT/Prologue. Reportedly all three were shot by firing squad in 1986, having been betrayed by Aldrich H. Ames, the KGB's mole in the CIA's Soviet Eastern Europe Division. Details of their cases emerged only after Ames and his wife had been indicted on espionage charges in February 1994.

Following his conviction and a life sentence, handed down in April

1994, Ames admitted to having sold many of the CIA's most treasured secrets for a total of two million dollars, including the identities of two high-ranking GRU officers, General Dmitri Polyakov, codenamed Accord, and a lieutenant-colonel, Million, and two KGB assets, Cowl, who was based in Moscow, and Fitness. In addition, he confirmed having compromised Oleg Gordievsky, codenamed GT/Tickle, who was SIS's star source inside the KGB *rezidentura* in London, and Blizzard, Weigh and Gentile, all of whom were executed by the Soviets.

Fortunately for Fitness, actually Lieutenant-Colonel Boris Yuzhin, he was only sentenced to fifteen years at a labour camp and has recently been freed and allowed to emigrate. A KGB First Chief Directorate officer who had undertaken two missions to California, first in 1975, masquerading as a postgraduate student at Berkeley, and then in 1978 under journalistic cover as a TASS news agency correspondent in San Francisco, Yuzhin confessed during a gruelling KGB interrogation to his recruitment by the FBI soon after his first visit to the US. He was sent to the notorious Perm 35 labour camp in the Urals, where he was released in February 1992 as part of a general amnesty of political prisoners. Now aged fifty-two, he works as a journalist in Movato, Marin County, where he lives with his wife Nadya and daughter Olga.

As well as betraying Adolf Tolkachev, a military researcher with access to the latest Soviet air force technology, Ames is believed also to be responsible for the arrest of a Hungarian security officer codenamed GT/Motorboat, a leading aerospace engineer, Vladimir Potachev, and a military analyst, Sergei Fedorenko, who were both supplying the CIA with military data.

Not surprisingly, none of these latter condemned prisoners wrote any account of their illicit activities and some doubt surrounds the authorship of *The Penkovsky Papers*, widely believed to have been assembled by an earlier defector, Piotr Deriabin, from the transcriptions of taped debriefings conducted at clandestine meetings with the GRU officer in London and Paris.

A question mark also hangs over Grigori Bessedovsky, the Soviet diplomat who defected in Paris in 1929 and subsequently enjoyed a very colourful career, much of which may have been spent in contact with his Soviet employers. Similarly, the journalist Yuri Krotkov never persuaded the British, to whom he defected in London in September 1963, that he was completely genuine. Certainly MI5 concluded that he was an example of that very rare phenomenon, a planted defector deliberately dispatched by the KGB. The only known, confirmed case of a 'plant' is

Oleg A. Tumanov, ostensibly a seaman who swam to the Libyan shore from the destroyer *Spravedlivy* in November 1966. He was recruited as an editor for Radio Liberty's Russian broadcasts in Munich, but disappeared suddenly in February 1986, following the defection of a senior KGB officer in Athens. According to his autobiography, *Tumanov: Confessions of a KGB Agent*, which was published in 1993 he, like the rest of his family, had been a KGB professional and his unscheduled return to Moscow had brought his penetration mission to a close. However, as he was, by his own admission, never truly a defector, he cannot therefore be included in this anthology. Nor can Oleg Bitov, formerly the deputy editor of the *Literary Gazette* who defected in Italy in September 1983, only to return to Moscow the following August, claiming at a press conference that he had been abducted by the British Security Service. During the year he spent in London Bitov had signed a contract for his autobiography, *Tales I Could Not Tell*, but as he never completed the manuscript, he too must be excluded from these pages. Whether he succumbed to the KGB's pressure, or suffered from acute depression, is unknown, but it is unlikely that he was a dispatched defector.

The idea that the KGB might send false defectors to the West, primed with disinformation, itself originated from an FCD officer. Twenty-one months before Krotkov defected a member of the KGB's *rezidentura* in Stockholm, Anatoli Golitsyn, had presented himself to the CIA in Helsinki and had undergone an intensive series of debriefings. Like several other defectors before him, Golitsyn's first interviews were conducted at Ashford Farm, a remote estate in Maryland overlooking the Choptank river. Significantly, Golitsyn claimed that an attempt would be made to discredit his evidence by the KGB dispatching false defectors to undermine his credibility. Although the CIA's Counter-intelligence Staff was to become obsessed with the concept of a 'plant', only Krotkov and Tumanov can really be proved to have fitted the bill.

Altogether twenty-five KGB officers have defected and have written unclassified accounts of their experiences which are in the public domain, thereby guaranteeing themselves a death sentence. Some have written long novels, others more personal autobiographies, while a few like Viktor P. Gundarev have emerged from hiding only briefly, settling for two interviews to the media given under strict security conditions. Gundarev, a KGB colonel based in Athens who came across to the CIA in January 1986 with his son and his Russian mistress, used the press to complain about his post-defection living conditions in the United States, and thereby to apply pressure to improve the generosity of his CIA protectors.

Having supplied enough information to the CIA for Oleg Tumanov to be pinpointed as the KGB's asset in Radio Liberty, thereby forcing the KGB to extricate him in an emergency operation, Gundarev believed he was entitled to better treatment and threatened to redefect unless he received it, but his value as an intelligence source diminished when an American naval officer he had accused of spying was arrested in England, and then acquitted on all charges.

Using the pseudonym Victor Orlov, another KGB officer also resettled in the US has limited himself to contributing articles to the *Washington Post* in 1988, exposing aspects of the KGB's totalitarianism. In particular, he performed the useful function of revealing the scale of the KGB's infiltration, to the point of control, of the Russian Orthodox Church. What distinguishes these individuals from the hundreds of other Soviets who have successfully fled abroad is that instead of accepting the transition and starting again in a new country, they have deliberately provoked the regime by publicizing their grievances and thus have been confirmed as permanent, irredeemable enemies of the state. To provide testimony before a Congressional committee, like that of Captain Nikolai F. Artamonov in 1960, and Colonel Yevgeny E. Runge in 1970, was to court disaster. Runge had defected in Berlin in October 1967 and, after having given his evidence, he slipped back into obscurity, declining to publish his memoirs. In contrast, Artamonov, the Red Banner naval officer who had crossed the Baltic with his Polish girlfriend in June 1959 to claim political asylum, had been persuaded to re-establish contact with the Soviets in the dangerous role of an FBI double agent, but he disappeared in Vienna in December 1985. According to Vitali Yurchenko, the KGB counter-intelligence expert who defected in August 1985, Artamonov had been killed accidentally by his colleagues.

Of the postwar defectors, more have come from the KGB than from any other Soviet organization, but that is not entirely surprising considering the greater opportunities for Soviet intelligence personnel to develop the necessary contacts in the West. As well as knowing the right agencies to approach with a view to negotiating terms, they were also more likely to possess the skills required to elude detection by the KGB's local security apparatus. Upon analysis it becomes evident that few defections are spontaneous, and most are well planned. In some cases there is an element of courtship, with the host agency cultivating a particular target perhaps for months prior to the act itself. This is what happened in 1954 to Vladimir Petrov who was reluctant to return to Moscow and preferred life in Australia. The fear of an unexpected recall home, which often heralded punishment for some perceived infraction, proved a significant factor, as was demonstrated by Piotr Deriabin who suspected he would not survive the transition of power after Beria's death. Similarly, when Vladimir Kuzichkin discovered in May 1982 he had mislaid some important documents, he realized his career (if not his life) would be terminated. The only alternative to a dreary desk job in Siberia, or perhaps execution, was resettlement with a new identity in England.

Considerable research has been undertaken to understand why defectors defect. Purely personal considerations can play a significant role to motivate potential defectors and there is a belief, supported by a CIA psychiatrist, Dr Alan Studner, that many defectors transform personal grievance into an issue of political principle. Certainly it can be demonstrated that several defectors conform to a pattern of family or professional problems which predated a decision to collaborate with a Western intelligence agency and then defect. A classic example is that of Oleg Gordievsky, whose first marriage was in the process of collapsing when he first made an offer to spy for the British in Copenhagen in 1973. Curiously, his second failed after he had been joined in his new life in a leafy London suburb by his second wife Leila, and their two daughters Anna and Maris, following their enforced separation which lasted from Gordievsky's exfiltration in 1985 to their eventual release in 1991.

Personal relationships are considered important factors in defection decisions, and there is a common strand of tangled affairs and personality clashes running through several cases. Mikhail Butkov, a KGB officer with seven years' experience, defected in Oslo in May 1991 under dramatic circumstances, having attempted suicide in the apartment of a British diplomat. He had spent two years in Norway under cover as the local correspondent of *Rabochaya Tribuna* and was recovering from an unhappy love affair at the time of his defection, although he left these details out of his book, *The KGB in Norway: The Last Chapter*, when it was published in Norwegian only in 1992.

In contrast to the KGB, relatively few officers are known to have defected from the GRU, and during the Second World War there were only very limited opportunities for defection. Indeed, only one is known to have made the move: Ismael Akhmedov, the GRU officer who disappeared from the Soviet consulate in Constantinople in May 1942, but did not emerge from hiding until 1948. He waited until 1984 before writing about his experiences, and only three other GRU officers have discarded similar inhibitions. This trio of GRU defectors includes Igor Gouzenko, the cipher clerk who was prompted by economic considerations to stay rather than take his family back to Moscow in September 1945; Grigori Tokaev, the scientist who crossed over to the West in Berlin in 1948; and Vladimir Rezun, the United Nations diplomat who spied for the British in Geneva for a year before his escape in June 1978.

The relative lack of knowledge in the West about the secret organs of the Soviet government meant that even those on the periphery of the intelligence had information that could prove useful. Thus Nikolai Borodin, the microbiologist who defected in London in August 1948, turned out to know little of value beyond a detailed order of battle for the Soviet embassy. Thus, although Borodin was a senior and trusted scientist who had been allowed to travel to the United States to study methods of drug manufacture, the main value of his information lay in what he had picked up about intelligence operations, rather than in any disclosure regarding Soviet technological advances. Indeed, his debriefings confirmed the West's lead in the field of scientific research, a conclusion endorsed by the rocket and jet propulsion specialist, Colonel Tokaev, three years later. Indeed, it is significant that during the entire period of the Cold War, only two other Soviets (apart from Oleg Penkovsky) are known to have handed useful information of a highly technical data to Western contacts: Lieutenant Viktor I. Belenko, who defected by flying his highly secret MiG-25 interceptor to Hakodate in northern Japan, and Adolf G. Tolkachev, the aeronautical engineer who was arrested in June 1985 and executed soon afterwards.

The ultimate goal for the Western intelligence agencies, of course, was the recruitment of a fellow professional in the opposition camp. Damage caused by intelligence defectors is invariably out of all proportion to their apparent rank. Anatoli Granovsky, who applied for political asylum in Sweden in September 1946, was not a simple seaman as his papers suggested, but a senior NKVD officer who had held an important post in Prague. When he appeared at the American embassy in Stockholm he was about to embark on an undercover mission in the Soviet merchant marine for the Third Chief Directorate. The disadvantage of receiving a defector after the event is simply that the validity of his 'meal-ticket' diminishes from the moment the Soviet authorities realize their loss and initiate a damage-control exercise. When Granovsky failed to return to his ship, his Soviet colleagues assumed the worst and took the necessary precautions on the basis that every secret with which he had been entrusted would be compromised. Thus the ideal is the recruitment of an asset who can be kept in place for as long as possible before defection becomes necessary. Rupert Sigl, an Austrian-born KGB officer, crossed into West Berlin in

April 1969 after several years of collaboration with the CIA and brought with him details of KGB assets in the West. Captain Aleksei Myagkov of the Third Chief Directorate, who defected in Berlin in February 1974, had worked with what he called 'Western contacts' for an unspecified period before he surrendered to the British, but his most useful knowledge, from a Western intelligence standpoint, was limited to the five years he had spent in East Germany, attached to the 6th Motorized Rifle Guards Division. Viktor Sheymov, of the KGB's Eighth Chief Directorate, who was arguably the single most important defector of the decade, had also developed a long-term relationship with his handlers. He was exfiltrated from Moscow in May 1980, together with his wife and daughter, having maintained contact with his CIA case officer since the previous November.

In contrast, Stanislav Levchenko slipped away from the Soviet embassy in Tokyo without having made any prior arrangements with the CIA, which was both astonished and delighted to arrange political asylum for the FCD major in October 1979, at extremely short notice. Like Levchenko, Ilya Dzhirkvelov operated under journalistic cover but he was, he admits, a reluctant defector when he sought resettlement in England. He had served the Soviet system faithfully for thirty-seven years, and his final defection, in Geneva in March 1980, was almost spontaneous.

Aside from the intelligence personnel, there are those defectors who were not themselves KGB or GRU officers, but Soviet officials with a useful knowledge of intelligence operations. Thus, as well as their propaganda value, their memory represented an asset of additional importance. Some, like Alexander Barmine, who disappeared from his legation in Athens in June 1937, and Aleksandr Kaznacheev, who walked out of the Soviet embassy in Rangoon in June 1959, had been co-opted to participate in particular intelligence operations and were therefore able to disclose useful material upon their arrival in the West. In the case of Arkadi Shevchenko, the most senior Soviet diplomat ever to defect, although he had only limited dealings with the KGB, he was able to identify several key former colleagues who had been operating under UN or diplomatic cover, and did so during two and a half years of contact with the CIA before his defection in 1978. Vladimir Sakharov, also a regular Soviet diplomat, had been co-opted to work for the KGB as well as having been recruited to spy for the CIA by the time he defected in Kuwait in July 1971.

Although in retrospect it may seem easy to understand why the Soviets mentioned in these pages defected to the West, the fact remains that even within the *nomenklatura* they maintained an enhanced status which meant they endured little of the privations experienced by most citizens in a totalitarian society. They had access to special facilities denied their fellow countrymen, and they enjoyed the opportunity to travel abroad. The intelligence professional, often known as a *sotrudnik* or privileged member of the state who enjoys the trust of the Party, carried even more prestige and benefits. To abandon a comfortable lifestyle for the permanent insecurity of an existence in a foreign country, under a new name, with the threat of execution, is a momentous step not taken lightly. For lesser mortals, the undertaking is still a dangerous one, as a young Lithuanian seaman, Simas Kudirka, discovered to his cost in November 1970 when he seized the opportunity to defect by jumping from his fishing vessel on to an American Coast Guard cutter off the coast of New England. Astonishingly, Kudirka was handed back to the Soviets, on the orders of a misguided Coast Guard rear admiral, to face ten years' imprisonment for his treason. Another seaman, Sergei Kourdakov, was more lucky when he swam ashore in Canada from the Russian trawler *Shturman Elagin* in September 1971. As well as being a naval cadet, the twenty-year-old Kourdakov had worked with the KGB to penetrate and break up groups of Christians, and his account of religious persecution, *The Persecutor*, was published soon after he had been granted Canadian citizenship, and had completed a lecture tour of evangelical churches across North America. Shortly before publication, Kourdakov shot himself.

A superficial glance at the literature of defectors might lead to the conclusion that it is characteristic only of the Cold War, and that the new democracy in Russia has drawn a firm line under the totalitarian excesses which allowed the KGB to acquire its notoriety. Whilst it is true that much of the old KGB had been dismantled, and responsibility for internal security passed to a new, democratically accountable ministry, there is plenty of evidence to suggest that not as much has changed as the optimists had hoped. The new SVR runs Russia's foreign intelligence operations from the old FCD headquarters on Moscow's ring road at Yasenevo and despite the end of the era of superpower confrontation no less than twenty Russians were arrested during 1993 and charged with espionage. Equally significantly, the SVR's *rezident* in Washington DC, Aleksandr Lysenko, was expelled in February 1994 when he was implicated as one of the handlers responsible for handling the KGB's mole in the CIA, Aldrich Ames.

However unpalatable, the occupation that has been described as the second oldest profession continues to thrive in the post-Cold War climate, and the authors mentioned in the pages that follow are those that made a perceptible difference, not to Russian literature in the tradition of Boris Pasternak, but, rather, to the Soviet culture of betrayal and treachery. Unlike Aleksandr Solzhenitsyn, whose exposé of Stalin's crimes *One Day in the Life of Ivan Denisovich*, was approved by Nikita Khrushchev, these are the outcasts who can never contemplate a return to their beloved *rodina*.

Grigori Z. Bessedovsky

Knowing Soviet customs I no longer had any illusions; my condemnation was signed. Going to Moscow meant going to my execution.

A French gendarme on duty outside the Soviet embassy in the rue de Grenelle was surprised early in October 1929 by the sudden appearance of a tall young Russian, who had climbed over the wall armed with a loaded automatic. He introduced himself to the astonished policeman as the temporary Soviet chargé d'affaires, and demanded political asylum, claiming that his wife and son were being held by OGPU thugs in the embassy. He was escorted to the Quai d'Orsay where Bessedovsky and his family, who were removed from the embassy by a squad of gendarmes, were promised protection.

Of Ukrainian Jewish extraction, from Poltava, Bessedovsky revealed that he had been active in the Social Revolutionary movement, and had become a diplomat in 1922, serving in Vienna, Warsaw and Tokyo. At the time of his defection he was thirty-two years old and held the rank of counsellor. According to the Soviets, he was an embezzler who had failed to return to Moscow as instructed; Bessedovsky insisted he was an ideological convert who had been singled out for assassination by the OGPU. Under intensive interrogation by the French, during which he made no mention of having been suspected of having stolen large sums from the Soviet Foreign Ministry, Bessedovsky revealed what he believed was the identity of a British civil servant who had visited a colleague at the embassy in July 1929 in a vain attempt to sell secrets, including copies of the Foreign Office's ciphers. The offer had been rejected, but Bessedovsky supplied enough information about the mysterious Briton, who had given a false name, that MI5 was eventually able to identify him, albeit posthumously, as a junior clerk in the communications department named Ernest Oldham who gassed himself in September 1933.

Within two days of Bessedovsky's defection he was interviewed by Commander Wilfred Dunderdale, the Russian-born SIS head of station in Paris, who formed a poor opinion of the man who claimed to be his Soviet counterpart, a member of the local OGPU *rezidentura*. He was described as 'smart and intelligent, but neither frank nor principled, and quite possibly not honest'. Nevertheless he was 'extremely talkative and indiscreet' so he was considered an important catch by the British and French security agencies.

Bessedovsky subsequently made a living as a journalist and wrote *Revelations of a Soviet Diplomat*, which was published in 1931. He continued to live in France, and there were rumours during the Second World War that he had been active in the communist resistance, and that he had also maintained links with the Gestapo. He was last seen in the South of France in the 1950s, where he was believed to have re-established contact with the NKVD, on whose behalf he is thought to have peddled numerous literary forgeries, including *J'ai choisi la potence* by General Vlassov, *Ma carrière à l'État-Major Soviétique* by Ivan Krylov and *Les Maréchaux Soviétiques vous parlent* by Cyrille Kalinov. Masquerading as Stalin's nephew, Budu Svanidze, he wrote both *My Uncle Jo* and *In Conversation with Stalin*, and under his own name wrote an authenticating foreword to both in which he vouched for the author's identity. As the French expert on communism, Boris Souvarine, later demonstrated, Svanidze never existed. In 1952 Bessedovsky pulled off his most impressive and ambitious coup, *Notes for a Journal*, which were attributed to Maxim Litvinov.

Notes for a Journal was an impressive hoax and, despite the many mistakes the Russian typescript contained, supposedly made by the Commissar for Foreign Affairs, concerning details he would have known, the distinguished historian Professor E. H. Carr endorsed it, described it as 'the most sensational work of its kind yet published' and concluded that 'it contains a substratum of genuine material emanating in some form or other from Litvinov himself', although he conceded 'that numerous and extensive passages bear the mark of having been retouched or invented for the supposed purpose of giving the document a popular appeal'. Litvinov, who had lived in London, working as a publisher's clerk before he returned from exile to Russia, had spent nine years as Stalin's Commissar for Foreign Affairs and the *Notes* presented both him and history in rather a new light. Actually, much of the material had appeared already in Bessedovsky's *Na Putyakh k Termidoru*, previously published in Paris in 1931. Carr went to Paris to authenticate the typescript on behalf of the publisher André Deutsch and, having held two long meetings with Bessedovsky, was satisfied by the assertion that it had been entrusted by Litvinov to the Soviet minister in Stockholm, Alexandra Kollontai, who had died in March 1952, two months after Litvinov. Unable to check the tale further, Carr had accepted it, with this qualification:

> External evidence failing, the issue of the character of the document must turn mainly on the uncertain ground of internal evidence. The hypothesis of a complete forgery or fiction cannot be dismissed out of hand. If this hypothesis is correct, the motive has been commercial, not political. While particular

statements in the journal may be regarded as favourable or hostile to the regime, the document as a whole serves no apparent propaganda purpose; the author appears as in many respects ambivalent in his judgments of the events described, and, in particular, in his attitude to Stalin. This gives the document, whether genuine or not, a certain value for the historian. If it is a fiction, it is a fiction written without *parti pris*, and much of it written by someone intimately concerned with party and with diplomatic events; many passages betray close and detailed knowledge which can be checked from other sources. That it is not marked by any depth of thought, that it contains many trivialities, some improbabilities, and some demonstrable inaccuracies, that it exhibits a strong tendency to 'show off' and, considering the position of the supposed author, an extraordinary degree of independence, does not necessarily constitute an argument against its genuineness.

In view of some scholars, particularly Bertram D. Wolfe, Carr may not have been duped completely, for he points out that although Bessedovsky was later revealed to be the source for *Notes*, Carr omitted his name completely from his introduction, without explanation, which suggests that he was reluctant to link the defector with the typescript.

In one memorable passage, Litvinov allegedly recalled a visit made by Mao Tse-Tung to Moscow in May 1926 and demonstrated a remarkable degree of prescience by noting his shrewdness. In fact, Mao never went to Moscow in 1926, when the future leader was still a member of the Kuomintang–Communist alliance, and the trusted head of the Kuomintang's propaganda department.

Ir this extract from his autobiography, Bessedovsky describes how he was accused of treason by a notorious member of the feared OGPU.

Revelations of a Soviet Diplomat

My last days at the Embassy were a hell on earth.

I was surrounded by Ogpu agents, secret and official. My every word and movement was spied upon. My wife was exhausted, but never tired of repeating that she hoped for the best. I never went out without two revolvers and spare ammunition. Often I heard suspicious sounds in the little corridor beside my office which I used as a library. Once I jumped up and fired some revolver shots at the ceiling. Someone hastily decamped. One or two weeks more and I should have lost my reason; I had riddled the ceiling of my room with bullet holes. The hours dragged on interminably.

At last October 2nd came.

On that day, at 3 p.m., I was informed of the arrival from Berlin of Roisenmann, a member of the Ogpu and of the Control Commission. He asked me to go at once to his room, No. 82. I answered that I could not do so until five o'clock. This reply was not to his taste, but my arbitrary tone intimidated him.

At the appointed hour I entered room No. 82. It was raining, and the sky was full of clouds.

'Good afternoon, Comrade Bessedovsky,' said Roisenmann. 'I am going to speak to you in the name of the Politbureau of the Communist Party. We have learnt that you have permitted yourself to criticize the Soviet Government, not only in conversation with non-party sympathizers, but also in your dealings with foreigners. Your criticisms are calculated to damage the prestige of the Soviet Government, and are tantamount to acts of high treason. Moreover, we have been informed that you intend to spend your leave abroad instead of on the territory of the USSR. The Politbureau had instructed me to demand an explanation.'

I found myself scrutinizing Roisenmann's long face, stupid and repellent. I could no longer contain myself. I resolved to finish it once and for all.

'You are right,' I said. 'I have criticized and I do criticize the Soviet Government. I have a right to. I have acquired that right by shedding blood for the proletariat. You know me. It was not to obtain influential posts that I became a revolutionary. I have never shrunk from dangerous duties. But if I have become a revolutionary I have not done so in order to substitute for the Tsarist regime a Stalin regime that depends on a gang of besotted lackeys directed by a megalomaniac Dictator. I never denied the necessity for a dictatorship during the Civil War, when it was a question of taking up a brush of iron and sweeping away the dross of Tsarism. We performed that operation quickly and well, better than others could have done it. That is our justification for all time. But there must be an end to everything. Now our task is to create a new regime, a regime of democracy. The system of a monopoly in the hands of a single party has had its day. The country must be freed, and we must destroy the last vestiges of a feudal system which oppresses the peasants, and not impose upon them the additional expenditure which is the result of the monopoly of foreign trade. The peasant must become the owner of his portion of land. Liberty must be given to trade and to the small industries. Every revolution must have its Thermidor. I am not afraid of the word; we need a Thermidor. That is the law of history, and those who will not recognize it are traitors and criminals. They are jeopardizing the revolution, and they must be rooted up from the sphere of government.'

As I spoke these last words I raised my voice. Then I stopped.

Roisenmann flushed crimson, his eyes wide and staring. Clearly he thought I was off my head. Full of malice, he walked up to me.

'You are mad,' he said. 'You don't know what you are saying, or what you have become. You are a disciple of Miliukov, nothing more. Everything that you have bawled at me is counter-revolutionary. But you forget that you occupy a position of great responsibility. You have not the right to utter such words, especially in a foreign country. It is high treason. You are a traitor to your country, and you will have to answer to Moscow, where I shall send you here and now.'

'I shall not go to Moscow,' I replied, 'as I should not be allowed to express my views. I shall stay here and do my duty as a citizen to the end. I shall know how to make the Russian masses understand the cry that is tearing my heart.'

'You will go to Moscow!' Roisenmann shouted, thumping the table. 'Surely you do not suppose that you will be permitted to remain abroad with all the secrets that have been entrusted to you in your capacity as a Soviet diplomat! Oh no, my friend!'

I was the calmer of the two, and this enraged him all the more.

'I am not such a fool as to go with you. You accuse me of treason, and I know what that means. I might go to Moscow as a sacrifice, just as I made sacrifices during the Revolution. But I know what you do with your antagonists when you have accused them of high treason. The dungeons of Lubianka await them. I should be shot without a trial, in secret, and I should not be the first to disappear in such a way. No, my life is not mine to give away; it belongs to my people – the people I have always fought for. I shall go on leave with the authority of the Commissariat for Foreign Affairs. During my leave I shall have time to think. I shall certainly not remain in the Communist Party. This conversation means that I have broken with your party, or rather with the Dictator who is at its head. Thousands and thousands of its members think as I do. You smother their voices with your despicable Ogpu. The slightest indication of what I have said and done today would mean exile for life.'

'I refuse to argue with you,' snarled Roisenmann, more and more beside himself with rage. 'You are a counter-revolutionary who has betrayed his party. But you know too many things to be allowed to live abroad. You will not be touched if you come with me. You shall be sent somewhere in the South, and you shall be paid a pension of 1,000 marks a month, like Scheimann. But you shall not stay here. I, the representative of the Politbureau, say so. The entire staff of the Embassy and the Trade Delegation are under my orders, as Tumanov and Ahrens know very well.

If you do not go voluntarily you will be taken by force, dead or alive.'

Then, changing his tone:

'Listen, I give you my word that you shall be safe in Russia. I was wrong to accuse you of high treason; I lost my head. We know that you have hereditary neurasthenia. Your father committed suicide; so did several of your cousins. They were all neurasthenic. You must have lost control of yourself. You did not know what you were saying. You have always been a man of high principles, most conscientious. No careerist considerations have ever influenced you. You command universal respect. I guarantee that nothing will happen to you in Russia. Think; the masses have fought a decisive battle, and at such a time you strike this blow against them. You are a revolutionary, not a disciple of Miliukov. You could never associate yourself with such scoundrels. You will end by quarrelling with them, and your whole life will be thrown away. Come with me, Bessedovsky. Do me this favour. I am fifty-one; you might have been my son – you shall be. Not a hair of your head shall be touched; I give you my personal guarantee. You are undergoing a nervous crisis. It will pass. We cannot lose you. Think of your future. You are eloquent, and may do great things in Soviet Russia.'

'No, Comrade Roisenmann,' I said; 'I will not give in. Henceforth I shall fight for my new political ideals, with just as much ardour as I fought in the Civil War. And these ideals are not new; they spring from the very essence of my political creed. I have always fought for democracy. Once I believed that democracy implied social equality; it was for that that I joined your party. But from my earliest experiences of Communism I was sickened by the brutality with which you crush down everything democratic. That is why in 1920 and 1921 I worked for the Communist Opposition, demanding that the Soviets should be made democratic. In the name of this principle I spoke at the Poltava local conference in February 1921. Ask Comrade Poraiko – he is now Commissar for Justice in the Ukraine. Ask Cohn; ask Manuilsky. It was as a democrat that I was sent abroad. But even from abroad I have always protested against this abominable centralization which has transformed the Party first into the fief of a few leaders and then into the personal property of Stalin, the embodiment of the most senseless type of Oriental despotism.

'But don't be alarmed, Comrade Roisenmann. Remember the Camo affair – the man who was run over by a car at Tiflis. Do you recall what Stalin did? He ordered the Ogpu to shoot a poor workman, a member of the Party, whose only fault was that he had run over one of Stalin's personal friends! And still you dare to speak of a government of workers!

There can be no such thing in a country where a Dictator could do a thing like that. And what have you done, you, the controllers, the "conscience of the Party"? You are all safely dug in. All you care for is your income, your political career, your promotions. Don't talk to me about decisive battles fought by the Russian peasants. There is such a battle, but it is being fought against you, for the economic freedom you suppress. The peasants have unimaginable difficulty in protecting themselves from the machinations of those you sent to snatch away their corn. You flourish your tractors before the peasant's eyes, but you rob him of his last goat. You buy his corn at not more than 16 per cent of its market price, and then hurry off to sell it at an exorbitant profit. You suppress all economic initiative in the countryside. You are the gravediggers of the Revolution. You are criminals, and from this day forward I shall fight relentlessly against you.'

Roisenmann was silent. On his face was an expression of infinite hatred. Then he said in a solemn voice:

'In the name of the Party Central Committee I call upon you to go to Moscow immediately. If you refuse I shall take extreme measures.'

He stopped for an instant, and then added:

'Do not forget that you are now on Soviet territory. I have given my instructions. Neither you nor your family can leave the Embassy.'

I left the room, slamming the door behind me. The corridor was badly lit. A carpet deadened my footsteps. From an open door came the sound of a popular song that was being bellowed out by Comrade Roisenmann's drunken colleagues. I took courage. If they were singing a fox-trot they could hardly be contemplating an assassination. I went to my wife's room and told her that she must prepare for immediate departure. I took two revolvers, with two lots of spare ammunition. A quick calculation told me that I had twenty-six shots to fire. Surely that should be enough.

I went downstairs. There was my office with its porcelain name-plate: 'Embassy Counsellor'. Soon I would have to put up 'Chauffeur'. So much the better. It was not for the sake of a career that I had joined the revolutionaries. Let Stalin's underlings cling to their jobs. I would cling to my fight for the people.

I went out into the courtyard. The gravel crackled under my feet. The song was still going on. Yes, revolution had become reaction. An end must be made of the sufferings of millions of my fellow creatures, and this was an aim to strive for with all the energy and enthusiasm that had been used against the Tsars.

I went into the waiting-room. The door of the concierge's lodge was half-open. One of the concierges of the Trade Delegation, a man named Jijin, stood in front of me. He was as white as the wall behind him, and his lips trembled.

'Comrade Bessedovsky, our orders are strict; please go back to your apartments.'

'You won't let me go out? What right have you to stop me? Do not forget that I am *chargé d'affaires*. Go away at once.'

Jijin became still paler, and raised a revolver.

'Comrade Bessedovsky,' he said. 'I have a great respect for you. But I am a member of the Party, and Comrade Roisenmann has ordered me not to let you go out. If you take another step you are a dead man.'

What was I to do? Shoot Jijin? But through the doorway I saw another concierge, also with a revolver in his hand. I turned my back on Jijin and went out into the courtyard. I tried to get out by the main gate, which was usually fastened with an ordinary bolt. This time it was locked.

I thought of the simplest form an attack on me might take. I should be overpowered during the night – perhaps my family as well. I remembered that on the same day two diplomatic couriers had brought in an enormous trunk, into which three corpses might . . .

Call for help on the telephone? No use. I should not be allowed to communicate with my friends outside. There was only one thing left – the wall.

It was not very high. I took off my overcoat and threw it over to the other side. Then, thinking of the exercises I used to do in my native Poltava when I was going on an expedition to steal fruit, I pulled myself up and climbed over.

I felt a smile playing on my face. 'Here ends a phase of my life,' I said to myself, 'representing sixteen years of struggles, sixteen years of work for the State in positions of great responsibility. Now a new phase is beginning.'

The ground on the other side was damp. I picked up my coat and walked towards the building in front of me. It was occupied; and the only way out of the garden in which I found myself was through the doors of the house. A new despair overtook me. At that moment I heard my wife's voice; the windows of our apartments were open. I resolved to persevere. The other wall was at least three and a half metres high. In the garden I found a chair to help me in another gymnastic feat. At length I got into the second garden. Lighted windows overlooked the *parterre*. One of them opened, and a powerful voice asked me what I was doing there and how I had got in. I explained in a few hurried words and requested permission to go through the house. M. Rambeau, the concierge, was good enough to accompany me to the police station and to the Prefecture. An hour and a half later I returned with M. Benoist, Commissaire of Police; we got my wife and son out, and I left the Embassy for ever.

Elisabeth K. Poretsky

Normally anyone allowed to leave the USSR was
warned not to publish anything detrimental to it.

Austrian by birth, Elisabeth Poretsky met her husband Ignace Reiss in Moscow in 1922 as he prepared for a secret mission to Lwow. A founder member of the illegal Polish Communist Party, Reiss was arrested and charged with fomenting Bolshevism among the ranks of the Polish army. He was sentenced to five years' imprisonment but after eighteen months succeeded in escaping to Germany where he was joined by his fiancée. Together they moved to Vienna where they both operated as agents under the direction of the military attaché at the Soviet embassy. After being detained by the Austrian police for two months in 1925 Ignace was recalled to Moscow to receive a decoration and a new assignment, to recruit networks into Poland from Prague. However, they stayed in Prague only a short time before being sent to Holland under commercial cover to run a network based in England. This task lasted until 1928 when Ignace's contacts with an Irish communist who was under surveillance led to his sketch appearing in a London newspaper. Compromised, Ignace asked to be recalled to Moscow where Elisabeth joined him with their baby son in 1929.

After three years in Moscow Ignace was sent abroad and Elisabeth moved to Berlin before travelling to Switzerland and settling in Paris, providing her husband with a safe-house in between his missions across Europe, procuring weapons for the Spanish Republicans. She was recalled to Moscow in December 1936 by which time Stalin's purges were under way, and when she returned to Paris in March 1937 she gave her husband a report of the terror that had gripped so many of their friends. She also talked to their old colleague Walter Krivitsky, who had been ordered to fly home from his base in The Hague, but he made the journey and was allowed to resume his post in Holland. However, his depressing account of his visit convinced Ignace that he should resign from the Party and go into hiding. He chose the tiny village of Finhaut in the canton of the Valais in Switzerland but in September he kept a rendezvous with a trusted friend in Lausanne and was shot dead. The police recovered a box of chocolates laced with strychnine from the hotel room used by Ignace's assassins, and this made Elisabeth realize that she and her son had also been targets. When the police investigation into her husband's murder had been completed she moved to Amsterdam and at the end of October met Krivitsky in Paris, who explained that he had defected and warned her that she was still in danger. She and her son adopted new identities and found an apartment in Paris where they lived until 1940 when they travelled to Lisbon, and obtained a visa to the United States, where they arrived in February 1941, on the day Krivitsky was found shot dead in a hotel in Washington DC. In America she found work at a university and in 1955 was interviewed by the FBI about her pre-war underground work for the Soviets. Soon afterwards she returned to Paris and her biography of her late husband, *Our Own People*, was published in 1969. Here she recalls how Ignace, who she called Ludwik, learned of his fate from Krivitsky.

Our Own People

Weeks had stretched into months and we had heard nothing from Krivitsky. By now Ludwik was certain he would never return. Then one day we learned that he was back in The Hague.

Early next morning I rang him. I asked about our friends. In every case the answer was the same: 'He is very ill, he is in hospital . . .' It was obvious that all had been arrested. I was perturbed that Krivitsky should have been allowed to leave, while everyone else was being arrested. Ludwik said he thought that Krivitsky had been 'trusted' enough to be sent abroad to avert a panic in the services, on the calculated risk that he too might not return.

Ludwik was glad he had not acted before and decided that now he and Krivitsky together could take the necessary steps. I reminded him that Krivitsky was a person who alternated continually between hope and despair, and that for the last two years he had shied away from a decision. After all, it was he who in 1935, after Ludwik's return from Moscow, had said: 'They don't trust us.' This sentence became a leitmotiv, often repeated: 'They need us, but they can't trust us. We are international Communists, our time is over. They will replace us with Soviet Communists, men like Zarubin to whom the revolutionary movement means nothing.' But when I asked him whether he intended to wait until they disposed of him Krivitsky would always answer: 'No. But the time is not ripe yet.' I was sure he would find some ray of hope, even now, to hang on to. Ludwik answered that he knew Krivitsky's character well enough, but that his main argument, the Spanish revolution, was gone.

Ludwik met Krivitsky a few days later, and they had a long conversation. Krivitsky told Ludwik of an interview he had had with Yezhov, the new head of the NKVD. He was convinced Yezhov was insane. In the middle of an important and confidential telephone call he would suddenly burst out in crazy laughter and tell stories of his own life in the most obscene language. After a few hours spent with Yezhov, Krivitsky said he had begun to doubt his own sanity. This was the man to whom Stalin had given the task of purging the party.

But Krivitsky had things of greater personal import to tell Ludwik. He said he had been asked why he had not reported to the party that Ludwik's brother had been killed serving in the Polish army against the Soviets. Had he not known that Ludwik's brother had been a Polish intelligence agent, and that the reason Ludwik had kept this secret was that he himself was carrying on his brother's work, had in fact been working for the Polish police during all the years he had pretended to be a loyal Communist? Had Krivitsky misled the party deliberately about Ludwik's brother? Krivitsky said he had answered that he knew Ludwik's brother had been killed during the war but he did not know which war – he did know, of course – and that he had always believed it was the First World War. Krivitsky added that his explanation had not been believed.

Ludwik now realized why Krivitsky had been 'trusted' to return. The old and almost forgotten story of his brother was a clear indication: Krivitsky had been sent abroad with the mission of bringing Ludwik back. At the same time, it was obvious that Krivitsky was deliberately sabotaging his own mission by telling Ludwik the story. Had Ludwik still had any intention of returning, this story alone would have kept him from doing so; it was obvious what his fate would be the minute he got there. Moreover, Krivitsky realized very well the consequences of his loyalty to his old friend. If Ludwik did not come back, Krivitsky's failure would not be forgiven.

There was only one thing to be done now. Ludwik told Krivitsky that he had been awaiting his return before announcing his break, and that now was the time for both of them to make it. Krivitsky, however, could not bring himself to that last step, and here his loyalty to an old friend ended. In his book [*I Was Stalin's Agent*] he says: 'I mustered all the familiar arguments and sang the old song that we must not run away from the battle. "The Soviet Union", I insisted, "is still the sole hope of the workers of the world. It is our duty to stick to our post." '

Krivitsky also adds that Ludwik left him 'with the understanding that he would bide his time and watch further developments in Moscow before making his contemplated break with the Soviet Government.' But he knew Ludwik had no intention of biding his time. He had waited long enough and he knew he had to act, even alone.

Soon after this Ludwik went to Amsterdam and telephoned Sneevliet.

He knew that in spite of the many years during which they had not seen each other, he could trust him completely. Sneevliet told Ludwik he had expected his call. It was high time, he said. He had been in Barcelona, looking in vain for Andreas Nin. They arranged to meet in a café. 'I will come alone to this appointment,' Sneevliet added, 'and should you ask me to ride in a car with you, I would. I trust you.'

Sneevliet urged Ludwik to make a public break and publish it in the left-wing press. Ludwik however believed it was his duty to notify the Central Committee of the Soviet Communist Party first. He intended to wait a week to publish his letter, a week being about the time he calculated it would take the letter to reach the Central Committee through Embassy channels. Meanwhile Ludwik urged me to leave Paris immediately; for, as he pointed out, through me he could be easily detected.

In fact I was the only one through whom he could be traced, since he avoided any other contact. He could move from one part of the city to another and make it harder for them to find him, but I had a permanent address known to the NKVD. Although I was terrified at leaving him in Paris without knowing what was happening to him, I had to agree he was right. I therefore wrote to the mayor of a mountain village in Switzerland which we had once passed through and liked, and rented two rooms. Thus I would have an address when I left, and not have to communicate with him by post. He told me he would join us in about a week, after he had attended to his business in Paris. He did not say what he planned to do, and I am not sure he himself knew exactly how he would proceed.

Ludwik saw Krivitsky again in Paris but did not tell him of his meeting with Sneevliet. They agreed to meet again in a few days. I myself saw Krivitsky once more before I left, but this very old friend had only one thing to say: 'I hope you are not encouraging Ludwik not to return to the Soviet Union. I must warn you against that.' We spoke of the numbers of people passing through Paris now on their way back to Moscow, and I said that their returning there now to be shot reminded me of those soldiers in the First World War who were killed an hour before the Armistice bugle sounded. 'Yes,' said Krivitsky, 'that is true. And yet there were some killed in that last hour.' When I asked Krivitsky what he planned to do, he answered: 'I will go back to the Soviet Union.' He must have believed even then that if he went back the NKVD would let him live. I wondered whether he really would want to live on after all his friends had been liquidated. Did he want to be the only survivor?

Walter Krivitsky

Even in the United States Stalin's long
arm of vengeance has tried to reach me.

Born Samuel Ginsberg in Galicia, he was known in The Hague, where he ran an art gallery on the fashionable Celebestraat, as the wealthy antiquarian bookseller Dr Martin Lessner. In fact he was the head of Soviet military intelligence for Western Europe and ran a large network of illegals that stretched right across the Continent. At the end of September 1937 he was ordered back to Moscow but, fearing that he was intended to become a victim of Stalin's purges like his friend Ignace Reiss, he fled to Paris where he sought political asylum. The French Sûreté extracted enough information from him to fill eighty volumes but he was unimpressed by their protection. He moved to the United States where he gave interviews to the *Saturday Evening Post* and testified before the Dies Committee, and then to Canada, and it was not until September 1939 that the British Ambassador in Washington DC, Lord Lothian, was told by the journalist Isaac Don Levine that Krivitsky could implicate a spy in the British Foreign Office.

The spy was identified as a cipher clerk, Captain John King, who was arrested, convicted of espionage and sentenced to a long term of imprisonment. Impressed by Krivitsky's evidence, MI5 brought him across the Atlantic to interview him in London, and then returned him to Canada where he was the subject of two assassination attempts. His book, *In Stalin's Secret Service*, was published in America in 1939 (and in England in 1940, as *I Was Stalin's Agent*) and was the subject of much criticism from his friend Elisabeth Poretsky who asserted that 'Krivitsky in his ghost-written book took credit for operations he had nothing to do with':

> Unable to write in English, he had to rely on ghost-writers, and he knew nothing of the American press. Whoever wrote his book cared only for one thing: to make it as sensational as possible. I am sure he simply gave the writers the information and then looked on, as he had always done, while they distorted it. The errors and exaggerations I have pointed out are only the most obvious ones; the omissions from the book are almost as serious as the distortions. It did create a sensation – a sinister one, in Europe, and for me.

Krivitsky was eventually found shot dead in his locked Washington DC hotel room in February 1941, apparently the victim of suicide; but many believe that, despite the note he left, he had finally been cornered by one of the assassination squads that had been sent to Canada to liquidate him. Whether self-inflicted or otherwise, Krivitsky had brought massive damage on the GRU and was known to have been a priority target. In addition to tipping off MI5 to Captain King's espionage, he revealed to the French Sûreté and the FBI the extent of the Soviet networks in Europe and America. In this passage he recalls the aftermath of the assassination of his friend Ignace Reiss in Switzerland.

I Was Stalin's Agent

I was now preparing to leave for Moscow on August 21, by the steamship *Bretagne*. From the moment the Reiss affair broke and while I was still at the Hotel Napoleon, I had observed that I was being shadowed. When my wife and child arrived and we moved to the Passy pension, the shadowing became even more assiduous. My wife would notice it even when she took the child for a walk in the park. It was, of course, the work of Spiegelglass. My wife, who was not well, was made worse by these worries, and moreover my child got the whooping cough. When the date of my departure arrived it was clear that I should have to leave my family behind. I made arrangements for them to follow me to Moscow several weeks later.

Bearing a passport under the name of Schoenborn, I arrived about 7 p.m. at the Gare St Lazare to take the eight o'clock train for Le Havre, where I was to board the boat for Leningrad. About ten minutes before departure time, after I had attended to my baggage and already seated myself in the railway coach, the assistant to the Paris agent of the Ogpu rushed in. He told me that a telegram had just come from Moscow with instructions that I should remain in Paris. I was incredulous, but a moment later one of my own men, all out of breath, came dashing in with the news of another coded message, similar in content. I asked to see the telegram, but was told that Spiegelglass had them. I had my baggage removed and got off the train just as it pulled out of the station.

It flashed through my mind that the whole business of my recall had been staged to test me, to see if I really would return to the Soviet Union. In that event, I had passed the test. But I resented that bit of chicanery deeply. A feeling came over me at that moment that I not only would end my service, but that I would never go back to Stalin's Russia.

I registered now at the Hotel Terminus, St Lazare, as Schoenborn, the Czech merchant whose name I bore. My wife was still at the pension as Mrs Lessner. I sent word to her that I had not left after all. That night I walked the length and breadth of Paris, all alone, wrestling with the question whether to go back or not.

During the next days I kept trying to figure out why my departure had been postponed at the last minute. Did Stalin want to give me another chance to show my loyalty? Yet the spying on me was palpably intensified.

The evening of August 26 I went with my Belgian aide and his wife to the theatre to see a farewell performance of Gorky's *Enemies*, given by a Soviet troupe visiting Paris. We sat in the second row. During the first intermission, a hand touched my shoulder. I turned around. There was Spiegelglass with some companions.

'You can leave tomorrow with these artists on one of our own boats,' he counselled me.

I turned upon him angrily and told him not to bother me. 'I'll go when I'm ready,' I said.

I noticed that Spiegelglass and his associates shortly thereafter disappeared from the theatre. I cabled Moscow that I would return with my family as soon as the child recovered.

On August 27 I moved to Breteuil, a couple of hours from Paris, and we lived there quietly for about a week while the child convalesced. On the morning of September 5, opening the Paris *Matin*, I saw a dispatch from Lausanne, Switzerland, reporting the mysterious murder of a Czechoslovak, Hans Eberhardt. So they had got Ignace Reiss!

The assassination of Reiss became a celebrated case in Europe and reverberated in the press of America and throughout the world. The Swiss police, assisted by Deputy Sneevliet and the widow of Reiss, did a remarkable piece of investigation lasting many months. The record of the case has been published by Pierre Tesne in Paris in a book entitled *L'Assassinat d'Ignace Reiss*. The following facts were established by the police investigations.

On the night of September 4, off the Chamblandes road running from Lausanne, the body of an unknown man about forty years of age was found riddled by machine-gun bullets. There were five bullets in his head and seven in his body. A strand of grey hair was found clutched in the hand of the dead man. In his pockets were a passport in the name of Hans Eberhardt and a railway ticket for France.

A motor-car of American make, abandoned on September 6, at Geneva, led to the identification of two mysterious guests, a man and a woman, who had registered on September 4 at the Hotel de la Paix in Lausanne, and had fled without their baggage and without paying their bill. The woman was Gertrude Schildbach, of German nationality, a resident of Rome. She was an Ogpu agent in Italy. The man was Roland Abbiat, alias François Rossi, alias Py, a native of Monaco, and one of the Paris agents of the Ogpu.

Among the effects left by Gertrude Schildbach at the hotel was a box of chocolates containing strychnine – now in the hands of the Swiss police as one of the exhibits in the case. Gertrude Schildbach had been an intimate friend of the Reiss family, accustomed to play with Reiss's child. She had lacked the nerve to give the poisoned sweets, as Spiegelglass directed, to the family she was accustomed to visit as a friend.

Gertrude Schildbach herself had been wavering politically since the beginning of the purge, and she could plausibly play the part of one ready to join Reiss in breaking with Moscow. Reiss had known of her waverings and trusted her. He went out with her to dine in a restaurant near Chamblandes to discuss the whole situation. So he thought. After dinner they took a little walk. Somehow they wandered off into an obscure road. A motor-car appeared and came to a sudden stop. Several men jumped out of it and attacked Reiss. He fought the attacking band, but with the aid of Schildbach, whose strand of hair was found in his clutch, they forced him into the car. Here one of them, Abbiat-Rossi, assisted by another, Etienne Martignat, both Paris agents of the Ogpu, fired a sub-machine-gun point-blank at Reiss. His body was thrown out of the car a short distance away.

Renata Steiner, born at Saint-Gall, Switzerland, in 1908, was identified as the person who had hired the American-made car employed by the assassins of Reiss. Miss Steiner had been in the Ogpu service since 1935, and had been assigned previously to shadow Sedov, the son of Trotsky. She was one of three accomplices in the assassination of Reiss appre-hended by the police. She confessed to her share in the crime, and helped the authorities to solve it.

There was an expensive sequel to the murder. The Swiss authorities demanded the interrogation of Lydia Grozovskaya, and, in spite of the terrific pressure from the Soviet Embassy, the French authorities had her examined on December 15. It will be recalled that it was Grozovskaya who had received the letters of Reiss on July 17, and turned them over to Spiegelglass. Two days after her examination she was arrested. The Swiss Government demanded her extradition. But once more Stalin's diploma-tic hand went to the assistance of his other hand, the hand engaged in secret murder. The French Courts gave Grozovskaya her freedom on bail to the amount of 50,000 francs, and upon her signing a pledge not to leave France. Needless to say, she disappeared without a trace. The last sight of Grozovskaya by the French police agents was when she shook them off in a high-powered limousine of the Soviet Embassy.

When I read of Reiss's death on September 5, I realized that my own situation was desperate. Stalin and Yezhov would never forgive my refusal to participate in this crime. To them it would mean that I shared Reiss's doubts. I had before me now the choice between a bullet in the Lubianka from Stalin's formal executioners and outside Russia a rain of bullets from a sub-machine-gun in the hands of his informal assassins.

Alexander G. Barmine

*When I work on my book I feel as though I were walking in
a graveyard. All my friends and life associates have been
shot. It seems to be some kind of a mistake that I am alive.*

Alexander Barmine, whose real surname was Graf, defected from the Soviet Embassy in Athens in June 1937, a few days after Ignace Reiss had disappeared in Paris. Barmine held the rank of chargé d'affaires and took the train to Paris where he went into hiding with the Greek woman who was to become his wife. In 1939 they made their way to America where he published his controversial autobiography, *One Who Survived*, in 1945.

A much decorated political commissar during the First World War, Barmine left the Red Army in 1923 with the rank of brigadier-general to take up the appointment of Consul General in Persia. Upon his return to Moscow he worked in the Department of Foreign Trade and in 1929 was director-general of imports, in Paris and Rome. In 1932 he moved to Brussels and the following year headed an official delegation to Warsaw. He was then made president of the Auto-Moto-Export Trust, 'tangled deep in the red tape of Soviet bureaucratization' controlling the export of all Soviet cars and aircraft, and in December 1935 was sent as a diplomat to the Soviet Legation in Athens with the rank of first secretary.

During a routine visit to Moscow in December 1936, in the midst of Stalin's notorious show trials, Barmine learned that many of his friends had been arrested, and by the time he returned to Athens more of his colleagues and superiors had disappeared in the purges. Fearful that his relationship with Màri Pavlides, the Greek architect who was his fiancée, would place him under suspicion, he resigned his post and fled to Paris. In 1938 he published his first book in London, *Memoirs of a Soviet Diplomat: Twenty Years in the Service of the USSR*.

Barmine joined the US army during the war was a private soldier and was later commissioned and transferred to the Office of Strategic Services as a linguist. In 1944 he was dismissed for having written an article in *Reader's Digest* without first having submitted it for approval. He headed the Russian section of the Voice of America radio station for much of the postwar period and his autobiography, subtitled *The Life Story of a Russian under the Soviets*, was published in New York in 1945. Here he recalls his last days in Moscow before his defection.

One Who Survived

The last days that I spent in that land of suspicion and abject sycophancy were extremely painful. I found myself avoiding both friends and acquaintances, seeing only those whom I had to see on official business.

On two different occasions, separated by an interval of about three weeks, I saw Krestinsky, the vice-commissar of foreign affairs, and Doletsky, the director of the Tass press agency. On the first occasion they were still both of them normal men, preoccupied naturally, but capable of smiling, joking, making plans, giving advice. Three weeks later they were gloomy and nervous, so absorbed in their inward thoughts that they spoke in dismal tones, stared inattentively, and hardly understood what I said to them. They knew themselves to be doomed men. They knew that the Piatakov trial, not yet announced in the papers, was to take place in a few days' time. Hundreds of arrests were being made daily of those in positions of authority. A few days later Doletsky, several of whose colleagues figured in the Piatakov trial, was actually arrested soon after I saw him. If rumor speaks truly, he killed himself in prison. He was a Communist of long standing, a conscientious official, and the kind of man who never got involved in political quarrels.

I went to take leave of Krestinsky the very day of my departure from Moscow at the end of January. It was two days before the opening of the trial. He was so tired and depressed that, in talking of my tasks in Greece, he would forget to finish his sentences. He begged my pardon, saying that he was overwrought, and bade me farewell. A few days later the Central Committee relieved him of his duties as vice-commissar of foreign affairs.

The last time Krestinsky spoke in public was at a meeting of the Communists of the Foreign Commissariat. Speaking very slowly, and obviously deeply moved, he said that, although he was wholly devoted to the Party which he had served conscientiously for years, he realized that his record as a member of the Opposition in the past made it advisable that, in the present circumstances, he should be retired. Men at the head of foreign affairs, he said, should enjoy the absolute confidence of the country and should be able to show a stainless Bolshevik past. He knew that, nine years before, he had committed the grave fault of joining the oppositionists who had set themselves up against the Leninist wisdom of our chief, Stalin. He approved, without reservation, the decision of the Central Committee, which for that reason had given him a new position in the Department of Justice. The loyal Communist must learn, he concluded, to serve his country where the Party thinks best to send him.

Krestinsky thanked his former colleagues, old and young, assured them that he would never forget them, and asked them to devote all their energies to the service of the Party. He must have known that his change of employment was but a stopping place on his way to prison, and from there to death. There had been too many examples to leave him in doubt. It was one of Stalin's regular methods of procedure to separate his intended victim by some new appointment from his customary surroundings – from those, that is, who know him and could vouch for his innocence – some months before striking him down.

My conversations with Krestinsky concerned an idea I had for drawing Greece away from the economic subjection to Germany into which she was being led, together with the other Balkan States, by Dr Schacht's ingenious 'clearing system'. The system grew out of the fact that Germany was in desperate need of foreign exchange and could not spare any gold for financing imports from Greece. The Nazis, giving as their reason that Germany would be a good outlet for certain Greek exports which had few markets at this time of crisis (for instance, Corinth raisins), concluded an agreement between the German Reichsbank and the Greek State Bank according to which the Greek bank put at the disposal of German importers large amounts of Greek *valuta* destined to pay Greek producers. The equivalent in German marks was put at the account of the Greek bank in Berlin, but these marks could be spent only on German manufactured goods. Thus, for general purposes, they were frozen.

Having lured the Greeks into this agreement as a means of getting rid of things they had difficulty in placing elsewhere, the Germans proceeded to buy all sorts of products, including those, such as tobacco, which Greece was selling for gold to English, American, and other importers. Inasmuch as they paid with practically worthless frozen marks, the Germans could offer higher prices than their English and American competitors and soon crowded them out. They bought everything they could lay hands on, in larger quantities even than was needed for consumption inside Germany. Being in need of foreign exchange, they resold Greek tobacco for gold to England.

The Greeks, not realizing the danger involved in this agreement, were surprised when at the end of the first term they found that the Germans owed Greece many millions of Reichsmarks, which they could not collect except by buying German goods. They tried to stop this worthless credit from increasing, but under pressure of Greek producers anxious to keep on with these sales at favorable prices, and of the German Government, they did not succeed. The balance unfavorable to Greece grew larger every month.

The rate of exchange fixed by the agreement was also unfavorable to Greece. And, moreover, having such a large amount frozen in Berlin, the Greeks were obliged to import almost all their machinery from Germany in order to get a part of their assets back. The Germans, realizing that the Greeks were trapped, set artificially high prices for this machinery. Thus the Germans got back many times over what they had overpaid on the goods imported from Greece. As a result the German stranglehold on the Greek economy grew tighter and tighter. Belatedly the Greek economists and statesmen became aware of the situation and appealed to the Western powers, France and England, to take measures to offset it. But it was peacetime; the French and English were going easy and did nothing.

I believed that German economic penetration in the Balkans was as great a danger for Soviet Russia as for the Western democracies and that we ought to oppose this penetration by any means we could. The line of thinking I presented to Krestinsky was this: The Soviet Government holds a monopoly of foreign trade. What the other governments cannot do, even if they want to, our government can do by a simple order to the Foreign Trade Commissariat. It is our only buyer abroad, and Russia is an enormous market which can absorb without difficulty all the exports that Germany is dragging out of Greece, paying for them either in cash or with wheat, which Greece is in real need of. As the Germans cannot pay in either of these ways, a decision of the Politburo would be enough to upset the whole German scheme and greatly increase Russian influence in the Balkans.

I had prepared in Athens a very detailed report on this subject, including a program of carefully planned action. At our first meeting Krestinsky was obviously impressed by my report and promised to back up my plan in higher circles. I got the same warm support from David Stern, director of the German and Balkan Department of the Foreign Office. When I called at the foreign bureau of the Central Committee of the Party some days later in connection with another matter, the head of the bureau unexpectedly mentioned my report. He asked me to give him a copy of it. He had already heard about my plan: he thought it very important, and said that he was entirely for it and would do his best to see it through. I was optimistic. By the way things were going I expected the question would be put before the Politburo and a decision made so that I could return to Greece with new possibilities of action. But I did not know that at this time (January, 1937) Stalin was already beginning to play the game which was to lead to his pact with Hitler.

At my last meeting with Krestinsky, he answered my inquiry about the report with an embarrassed silence. In the foreign bureau of the Central Committee it was answered with a gay slap on the back.

'All right, Barmine. You go to Athens; we'll take care of all that.'

I never heard any more about the fate of my report. Krestinsky and Stern soon disappeared in the purge, and I was left to guess that perhaps my scheme had been found too expensive. Only later, when I got wind of the mysterious conversations between Moscow and Berlin, did I realize why the whole idea was buried. It was not convenient to irritate Hitler in that delicate situation.

I left Moscow with mixed feelings of sadness and relief. Sometimes in a dream you find yourself in familiar surroundings, and yet they are also alien and unreal; they are not the same; they oppress you. That is the way I had felt in Moscow, and to leave the country was to lose the old familiar scene and yet also to retain reality. It was like waking up from a gruesome dream of that kind.

On my way to Athens I met two more men who were to be purged shortly afterward. One was our new minister in Lithuania, Podolsky, who was on the same train with me, getting off to take up his duties at Kaunas. He disappeared some months later and is believed to have been shot. At Budapest I stopped for a day with our ambassador, Bekzadian, an old acquaintance and an excellent fellow, a tasteful collector of illumined manuscripts and rare editions. He had, too, a cellar full of the very best Hungarian wines. Soon after I left him he was recalled without any explanation and disappeared.

At Athens I found Kobetsky in a state of heavy depression. The execution of Zinoviev had broken his spirit. He was impatiently awaiting my arrival, to hand the post over to me and leave for Moscow.

When I went to see Màri I was torn by a painful inward conflict. After what I had seen in Moscow, I realized that in taking her to Russia I would be involving her in danger. No amount of loyalty or devoted work on her part could save her if the maniacs of the GPU decided to include her in their witch hunt of foreigners. All my efforts and those of my influential friends would avail her nothing. All I could do then would be to share her fate, but that would not help her. Ought I to warn her against this danger and say goodbye to her forever? Every time we met, this tormenting question assailed my mind. I did not speak of it but it preyed on me continually. Instead of bringing happiness to her with my love, I might be bringing her into trouble. Often after an evening with her I went back to the legation feeling lonely and desperate. Have I the right to keep my love when it means such a risk to her?

Finally one day I spoke my thoughts. I told her that foreigners were not well received in Moscow now, and, although I still longed to take her with me, I was anxious about what might happen to her.

She was not much impressed by this, except as an opportunity to say that she too had been worrying about our plan for a very different reason.

'Is it true,' she asked me, 'that Soviet officials lose favor with their government if they marry foreigners? People have told me that in Moscow they strongly disapprove of this, and that such a marriage almost always ruins a man's career. If that is so, I would not want you to do it.'

I told her that I did not think it was so, but in any case I was not disturbed about my career.

'We can get along with any kind of job,' I said. 'There is plenty of work crying to be done.'

Màri insisted that she could not bear to ruin my career.

Her future was the only thing to worry about, I answered.

Finally we agreed on a simple solution – not to worry at all. Whatever fate had for us, we would meet together.

'So long as I have your love, I am ready for what may come,' she said.

But I cannot honestly say that I lived up to my side of the agreement.

Ismael G. Akhmedov

Under Soviet rule, to think contrary to the official line
is considered a crime, and one has to suffer for it. Not
only did I not want to suffer for freedom of thought and
action, but also I knew from the many terrible experiences
of friends and acquaintances that my personal imprisonment
or death would serve no really useful purpose.

In May 1942 'Lieutenant-Colonel Grigori Nikoyev' disappeared from the Soviet consulate in Ankara, where he had been operating under press attaché cover, and he remained in hiding under the protection of the Turkish Security Inspectorate until 1948. He had initially approached the British but at the last moment had opted for sanctuary with the Turks, who provided him with a new identity and a bodyguard. When eventually he made himself available for debriefing by Western intelligence agencies, in an effort to move to England or America, his information was largely out of date. Under interrogation he revealed that his true identity was Ismael Akhmedov and, by a curious coincidence, the SIS officer assigned to interview Akhmedov was the SIS head of station in Istanbul, Kim Philby, who reported that the defector had nothing worthwhile to offer.

Although he had only limited value, he was resettled in America by the CIA and in 1953 he gave evidence to the Senate Committee on the Judiciary under the name Ismail Enge. His book, *In and Out of Stalin's GRU*, was not published until 1984, and in this extract he describes his encounter with his SIS debriefer, a counter-intelligence expert named Philby.

In and Out of Stalin's GRU

There in the beautiful city of Istanbul, a mixture of many cultures, a sort of melting pot, I was formally introduced to the Englishman, the visitor to Manisa. Mr J presented him as 'Mr Philby, the chief of British Secret Service in Turkey. Mr Philby is the son of the respected and honorable Arabic scholar St John Philby, who became a Moslem. It is the desire of Mr. Philby to have a very long interview with you, an interview which perhaps will take several weeks to complete. Mr. Philby specifically asked our permission that none of our representatives take part during your conversations together. This we have granted. You are absolutely free to move in Istanbul and arrange your meetings with Mr Philby. Here are fifteen hundred Turkish liras, an equivalent of five hundred US dollars, for your expenses in Istanbul. They were advanced to us by Mr Philby. For your convenience we have reserved a suite in a nice hotel.'

Then, there it was. My visitor of the recent past in Manisa was Philby, the head of British Secret Service in Turkey, the son of the famous St John Philby. Some day in the future I would ask myself: how could I have suspected him of being an agent of the dreaded KGB? His own service did not suspect him, neither did the Turks. He was so courteous and pleasant, always smiling. For me he was a legitimate British intelligence officer interested in Soviet affairs.

It was arranged with Philby that a member of his staff, a nondescript character, would pick me up every morning at nine and drive me to a place for our interview. He would also drive me back to my hotel in the evening after our day's work. Meanwhile, Mr J – whom Philby would later refer to in his book, *My Silent War*, as an 'easy-going Aunt Jane' – relayed to me a private message which read, 'Ismail Bey, don't be afraid for your safety. You are under our custody and all necessary measures are being taken to protect your life.' That message put me at ease.

The next morning, exactly at 9 a.m., the nondescript character drove me to the place of our meeting. It was a luxury apartment building in Jihangir, overlooking the Bosphorus and Marmara with a wonderful view. The door was opened by a giant Kurd of dark complexion. One look at this ruffian on a dark corner at midnight would have given a person quite a scare. He gave a servile look to my escort and glanced at me with a look full of unexplained hostility. 'Well, well,' I said to myself, 'this one could easily strangle a person and carry his body away in a bag to the Bosphorus.' We entered the apartment. This was Philby's safe house. I have seen many safe houses in my lifetime, but this one was more than the usual run-of-the-mill type. Above all else it was very comfortable, richly furnished with taste and understanding. The floors were covered with expensive oriental rugs, and in the center of the living room floor there was a polar bear skin of good size. As soon as we entered the living room I was met by Philby, who introduced me to a young and charming English lady who was going to act as our hostess and stenographer for the days ahead. The nondescript Englishman retired with the reminder that he would pick me up in the evening.

Philby was all smiles and courtesy: the impeccable English gentleman full of attention. For starters we had a drink, and then got down to business, business which was going to last approximately four weeks – each day from nine to five, with short interruptions for lunch, which was served in the same room.

Oh, my God. If I had only known that this smiling, courteous Englishman named Philby was the man who had tipped the KGB about Soviet Vice-Consul Konstantin and had him sent to certain death!

If I had only known that here in the most luxurious apartment I was actually sitting in a KGB den and was being interviewed by a KGB agent!

How could I? Even so, when my interviews were completed and I left immediately for my return to Izmir by boat, I had some vague misgivings about this man Philby, but I managed to subdue them. To whom could I tell and discuss my misgivings? To suspect a senior officer of the British Secret Service was one thing, but to talk about it was suicide. Who would listen and even if I could find someone to listen – who would believe me? One would immediately accuse me of causing a Soviet provocation, or of being slightly 'off my rocker'. And what proof had I except rationalizing? Therefore, on my return to Izmir, I made up my mind to keep my misgivings about Philby to myself until the proper time.

Now, looking back in retrospect and reviewing my conversations with this master of deceit, and after so many years, I see certain flaws in the strategy Philby used in questioning, certain flaws in Philby's behavior, and most vividly of all now, the biggest mistake he made in my case.

Of course from our earlier, brief conversations, Philby had learned the scope and value of my information. Much, much later it became clear that while seeing me in Istanbul, Philby had received KGB instructions to learn my motivations, how much I knew of the Soviet military, diplomatic, intelligence, and technological secrets, to whom and on what I talked on these matters.

Accordingly, the program of my interview was outlined by Philby approximately as follows:

- My background and biographic data.
- My motivations for defection.
- Step-by-step details of my defection to the Turks.
- All Soviet high-ranking military officers and other public figures known to me, and their characteristics and style of working.
- Soviet High Command, the General Staff, the political directorate of the Soviet army and navy, their organization, policy, control, strategy, and doctrine. Military schools and academies. All personnel known by name, and their characteristics. Soviet military, scientific, and research organizations, their tasks, personnel, and their characteristics, and so on.
- Signal corps of the Soviet army.
- Border troops.
- Purges in the Soviet armed forces; Soviet invasion of Finland in 1939.
- Soviet military intelligence – functions of the GRU, strategy, operations, tactics, its history, chiefs and deputies, and organization. Intelligence objectives, political aspects; that is, the relationships between the Party, Soviet government, and the GRU. Finances, operational doctrine, and methods of operation, agent handling and modus operandi, and communications. Soviet diplomatic, commercial, and some other establishments, such as *Tass*, as cover for Soviet espionage activities. Professional standards, efficiency, security, and so on; training establishments.
- KGB history, organization, the relationship between GRU and KGB.
- GRU activities abroad, the legal and illegal networks in Turkey, Europe, USA, Asia.
- The state of my mind and my plans for the future.

All conversations took place in a smaller room, a sort of anteroom, with my chair placed behind a glass door leading to a balcony overlooking the Bosphorus. I believe we were on the fifth or sixth floor, and the narrow cobblestone street was far below – an ideal spot for a so-called suicide jump.

The charming young English lady took notes in shorthand, but I felt certain the place was wired, and perhaps somewhere in the front of me there was a concealed microphone.

Our discussion of my background and the talks covering my biographic data were suprisingly short. Perhaps they would add up to a few hours. As a rule, any intelligence service (and certainly the KGB) would take a long look into a person's background. Nothing is overlooked in this respect. A complete family history of parents and relatives would be taken. Then a thorough interrogation covering friends, associates, education, professional skills, languages, military duty, names and dates of schools attended, service record, classmates, transfers, and moves from place to place; everything would be examined and sifted to the most minute detail. It would take several days, sometimes a week or more, to effectively evaluate a person of interest. The more mature the person under scrutiny, the more information he has; the more experienced he is, the more time it takes to discuss and evaluate him. This is done in order to understand him, to establish his *bona fides*, to evaluate the materials and information he provides.

In short, it takes a great deal of time to check out a person from all angles. Yet, here I was, the former chief of the Fourth Division of the GRU, a Soviet General Staff officer, a lieutenant colonel, sitting face to face with the head of the British Secret Service in Turkey, and he showed virtually no interest in me, my background, my *bona fides*. I was both puzzled and hurt, because I had hoped that this high-ranking British intelligence officer would understand my problems and perhaps be able to assist me in my plans to go to the West.

Many years later it would become clear to me why Philby had not the least interest in my background. It was already fully known to his masters in Moscow, and Philby had no reason to spend much time on the subject. This was the big mistake made by both Philby and his masters. Every game must be played all the way, according to the rules. And of course on this point, he would never have helped me leave Turkey. On the contrary, he would and did do everything to prevent my move to the West.

Even though my personal history was just touched lightly, Philby did not forget to ask about my close relatives in Moscow. He wanted their names and addresses; when I mentioned the name, address, and place of employment of my sister-in-law, a most charming and beautiful lady of high culture, Philby immediately asked if I would write her a short letter. 'Someone from the British Embassy in Moscow will find her and deliver your note.' Delighted with the opportunity to inform her of my freedom, I wrote a short note and gave it to Philby. She and her husband were in opposition to Stalin's dictatorship, though they were not anti-Soviet. Much to my sorrow, I realized years later that this dirty trick was used by Philby to victimize a poor innocent lady.

Victor A. Kravchenko

The Russian raised under the Soviet tutelage, emerging into the non-Soviet world for the first time, is a bewildered and almost helpless creature.

Born in Ekaterinoslav in the Ukraine to a revolutionary activist in 1905, Kravchenko started his career as a miner before he joined the Party and attended the Technological Institute at Kharkov. Having received a diploma for the design of a pipe-rolling fabricator he was sent to manage a steel factory in Nikopol. Here he experienced continuous surveillance by the omnipotent OGPU and, as he later claimed, he began to develop doubts about the regime that had originally emerged during Stalin's purges.

Following the evacuation of Moscow in August 1942 Kravchenko supervised the dismantling of his factory and its removal to a new, safer site in the Urals. Once completed, he was drafted into the Red Army and assigned to an engineering company which liaised closely with an NKVD demolition battalion. These duties lasted until November when, following treatment in Moscow for an infected jaw, he was transferred to Sovnarkom, the centralized bureaucracy that ran what was left of the Soviet manufacturing and heavy industry.

In January 1943 Kravchenko was nominated to travel to the United States as a metallurgical specialist on behalf of the Ministry of Foreign Trade to help negotiate details of the lend–lease agreement. For six months he was investigated by the NKVD to ensure his suitability for the appointment, and when he had won approval he went by train to Vladivostock and thence to Vancouver by ship.

Canada, and then Washington DC, proved to be revelations for Kravchenko, who had been instructed by the NKVD to deny his party membership if questioned by American officials while en route to join the Soviet Purchasing Commission on 16th Street. Although not co-opted to assist the NKVD in espionage, during the seven months he was based at the Commission he acquired a comprehensive knowledge of the NKVD's local structure. At the end of March 1944, following official inspection visits to Pennsylvania and Chicago, he abandoned his rented room in Washington and took the train to New York where he surrendered to the federal authorities. Within a couple of days his 'resignation' was front-page news, but the Soviets responded by charging Kravchenko, who held the Red Army rank of captain, with military desertion.

Kravchenko gave evidence before the House Un-American Activities Committee in 1947, soon after his book, *I Chose Freedom*, had been published. In it Kravchenko gave a harrowing account of police terror in the Soviet Union, and of the gulags. As soon as it was released it was denounced as a forgery by the Soviets and similar allegations were circulated in Leftist journals in Europe, although Kravchenko admitted only to having had professional editorial help. Incensed by an article in the Paris weekly magazine *Les Lettres Françaises*, entitled 'How Kravchenko Was Manufactured', which called him a traitor and a liar, the author brought a defamation suit. The communist periodical's story claimed that Kravchenko had stolen papers from a safe in the Soviet embassy in Washington DC and had sold them to officials from the State Department. The correspondent credited with the story, an American named Sim Thomas, also asserted that he had been told that the US Office of Strategic Services had fabricated the entire book.

Kravchenko's litigation, which was concluded in March 1949, effectively proved that there was no 'Sim Thomas' and that the magazine publishers had no evidence to substantiate their libels. Although the court awarded Kravchenko barely enough to cover his costs, he capitalized on his experience by releasing *I Chose Justice*, an account of the trial, the following year.

In February 1966, perhaps a greater target than ever, Kravchenko was found shot dead in his New York apartment, apparently the victim of suicide.

In this passage from his autobiography Kravchenko describes how he encountered the NKVD in his factory, an episode that helped persuade him to defect whenever the opportunity presented itself.

I Chose Freedom

In town one night I caught sight of my old-maidish secretary, Comrade Tuvina, coming out of the Nikopol NKVD building. I never doubted that she was reporting on me; spying on the boss is the main job of Soviet secretaries. But knowing it was one thing, stumbling on the proof was another. The very next day I instructed our Personnel Department to remove this woman from my office and to recommend someone else, preferably a man.

In a few days a man of about thirty-two came to me with a note from the Personnel chief. His appearance was remarkable. The first word that came to my mind as I looked up was 'scarecrow'. He seemed a skeleton hung with rags. His shoes were torn, his trousers patched, his jacket a crudely tailored thing made of sacking. Even under our Soviet conditions he was an extreme specimen of squalor. But his starved features were cleanly cut and even attractive, under reddish hair gray at the temples.

'I know what I look like, Comrade Kravchenko,' he said, 'but I beg you not to hold it against me. You see, I've just come from a prison camp, after finishing a four-year term. The Personnel Department knows this. If you give me a chance, I know you'll find my work satisfactory.'

He spoke like an educated man. My initial revulsion turned to pity. The poor fellow had evidently passed through some fearful ordeal. I rang for tea and sandwiches. He tried to restrain himself, eating slowly and casually, but it was evident that he was famished. As we talked, my phone rang. It was Romanov, an important and likable official from another department. Though he was not a Party man, Romanov enjoyed the confidence of the administration, from Kozlov down.

'Victor Andreyevich,' he said, 'I would consider it a personal favor if you hired Citizen Groman, who's in your office now. Despite his misfortune, he's a reliable fellow.'

'Have you known him long?'

'No, but I'm in a position to vouch for him.'

'Thanks, it's kind of you to let me know.'

While Groman waited in the reception room, I telephoned the NKVD and was connected with Gershgorn. It was my duty to inform him, since my secretary would handle important official documents. When I told him the story, he asked me to wait a minute. After a brief interval, he returned to the phone and assured me that he had no objection if I found the man otherwise acceptable.

When I told the dilapidated ex-prisoner that he could show up to work in a day or two, he smiled for the first time. He was embarrassingly grateful. I gave him enough money in advance and instructed the plant store to give him essential clothes. I also helped him, through my assistant, to find a livable room in one of the factory apartments.

Groman proved himself quickly to be both intelligent and efficient. He took many details off my shoulders. Better dressed, his bones slowly taking on flesh, his eyes coming alive, he seemed a man reborn. He came to my house often for work, and occasionally I drove him home after work. Our relations were on an easy human basis. I thanked Romanov for his recommendation of a first-rate secretary.

Many weeks passed. One morning Groman failed to appear for work. I assumed that he was ill. When he didn't show up next day, I became worried and decided to send someone to his house at the end of the work day to see what was wrong. He had no telephone. As I was going through some papers stacked in my desk, I came to a batch of sheets, hand-written and clipped together. I recognized Groman's handwriting. Instinctively I avoided touching the sheets as I read the opening words:

'Dear Victor Andreyevich, when you read these words I shall no longer be in Nikopol. I am trying to escape this land of horror. Even death will be better than life as a slave . . .'

I broke out in cold sweat. Nervously I locked my door. Then I put on gloves and picked up the letter. It was an extraordinary document. Though I do not remember all the words, the subtance remains engraved on my mind:

'Thank you from the bottom of a true Russian heart for all you have done for me. Your kindness has awakened in me feelings of humanity which I thought were dead beyond recall. That, in fact, is one of the reasons why I decided to run away. If God is with me, I shall cross the frontier. If I'm caught, I'll be shot, of course.

'I hate the Soviet regime and its police with a deadly hate. Though I have committed no crime – unless loving freedom is a crime – I have been through their torture chambers and prison isolators. When I was released, I realized that my freedom would be short-lived and that I could not even find work unless I put myself at the service of my torturers.

'The evening before you met me I had just arrived in Nikopol from concentration camp, as I had been ordered. I went to the NKVD and was taken to Gershgorn. That's how I came to you. All that happened – including the recommendation by Romanov – was part of an ugly comedy of which you were the victim.

'I did not mind working as a spy. Hating all Communists, it seemed to me a chance to revenge myself by getting a few of them into trouble, the deeper the better. I looked on you as my first victim. But very soon I came to respect you and loathed myself for what I had planned to do to you.

'I want you to know that after a while I became the main informer so far as you are concerned. Once a man has been through the purgatory of the NKVD he is trusted. Those devils know that fear will keep their human tools loyal. Every day the other agents who fill your plant and offices reported to me. About once a week I assembled their information into a comprehensive report about your work, your words, your friends, even the expression on your face, along with defects in the work of your plant.

'Though the spies did not know one another, I knew them all. The least I can do, in gratitude for your sympathy, is to reveal them to you.'

A list followed. It included Romanov, the genial Romanov whom we all liked and trusted for his soft, paternal ways. It included several of my closest colleagues in the plant, foremen, plain workmen, clerks in the commissary. The network of informers was spread through every shop and office in the factory, covering all stages of the technological process.

'Beware of these people, Victor Andreyevich! They have no respect for truth. Their careers depend on uncovering plots, and their temptation is to invent plots to uncover. You should know that men who have been physically broken and psychologically demoralized by the Chekists will do anything, confess anything, accuse anybody. There are several such around you' – again he gave me names – 'for I was not the only one.

'I assume you will suspect this letter to be a trap. I cannot blame you. I can only swear by God and my sainted mother that I am telling the truth, that I am trying to expiate the weeks of spying on a man who was kind to me and considerate of the human spark in me. Whether you will believe me I leave to your instincts.

'If you turn this letter over to Gershgorn, he will say I'm a liar and will immediately reshuffle the network of informers. But if you can bring yourself to trust me, destroy the letter, pretend to be indignant over my mysterious desertion, and they will never suspect that I have betrayed them.

'Whatever you decide, I beg by all that's sacred to you to give me at least one day's leeway before reporting my absence. The extra day may be the difference between life and death. I implore you on my knees, dear Victor Andreyevich.

'Thank you for all you have done for me. Thank you for having helped to revive the decent human being whom the torturers had nearly wiped out. If I remain alive I shall pray for you always.'

Some inner feeling prompted me to trust the fugitive. Perhaps I had come to trust the kind of mind he had unveiled to me in our random talks during the past weeks. Despite this inner assurance, I felt as if I were gambling with my very life as I copied out the names he had given me. Then I burned the letter, carefully removing every trace of ash.

Toward the end of the day I sent a messenger to Groman's residence. He reported the following morning that the family with whom Groman lived said he had not been home for two days. I thereupon called the Personnel Department and in simulated anger asked why they couldn't find me a more dependable secretary. This was the third day he had absented himself, without so much as an explanation, I complained.

Within the hour, Gershgorn himself, accompanied by a uniformed man, arrived in great excitement. They asked me questions, ransacked Groman's desk, and departed. Whether the fugitive escaped I could not ever know. The chances of stealing across a Soviet frontier are very slight, yet hundreds have accomplished the feat.

The information about the spies around me was helpful. It enabled me to safeguard myself and sometimes to protect others. If I wanted something to reach the ears of the police without delay, I needed merely to mention it casually within earshot of the informer at the furnaces, the one in the tool department, the head of the finishing department, the engineer Makarov, the foreman Yudavin, the trade-union official Ivanov, who was Starostin's assistant. Social contact with Romanov became a painful chore, yet I could not drop him without arousing suspicion.

Groman's successor was a young, pretty and hard-working Comsomol. No doubt she picked up the espionage threads where the unhappy Groman had dropped them.

My chauffeur's name had been on Groman's list, which hardly surprised me. He reported directly to the Informational Division of the NKVD rather than to Gershgorn's Economic Division. But my maid Pasha's name was not on list. In time, however, I learned that this was an oversight or that Groman simply did not know about her.

One day, when Pasha had been in my home for nearly a year, I returned from a visit to Moscow. She helped me unpack two suitcases. I had bought her a few presents – a garishly printed shawl, several pairs of cotton stockings, a pair of house slippers. She accepted these, it seemed to me, with strange reserve.

'Don't you like them, Pasha?' I asked.

'Oh yes, I do, and I am most thankful, Victor Andreyevich.'

But that same evening, after serving my supper, Pasha came into the dining room carrying the gifts. She was crying noisily in peasant fashion. I looked up in questioning alarm.

'I can't accept these things, Victor Andreyevich,' she sobbed. 'Please, please take them back.'

'All right, but tell me why. What's the mystery?'

'God forgive me,' she crossed herself, 'but I can't tell you. Only don't make me take these gifts.'

After some urging and a pledge of secrecy, however, she did tell me. It added up to this: that she could not take gifts from a good man while acting as informer against him.

'Yes, ever since I came here I've been reporting once a week to the NKVD,' she said. 'I came from the village and got the job. But no sooner was I settled in your home than I was ordered to come to the NKVD and told what to do. I refused and cried and said that it was against my religion but the uniformed man only said: "Pasha, don't be an idiot. You want your father to come back from his banishment, don't you? Well, if you serve us right and loyally, we'll see about it."

'Once a week I go to a private house in Nikopol and tell all I know, especially who comes here and what they say. "And did they curse the government?" they ask me, and always I cross myself and say, "No, on the contrary." They laugh when I make the sign of the cross, the infidels!'

I assured poor Pasha that she had my forgiveness. I would never mention what she had told me, provided she, too, held her tongue. I even convinced her that it was proper to accept my gifts, now that she had taken me into her confidence.

For the rest of my stay in that house Pasha continued to report on me. We never referred to her tearful confession. But several times she asked me questions intended, I was sure, to ascertain whether it was desirable that she report certain incidents. I made it clear that I had nothing to hide and that, in my case, what she overlooked would be communicated by others.

Igor S. Gouzenko

Doubts began to assail me about the wisdom of my
decision to steal documents on the spy ring activities.
It would be so much easier to take Anna and Andrei,
now two years old, and disappear.

A twenty-six-year-old GRU cipher clerk based at the Soviet embassy in Ottawa, Igor Gouzenko was scheduled to return to Moscow in September 1945 at the end of a tour lasting three years. However, he decided to stay in Canada with his wife, Svetlana, and his daughter, and over a period of weeks he smuggled documents from the closely guarded *referentura* in which he worked to give himself something to bargain with. In total, he removed from the building and hid in his home 109 items, which included copies of telegrams to Moscow and file entries relating to individual NKVD and GRU sources, among them a member of Parliament, Fred Rose, and numerous communists.

As soon as the Soviets realized Gouzenko had gone missing they broke into his apartment and reported to the Canadian authorities that he was wanted for the theft of money. Belatedly the Canadian government realized Gouzenko's value and he was granted full protection. The implications of the material he had purloined were far reaching: the atomic scientist Allan Nunn May was identified as a Soviet spy and in February 1946 more than a dozen others were arrested and accused of supplying secrets to the Russians. A Royal Commission was empanelled to examine Gouzenko's compelling evidence, and when its report was published, complete with facsimile reproductions of secret Soviet files, twelve suspects were convicted.

Gouzenko enjoyed his new-found fame and courted publicity. He sold interviews to magazines, appeared on television with a pillowcase over his head, and even sold the movie rights to his story, *The Iron Curtain*, to Twentieth Century Fox. However, for his Royal Canadian Mounted Police bodyguards, he proved very difficult to handle. With the help of his RCMP interpreter, Mervyn Black, and two journalists, John Dalrymple and Laurie McKechnie, he wrote a novel, *Fall of a Titan*, and an autobiography, *This Was My Choice*, both of which were bestsellers. His wife also wrote a book, *Before Igor*.

The question of exactly what motivated Gouzenko to defect remains unresolved. At different times he said it was the burden of knowledge he had accumulated, but this was not what he said in *This Was My Choice* or what he had told the Royal Commission. According to one transcript, in October 1945 he claimed that:

> Convinced that such double-faced politics of the Soviet Government towards the democratic countries do not conform with the interests of the Russian people and endanger the security of civilisation, I decided to break away from the Soviet regime and announce my decision openly.

In his 1948 autobiography, Gouzenko had stressed the ideological nature of his conversion: 'instead of convincing myself that doctrines instilled by the Soviet Union were still sound, I had found my thoughts drifting towards the democratic way of life'.

The most likely explanation is that Gouzenko, who was from typically Slav peasant stock, simply wanted to improve his life and that of his family. He knew that only austerity and hardship awaited him at home whereas Canada offered living conditions that could never be matched in the Soviet Union. In terms of the damage Gouzenko inflicted, his testimony and the evidence of his stolen files probably did more than any other single event to alert the West to the nature and scale of the espionage offensive waged by the Kremlin. Apart from the dozen or so defendants convicted of spying, Gouzenko wrecked an organization which had taken years to develop, exposed the penetration of the Manhattan atomic weapons project and demonstrated the very close relationship between the Canadian Communist Party and Moscow. Surprisingly, although Gouzenko's subsequent whereabouts in Canada were something of an open secret, no attempt on his life was ever uncovered and, despite the dangers, he frequently courted publicity. In 1955, for example, he volunteered testimony to the US Senate Committee on the Judiciary.

Gouzenko was provided with the identity of a Canadian of Ukrainian extraction who had been born near Saskatoon in Saskatchewan, and lived off his royalties and a generous government pension. He died at his home outside Toronto in June 1982, blinded by a combination of diabetes and alcohol, and embittered that his literary merits, which he regarded as on a par with Tolstoy, had gone largely unrecognized by anyone apart from his loyal wife and children. Here he gives his version of his defection, an episode that nearly ended in tragedy when the Canadian authorities briefly contemplated returning the cipher clerk to his employers.

This Was My Choice

Anna and I had decided long since that it would be necessary to make my escape during a weekday although a Saturday night would have been ideal, allowing me until Monday morning to make good my getaway. But the newspaper offices would not be open Saturday night and we had decided I should take the documents and my story to a newspaper.

There was no thought of going to the police. That was a natural result of our experience with the thoroughly corrupt NKVD police. I naturally thought the local police would sell out to the Soviet Embassy. At the same time, we had been impressed with the freedom and fearlessness of the Canadian press.

Other factors were involved in the Wednesday night choice. I knew this was Koulakov's assigned night to sit up on watch at the Military Attaché and, in consequence, he was permitted to sleep until noon next day. This would allow me more leeway because Koulakov would be the most likely one to first report me as missing. Since the cipher section work was so secret, the rest of the staff, with the exception of Colonel Zabotin, knew little of the hours I was supposed to be on or off duty. And I knew that Zabotin, who was scheduled to attend a moving picture show at the National Film Board that night with Rogov, would hardly turn up before noon.

What made the forthcoming ordeal all the more hazardous was that I would have to go to the Military Attaché's ostensibly to complete some work and then go to the Embassy where most of the really important documents were kept. As a trusted cipher clerk, I was admitted without question at any hour of the day or night.

Finally I turned into Range Road, and curiously, I felt a sensation of exhilaration. The suspense of recent weeks had put my nerves on edge, but now that the moment of action was upon me I felt strangely relieved.

As I entered the hall I noted Koulakov had already taken his place at the night-watch desk. That was good. A switch in Koulakov's plans would have hurt mine for the morning.

Captain Galkin, supposedly a door guard but in reality an extremely well trained Intelligence operator, appeared as I entered.

'How about coming to a movie with me?' he asked.

I tried to appear interested. 'Which one are you going to?'

Galkin mentioned a neighborhood theatre. The thought occurred to me that this would provide an ideal opportunity to leave the Military Attaché since I had really wanted only to see if Koulakov was on the job.

'That's a good idea,' I said. 'It's too hot to work anyway.'

Galkin said some of the other members of the staff were coming and we waited outside until they joined us.

We walked to the theatre, where I pretended disappointment.

'Damn it, I've seen that show! You fellows go ahead because it's a good picture. I'll take a streetcar and go to another show downtown.'

I walked in the direction of a car stop but veered when they vanished into the theatre. So far so good. I turned toward Charlotte Street, walked deliberately to the Soviet Embassy, mounted the steps and nodded to the guard, who nodded in return as I signed the book. As I was putting my fountain pen back in my pocket I glanced toward the reception room and my blood seemed to freeze.

There sat Vitali Pavlov, chief of the NKVD in Canada!

Somehow I managed to act naturally and walked by the reception room seemingly concerned with the clip of my pen not fastening into my pocket the way it should. From the corner of my eye I noted that Pavlov had apparently failed to notice me. I pressed the secret bell under the banister, mounted the stairs leading to the secret cipher room, pulled aside the curtain and held my face in front of the small opening in the steel door.

The attendant inside unbarred the steel door. It was Ryazanov, commercial attaché cipher clerk and a friend of mine. I noted with relief that he was alone.

We exchanged a few remarks on the weather. Ryazanov asked if I was working late again.

'No,' I replied, 'there are just a couple of telegrams to do and then I'll catch an 8.30 show.'

Ryazanov said I was being sensible and turned to his own work.

I entered my little office and closed the door carefully behind me. I went to my desk, opened it and removed Zabotin's cipher pouch, which I had left there that afternoon. Most of the documents I wanted were there. The others were in the files. All were marked by the turned down corners.

Some of the documents were large sheets of paper. Others were small scraps. Later, the police count showed a hundred and nine items.

I opened my shirt and carefully distributed the documents inside. Then I completed the telegrams which represented my reason for being there.

They dealt with information supplied by Emma Woikin, an agent in the Canadian External Affairs Department.

Originally these 'excuse' telegrams hadn't seemed very important, but on second thought I saw they fitted in with other data. It was too bad for Emma that I stopped to reconsider them. Those telegrams cost her a three-year prison sentence.

Once the ciphering task was finished I stood up and gingerly examined my shirt, which to me appeared to bulge suspiciously. However, the evening was so warm I felt a sloppy-looking shirt wouldn't arouse undue interest.

I walked across the corridor and handed the telegrams to Ryazanov for dispatching to Moscow. I also handed him Zabotin's sealed pouch to be placed in the safe.

I watched Ryazanov's face for any evidence that he noted anything unusual in my manner or appearance. Certainly, I felt conspicuous around the waist. But Ryazanov displayed no undue interest. Casually I stepped into the men's room and washed my hands.

While doing so I called out:

'It's too hot to stick around here. Why don't you skip out with me to the show?'

Ryazanov grunted.

'Fat chance of getting away with anything around here. Besides, Pavlov is downstairs. Thanks just the same, I'd better stick around.'

Mention of Pavlov left me a little weak around the knees. I had momentarily forgotten him. But there was no turning back now. I adjusted my shirt again and stepped to the door. Ryazanov opened it and I bid him goodnight.

I was careful about walking down the steps, afraid that I might disturb the documents and cause an extra large bulge. There was also danger that a smaller document might slip through my belt and drop from a pant leg on the floor.

Sweat was standing out on my brow and I felt my chest tightening as I approached the reception room. This will never do, I thought. I didn't even dare reach into a pocket for my handkerchief lest the movement might disturb something.

The street door seemed miles away. Gradually I neared the reception room. Then I was passing it. My heart leapt with joy. The room was empty. Pavlov had gone. A good omen. I was very much in luck. I signed myself out in the book, bid the attendant goodnight and walked out into the night. It was still humid but I sucked in the air gratefully.

I took a streetcar downtown and went quickly to the office of the *Ottawa Journal* newspaper.

I was trembling like a leaf. I couldn't figure just why, except that it must be due to nervous reaction. Outside the building I stopped to mop my brow and make sure nobody was following me. Finally, I entered and asked the elevator man where I could find the editor.

'Sixth floor,' he said, and slammed the door shut behind me.

At the sixth floor I walked toward the door marked 'Editor' but just as I was about to knock something happened inside me. Grim doubts filled my mind. Surely, I thought, every big newspaper must have an NKVD agent working in it. Was I doing the right thing? Hurriedly I decided to think it over and turned back to the elevator. The door opened to let somebody out and the operator yelled:

'Down!'

I stepped in. The elevator descended a few floors and stopped to pick up some people. Among them was a girl who looked at me and smiled.

'What are you doing here? Is there news breaking at the Embassy?'

I was panic-stricken. Her face was familiar. Where had I seen her before? What would I do?

The elevator reached the ground floor. As the door opened I muttered an apology to the girl, said something about being in a big hurry and walked quickly to the street. Outside I ran to the first corner and then slowed to a fast walk. This went on for blocks, as I tried to calm my burning mind. What would I do now? I boarded a streetcar and went home to Anna. We would talk it over.

Anna answered my code knock. Her face was drawn and white.

'Did something go wrong?' she whispered tensely.

I sat down heavily on the sofa. Anna came over and sat beside me. I told her the whole story, finishing up with the account of being spotted by the girl in the elevator.

Anna listened attentively. After I finished, her voice came absolutely unruffled:

'Don't worry about her, Igor. She must be a journalist or she would not have been in the office. Many journalists were entertained at the Embassy and that is where she probably met you. They have good memories. But even if there is an NKVD agent in the newspaper office, it needn't matter. What could he do in time to stop you?'

I took renewed strength from her confidence.

'What now?' I asked.

'Go right back to the newspaper office and see the editor. You still have several hours before the Embassy learns what has happened.'

I opened my shirt and removed the documents. They were soaked with sweat. Anna tried to dry them a bit by waving them. Then she wrapped them in a paper.

Anna kissed me as she opened the door. I squeezed her arm and went out into the night again. At the *Ottawa Journal* the same elevator man took me up to the sixth floor. I stepped quickly to the editor's door and knocked. There was no answer. I knocked again. Still no answer. I tried the door. It was locked. I walked down to a door leading into a large room. It was the City Room and it was filled with busy people. Nobody paid any attention to me. I saw an office boy hurrying in my direction. I asked him where I could find the editor.

'Gone for the night,' the office boy said and dashed past me.

I walked to the nearest desk and told a man working at a typewriter that I wished to see whoever was in charge.

'It is extremely important,' I said.

He looked at me inquiringly, then took me over to a desk at the other side of the big room where an older man wearing a green eyeshade told me to sit down.

I took out the stolen documents and spread them on the desk. As I did so, I explained who I was and that these were proof that Soviet agents in Canada were seeking data on the atomic bomb.

The man with the eyeshade stared at me, then picked up several of the documents. But he looked at them only for a moment. They were written in Russian.

'I'm sorry,' he said finally. 'This is out of our field. I would suggest you go to the Royal Canadian Mounted Police or come back in the morning to see the editor.'

I hastened to explain that by morning the NKVD might be on my trail and even kill me. But as I spoke my heart was falling. I could see from the man's expression that he thought I was crazy.

'Sorry,' he said. 'I'm busy.'

He stood up and walked away, leaving me sitting there. I felt helpless and confused. Out on the street I leaned against the wall and tried to collect my thoughts. There was only one thing to do and that was contact a high official. The Minister of Justice seemed the logical person. I walked to the Justice Building on Wellington Street, where a tall man in RCMP uniform stopped me at the door. I hesitated for a moment but realized things were getting desperate. I said it was most important that I see the Minister of Justice immediately.

The policeman replied politely but firmly:

'It is almost midnight. You can see nobody until morning. Sorry.'

Sorry. That word was getting on my nerves. 'But,' I repeated, 'it is desperately necessary that I reach the Minister right away – by telephone at least.'

He shook his head. 'It can't be done.'

I returned home, thoroughly subdued and more than a little frightened. Anna, however, bolstered me again.

'Don't worry about it. You have the whole morning to reach the Minister. Have a good sleep and you will feel better.'

She tucked the documents in her handbag and put it under her pillow. But neither of us slept that night. We just lay there thinking and talking until the first light of dawn was filtering through our bedroom window. I raised myself on one elbow and looked out. There was a tinge of red in the eastern sky. Somehow, it comforted me immensely to know there was a nice day coming.

'Anna,' I said, 'we will all go to the Minister of Justice's office as soon as it opens, around nine o'clock. I might be kept waiting and the suspense would be unbearable if I wasn't certain about your safety. I'll dress Andrei. Do you think you could stand the strain . . . even if you are ill when you get up?'

'I will be all right, Igor,' she replied instantly. 'We will all go together and you will have nothing to worry about once we are all in the Minister of Justice's office.'

I lay back with a sigh of relief. Things were clearing somewhat. The next thing I knew, Anna was shaking me.

'It is seven o'clock, Igor.'

I had dozed off into heavy slumber, but the sleep had done me a world of good. I shaved and put on my good brown suit. Anna was already feeding Andrei and had a pot of coffee boiling on the stove. It was a bright, sunshiny day without the clamminess of yesterday. I felt prepared for anything that lay ahead.

But even my immense optimism would have wilted if I had been able to foresee the staggering disappointments in store for us.

Before leaving the house we decided that Anna should carry the documents in her purse, because if the NKVD caught up with us they would go after me. I would try to create a diversion and Anna might have a chance to slip away. The documents would be a passport to protective custody with the Canadian Government, I thought.

At the Justice Building, I explained to the man at the reception desk that

I had to see the Minister of Justice on a matter of absolute emergency. The man looked at me doubtfully, then spoke for some time into the telephone. We were escorted to the Minister's office, where a courteous secretary asked what was the nature of my business.

I did my best to tell him the matter was of such urgency and importance that I dared not speak to anybody but the Minister. The secretary glanced from me to Anna to the child. I could imagine what was running through his mind; this man may be off his head but if that is the case why would he bring along his wife and child? I had not thought of that angle in my planning but it seemed a fortunate one. The secretary went into the inside office and I could hear him telephoning somebody.

The secretary finally returned.

'The Minister is in his other office in the Parliament Buildings,' he said. 'I will take you there.'

Anatoli M. Granovsky

In my own country my true being found no intrinsic value,
my life was not worth a kopec for itself, my individuality
was a dangerous thing, indeed my own worst enemy.

Assigned to the Soviet ship *Petrodvorets* in July 1946, Granovsky's responsibility, as a captain in the NKVD's Third Chief Directorate, was to act as a security officer for the crew and ensure their loyalty. The ship underwent repairs in Stockholm while en route to the Black Sea, and Granovsky seized the opportunity to approach the US military attaché in Sweden for political asylum. Having previously worked for the First Chief Directorate in Czechoslovakia he had useful information to offer, and he was resettled in the United States, where he wrote *I Was an NKVD Agent*, which was published in 1962.

The son of a member of the Central Committee, Granovsky had joined the NKVD in 1942 at the age of twenty. His father had been arrested in a purge in November 1937 and Granovsky also was imprisoned when he tried to discover his father's fate. However, instead of being executed, after six months' imprisonment Granovsky was offered the opportunity to become a secret agent. This required him to join the Red Army and receive training at an anti-aircraft school, but this was merely to develop his cover. In September 1942, after a year in the role of undercover informer, Granovsky attended the NKVD academy at Bykovo and was dropped behind enemy lines to a group of guerrillas based near Drogobich in the Ukraine. He returned to Moscow to learn that his girlfriend, who had also worked as a partisan, had been captured by the Nazis and hanged. This prompted him to try to desert but before he had an opportunity he was transferred first to Poland and later to Ruthenia in Czechoslovakia where he screened former prisoners who had been repatriated.

In April 1945 Granovsky was posted to Berlin, to recover NKVD files captured during the Nazi occupation of Kiev, and was then transferred to Prague. While there he impulsively interceded with the Soviet ambassador on behalf of a friend who had been arrested, and had been singled out for liquidation, but the incident caused him to be recalled to Kiev to be disciplined. However, a colleague agreed to assign him to Odessa to keep him out of the way for a while, and when in July 1946 he joined the *Petrodvorets* he at last found a chance to defect. He died in America in September 1974, always mindful of his experience at the hands of the NKVD during his detention in 1939.

I Was an NKVD Agent

Some days afterwards, also at about midnight, I was ordered to get up and accompany the gaoler to the interrogation room.

The interrogator, a State Security lieutenant, looked a contented man. His words to me were very polite.

'Please sit down, Citizen Granovsky,' he said.

He handed me five typewritten sheets of paper headed 'Report on Interrogation of Accused, A. M. Granovsky', and dated January 30, 1939. That was the date of my first interrogation in the building of the NKVD of the USSR. On reading the pages I saw that there were several questions written down which had not been made, as well as replies to these questions which, obviously, I had not given. According to this paper I was guilty of spying on Soviet authorities with the intention of finding out who guarded the Politburo members and how they were guarded, discovering the layout of the streets which were used as government thoroughfares and discovering which types of cars were used by the various members of the Politburo. This information was supposedly sought and collected by me in preparation for terroristic acts against the lives of Politburo members. It was stated that I had been arrested in the act of carrying out careful observations concerning the movements of Politburo members to and from the Kremlin. It was declared that I had freely confessed guilt on all points on the occasion of my first interrogation and was therefore accused of anti-Soviet activities in accordance with paragraph 58 of the Soviet Criminal Code.

At the bottom of the fifth and last page of the report was my signature which I had been obliged to append to a blank sheet of paper during my first interrogation.

When I had finished reading this interesting document the interrogator ordered me to put my signature to each separate page. I naturally objected to this and tried to explain that, even on the last page, the signature had come first and the text later. He told me calmly that I was a liar, and said that if I did not wish to sign the other pages as I had signed the last, then he would find a way to force me. Though afraid, I nevertheless persisted. The interrogator then pressed a button on his desk and another State Security lieutenant came into the room. The two of them approached me and started to give me the severest beating up I have ever had. I was kicked many, many times, whipped with a rubber hose and beaten with a truncheon and an iron bar.

In the West very few people know what it is to be beaten up thoroughly. You are hit once, and you grit your teeth and swear you will not scream or show that you are hurt. But you are hit more and more, you fall down, blood comes, you get terribly hurt everywhere and your mind can scarcely function, then you can't grit your teeth any longer, your jaws come apart – and you scream. You try to dodge the blows, to crawl away, to protect yourself, but your muscles no longer react properly. You ache terribly, and every blow is worse than the last.

When they had finished with me I could not stand without support, but I had not signed the papers – I do not think I could have signed. I was thrown back into my cell. The beating had lasted almost one hour.

In the cell, when I had begun to feel a little better, my comrades offered me some advice. I was still young, they said. If I were to sign what they wanted me to sign, and cause them no trouble, I would get about ten years in Siberia. I would be out at less than thirty years of age. But if I refused, I could see for myself, they would end up by crippling me. I thought of Gorodietsky. For him it was harder than for me to refuse a 'confession', but he had refused, and I admired him immensely for it. I wondered if I would be able to last out.

There was a strange thing I had frequently noticed about my comrades. Bitter as they were about their fate, they were not as resentful as I would have expected. They all still seemed to have a vague, tenacious hope that they would one day be freed and return to favour once more. They never openly criticised the Stalinist regime but made unconvincing efforts to justify what had happened to them and others like them. 'When the forest is cut down,' they would say, 'the little twigs fly.'

Boris I. Bakhlanov

I no longer wanted to assist in the realisation of our
magnificent aim, in the cause of destroying the old
world and creating the new.

The son of a Cossack who became a revolutionary, Bakhlanov attended the school of artillery at Gorky and then served in an NKVD demolition battalion before going to an intelligence school in Moscow. He was later transferred to the counter-intelligence organization known as Smersh ('death to spies') to train saboteurs and to supervise partisan operations behind German lines in the Ukraine.

After the war he was sent to Baden in Austria, where he specialized in the recruitment of Western citizens, but he was becoming increasingly disillusioned with the regime. In 1945 he was posted to Budapest to process refugees in an attempt to identify war criminals and, during a home leave to Kiev, he realized he would never be allowed to leave the NKVD, despite the wishes of his father, who had wanted him to have a university education. Having decided to defect, and having taken some precautions to protect his father and his Austrian girlfriend from accusations that they knew of his plans, Bakhlanov approached the Americans in Vienna in 1947. His intention was to go to England but he had reckoned that escape would be easier through the American zone of occupation in Vienna. In this judgment he was proved correct, and he was passed on eventually to the British. He anglicized his name to Boris Haddon and in 1971, under the pseudonym A. I. Romanov, wrote *Nights are Longest There*, which was translated from Russian by Gerald Brooke, the university lecturer imprisoned in Moscow in 1964. Bakhlanov is reported to have committed suicide by drowning in London in 1984.

In this passage from his autobiography Bakhlanov explains what motivated him to escape the Soviet system.

Nights are Longest There

During my first night in the NKVD school in Babushkin I spent a lot of time thinking about the papers I had signed that evening, particularly about the last one which had Stalin's signature on it. All the events of my life hitherto, my service in the NKVD demolition battalion and the paper I had signed undertaking not to divulge any battalion secrets, now seemed like a joke or a children's game. One thing at least was clear: I should have to keep a very close watch on myself and keep my mouth tightly shut all the time, everywhere and in all kinds of company. If I didn't, I could expect short shrift from the authorities.

'How does one tell what is secret and what isn't? How best keep a secret so as not to get into trouble?' exclaimed our instructor at a special subject lesson the following day. He went straight on to answer his own question. 'I trust that you all read our newspapers, magazines and books regularly. Well, everything that's printed there is for the masses and for general consumption, and it isn't secret. All that you will learn in the course of your studies and your service, none of which you will ever find in any of our magazines or books, is totally secret. Consequently, in your dealings with the masses, you must always, in any speeches, conversations, talks, confine yourself to exactly what is in the press – in our newspapers and journals. This is the only way,' our instructor concluded, 'that you can safeguard yourself from all kinds of unpleasantness.' This was my first encounter with this instructor – the man who taught us special subject No. 1 – dealing with the rights and obligations of the State Security bodies of the Soviet Union. The instructor was a middle-aged man, or so he then seemed to me, with greying fair hair, and he was known as 'Lord' among the cadets. He had come by this nickname because of his impeccably straight parting, and also because his suits were magnificently pressed the whole year round. From the very first lesson I was terrified about 'Lord'. For many of his remarks he could easily have been prosecuted at least on the basis of a series of sections of article 58 of the Criminal Code [of the RSFSR, as it was then] for counter-revolutionary agitation and propaganda.

'Lord' upset all our time-honoured ideas about the Soviet press, for which he hadn't the slightest respect, and about the Party and the government, which I had always thought never concealed from the people even the very worst items of news. I gradually got used to this kind of conversation and became convinced that neither 'Lord' nor the other teachers were trying to be provocative but were simply communicating facts to us which would be essential in the work we would have to do.

In many respects the school's daily time-table reminded me of the one in the Gorky gunnery school. Much to my annoyance, here too a bugler sounded the reveille, here too a sergeant-major chased us out for a physical training session for which, winter or summer and whatever the temperature, we had to strip to the waist. In many other respects the NKVD school was vastly different from the army school. The first time I had breakfast I could not believe my eyes when I saw the huge plates of bread, ready sliced, on the tables. Each cadet took as much bread as he could eat and there was no hint of any rationing! Bread had been strictly rationed both in the army hospital and in the gunnery school. I can't claim that I went hungry in either of these places, for on the whole we weren't fed too badly, but I was always dreaming of food, particularly in Gorky. My friends from among the cadets consoled both themselves and me by quoting a remark of Voroshilov's: 'A cadet is made up of bone, sinew and muscle.' The quotation didn't seem to help much.

In the NKVD school I soon stopped thinking of food. In hospital we were given People's Commissariat of Defence ration No. 10 and in the anti-aircraft artillery No. 9 (a special ration for cadets). Here in the NKVD we received special internal rations which had neither name nor number.

After the first breakfast I disgraced myself somewhat. Seeing the unbelievable abundance of the dining-room, I threw myself upon the food and gorged until I was fit to burst. The first lesson after breakfast was political affairs. The huge quantity of food had made me drowsy and as I listened to the monotonous voice of the platoon commander, who was taking the period, I began to doze off. Nothing dreadful happened, but I was politely roused by my neighbour saying, 'Wake up, he's almost finished.'

During the whole of my time at the NKVD school I don't recall a single occasion when the political affairs period lasted for more than ten or fifteen minutes. They used to read out to us the Soviet Information Bureau communiqué concerning actions in the various theatres of the war, after which first the *partorg*, then the *komsorg*, announced forthcoming Party and Komsomol meetings. At these meetings either new candidate members of the Party were received from the Komsomol or candidate-members of the Party were received into full membership. We all already belonged either to the Komsomol or to the Party, and indeed people without such affiliations are not considered for work in the field of State Security. Moreover, in the NKVD school political affairs had no special importance. Even in the ten-year school far more time was devoted to the subject. At the beginning of the course I was amazed by this discovery, but I gradually realised that it was no malicious omission on the part of an individual, but a well-conceived practical plan. Really, what was the point of wasting time, which was short anyway, on long talks about successes in the fields of the collective farms or the factories, or even about the splendour of Marxism-Leninism, when in all the special subject lessons we were taught hard facts about the essential nature of both the Soviet State and communism, about difficulties and mistakes and plans for the future, in any case without any dull, long-winded routine propaganda.

At a lesson in special subject No. 1 the instructor 'Lord' was listening hard to how a cadet answered a question which he had just put to him. The cadet, who, like myself, had arrived at the school not long before, was talking about the official links between State Security bodies and the regional party committees. His speech was peppered with such expressions as 'Thanks to the wise leadership of our father and teacher the great Stalin,' or, 'Our field HQ is Stalin's Central Committee.' As usual, long-suffering 'Lord' began by drumming with his fingers on the table, then he started to put in remarks like 'Make it brief', 'Stick to the point' and finally 'This isn't a collective farm meeting.'

After the end of the lesson, when the instructor had left the room, the platoon commander made us all stay behind and turning to this particular cadet said, 'Now tell me whom do you think is the bigger fool, yourself or our instructor?'

'I can't see the point of this question,' said the cadet, his eyes goggling.

'I'll explain,' the commander went on. 'Of course, it's a very good thing that you are absolutely devoted to Comrade Stalin and that you trust in the leadership of our Party, but if that weren't the case you wouldn't have been sent to this school in the first place. Do you really think that our instructor, a tried and tested Chekist, trusts in Stalin and our Party any less than you do? To answer as you did, even if we discount the valuable time you wasted, means that you regard him as an utter fool. Who are you grovelling before? Before your own brother Chekists. We need deeds not words. All we want from you for the time being is that you should study well. Do you understand now?'

'Understood, Comrade Second Lieutenant of the State Security,' answered the cadet, by now as red as a beetroot.

Grigori A. Tokaev

*I had no conception that my effort to assist the regime
by speaking the truth would land me in the opposition,
and still less idea that many of the people I knew who
made public speeches in defence of Stalin's interpretation
of the Dictatorship of the Proletariat were really engaged
in underground anti-Stalin work.*

A lecturer in jet engine technology and rocket propulsion at the Zhukovsky Air Force Academy in Moscow, Colonel Grigori Tokaev was an Osset who had spent much of his career at the elite Institute of Engineers and Geodesics. However, at the end of the Second World War he was transferred to Berlin with instructions to recruit as many German scientists with a knowledge of missile research as he could find. In this context the NKVD's reference to recruitment meant kidnapping, and when Tokaev discovered that Professor Kurt Tank, Focke-Wulf's chief aircraft designer, was listed for abduction, he underwent a crisis of conscience.

Appalled by the ruthlessness of the NKVD, Tokaev was also preoccupied by the fear that he himself might be kidnapped by an émigré organization, and by the worry that the NKVD had learned of his support for Trotsky. Unable to bear the pressure any longer, Tokaev crossed into the British sector in Berlin with his wife and daughter in 1948 and surrendered to SIS. In London he was debriefed at a Special Liaison Centre and his interviews formed the basis of his two autobiographies, *Betrayal of an Ideal*, published in 1955, and *Comrade X*, released the following year. Tokaev subsequently changed his surname to Tokaty and pursued a distinguished academic career at the City University in London. Among his many publications are *Rocketdynamics* and *Cosmonautics-Aeronautics*. His most recent is *Theoretic Principles of Spaceship Design*, published in 1989. In this passage Tokaev recounts his first experience of falling out with his communist colleagues.

Betrayal of an Ideal

Early in 1928 the Central Committee of the Party decided to banish Trotsky from the USSR. Over Stalin's signature instructions went to all parts of the Union calling for demonstrations in support of the decision. We too in the North Caucasus demonstrated. There were endless compulsory marches of 'spontaneous' demonstrators, over whom waved a regular forest of flags, pennants, banners, portraits and caricatures. The procession tramped past the building of the Provincial Party Head-quarters. Here the right slogans were chanted: 'Down with Trotsky!', 'Long live our leader, Comrade Stalin!', and there were bursts of cheering. But, just as my group were passing under the balcony of the Headquarters a voice quite close to me shouted: 'Long live Comrade Trotsky, leader of the World Proletariat.' A scattered 'Hurrah' followed and the procession was thrown into confusion.

I neither shouted nor cheered. I merely watched the ultra-Stalinists and the Trotskyists come to grips. The Trotskyists were in a minority, but there were bloody faces and torn clothes before the police broke up the fight and swept some fifteen people into the prison courtyard. I was among them!

We were cross-examined in alphabetical order. I insisted truculently on my rights as an individual, and so exasperated the magistrate that he shouted at me that it was obvious from my florid handwriting that I was a Trotskyist. Very well, I asked, if that was so, why need he examine me? If he wanted to pursue a real political enquiry, let him look into my known political convictions.

He then spoke to me calmly, but still assuring me that all I said proved I was a Trotskyist. He fully understood me: 'My leader', Trotsky, was being banished and sent to 'our' masters, the capitalists of the world, so naturally we were all very disturbed and in a state of high tension. This tried my patience beyond what were then its limits. I shouted at him to go to hell with his fantastic arguments. He too lost his control. 'You Trotskyists,' he cried, 'want ploughing in. What we can't get into your thick skulls should be stuffed in your . . .' This indecency I took as an insult not only to myself but to the ideals of the regime in which I so passionately believed, and I fired a volley of extremely strong expressions at this man who was a magistrate and three times my age. To this day I cannot forgive myself for this folly.

I remember how he rose from his chair and paced the room, deep in thought. Then he turned to me and delivered a lecture, not on Trotskyism but on manners. Coarseness and hooliganism of this sort merely debased a man. I, a young Comsomol, had used the foulest language to him, a man getting on in years, a magistrate who was doing his duty, a Party member since 1917, who had been a prisoner of the Tsarist regime released by the Revolution. He would not continue the enquiry: I could walk out and everyone would know that he refused even to examine me.

I now made some effort to convince him that it was not I who had shouted the Trotskyist slogan, and in fact I succeeded. He was very human. Later on he himself was to go to Siberia for *his* own Trotskyism! I met him when he returned to Moscow in 1932 and we became fast friends, but in 1935 he was again arrested; since then his fate is unknown to me.

I have often asked myself what exactly was my attitude to Trotsky at this time. I was certainly opposed to him. Trotsky's conception of the Revolution had never been mine. For in my view Trotskyism could be summed up as a belief in a system of *imperialist-revolutionary dictatorship*. It was in fact a doctrine of one-party tyranny based on a concentration of forces along imperialist lines. *In this respect it was indistinguishable from Stalinism.* Viewed from another aspect it was neither more nor less than a revival of the tradition of territorial expansion of the Russian Tsars, only under a new banner. One distinction, however, between Trotskyism and Stalinism was that on the nationalities question Trotsky was even more reactionary. How could I possibly be thought to have subscribed to such a view, when the very springboard from which I and my family had leapt into the revolutionary stream was the national aspiration of the North Caucasian peoples!

But the accusation of being a Trotskyist at this time is interesting. The practice had already begun of identifying any kind of independent thinking with an extremist form of opposition to the regime. While freedom of discussion was a slogan, in practice any dissident opinion was treated as heresy. I was being treated as a delinquent without even having expressed any dissent.

It was only later, however, that I came to see this development as significant. At the time I was still wholly *inside* the Soviet process, and though its workings filled me with indignation, I continued to ascribe them to the mistaken zeal of individual officials and failed to understand them for what they were.

Piotr S. Deriabin

*I have never regretted for a moment
my decision for liberty.*

On 15 February 1954 Piotr Deriabin, a thirty-three-year-old Siberian from Lolot, walked into the American military headquarters in Vienna and asked for political asylum. He identified himself as a case officer in charge of security at the local NKVD *rezidentura* and described his background as a career intelligence officer with experience as a member of Stalin's personal bodyguard, as a veteran of the siege of Stalingrad and as a graduate of the Red Army's Higher School of Counter-Intelligence.

Wounded four times and decorated five times during the war, in which he served as an infantry officer, Deriabin had been recruited by the NKVD as a security officer in Barnaul before he joined the elite Guard Directorate of the Kremlin in 1947. To his credit was his long membership of the Komsomol and his pre-war career as a teacher, as well as his surveillance work in the Altai Kray province of his native Siberia, but these assets did not prepare him for what he learned about the Soviet heirarchy. 'Neither the betrayal of Party principles, as he thought he had learned them years before, nor even the unjust condemnation of the innocent revolted him so much as the gross moral double standard of his leaders. The Soviet leaders' dedicated obsession with pleasure and power illustrates as nothing else could how completely the early ideals of the Revolution have vanished,' he said in his autobiography, written in the third person.

After six years in Moscow, during which his first wife died and he married for a second time, Deriabin attended the Marxism-Leninism Institute and in May 1952 was transferred to the Austro-German section of the Second Chief Directorate. Here, in July 1952, he supervised the abduction of Dr Walter Linse, the anti-communist lawyer based in West Berlin. A refugee who had fled from East Germany in 1947 to head the Association of Free German Jurists, Linse was tried in secret for treason and sentenced to twenty-five years in the labour camps. In September 1953 Deriabin was posted to Vienna, accompanied by his wife and daughter, to concentrate on the West German security service, the BfV, headed by Otto John. However, in February the following year he was implicated in the defection of a visitor, Anatoli I. Skachkov of the Soviet Petroleum Administration. Skachkov's defection to the Americans, while under Deriabin's jurisdiction, would have led to a reprimand or perhaps a worse punishment. He had a row with his wife and, apparently on impulse, took a taxi to the American Kommandantura.

Deriabin was the only Soviet defector to become an established CIA officer, and at the time of his death in September 1992, aged seventy-two, after a long battle against cancer, he was still making regular visits to Langley from his home in nearby northern Virginia. He testified before Congressional committees four times, taught at the Defense Intelligence College after his retirement from the CIA in 1981, and completed graduate studies at the University of Michigan and the University of Virginia. He married for a third time in the United States and had a son, Peter junior.

Five years after his defection Deriabin teamed up with an experienced *Time* and *Newsweek* journalist, Frank Gibney, to write *The Secret World*, which was based upon two *Life* articles published in March 1959. Although only Gibney was credited with having edited *The Penkovsky Papers*, Deriabin also played a major role in the book's preparation. In this extract from his memoirs, written characteristically in the third person, he gives a glimpse of life in the Kremlin under Stalin and Beria.

The Secret World

One of the principal duties of the State Security is to screen the private lives of the New Class magnates and their friends from the view of the Soviet people. It is probably more merciful to do so. At least it is a service to the cause of public morality. The excesses of the New Class go far beyond cases of simple wantonness, like the son of Mikoyan who repeatedly smashed up the state cars that were given him. In fact, a clinical study of Soviet social life might easily dwarf *The Lost Weekend* and make the Kinsey Report look like a *Parents' Magazine* anthology. The few lurid revelations which have reached the outside world deal mostly with the immoral excesses practiced under 'Stalinism', the implication being that such things have now been corrected. They have not. The same people are running the Soviet Union now as then, and they have the same habits.

In his duties with the State Security, Deriabin got recurrent glimpses into the private lives of the men he protected. Neither the betrayal of Party principles, as he thought he had learned them years before, nor even the unjust condemnation of the innocent revolted him so much as the gross moral double standard of his leaders. The Soviet leaders' dedicated obsession with pleasure and power illustrates as nothing else could how completely the early ideals of the Revolution have vanished.

The standard originated with Stalin. He is presumed to have murdered his beloved wife Alliluyeva in 1932 in a fit of sudden drunken rage. She had been appalled by the developing excesses of his forced collectivization campaign. He admitted his crime before a special session of the Central Committee, which was already heavily peopled with his creatures. The Committee limited its punishment to an 'admonition', and the death was listed as a suicide, when it was mentioned at all. As late as 1950 Stalin used to visit the Novo Devichye cemetery daily between 5 and 6 a.m., where he would sit as long as thirty minutes at a time staring at his wife's grave.

Stalin rarely if ever took action to curb the off-duty rowdiness of his disorderly bodyguard, and he was similarly indulgent with the immoralities of higher-ups. One of the most notorious primal urges in the Soviet Union belongs to Marshal Konstantin Rokossovsky, until 1956 the Soviet proconsul in Poland. Rokossovsky was 'unofficially' married several times and brought relays of girl friends to share his quarters wherever he happened to be serving. A stream of reports and complaints about Rokossovsky's conduct landed in the files of the Central Committee, specifically with the Conduct Supervision Committee, one of the most overworked administrative bodies in the Soviet Union.

In 1948 Matvey Shkiryatov, then chairman of the Party Control Commission, asked Stalin to take action against Rokossovsky. Although he read his report Stalin refused. 'I have no Suvorov,' he said, 'but Rokossovsky is Bagration.' He said this in obvious reference to the famous statement attributed to Catherine the Great, when her ministers asked her to punish the great General Suvorov for insubordination. Reminding them of Suvorov's victories, Catherine had replied: 'Conquerors do not stand trial.'

Marshal Zhukov was another prominent ladies' man on the General Staff, and even the chambermaids in his residences were not safe from his advances. Marshal Timoshenko, on the other hand, was best known as a drinker. His prolonged vodka bouts were notorious, and Guard officers assigned to Timoshenko's house or *dacha* needed strong stomachs, as they

were invariably commanded to participate. The drinking sessions sometimes lasted for days. One Guard Directorate captain was hastily
transferred to Moscow after hitting the Marshal with a bottle in the
course of an early morning brawl.

For all-round dissipation, however, few could approach the exacting
standard set by Stalin's own son, Vasiliy. For years Vasiliy's quarters on
Gogolevskiy Boulevard were the scene of lavish debauches, complete with
all the classic touches, down to naked dancing girls performing on the
banquet table. The Guard Directorate officers assigned to Vasiliy took an
incredible amount of punishment, subject as they were to constant calls
for a weekend or longer of heavy wining and wenching on Vasiliy's estate.
In most cases they ended as depraved as their boss.

Vasiliy broke up both of his own marriages – the second was to the
daughter of Marshal Timoshenko. It was after this that his father finally
took a disciplinary hand to him, demoted him to the rank of colonel from
lieutenant general, and cut down heavily on the scope and intensity of his
entertaining. After Stalin died Vasiliy was dismissed from the Air Force
Staff Academy for drunkenness and misconduct. (He was once found
lying insensible in a Moscow gutter.) He was finally put in a treatment
center for alcoholism.

Stalin's daughter, Svetlana, on the other hand, was a plain and rather
quiet girl. But she was a victim of politics. In 1948 she was forced to
divorce her first husband. He was accused of being a 'cosmopolite' and
associating with foreigners and was sent away, never to be heard from
again. In actual fact, his principal offense was being Jewish. Stalin was
always a leader in the regime's recurrent anti-Semitic outbursts.

Svetlana's second husband was Yuri Zhdanov, son of Stalin's collaborator, Andrey Zhdanov, who died in 1947. After Svetlana's father died
Zhdanov divorced her, anxious to weather the de-Stalinization storm. She
was allowed to return to Moscow, where she retained her apartment and
one of Stalin's estates in the Moscow suburbs. Her most intimate friend
was the daughter of Nikolay Shvernik, the trade union boss. Aside from
this she had few contacts even with other members of the New Class. Nor
has she now.

At least during the dictator's declining years Lavrentiy Beria was
probably Stalin's closest friend. They often took their holidays together,
happily drinking and cooking *shashlik* on one of the Caucasian estates.
Beria was the most depraved of the Soviet leadership, excelling even such
pillars of immorality as Viktor Abakumov, who maintained a string of
private brothels, or Lieutenant General Vlasik, the brutal head of Stalin's

personal guard. The stories circulated about Beria's sex vices by Khrushchev and Co. after they got rid of him have a substantial basis in fact. He had no compunction about the women he debauched. The wives of several State Security officers, among others, were ordered at various times to spend the night with Beria, under pain of their husbands' arrest. After his arrest the names of two hundred call girls and worse were found among his personal files, and this was just the Moscow file. Whenever or wherever Beria happened to see a woman who struck his fancy he would send an officer of the Guard to 'get' her for him. But his peculiar failing was a liking for very young girls.

The most egregious case of Beria's Lolita complex involved an innocent thirteen-year-old girl, a student in high school. Beria spotted her on a Moscow street while driving past in his car. He sent the chief of his personal security staff, one Colonel Sarkisov, to get her. Sarkisov followed the girl and told her that an important person wished to speak with her. Because her mother was sick and needed her the girl refused to go. At which point the Colonel produced his identification and ordered her to come with him.

Inside his house Beria gave the girl some food and liquor and asked her to sleep with him. When she refused, fighting and screaming, Beria had her drugged. The next day she woke up in his room, where she spent the next three days. She was sent home with instructions not to tell anyone of the incident unless she wanted her mother shot.

She did tell her mother on returning home. The mother rushed to Beria's house with the girl and somehow got in (the guard thinking she had returned on order). When the mother threatened Beria with a protest to the Central Committee he told her she would not live to see its outcome. So she did not report the matter until after his arrest.

The closest thing to an outdoor type among these bloated gentry was probably Lazar Kaganovich, who has been mouldering in a provincial limbo ever since his denunciation by Khrushchev as part of the 'anti-Party' group. Kaganovich was fond of taking long walks in the country. It was not unusual for him to walk for several miles along a country road, followed at a respectful distance by a car full of his State Security bodyguard. He did not go overboard completely for the rugged life; whenever he got a sharp pebble in his shoe the Guard had to make a breakneck automobile dash back to his *dacha* to procure another pair. He was also something of a do-it-yourself man, almost the only member of the leadership who occasionally took the wheel of his own car. (He once pursued a taxi-cab driver for half an hour through the streets of Moscow after the cab had hit a pedestrian without stopping. When Kaganovich caught up with him justice was swift.)

To complement his foible for exercise Kaganovich had one of the most luxurious sauna-baths in the Soviet Union on his estate, liberally supplied with brandy and other comforts. In the course of an inspection trip around his *dacha* a group of State Security officers, Lieutenant General Rumyantsev and three of his colonels, found the bath irresistible. They stripped, went through the birch-twig-and-steam routine with abandon, and liberally solaced themselves with the brandy and *kvas* chasers to the point where they were almost hopelessly drunk. At this moment the phone rang in the Guard headquarters on the estate. A worried voice conveyed a message: 'The owner is coming home. He'll be there in five minutes.' There was nothing for it but to bundle the General and the colonels, clothed only in towels and brandy fumes, into a car, throwing their uniforms in after them. Kaganovich, as it happened, was never the wiser.

Nikolai E. Khokhlov

In the winter of 1954 I had to make an extraordinary decision. On the scales three human lives were being weighed against two consciences. I do not regret the decision, for there could be only one.

During the Second World War Nikolai Khokhlov had operated behind enemy lines as a partisan and had played a role in the assassination of Wilhelm Kube, the Nazi *Gauleiter* of Minsk. In 1952 he had married Yana Timashkevits, who came from a strong Christian Uniats family, and fell under her influence. After a period of four years in Romania, where he was sent to perfect his cover, he was ordered to travel to Frankfurt to murder Georgi S. Okolovich, the leader of the exiled NTS Ukrainian nationalists. However, inspired by his wife, in February 1954 he gave himself up to his intended victim at his apartment.

Okolovich persuaded Khokhlov to surrender to the CIA but he was reluctant to do anything that would jeopardize his chances of smuggling Yana and their young son Alushka to the West. Nevertheless he gave the CIA the name of Nikita Khorunsky, the Soviet mole inside the NTS organization, and helped his contacts entrap two of his colleagues, Kurt Weber and Hans Kurkovich. Both men also agreed to defect, but an attempt to ensnare their handler, Colonel Oleg Okun, failed.

Khokhlov was overcome with remorse when, instead of joining Weber and Kurkovich in the West, Okun had fled to Moscow. Khokhlov's wife and son were arrested soon afterwards, and when this news filtered to the defector in April he called a press conference in Bonn, at which he displayed a silenced gun, loaded with cyanide-tipped bullets, disguised as an innocent-looking packet of cigarettes, in the hope that publicity might give his family some protection. Whether the ploy succeeded is doubtful, but Khokhlov moved to Switzerland where he wrote his melancholy memoirs, *In the Name of Conscience*. In 1954 and again in 1956 he gave evidence to the Senate Judiciary Committee.

In September 1957, while attending a conference in Germany, he was injected with a tiny but highly toxic quantity of radioactive thallium, but he survived the attempt on his life and, after his recovery, moved to America where he now lives under yet another identity. According to another FCD defector, Oleg Gordievsky, the KGB did trace Khokhlov to his new home in New York in 1977, but failed to obtain permission to have him liquidated. In this passage Khokhlov breaks it to Yana, his future wife, that he is a member of the feared Soviet intelligence apparatus.

In the Name of Conscience

Several days had passed since the evening of November 13. Again I was visiting Yana, sitting comfortably on the sofa among the small pillows that had probably been embroidered by her mother.

Yana had returned from work only a short while before and was busy with a lot of little household chores.

Now she was ironing on an improvised board, a folded grey blanket on an oval table. The iron made a melodic clink as she set it on the metal stand, while she straightened the small white cuffs for Masha's school uniform. Yana pressed them, folded them neatly, then started on the blue ribbons.

I watched the smooth, sure movements of her arms, saw the carefully darned elbow of her worn blue jacket, looked at the pale face dimly lighted by the reflection from the table lamp, and thought of how warm my feeling towards her had grown during these past few days.

An instinctive sense of caution still restrained me from touching on the question of my work. Yana did not ask me about it. Five years ago I had told her something of my participation in partisan warfare at that time. Now I no longer had reason to be proud of my official status – most likely the contrary. Involuntarily I feared Yana's possible reaction to frankness on my part. What if she should become cool, as my other friends had done? What if our friendship – the friendship of two people, which, though not intimate, covered a long acquaintanceship – should vanish at the first mention of the truth?

I now knew that a year before the war she had completed her course at the Engineering Institute. I knew that she was working as a metallurgical engineer in the 'Promep' (Industrial Energy Planning) and Construction Bureau of the Ministry of Power Stations. I was even familiar with the routine of her daily life. Early in the morning she took the underground to the Bauman District, at the outskirts of the city. For nine hours without interruption she designed metal frameworks for hydro-electrical stations in many parts of the Soviet Union, edited construction prospectuses, checked production blueprints. In the evening Yana rode back across Moscow, did her necessary local shopping, and took care of household chores. Not the least of these was looking after her little sister, whom she must help to raise to become educated – to dress neatly, even to freshly pressed blue ribbons. Often after Masha went to bed, and the lights in neighbouring flats went out, Yana would spread blueprints on the oval table for the overtime work that brought additional income. In the economy of a Soviet engineer extra money was very much needed.

About the rest of her family I knew almost nothing. Her brother Andrei, disabled in the war, had gone to Murmansk hoping to find work in the fishing industry. Other relatives we had not discussed.

But even if I knew approximately how Yana was living, it was difficult for me to guess how she was thinking. Specifically – how she would react to my status as an employee of Soviet intelligence.

Apparently it was going to be necessary to take that risk. Lately I had been trying so hard to find someone with whom I could at least share my doubts and problems – someone who would listen to me without becoming afraid, who would want to understand and help me. Was it not the secret hope that Yana could be that person that kept bringing me again and again to her home?

Certainly it was the fear that this hope might not be justified that had been holding me back and forcing me to keep silent. But it was impossible to delay indefinitely this inevitable step.

I gathered up courage.

'Yana, you haven't even once asked me where I work. Is it of no interest to you?'

'Of course it is of interest to me, Kolya. But I've been waiting for you to speak of it yourself. I don't know whether you even have the right to talk about it.'

I smiled awkwardly, and tried to find the correct words. 'No particular right . . . but I want very much to tell you. You know – well, as a matter of fact, I'm in the intelligence service.'

She raised her head and looked at me attentively.

'Yes,' I plunged on. 'Intelligence service, in the Ministry of State Security, MGB.'

A shadow passed across Yana's face. She lowered her head and silently continued to iron. I waited. Apparently neither of us knew what to say next.

I was the first who could stand the silence no longer. 'Perhaps it would be better if I didn't talk about it? My frankness, evidently, did not please you–'

'Oh, no, it's not that,' she protested in a clear voice. She gave a little shrug. 'I felt that your work was connected with something out of the ordinary – but, of course, I didn't know it was that bad.'

She picked up the iron and left the room, then returned with a cardboard box and started to prepare Masha's lunch for the morning.

Again we both remained silent.

I sat, mechanically examining the embroidery on the sofa pillows, unable to rid myself of the feeling that I had become unwanted in this room. Suddenly, as though to myself, I asked Yana almost defiantly, 'In your opinion, is this profession so shameful?'

'I don't know,' she replied slowly, as though pondering her answer. 'I've had no occasion to come in contact with the work of MGB. But decent people don't . . .' She hesitated a moment, then immediately continued firmly, 'For decent people there are many more honourable occupations.'

Yana sat down in the armchair opposite me and assumed her favourite pose – elbows on the table, chin in her palms, her eyes regarding me earnestly.

I realized that she was waiting to hear my side of the story, but I forced myself to get up.

'Well,' I said slowly, 'it's time for me to go home.'

'As you like.'

In Yana's voice sounded that same note of sadness. She rose and walked into the hall. At the very threshold I joined her and turned her towards me. She leaned back against the wall, arms behind her, and lifted an inquiring eyebrow.

I leaned over her very close. 'Why are you silent?'

'What can I tell you, Kolya? Is it really possible that you yourself don't understand?'

I took Yana's elbow and pulled her towards the living room. She carefully freed her elbow but came with me.

Again we sat opposite each other, but I no longer avoided her eyes.

'Yana, you're wrong. You're very wrong. It is not at all as you think. I am listed as a worker in MGB, it's true, but I came to them in wartime and for very special reasons. The main point is that I have decided to leave them.'

I told her how at first I did not question and could not make comparisons; how gradually there dawned upon me an understanding of the truth and how I came to the inevitable decision. During my long and frank story I was afraid of only one thing – that Yana would not understand and believe. But the reverse happened. She understood and believed.

Vladimir M. Petrov

Fear is the master wherever the power of the Kremlin can make itself felt. That fear ruled our lives in the Embassy at Canberra and drove us to seek refuge and freedom from fear in Australia.

The operation launched by the Australian Security Intelligence Organization (ASIO) to cultivate a source in the Soviet embassy in Canberra lasted from April 1951, four months after the arrival of the Soviet Consul, to his defection in April 1954. During that period ASIO had placed an agent of long standing, a Polish refugeee and physician, Michael Bialoguski, close to Petrov, who was the NKVD's *rezident*, in the hope of persuading him to defect.

Petrov, whose real name was Proletarsky, enjoyed life in Australia and when in May 1953 he was recalled to Moscow, Bialoguski arranged to diagnose an eye complaint to give the diplomat an excuse to stay. Unaware of Bialoguski's dual role, Petrov confided in him that his strong-willed wife, Evdokia, had quarrelled with the wife of the new ambassador, and that the atmosphere in the embassy was intolerable. He arranged to buy a small farm near Sydney and Bialoguski tape-recorded the conversation in which he declared his intention to complete the sale in April 1954.

Petrov had not confided in his wife, the *rezidentura*'s code clerk, who was also an NKVD professional with twenty years' experience, so when he disappeared without warning she was held captive in the embassy until she could be flown back to Moscow. Her Soviet colleagues told her that Vladimir was dead, but on the plane home she was informed by the crew that her husband was alive and had applied for political asylum. When the aircraft was refuelled at Darwin her two escorts were disarmed and she spoke to her husband on the telephone. He had no difficulty in persuading her to stay, and they adopted the identity of a Greek couple named Cronides.

On the strength of documents removed by Petrov from the embassy's *referentura*, the Australian government empanelled a Royal Commission to investigate Soviet espionage and it listened to 104 hours of testimony from the Petrovs. According to Ron Richards, ASIO's former Deputy Director, their evidence resulted in the identification of 600 Soviet intelligence officers and their agents around the world. They also disclosed, for the first time, that the missing British diplomats, Guy Burgess and Donald Maclean, were ideologically motivated spies who had served the Soviet cause since their days at university, and that they were now living in Moscow.

Petrov, who together with his wife wrote *Empire of Fear*, suffered from poor health, aggravated by alcoholism, and died in June 1991, aged eighty-four. Evdokia, who survived him, still lives in Australia. In this extract they assess the impact of previous Soviet defectors, including Igor Gouzenko, Victor Kravchenko and Yuri Rastvorov.

Empire of Fear

A Soviet official who escapes from the Soviet service to refuge in a Western democratic country passes from one world to another. It is difficult for people who have lived all their lives in the free world to understand how formidable that step looks from the other side of the Iron Curtain. So many fears hedge it round that it is rarely taken, except under the impact of an even greater fear.

But I can hope that more people in the non-communist world will understand what it means when they have heard our story. They will understand how such a step, for Soviet officials, even though, like ourselves, they have served for years in foreign countries, remains a huge leap in the dark, a launching into the unknown, a hazard whose end cannot be foreseen. This uncertainty is perhaps the greatest barrier of all to those who contemplate crossing this dangerous frontier. It is a barrier the Soviet Government strives desperately to maintain. It was a major obstacle in my own case.

Others before me had dared to cross this frontier. Though the names of such people are never publicly mentioned inside the USSR, I knew some of their stories. While in Sweden, I had read in English newspapers about the flight of Igor Gouzenko from the Soviet Embassy in Ottawa. In Canberra I saw Kravchenko's book *I Chose Freedom*, a copy of which had been left by some curious chance in our secret MVD office in the Embassy. And on 2nd February 1954, when my own crisis was reaching its climax, the Australian press carried an account of the flight from the Soviet Embassy in Japan, of Yuri Rastvorov (whom my wife and I had known as an MVD officer in Moscow) to refuge with the Americans.

Knowledge of the existence of this way of escape lies in the background thoughts of every Soviet official, and remains a permanent spectre to the Soviet Government wherever contact between Soviet citizens and the outside world is concerned.

How was my own decision conceived and born? The Ambassadors in Canberra were its parents. The Australian Security Organization played the part of midwife.

Gouzenko's experience was very different from my own. When he walked out of the Soviet Embassy in Ottawa with his bundle of documents, he threw himself on a society that was busy with other problems and had hardly heard of Soviet espionage. He has described how, for two anxious days, he trudged round newspaper offices trying to get someone to take an interest in him before it was too late. That was the world of September 1945, when the USSR and the West had just emerged as victors and allies in the struggle against Fascism. But, on the 3rd of April 1954, when I stepped into Mr Richards' car in Sydney and drove away to political asylum in Australia, the Australian Security authorities had been able to prepare in detail for the possibility of my defection. Once I had made up my mind to stay in Australia, everything went, to a surprising degree, according to plan. The agonies of fear, doubt and conflict which led up to my decision are another story.

I suppose it really began far back in my native Siberia, when, as I have described, I saw the sufferings of my own peasant folk under collectivization, and the ruin of my native village of Larikha. After that, the horrors of the purges, the victimization of innocent people, the desperate poverty of the Soviet masses, followed by the striking contrast of conditions in other countries – all these had destroyed my faith in the professions of our regime, long before I came near the point of action. I had reached a disillusionment, even cynicism, which today is general, though concealed, among Soviet officials who have seen the outside world and allow themselves to think honestly.

Whenever I travelled from Canberra to Sydney to meet the diplomatic couriers or other new arrivals from Moscow, I was reminded of the true state of affairs. These couriers always asked me to take them around the shops to spend their precious foreign currency on articles unobtainable in the Soviet Union.

Once I asked one of these visitors how things were at home. This man knew me well and, carried away by his feelings, threw discretion to the winds.

'Oh, — awful!' he exclaimed. 'High prices and poor quality.'

The persistence of shortages down to the present moment is confirmed by the American journalist, Stewart Alsop, who took up Krushchev's invitation to foreign journalists to visit the USSR and wrote from Moscow (5th July 1955) that 'all consumer goods are snapped up almost regardless of price, as soon as they appear in the shops'.

But for myself and my wife personally this difference was immaterial to our decision to stay in Australia. We left behind us in Moscow a comfortable flat, clothes, furniture, a bank balance equal to £A13,000, excellent jobs and a position among the privileged bureaucracy. Money was not our motive.

Fear drove and a way of escape was offered.

I will begin at the beginning.

Aleksandr R. Kaznacheev

I knew my Soviet masters would denounce me as a traitor, but my conscience would be clear, for I would be betraying 'them', not my country. I would tell to all the world the truth about the dirty game of the Soviet government in Burma.

A regular diplomat at the Soviet embassy in Rangoon, Aleksandr Kaznacheev defected to the CIA in June 1959. He was twenty-seven years old and he revealed to the CIA that he had been co-opted by the KGB to assist in local intelligence operations.

The son of an electronics engineer, Kaznacheev graduated from the Moscow Oriental Institute and the prestigious International Relations Institute. Fluent in Burmese, he was posted to Rangoon in March 1957 and was quickly captivated by the country and its people. He was appalled at the clandestine support given by his embassy colleagues to the local Communist Party and the communist insurgents and, as his first tour of duty drew to an end, decided to remain in the West, even though he had been assured of a promotion and a swift return to Burma. Curiously, he was inspired by the experience of the Soviet military attaché, Colonel Strygin, who attempted suicide after having been criticized at a Party meeting in the embassy. When he recovered from his overdose in hospital Strygin tried to escape by jumping out of a window but he was caught and escorted on to a Chinese plane bound for Peking, and then the Soviet Union. Undeterred by Strygin's fate, two months later Kaznacheev drove to the US Information Service's library and asked the head librarian to seek political asylum on his behalf. By the following morning Kaznacheev was accommodated in a CIA safe-house, and then moved into the embassy building to attend a press conference which was intended to cause his former colleagues maximum embarrassment.

After five days of interrogation Kaznacheev was flown out of Burma on an American military aircraft. His autobiography, *Inside a Soviet Embassy*, was published in 1962, and here he reveals the extent of the KGB's clandestine activities in Rangoon, a disclosure that was to influence the Burmese for a generation.

Inside a Soviet Embassy

Our Political Intelligence group, in which I came to be accepted as a junior colleague, was definitely the most dangerous and the most elite of all Soviet Intelligence units operating in Burma. It was a part of the Political Intelligence Service – *Politicheskaya Razvedka* – a section of the State Security Commitee (KGB), which in turn was directly subordinate to the Soviet Communist Party's Central Committee. From talks with my colleagues and through observation of our group's operations I could learn that the Political Intelligence was a product of some recent reorganization of the KGB's infamous Foreign Section, which followed adoption of Khrushchev's new foreign policy line of massive Soviet thrust into the so-called 'underdeveloped areas'. The Political Intelligence was designed to meet new conditions and new requirements of the cold war in those areas, where traditional diplomatic methods proved to be useless, and where anything less than ceaseless and ruthless interference in the internal affairs could mean a defeat for the Soviet political goals. The primary objective of the Political Intelligence operations was penetration and subversion of local regimes, direct and active participation in the struggle between different political parties. The gathering and analysis of information was only a secondary aim.

The Political Intelligence's targets in Burma, as I found out, were along the general lines described to me on the very day of my recruitment in Moscow. The main targets were the Burmese major national political parties, Trade Unions, and youth groups. Vozny's officers were assigned to penetrate each of them, to establish contacts with their rank and file, and to cultivate the most promising and important of their people to the point of recruitment. Simultaneously, attempts were made to plant trusted Soviet agents at strategic places within a party, and all these efforts taken together were expected to give the Soviet Intelligence the chance to influence the policies of a party in the way most beneficial to the Soviet government. The other side of this political game was the relentless struggle against Burmese anti-Communist forces and leaders, the attempt to isolate them and to undermine them from within. Through my translations of Intelligence materials I came to appreciate fully the vigor and persistence with which our Intelligence group pursued this goal.

The former Prime Minister of Burma, U Nu, was usually labeled in the Soviet Embassy as a notorious anti-Communist and the most hypocritical and dangerous enemy of the Communist cause. Accordingly, no efforts were spared to undermine his political status in Burma and especially to infiltrate his Union Party. The following small incident is an illustration of the effectiveness of Soviet Intelligence efforts. In late March, 1959, the Executive Committee of the Union Party (Clean AFPFL), which was at that time in bitter opposition to the military government of General Ne Win, discussed in great secrecy the text of a very important political speech to be delivered by the chairman of the party, U Nu, at the May Day rally one month later. The leftist faction of the Union Party, over the opposition of U Nu, insisted on including in the speech a strong criticism of the military government. When only a week later the unsuspecting U Nu went to the United States to take part in a religious convention, high-placed Soviet agents from his immediate surroundings brought a copy of his May Day speech to Soviet Intelligence in Rangoon. The secret text was in Vozny's hands prior to April 3, 1959, which was the first day I saw the speech. A report from an agent was attached to it, describing in great detail how the leftist faction of the Union Party intended to use U Nu's speech in order to provoke the Burmese Army into arresting him, thus giving the militant leftists full control over the Union Party and making U Nu a popular martyr at the same time. Vozny ordered me to translate both papers as fast as I could so that we would have enough time to prepare for the 'great' event. I made the translations and they were immediately sent to Moscow. When one month later the speech was delivered it contained no surprises for Soviet Intelligence, but to our utter dismay the Burmese Army had seen through the Communist plot and took no steps against U Nu.

During my Intelligence career in Vozny's group I learned another important thing: the Soviet government gave to the Political Intelligence an almost complete monopoly over contacts and behind-the-scene negotiations with national political parties and groups. Contacts with Burmese Communists above- and underground were also a monopoly of the Political Intelligence. The group conveyed to Burmese Communists all instructions and financial assistance that was forthcoming from Moscow and delivered to Moscow all messages received from them in return. Since

1958 the Political Intelligence has also been assigned the difficult and highly delicate task of subtly struggling against the Chinese for influence and control over Burmese Communists. As for the relations between Soviet and Chinese Intelligence people in Burma, the appearance of friendliness and cooperation was fully maintained, though I did not know how real they were. I noticed that during diplomatic receptions in our Embassy Vozny was often in the company of his Intelligence counterpart from the Chinese Embassy, and the two men seemed to know each other quite intimately. Probably of some significance was also the fact that even in 1959 we were still instructed to refrain from recruiting to our service local overseas Chinese.

Penetration into foreign Embassies in Rangoon, especially the American Embassy, and recruitment of their personnel provided another major target of Political Intelligence operations in Burma. I knew that practically all members of the group at one time or another had tried their hands at this line of operations. From talks with the Sovfilmexport representative, Ivan Rogachev, who was an important Intelligence personality, and especially my 'colleague' Boris Galashin, I learned that the usual technique used by them for establishing contacts with foreign Embassies' employees was one of striking up 'friendship' at Rangoon's few social gathering-places such as swimming pools, horse-race courses, tennis courts, chess clubs, etc. Our Intelligence boys were not above even such petty tricks as taking seats in the movie houses near foreigners, or driving near the residences of foreign diplomats and proposing a lift to anyone who might happen to walk in the street.

Our Intelligence group apparently was not always successful in its operations against foreign Embassies. Boris Galashin, who often discussed Intelligence problems with me, admitted that although it was not difficult for him to establish contacts with interesting people from the British and Australian Embassies, all his attempts to get acquainted with Americans had failed. He also told me that he had found Rangoon social gatherings a poor place for Intelligence work. As he put it, 'fifty eyes follow your every step at the swimming pool, and you simply can't have a confidential talk with anybody there.'

Although on my recruitment I had been told that the work with foreigners would be one of my duties, my chief Vozny did not give me any specific assignment in this line. Apparently, he intended to use me entirely for translations and the work with Burmese political parties. As for me, I was only too glad to avoid contacts with Americans or any other foreigners, for I was afraid that they might endanger my rather free way of living in Rangoon. Only in early 1959 did Vozny and Galashin begin pressing me to take part in these operations. They particularly urged me to strike up acquaintance with just any American, saying that no expenses would be too large for the purpose. Somehow I avoided this work to the very end.

Anatoli M. Golitsyn

The scope and scale of disinformation activity by communist regimes is virtually unlimited.

Shortly before Christmas in December 1961 a Soviet diplomat identifying himself as Anatoli Klimov called on the CIA station chief in Helsinki, Frank Friberg, and demanded political asylum in the United States. Accompanied by his wife and daughter, he revealed that his true name was Anatoli Golitsyn, a member of the KGB's First Chief Directorate. Although he claimed to be inspired by political considerations, he admitted to having quarrelled recently with his *rezident*, Colonel Zhenikhov, an incident which he knew would not enhance his career prospects.

Golitsyn's credentials were confirmed at the CIA headquarters by Piotr Deriabin, who recalled having served with him in Vienna, where he had remarked that Golitsyn and his wife had a reputation for being difficult. A graduate of the FCD's counter-intelligence school in Moscow, Golitsyn had worked as a line PR officer in the Third Department, the section dealing with British and Scandinavian affairs. Upon his defection he identified various individuals as KGB sources, and confirmed that he had seen classified British Admiralty documents supplied by a source who was subsequently confirmed as John Vassall. Among the other KGB assets 'neutralized' by Golitsyn's disclosures were Barbara Fell (who received a three-year prison sentence in England), Georges Paques, then deputy head of NATO's press department, who received a gaol term of twenty years; John Watkins, a Canadian diplomat who died of a heart attack; and the French politician Jacques Foccart who went into self-imposed exile.

Because of the quality of his information, Golitsyn acquired a near guru-like status within the West's counter-intelligence community and travelled the globe to advise security agencies on measures to inhibit Soviet penetration. His assertions to Philippe Thyraud de Vosjoli regarding the KGB's comprehensive penetration of SDECE were to have profound consequences on the French officer. Always controversial, Golitsyn's political analysis was rather more eccentric than reliable, for he remained convinced of a massive, Kremlin-inspired deception scheme to destabilize Europe. He insisted to all those who were willing to make the journey to his hideaway farm in upstate New York that the Sino-Soviet split was an elaborate sham and maintained that Tito's break with Moscow in 1948 was further evidence of a Machiavellian plot. He encapsulated many of his bizarre theories, which bordered on the paranoid, in *New Lies for Old*, which questioned Penkovsky's *bona fides*, and is presently working at his home in Florida on a sequel. His principal supporters, like the CIA's Jim Angleton, now discredited as having succumbed to a wholly unjustified interpretation of the KGB's omnipotence, Golitsyn remains a lonely and sad reminder of how the Cold War beguiled many into the 'wilderness of mirrors' from which there was no escape. Sentenced to death *in absentia* in July 1962, he remains convinced that he is still a target for assassination. In this perceptive passage from his book he gives an insider's assessment of the KGB's relative strengths, but omits to take the credit for identifying John Vassall and Georges Paques to the CIA.

New Lies for Old

At present, Western efforts to obtain secret political information on the communist world, Western attempts to analyze information from communist sources, and Western ability to distinguish between reliable and unreliable sources – between genuine information and disinformation – all appear to be suffering from at least a temporary loss of effectiveness. This state of affairs is symptomatic of the penetration of Western intelligence services by their communist opponents.

Western intelligence has not always been unsuccessful. During the post-Stalin crisis, the communist intelligence and security services were weak. More people were disposed to help the West; five officials of Soviet intelligence defected in 1954. Although the West has never fully uncovered the extent of communist intelligence penetration of its governments and societies, Western intelligence did nevertheless have some reliable sources with access to policy-making bodies in the communist countries. But as the communist world recovered from its crisis, so its intelligence and security services regained their strength and effectiveness. The effort to penetrate Western governments in general and Western intelligence and security services in particular, which had been continuous from 1917 onward, was revitalized with success. This is not the place for a detailed study of the problem; nevertheless, some examples to illustrate the argument must be given.

From his service in the NATO section of the Information Department of the KGB's First Chief Directorate in 1959–60, the author knows that at that time the Soviet and bloc intelligence services had agents in the foreign ministries of most NATO countries, not to mention those of many of the non-NATO countries. This meant that the Soviet leaders and their partners were nearly as well informed about the foreign policies of Western governments as were those governments themselves.

Symptomatic of the depth and scale of penetration were the cases of the former British Admiralty official, Vassall; the former Swedish military attaché in the Soviet Union and later in the USA, Colonel Wennerström; the former senior official in NATO headquarters in Paris, Colonel Paques; and the forty concealed microphones belatedly discovered in the American Embassy in Moscow in 1964.

There is also striking public evidence of communist penetration of Western intelligence services. The British security and intelligence services, the oldest and most experienced in the West, were gravely damaged by Blunt, Philby, Blake, and others who worked for Soviet intelligence inside them for many years before being discovered.

The exposure of the Felfe ring inside the German intelligence service in 1961 showed that this service had been penetrated by the Soviets since its rebirth in 1951.

The author's detailed information on extensive Soviet penetration of French intelligence over a long period of time was passed to the appropriate French authorities, who were able to neutralize the penetration.

American intelligence suffered from Soviet penetration of allied services with which it was collaborating. In 1957–58 American intelligence lost an important secret agent in the Soviet Union, Lieutenant Colonel Popov, as a result of KGB penetration.

Particularly because the problem of disinformation has not been understood, it is doubtful if adequate account has been taken of the compromise of sources resulting from known instances of communist penetration of Western intelligence.

Oleg V. Penkovsky

I am joining the ranks of those who are actively fighting against our rotten, two-faced regime, known by the name of Dictatorship of the Proletariat or Soviet Power.

Married with a daughter, Oleg Penkovsky was a much-decorated, well-connected, senior GRU officer, with an apartment overlooking the Moscow River, who was destined for further promotion, but he was constantly troubled by an offence he had committed many years earlier. He had concealed the fact that his father had fought with the White Russians in the civil war, and he was convinced that if his father's record was ever discovered, his career would be ruined.

Perhaps motivated by this guilty secret, Penkovsky made two direct approaches to Americans in Moscow, and a Canadian businessman, which were rejected by the CIA as rather crude provocations orchestrated by the KGB. However, SIS proved more receptive and in December 1960 he made an offer to Greville Wynne, an SIS asset who frequently visited the Soviet Bloc as an entrepreneur seeking business deals for British engineering companies. Penkovsky's role as the GRU liaison officer with the State Committee for Scientific Co-ordination gave him an authentic reason to continue to meet Wynne, and to travel abroad. While in London in April 1961 he underwent a lengthy debriefing by SIS case officer, Harold Shergold, in the presence of two CIA officers, George Kisevalter and Joe Bulik, who had been dispatched for the purpose.

Penkovsky made a second trip to London in July 1961 and later in the year flew to Paris where more sessions were held with his CIA and SIS contacts. Upon his return to Moscow his communications relied upon supposedly chance encounters in a park with Janet Chisholm, the wife of the local SIS station commander, and then through a complicated system of signals and dead drops. This arrangement appeared to work well until October 1962, when an American diplomat was arrested by the KGB at the site of one of the dead drops, in the act of retrieving a message from Penkovsky.

Ten days later, on 4 November, Wynne was taken into custody by the Hungarian security police while in Budapest and sent to Moscow, where he was charged with espionage and tried, in May 1963, alongside Penkovsky. Both men pleaded guilty to treason and the trial lasted four days, at the end of which Penkovsky was sentenced to death and Wynne received eight years' imprisonment in a labour camp. On 16 May an official statement announced that Penkovsky had been executed by a firing squad. Eleven months later Wynne was swapped in Berlin for the KGB illegal Konon Molody, known as Gordon Lonsdale, who had been released from prison in England.

It was only after Wynne had been freed that a book purporting to be Penkovsky's autobiography, *The Penkovsky Papers*, was released. Edited by Piotr Deriabin and Frank Gibney, who had previously collaborated on *The Secret World* (published by the same publishers, Doubleday, in 1959), the book struck many intelligence professionals as odd. After all, what spy with any sense of self-preservation would leave reams of incriminating material in his apartment where they might be found at any time, not least by his family, who had no knowledge of his duplicity? In fact Deriabin and Gibney had been directed to reconstruct the autobiography from the transcripts of taped information that Penkovsky had provided over the eighteen months he operated as a source. Certainly there were some odd passages in the book, including some rather old-fashioned phrases that made it unlikely Penkovsky had written them.

Regardless of the exact origin of his book, there can be no doubt that Penkovsky delivered to the West technical intelligence of the most important kind. Apart from looting the GRU's files, he also provided a detailed analysis of the Soviet strategic arsenal at a critical time when Nikita Khrushchev was planning to deploy nuclear weapons in Cuba.

Despite the court's sentence that he should be stripped of his assets, Penkovsky's widow continues to live in their apartment, and her daughter is now employed by the GRU.

In this passage Penkovsky expresses his views on the Soviet leadership in typically disparaging way, which makes it unlikely that he really had been the sole author and had committed details of his treason to paper in his Moscow apartment.

The Penkovsky Papers

During the time when Khrushchev denounced the personality cult and had the intra-Party struggle with the Molotov–Kaganovich–Malenkov group, Marshals Timoshenko, Rokossovskiy, and Konev had many points of disagreement with Khrushchev, while they often agreed with Molotov, Malenkov, and Kaganovich. In many cases Voroshilov, too, was in disagreement with Khrushchev, as was Pervukhin. But because all these leaders were quite popular and well known among the Soviet people, Khrushchev was afraid to have them arrested or take other strong measures against them. He just said: 'Let them stay; the time will come when I can get rid of them.'

Of course, he did get rid of Zhukov in the end. More on this. Georgiy Konstantinovich Zhukov is loved by all Soviet officers and soldiers as well as by the entire population. Our people call him 'today's Suvorov' and 'the military genius of our time'.

At first Khrushchev bestowed on Zhukov the honors which he fully deserved. Zhukov was both Minister of Defense and a member of the Presidium of the Central Committee CPSU. Zhukov helped Khrushchev to consolidate full power in his hands at the time of the struggle against the anti-Party group. He supported Khrushchev. Later Khrushchev got scared of Zhukov. When Zhukov was still in power, Khrushchev began to reduce the supplementary pay for officers in order to save money for the production of armament. Zhukov opposed this and declared: 'I do not want my officers to become beggars. If they become beggars, they will not fight; indeed, nobody will be able to recognize them as officers. An officer must be well fed and be able to provide more or less adequate support for his family.' Zhukov hated Marshal Bulganin intensely. When Zhukov was

Commander of the Sverdlovsk Military District, Bulganin telephoned him and said, 'This is Marshal Bulganin speaking.' Zhukov answered, 'I do not know any such marshal,' and hung up.

Zhukov was for centralization of authority in the Army. He also reduced the time used for political indoctrination. As I said, he tried to lower the political workers to the second echelon. All these things, however, were not the main reason for Khrushchev's fear. A case in point: General Shtemenko, who at that time was Chief of the GRU, had organized a sabotage school near Moscow, where about two hundred inveterate cut-throats were being trained as saboteur agents and terrorists. Zhukov knew about this school, but he had not reported its existence to Khrushchev. At least this is what Khrushchev claimed. Actually I think this school had been in existence for years. Besides, Zhukov had once stated, 'The Army will always follow me.' All these things scared Khrushchev, and he decided to get rid of Zhukov. This question was decided secretly while Zhukov was in Yugoslavia.

When Zhukov returned from Yugoslavia, it was announced to him right at the airport that he had been removed from his post of Minister of Defense. After this, large meetings of Party activists were held in all cities, and Zhukov's 'cult of personality' was discredited on Khrushchev's orders. A large meeting of the Moscow party *aktiv* was held which I myself attended. It was held in St George's Hall of the Grand Kremlin Palace. It began with a speech by Khrushchev, who then left the hall. Next came a speech delivered by a minister, who also left the hall several times. Then came the regular propaganda speeches directed against Zhukov. Finally the minister returned once more and apologized for leaving the hall so many times but said that he had been called to the government.

In his speech at the meeting in the Kremlin, Khrushchev tried to prove that Zhukov was creating a new cult of personality, was displaying some Napoleonic ways, and was underestimating the role of the Party organs in the armed forces. As an example of Zhukov's cult of personality, Khrushchev cited the fact that there was a large picture of Zhukov on a white horse hanging on the wall at the Soviet Army Club. 'What else can it be called but Zhukov's cult of personality?' But when Khrushchev had seen this picture before, he had always admired it, saying: 'A fine picture! Zhukov is our hero and he has earned this honor!'

That is how this scoundrel Khrushchev operates. When he needed Zhukov, he called him a hero, but as soon as he felt that full power was in his own hands, he decided to get rid of this popular hero. Zhukov's cult of personality really scared him. But what about the cult of personality he has created for himself? There is not a word about it from him! Many people have already lost their heads for criticizing Khrushchev's cult of personality. So, here is truth for you, here are Lenin's standards of Party life! My poor Russian people!

Khrushchev criticized Zhukov also for his alleged attempt to fill government civilian posts with military personnel. Zhukov, ostensibly, had proposed that Serov be removed from the post of KGB Chairman, to be replaced by Marshal Konev. Khrushchev talked about this at the meeting of the *aktiv* of the Moscow Military District held on October 24 or 25. In the same speech Khrushchev accused Zhukov of creating the sabotage school, etc. Actually the school had existed long before Zhukov's time, and it exists now, and continues to train assassins for Khrushchev's purposes. This, of course, is all right! This is permissible! How I would like to see these cutthroats attack Khrushchev and the Presidium one fine day.

Soon after Zhukov's removal by a special decree of the Council of Ministers he was permitted to retire from service. He was given a pension of 5,500 old rubles a month. (This was not a large sum of money. A good pair of shoes, for instance, cost 400 rubles at that time.)

Zhukov has a nice apartment, on Granovskiy Street, house no. 3, but he spends most of his time at his country house near Moscow, on the Rublevskoye Highway.

Later, in 1961, during the Berlin crisis Khrushchev proposed that Zhukov, Sokolovskiy, and Konev, to prove their loyalty to the Party and the country, return to active work with him. Sokolovskiy and Konev agreed, but Zhukov refused although he is still in good physical condition and could still do some work.

See what a scoundrel Khrushchev is! When Zhukov was needed, he gave him a fourth star of Hero of the Soviet Union. Then he dismissed him. Then for propaganda purposes he wanted to use Zhukov once more. Zhukov did the right thing by refusing.

The disagreement between Marshals Timoshenko, Konev, Rokossovskiy and others on one side and Khrushchev on the other began after Zhukov was removed from his duties. Another source of friction: Khrushchev had reduced their pay and discontinued payments of the additional money which they and other officers of the Soviet Army had been getting; he had also reduced generals' and officers' retirement pay. In addition, the marshals and generals mentioned above did not agree with Khrushchev's policy of cutting the Air Force, the ground forces, and other forces – including the Navy – in favor of missile armament.

In 1960 Sokolovskiy went to see Khrushchev and told him: 'Just look at the military forces which are needed, and the money allocated for them. Under these conditions I cannot provide adequate defense for the country. Look how many enemy bases surround our country. I cannot maintain the strength of the troops at the level at which it should be especially in case of an enemy attack.' Khrushchev answered him: 'If that is what you think, then get out of here.'

After that, Khrushchev recalled Zakharov from East Germany and appointed him Chief of the General Staff in place of Sokolovskiy. He also recalled Chuykov from Kiev, where he was Commander of the Kiev Military District, Grechko by that time was already in Moscow. Sokolovskiy, however, had prestige among the generals and within the Army as a whole. Khrushchev therefore had to play his game carefully, removing his adversaries one by one, until finally he had got what he wanted. He defeated the anti-Party group, then fired Zhukov, and also got rid of the unwanted marshals, moving those who disagreed with his policies to less important posts.

Yuri V. Krotkov

Despite what may legitimately be viewed as my present
advantageous position and relative personal safety, –
though the revengeful arms of the KGB reach everywhere
– I must bear the relentless inner agony that possesses
a forty-six-year-old man who has foresaken his native
land forever.

A well-known Soviet playwright, and the author of the anti-American play based on the life of Paul Robeson, *John – Soldier of Peace*, Yuri Krotkov's name first became known when he was implicated in a scheme masterminded by the KGB's Second Chief Directorate to discredit the French ambassador in Moscow, Maurice Dejean. He and his wife had been targeted for a honeytrap and as soon as Krotkov revealed the plot, to MI5 interrogators in September 1963, the diplomat was recalled to Paris.

A Georgian by birth, his parents were an actress and an artist. After university in Tbilisi Krotkov moved to Moscow in 1938 and joined the Literary Foundation of the Union of Soviet Writers. He served in the Red Army during the war and as a TASS correspondent. In 1959, as a favoured intellectual, he made a journey by car across Poland, Czechoslovakia and East Germany. In 1962 he visited Japan and

India, and the following year defected in London while on an approved visit, accompanied by the usual contingent of KGB escorts. He arrived on 4 September and while staying at a hotel in Bayswater he alerted an English acquaintance of his decision not to return home; the acquaintance contacted the Security Service, which kept him under discreet surveillance and ensured his plan to elude the KGB went off uninterrupted. After his defection in London, Krotkov continued to write and in 1967 published *The Angry Exile*, a critique of postwar social conditions in Moscow. Two years later he gave evidence to the Senate Judiciary Committee under the name George Karlin and in 1979 published *The Red Monarch*, a semi-satirical biography of Stalin. Krotkov was allowed to settle in the United States but he was never accepted as an authentic defector, and he eventually died in Spain. In this passage he addresses the Soviet view of treason.

The Angry Exile

A Russian cannot emigrate in the normal way. That simple act, the ancient and common prerogative of all people, is, according to Soviet law, a form of treason, a betrayal of the motherland; in other words, the most heinous of crimes. But for the defectors themselves the reality of escape is immeasurably more serious and agonizing than it is conceived to be in the harsh formulations of Soviet law, because these ignore the most essential and painful aspect of this act – the human, psychological aspect. A terrible, complex burden of doubt and longing, fear and hope, guilt and elation, self-recrimination and self-justification, accompanies the fateful option for freedom: the soul stands tormented between two worlds.

Among defectors can be found publicity-seekers and opportunists, but it is not they who determine the nature of an indisputable historical phenomenon. Deserters from the Communist camp are noted primarily for their *ideological* fervour. Remember what happened during Hitler's occupation of Russia? An enormous number of people driven to the West, so-called displaced persons, refused to be repatriated to their homeland, preferring a difficult and sometimes tragic life in a foreign land. One cannot disregard these millions. It is not Nureyev who is the spearhead of this new emigration, or even the defectors from the KGB, although today they also are an integral part of the story.

After reading here in the West a vast body of literature about political emigrants from every country under the Communist yoke, I have come to believe that the act of the defector illustrates a tragic but very basic conflict in life: the clash between a strong, ineradicable feeling for one's native land, of belonging to one's own earth, and the need of a man to be above all free, to have the right to independent thought, unlimited by dogma.

The act of defection is unnatural, and nature takes its revenge. The defector is deprived of something essential; it is almost as if his body loses its correct working temperature and is forced to function at an unfamiliar one.

The very fact that the number of defectors from Communist countries increases each year is proof of the existence of an insoluble conflict. It is the most vulnerable spot in the policies of the Communist leaders. It is why they still, as in the past, resort to political murders; why they become so 'angry' and 'suffer' because of each escape. How else can you explain the fact that the borders of the Communist countries are 'locked', that it is impossible to cross them of your own free will? It is all exactly the same as it was under Stalin.

It is another matter in the West. If you want to live under Communism, go there and live. That is your right. If you do not like capitalism, try Communism.

Rupert Sigl

I never felt like a hero and I did not feel any
inclination to become a martyr. My actions were
dictated only by the existing circumstances.

Austrian by birth, Sigl worked as a carpenter at Ybbs, near St Poelten, until his army service with the Wehrmacht. He was wounded in the arm and subsequently recruited as an NKVD informant in his village, which was then in the Soviet zone of occupation. In 1952 he was recommended for promotion and flown to Moscow for training and induction as an officer in what was to become the KGB's First Chief Directorate.

Sigl was trained as a KGB illegal and was posted to Germany where he undertook several missions to the Federal Republic. His principal task was to establish contact with former prisoners of war to remind them that they had been granted their release on condition that they responded positively when asked to help the KGB in an intelligence operation. Sigl claimed that he had never been ideologically suited to his work and that he had co-operated with the KGB so as to escape to the West. His initial efforts to link up with the CIA and the BfV in Germany were rebuffed as provocations, but eventually he did succeed in defecting in 1969, using as his 'meal-ticket' the identities of those agents he had handled personally. He denounced a well-known East German television journalist, Fritz Moellendorf, as a KGB asset and also identified Alfred Lomnitz, a chemist who had subsequently acquired American citizenship, and was then living in England, as a KGB source. His book, *In the Claws of the KGB*, which was published in 1978, amounted to an account of his own life and, more significantly, the case histories of dozens of his contacts. Here he identifies Dr Alfred Laurence as a contact, thus precipitating his arrest by Special Branch detectives. He was released without charge, and now lives in the Isle of Wight, surprisingly sanguine about Sigl's allegations.

In the Claws of the KGB

In 1963 I met my former instructor from Moscow – Max – once again in Berlin. We had not seen each other for ten years. Except for Viktor, who brought me from Vienna to Moscow, Max was the only one from those days whom I met again. He told me that Viktor had in the meantime gotten ahead and had a leading post with counterintelligence in Leningrad. Max did not have anything happy to report about my former political instructor Volodya, who tried to make a communist out of me in Malachovka and Moscow. He had become mentally ill and would have to spend the rest of his life in an institution because he probably could not be cured. Max asked me whether I was already informed about my family in Austria or whether my section had made contact. He said that he had nothing to do with that, and therefore did not know anything about them. I complained that nothing had been done in that direction, that nobody was telling me anything. Max acted astonished and promised to bring up the matter at headquarters and if necessary take action himself.

During that year I only saw him a few months and then I never saw him again – and headquarters continued to be silent. I only had one case to work on with Max in the GDR.

The domestic servant of an American diplomat in Bad Godesberg was to be recruited using all possible means. With the help of her brother, who lived in the GDR and who was a loyal SED member, she was enticed into the KGB net and trapped into the bed of a German operative. They even got engaged. The girl was to get married, and for this reason she was even to move to the GDR. At that point trouble developed. She was to get her entry visa if she were prepared beforehand to prove her loyalty to the GDR: she would have to pledge to work for one year with the state security organs of the GDR. The girl was completely shaken up; she was constantly close to a nervous breakdown and the case had to be dropped as a result. The 'bridegroom' – the poor, unsuspecting girl did not know that he slept with her only in the line of duty – withdrew discreetly, giving some personal reason.

My new boss, Eugene – he was introduced to me in September 1963 in the safe house (conspirative apartment) at 75 Hermann-Dunker Street in Berlin-Karlshorst – started off with a specific recruitment assignment for me: 'We have for a long time been trying to recruit an American citizen who lives in England. We already have all the information concerning him personally and the circle in which he works. He has a very large circle of international acquaintances and some highly interesting connections. He is an industrial expert, and, according to our latest information, he has the intention of getting a job with the UNESCO in Paris. He has a perfect knowledge of English, French, and German. This fellow is very important to us, and it would be a big success if we could recruit him. His name is Dr Laurence.

'As I said before, we have been working on this case for quite some time, and one of our contact men is already in touch with him. He arranged for Dr Laurence to come to East Berlin, and he put him up in the Adria Hotel. He told Dr Laurence that a CEMA staff member wanted to talk to him. Laurence agrees to this meeting. For this purpose he will turn up tomorrow afternoon in the lobby of the Johannishof Hotel and government guest house.

'In your capacity as CEMA staff member, you have the ticklish task of bringing our efforts around Laurence to a good conclusion and conducting the decisive recruiting talk with him. We took the precaution of setting up this CEMA connection in order to be able to withdraw to neutral ground, that is to say, without having shown our colors, if Laurence should turn us down. But it is my great hope that this precautionary measure will prove to be superfluous.

'The essence of this recruiting talk consists of winning him not only for more or less official collaboration with the CEMA in informal terms but also to pin him down for unofficial, secret, illegal, and conspirative collaboration. If he agrees, then we all have gained.

'If you should be successful, immediately arrange as the next step, a meeting with me for the following day. Tell him that you will introduce him to a higher-ranking, leading Soviet representative of the CEMA with whom he could discuss all further details.'

After Eugene had briefed me on the Dr Laurence case with this background information, we discussed procedural questions in detail, and Eugene concluded my first meeting with me, wishing me every success.

As anticipated, Dr Laurence turned up in the Johannishof Hotel the next day. Earlier I had gotten a precise description of him so that I did not find it difficult to recognize him. Dr Laurence was very talkative, uncomplicated, and frank. After the usual exploration through topics of a general nature, we finally got down to specifics. A series of negative experiences had made me a pessimist, but I found him easier than I had expected. He was most understanding with regard to unofficial collaboration which would be in our interest. He established only one condition: 'Before I decide, I would like to know one thing from you: am I really valuable – really useful – to you?'

No obstacle would have been easier for me to take than this one.

'You would not only be useful to us,' I assured him, 'but you would be *extraordinarily* useful; and I can assure you that this evaluation will be expressed in magnanimous rewards for your information.'

Dr Laurence was so impressed by my offer that, in his readiness to collaborate, he went even further than we had hoped. 'Do my efforts to get a good job with UNESCO fit in with your plans or do you have some other ideas?' he asked.

'Basically that does not bother us – on the contrary. But if you are prepared to collaborate with us, then this question and others can be discussed.'

'Fine. If I am really of use to you, then I would be glad to be available to you.'

We had achieved our objective.

Dr Laurence was, of course, a skillful negotiator and a good business-man. He emphasized the question as to usefulness so much only in order to push up the price. Since I promptly spoke of 'magnanimous rewards', he saw that his purpose had been attained and agreed to go along.

Everything else was only a formality. I arranged the meeting with Eugene – Laurence immediately agreed – and he himself suggested that his hotel room would be the best place for this conference with the Soviet representative because they would not be disturbed there. In other words, he understood what we were after.

Eugene was extremely enthusiastic and he would almost have embraced me. On the next morning we met Dr Laurence in the latter's hotel room for breakfast. Under some pretext I withdrew after awhile and left the two of them alone, as had been agreed on in advance with Eugene.

During the next meeting with Eugene, he again displayed the greatest satisfaction with regards to Dr Laurence, and he himself took the case over.

I did not hear about Dr Laurence again until after his arrest by British security agencies in April of 1969. During the interrogation, he admitted his meeting with me and Eugene, a conference in Berlin-Karlshorst with a 'leading Russian', and several meetings with Soviet citizens in London; but he denied ever having delivered secret information to the Soviets. The British press, by the way, played up the story in a big way.

Vladimir N. Sakharov

*I was encouraged in my belief – derived from family and
cultural experiences – that I had rights, dignity, worth.
At the same time I found myself subject to a psychologically
dehumanizing environment. Just because I was fortunate
enough to circumvent the system didn't make me like it.*

While training in Moscow in 1963 to join the Foreign Ministry as a regular diplomat, Vladimir Sakharov had volunteered to work for the CIA in Moscow. He also found himself co-opted to assist the KGB, which greatly enhanced his value to his CIA case officers. His first assignment, in March 1967, was to the Soviet consulate at Hodeida in the North Yemen, where he undertook some minor errands for the KGB *rezident*, Vladimir Ivchenkov. These were successful and in April 1968 he was sent with his wife and daughter to the consulate in Alexandria for a tour of duty that was to last two years, during which he held regular meetings with the CIA. He returned to Moscow in July 1970 and was flown in November as an attaché to the Soviet embassy in Kuwait City.

In July 1971, while posted to Kuwait, the KGB discovered the existence of a mole within its ranks in the Middle East and began to close in on Sakharov, who left an emergency signal (a bunch of flowers in the back of a Volkswagen) for his CIA contact, who arranged for him to be smuggled out of the country. After the usual lengthy debriefings, he was resettled in California where he worked briefly as a taxi driver before he joined a hotel management course which went bankrupt. He eventually obtained a Ph.D. from the University of Southern California but remains critical of the CIA's skill at resettling defectors. In his book, *High Treason*, which he wrote with Umberto Tosi in 1980, he recalls his last encounter with George, his CIA case officer.

High Treason

By the summer of 1971, I fully realized, and so did George, that my time as a CIA agent-in-place was running out. Developments were conspiring to make my balancing act more and more difficult and dangerous – the anti-Soviet counter-coup in Egypt and the inevitably resulting security invest-igation in Moscow of all Soviet personnel who had been involved in the

Egyptian missions; the fact that my term abroad was over and I'd have to remain stationed in Moscow for at least two years; and my marital crisis. The pressure, increased by the paranoid atmosphere in the Soviet Embassy in Kuwait, was beginning to get to me. Both George and I knew that I would have to get out soon and we had discussed my escape plan carefully. The immediate incident that precipitated my having to flee, however, is something I am not at liberty to discuss. Although it was minor in nature, the details of it could compromise ongoing operations and people still in the field.

The escape plan had been worked out so that if I had to get away in a hurry no further contact with my friends or the US Embassy itself would be necessary. I could activate it at my own discretion or if I got a signal from them. One hot, humid summer afternoon – July 11, 1971 – I got just such a signal.

I felt detached, pulled into a vacuum. It was the same feeling of alienation I'd had a year earlier in Moscow when Natasha had told me of my grandfather's death. Then I had immediately gone up to the Pirogovo reservoir and taken off on my boat for two days to be alone.

But now I couldn't leave just yet. I drove back to our apartment first. Natasha was there having a drink with an Arab businessman of our acquaintance. Katya was napping in her room. I stormed in, barely nodding hello to the Arab, and marched into our bedroom, asking Natasha to come with me.

She followed and shut the door behind her. 'I don't want anybody here when I'm not home,' I hissed at her. I hadn't played the enraged jealous husband role since that night long ago in Moscow with the five-thousand-nik, but this opportunity suited my purposes. I had planned to pick a fight anyway. It would be easier that way. 'I don't care what you do,' I said, 'but don't pull any of your stuff in my house. So get him out of here. I want to talk to you.'

'What do you mean?' she yelled. 'Who are you to tell me anything, you motherfucker. Who do you think you are? I have my own life. When I get back to Moscow, I'm getting a divorce and that's final. We've got nothing to talk about.'

'Thanks.'

'I want my airplane ticket tomorrow!' she shouted.

'I'm not going to get you any ticket,' I told her. 'You go to your precious sucker the ambassador and you talk to him about it. I don't care anymore. You can tell him all about me, how badly I treat you, how arrogant I was.'

I heard Katya crying in the other room. We'd awakened her. I went back into the living room and told our Arab friend, 'I'm sorry, but would you mind leaving? I'll call you and we'll get together another time.'

'That's all right, I understand,' he said. 'I'll see you. Goodbye.'

I went into Katya's room. She was sitting on the bed, rubbing her eyes. 'Katya, would you like to go for a ride?'

'Yes, Papa, where are we going?'

'We'll just go out for an hour while Mama cooks dinner.'

We drove in the direction of Mina al–Ahmadi; the bright lights of the oil installations and loading docks were already on as the sun was setting.

'Papa, can we go closer to all those lights?'

'All right.' We took a turn and went along the ocean. Finally we stopped at a place where the beach was accessible, got out of the car and walked along the surf in the dusk. Katya played in the sand. I didn't say anything.

'Papa, I'm getting tired, can we go home?'

'Yes,' I said, and picked her up and carried her back to the car.

Natasha was in a rage. 'It took you two hours. Where did you go? Dinner is cold.' Katya went into the bathroom to wash up.

'You can stick your dinner up your ass,' I said quietly. 'I'm leaving. I'm going to eat out. All right?'

I walked out.

I went back to the embassy and rang the bell. The guard let me in and I went through the lobby to my office. There was a safe there which I locked every day. It contained the latest classified information about the embassy and other diplomatic posts. I took one last look at the papers, memorizing all I could.

I also read over a letter from my father that had arrived in the last mail. My family was disappointed in me, he wrote; I didn't seem to be working hard enough any more. I was not fulfilling their expectations. An embassy employee while on vacation in Moscow had filled them in on my recent behavior. There were complaints about my not attending weekly propaganda meetings. My father advised me strongly against this – not good politics. He also advised me against entertaining too many Kuwaitis and other foreigners and to concentrate more on what was happening inside the embassy.

Otherwise the letter was warm. Everyone was looking forward to my upcoming vacation in Moscow. My new cooperative apartment was ready. We would all go to the Black Sea. Mother was in good health. Asking about Katya and how things were going with Natasha, he closed saying we'd all have a marvelous time upon my return home.

There was a knock. It was the GRU chief, Zimin.

'What are you doing here so late, Vladimir?'

'Just checking on some papers, a report I have to do in the morning. I have to review my files.'

'Very well, young man. You want to play a little pool?'

'No, thank you very much. I will join you later. Why don't you go ahead? I've got about another half hour here. I'll join you.'

'Fine,' he said and left.

I put the papers back into the safe. My hands were trembling as I took a small box containing gold rings and bracelets that I had purchased in Kuwait and had been keeping in the safe, meaning to bring them to Moscow on my return from Kuwait and give them to Galya. Since our romance at the Soviet resort a year ago, we had continued to correspond, she sending me letters that were masterpieces of double meaning under the code name of 'Nikolai' that we'd agreed upon. I put the box in my pocket, not out of any hope of seeing her again, but thinking that in case I ran into trouble during my escape, I might be able to use the gold to buy my way out.

The embassy was dark as I walked out and up the street past a grocery store and past the innermost of Al-Kuwait circular drives, the one nearest the embassy. I kept walking faster past the second, then the third, finally the fourth circle. Then I continued into the desert. I kept walking until I reached the point where the radio receiver was supposed to be. I was wearing a green sports shirt, an old jacket, and a pair of baggy slacks made in India that I'd purchased only a few days earlier. I'd taken to wearing casual attire in Kuwait.

I had a small flask of Scotch in my jacket pocket and I stopped to take a swig. I must have looked comical in that outfit there in the desert in the middle of the night. Miraculously I found the radio. I was worried that the shifting sands would have obliterated its location.

The little transistorized receiver was wired with a directional antenna and tuned to one frequency, so that by rotating it I found the signal that would guide me. I started walking. The signal was on a very narrow band so that if I turned off course I'd lose it. One song was playing on it, over and over. It was 'The Girl from Ipanema', sung by Astrud Gilberto. Was this a coincidence or a touch from George?

I kept walking across the desert. Hours went by. The dark sky and black sand seemed to turn upside down and back again, rotating slowly. I walked long into the night.

At one point I heard a helicopter. I lay down on the sand, hoping my gray slacks and jacket would camouflage me. The chopper passed nearby at low altitude, its searchlight probing the low dunes. I couldn't be sure what that chopper was looking for. I didn't think the Soviets would have detected my absence until I failed to show up at the embassy in the morning. By then I had to be out of Kuwait. As soon as the thudding of the copter faded into the darkness, I got up and kept walking.

From my instructions I knew that as soon as the escape plan was activated, a jeep filled with gasoline and equipped with a two-way radio would be left somewhere along the line of the radio frequency for me to find and drive the rest of the way. There would be dirt tracks in the desert that were far from the main Kuwaiti highway, where Soviet agents might be looking for me as soon as my absence was discovered. The Soviets likewise would immediately send men to the Kuwait airport and to the seaport, so my departure from the country had to be from the back door. All I had to do was reach the jeep before KGB and GRU security got a start on combing the desert outlands. Once I'd found the jeep I was to receive further directions on its radio.

I drank the Scotch, which only made my mouth drier and turned my stomach to fire. The song repeating on the radio took on a nightmarish quality, with no ending or beginning, the notes dissociating from themselves chaotically. Then things were very quiet. I felt relieved for a moment, then froze. I realized that I'd wandered off course and didn't know how long I'd been walking without the sound. Without any reference point in the dark I had no idea which way to turn. I tried walking in a zig-zag pattern, but was unable to pick up the signal again. I stopped to think. There was no breeze and all I could hear was the sound of my own breathing. I figured it was safe enough to use my cigarette lighter for a moment so I could get a look at my Seiko wristwatch. It was four in the morning.

I put the lighter back in my pocket and then heard a click, the unmistakeable sound of a gun being cocked.

'Stop, don't move,' said a voice in Arabic.

I pulled the little radio receiver out of my upper left jacket pocket and dropped it on the ground, pushing sand over it with my foot.

Three Arabs approached me. I realized they were Bedouin when I made out the camels in the darkness behind them. When they got up close enough to have a good look at me, one, who had been pointing the rifle at me, slung it back over his shoulder. Apparently I looked harmless.

'Hello. I'm an American,' I said in English, then switched to Arabic. 'I'm lost, can you direct me back to the road? I know my car is up there somewhere. I got out to pick up some rock samples and lost my directions, I'm a geologist.'

It was an unlikely story, but the only one I could think up at the moment. I figured that Bedouins liked to keep to themselves and didn't worry over the strange activities of the foreigners they occasionally encountered in their deserts.

'Ah, the jeep,' one of them said after a moment. 'We passed it a couple of kilometers back.' He pointed into the night behind him.

'Thank you very much, *Salam Alaykum*,' I said and started walking in that direction without further conversation. I was greatly relieved and soon found the jeep. Keys were in the ignition and I started it and switched on the radio, tuned to our prearranged frequency, and said in English, 'Seid Ahmed has arrived safely.' That had been my code name in Kuwait. 'Request directions.'

'Drive straight for the next two hours and you'll be met.' I switched on the jeep's headlights and started driving slowly over the dirt road.

By the next day I was very far away – on an island in the Mediterranean, talking to George, being briefed, debriefed, and processed for entrance to the United States.

The Soviet Embassy in Kuwait shut its doors for a week. Two KGB counterintelligence experts who were urgently flown in from Moscow began their investigation.

Vladimir B. Rezun

All those who tried to put up resistance to the system have been placed by history into the category of foul traitors. So I was faced with a choice: to surrender without a fight, like a lamb, or to become a foul traitor.

On 10 June 1978 Major Vladimir Rezun, a thirty-one-year-old GRU officer working under United Nations cover in Geneva, was smuggled out of the country to England with his wife and two young children. A career soldier, he had participated in the invasion of Czechoslovakia in 1968 and later had supervised the training of the elite Spetsnaz special forces. After he had been recruited by the GRU he was shown the film of Piotr Popov being pushed live into a furnace and given the standard lecture on defection to the West:

Some of us flee to the West in the hope of having a magnificent car, a mansion with a swimming pool and a lot of money. And the West really does pay well. But once he's got his Mercedes and his own swimming pool, the traitor suddenly realises that all the people around him also have nice cars and pools.

Rezun is deliberately vague about his career but he undertook missions in Munich, Rome, Basel, Amsterdam, Vienna and Hamburg. Using the pseudonym Viktor Suvorov he has written several books about the Soviet military and his experiences. The first was *Inside the Soviet Army*, which discussed the relationship between the KGB and its military counterparts, the GRU. This was followed by *Inside Soviet Military Intelligence*, his autobiography, *Aquarium* and *Spetsnaz*.

Whether Rezun wrote all four books, in the space of five years, has been questioned, particularly since some of his assertions have proved inaccurate. For example, his claim that the head of the GRU in 1940, I. E. Proskurov, was deposed in July 1940 and shot is definitely wrong. In fact Proskurov was appointed to the Far East Air Force in August 1940, and at the end of September 1940 he was transferred to Strategic Aviation. He was arrested in April 1941 and executed in October the same year. A minor slip in detail, or evidence of a fabrication composed by several different intelligence analysts? According to Michael Parrish of Indiana University, Rezun has made other mistakes about the careers of Ivan Serov, A. P. Paniflov, I. I. Il'ichev and I. F. Dashichev.

In 1993, still using the pseudonym Victor Suvorov, Rezun released *Icebreaker* in Russia, a controversial interpretation of the origins of the Second World War which concluded that Stalin had always intended to go to war against Germany in July 1941, a theory not entirely unknown in Western academic circles. Nevertheless it is a proposition that was demolished convincingly by the scholar David M. Glantz writing in the *Journal of Military History*.

In this passage Rezun admits that he has always been haunted by the face of Major Piotr Popov, the GRU officer who spied for the CIA until he was executed by being burned alive in a furnace, a harrowing event that was witnessed by a selected audience and filmed to deter GRU recruits from following his example.

Aquarium

I thought that his face would pursue me in nightmares throughout my life. But that was not the case. I never dreamt of him. But I often thought about him, and there was something about the affair that I couldn't understand. The official version said that a GRU colonel sold himself to the British and American intelligence services because he was fond of the opposite sex and that that was why he needed a lot of money. Let us suppose that was true. But if it was just a question of women why on earth did he not simply defect to the West? In America or Britain he would have had enough money and enough women to last him all his life. A man with the information he had would have been welcomed and treated at his true worth. He had plenty of opportunities to defect. But he didn't do it. He went on working in Moscow, where he had no opportunity to spend that sort of money. Which meant that it wasn't a matter of money or of women. So what was it then?

If he had been nothing more than a womaniser he would have escaped and settled for women and money. But he didn't. He finished up in the crematorium, the man I had seen silently screaming. But why, for goodness sake? I twisted and turned on the hot pillow and just couldn't get to sleep. It was my first night without examinations. But was I being observed at night by closed-circuit television? Oh, to hell with it! I got out of bed and made a rude gesture to each corner of the room. If I was still being watched they wouldn't be taking me to the Central Committee of the Party tomorrow. Then I decided that it wasn't enough simply to make rude gestures, so I exposed to the camera, if there was one there, everything I had to show. We would see next day whether they would throw me out or not. Having displayed what I could I got back contented into bed and went straight to sleep, firmly convinced that I would be shipped off to Siberia the next day to command a tank company.

I slept in that bed like a babe. A really deep sleep. I knew that, if I were accepted into the Aquarium, it would be a big mistake on the part of the Soviet Intelligence. I knew that, if there remained only one exit and that through the chimney, my departure would not be an honourable one. I knew that I would not die in my bed. No, people like me do not die in their beds. It would really have been better for Soviet Intelligence if it had despatched me through the chimney right away!

Stanislav A. Levchenko

Like anyone anywhere, I tended to confuse loyalty to a country with loyalty to a regime and therefore to wonder if the act of becoming a political refugee was not an act of treason against my people.

Born in Moscow at the outbreak of the Second World War, Stanislav Levchenko's mother died when he was a child and he was brought up by his stepmother. Immediately after the war his father, an officer in the Red Army, was posted as an adviser to Belgrade, but in 1948 he was ordered home.

A decade later his son graduated from high school in Moscow and was accepted as a student by the Institute of Oriental Languages at Moscow University. Later he switched to the Institute of Oceanography and Fisheries, where his work on the Japanese fishing industry brought him to the attention of the KGB, which sponsored his first visit to Tokyo in April 1967 in the role of an interpreter for a delegation of trade unionists, and of the GRU, which gave him military training.

Three months later he escorted a group of Komsomol students to a youth festival at Lake Yamanaka. During the following three years Levchenko returned to Japan several times, usually as a translator, but in 1970 he was posted for eight months to Expo '70 at Osaka under *Novosti* cover. Upon his return he was deployed by the KGB against two Japanese diplomats, who declined to be recruited or entrapped, and he formally joined the organization in 1970. Four years later he was an accredited *New Times* correspondent and in February 1975 he was posted to Tokyo with his second wife and their young son. Levchenko completed his first tour of duty but he had made an enemy of Vladimir Pronnikov, the deputy head of the FCD's Seventh Department, whose decision not to authorize the recruitment of a particular agent, a well-connected Japanese newspaper columnist, had been overruled by the FCD's deputy director, Major-General Popov. Having made an enemy of Pronnikov, Levchenko realized his career would suffer and, influenced by his conversion to the Orthodox Church and his failing marriage, he opted for defection. 'Once I had made the irreversible decision to request political asylum in the United States, I was the perfect KGB officer, facing the moments of danger with a coolness I had never before experienced as I went about preparing to take the final step.'

In October 1979 Major Levchenko defected from the KGB's *rezidentura* in Tokyo to the CIA by walking into a diplomatic reception at the Hotel Sanno and surrendering himself to an astonished American naval commander, who alerted the CIA. His main meal-ticket was the identity of Yukihisi Miyanaga, a retired major-general and a GRU asset who had been recruited in 1974. He was consequently sentenced to twenty years' imprisonment and his contact, Colonel Yuri N. Koslov, the Soviet military and air attaché, was expelled. Two other Japanese officers of the Ground Self-Defence Force, were also imprisoned for passing secrets to the GRU, and in 1982 *in absentia* Levchenko was sentenced to death by a military tribunal.

In 1991 Levchenko married Alexandra Costa, formerly Yelena Mitrokhina, the wife of the Soviet First Secretary stationed in Washington. She defected in August 1978 with her two children and wrote *Stepping off the Star* in 1986. Levchenko's autobiography, *On the Wrong Side*, was published in 1987 and here he describes his defection.

On the Wrong Side

Although my tour of duty in Japan was scheduled to end in October 1979, if I had stumbled the least little bit or made some embarrassing political blunder along the way, I could have been yanked out and sent home at a moment's notice. I also knew that time was slipping away entirely too fast for me to delay much longer, but I simply wasn't yet ready to make a final commitment. Then something happened that made me realize just how short the time was getting.

I was in the resident's office one morning when his secretary buzzed through on the intercom. The resident listened a moment, then said, 'Send him in.'

'Shall I leave?' I asked.

'No, this will only take a moment.'

The door opened to admit an officer whom I knew by sight only. I think he worked in communications somewhere.

'Come in, come in,' said the resident with what I thought was a false heartiness. 'We've just received a special message from Moscow, and they need you back as soon as we can get you there. Here's your plane ticket. There's a driver waiting downstairs to take you to the airport.'

'What about my family? Will I be coming back? What—,' he sputtered before the resident interrupted him.

'Just call your wife. Tell her you're on your way to Moscow and that she and the children will follow in a few days. We'll see to packing and returning your household effects. Now, you must hurry. Maybe you'd better wait until you're at the airport to call. You mustn't miss that flight.'

As soon as he had hurried from the room, I asked, 'A promotion?'

'No,' he explained, shaking his head sadly, 'the poor devil's in serious trouble of some kind. He just won't know it until he walks into headquarters.'

I too could be returned to Moscow at a moment's notice. I'd just seen it happen to another with my own eyes. As a consequence of that incident I took pains to maintain my high level of work. I was under the sword of Damocles; I had to keep all risks to a minimum. By late spring and early summer Pronnikov was so firmly entrenched in the Seventh Department in Moscow that those of us in Tokyo were often made aware of his interest in us. I was particularly aware of his far-reaching and unsympathetic interest in me. I knew that the caliber of my work could not falter, or I would be whisked back to Moscow before I could have a chance to think through my personal dilemma. I had no intention of becoming one of the expelled officers. Even if I were to return to Moscow in the normal rotation, Pronnikov was still there gunning for me. As events unfolded during my last months in Japan, I became increasingly aware that he was just waiting to pounce.

The incident regarding agent Thomas was the final proof I needed that Pronnikov was my enemy. Thomas was a senior correspondent with Japan's largest newspaper, a successful author, and a well-received political analyst. He had been wooed by various KGB officers for about eighteen months before being turned over to me for what we all hoped would be a successful recruitment. He knew everyone of importance, including Japan's high-ranking government officials. When I took him over, I found to my delight that I thoroughly enjoyed my conversations with him. He was sophisticated and witty, cultured and urbane. He lived well, wore expensive clothes, and obviously liked the finest restaurants and meeting places. I judged early on that Thomas would welcome some additional income, so I offered him the opportunity to contribute articles to the non-existent newsletter, the same one I had used so often before to lure potential agents. 'For a fee, of course,' I told him. 'We really need your expertise.'

He accepted; this was the same man who had resisted various other KGB officers. The only way I can account for his change of heart is that I must've caught him at a moment when he needed money badly. (Money – the first weakness to look for – as in MICE [Money, Ideology, Compromise, Ego].) Because I still wasn't sure that Thomas was willing to go all the way with us, I asked him to plant certain stories in the press. He did so without any questions whatsover. The more he aided us in this way, the more I suspected that he knew he was dealing with Soviet intelligence. Then Thomas told me something straight out of a spy novel.

'The US government is going to announce that the Lockheed Aircraft Corporation has paid huge sums in bribes to highly placed Japanese officials to guarantee that they will win Japanese contracts.'

When I reported what Thomas had told me, my superiors were skeptical. 'That can't possibly be true,' one officer protested. 'It's too sensational to be the least bit credible.' 'My God, such a scandal would cause heads to roll all over Tokyo,' said another.

Several weeks later the Lockheed story broke, proving that Thomas was correct. The story behind the scandal caused political upheaval in Japan and political repercussions in the United States. During the mid-1970s Lockheed Aircraft Corporation had received large sums of money from the US government in order to keep it solvent. The scandal from the US point of view was that Lockheed was using American taxpayers' money to bribe Japanese officials for Lockheed's profit. By extension, the American taxpayers could be said to be bribing Japanese officials, with Lockheed merely acting as the middleman. The American government was furious, the Japanese government was embarrassed, and the Soviets, because they hadn't believed my agent Thomas, had missed the opportunity to capitalize (if you'll pardon the expression) on the scandal.

I had already been convinced that Thomas was genuine and that he could be extremely useful. After this incident I recommended that Thomas be included in the embassy's network. The new resident concurred, so I submitted a formal recommendation to that effect, and we sent it on to Moscow.

After Pronnikov's departure for Moscow, the new resident, Colonel Oleg Guryanov, had taken over control of the Tokyo residency. He wasn't from the Seventh Department; he had served as the resident in the Netherlands and, later, as the senior officer in Havana. I liked him. He was personable, clever, and capable. From the first meeting he'd had with us after his arrival, he'd established an *esprit de corps* that had been totally lacking under Pronnikov. He never mentioned the upheavals that had resulted in the recalls of Yerokhin and Yevstafyev to Moscow and that had coincidentally propelled Pronnikov into the upper echelons of the Seventh Department. It was clear that Guryanov was the kind of troubleshooter who could establish order. In no time at all, he had the residency in shape and all of us working together smoothly.

Several weeks after I'd recommended Thomas, Guryanov called me into his office. 'Well, Stanislav, it's bad news. Now don't lose your temper . . .'

'What's happened?'

'Your request for the inclusion of Thomas in the network has been turned down,' he answered, 'and turned down in a thirty-six-page diatribe the likes of which I've never seen in my life.'

'Over whose signature?'

'Vladimir Pronnikov's.'

'It figures,' I answered.

I was mad as hell. That son of a bitch knew I was right. I knew he knew it, and back in Moscow he'd be sitting at his desk gloating over having put me in my place.

'Never mind,' said Guryanov. 'Our time will come.'

It wasn't long after that incident that my high-ranking advocate, First Directorate Deputy Director Major General Popov, visited the Tokyo residency. Having met him at the center in Moscow, I was gratified that he remembered me and flattered that he took the time to look me up at the residency. After a few minutes of small talk, he adopted a serious tone. 'Does all go well here with you?'

On the spur of the moment I decided to bring up the Thomas case. 'Well, sir, there's something I don't understand,' I began, providing him with a complete rundown on what kinds of information Thomas had supplied, the work he'd done as an agent, and his reliability in general. I finished by showing Popov the center's reply to my request that Thomas be included in the residency network.

'And look at this,' I said when he'd finished reading Pronnikov's reply. 'Resident Guryanov was interested enough in Thomas's reliability to research these statistics. Roughly half of the intelligence supplied by Thomas has been so valuable and accurate that it's been sent from the center directly to the Politburo.'

'That damned Pronnikov!' responded Popov, almost spitting out the words. 'He gave me this bloody paper to sign one night when I was so damned tired I was groggy. I did what I try never to do, initialed it without reading it. This is a terrible injustice.' After he and I had both calmed down a little, he added, 'Trust me to set this right, Stanislav.'

When I reported the meeting with General Popov to Guryanov, he said 'Let's hope Pronnikov doesn't talk him out of it once he's back in Moscow.'

'I don't think he will, sir.'

'Why not?'

'Because he was still calling me by my first name when he left. In the center they used to say that when Popov used a person's first name, it was a commitment.' As it turned out, only a few days after Popov's return to Moscow, the center cabled its approval to include Thomas in the network and offered congratulations to me.

That happened in the early summer of 1978, just before we went back to Moscow for our last leave before my tour of duty was scheduled to end in 1979. When I arrived in Moscow, my first duty was to report to the center for debriefing by my superiors. Traditional though this visit might be, I knew that it occurred not only for reasons of protocol, but also as a visit that could have a profound effect on a person's career in many ways. If a man were in trouble, sometimes he would receive no hint of it at his residency. But when he made his call at the center – ah! Then the axe would fall.

When I got to the First Directorate building, I was filled with trepidation. I knew that the agent Thomas incident would be fresh in Pronnikov's mind. The most nerve-wracking thing of all was that he was the first man I'd have to face.

As I'd expected, Pronnikov was cool, terse, and businesslike in the preliminary conversation. As our talk was drawing to a close, he leaned towards me and said, very softly, 'I underestimated you.'

Here it comes, I thought. He's getting ready to move in for the kill.

'You shouldn't have gone over my head to Popov.' He let the silence stretch. I didn't do a thing to break it.

'For that alone I should strike back.' Another silence. 'But I'm too big a man to harbor grudges.' Another silence stretched on and on. Finally he added, 'Enjoy your vacation.'

I had survived. I got out of his office and took a deep breath. This time, I would be going back to Japan. But sooner than I wanted to accept, I would be reassigned to Moscow, and Pronnikov would be there, waiting like the spider in its web. I didn't like one little bit the image of myself as the fly.

I often think about Pronnikov because his type isn't uncommon; certainly it isn't limited to the Soviet Union. That he was brilliant and good at his job is undeniable. Equally undeniable is that he saw those who worked for him as mere appendages to his own life. When his subordinates performed well, it was proof to him that he himself – the brain of that extended body – had given the proper directions. On the other hand, when his subordinates thought, reasoned, or acted independently, they became threats to him. This attitude alone, I believe, accounts for the antagonism that existed between us. He thought I was different because I thought too much. To him, I was an enigma that he could never stop trying to solve and understand or destroy. This made him as big a threat to me as I was to him, mainly because I hadn't yet solved the puzzle of my own intentions. I couldn't let him probe too deeply because I didn't know myself what was really inside me. Until I did, I'd have to resist his probes.

Time, meanwhile, was ticking away too quickly. I was working long, exhausting hours, which, combined with my inner anguish, took a toll on my health. More and more, I suffered from cardiac arrhythmia in reaction to the stress I was under.

Even now, I can't pinpoint the moment when I knew I'd ask for political asylum in the United States. All at once, it was simply a fact, it seemed I'd intended to do it for a long, long time. Once my decision was finally made, my good health returned.

Ilya G. Dzhirkvelov

I was moved by purely personal feelings – above all by a sense of the cruel injustice of a regime that could treat a loyal servant with such contempt and inhumanity. I chose to defect rather than suffer any further indignities at the hands of the Soviet bureaucracy.

In 1943, while still a teenager, Ilya Dzhirkvelov joined the NKVD, having played a role in the resistance to the German invasion of his native Georgia. Both his parents had been active Bolsheviks and he was also a committed member of the Party. By April 1944, when the Nazis retreated from Sevastopol, he had been appointed a cadet officer in a small commando unit assigned to clear up what was left of the Waffen SS in the newly liberated areas. He also participated in the ruthless deportation of the Crimean Tartars who had fought alongside the Germans.

During the Yalta Conference in February 1945 he was one of the guard detachment which maintained security for the visitors, and later in the war he operated against nationalist guerrillas in Latvia. By the end of the war he was back in Tblisi, only to be selected in September for a course at the NKVD's training school in Moscow. After two years he and his wife were sent on a short assignment to Romania, which lasted six weeks. He was then posted to the Iranian section of the FCD's Middle East Department, and in 1949, having learned Farsi, was transferred to Tehran. One of his first missions was to assist in the abduction of a Soviet diplomat named Orlov who was believed to be about to defect to the Americans. He was seized on the street, apparently on his way to the US embassy, and taken to the Soviet embassy where he was interrogated and killed, bludgeoned to death with the leg of a piano. 'Even today,' observes Dzhirkvelov,

> an official who defects to the West is signing his own death sentence; and it is only a question of when he will be discovered and when the possibility will arise of carrying out the sentence. Exactly how it is done is of no significance – whether it is with an axe, a gun, a dose of poison, a poisoned umbrella or a car accident.

Upon his return to Moscow Dzhirkvelov worked in the KGB's archives and attended the Higher Party School in the evenings. His career had taken an unexpected turn following the disclosure that his father, whom he had never known, had not died at sea in the way described by his mother. In fact he had been executed in 1937, while serving a ten-year prison sentence for undefined political offences. Nevertheless, in August 1952, he was rehabilitated and transferred to the FCD's American department. Later he moved to the newly formed Second Chief Directorate, responsible for the surveillance of suspect foreigners in Moscow, specializing in diplomats from Iran, Egypt and Turkey. In 1955 he returned to the FCD's Tenth Department, monitoring the Turkish frontier and liaising with the Georgian KGB in Tblisi, and in August 1957 was back in Moscow with the Second Chief Directorate.

As part of his cover, Dzhirkvelov worked for *Soviet Sport* and became General Secretary of the Union of Journalists of the USSR, a post he held from 1957 until September 1965 when he joined TASS. He was assigned as the agency's correspondent to Zanzibar, where he arrived with his wife in September 1967. There they remained until early 1970 when they moved to Dar-es-Salaam temporarily before taking up a permanent post in Khartoum in May. The Dzhirkvelovs spent just over two years in the Sudan and in April 1974 flew to

Geneva, he as a press officer for the UN World Health Organization. This attractive posting came as a surprise because in that year Dzhirkvelov's name had been listed in John Barron's *KGB: The Secret Work of Soviet Secret Agents* as a KGB asset who had been expelled from Turkey and had been spotted in the Sudan in 1971.

Dzhirkvelov's mission to Geneva remained uneventful until New Year's Day 1980 when, after a minor traffic accident, he was accused of drunken driving. Dzhirkvelov denied the charge but when he declined to resign and insisted on completing his contract, which was due to run until May 1981, he was recalled to Moscow in March. Within hours of landing he learned that his career was in ruins so, without waiting for the final interview at which he knew he would be confined to Moscow, he hastily flew to Vienna and took a train back to Geneva where he explained his predicament to his wife and daughter. The same day, all three were granted political asylum in Britain. In his book, *Secret Servant*, published in 1987, Dzhirkvelov described himself as a reluctant defector. 'I was lucky. Had I failed the penalty would have been very severe. As it is, I am listed as a traitor.' The fact that he is regarded as such by the KGB is hardly surprising, considering the detail displayed in his account of Soviet penetration of the United Nations and its institutions.

Secret Servant

It is not just the KGB and the GRU that are engaged in collecting information and documentary material. All Soviet officials employed in international organizations, even one so seemingly remote from politics as the WHO, are drawn into this work. I could not conceal my amazement at a meeting of Soviet employees of the WHO to learn that some 900 reports running to several thousand sheets of paper had been sent to Moscow in the course of one year.

The reports consisted in the main of all the more important documents issued by the WHO in connection with medical and other problems. They were conscientiously copied by the Soviet employees on the photo-copying machines available on every floor of the WHO building (at the WHO's expense, of course) and sent with comments and notes to the medical institutes and the Ministry of Health in Moscow to speed the progress of Soviet medical science. Such activity is, of course, a blatant violation of the rules of the international organization, but that doesn't bother the heads of the Soviet mission who direct this activity.

The constant supervision and pressure on Soviet employees to obtain information forces them to find ways of resisting. In practice the preoccupation with gathering information leads to the creation of disinformation. Faced with the impossibility of producing all the material demanded, people start making up conversations they are supposed to have had with foreigners along lines they think will suit the Soviet mission and Moscow. For example, after the invasion of Afghanistan by Soviet troops we were asked to sound out our foreign colleagues' reaction. Every normal person realized that no foreigner was going to approve of the Soviet invasion, yet Moscow received several reports signifying approval of the developments in Afghanistan.

In the autumn of 1979 the Soviet mission received a secret document from the Central Committee concerning steps to be taken to combat Chinese expansionism and China's steadily increasing influence in world affairs. It was a long and sharply worded letter demanding action on our part against Chinese representatives and proposing steps to discredit their political and scientific ideas. Hardly a month had passed when a recently arrived employee of the WHO, G. Podoprigora, who knew no foreign language, wrote a detailed report about Chinese penetration of the WHO, which was highly appreciated in the Far Eastern Department of the Foreign Ministry. Consequently most of us reckoned that it didn't matter what you wrote about so long as you wrote something that had some claim to be serious and was likely to please your superiors.

D. Benediktov, the Deputy Soviet Minister of Health, who was a frequent visitor to Geneva, told us more than once that we must establish where the WHO was going and who was behind its general director Halfand Mahler, so that the Soviet authorities could determine a definitive attitude to the WHO. They had been trying to get Mahler to agree to make the WHO into a scientific centre which would receive all information about all the latest discoveries in medicine. This was much more important, Benediktov said, than taking part in the WHO programmes for the developing countries, which cost the Soviet Union money with no return in economic or political terms. In any case, we were in no position to compete with Western countries in this field because we hadn't the resources, the equipment, the medicines or the trained personnel.

At the same time Soviet employees of the WHO were instructed to find ways of getting as much as possible of the Soviet contribution to the WHO returned by setting up programmes of work that the Soviet Union could carry out. Apart from the financial aspect, the idea, though not properly thought through, was that if some of the developing countries could be persuaded to apply the experience of the Soviet health service this might make it possible to influence the politicians in those countries to change their political systems.

Special attention was paid by the Soviet mission to contacts with foreigners working in the international agencies. All such contacts had to be supervised by KGB officers responsible for carrying out counter-espionage work in the Soviet community. Every six months all Soviet employees of international bodies have to submit to the mission lists of the foreigners they know and with whom they maintain contact, with details of their official positions and any other information by which their potential use to the Soviet Union can be assessed. This is done not only for the purpose of exercising control over such contacts but also to enable the mission to have some idea of what Soviet employees can do if Moscow demands to know the reaction of foreigners to some move it has made.

In spite of these efforts the KGB is unable to exercise complete control over all the foreign contacts the Soviet employees have. Everyone has acquaintances he does not reveal to the mission. But if the KGB gets to know about such contacts and thinks they may have unpleasant conse-quences, the Soviet employee is warned and instructed to break off the connection. If he fails to do so he may be sent back to Moscow.

It is not only the clean Soviet employees who are kept under observation by the KGB's counter-espionage service. It also keeps an eye on people working for GRU, to whom similar disciplinary measures may be applied.

Every serious conversation with foreign colleagues has to be reported in writing, in a special room in the mission, on paper usually marked 'Secret'. The reports are handed in to the KGB officer in charge of the secret registry, who extracts matters of sufficient importance to send on to the Centre.

Conferences and Party meetings are held in premises which are equipped with special electronic devices making it impossible for anything to be overheard from outside; there is no possibility of any eavesdropping devices being set up by outsiders. Folders and attaché-cases have to be left in a special place in charge of the mission's duty officer.

In 1979 it was reported that a Soviet citizen working in one of the international organizations in London but visiting Switzerland on busi-ness had committed suicide in his hotel. His name was Panchenko.

From my friends in the KGB and GRU *rezidentury* in Geneva I learnt that Panchenko was an officer in Soviet military intelligence with the rank of major. My friends were quite convinced that, as had been announced officially, Panchenko had indeed committed suicide when he was very drunk. At the same time they did not exclude the possibility that, as a result of his addiction to strong drink and consequently to women, he might have been hooked by a Western intelligence agency and, realizing that if his weaknesses and offences were to be discovered by the Soviet authorities he would be severely punished, he had chosen the best way out in the circumstances. Better a terrible end than terror without end, as they say.

That was what we thought, but the Soviet authorities thought differently and accused British intelligence and the Swiss authorities of responsibility for Panchenko's death. To refute these charges the Swiss, assisted by some British criminologists, made a film for television which made it clear that Panchenko was not killed by Western 'special services' but had committed suicide. This version did not suit the Soviet authorities, in spite of the fact that there was documentary film which made it clear that Panchenko had cut his wrists in the bath. The Soviets insisted that British intelligence had murdered Panchenko because he refused to collaborate with them, and had dressed it up as suicide.

These accusations may have been convincing to the uninformed layman. But I had been told, even when I was at the KGB training school, that there were now poisons that left no traces after killing a man and gave the impression of death by natural causes, from a heart attack or food poisoning. Was it likely, so many years later, that British intelligence would kill a man in such a primitive manner? In October 1979 the film was shown on Swiss television, in spite of efforts by the Soviet mission to prevent its showing, and it was at that point that a piece of instant disinformation was brought into circulation – disinformation mixed with blackmail.

Arkadi N. Shevchenko

I am still puzzled as to why the plight of political defectors
is so much harder than that of artists or writers, whose
motives for defecting are always taken on faith.

As a disarmament specialist and Under Secretary General at the United Nations, Arkadi Shevchenko enjoyed access to all but the very highest classifications of Soviet diplomatic telegrams, and in April 1975 he made contact with the CIA's station in New York with a view to defecting. There, in a mid-town brownstone safe-house, he was received by Kenneth Millian, a former station chief in Argentina and Costa Rica, and latterly Chief of Covert Action for the whole of the Latin American region.

For the next thirty-two months his CIA case officer, Millian's deputy, liaised closely with him, arranging a regular schedule of meetings every ten days, and made the arrangements for his eventual escape from his apartment building in April 1978. Thereafter Shevchenko's resettlement, a lonely business because his wife Lina died of an overdose in Moscow soon after his defection, was to cause considerable anxiety. In an effort to supply him with female companionship the FBI searched the Washington DC yellow pages for a suitable escort service. Their eventual choice, a twenty-two-year-old Georgetown prostitute named Judy Chavez, later wrote *Defector's Mistress*, much to Shevchenko's embarrassment. She became his constant companion within three weeks of his defection and remained until October 1978, when she sold her story to the media.

Shevchenko's autobiography, *Breaking with Moscow*, published in 1985, was criticized in an article in the 15 July 1985 edition of *The New Republic* by the American author Edward Jay Epstein, who pointed out that certain episodes could not possibly have taken place as described. He also suggested, incorrectly, that Shevchenko had invented his pre-defection collaboration with the CIA to enchance the interest of his manuscript which, allegedly, did not contain the relevant material when it was first submitted to his original publisher, Michael Korda of Simon & Schuster. He later rewrote it with the help of his American wife Elaine, whom he married in December 1978, and the revised version was published by Alfred A. Knopf in New York. Epstein dissected the book line by line and concluded that the author had embellished many episodes and invented others to make his story more interesting.

In fact Shevchenko's story was largely true although he had embroidered some incidents, including the dramatic circumstances of his defection. After twenty years in the Soviet foreign service, including three as one of Foreign Minister Andrei Gromyko's personal advisers, his conversion represented a considerable coup, particularly since Millian and the small circle indoctrinated into the secret had managed the case for so long without a leak. According to Millian, 'the intelligence product was phenomenal. He was much better placed than Penkovsky. It was our first opportunity to get right to the top of the Soviet decision-making machine. He had complete access . . . he could even go into their coderoom and look at all the latest cables.'

Shevchenko, whose son Gennady and daughter Anna stayed in Moscow, now lives openly in Washington DC under his own name. In this passage the author describes how he was debriefed by his CIA handlers, Tom Grogan and Bert Johnson, after an encounter with Boris Solomatin which Epstein demonstrated could not really have happened in the way suggested, for the KGB *rezident* had already left New York at the time mentioned, in July 1975.

Breaking with Moscow

As I looked at the files Grogan brought with him, I saw I could give him a number of answers. I balked, however, at his suggestion that I improve my ties with the KGB. Grogan was especially persistent in this recommendation. The KGB, he argued, could be valuable sources and dangerous enemies: 'You'd be better off staying on their good side.'

'It can't be done,' I told him. 'Most of them are arrogant and vicious and some are just plain stupid. I try to maintain reasonable working relations, but that's never enough for them. They want to control everyone around them, to make all of us do their work and dance to their tune.'

I said to Grogan I didn't intend to make KGB friends to help him out. I would tell him what I knew; beyond that he would have to use other resources.

I began by describing the KGB chief in New York, Boris Aleksandrovich Solomatin, a short, stocky major general, the *rezident*, as Soviets called him. After my appointment as Under Secretary General, Solomatin invited me again and again to his apartment for drinking sessions and 'friendly talks'. He was cynical, boorish, and a drunk besides. He holed up in his smoke-filled apartment, where he summoned others to him.

He did not participate in any operations outside the walls of the Soviet Mission, but he directed the agents who did. Solomatin lived in reclusive safety, seldom venturing outside the Mission, except to Glen Cove. His safety was further enhanced by the diplomatic immunity conferred by his cover title of Deputy Permanent Representative of the USSR to the UN, and a minister's rank.

The two-room apartment in the Mission he shared with his wife, Vera, was not quite as much of a fortress as the *referentura*, but it was secure nonetheless. To thwart American bugging of his apartment, which he was convinced was thorough, permanent, and effective, Solomatin had two television sets and a stereo system, at least one of which was always on. Since he had virtually no contact with Americans, he lived by his television sets. He particularly liked news programs and would watch the CBS and ABC news simultaneously. Another of his favorite pastimes was listening to tapes of Russian patriotic songs from World War II and recounting his wartime experiences as an infantry officer.

Now in his early fifties, he was also a graduate of MGIMO, and I had known him for years. Soon after my arrival in New York in 1973, he was openly trying to involve me in the KGB's espionage activities. On one occasion, sprawled out on the sofa, a cigarette between his teeth, he fixed me with a stare and said, 'You can be one of our most important intelligence officers.' He reeked of vodka as he leaned confidentially closer. 'You go everywhere. You talk to everyone. All you have to do is tell me what you hear. After all, we both work for the Soviet state.'

He said that any interesting information I provided would be sent to KGB headquarters in Moscow, where it would undoubtedly receive attention from the Politburo.

'We know how to work,' he said smugly. 'We're not like your Foreign Ministry bureaucrats, forever sitting on valuable information like a brooding hen who never produces any chicks. Collaboration with us will advance your career.'

Solomatin's assurances were lies. It was true that the *rezident* had an independent communications connection to KGB headquarters in Moscow and that he was absolutely free to choose whether or not to share any information with Ambassador Malik before forwarding it. But when the KGB transmits information to Moscow, it never identifies the person who procured it. Not even the *rezident* who generates a cable uses his own name. He simply signs as the *rezident*.

Solomatin merely wanted me as another foot soldier. I told him that Gromyko would judge my performance by the work I did for the ministry, not on what I did for the KGB. He rubbed his temples as if he were deep in thought. I ought to consider his proposal seriously, he said.

I had no intention of being drawn into his network, but I was compelled to make several concessions to him during his tenure as *rezident*. In the fall of 1973, Solomatin introduced me to Valdik Enger, a tall, handsome Estonian. Solomatin insisted that I arrange a job for Enger in my office, where there was a vacancy. At first I refused, saying I needed an assistant who would really assist me, not someone who would be his man. The *rezident* was persistent, and finally I agreed to take Enger on, with the condition that after a few months in my office I would transfer him to another position in the Secretariat. Solomatin did not object.

Solomatin's chief aide was Colonel Vladimir Gregorievich Krasovsky, the deputy *rezident*. He was a steady and experienced KGB professional who had served several years in New York. Solomatin's close associates also included his frequent guest Georgy Arbatov, the director of the Institute of the United States and Canada of the Soviet Academy of Sciences, who often traveled to the United States. In fact, Lina and I had seen him recently at a dinner party at Solomatin's apartment.

Johnson said, 'A lot of people think he's very close to Brezhnev, practically the Kremlin's spokesman. And it seems like every time he's over here he's being interviewed in the papers or on TV. Do you know him well?'

I knew Arbatov very well; in fact, I had known him since the beginning of my career. When we met at the Solomatins' dinner party he was on one of his regular scouting missions. Then, in 1976, his purpose was to sift through the political underbrush prior to the American presidential election.

President Gerald Ford was thought to be continuing Richard Nixon's policy toward the USSR. The Soviets, therefore, preferred him to any other contender for the presidency, concerned as they were with what they perceived as a threat from the right wing of American politics. Ford's challenger for the Republican nomination was Ronald Reagan, a hard-line anti-Soviet and anti-Communist. The Soviets knew, of course, that even if Reagan were to win the nomination and then the election, he would eventually have to deal with Moscow, just as Nixon had. Nevertheless, the prospect of a Reagan presidency was not one they found pleasant. As Gromyko put it, 'No one knows what kind of surprise this actor might spring.' There was an air of uncertainty and dissatisfaction, even confusion, that affected general trends in the superpowers' relations at the time of the Solomatins' dinner.

Lina and I were the first arrivals. Vera Solomatin, a onetime research assistant at Arbatov's institute, was celebrating her enrollment as a lieutenant in her husband's organization. There was nothing unusual in that; there were many women KGB officers. The wives of many KGB professionals also worked for it, including Irina Yakushkin, the wife of Washington's *rezident*. Moreover, some of the wives of my fellow diplomats in New York were KGB officers.

As Solomatin put glasses and plates on the table in the small foyer of his apartment, which also served as a dining room, he told me to go into the living room and pour myself a drink; he would join me in a minute. As I looked around, waiting for him, I noticed four copies of John Barron's book, *KGB*, sitting on a bookcase. I asked Solomatin why he had so many. He said that people in Moscow kept requesting it.

'But it's not so hot,' he said. 'My name and Vladimir Krasovsky's aren't even mentioned in it.'

I couldn't tell whether this was an expression of regret or pride on Solomatin's part.

Krasovsky and his wife arrived with Arbatov. After several rounds of vodka toasts had warmed the conversational chill I always sensed in Solomatin's presence, Arbatov agreed to summarize the report he would be making to Moscow.

Gerald Ford had a fairly good chance of winning the 1976 election. 'Of course, right now he does the usual zigzagging, taking hard-line positions, but that doesn't worry us very much. It's just the usual campaign bluster. After it's over, he'll be good old Jerry again,' he said.

Neither Solomatin nor I disputed this assessment when Arbatov asked for our opinions. We and he knew that Moscow wanted reassurance on Ford's continuing in the White House, and none of us wished to be the bearer of bad news, even if we had strong presentiments of Ford's defeat. I turned the talk to my special interest, arms control, and asked Arbatov if there was anything new in that area.

Arvatov acknowledged that the negotiations' momentum had dissipated. 'It's too close to the elections for the Americans to move on something as controversial as SALT,' he said with evident unhappiness. 'We understand that reality. It's the way things are, but it's too bad.'

Solomatin, whose interest was espionage, not disarmament, broke in. 'Does it really matter that much? Why should we want to speed up the SALT business anyway?'

'I know what you mean,' Arbatov said, 'but things are serious.' He then reiterated arguments about the connection between arms-spending and the failing health of the Soviet economy. The difference was that three years after the Nixon–Brezhnev breakthrough the domestic situation was even graver. Solomatin and I listened as Arbatov ticked off the depressing list of chronic shortcomings in management, in farming, in transport and distribution.

'Zhora-sha,' Solomatin finally burst out, using a nickname for Georgy common in his native Odessa, 'you're a pessimist. We've survived worse. Don't forget the war. We came through that, after all.'

It was the standard, patriotic, orthodox, unthinking rebuttal to any hint of criticism. Solomatin, like so many veterans who looked back to the war with a nostalgic glow, used this retort to effectively shut off serious talk.

Vladimir Krasovsky broke the awkward silence by reminding us that this was a celebration. He suggested that we put on some music and dance. Our wives enthusiastically agreed. Krasovsky clicked the heels of his gleaming, brand-new shoes.

'Look at my *baretki*,' he exclaimed, using underworld slang for shoes. 'Expensive. I paid more than seventy bucks for them,' he said with pride.

Lean, tall, and good-looking, Krasovsky, unlike Solomatin, engaged daily in real espionage activity. He loved to dance and was very good at it. He clicked his heels again in front of Lina and kissed her hand in a gesture of burlesque. Watching them dance, half listening to Solomatin's heavy laugh and Arbatov's banter with the other women, I was grateful that even in the age of technological miracles no one could yet read thoughts.

Soon after I described that evening to Johnson a new *rezident* came to New York to replace Boris Solomatin. Muscular and bald, with the eyes of a basilisk, Colonel Yuri Ivanovich Drozdov struck me as a formidable adversary. Solomatin had been a pompous recluse who lived like a bear inside the mission, but at least he was occasionally convivial.

Drozdov appeared to have no human failings. Moreover, he was a bolder and more intrusive presence in the Mission. Although he spoke poor English and, having specialized in China, knew little about the United States or the United Nations, he tried to take an active part in diplomatic work. His ignorance, however, only seemed to make him more demanding and cocksure than Solomatin had been. I found him not just unpleasant but menacing, and made it a point to keep a distance between us.

Shortly after he arrived, however, I got a late-night summons from him. I had been working in a *referentura* cubicle going through the code cables in hopes of finding a nugget or two to pass on to Johnson. It was after eleven o'clock. I was tired and, as always when engaged in such searches, jumpy.

'Arkady Nikolaevich' – a *referentura* clerk abruptly materialized at my elbow – 'you are wanted on the telephone.'

I must have shown my surprise and anxiety, for the clerk repeated himself. 'It's a telephone call for you.'

No one except Lina and the Mission guards downstairs were aware that I was in the building. Only the code room personnel knew which room I was in. I walked in worried confusion to the telephone. My muscles tensed at the sound of Drozdov's voice on the line asking me to report to his office.

'Upstairs?' I asked, envisioning the deserted corridors of the eighth floor, given over entirely to the KGB, hallways where the blank doors were locked even during the day, a sanctum from which there could be no escape.

'No, no.' Drozdov sounded impatient. 'I'm on the sixth floor. Could you come down now? There's a matter I'd like to discuss.'

I consented.

All I really knew of Drozdov at this point was that he looked malevolent and appeared efficient. What if he had been culling old reports on me and noticed something which Solomatin, in his haste to depart some months before, had overlooked? I found the *rezident* hunched over a stack of papers when I entered his room. Only a single desk lamp illuminated the small chamber. It was a setting for an inquisition, but Drozdov, it turned out, had not mustered me for questioning. What he wanted was a favor.

'Thanks for coming at this hour,' he began. 'I need your assistance. It's about Enger. Can't you let up on him? He's doing valuable work for us. I know he's sometimes too busy for other jobs, but we have to strike a balance. I hope you'll oblige us in this business.'

I was simultaneously relieved and angry: Valdik Enger again. To hear his name mentioned was, of course, far better than to be confronted with accusations about my own conduct. But it reminded me once more of the ways in which the KGB had used me, had forced my acquiescence to their wishes. I complained that each time I warned Enger to put more effort into his UN work and to be more discreet about his conspiratorial activities, he apologized and promised to mend his ways, but he never did. And when I'd returned from my New Year's vacation with Lina, I had found that he was even neglecting the less-demanding job I had provided him, that of supervising the preparation of a press digest that was circulated to fifty or sixty senior Secretariat officials four times a day.

The quality of the summary had noticeably deteriorated. Inaccuracies grew. Important news articles or commentaries were omitted. Other employees told me Enger was at fault. He paid almost no attention to the work. I called him into my office for what became an angry encounter, ending with my threat to take him off the UN payroll unless he began to earn his keep legitimately.

It was that argument which had been reported to Drozdov and had prompted his call to me. In response to his appeal that I give his agent the benefit of the doubt, I decided to take what advantage I could from a situation in which Drozdov, not I, was at a disadvantage.

'I've tried to be accommodating,' I told the *resident*, 'but you may not know what sort of man we're talking about. He hasn't lived up to his word. It wouldn't take much time to do the job he has now but he won't give it any. He's too blatant about his work for you. It's causing talk and trouble and I don't see how I can go on covering for him.'

Drozdov thought for a moment before replying. 'I can't see that his mistakes are so important, but' – he paused again – 'I'll try to look at it from your point of view. We really want him in the UN. Do you have any ideas?'

'Well, I get nowhere with him,' I answered. 'Maybe you can get him to do his job. Tell him it's important. He ought to listen to you.'

Drozdov seemed relieved. He accepted my idea right away and we parted amicably. He never knew the fright his call had caused me.

Perhaps that incident was what triggered that night vivid dreams of my childhood. I woke several times drenched with sweat, my heart pounding. I was reliving the beginning of war in 1941, when the heavy bombing began and my mother and I hid night after night in the potato cellar under our house by the Black Sea.

Viktor Sheymov

Communism is not only an ideology, it is also a mentality, a mind-set that is alive and well.

A born Muscovite, and a graduate of Moscow's Technical University, Viktor Sheymov joined the KGB in 1971 at the age of twenty-five, having been recommended by friends of his father, a doctor. After training Sheymov was assigned to the elite Eighth Chief Directorate, responsible for all the KGB's communications. Initially he worked as a cipher clerk and then was posted temporarily to the FCD's new headquarters in Yasnevo to assist in the installation of a new mainframe computer. Having gained a reputation as a computer expert Sheymov became the Eighth Chief Directorate's troubleshooter, checking on the security systems protecting KGB facilities across the globe. In particular, he scored well in Warsaw where the local *rezident* had fallen foul of the ambassador over a dispute concerning the size of the *referentura*. Sheymov overruled the ambassador and ensured the KGB's prestige was untarnished.

Late in the autumn of 1975 Sheymov was promoted to the Third Department, dealing exclusively with security systems, and there acquired an unrivalled knowledge of the precautions taken by the KGB to prevent hostile interception of its machine ciphers. However, the more he learned about the KGB the less satisfaction he found in his job, and he was suspicious about the circumstances of a friend's death in which he suspected the KGB had played a part. He was particularly disillusioned by the scale of the KGB's penetration of the Church and, as a minor Party official within the KGB he realized through the required study of communism that the leadership had betrayed the Party:

> What I've learned so far has shocked me deeply . . . It's clear that ever since the Revolution the leaders of the Communist Party have deviated more and more from the original Party goals. Now all we have is a bunch of bureaucrats who have usurped all the power and are doing nothing for the good of the country.

Sheymov obtained his wife's consent to defect and he established contact with the CIA in November 1979 while on a visit to Warsaw. In May 1980 he was smuggled through Czechoslovakia to Austria by car with his wife Olga and their five-year-old daughter Elena. Their disappearance went unreported in the West for ten years while Sheymov underwent a lengthy debriefing, and his autobiography was not published until 1993. Here he recalls, in the third person (as 'Victor'), the moment he decided to defect.

Tower of Secrets

He needed to be alone. Using familiar paths, he went to a remote part of the magnificent estate. Not that it was formally grand; it was simply a perfect country retreat. The most attractive time here was the fall, but even now the color of the foliage had become just a shade warmer. In a short while the leaves would turn to gold. The natural and unregimented beauty of the park slowed Victor's pace and brought his wandering thoughts into focus.

Yes. The decision had been made. They'd have to defect. There was no other way that would give him a shot at the profoundly evil system.

Victor found himself in an unfamiliar moral territory. So far, when he'd taken chances, he'd put only himself at risk. Now it was very different. Victor was talking to himself: 'Now, calm down. You've got to be absolutely cold-blooded. Cool as a cucumber. No emotions. Any emotion can cause an error. Any error can kill you. And your family. Yes, your wife and daughter. You certainly have a right to risk your own head, but do you have a moral right to risk your family? Especially when they aren't capable of comprehending the level of risk. Even Olga, no matter how much you tell her about the KGB, doesn't have a chance of understanding it. You have to be in the system, and high up, for that. So there's no way even Olga can make her own relatively informed decision.'

A long time ago his father had given Victor a good maxim: 'If you have something worthwhile to risk for, go ahead, take the chance. Even if it's one in a million. If the goal isn't worth the risk, don't take nine to one.' Good guideline. For yourself. How about others? How about those you love? Easy, when you're a commander and you have to send your troops to an almost certain death. Soldiers know what they're in for. Children do not. Soldiers can fight. Children cannot. *Here we go again. Moral choices.*

Victor came upon a large tree stump and sat on it. The possibility of failure weighed on him. The possibility of being cut down by the system, of going down the well-traveled path followed by so many. Leo Tolstoy had philosophized, using an oak as a model. 'Our generation has to settle for an oak stump,' Victor mused. He put his hand on the wood. 'This used to be an old oak. Cut down. But the more you grow before being cut, the better foundation you make for someone else. And you never know in what way. If I'm lucky, even having failed, I can be of use to somebody down the road, in some unpredictable way, like this stump, so comfortable for my butt. At least that's something.'

OK, let's stop wobbling. Sort things out. Make decisions and act.

'So, the Number One question is: Do I have a moral right to put my family at risk, and to a degree they cannot comprehend?' Victor considered this for a while. Then the answer came to him: 'For lack of any better idea, let's consider the alternative. If I want to avoid the risk to my family, I'll have to continue working for the communist system, contributing to its strength. I simply cannot do that. And if I didn't, my family would suffer almost as much as if we failed to defect. Moreover, even if I could keep on doing business as usual, my daughter will continue getting those massive doses of brainwashing and, God forbid, will become a devoted communist. So the answer has to be yes, at least by default. But in the end I'll probably never know the answer to the big one. And God help me not to have to face it when it's not academic.

'Now, to question Number Two: Where to defect to? Given that the goal of the defection is to fight the communist system, it only makes sense to defect to a country strong enough to do so. Besides, there are practical operational restrictions. There are only a handful of countries in the world with intelligence services really capable of pulling off an exfiltration operation from the Soviet Union: the United States, Great Britain, West Germany, and perhaps Israel. Realistically, that's about all,' he concluded.

Israel would not fit the bill overall. Victor also knew that West Germany was thoroughly penetrated through the East German service, and the danger of walking into a waiting trap was too great even for Victor's taste. On top of that, even knowing it was wrong, Victor couldn't overcome his prejudice, the aftertaste of World War II. To say nothing of the fact that it was the Germans who had played a major role in helping the communists to usurp power in Russia during World War I. So, the last two on the list were out.

Choosing between the United States and Great Britain was difficult. To some extent it might well be academic since the whole approach was chancy at best, and it was impossible to predict what kind of opportunity would come Victor's way. But still, priorities should be set.

There was no clear-cut choice between the CIA and MI6. On the one hand, being much bigger, the CIA should statistically have the larger set of operational alternatives. Also, the famous British 'fifth man' had still not been located, nor had other possible 'deferred payments' Great Britain might yet make for some of its elite's flirtation with Communism. On the other hand, in a large organization like the CIA there was a much greater chance of a bureaucratic slipup, which could prove deadly in an intelligence operation. Besides, the fact that no 'four men' had been discovered in America didn't mean that 'all five' weren't happily operating there. So Victor felt it was hard to choose between the two organizations. *Let it be a draw for now.*

When it came to weighing the pros and cons of the two countries themselves, Victor felt distinctly at a loss. Even though he was better informed than most on the Main Enemy's positions on geopolitical issues, he was appalled at how relatively uninformed he was about real life in the West. He'd never even spoken to an Englishman or an American. Now more than ever he was irritated by the fact that what he did know was based on communist propaganda. Finally, to his dismay, Victor had to admit that the only sense he had of the difference between the two countries was that America had a tradition of offering a relatively safe harbor to foreigners, most of whom were fleeing trouble in their native lands, for one reason or another. English society, he reckoned, based on his limited knowledge, was notorious for being static, structured, and elitist – a tough place to start from scratch. On the basis of these superficial impressions, Victor concluded that he and his family would probably adapt more easily to a new life in America.

One more consideration crossed Victor's mind. He recalled that Oleg Penkovsky, the army colonel executed in Moscow for espionage, had initially worked with the British. Later, that became a joint operation with the Americans. Considering the extreme sensitivity of the matters Victor was involved in, it was absolutely essential to limit the number of people in any intelligence service who even knew of his existence. He concluded that the British were very likely to get the Americans involved, while the Americans most likely would not even give a hint of his existence to the British. If you double the number of people 'in the loop', you at least double the risk.

OK, the Americans are the first choice. The British will be our backup.

Victor stood up and started walking slowly, in no particular direction. *Two down, a hundred to go.*

Now, question Number Three: How to contact the Americans? His wife and daughter were hostages, forever forbidden to leave the country. They couldn't even travel into the Soviet Union's own backyard, such as Bulgaria. So, there was no point in even considering the three of them simply walking into an American embassy anywhere in the world – which would have been nice and easy. The American embassy in Moscow was too heavily guarded around the clock: it was out of the question to try to penetrate its KGB guards – even alone. A lot of people tried that without knowing what they were up against, and paid dearly. If all else failed, which was inconceivable, the guards simply shot to kill. Even if somebody were to have the incredible luck of getting inside, then what? Sit out the rest of your life in the embassy? No, that was no way to go.

Bearing all of this in mind, he still had no choice but to contact the Americans and make the arrangements for all three of them to get out at a later date through by far the most tightly guarded border in the world.

Generally, outside of the Soviet Union, Americans are much less intensely surveilled, and their embassies are much less closely guarded by the host country. That seemed to present a possible opportunity. However, because of his job, Victor had to stay on the premises of the Soviet embassy during his trips abroad, and could go outside it only if he was accompanied by a KGB guard, usually the Chief Security Officer of the embassy. The prospect of attempting to contact the Americans under such conditions, and on top of that to return back for his family, made Victor shiver. 'No, no, too crazy even for my taste,' he mumbled.

Well, the only thing left is Moscow. I've got to contact an American here. So be it.

There were hundreds of Americans in Moscow. But Victor knew that there were Americans, and there were Americans, with a world of difference between them. Some of them were intelligence officers, some were diplomats, some were businessmen or tourists. Some of them were honest, some were not. Some of them came on their own, and some were lured or just brought in by the KGB. And the KGB was working on all of them. Relentlessly.

With the problem of Soviets' traveling abroad well under control, the KGB's biggest problem in Moscow was the physical proximity of foreigners to the Inner Ward Members, the 'carriers of the secrets'. That proximity suggested possible opportunities to those who would want, for whatever reason, to volunteer to cooperate with the West. The KGB took this problem extremely seriously and devoted a great deal of energy to it. As with most things the KGB focuses on, its efforts were remarkably effective.

Characteristically, the KGB attacked the issue from both ends, intimidating Soviets and foreigners alike. Unless they happened to be a KGB officer or an informer, Soviet citizens were aggressively dissuaded from any contact with foreigners. And any foreigner who in the KGB's view was too active in his contacts with Soviets was given a really hard time. As a result, people on both sides developed a Pavlovian reflex, and became extremely cautious about their contacts with one another.

Suppose Victor did manage to contact an American. The first danger awaiting him was that the American might be 'friendly' with the KGB. The second danger was that the American might be justifiably frightened of a KGB provocation and make a big stink out of Victor's approach. Then the KGB would unquestionably find Victor, and quickly. The third, and more likely, possibility was that the American might just be someone who wanted no part of any spy games. And then all the risks he had taken to establish the contact would have been for naught. Victor had no illusions that if any attempt by him to contact an American were noticed it would be misinterpreted. Any professional would know there could be only one reason for Victor to try to contact a foreigner, especially a NATO-country native: Espionage. He'd have zero chance of getting away with it. So the only type of contact Victor was interested in was an intelligence officer.

So, Victor concluded, here's my immediate task. Contact an American KIO – known intelligence officer – and offer my expertise in exchange for exfiltration and political asylum for me and my family. He realized that this mission, far beyond any other he had ever attempted, should be classified 'impossible'. *What the hell, why not pull off one of these for a good cause for a change?*

Vladimir A. Kuzichkin

What about Russia? I asked myself, for Russia does not
like traitors. But the Russia that I was trying to serve,
living on a diet of illusions, existed only in my head.

A member of the KGB's elite Illegals Directorate, Kuzichkin spent five years at Moscow University studying Iran, followed by the usual two years at the FCD's Red Banner Institute, before he was posted to the Soviet Consulate in Tehran in the summer of 1977 under diplomatic cover as a Line N officer specializing in handling illegals. Fluent in Farsi and English, he ran a small network of KGB illegals, but in September 1981 his two best agents, a husband and wife team operating on West German passports, were arrested in Switzerland. Not long afterwards, in the following May, Kuzichkin realized that an undeveloped roll of film, on which secret documents were routinely stored in the *referentura*, had disappeared while in his care.

Faced with the extreme penalties for the loss of classified documents, Kuzichkin made contact with SIS and was exfiltrated early in June 1982. His motives seem to have become clear only after he had been resettled in London for, as he admits,

> I had never been pro-Western. I always thought that the West had its own interests, and that it needed a strong Russia like a hole in the head, whether it was a communist Russia or a free Russia. I believed that we, the Russians, had to solve our own problems, and that changes in the Soviet structure were possible only from within, and absolutely not from outside. Interference from outside would always unite the people and only strengthen the regime.

As well as identifying the complete KGB and GRU order of battle in Iran, and the identities of those illegals he had handled personally, he was to give SIS an authoritative account of the KGB's role in supporting the Tudeh party, then the subject of considerable repression by the Ayatollah's regime. Kuzichkin was resettled in London where he now lives with a new wife, and his autobiography, *Inside the KGB*, was published in 1990. In it, he lifts the lid on the KGB's operations in Tehran.

Inside the KGB

By the beginning of 1982 the Soviet Union had decided on its policy towards the Iran–Iraq war. This policy favoured Iraq, which the Soviet Union began overtly to supply with arms, while showing itself increasingly contemptuous towards Iran. On several occasions the Soviet air force made raids on Iranian territory from Afghanistan, in order to strike at camps where Afghan partisans were undergoing training. No one fell over backwards to apologize.

It was obvious by now that as a result of the policies it had been pursuing, Iran had virtually isolated itself from the rest of the world. So long as Khomeini was alive, Iran would never return to the American fold. That was the prospect which had worried the Soviet rulers most of all. The Soviet Union was far better off with an Iran that was weak and stewing in its own juice. From the Soviet Union's standpoint, Iran was no longer an important country. This also found expression in the appointment of the new ambassador to Tehran. Vinogradov had been a member of the Party's Central Committee; Boldyrev, the new ambassador, had held the very modest position of head of the Middle East Department in the Soviet foreign ministry. Vinogradov left Iran in the spring of 1982, and he was given some high ceremonial post in the governing establishment.

Oddly enough, and much to our surprise, Iran reacted to the cooling Soviet attitude in an almost placatory way. The Iranian authorities grew less truculent. The press adopted a softer tone towards the Soviet Union.

The slogan 'Death to the Soviet Union' was almost dropped. Furthermore, the Iranian–Soviet negotiations on economic cooperation were renewed on the Iranians' initiative. A new treaty on the further development of economic cooperation between Iran and the Soviet Union was signed in Moscow in February 1982. Soviet specialists began to return to Iran.

Against that background, the conditions around the Soviet embassy began to return to normal. Anti-Soviet Afghan demonstrators went on parading in Tehran, but this time we were very well protected. On the next anniversary of the Afghan revolution in April 1982, the demonstrators were not even allowed near the embassy, which was ringed by a remarkably large number of police and Revolutionary Guards. The Iranians were now afraid that something might happen to us, and were doing everything possible to carry out their promise, given earlier in Moscow, to guarantee the safety of Soviet citizens.

In these circumstances I decided that there was no longer any point in keeping the film of secret documents in the cache, and that it should now be taken out and destroyed. I went into the Impulse station premises during the lunch-break, when no one was there, and went to the cache. Then I squatted down and began to prise at the skirting board. To my surprise, it fell away from the wall at the first touch. That is a part of it fell off, near where the cache was. Under the skirting board gaped an empty hole. The container and the film had disappeared. I could not believe my eyes and checked everything again, but with the same result. The cache was empty. Only then did I realize that the skirting board had not been fixed tightly in place, as we had left it when we filled the cache, but had only been leaning against the wall. Whoever had removed the film in haste had not had time to stick the skirting board back.

I sat there in a state of shock still squatting, and stared long and hard at the empty opening in the wall. For me, this empty space was a tragedy. It was the end of the road. Under Soviet law, seven years in jail is the minimum sentence for losing top-secret documents. Whoever stole the film must have known this. In a mean, low-down way, in the Soviet way, someone had dealt me a fatal stab in the back. As to who it could have been, I could only guess. Officially, only Resident Sherbarshin knew of the cache beside myself. Whom else he could have told about it, I did not know. But that no longer mattered. Whoever did it had created an irreversible situation. He could not put the film back in the cache, or, let us say, give it surreptitiously to the resident. That would be a clear indication that I had nothing to do with it. He could only destroy the film and sit and wait until its loss was officially discovered. It any event the responsibility for the loss of these top-secret documents lay on my shoulders.

My brilliant career was over. And that career had indeed been brilliant. I had been promoted three times in military rank, rising from lieutenant to major in the course of only one tour of duty in Iran. But more important than rank was promotion in the posts I held. In these too I was promoted three times during my tour of duty. From junior case officer I rose through the posts of case officer and senior case officer to that of assistant head of department. In addition, I had been given to understand unofficially in the Centre that my candidature was being seriously considered for the post of head of a geographical section after I had finally returned from Iran. In the KGB, such quick promotion in the course of only five years' service does not happen often. Now everything had come crashing down. And not only that. It was the ruin of all my secret plans for what I intended to do after I got back to the Soviet Union.

My first impulse was to go to the resident immediately and tell him everything, and then to find and punish the rat who had done it. But I realized that this would lead nowhere and would amount to virtual suicide. The resident would have to report it to the Centre, whose only possible response would be to recall me to Moscow for an inquiry. I decided to wait before reporting.

At that moment Arkadi Glazyrin, the Impulse station operator, returned from his lunch-break. When he saw me sitting there at the wall, he asked me what I was doing. I gave him the straight answer that I had opened my cache and had not found what should have been inside, but added that its contents were not too important. Arkadi inspected the empty cache, dug around inside it with his hand, and then, after muttering something, went off into his room. He cannot have attached any great importance to it. It was just as well that he did not.

I was in a strange state in the days that followed. I was one person who went to work, wrote telegrams to the Centre, and talked to my friends. At the same time I was another person who could think constantly of one thing only – WHAT CAN I DO? I could not eat. My body refused food. At night I was tortured by nightmares, or rather always by the same dream – a man dressed all in black, with an axe raised over his head, approaches my bed to finish me off. At that point I awoke in terror.

What could I do, I thought. Report it, or equally, sit and wait until it was discovered and then begin to prove my innocence? But that was no use. In my country, those who stumble and fall are trampled to death. To scorn danger and proudly take your punishment, while you fight on to prove your innocence, means adding your name to the list of the millions of victims of the Soviet system. And for the sake of what? For I already hated all that with all my heart. Nobody would appreciate my sacrifice, nobody needed it, and what did I have to prove to a system I despised?

'What would Comrade Lenin have done in your place?' I suddenly recalled the comical question often asked by the positive heroes of Soviet literature. All right, I thought, what would he have done? 'He would have emigrated,' were the words that sounded lucidly and clearly in my head. It seemed to me at that moment that it was not really my response, but that somebody else had said it. No, I thought. That's not for me. I had never been pro-Western. I always thought that the West had its own interests, and that it needed a strong Russia like a hole in the head, whether it was a communist Russia or a free Russia. I believed that we, the Russians, had to solve our own problems, and that changes in the Soviet structure were possible only from within, and absolutely not from outside. Interference from outside would as always unite the people and only strengthen the regime.

But the more I thought about this, the more I came to the conclusion that I had no other way out, no matter how I might try to avoid it. And in the West I should be able in some way or other to realize my plans. The thought again occurred that most of the Bolshevik leaders, who knew a thing or two about resistance, had spent a great part of their pre-revolutionary lives as emigrants abroad, and derived only advantage from it. What about Russia? I asked myself, for Russia does not like traitors. But the Russia that I was trying to serve, living on a diet of illusions, existed only in my head. The fact is that what has existed in Russia from the moment the Bolsheviks took power is hostile to her, and to fight it is the sacred duty of all Russians. So why waver now? That is what was going through my head at the time.

My nervous tension was so great that I began to take to the bottle to get rid of it. That helped. Then one evening I happened to run into Mylnikov, our Party leader. We met in the embassy grounds. He was drunk as usual, and when he saw me he invited me round to his flat to sink some more. I did not like the man, and it was never my habit to drink with his kind, but that evening something impelled me and I agreed. After a couple of drinks in Mylnikov's flat we had an argument, and at that point my dam burst. I told Mylnikov everything I thought about the Party, communism, the KGB, everything. For me at that moment, Mylnikov was the embodiment of everything I hated. That encounter would have ended fatally for Mylnikov had Levakov the security officer not arrived at the flat. The neighbours had complained about the racket from Mylnikov's flat. It turned out that Mylnikov had already had two rows with other people that day before he met me.

Levakov was surprised when he saw me, and said that he never expected that I might keep such company. 'I didn't expect it either,' I answered him. But it had happened, and a good many neighbours must have overhead our conversation. Sound carried far in the embassy block of flats. It was like talking face to face with everybody. I was certain that I would be reminded in due course of my candid revelations.

One day in a private conversation, one of our cipher clerks told me what he thought was a funny story. Friends in the Centre had told him that the commission that oversees the security systems for storing KGB documents had visited embassies in several Latin American countries and had found so many security breaches that it had now been decided to screen all Soviet embassies abroad. The cipher clerk said that it would be our turn soon, but there was nothing for him to worry about – he had all his records completely in order. If his story appeared funny to him, I for my part saw little in it to laugh about. The loss of my documents could be discovered even before the commission arrived, for our cipher clerks would begin their own check before the appearance of the commission. When I asked him when the commission was due, he replied that he didn't yet know exactly, but they were planning to come in the summer.

I had to act at once, since the preparations for my move could take a great deal of time. The first thing to decide was which route I should take to leave Iran. Of the existing passport check-points on the Iranian frontier, those on the Soviet, Afghan, Pakistani and Iraqi borders were out for a start. That left only Mehrabad airport in Tehran and the Bazargan check-point on the Turkish-Iranian frontier.

It would have been tempting of course to board an aircraft and fly off from Iran to the other end of the world. But there were serious objections to my using Mehrabad airport. First, practically everyone there had known me for several years, as I appeared there about once a week. Second, there were always many Soviet nationals knocking about in the airport. This meant that, if the airport were chosen, it would only be possible to fly out on my personal Soviet passport. Even buying the tickets on that passport would be very risky, as it would be noticed. It does not happen often in Iran that a Soviet official flies off to Europe on his own. But were it to happen, news about it could reach the Aeroflot representative. And it would have been quite stupid for me to use a foreign passport in Mehrabad airport, since everybody there knew me.

My work with illegals taught me to think out everything, down to the last detail, and to pre-empt all possible contingencies. Mistakes lead to failures. In my case, they would have led to catastrophe. There was only one way left – Bazargan, the check-point on the Turkish–Iranian frontier. The unfavourable factor here was that Bazargan was 900 kilometres from Tehran. In other respects, nothing could have been better. I had a solid reason to give to the Iranians for making a trip to the north-west. There were Soviet specialists in Tabriz, which is no more than 200 kilometres from Bazargan, and as a consular official I had the right to make a trip into that area. Also, I knew the procedures at the Bazargan check-point very well, as it was part of my duties to gather information of this nature. So that was to be the crossing point.

Now for the documents. Unfortunately I could not use a Soviet passport. Had it been an official journey, the Iranian foreign ministry would have given prior notification to the local authorities that a Soviet diplomat would appear at the Bazargan check-point. That meant that I should have to provide myself with a foreign passport. Here I had to summon up all the knowledge I had accumulated as an officer of the documentation department of illegal intelligence. I obtained the passport.

CHAPTER III

The Soviet Bloc

*All Socialist intelligence services are, of course, under
the supervision and command of Soviet intelligence operatives.*
Ladislav Bittman

The Iron Curtain that fell across Europe at the end of the Second World
War ensured that much of Eastern Europe remained in the grip of
totalitarian regimes, and in the forty years of Soviet domination that
followed only a handful of escapers made the hazardous journey to the
West to write books that seriously undermined the communists' grip on
power. When Cuba effectively joined the Soviet Bloc in 1959 it adopted
the Soviet model already established in Poland, Hungary, Bulgaria,
Romania and Czechoslovakia, where in each case a ubiquitous and
ruthless security apparatus directed by the NKVD had ensured compliance from a subservient population recovering from the ravages of war.

The exception to the rule was Yugoslavia, where Marshal Tito's very
public split from Stalin ensured that the country and its intelligence
service, the KOS, retained a unique measure of independence. Plenty of
anti-Tito literature has been published in the West, including some
trenchant contributions, such as *The New Class* and *Memoir of a
Revolutionary* from Milovan Djilas, the ex-partisan who was once vice-
president, but was expelled from the Communist Party in 1954. While his
views commanded widespread respect, they inflicted no perceptible
damage on Belgrade's grip on Yugoslavia. Similarly, although Arthur
Koestler and Franz Kafka did much to enlighten the free world to the
realities of post-Nazi totalitarianism in Eastern Europe, neither really
harmed the regimes they so detested. There were, however, a few authors
that can be seen to have caused sufficient damage to merit the injured
parties to seek redress.

Despite the authoritarian nature of the puppet governments sponsored
by the Kremlin, which rarely tolerated any opposition, a few individuals
with inside knowledge did flee to the West during the years of the Cold

War and published accounts of their own experiences which, in retrospect, can now be seen to have had a serious impact on the principal organ of repression. In Bulgaria, where the feared Drzaven Sigurnost enforced the absolute, tryannical power of Todor Zhivkov, Vladimir Kostov was a unique example of a DS officer seeking political asylum in the West, which was granted in Paris in June 1977. His subsequent broadcasts on Radio Free Europe attacking the dictator ensured that he became a target for assassination. Although he escaped an attempt on his life in September 1978, another troublesome and vocal exile, Georgi Markov, who worked for the BBC World Service in London, was not so lucky and his memoirs had to be completed by his widow and published posthumously. Nor were these isolated incidents. Vladimir Simoneoff, another dissident who worked for the BBC in London, was found dead at his home in September 1978, apparently the victim of a fall. Once again, there was good reason to believe the DS had disguised a murder as a household accident.

Nicolae Ceauçescu was a despot in much the same Zhivkov mould who relied upon the notorious Securitate to maintain his grip on power, but rather lesser known was the Departmentul de Informatii Externe (DIE), its overseas counterpart, which monitored the activities of the regime's opponents abroad. The full extent of the DIE's operations remained unknown until its head, Lieutenant-General Ion Pacepa, defected in Bonn in July 1978. After three years of intensive debriefing by the CIA he was revealed to be the most senior Eastern Bloc intelligence officer ever to switch sides. However, unlike the Czech StB, which also concentrated its operations abroad, the Romanian DIE was never regarded as a serious threat to Western security, but merely to dissidents living in exile. Further evidence of Ceauçescu's paranoia, and his sensitivity to criticism from exiles, was presented by Colonel Matei Haidecu, who had been ordered to murder two troublesome dissidents based in Paris: Virgil Tanase, who had written a magazine article attacking the President and his wife, and Paul Goma, the author of *The Dogs of War*, in which he had described political repression in Bucharest. Rather than carry out his instructions Haidecu, who had acquired French citizenship, confessed to the French DST in April 1982 and surrendered a vial of poison concealed in a fountain pen that he had been supplied with to complete his assignment. With Haidecu's co-operation the DST organized an elaborate scheme with the dual intention of persuading the DIE that the colonel was still operational, thereby allowing his wife and children to travel to France, and of luring Pacepa's successor, General Nicolae Plesita, to the West. Ostensibly, Tanase was abducted by a gang of men in broad daylight, but in reality the journalist had allowed the DST to hide him in a safe-house in Brittany while Haidecu reported the success of his mission to Plesita, but premature press speculation about the bogus kidnapping forced the project to be aborted, leaving Haidecu to write a book, *I Refused to Kill*, which was published in France in 1984.

The combined effect of the revelations made by the DIE defectors was to undermine the grip on power of Ceauçescu's regime, and they may have hastened his fall. However, Romania's new security organization, the SRI, headed by Virgil Magureanu, is not unlike the notorious old Securitate. Magureanu was himself a career Securitate officer, and there have not been any prosecutions of the Securitate personnel responsible for Ceauçescu's twenty-five-year reign of terror.

In Czechoslovakia, the Statni tajna Bezpecnost, to give it the full title under which it existed until it was officially wound up in December 1989, was considered rather more sophisticated than the DIE and often acted as a surrogate for the KGB, running sophisticated spy-rings in Europe on behalf of the Soviets. The historically close relationship between Czech and Russian communists has been described by Joseph Heissler, a former agent who took British citizenship, adopted the name J. Bernard Hutton, and wrote a series of books based on his own investigations and experiences. Heissler warned continuously of the dangers of Soviet-inspired subversion, but it was not until Frantisek Tisler, an StB officer at the Czech embassy in Washington DC, started handing StB secrets out of his office window to his FBI contacts that the scale of his service's activities came to be recognized. Code-named Arago, Tisler tipped off the FBI to the existence of an important spy in London run by the local military attaché, Colonel Oldrich Prybl, and this led MI5 to a British traitor, Brian Linney, who was arrested and sentenced to fourteen years' imprisonment in July 1958. Two years later Tisler gave evidence before the House Un-American Activities Committee, the first insider to reveal the StB's secrets and expose it as a highly professional intelligence agency.

Tisler's testimony literally provided a window for the FBI into the StB, and he then disappeared into American society, which was already providing safe haven for another refugee from the Czech intelligence community, General Frantisek Moravec. Regarded for many years as a hero, a key figure in the Allied fight against the Nazis, when he was the Czech Director of Military Intelligence, and then a focus of dissent after his escape from Prague a fortnight after the communist coup of March 1948, Moravec has only recently been exposed as a Soviet mole. Although it is now confirmed that he worked as a Russian agent in London during the Second World War, the question that remains unanswered is for how long he maintained contact with his controllers afterwards, a subject that he omitted to address in his autobiography.

It was not until the brutal Soviet invasion in the summer of 1968 that clear evidence emerged of the scale of what the StB had accomplished, both at home and further afield. The collapse of the Dubček government and the suppression of the short-lived liberal era of the 'Prague spring' proved to be the catalyst for the defections of several key StB officers, three of whom subsequently wrote about their experiences. Ladislav Bittman was attached to the Czech embassy in Vienna when the Warsaw Pact tanks rolled into Prague, and he promptly sought political asylum in the United States, where he started an academic career. A year later he was followed by his colleagues Josef Frolik and Frantisek August. Together this latter pair were responsible for the identification of numerous StB assets in the West, particularly in England, and their achievements in the intelligence field were matched in the more overtly political arena by General Jan Sejna, the most senior Warsaw Pact military commander ever to defect. His authoritative account of Soviet hegemony had a significant political impact, particularly on those who had been inclined to interpret the period of détente as proof of change in the Kremlin's strategy of world domination. According to Sejna, Soviet Bloc communism's ultimate goal had remained unchanged and peaceful co-existence was nothing more than an expedient sham. Sejna's defection was a considerable propaganda coup for the West, and may have influenced Vaclav Havel, who almost completely dismanted the StB after the velvet revolution. The new playwright president installed another dissident, Jan Langos, as Minister of the Interior and he created a new agency, the FBIS, employing staff trained in the West. Significantly, the FBIS has retained only thirty former StB officers. Following the country's division, in December 1992, Slovakia has built its own intelligence service, headed by Igor Cibula.

The defection of Orlando Hidalgo from the Cuban embassy in Paris in March 1970 inflicted similar damage on the Cuban Direccion General de Inteligencia (DGI). Hidalgo boasted that he had exposed more than 150 DGI officers and agents and he certainly provided the CIA with a detailed breakdown of the organization's internal structure which did much to compromise operations that, hitherto, had maintained an impressively high degree of security.

Of all the members of the Soviet Bloc, the weakest link has consistently been the Polish Urzad Bezpieczenstwa (UB), which has been dogged by numerous defections over a long period. Among the first was General

Izyador Modelski, a former military attaché who gave evidence to the House Un-American Activities Committee in 1949. He was followed by Colonel Pawel Monat, who had also operated under military attaché cover and accepted political asylum in Vienna in June 1959. Whereas Modelski never wrote his memoirs, Monat gave a full account of his work in *Spy in the US*. The appearance of Michal Goleniewski in Berlin the following December was probably even more valuable for the CIA for, as well as being a senior UB officer, he revealed that he had also worked undercover for the KGB and therefore had enjoyed access to many secrets belonging to both organizations. Goleniewski, who betrayed the existence of the Portland spy-ring in England to prove his *bona fides* before his defection, did not write a book himself, but he was the subject of a biography which was prompted by his claim to be a direct descendant of the Russian Czar. In the same year that Goleniewski defected, another UB officer, Adam J. Galanski, gave evidence before the House Un-American Activities Committee, and in 1966 Wladyslaw Tykocinski, who had until a few months earlier been the head of the Polish Military Mission in Berlin, testified before a congressional committee. Although not a member of the UB himself, Tykocinski's knowledge was extensive.

In February 1967 Janus Kochanski, a UB officer with the rank of lieutenant-colonel, defected in Copenhagen and released his story, written with an American journalist, calling himself Mr X. The blow felt hardest by the UB, however, was the loss of the Polish ambassador in Tokyo, Zdzislaw M. Rurarz, who defected in December 1981, motivated by the sudden imposition of martial law, and when he was debriefed by the CIA he revealed that thoughout his diplomatic career he had worked as an informant for the UB, as he confirmed in *An Ambassador Speaks*.

Rurarz's defection had a profound impact on General Jaruzelski and on public opinion in the West, but the betrayal which hit the communist president hardest was that of Colonel Ryszard Kuklinski, the senior military staff officer who spied for the CIA for a decade until his exfiltration in November 1981. 'He knew the secrets of the kitchen,' said Jaruzelski:

> I had full confidence in him. His lifestyle, behaviour and manners gave no hint that he . . . could be a spy. I even liked him. So what occurred was a double disappointment for me, first of all because of the military and political consequences, and secondly because of my personal disappointment: someone you trust is betraying you.

Even after the fall of communism and the introduction of democracy, Kuklinski's conviction and death sentence, for having turned over film copies of more than 30,000 Soviet documents to the CIA, are maintained and his motives continue to be the subject of much public debate in Warsaw. The CIA awarded him the Distinguished Intelligence Medal, a rare honour, but Aleksandr Bentkowski, the Minister of Justice in Lech Walesa's government, condemned him: 'Despite the fact that Poland was then an unjust state, it remained our motherland. There are certain army principles which cannot be ignored.' The Defence Minister, Janusz Onyszkiewicz, also acknowledges the dilemma: 'Maybe he was motivated by some noble motives, but he should not be seen as somebody who should have a monument.' Since Kuklinski's defection the Polish external intelligence service has undergone considerable change, most recently under the leadership of Gromek Chuimpinski, and has developed close links with its Western counterparts.

Like the Polish UB, the East German Hauptverwaltung für Aufklarung (HVA) maintained the closest of ties to the KGB, but it enjoyed rather better security, with only a single example of Markus Wolf's officers defecting to the West and writing a book. That accolade goes to Werner Stiller, who collaborated with the Federal Republic's BND for two years before escaping in January 1979 to produce *Beyond the Wall*, which was published rather more than thirteen years later.

Although the Hungarian Allami Vedelmi Hatosag (AVH) is also known to have had a liaison relationship with the KGB, it was not, according to Laszlo Szabo, completely in the pocket of the Soviets and it invariably exercised an unusual degree of independence. Szabo, who had served in London under second secretary cover until 1965, gave evidence to the US House Committee on the Armed Forces in 1966 and is believed to be the most senior AVH officer ever to defect. Although Szabo's fellow Hungarian, George Mikes, was not a member of the intelligence establishment, he did base his book on files removed from the headquarters of the secret police during the uprising, and as well as being a damning exposé of the organization's activities, it represents the only significant literature of its kind.

As a somewhat freer regime and economy than other Soviet satellites, Hungary has been relatively free of high-ranking defectors during the postwar era. The moment the situation changed was towards the end of the Vietnam War, when a senior member of the International Commission supervising the ceasefire negotiations between the Vietcong and the Republic of South Vietnam, who happened to be Hungarian, took the opportunity to defect to the CIA Station Chief in Saigon, Tom Polgar, who was himself of Hungarian extraction. That unpublicized episode had been preceded by the application for political asylum made in May 1967 by Janos Radvanyi, the Hungarian chargé d'affaires to Washington DC. A professional diplomat who had acted as an intermediary between Hanoi and the Americans, Radvanyi realized that his Foreign Minister, Janos Péter, was more interested in serving Moscow's interests than in finding a formula for peace in south-east Asia. As he described in his 1978 memoirs, which concentrated on his role as a go-between, this discovery obliged Radvanyi to resign his post and alert Dean Rusk to the lack of authority from Hanoi for Péter's misleading offer of a temporary ceasefire. After his defection Radvanyi was resettled in California, and was later appointed professor of history at Mississippi State University. Radvanyi's intervention served to disillusion the US State Department, which hitherto had been convinced that the Soviet Politburo had been acting as an honest broker. Although Radvanyi's book is largely a scholarly analysis of the conflict and the peace process, it does shed light on how a diplomat, once described as 'someone sent abroad to lie for his country', coped with the challenge to his personal integrity, and placed political considerations in second place.

Since Radvanyi's defection Hungary has undergone a transformation, and its intelligence service, now run by Kalman Kocsis, who had previously operated as the AVH station chief in Athens, works closely with its old adversaries in the West.

Of course, the individuals mentioned here are by no means the only dissidents to publish books critical of the regimes in their home countries, but the difference between them is in both the level of risk involved and the actual impact of each on the respective regime. It is now known that Ion Pacepa's defection was seen by Nicolae Ceauçescu as an intensely personal betrayal of the tyrant's family, and quite apart from the damage his information did to the DIE, his decision to speak out and publish a devastating critique of the dictator and his entourage placed the author in considerable jeopardy. Most of the Soviet Bloc defectors have undergone the full resettlement programme, adopting a new identity and starting completely afresh with a set of rigid rules concerning personal protection. The StB defector Josef Frolik, for example, has completely dropped from sight since the publication of his memoirs, and even the establishment of a democratic government in the new Czech Republic has not persuaded him to emerge from hiding. As the Bulgarian DS demonstrated very publicly on several occasions, the danger of retribution is far from imagined. It is believed to have been behind the murder of a Bulgarian rocket technician in Vienna and the mysterious death of the editor of an émigré newspaper.

Doubt still surrounds the Bulgarian connections of Mehmet Ali Agca, the Turkish terrorist who shot Pope John Paul II in May 1981, the incident which led to the arrest of Sergei Antonov, the senior DS officer in Rome, who had been masquerading as manager of the Bulgarian state airline offices. According to Colonel Stefan Svredlev, a high-ranking Bulgarian police officer who defected in 1971, the DS has always been willing to perform deniable killings for the KGB, which is an opinion that has subsequently been confirmed by the FCD's Oleg D. Kalugin. Even in the supposedly civilized and safe environments of Paris or London, the fear of retribution was very real indeed for those who dared to irritate the hard men of the Soviet Bloc.

Vladimir Kostov

Until the 1960s, the DS had considered every émigré to be an enemy of the Communist regime, a 'traitor to the Socialist Party', an 'enemy of peace'.

After graduating in literature from the University of Sofia Vladimir Kostov was active in the communist youth movement and was quickly appointed head of a propaganda section based in Sofia. He was granted full membership of the Party in 1956 and the following year joined the communist daily *Rabotnichesko Dela* as a journalist.

Four years later, in January 1962, Kostov was sent to Paris as the newspaper's local correspondent and he remained in France until December 1964 when he returned to Sofia. During this period, when he was exposed to life in the West, Kostov began to experience a conversion. 'We kept finding ourselves faced with events, circumstances and attitudes born of the policies of the regime, which seemed quite unacceptable to us.' In 1966 he joined the editorial staff of a new magazine, *Pogled*, to write an international column, and this brought him into closer contact with the DS, for whom he worked on an occasional basis. In March his recruitment as an informer was completed and he began to travel abroad extensively, and wrote three books.

In June 1967 he toured the Middle East during the Six Day War and the following year he was interviewed by the head of the DS, General Dimitar Stoyanov, and asked to join the DS as an undercover intelligence officer. One of his first assignments was to Czechoslovakia, to report on Dubček's Prague spring, and thereafter he continued to work as a roving reporter. In 1973 he wrote a book on the Yom Kippur War, and in April 1974 he was posted to Paris for Bulgarian radio and television. In reality he was working for the local DS *rezident*, Colonel Dimo Stankov.

Finally, in June 1977, Kostov applied for political asylum in Paris together with his wife, Natalya, and his two teenage children, Clement and Maya. Their decision had been prompted by Todor Zhivkov's recent visit to Moscow to sign a secret agreement with Leonid Brezhnev. In Kostov's view, 'it amounted to making more active, by every possible means, the process of Russification and Sovietisation of Bulgaria'.

Just over a year later, after he had started broadcasting from Radio Free Europe, he was stabbed in a Paris métro station and suffered a cardiovascular collapse. It was later established that he had been injected with the deadly toxin ricin and he had been extremely lucky to survive. In this extract he demonstrates why the DS was so anxious to stop him haemorrhaging its secrets to his Western debriefers.

The Bulgarian Umbrella

The Bulgarian Embassy in Paris was, in fact, nothing else but an annexe of the Soviet Embassy. From the earliest days of the establishment in power of communist regimes in its satellites, Moscow had made use of them on the international scene as 'errand boys'. And yet the style of the relationship between the Bulgarian and the Russian Embassies had something special about it and, in a certain sense, something new. Was it the involvement (thanks to the agreed practices of 'organic integration' between the two countries) of all of the chief Bulgarian officials in this coordination which amounted, in fact, to placing themselves directly at the service of the Soviets? Was it the cynicism with which the Bulgarian leaders (Ambassador Athanassov was only copying the behaviour of Zhivkov and other Party bosses) paraded their subservience to the Soviets to whom they had made a gift not only of the Bulgarian Communist Party, but also of the Bulgarian state? Or was it a consequence of the mobilisation the Soviets had already set in motion for the decisive attack against the West, scheduled to take place in the course of the next twenty or thirty years?

The beginning of 1977 saw the start of the preparations for a 'great Bulgarian initiative': the International Writers Conference. The decision to hold this conference had been taken two years earlier in Moscow. The KGB wanted new ground for contacts and, above all, to find 'new faces'.

Bulgaria seemed to be the ideal sponsor country for such an event. Moscow kept in the background: echoes from the publication of Solzhenitsyn's *Gulag Archipelago* had not yet died away. And again, the Bulgarian migrations to the West had not caused the same stir as those from Poland, Czechoslovakia and Hungary. There was consequently less of a risk in our country of such an initiative being attacked head on.

Another detail of some importance: the Union of Bulgarian Writers had been for many years a tried and tested 'cover' for the activities of the DS.

The preparations for the International Writers Conference began badly in France. French writers who had been invited by the Bulgarian Embassy to take part, had declined. The Ambassador and the Resident of the DS sent off frantic telegrams to Sofia: if we do not succeed in securing a suitable French representation should we alter the conditions?

One of the members of the Central Committee of the Communist Party, a leading member of the Bulgarian Writers Union, came to Paris. He lectured the Embassy people for their defeatism and declared, tapping his briefcase: 'I have in here all I need to be sure of French representation at the Conference in Sofia: money, publication contracts, free air tickets, invitations for Black Sea holidays – absolutely everything!'

He was right. The obstacle of 'this impossible task' was soon overcome and a 'French delegation' was quickly formed.

Perhaps this had happened in the most perfectly natural manner possible. Had each member of the delegation found, in this conference, a personal interest, in sympathy with the noble ideals of the struggle for peace, for amity between peoples, etc.? I merely testify to the way in which things were seen from the Bulgarian side.

Western intellectuals forget that relations with Eastern bloc countries are established on a rather special basis: in the West, writers, journalists, research workers, work independently; in the East, state employees – wearing different 'hats', as journalists, writers, poets – are under the guidance, in the first place, of the directives they receive *as employees*. Among these people, in their various occupations, are the more or less discreet 'invisible' DS agents. Western representatives never have either the means or the common viewpoint of their counterparts in the East. For this reason they are often 'innocents' in the concerns which interest Moscow most – the establishment of confidential relations with certain Westerners.

Shall we try to imagine how many French writers would have accepted an assignment, however harmless, to work for the French Intelligence Service? I am not speaking of war-time or of some other exceptional situation. Every single French writer would shy away from having anything to do with the everyday routine work of that Service and say: 'You do your own dirty work!' French writers are not answerable to the Intelligence Service nor even to the French state except within the limits of their duties as citizens. But which Bulgarian writer would take it on himself to refuse a mission for the DS? I would not give much for his chances of foreign travel or of having a book published after such a refusal. How can one compel private individuals to seek a *quid pro quo* when the state does not feel inclined to offer it?

In 1977, there were five accredited Bulgarian journalists resident in Paris. Four of them were affiliated DS collaborators. The fifth would on no account whatsoever have refused to cooperate. How many French journalists were there on assignment in Sofia? Not one – except for the correspondent of *Humanité*, who was being 'looked after' by the Central Committee of the Bulgarian Communist Party. How can one explain such a difference? Can one possibly suppose that France was deriving some sort of profit from a similar reciprocal arrangement?

Naturally, each of the Bulgarian journalists was renting a flat in Paris. Each of them went shopping, partly in the French markets. Was the image of France and French life better presented to the Bulgarian public? In spite of its five journalists in Paris the situation remained the same as it was when there was only one, as had been the case until 1961: the Bulgarian press, radio and television authorities decided that the coverage to be given to French affairs should correspond to the Soviet model – in content and quantity.

One may well believe that the French press does not think it necessary to post a permanent correspondent in Bulgaria when there are few, if any, events that take place there of any interest to the French public. That is very possible. But why does the French government permit a group of DS collaborators to settle in France and work there with complete impunity without some reciprocal arrangement?

In 1984 one of the correspondents of the France-Presse Agency in Vienna was accredited to the Bulgarian Ministry of Foreign Affairs in his capacity as the Agency correspondent. In September he travelled to Bulgaria. There he learnt that, early that month, a number of terrorist attacks had taken place. After verifying his sources and receiving assurance that it was not a question of false rumours, he published an article on the subject.

His article was the first news account to appear in the world press on the terrorist attacks in the first days of September 1984 in Bulgaria. Thanks to this correspondent of the France-Presse Agency, the whole world learnt that events of a serious nature had taken place in Bulgaria. The Bulgarian authorities remained silent. Two weeks later a first semi-confirmation was issued by the Bulgarian Telegraphic Agency (BTA) – but only for publication in the West. Two months later, the France-Presse Agency news item was fully confirmed – again exclusively for Western consumption. Confirmation on this occasion came from the Vice-President of the Council of Ministers acting in his personal capacity. The Bulgarian public was indirectly informed in the following spring. The Bulgarian National Assembly adopted measures against terrorism, and the Public Prosecutor acknowledged in the press that such incidents had taken place in the country; hence the new repressive measures.

What were the consequences for the correspondent of the France-Press Agency? His accreditation was cancelled. He was henceforth banned from entering Bulgaria because 'he had libelled socialist reality'. To have supplied an item of news recognised by the highest authority as a true account of what had taken place amounted to 'libel'!

What was the reaction of the French authorities? Did the French Embassy in Sofia protest? I saw nothing in the press on the subject. On the other hand, in the Bulgarian newspapers one could confirm that Bulgarian journalists, accredited to Paris, calmly continued their work without harrassment of any kind.

Georgi Markov

Had I possessed real national courage and integrity, its most logical expression would have been to remain in Bulgaria and to attempt to struggle there, as do far braver and more honest people than I.

The son of an officer in the Bulgarian army and born in 1929 in Sofia, Georgi Markov was a successful novelist and playwright in his own country before he defected to Italy in June 1969 and took up residence in London in 1971. He studied chemical engineering and published his first novel, *Men*, in 1963. During the following seven years his novels and plays were received with official approval but after the invasion of Czechoslovakia Markov's attitude changed and he was summoned by the Party's Cultural Committee to explain his new satirical play, *The Man Who Was Me*. Instead of attending the meeting Markov fled to Bologna where, in 1974, his brother Nikola also defected. Nikola later moved to the United States.

Using the pseudonym David St George, together with his co-author David Phillips, Georgi Markov wrote a political satire, *The Right Honourable Chimpanzee*, in 1978 and his broadcasts for Radio Free Europe in Munich were considered sufficiently damaging by the Bulgarian dictator Todor Zhivkov for him personally to order the author's assassination. In September 1978, while walking to the BBC (where he worked as a culture correspondent), he was stabbed in the leg as he crossed Waterloo Bridge by a pellet gun concealed inside an umbrella. A tiny pellet, visible only under a powerful microscope and made of a rare platinum and irridium alloy containing traces of ricin, was later recovered from a wound, but he died in hospital four days later. According to Colonel Stefan Svredlev, a DIE officer who defected in 1971, the agency compiled lists of seventeen different categories of suspect Bulgarians, and Markov's death conformed to the pattern of executions carried out by the DIE's hitmen.

> From my own experience I know of cases of kidnapping and murder of Bulgarian exiles abroad by the state security. The organisation that killed Georgi Markov was the Bulgarian state security. And, from my experience, the assassin would have been someone sent from Bulgaria. In that way it's much easier to conceal all the clues in the crime.

Later in 1989 Zhivkov was arrested, and a lengthy investigation into Markov's death was launched by Leonid Katzamunski, the head of the new government's investigation department. In October 1993 General Oleg D. Kalugin, a former KGB counter-intelligence expert who had boasted of having supervised the DIE operation, was briefly detained in London and interrogated about his knowledge of the murder. As yet, no one has been charged with Markov's murder. In this passage from his autobiography, Markov describes the events that led to him crossing the Yugoslav frontier by car.

The Truth that Killed

It was Sunday, 15 June 1969 – according to the astrologers a fateful year for those born under the sign of Pisces. At eleven-thirty in the morning at the State Theatre of Satire in Sofia, the preview of my play *The Man Who Was Me* was just beginning. At eleven-thirty that evening, I was at the Hotel Excelsior in Belgrade. One of the fundamental principles according to which all my plays were constructed was that they consisted of only two acts, with the second act invariably negating the first. After all that has happened since, I can say that these twelve hours were not the divide between two different plays, but were simply the end of the first and the beginning of the second acts of one and the same play: a play I would define as a 'contemporary tragi-comedy with farcical interludes'. Put more simply, it was one of those plays where the spectator often 'does not know whether to laugh or to cry'.

In spite of the long journey and the tense hours which had preceded it, I did not feel tired on my arrival in Belgrade. My agitation, compounded by the events of the morning, the parting from those dearest to me, and the strange last drive through Sofia, had been replaced by a large question-mark about what was to follow.

It was not the fate of my play at the Satire Theatre which concerned me. For me, as for everyone else, it had been obvious that it would be banned. After all, the theatre belonged to *them*. The crux of the matter was that I had never been able (despite my attempts) to identify with *them*. I had always felt with compelling clarity what was *mine* and what was *theirs*. Moreover, this difference often seemed to approach the mutual exclusion of fire and water, with only two possible alternatives resulting from their forced union – either the fire would be extinguished or the water would evaporate.

The preview of my play before a restricted invited audience had been planned by the theatre management with two aims in view – to sound out the authorities and to seek the public's support. The director was Metodi Andonov, while the producer, Neicho Popov, had come out of hospital especially to watch our performance. Poor Neicho, he still believed it was possible to create an honest, hard-hitting satire without offending a regime which had always been against any fundamental criticism. For me, and I think for Metodi too, there were no illusions. Of all the principles that any form of art can follow, the least valid is that which, in the words of the Bulgarian proverb, wants to have both 'the wolf replete and the lamb intact'. Indeed all great literature, like all great art, has always been based on the principle of clear choice: either the wolf or the lamb.

The audience's reaction exceeded our most optimistic expectations. The actor Partsalev was magnificent and the theatre echoed with laughter. But the funnier the first act became, the gloomier looked certain faces in the hall. During the interval a well-known colonel in the State Security pushed his way towards me.

'Why have you written such a Czech play?' he said.

I retorted that the play was Bulgarian and moved on. Then came Stefan Tsanev, one of the theatre's playwrights, who told me that there would be a special meeting of the theatre council after the performance, which would include the members of its Communist committee, to decide the fate of the production. I told him that I did not wish to attend the meeting, as I had a pretty good idea of the way things would go. I asked him to represent me. The final curtain was greeted by enthusiastic applause from the audience.

Outside on the pavement, my father, who had watched the performance, said to me: 'This play will bring you nothing but trouble!'

I went to have lunch at the Russian Club. Three months earlier, I had obtained a passport and a visa for Italy, but I had been putting off my departure because of the play. Nevertheless, I had decided that one of these days I would leave. At about two-thirty, Stefan came over from the council meeting to say that things had gone very badly. The play was being taken off for the time being. He looked depressed but sounded resigned. Then one of my more important friends arrived at the Club. He took me aside and asked: 'Are your passport and visa in order?'

'Yes', I replied.

'Then I advise you to go immediately. I think you might find yourself in trouble tomorrow because of today's performance and then you might not be able to travel. Stay away for a month or two – until it all blows over.'

I went home to pack some things. My father and mother saw me to the car. I told them that we would see each other again in a few weeks. And then I left. When I reached the ring-road, the clouds had cleared after a downpour of summer rain, and the sky above Vitosha and the lovely verdant landscape shone with sunlight. On a sudden impulse I decided that instead of taking the direct route out of the city, I would drive around the whole of Sofia on the ring-road. The car sped along the drying asphalt and everything around me seemed strange and inexpressibly beautiful. Mercilessly beautiful. It was as if nature had decided to show me the priceless riches of a country that I was destined to lose. Perhaps men condemned to death meet the last sunrise with the same cruelly persistent feeling of seeing everything for the last time.

'Look! You will never again set eyes on this land, this nature!' cried a fierce voice within me.

As yet I hadn't decided on anything. One of the few lessons life had taught me was not to take preliminary decisions, but to let things follow their own natural course. This time, however, as I drove around Sofia, I felt that the decision had already been taken – by the angels or the devils who determined my fate.

Towards six-thirty I reached the frontier. All the railway and customs officials were huddled round the television set watching the World Cup match between Bulgaria and Poland. The officer on duty recognized me and very politely invited me to join them. I made some excuse about being in a hurry. Then, on the other side of the Yugoslav barrier, I stopped by a meadow. I looked back towards Bulgaria and it seemed to me that even its natural beauty sharpened the feeling of how unbearable it was to have to live the ugly life which I and many others like me were forced to endure. It was as if nature, history and the national spirit had established a very precise standard for judging the beautiful and the ugly. I felt that I could no longer bear the atmosphere in which I lived, the work I did, the relationships in which I found myself ensnared. I had a sense of the unbearable about the outside world as well as about myself. I realized that for many years I had been unable to enjoy anything, that everything was not only poisoned in advance, but doomed to be poisoned by this sense of the unbearable. If you have entertained a certain idea of yourself, if you have imagined that you are one thing and discover that slowly but inexorably you are being turned into quite another, then the moment is likely to come when you want to smash either the mirror or your own head. In a purely moral sense, this was a feeling of two-fold treachery – towards others and towards myself. Quite apart from morals, it was a sense of an impasse.

Walking the Belgrade streets at night, I reflected that it really was impossible for me to stay in Bulgaria and remain myself. The very act of living in the country represented an endless chain of compromises. Even the struggle against compromise was not without compromise. The relationship between the individual and society was almost negligible. And it seemed to me that the ancient rule according to which man gradually acquires the features of the thing he is fighting against functioned faultlessly. More and more often I discovered in myself (even if they were directed the opposite way) the same elements of primitiveness, instinctiveness, indifference and even ruthlessness that were typical of those I hated. Unlike many others who realized that the same thing was happening to them, but believed that it was temporary, that things would get better, I had no illusions whatsoever that things could improve where I was concerned. Perhaps my feeling was more selfish, perhaps I was too preoccupied with the division in my own mind.

Ion Pacepa

The Western intelligence community was later in agreement that the DIE had become the first espionage service in history to have been entirely destroyed by the defection of a single man.

The most senior intelligence officer ever to defect from the Warsaw Pact, Lieutenant-General Pacepa had headed Nicolae Ceauçescu's feared DIE until he was granted political asylum by the United States at the end of July 1978. Prior to that date, his organization had not been immune to defection. Among his subordinates who had fled to the West had been Ion Iacobescu, based under UNESCO cover in Paris, in 1969; Constantin Dumitrachescu, the Tel Aviv station chief, in 1972; Constantin Rauta, a DIE engineer who went to the CIA in 1973; Virgil Tipanudt, who defected in Copenhagen in June 1975; and Colonel Ion Marcu, who had managed to move his entire family from Tehran, where he had been based under commercial cover, to Canada in 1977.

After Pacepa's defection, which was entirely unexpected, his wife and daughter were placed under intensive surveillance in Bucharest. Only after the revolution of December 1989 did his daughter Dana choose to join her father in the United States. Pacepa has been sentenced to death *in absentia* and remains liable to arrest under the current regime. According to rumours circulating in Bucharest, Pacepa is suspected of having been a CIA agent for many years, possibly since his period in Germany when his recruitment is believed to have taken place.

Among Pacepa's revelations was the DIE's recruitment of Yasser Arafat's intelligence chief, Hani Hassan, who was assigned the code-name Annette in 1976 and thereafter ensured that the PLO enjoyed the closest relationship with the DIE. The purge that followed his defection involved the replacement of twenty-two ambassadors and the dismissal and disappearance of more than two dozen senior Securitate officers. The extent of the damage inflicted by Pacepa's disclosures can be judged from this vignette of life under Ceauçescu, taken from his 1987 autobiography.

Red Horizons

To the ordinary Romanian people, the word *nomenclatura* means the elite, a social superstructure recognizable by its privileges. *Nomenclatura* people do not travel by bus or streetcar. They use government cars. The color and make of the car indicate its owner's status in the hierarchy: the darker the color, the higher the position. White Dacias are for directors, pastel colors for deputy ministers, black for ministers; black Audis for Nicu; black Mercedes for the prime minister and his deputies; and black Mercedes 600, Cadillac, and Rolls-Royce limousines for Ceausescu. *Nomenclatura* people do not live in apartment buildings constructed under the Communist regime. As I did, they get nationalized villas or luxury apartments that previously belonged to the capitalists. *Nomenclatura* people are not seen standing in line to buy food or other necessities. They have their own stores, and black car people can even order by telephone for home delivery. *Nomenclatura* people are not seen in normal restaurants fighting for a table or listening to a disagreeable waiter saying, 'If you don't like it, stay home.' They have their own special restaurants, and they can even go to the ones for Western tourists. During the summer, *nomenclatura* people are not seen on Bucharest's crowded, sweaty public beaches. They either go to special bathing areas or have weekend villas in

Snagov, a resort located 25 miles outside Bucharest. *Nomenclatura* people do not spend their vacations packed like sardines into Soviet-style colonies. They have their own vacation homes.

The darker the car, the closer the house is to Ceausescu's vacation residence, and black car people also get cooks and servants. They do not stand in line outside Soviet-style polyclinics, where treatment is free but you are yelled at by everyone from the doorman on up and may not spend more than 15 minutes with the doctor, who has to see at least 30 patients in his eight-hour shift. They do not go to the regular hospitals, where people may have to double up two to a bed. They have the luxurious, Western-style Hellias hospital, built as a private foundation in the days before Communism.

The microphone coverage on top members of the *nomenclatura* is without doubt the best kept secret in the Soviet bloc. 'For us, only Comrade Brezhnev is tabu,' KGB Chairman Yuri Andropov told me when I was visiting Moscow in 1972. 'Keeping a close watch on our *nomenclatura* is the KGB's most delicate task. Take Shchelokov, for example.' General Nikolay Shchelokov was the Soviet minister of interior. 'We all respect him, but through the microphones we learned that he was drinking too much. I reported it, and Comrade Brezhnev is now trying to help him. The same thing happened with Ustinov.' Marshal Dmitry Ustinov was the Soviet minister of defense.

The KGB's *nomenclatura* coverage is imitated throughout the whole Soviet bloc. Every East European country has its own top secret 'Iosif's unit', where a faceless army of little security people record everything for the supreme leader, even the way a *nomenclatura* man moans when he is making love.

Frantisek Moravec

When the USSR was attacked by the Nazis in 1941 the Soviet military attaché in London visited me at once and very politely, almost humbly, asked me for information which would be of interest to his government. I consulted my British friends, who agreed on condition that I inform them of everything I gave to the Russians.

Born into the Austro-Hungarian Empire, Moravec was decorated for gallantry during the First World War and in January 1916 distinguished himself by leading his platoon over to the Russian lines and surrendering. He then fought with the Russians on the Bulgarian front, where he was wounded. Once recovered, he was evacuated via Vladivostok to fight at Verdun, and was sent to Greece to defend Salonika. At the end of the war his unit was near Venice, and when Czechoslovakia was created Moravec accompanied President Tomas Masaryk to Prague.

Moravec remained in the new Czech army and in 1928, having graduated from Prague's military college, he was assigned to intelligence duties. By the outbreak of the Second World War in 1939 he was Director of Military Intelligence, running some highly successful agents in Germany, among them the legendary A–54, but when the Nazis occupied Prague he fled to London where he became a significant figure in the Allied intelligence community.

After the Liberation Moravec remained in his post as DMI but when the communists staged a coup in March 1948, and after the murder of Jan Masaryk, he took his wife to London where his daughters were living. He later moved to the United States and died in 1966, aged seventy-one, while on his way to work in the Pentagon. His memoirs were released in 1975, having been completed by his daughter Hanyi Disher, and were published with a foreword written by Sir John Masterman, the wartime MI5 officer and chairman of the XX Committee.

After the collapse of the Soviet Bloc various former intelligence officers revealed that Moravec had worked for the NKVD, and this was confirmed by General Oleg Kalugin. As Moravec mentions in his autobiography, he had been in contact with the NKVD on an official level since the summer of 1936, when he visited Moscow, but the question was whether his overt relationship had developed into something more sinister. In this passage from *Master of Spies*, Moravec describes how he was instructed by Edvard Benes to cultivate an NKVD officer named Cicajev. This was probably Ivan A. Chichayev, and the question that remains is exactly how far Moravec allowed himself to come under the formidable Chichayev's control, and to what extent this liaison was approved or even sponsored by the British Security Service.

Master of Spies

When the USSR was attacked by the Nazis in 1941 the Soviet military attaché in London visited me at once and very politely, almost humbly, asked me for information which would be of interest to his government. I consulted my British friends, who agreed on condition that I inform them of everything I gave to the Russians.

Later that year there appeared in London another representative of Soviet Intelligence. His name was Cicajev and he was obviously a NKVD man (later KGB). He too began our co-operation in a suppliant mood. Russia was losing.

But our co-operation with Soviet Intelligence was always unilateral; we were giving information and receiving only requests. There was no real Intelligence co-operation between West and East. For instance, no Intelligence collaboration existed between the British and the Soviets in practice; they did not exchange even information which was important for the co-ordinated conduct of the war, a state of affairs injurious to the common cause, and therefore also to us. When I reported this to Benes he ordered me to transmit to the Soviets in future even information gained from our other Allies. Thus, according to Benes, we would show the Soviet Union more than good will. Among such transmitted Intelligence was much that had, or could have had, a really serious impact on the outcome of war, not counting the mass of important daily reports.

It is ironical that it was our detailed report on Stalingrad which made the Russians' first victory possible, because it was this event which brought to an end the first, or 'friendly', stage of Intelligence co-operation between us. Naturally there was a transitional period between the soft-glove approach of the first stage and the no-holds-barred of the second. We were still needed. But the forewarning of things to come was there, although it went unheeded except by a few.

After Stalingrad the Soviet smiles faded. As the Russian military situation improved Cicajev's attitude changed completely. Whereas before he had come to me every day and thanked me for whatever he received, he now became critical, imperious and even threatening. Although we were giving him all the Intelligence reports at our disposal, he was never satisfied, always asking for more and often categorically demanding information which there was no possibility of our getting. He was no longer fastidious about interfering in our internal affairs. He criticised the activity of our underground, demanded its intensification into open guerrilla warfare and could not be persuaded that conditions in Bohemia and Moravia were simply not suitable for it.

Some months after the assassination of Heydrich, Cicajev came to me with a demand that we organise a massive sabotage action at our Skoda works in Pilsen where, as he pointed out with a sneer, Czech workers were obediently and efficiently manufacturing arms later used by the Germans to kill the soldiers of the Red Army. The sabotage operation, said Cicajev, should be on a scale to bring the huge Skoda factory to a stop for a considerable time.

I told him that as a small nation we could not afford such an action. The German reprisals would far surpass the sacrifice extorted as the price of Heydrich's life.

'How much did Heydrich cost you?' Cicajev asked.

'Five thousand of our best,' I replied.

'And the Skoda works are worth 20,000,' said Cicajev.

In vain I explained that such losses would be unbearable for our nation, that the Germans intentionally chose our best people for execution. Cicajev's retort was that the peace-time agriculture reforms cost the Soviet Union several million lives and that the present war, up to now, had cost as many more. What was 20,000 people in a struggle of such dimensions?

Finally I asked Cicajev why the Soviet underground did not carry out something of what he was proposing to me in the munitions factory of Odessa, the Black Sea port then occupied by the Germans. I told him I had reports that in Odessa Soviet engineers and workers were also industrious, producing, under the supervision of the Gestapo, weapons with which Red Army soldiers were being killed. To this Cicajev said not a word, and left in injured silence.

At the time of President Benes's visit to Moscow at the end of 1943, the Soviet armies were at Rostov. In 1943, we managed to have several secret transmitter contacts in Bohemia, Moravia and Slovakia. They were well-placed and produced good political and military information. One day, shortly after the President's return (January 1944), Cicajev came to me and demanded, on behalf of his superiors, all the necessary technical data which would enable the Russians to get into direct contact with our sources at home.

I was so surprised that for a moment I was unable to speak. When I recovered my composure I told him that such a great decision was not mine to make, but was up to President Benes. I informed Benes, who was not as surprised as I was but nevertheless instructed me to reject the demand. I did so, making excuses about 'technical difficulties'. Cicajev then approached Benes directly. The President told him he 'agreed in principle' then diplomatically referred him to me to make a decision in the matter.

This incident showed clearly what we could expect from the victorious Soviets after the war. But my efforts to convince Benes that we could not trust them were in vain.

Joseph Heissler

*I personally received extensive schooling during my four years'
stay in Russia and whilst I was there, as well as later on,
obtained first-hand knowledge on the complete structure,
recruiting and training of the Soviet Secret Service.*

Born in Chrast, Czechoslovakia in July 1911 and educated in Germany, where he
lived until 1933 when he was forced to return home by the Nazis, Joseph Heissler
was a member of the Central Committee of the Czech Communist Party, and on
the editorial staff of Prague's communist daily, *Halo Noviny*. He was trained at
the Lenin School in Moscow and worked there as a foreign editor on the
Vecherniaya Moskva newspaper. In 1938 he fled Moscow, having been marked as
a dissident, and returned to Prague where he became an adviser to the Czech
government. However, in May 1939 he escaped to Poland where he made contact
with the British Committee for Refugees from Czechoslovakia, and made his way
to London. There he broadcast for the BBC and used the name Jan Cech to publish
Death Stalks the Forest, *Thirty Thousand Miles* and a play, *The Third Front*. He
won the Military Cross in 1943 and at the end of the war he was press and cultural
attaché at the embassy in London. When the Czech Foreign Minister Jan Masaryk
was murdered in March 1948 Heissler made his home in Sussex and took the
name Joe Bernard Hutton, under which he wrote more than twenty books,
including *Out of this World*, *Danger from Moscow*, *The Traitor Trade*, *Struggle
in the Dark*, *Healing Hands*, *Women Spies* and *Stalin: The Miraculous Georgian*.
The majority of his books dealt with the Soviet threat but, despite his own first-
hand experience, were of doubtful reliability. He was particularly preoccupied by
the case of Commander Lionel Crabb, the British diver who in April 1956
disappeared under the visiting Soviet cruiser, the *Ordzhonikidze*, in Portsmouth
harbour. Heissler wrote two books about this embarrassing incident, *Frogman
Extraordinary* in 1960, and *Commander Crabb is Alive* in 1968.

   In the first book Heissler claimed to have discovered a secret Soviet dossier,
typed in German, in which it was alleged that Crabb, who had been captured alive,
had admitted under interrogation to have been undertaking a clandestine survey
of the *Ordzhonikidze* on behalf of an American naval intelligence officer using the
convenient pseudonym of Mr Smith. In reality, although Heissler could not have
known it, Crabb had been supervised by two SIS officers, Bernard Smith and Ted
Davies, and Heissler had mistakenly assumed that these innocuous names must
have been false, which they were not. In his second account Heissler suggested that
Crabb had been given the name Lev Korablov and, until his purported death in
1962, had been an officer in the Soviet navy.

   Heissler worked for Thomson Newspapers as diplomatic correspondent until

1961 and then joined *Topic* magazine before returning to freelance writing and psychic research. In 1970 he published his autobiography, *The Great Illusion*. In this passage from *School for Spies*, a book in which he made a series of spurious claims regarding Soviet training camps for KGB agents, and fabricated some entirely bogus case histories of Soviet espionage, he gives an apparently authentic account of a non-existent KGB facility.

School for Spies

The most unique and unheard of school for Soviet spies is a specialised establishment known simply as Gaczyna.

It lies some hundred miles south-east of Kuibyshev, and the school grounds, covering an area of some 425 square miles, stretch along the south of the Tatar Autonomous Soviet Republic to the Bashkir Autonomous Soviet Republic.

Without a Secret Service permit no one can get near to Gaczyna, for the whole zone is guarded by crack State Security detachments who, from an outer ring thirty miles away, seal off the whole terrain.

Soviet Intelligence bosses take every precaution to blanket this top-secret establishment which does not appear on any map, and, to the peoples of Russia and the world, does not even exist.

Future Soviet spies – flown in special MVD aircraft to Gaczyna, knowing that for the next ten years they will be undergoing specialised training for service abroad – never even guess what type of institution this is. On arrival at Gaczyna, they find themselves in foreign surroundings.

And foreign is the only word. Gaczyna is the school in which future Secret Service agents for the English-speaking world are trained. To give each pupil the most thorough education in the English-speaking world, Gaczyna is divided as follows:

In the north-west; North American section.
In the north; Canadian section.
In the north-east; United Kingdom section.

In the southern part are the Australian, New Zealand, Indian and South African sections.

Each division forms an entirely independent zone and is completely separated from any of the other 'countries', for Moscow Secret Service Headquarters want each cadet spy from the start of his or her super-schooling at Gaczyna to live in the atmosphere of the country which, from then on, is to be their native one.

Though most newcomers to Gaczyna know hardly more of the English language than that which they have learned at school or during the language courses attended while on 'assessment duties' in Moscow, they are under orders to speak only the language of the chosen country, even if they can hardly make themselves understood.

Another equally strict order is that once and for all, they must forget their Russian identity. Instead, they change to their new identity. Russia's Secret Service bosses believe that after ten or more years a man's or woman's brain becomes completely accustomed to being the new person. Consequently they are convinced that even if any agents are ever caught by foreign counter-espionage, they would always stick to their adopted identity and would never give away who they really are, not even under torture, brainwashing or injections with truth drugs.

It has been proved that the Gaczyna schooling is successful. Not only do Soviet spies in all parts of the English-speaking world manage to be accepted as natives of the countries from which they claim to have come, but they also stick to their adopted identity when caught and questioned. Here again the recent Lonsdale case is a good example. When caught and questioned, and also throughout his trial at the Old Bailey, he continuously insisted that he was Gordon Lonsdale, although Scotland Yard's Special Branch had been able to establish that he is a Russian.

On their arrival at Gaczyna the students are at once taken to the 'country' for which the Selection Board of the Recruiting Division in Moscow has assigned them. For the duration of the ten years' schooling they never leave their sector.

Every division of Gaczyna is a true replica of streets, buildings, cinemas, restaurants and snack bars, public houses and other typical establishments in countries of the English-speaking world. Everyone is dressed in the clothes particular to these countries, and life in Gaczyna is in every respect true to style. The inhabitants occupy rooms in boarding houses or hotels, flats or houses which are identical to those in America, England and elsewhere. So, from the first day of their arrival they find themselves in typical Anglo-Saxon surroundings.

In order to keep to the normal conditions of life in each of the chosen countries, the male and female inhabitants of Gaczyna share the same hotels, flats and houses, and are no longer expected to avoid personal friendship, as had been the case in the Marx-Engels School, Gorky and at the Lenin Technical School, Verkhovnoye. But, when alone, they are still under strictest orders to speak English with each other. If ever an instructor or senior student overhears 'first formers' speaking Russian together, they are reported immediately for disobedience. Culprits are fined, and warned that another such occurrence will end their career.

The first five years for every newcomer to Gaczyna consist only of continuous tuition in the English language. They are not only taught grammar, the right construction of sentences, and special idioms, but great weight is also laid on pronunciation. They listen to tape-recorded BBC, CBC, NBC, and other broadcasts, and work on perfecting the language until they are fit to be passed as sons or daughters of the country from which they are supposed to originate.

All the language masters at Gaczyna are rigidly selected Communist Party members who have come from America, England, and other countries of the English-speaking world, and who have been entrusted as expert teachers at this extraordinary school for master spies since they first became Soviet citizens and thus broke off for ever all ties with their countries of birth.

They are, of course, by no means the only foreigners employed at Gaczyna. So that students may live in perfect Anglo-Saxon surroundings, waitresses, shop assistants, bus conductors, and people of many other professions, are also ex-citizens of the particular country. They too have been foreign Communists who became Soviet citizens and thus qualified for these special jobs. But they are all life-timers in Gaczyna because the Soviet Secret Service will not risk their talking. Even though most devoted Communist Party members, the Russians never fully trust their foreign comrades.

From the start, every newcomer is, so to speak, in the hands of genuine ex-citizens of the country of their 'adoption', and hears the right pronunciation, sentence construction and intonation, which is so vastly different from Russian intonation. Not only the actual language teachers, but also all the other born Anglo-Saxons are under strict orders to correct every student whenever he or she makes a mistake or pronounces a word badly.

Ladislav Bittman

There is not a single operation that would be unnoticed by the Soviets. They control the whole process of initiating, conducting intelligence operations, and getting the results.

Based at the Czech embassy in Vienna as the Soviets crushed Alexander Dubcek's liberal administration, Ladislav Bittman immediately sought and was granted political asylum. His status as a deception specialist with the Czech StB ensured that his information was highly prized by the CIA, which also received another StB defector, Captain Marous, almost simultaneously. The impact that the loss of this pair had on the Czech intelligence agency cannot be underestimated, for in the Federal Republic of Germany its principal network began to self-destruct in anticipation of arrest. Rear-Admiral Hermann Luedke, SHAPE's logistics chief, shot himself, and the next day the BND Deputy Chief, Horst Wendland, committed suicide in his office. A few days later Hans Schenke of the Ministry of Economics hanged himself, as did Colonel Johann Grimm of the Ministry of Defence. Finally, Gerhard Boehm, also of the Ministry of Defence, was found drowned in the Rhine near Cologne. All had been implicated in an extensive spy-ring run by the StB and had feared exposure. The one member to be caught and imprisoned was Alfred Frenzel, of the Ministry of Foreign Affairs, who was sentenced to seventeen years' imprisonment.

Bittman was resettled in the United States, where he became an academic, using the name Dr Lawrence Britts. In 1971 he emerged to give testimony to the Senate Judiciary Committee and the following year his book *The Deception Game* was published. In 1985 he returned to the same subject with *The KGB and Soviet Disinformation*, and he now lectures on the American university circuit under the name Dr Lawrence Martin. He remains sensitive to the ethics of espionage, as is clear from this passage.

The Deception Game

The ethics of special operations is closely entwined with the ethics of intelligence work in general in which Communist-bloc intelligence agencies do not differ significantly from their Western counterparts. The activities of every intelligence agency are amoral because they involve daily infringement of foreign and sometimes even domestic laws and because they conflict with the precepts of generally recognized humanistic principles. In the conflict between legal and ethical criteria and practice, it is the goal – the initiator's practical interest – that has priority. If intelligence agencies are to function as effective components of the state apparatus, they must perpetrate actions abroad that often violate the enemy's legal norms. It would seem that an action's effectiveness is proportional to the extent to which it breaks the enemy's laws. The highly confidential and complex nature of intelligence operations and the difficulties of establishing adequate control by supreme state organs sometimes even lead intelligence services to violate the laws of their own countries.

The very essence of intelligence work clashes with generally accepted humanistic principles. No more than a small percentage of the agents recruited by intelligence agencies of East and West decide to work for the enemy of their own free will as a result of pure idealism or faith in the enemy's ideals. Anyone offering his services has little chance of being welcomed into the fold, for he may have been sent over by the other side. The intelligence service must therefore seek out agents on its own, and when it finds a likely candidate, it must bring all sorts of pressure to bear on him, beginning with the prospect of a good salary and ending with blackmail.

Ethical problems provide no barrier for special operations. A proposal submitted by a Department D official in 1965 to blow up the Andreas Hofer monument in Innsbruck in order to aggravate nationalistic tension between Italy and Austria in their dispute over South Tyrol was refused not because of the monument's cultural value. The Austrian press had mentioned possible Communist involvement in the Italo-Austrian controversy, and the intelligence service's smallest mistake indicating Czechoslovak connection with it could have had very unpleasant political consequences.

Although every proposal is reviewed at several stages, criticism is continually made of the proposal's practical aspects – the techniques employed and the risks involved – rather than of its ethical validity. Whoever voiced objections of an ethical nature would be suspected of being politically unreliable. The ethical criterion for special operations is none other than the old stand-by that the end justifies the means, a fact which naturally influences the moral standards of every intelligence officer. Cynicism is a part of the working atmosphere of the service. But not all Communist intelligence officers are alike.

Frantisek August

Moscow viewed indigenous Communist Parties first and
foremost as instruments of Soviet power and policy.

Born near Prague in 1928, Frantisek August was the son of an anti-Nazi who survived imprisonment in a German concentration camp after his arrest for helping a resistance group engaged in sabotage. After the war both father and son joined the Communist Party, and after the coup of February 1948 the younger August joined the National Security Corps. Five years of training followed, and then he was posted with a commission as an intelligence officer to a battalion of the Czech Border Guards.

In 1953 August took a course at the Counter-Intelligence School in Prague and the following year was sent to Moscow for training by the Soviet MVD. Upon his return to Prague in early 1955 he was appointed head of the intelligence department at the Border Guards Brigade headquarters. In January 1958 he was promoted to the StB's British desk and in December 1961 arrived in London under consular cover for a tour of duty which was to last two years, until October 1963. Later, in July 1966, he was to serve as the StB's deputy *rezident* in Beirut, under third secretary cover.

Appalled by what he discovered in the StB's files concerning the Soviet-inspired coup of 1948, August was a supporter of the reform movement which gained the ascendancy when Alexander Dubcek deposed Antonin Novotny in January 1968. He survived the purge of the StB conducted by Dubček, which cost the StB's hardline chief, Colonel Josef Houska, his job in July 1968, and had watched from Beirut when Houska had been reinstated by the Soviets after the invasion by 5,000 Warsaw Pact tanks in August. When the news first reached his embassy he unwisely had sent a cable in support of the reformers. In April, while on extended sick leave, he received a tip that he had been judged unreliable and, to force him to return home, his wife and children were to be abducted. Instead, at the end of July 1969, he sought political asylum.

August's disaffection from the StB had begun in the early 1950s, at the height of Stalin's power, according to his memoirs (published in 1984, and written largely in the third person by David Rees). They also contained the most detailed breakdown of the StB's structure, and identified dozens of the organization's personnel. In this passage he describes the entrapment of a source he refers to by his StB code-name Lora, who was actually Edward Scott, formerly the British Chargé d'Affaires in Prague. Scott was never prosecuted for passing classified information to the Czechs, but merely allowed early retirement.

Red Star Over Prague

Not only accredited diplomats, but secretarial and technical personnel naturally were targets of the CI service. Before arrival in Prague, their apartments were lined with microphones, not only in the bedroom and living room, but in the bathroom and toilets as well. All Czechoslovak domestics, cleaners, drivers and other servants were recruited as inform- ants for the CI service. Counterintelligence was aware that it only had the relatively short time of two or three years – a standard tour of duty – to recruit and develop potential agents from amongst these foreign officials. Another major task of the CI service was to identify British Embassy Intelligence and Security officers who were buried under cover in the often innocuous Embassy listings.

In this context, the wives of diplomats and Embassy typists were also a target of co-ordinated activity by Foreign Intelligence and Counterintelligence. Recruitment of a British Foreign Service typist was regarded as a significant success. On the other hand, the Czechoslovak Counterintelligence discovered this fact for itself when it found that the typist – and subsequently secretary and mistress – of the late President Antonin Novotny was an agent of the French Intelligence service!

Of course, the British tried to prevent eavesdropping or 'bugging' of their Embassy staff by sending out technicians from London to discover the hidden microphones and other electronic devices. These men were mostly employees of the Ministry of Public Buildings. Thus when the official application for a visa was received the fact was instantly reported to the Counterintelligence section. The Czechs then dismantled or switched off their listening devices for a short period.

In one case the report of the British technician's arrival was held up, and at only the last minute was the listening device disconnected. But a story is told how at that time the Czechoslovak technician and his British counterpart had a tug of war from opposing sides over the wired listening device implanted in the wall of a British diplomat's flat. But there is no stereotyped pattern in Counterintelligence work. Take the case of the Czech chauffeur hired by a British Military Attaché in Prague. The chauffeur in question had relatives in England who were pro-British, and the driver himself made no secret of his disapproval of the Prague regime. The British Attaché would understandably expect that the driver must be a Counterintelligence informant.

A few months later, the driver told the Briton that the police were forcing him to be an informant about his job and the situation in the British Embassy. The driver emphasised he was opposed to the informer's role, and did not like the situation. Then, however, acting on the principle that a known informer is better than an unknown one, the Attaché asked him to continue as his chauffeur. The whole episode in fact was planned by the CI section, who in this way strengthened the Military Attaché's confidence in their agent for further exploitation.

Not all operations run by the Czechoslovak security services ended as simply as the above affair. The case of 'Lora', for example, shows the interconnection between the Czechoslovak Foreign Intelligence and Counterintelligence. Lora – as he was known to Czechoslovak Intelligence – was a senior British diplomat based in Prague. He was a married man with several children. Suddenly he fell passionately in love with a younger woman, and tried at all costs to get his mistress out of the country, quite legally, to Austria.

FRANTISEK AUGUST

After a while, Lora was contacted by two members of Czechoslovak Intelligence. One was from the British desk of the Foreign Intelligence Service, the other from Counterintelligence. In return for being allowed to take his mistress abroad, Lora handed over information.

According to the agreement, this was supposed to be a one-off operation which did not commit Lora to permanent collaboration with the Czechs. But it was naive on Lora's part to expect this agreement to be kept. Soon after delivering the information, Lora returned to the Foreign Office in London. Here he was contacted by officals of the CIS from their London Station at the Czechoslovak Embassy. Lora told them that he regarded the episode as over, and refused further co-operation. Again the contact was renewed, and this time the meeting ended in dramatic circumstances as Lora tried to escape by car from his CIS contact. At the last minute Lora stopped his car, afraid that he had injured the Czech officer; he then agreed to further collaboration.

However, Lora did not come to the next meeting, or appear on any of the alternative dates. His name vanished from the internal Foreign Office telephone directory of which the CIS had a copy.

Two particularly interesting case histories from the post-1948 period illustrate the unceasing struggle between Czech and British Intelligence in which the CIS London Station played an important part.

The first is the story of the 'Czech Intelligence Office', or CIO. This episode begins in 1948, when a Czechoslovak Army staff officer, Colonel Prochazka, escaped to London. Colonel Prochazka decided to set up an anti-Communist Intelligence network in his country, based on members of the former Free Czechoslovak Army and Air Force in England during the Second World War. The self-styled CIO was run from a discreet office in Hampstead, and its work was supervised and financed by the British Secret Intelligence Service (SIS).

As the Communists imposed their rule on Czechoslovakia in the late 1940s and early 1950s, so the work of the CIO expanded, with hundreds of agents throughout the country, including the government apparatus. The CIO also had stations in West Germany and Austria, and its networks now became a major penetration of Communist Czechoslovakia by the SIS.

However, one of the CIO's filing clerks was a man named Mr Karel Zbytek. In the mid-1950s, Mr Zbytek (alias Light) came into contact with the London Station of the CIS, and began to pass over the innermost secrets of CIO operations. The motive was quite simple: money. Soon, the networks of the CIO were rolled up by the STB Counterintelligence section in Prague, and scores of agents arrested. Mr Zbytek also turned over a list of CIO officials working in Belgium, Holland, Scandinavia, Austria, West Germany, Switzerland and the Middle East.

This material also included a roster of 120 CIO agents in Britain, and 300 talent-spotter reports on Czechoslovak nationals, mostly foreign trade officials, who travelled to Western Europe. The material also named the SIS liaison officers with the CIO. One of the largest positive intelligence operations of modern times was now destroyed.

It was the original intention of the Czechoslovak Intelligence Services not to arrest all the CIO agents but to set up a special department of their own to control and run these spies. However, this was 1956, the year of the Poznan riots in Poland and the Hungarian Uprising. The KGB was afraid that something similar might happen in Czechoslovakia. Because of this, General Medvedyev, Chief KGB adviser to the Prague Minister of the Interior, Mr Rudolph Barak, insisted that all identified CIO agents should be arrested.

Mr Medvedyev rejected the Czech idea, saying, 'After all, we are not going to play the snake in our own bosom.' His decision invoked indignation in Czech Intelligence, who considered this a narrow police mentality. When the mass arrests of CIO agents began, the SIS correctly reached the conclusion that their operations had been 'blown' and decided to write off the CIO. The CIO was disbanded.

Mr Karel Zbytek now told the London Station of Czech Intelligence when the files were to be removed from the CIO office. Consequently, Czech Intelligence was able to set up surveillance of the cars transporting these files, and thus locate the new SIS premises in question. In the meantime, some of the Czechoslovak nationals who had featured on the list of the CIO talent-spotters in London were re-recruited by Prague. They were now sent abroad as Czechoslovak agents, and in some cases they were approached and enlisted by the SIS. The aim of this operation, of course, was to discover SIS objectives in Czechoslovakia, and this was partly achieved as a result of these planted agents.

Altogether Mr Karel Zbytek was paid about £13,000 and apparently bought a boarding house in Folkestone, Kent. But Mr Zbytek was not the only betrayer of the CIO. In 1960, the KGB began to hand over to the STB top-secret lists of Czech nationals who had been spotted for possible collaboration with the British SIS. Most of this was CIO material. This confirmed the earlier conclusion of Czech officials that the KGB was fully informed independently of the activities of the CIO. Part of the material had in fact been supplied by the former SIS official, George Blake, an in-place agent of the KGB in British Intelligence.

The ripples continued to spread long after the dismantling of the CIO. From the time that Mr Karel Zbytek began to pass information, the Prague Ministry of the Interior set up a special section for retaining all the addresses of the CIO agent network and also the addresses of all CIO officials. All correspondence sent from Czechoslovakia to these latter addresses was checked.

Josef Frolik

Not to put too fine an edge on it, I am a traitor, who fled his native country, bearing with him important secrets, which could only injure that country's security and intelligence services.

Josef Frolik joined the Ministry of State Security in December 1952 and eight years later had risen to be head of the department supervising the StB's espionage in Britain. In 1964 he began a two-year tour of duty in London, attached to the Czech embassy under diplomatic cover as labour attaché.

In mid-1968, having returned to headquarters in Prague, Frolik was informed that his career in the StB had come to an end and that from August he would be unemployed. This news prompted him to contact the CIA in Prague, which arranged for the exfiltration of himself, his wife and his son while they were on holiday in Bulgaria. Together they kept a rendezvous with a fast speedboat which collected them off the beach and carried them across the Black Sea to Istanbul, whence they were flown to the United States.

During his debriefing Frolik identified several StB assets in London, including three Labour members of Parliament, Sir Barnet Stross, John Stonehouse and Will Owen. Although Stross had died in May 1967, and Stonehouse denied any contact with the Czechs, Owen was charged with having sold secrets from the Defence Estimates Committee to Frolik's colleagues, Colonel Jan Paclik and Robert Husak. He was acquitted, but later admitted his guilt. Also arrested was Nicholas Prager, a former RAF technician who had betrayed details of various classified radar systems. He was sentenced to twelve years' imprisonment and deportation to his native Czechoslovakia.

Frolik's autobiography, *The Frolik Defection*, published in 1975, was heavily sanitized by the British Security Service because several of the StB and KGB assets identified by the author, particularly those within the trade union movement, had been run by MI5 as double agents. However, while he was *en poste*, as is evident from this extract, Frolik found some obstacles in his attempts to approach union leaders like Ted Hill.

The Frolik Defection

The British Communist Party, as we all knew in the Embassy, was a downright failure. After half a century of really hard work in the United Kingdom, it had never had a membership larger than – say – sixty thousand; and at general elections it had never polled more than one hundred thousand votes. The number of MPs it has had in Parliament can be counted on the fingers of one hand. Yet, in one particular field, it has shown outstanding results, in relation to its exceedingly small numbers – the trade union organizations.

By virtue of a great deal of hard work and the intensive training of the communist organizers in the union movement, most of whom leave the normal non-communist union leader standing when it comes to any kind of debate or discussion, and sheer twenty-four-hour devotion to the job in hand, communists had begun to penetrate union leadership very effectively by the early 'sixties. So much so that today communists control over 10 per cent of the important posts in the major unions: a figure ludicrously out of proportion to their actual numbers. Thus communists virtually control the Scottish and Welsh (and probably the Yorkshire) sections of the National Union of Mineworkers; are especially strong in the Amalgamated Engineering Union, with 27 communists or 'Marxists' in its 52-strong national committee; and have an important say in the affairs of the giant Transport and General Workers' Union.

And the communist trade unionists make little attempt (especially those at the lower level) to hide their sympathies. In January of 1974, for example, that veteran communist, one-time miner Idris Cox, who has been the secretary of the CP's International Department since the 'thirties, stated publicly at a party meeting: 'Our comrades hold key positions in influential organizations at a regional and national level and the stand of some of the unions on fundamental issues is shaped under their influence.'

But it took Mr Bert Ramelson, the Ukrainian-born Industrial Organizer of the British Communist Party, to reveal the real significance of the communist infiltration of the unions, when he boasted that the CP only had to 'float an idea early in the year and it can become official Labour policy by the autumn'.

Why? Because if the communists can dominate the unions, they can also dominate the Labour Party. Thus the two big unions, the Transport and General Workers, and the Amalgamated Engineering Union between them can play a decisive role at any Labour Party autumn conference where they control no less than forty per cent of the vote!

Naturally, we were already aware of the trend within the unions way back in the mid-sixties; and our people in London actively encouraged the contacts between the TUC and officials of the communist-controlled World Federation of Trade Unions. As I write these very lines, we are informed by the press that secret talks have been going on between the TUC and the WFTU, and that a delegation of key union leaders is to tour Hungary and Czechoslovakia, perhaps as a follow-up to those talks.

And who arranged the key talks? No other than two former colleagues of mine, Mr S. Ulik and Mr Josef Lebl, respectively Second and Third Secretaries at the Czech Embassy in London – *officially*! Unofficially they were something else, as the British Government's expulsion of them earlier in the year shows; they were both accused of spying!

But to return to 1963. By that time, I had been in London nearly a year and in spite of my only average English, I was, I think, a welcome guest at TUC parties and receptions and in the private homes of some trade union leaders. With most of them I was on a first name basis – they had downgraded my Czech Christian name to the chummy English 'Joe' – and some of them even came to my own home for food and drinks, especially drinks!

There was —— of the —— Union, whom I first met at the TUC Conference in Brighton. We were soon firm friends and I was often invited to his home, where I met his wife. She herself was a communist, as was her husband, though he kept his Party membership secret. Why? I can only conjecture that a notorious friend of the family had something to do with it. He was none other than Lieutenant-Colonel Nikolai Berdenikov, whose name first attracted attention in connection with the Penkovsky affair.

I had first met the charming Russian Colonel, who, like myself, was an Intelligence officer with a diplomatic cover, at the Brighton TUC Conference in 1965, where I was seated at a table with Ted Hill, Harry Nicholls, the General Secretary of the Transport and General Workers' Union, and Mr Callaghan. After the dance that night, Berdenikov, who officially was Soviet Labour Attaché, returned with me to my hotel near the front. Naturally he knew what my real job was in England, just as I knew his. We chatted about general Intelligence matters for a little while; then I remarked that we were missing a great opportunity for Intelligence by not using the Irish Nationalist Movement, the IRA. Berdenikov laughed and promptly proceeded to fill me in. In 1945 the NKVD had seized all the Abwehr files in Berlin, including those concerned with the Abwehr apparat within the IRA during the war. The Abwehr was the German Intelligence Service, which regularly ran agents into Ireland during the war, although they were never very successful because their IRA collaborators were usually more interested in the money they brought with them (and the resultant drinking parties) than in carrying out espionage missions. Boastfully he said, 'We won most of their people over to our side and we could unleash a national liberation struggle against the British at any time. We would consider ourselves fortunate if we had a network similar to the one we have in Ireland here in England.' At the time I thought he had drunk too much Scotch. Today's headlines make me think differently.

This, then, was the man who was a frequent guest at the —— home, a powerful man who jealously protected his own contacts and agents; for when I asked Prague for permission to recruit —— for Intelligence purposes, I received a very smart reply: 'Hands off! That particular mare is being run from another stable close by.'

One didn't need to be clairvoyant to realize where that stable was and who was running the mare. The owner of the stable was undoubtedly Colonel Berdenikov.

Jan Sejna

By the time you get around to wondering whether what you are doing is wrong, it is too late; you are already enmeshed in the Party machine, a part of the system. You have only two choices: either to go on as before; or to speak your mind, be expelled from the Party, and finished for life.

Born in May 1927 to a family of peasant farmers at Libotyen, near the Bavarian Czech border, Jan Sejna worked as an agricultural labourer before being pressed into service by the Wehrmacht to build anti-tank obstacles. At the end of the war he resumed farming, on a property confiscated from a Sudeten German, and joined the Communist Party.

In 1950 Sejna was called up for military service and by the age of twenty-seven he had been promoted to the rank of lieutenant-colonel and had been appointed Commissar to the Corps of Engineers. As Chief of Staff to the Minister of Defence he gained access to documents relating to past purges which appalled him and sowed 'the first seeds of disillusion with the Communist system'. Nevertheless his rapid promotion continued and by forty he was a member of Parliament, a general, a member of the Central Committee and, more significantly, secretary to the Czech Defence Council.

Sejna's disaffection was confirmed when he was allowed to read the Soviet Strategic Plan, which amounted to a timetable for world domination and left no room for a free, independent Czechoslovakia. He was also convinced that Alexander Dubček's liberal administration had not fully appreciated the Soviet determination to prevent the Czechs from ideological backsliding. When he tried to warn Dubček he was accused of sabotage and treachery. He decided to defect and in February 1968 his eighteen-year-old son, and his son's younger girlfriend, agreed to join him. Over a weekend the trio drove through Hungary to Yugoslavia and bluffed their way across the Italian frontier to Trieste. There they applied for political asylum at the American consulate, and were promptly flown to the United States.

When the defection of Major-General Jan Sejna was announced it had considerable repercussions in Prague for he was the highest-ranking military officer of the Warsaw Pact ever to switch sides. His autobiography, *We Will Bury You*, was published in 1982 following the failure of his CIA-financed restaurant in Chicago, and provided a synopsis, country by country, of the Soviet Strategic Plan. In this passage from his memoirs Sejna reveals how he became disenchanted with the Party.

We Will Bury You

At the beginning, between 1947, when I joined the Party, and 1956, I did not consider I was exercising personal power. 'It is Party power,' I thought. And that continued to be my view, even when I was elected in 1954 to the Central Committee, the highest position in the Party, I was told. By then I had learnt that there were two Marxisms: one for the Party leaders and the members of the Central Committee; the other for the Party rank and file and the people. That was when I began to change, for I realized that the first kind of Marxism was not what Marx and Engels had taught me; it was simply the bourgeois life of enjoyment. Even so it took me time to change.

I concluded that I had two choices: either to continue to work hard, as a fanatical Communist, which would be a stupid choice; or to relax and enjoy life like the other Party leaders; in fact, to cash in on the great deception. But I changed more rapidly after 1956, when I had been in the USSR and talked every day with Soviet military and political leaders. I was shattered when I saw that their lifestyle was the same as that of the nobility in Tsarist days. I am sure that they treated the poor worse, and spent money with more abandon, than in the West. This was a genuine shock to me, for I had always thought that the Soviet leaders lived as simply as the workers; I could hardly believe my eyes when I saw their way of life.

Again, I had only two choices: either I could quit, in which case not only would I myself be finished but so would my family, especially as I knew too much; or I must lead a double life – on the surface, the official Party life, but privately the life of a pleasure-seeking bourgeois. I chose the second alternative, the double life.

But inside I was very disillusioned, more so after I had learnt about the Soviet Strategic Plan for my country. I often discussed it with my close friends, and all of us were deeply pessimistic. Knowing the plans of the Soviet Marshals as we did, we had to admit there was no chance of Czechoslovakia becoming a free country in five, ten, or even twenty years. Even the most pro-Soviet members of our military establishment were bitterly disappointed; but they knew there was nothing they could do.

The further I advanced in the Communist Party, the more I understood that the Communist system was a self-serving bureaucracy designed to maintain in power a cynical elite. During my early years of struggle for the Party I believed firmly in Marxism-Leninism, and closed my eyes to practices which later became abhorrent. I have written about my campaigns for the Party as a young man before the coup of 1948, when it was engaged in a life and death struggle with the Social Democratic Parties. Even after the coup of February 1948, we lived in a continuing atmosphere of crisis and fear that we were surrounded by enemies, as indeed we were – enemies of our own making!

It stimulated my idealism during this period to know that more than 70 per cent of the new settlers in my region of Horosovsky Tyn were Communist sympathizers. We had no problem in recruiting cadres and there was genuine competition for places in the Party, a marked contrast to the tired system of 'democratic centralism', or central selection of candidates, which prevailed throughout the country later on, when the Party was firmly established.

By 1950, when I was conscripted into the Army, I had made up my mind to seek a career in the Party. Like most young men, I found the Army a tedious but unavoidable duty, and looked forward to getting it behind me as soon as possible. I welcomed my transfer to the Commissars School in January 1951. I was interested in Party affairs and felt the School would help to compensate for my lack of formal education. Most of our time there was devoted to political studies. This was a more attractive opening than the only alternative, the School for Commanders. I had no interest in military affairs, and my slight build hardly suited me for field command.

I had some illustrious fellow students. In my class of ten was Professor Vladimir Ruml, already a leading Party ideologist then and later a member of the Central Committee and Director of the Institute of Marxism. In the next bed to me was Karel Kosik, who later became a leading liberal Marxist and fell into disgrace after the Prague Spring. Across the room was Voytech Mencl, who was the most prominent liberal in the Czech armed forces before the Soviet invasion of 1968. Another student with considerable Party experience was Jaromir Obzina, later Minister of the Interior and a member of the Central Committee.

I was the only country boy in this collection of young Party talent, but a common bond between us was our desire to return to civilian life. I learned a great deal from my association with these colleagues, and even taught them a little in return. Only Obzina had as much experience as I in the practical side of Party organization and in the struggle for power in the streets. After Commissars School we all dispensed to regimental duties as political commissars or propagandists, to complete our two years of service.

My rustic naivety managed to survive the cynical way in which I was elected to Parliament and to the Central Committee in 1954; but it received the first of a series of shattering blows in 1955. The occasion was a meeting of the Central Committee to discuss agriculture and nutrition. The Government had closed a large number of sugar refineries, a move that obliged the peasants, including many in my own constituency, to transport their beet to distant mills for processing.

I criticized Ludmila Jankovcova, Deputy Prime Minister and member of the Politburo with special responsibility for food and agriculture, for this short-sighted policy, and I received some open support from other members of the Central Committee. But Jankovcova cornered me at the first coffee break.

'Who gave *you* the right to criticize a member of the Politburo?' she demanded, and continued in a caustic tone, 'You only see the local view, you don't know the national picture.'

'I'm here in Prague to defend the interests of my constituents,' I answered stoutly, 'not to sympathize with your problems.'

This was heresy. Jankovcova was formerly a Social Democrat, but she had learned a lot from her new comrades. 'You're practising "mass policy",' she told me grimly. 'Your job is not to tell the Party what the masses want, but to explain the Party's policy to the people.'

Novotny, though I scarcely knew him then, adopted a more paternal attitude, and took me aside for a few words.

'Really, Jan,' he said gently, 'you must get to know the difference between a local Party meeting and the deliberations of the General Committee.'

Much more direct advice came from General Zeman, Chief of the Main Political Administration: 'If you want to continue your career, shut up!'

I began to wonder if I really understood Marxism. Nevertheless, it marked the start of my apprenticeship in the mechanics of power and the making of Party policy.

Khrushchev's famous speech about the evils of Stalinism came as a severe shock to my faith in the Party. But this was nothing compared to the horrors I uncovered when I opened the fourteen safes used by Cepicka. I have already mentioned the list of names of people falsely imprisoned, many of them Communists, and the harrowing letters from the death cells and from the families of the condemned. Some cases were described in clinical detail.

I recall the affair of Colonel Vasek, an officer on the General Staff whom the Secret Police considered dangerous because he was not in sympathy with Communism, though he was highly regarded by his brother officers. Two members of military counter-intelligence visited him one night in 1949 when he was working late. They let themselves into his office, where they accused him of being a British spy. When he protested his innocence, they beat him unconscious, only to revive him with cold water. They repeated the process five times until, as dawn broke, they realized he would never confess. And so they dragged his unconscious body to an air shaft and threw him five storeys to the ground; then they backed a truck into the inner courtyard of the General Staff building, retrieved the body, and took it to the crematorium, where they burned it and scattered the ashes.

The Secret Police visited Vasek's wife, by whom he had two children, and told her he had defected to West Germany with his secretary. They were very convincing, and in her anger and distress she accused him of pro-Western sympathies and activities. Her accusations were, of course, taped, and they appeared as evidence that afternoon before a hurriedly assembled military tribunal, which found Vasek guilty of treason and condemned him, retrospectively, to death. The murder was legalized in just eighteen hours.

Another innocent officer who had played an active part in the anti-Nazi underground was arrested on his way home from work, and given the 'step by step treatment'. Bound hand and foot, he was shoved into a potato sack and dropped into the river; after each immersion he was invited to confess. Few people can endure this for long, but this man drowned at the second immersion.

The Zalocnici case involved twelve officers of the pre-war Czech Army who were arrested by the Gestapo and imprisoned in a concentration camp in Germany; among the inmates was Cepicka. These officers became members of the underground Communist Party in the camp, and after the war they rejoined the armed forces, where they held ranks from Army major to colonel in the Air Force. One Sunday in 1949 they were invited individually for personal interviews with the Cadres Administration of the Defence Ministry in Prague. On arrival they were arrested, tried as Western spies, and executed that day, after digging their own graves in a forest about fifty kilometres from Prague. The link between them was their suspicion that Cepicka had collaborated with the Nazis in the camp. In 1953 Cepicka had the bodies exhumed and secretly cremated.

Novotny's refusal to take action against Cepicka and his decision to cover up the evidence fed my disillusionment, which grew gradually into cynicism and disaffection. The Cepicka affair changed my idealistic view of our Czech leaders, and indeed of the Party, for it was clear to me that the whole Party apparatus had been responsible for these murders. With shame I recalled the lists of bourgeoisie to be imprisoned which our district committees had compiled in 1948. Novotny's attitude showed that Khrushchev's 20th Party Congress had changed nothing; 'the dictatorship of the Proletariat' meant no more than the tyranny of the Party and the Secret Police.

Janusz Kochanski

The brutal elimination of Mroz – a sickening episode that still gives me nightmares – was a key factor in what was to be my decision to become a double agent for the West. Ultimately, I was forced to escape to the United States. Today, I too am under a death sentence for treason against the Polish regime.

A Catholic born in Warsaw in 1930, Janusz Kochanski spent the war in the capital and was instrumental in the escape of many Jews from the ghetto. While at university he became a Communist Party activist and when he graduated he was recruited into the Urzad Bezpieczenstwa. Having completed his training at the UB's academy, he was assigned to the British and Scandinavian desk, handling reports from agents. In 1956 he was posted to the embassy in Stockholm under diplomatic cover, and in 1958 was expelled for espionage.

After two years at headquarters he was sent to Paris to supervise the assassination of Wladyslaw Mroz, the senior Polish intelligence officer operating illegally and suspected of having been recruited by the French. Once the murder had been completed, Kochanski returned home but became increasingly disillusioned with the regime. When, in 1964, with the rank of lieutenant-colonel, he was posted to the embassy in Oslo in the role of first secretary he made contact with the local CIA station and worked as a valuable spy until he fell under suspicion in December 1966 and was recalled to Warsaw, ostensibly to receive a promotion. However, he quickly learned that he was under investigation for pro-Western sympathies, and was to be dismissed from the service. In February 1967 he eluded his surveillance and, leaving his wife and son behind, flew to Oslo where he reported to his CIA contacts and accepted political asylum in the United States, where he now lives as a corporate accountant, having used the names John Kruspin, Jos Glucek and Bleslaw Kowalski. In May 1988 he was sentenced in his absence to death for treason and in his autobiography, published in 1979, he referred to himself only as 'Mr X', but revealed the background to Mroz's death.

Double Eagle

Of the Eastern European spying organizations, by far the most important is the Polish Intelligence Service. The reason is rooted in a historical phenomenon – the traditional exodus of Poles to other lands because of their own country's poverty, political instability, and unfortunate geographical position between larger, more powerful European neighbors who have repeatedly overrun Poland in their wars with each other. At least twenty-five percent of Poland's native-born population is living abroad, the vast majority emigrants.

This fact is a unique asset to the Polish Intelligence Service and, in turn, the Russian KGB. Because of the number of Poles living abroad, the Polish UB has more opportunities than the intelligence services of other Eastern European nations to recruit individuals who are already living in strategic countries in the West.

Thus Poland is deeply involved in the cloak-and-dagger Cold War being waged unremittingly, if clandestinely, between the espionage apparatuses of East and West. It was this fact that spelled the end for Wladyslaw Mroz.

I first met Mroz in 1953, when he was a part-time instructor at the Polish Intelligence School in Warsaw, which I was attending at the time. Even though he was only a little over thirty, he was already an experienced intelligence staff officer. As I was later to discover, during this period he was also the officer in charge of the illegal Polish espionage network in Scandinavia. He had been among those who, in 1947–49, had organized our net in the northern countries.

Not only for the younger officers such as myself, but for the old-timers as well Mroz was an example. Born in Eastern Poland, he had fled with his family to Russia during World War II. He had been the youngest student ever to graduate from the Polish Intelligence School organized by the Russians during the war in the city of Kujbyszew, in the Soviet Union. After the war he returned to Poland and began his working career in his native country's intelligence service.

Mroz's wife – they had two children, and at the time of his assassination his wife was pregnant with their third child – was born in France. She thus helped Mroz become familiar with the French language and French customs. He traveled abroad a great deal, always using a fictitious foreign identity and a foreign passport, even when departing from Poland. At the beginning of his career he was especially active in Scandinavia; later, his work spread to France, West Germany, Belgium, and Switzerland.

In 1953–54, Mroz was instrumental in helping organize Branch 1, which was designed to be a new, all-embracing arm of the Polish Intelligence Service in Western Europe that would function underground, or illegally. In the future, it was projected, this branch would replace the other branches of the service that worked from so-called legal positions, such as diplomatic posts. The objective was to eliminate contact between official Polish installations abroad and our agents. I hardly need to emphasize the importance that this reorganization had for our operations. It was carried out in almost total secrecy, and those involved in Branch 1, with the exception of Mroz and a few others, were completely unknown to the rest of our staff officers.

In 1957 it became obvious that Mroz would be the leader of the entire Branch 1 operation. It was decided, however, that he would function from a cover position outside of Poland. In November 1958 I replaced Mroz in headquarters, where he had been engaged in logistical support of illegal activities, operating under what was known as Branch 1-A. He began an intensive training program that was to prepare him to leave Poland for a minimum of ten years and, if necessary, forever.

In the early summer of 1959, Wladyslaw Mroz, according to plan, 'disappeared' from Poland. Only I and a few other persons knew that he was surreptitiously posted to Paris. I can personally confirm that the whole program was completed satisfactorily. Everybody interested in it was extremely pleased.

During the summer of 1960, nevertheless, we received an alarming report from the Russians that the French had an agent in the Polish Intelligence Service who was supplying them with valuable information, including details of our underground operations in the West. Everybody was suspected *except* Mroz. At approximately the same time, Colonel Bryn, who had allegedly been kidnapped by the Americans in Hong Kong, appeared at the Polish embassy in Paris asking to return to Poland.

During the investigation of his case by the Polish authorities, it became clear that he had been told, by someone, many important things that he had not previously known. We were now sure beyond a doubt that Western counterintelligence was learning far too much about us. Yet we still did not suspect Mroz. On the contrary, we were concerned that he was in great danger, since the Americans or the French were quite possibly aware of his work.

It was concluded that we would recall Mroz to Poland. Everybody was surprised when he tried to invoke a thousand reasons to delay his return to his homeland: his wife was sick, pregnant, etc. In spite of the urgency of the situation, he failed to appear for several appointments at head-quarters; after ignoring half a dozen calls, he didn't even show up for the last call, which was worded in the most urgent terms. We were now certain that it was none other than Wladyslaw Mroz who was supplying the information to the West.

The decision was quick and final. Mroz had to be killed before he could compromise everything and everybody, if he had not already done so. It would have been unfeasible if not impossible to take him out of France against his will. In a smaller country, such as Sweden or Holland, we might have been able to smuggle him out on a Polish boat, but such things are more difficult in France. And if we had been caught, it might have blown our entire intelligence operation in France and precipitated a diplomatic crisis between Paris and Warsaw. No, much simpler to eliminate Mroz on the scene. The assassination was organized by the resident chief of Polish intelligence in France at the time, whose cover was that of an officer in the Polish embassy in Paris. (Our planned separation of illegal operations from legal cover positions, while proceeding apace, had not yet been completed in France and several other countries.)

A group of our intelligence officers was about to return from South Viet Nam, where they had been stationed under the cover of the International Control Commission, a body set up by the 1954 Indochina Peace Conference at Geneva and made up of representatives from Poland, India and Canada. In Saigon, a special team was organized to liquidate Mroz. Simultaneously, preparations were underway in Paris. The main problem was how to get Mroz into our hands, because he was probably under French or American protection. It was concluded that we had to use his father, who was still in Poland, and one of Mroz's best friends.

Mroz was informed through the normal channel of communication that his father had been involved in a serious car accident. A few days later, by careful design, one of Mroz's old friends from Warsaw 'accidentally' met him on a street in Paris. Both were interested in talking, and they drifted into a coffee shop. Mroz's friend said that he did not have time for an extended conversation just then; he suggested a place to meet two days later at 11 p.m. Wladyslaw Mroz would never arrive for this meeting, which was to have taken place on October 24, 1960.

On the evening of October 24, a functionary of the Polish embassy in Paris, W, had dinner at Restaurant B with a member of the Polish Parliament, Z, who was on an official visit to France and knew nothing of the plan to assassinate Mroz. The dinner between the embassy official and the visiting Polish parliamentarian was a backstop in case something went wrong. If, after abducting Mroz, it had been discovered that those carrying out the plot were under surveillance, Mroz would have been taken to the dinner.

They knew that Mroz would travel by auto to a particular subway station. The idea was to abduct him at a parking lot adjacent to the underground station, or to cause him by some other means to stop his car long enough that he could be forced into another car. Everything went according to plan. He was successfully forced into another auto at the parking lot.

At the beginning he was told that he was to be taken to meet with one of the chief deputies of the Polish parliament in a place in Paris convenient for the Poles. The well-known name of Wladyslaw Wicha was mentioned to him. Wicha – who had nothing to do with the assassination – was at the time not only a member of the Polish parliament, but also Poland's Minister of Interior and a member of the politburo of the Polish Communist Party. Mroz's abductors then told him that he was being taken to Warsaw. He said that he would refuse to go, invoking various innocuous explanations.

Of course, both stories about where he was going were only ruses to gain time, so that the kidnappers could make certain that they were not being followed. After they were sure that everything was clear, Mroz's escorts took him to the city dump. Only then did he realize what was going to happen to him. Up to that point, he evidently had not sensed just how much evidence his former comrades had against him, and perhaps he hoped that he could still maintain his innocence.

Mroz was about forty years old, approximately five feet, ten inches tall, relatively slim, with a dark brown crew-cut. Generally speaking, he was a good-looking fellow; one could say almost handsome. The assassination team's car was a German Mercedes belonging to the Polish embassy in Paris, with diplomatic plates. The driver of the car was M, an attaché of the Polish embassy. On one side of the back seat of the car was J, code clerk of the Polish embassy in Paris and an officer of Branch 1 of the Polish Intelligence Service. On the opposite side of the back seat was S, who was the overall leader of the group in the car. S was at the time a member of the Polish consular staff in Paris, and deputy chief resident agent of the UB. Sitting between J and S was Mroz.

They had several guns, all of them equipped with silencers. Until the last minute the guns were kept by J in a special diplomatic pouch, protected by the proper seals.

After they left the car and dragged Mroz a couple of yards away, he was beaten and kicked. Then J opened the diplomatic pouch and handed guns to two of the group. At this point M, who had remained in the car as lookout, joined the two with Mroz, after checking with the surveillance in the area to make sure that everything was okay.

S started reading the very short verdict informing Mroz that he was going to be killed because of the death sentence imposed on him by the Polish government. The accusation was treason. It was now quite obvious to Mroz what was going to happen. In spite of several blows and kicks, he went down on his knees and begged for the opportunity to have more time. He would explain, he pleaded, exactly what had been happening and why he had had no choice except to cooperate. He said that he had been blackmailed and forced, that he had been doing it in order to protect his own life and those of his pregnant wife and his children.

Of course it was too late. They were under orders; they did not have a choice. J, who was obliged to carry out the execution, told all present – as he had even before Mroz was kidnapped – that he wanted everybody in the car to participate in the execution. He felt that Mroz deserved this from all of them and that he, J, should not be the only one doing the shooting. At this point the others were nervous and angry but at the same time also felt a little sorry for J, who didn't want to take the whole blame for the killing.

At the very last second J said to Mroz: 'You will die, son of a bitch, like a dog, a dirty, dirty dog. You do not deserve anything better—' Before he had finished the sentence, J shot Mroz somewhere in the forehead or between the eyes. Mroz fell down on his face, and, at this time, several other shots were fired, mainly into his chest and head, from a very close range. It is difficult to say for sure which shot or shots really killed Mroz.

But there were at least two or three shots fired by each of the people surrounding his body.

A moment later, S, who was obviously very familiar with the area, yelled: 'Help me!' They grabbed Mroz's legs and started dragging him to an empty well approximately twenty-five yards away. At this point J went completely berserk and started kicking Mroz's inert body. When they reached the empty well, all of them together pushed the body of Wladyslaw Mroz in. S gave orders to throw as many different objects as possible into the well to cover Mroz's corpse. So they threw pieces of brick and rocks and empty containers – more or less what you would expect to find in a garbage dump – over the body, which was lying probably sixty feet down in this empty, dry well.

After a couple of minutes, S said: 'Let's get the hell out of here!' They ran to the car, and J demanded the guns, all of which were dropped into the diplomatic pouch. J was very, very busy trying to seal the pouch again. They took the same places in the car they had had before and sped away from the area, driving directly to the Polish embassy. There they were invited to the office of W, where a couple of bottles of French cognac – Martell and Hennessy – were opened, and everybody had a drink. J left immediately for the code room to send the cable to Warsaw. A few minutes later it was confirmed that the twelve to fourteen people in the four surveillance cars were safely back in the Polish embassy compound. The action was over.

Perhaps three-quarters of an hour later, I was at the hotel where I was staying. There I encountered Z, the member of the Polish parliament who had had dinner with W. Z was returning from the dinner, and was very happy about the evening with W. He didn't realize, and maybe he has never realized, that he was used as a front for the whole operation.

M, J and S were shortly afterward recalled from Paris to Warsaw – one by one, over a period of time, in order not to arouse suspicion. To the best of my knowledge, none of the three ever left Poland again. As far as I know, they completely disappeared from the Polish Intelligence Service and the Polish Foreign Service. This is significant, because it indicates that even though they were selected to carry out the Polish government's orders to assassinate Mroz, the government obviously never trusted them to station them abroad again. I am the only one who knows the story who was lucky enough to be able to leave Poland again.

Two days after the elimination of Mroz, I returned to Warsaw. In the airplane I opened a French newspaper and saw a story about the assassination of Mroz. There was a picture of him, but he was identified only as a Polish immigrant who had for some reason been murdered. I couldn't understand the article too clearly because I couldn't read French well. With the help of Z, who was leaving France with me and who was proficient in reading French, I was able to absorb the contents of the story. While assisting me in this, Z was at the same time asking me whether I knew the man and whether I knew anything behind the story. To which I replied: 'No, I do not have the slightest idea about the man or the story. I am surprised. I feel that it is some kind of provocation or fabrication.' And I concluded: 'Well, we'll find out later on in Poland.'

The French press later described the episode somewhat more accurately – that the victim had been a Polish intelligence agent, and had probably been eliminated by his own people because he had become a double agent. The intimation was that perhaps the CIA was involved, not French intelligence.

The case was handled extremely badly by the French authorities, in terms of both counteraction and propaganda potential. Investigating the assassination, the French counterintelligence service arrested more than a score of persons on espionage charges. However, none were Polish intelligence staff officers. All of our espionage staff officers from France, Belgium, West Germany and Switzerland not involved in the assassination had returned to Poland under orders at least twenty-four hours before Mroz was killed, precisely to avert any possibility of reprisals against them. Thus the Polish agents arrested by the French could say little if anything, and then only about their individual activities, because each had as a contact only a single staff officer – who was no longer in France. Because of the lack of evidence, all of our arrested agents were eventually either released from custody or given very short terms of imprisonment. And the French have never captured the killers of Mroz.

Why France did not make more of the case I still do not understand. They could have made a great scandal, but instead they said nearly nothing about it. As a result, the episode has been, up to now, one of the untold stories of the clandestine Cold War.

To me personally, the murder of Wladyslaw Mroz has been much more than that. It was instrumental in my decision to reject the Communist system. I must admit that at the time of Mroz's death, I was part and parcel of that system. But even then I was having growing doubts about Communism, and after the killing of Mroz these doubts began gnawing on me with an intensity that finally I could not bear.

He had once been my friend. I had followed his example when he was a young, enthusiastic, active Communist. I will never know for certain whether he was indeed a traitor, whether he had really changed his mind. I do know that I have changed my mind and that I was a traitor. Therefore, I don't have any reason whatsoever to condemn him. He had been exposed to more or less the same kind of life that I had. As my experiences changed me, his may have changed him. But in this kind of business, when you are a traitor you have to be aware of the danger of assassination, as Mroz knew very well.

There is a small doubt in my mind that he was a traitor at all. Whether he was or not, he was assassinated without proof of the facts. The mere suspicion was enough for him to be sentenced to death, without any formal investigation or trial, and to be killed in the most brutal, barbaric way.

Mroz's death forever forces me to think about my own life and my own experience with bitterness, pain, shame. Because somebody somewhere decided that it was proper to kill Mroz, he was killed. The decision could not be questioned, at least openly. A man was murdered, even though nobody had any real guarantee or assurance that this man had to be killed.

In the wake of that event, the thought went through my mind that this could happen to any of us in the Polish intelligence apparatus. That it had probably happened many times to many others. That it could happen to anybody, because the battle for individual rights, the war for the human spirit, does not count in a Communist system.

I could only imagine how the wife and children of Mroz were going to feel. How were they ever going to understand what had happened to their husband and father and why?

Many years earlier, when I had been very young and very enthusiastic, I was perhaps ready to kill anybody if ordered to do so. But by 1960 it wasn't the same. Mroz's liquidation was a turning point in my life.

Pawel Monat

Nobody won the Korean War, but before it was over Communism had come close to losing me. It was the war, in fact, which planted the seeds of my defection.

Born close to the Soviet border in Galicia in 1921, Pawel Monat intended to become a doctor but was obliged to drop out of the medical school at the University of Lvov when his father died. He was then drafted into the Red Army. He was selected for officer training at the artillery academy at Sumy, in the

Ukraine, but in June 1941 was sent to the front as a cadet, where he was wounded.

During the war he was wounded four times, the last occasion being during the liberation of Warsaw. At the end of the war he remained in the Polish army and in 1947 attended staff college. In February 1950 he was transferred to the military intelligence branch known as Z-2. After training at the intelligence school at Sulejowk he was assigned to Z-2's American section at headquarters, in Warsaw.

In September 1951, following the death in Korea of the Polish military attaché in Pyongyang, Monat was sent to Beijing, and in July the following year he was posted to North Korea. At the end of the war in Korea Monat returned home for a new assignment, to Washington DC, where he arrived in September 1955. It was during his period in the United States that Monat and his staff of eight were required to act as a surrogate for the Soviet GRU and he participated in numerous operations for the Soviets. However, his ideological commitment underwent a transformation following the publication of General Alexander Orlov's memoirs, *The Secret History of Stalin's Crimes*, in the United States. Whilst he initially had been inclined to dismiss the book as worthless Western propaganda, he interpreted Khrushchev's secret speech, in which he denounced Stalin, as confirmation of Orlov's charges. Upon his return to Poland in spring 1958 Monat became increasingly disillusioned with communism, and by December had decided to defect, together with his wife Maria and their thirteen-year-old son. As the recently appointed head of the military attaché's liaison department in Z-2 he suggested a tour of Warsaw Pact countries, and this he undertook in June 1959, accompanied by his family. When they reached Vienna Monat approached the American embassy and was granted political asylum. Six days later, he was flown back to Washington DC under the protection of the CIA. His memoirs, co-authored with the *Life* magazine journalist John Dille, were published in New York in 1961, and in this passage he describes his relationship with the UB at the Polish embassy on 16th Street.

Spy in the US

The agents from UB had a triple-threat job: (1) to carry out special political and economic espionage against the US; (2) to provide security for our embassy and annex; and (3) to keep an eye on our own people. To carry out the first mission, the UB was especially active in Chicago (which has a half-million residents of Polish descent whom the UB thought might be useful sources of information) and Detroit (with two hundred thousand Polish-Americans). But these two cities were not the UB's only stamping grounds. Approximately three-fourths of the Polish delegation to the United Nations, which is bedded down in New York, is made up of UB agents who form the strong-arm branch of Polish diplomacy. And to take care of its third mission, the UB also had a good deal of work to do right in our embassy and annex, among us Communists. The reason for this was simple.

The imposition of a police-state system like Communism on any people calls for the deployment of an immense number of undercover agents and informers to protect the system and hold the people in line. This is true on all levels – from the lowly crowd of the governed to the exalted elite of the governors. Intrigue, cunning and deceit are inevitable ingredients of Communism wherever it is found. And no one ever really trusts anyone else. This is especially true among the Communist cadres which have been plunked down inside the US. The easy American way of life and the heady influence of freedom and justice which we saw all around us might have tempted any of us to defect at any moment. And a defector from an embassy can take important secrets with him. It is the job of the UB – which is made up of some of Poland's most trusted Communist cops – to see that this does not happen.

Most of us in the embassy knew who most of these UB agents were. We knew that the embassy's Chief of Registry, who was responsible for the mail and the diplomatic pouches, was a trusted UB agent. We knew that the code clerks, guards and chauffeurs – who were there to protect us – were all UB men. And we knew that the embassy's First Secretary was their chief. But the UB also had representatives scattered among us whose membership in the secret police was a secret to all of us. Their mission was to watch us all – including the ambassador himself – and to report any sign of instability or wavering loyalty to Warsaw immediately. These men showed up at our parties as friends, listened to our most private conversations and kept a secret score on our spoken thoughts. If any one of us did not fill the UB's quota of appropriate anti-American, anticapita-listic and pro-Communist remarks in any given period, he was immedi-ately suspect, and the UB would start watching him in earnest.

But this system of intrigue could work both ways, and one day I decided to try a little intramural espionage of my own. I had a good reason. The consular office downstairs processed a good deal of mail from Americans, especially from people who wanted visas to visit Poland. It occurred to me that some of these people might be good sources of military information. An American who worked in a defense plant, for example, or an officer or enlisted man at a classified installation might be very useful to me – especially if I knew ahead of time that he was about to visit Poland. If we could manage to compromise or embarrass him in some way while he was there – and Z-2 had ways of doing this – I might be able to get him on the hook and pry some secrets out of him when he got back home.

But, in order to accomplish this, I would have to have complete control over the man's travel plans. I would have to take him out of the regular consular channels, and I would have to do all this without letting the consulate know what I was up to. The UB men who were planted there were also involved in espionage work, and if they happened to spot a likely informer or a good candidate for recruiting before I did, they would probably line him up for themselves before I could even get started. I had to get the jump on them in order to compete with them.

I decided to go about this in two different ways. The first approach was quite simple – I would read the consular mail before it ever reached the consulate. This was not hard to arrange. The mail for both offices in the annex was delivered to the building every day in one bag. By embassy custom, it went to the consulate first for sorting, and then I got whatever mail was addressed to me. I called on the ambassador and explained to him that I considered this routine very risky and would like to have it changed. I told him that since some of my mail was extremely sensitive and even secret in nature it was vital for me to protect it from all eyes, and I suggested that the best way to accomplish this would be for the embassy to send the bag of mail to me first. I would see to the sorting and would then forward whatever did not belong to me to the consulate. The ambassador agreed, and my plot had official sanction.

From then on my staff opened and read all of the mail – including letters addressed to the consulate, which we then sealed up again and sent downstairs where they belonged. But we held back anything which seemed promising – like a visa application from a scientist, an engineer or a missile worker – and processed this business through our own channels.

My second plan for keeping a jump ahead of the consulate and getting first crack at Americans who might be useful to me was to recruit one of the men on the consulate staff who had official dealings with Americans and could keep me posted on the best prospects. I looked over the people downstairs and decided to work on a young man named Witek who had come to Washington as acting consul in 1956.

It was Witek's job to keep in touch with Polish-American groups around the country, to help Poles who were living in the US look after their relatives in Poland and to advise American tourists who wanted to go there. If anyone could help me, I decided, Witek was the man. He was also an extremely friendly fellow. And I judged, from observing his habits, that he could use the extra money. He was on the Foreign Ministry payroll, but if he worked for me – on the side – he would get an additional salary from

Z-2. I sent a coded message to Warsaw asking Z-2 to check his file and verify his security clearance.

Two weeks later, Z-2 cabled back: 'Continue with Witek; security cleared; we are interested; proceed as if in Poland.'

This meant that I could go straight to the point with Witek without too much shilly-shallying or needless double talk. I invited Witek to my apartment for dinner and asked him up to my office several times to sound him out. Then I asked him point-blank if he would like to work for me. I explained the extra pay, in passing, but I made an especially strong appeal to his sense of patriotism. I really worked on him.

'You are already doing valuable work for Poland,' I told him, 'but if you also work for me you will be doing double duty for our fatherland.'

Witek listened politely and kept nodding his head as I talked. I went on, to make sure he understood the details of his new job, and told him that he would have to sign a few papers agreeing to keep the new arrangement completely secret.

Again Witek smiled and nodded. Then, without changing his expression, he interrupted me.

'Colonel,' he said, 'I must tell *you* a secret – and for God's sake please keep it. You see, I signed a paper before I ever left Warsaw, committing me to work for the UB. I do not believe I can hold *three* jobs for Poland.'

I tried not to show it to Witek – I thanked him and apologized for taking up his time – but I was so angry with Warsaw for letting me make a fool of myself that I sent off a cable immediately:

'You badly misinformed me,' I said. 'Man you cleared works for UB.'

Warsaw did not answer, but I could guess what had happened. Z-2 had confirmed Witek's clearance, but it had neglected – on purpose – to consult with the UB. Z-2 knew that if Witek was really a good man, and the UB did not have him, the secret police would snap him up for their own outfit before I even had a chance to see him again. I could only hope, after all the trouble I had gone to, that Comrade Witek had some nice things to say about me in *his* reports.

Orlando Castro Hidalgo

*To defect is to alter drastically one's whole life, and
the lives of all members of the family. To defect is not
merely to abandon an ideology, or to exchange one ideology
for another.*

A young *campesino* from Puerto Padre in Oriente province, Orlando Hidalgo joined Fidel Castro's guerrillas in the Sierra Maestra mountains in 1956. After Batista had been overthrown, Hidalgo joined an elite police battalion and was deployed against anti-Castro rebels in the Escambray mountains. In April 1961 he fought against the CIA-backed invaders who landed in the Bay of Pigs and was wounded. Later he joined the Ministry of the Interior in Havana and then was selected for recruitment by the Direccion General de Inteligencia (DGI).

After nine months of training Hidalgo was assigned to Section III of the DGI, responsible for illegal intelligence operations in Canada, Mexico and the United States. He served in the personnel and counter-intelligence branches before being transferred to the European section for a mission to Paris.

Soon after his arrival in Paris Hidalgo's wife Norma, a teacher, was accused of not being sufficiently revolutionary because she had refused to participate in a voluntary teaching programme, and in November 1968 the couple decided to defect with their two boys. They made contact with a Cuban exile who agreed to act as an intermediary and negotiate terms with the CIA, and in March 1970, while on Sunday duty at the embassy, Hidalgo emptied the DGI *rezident*'s safe of classified documents. After spending the night at a safe-house they drove to Luxembourg, where they were granted asylum by the US embassy. During his debriefing by the CIA, Hidalgo identified more than 150 DGI agents and gave a detailed account of the organization's operations, as he admitted in his autobiography published in 1971.

A Spy for Fidel

My decision to defect was rooted in the very Revolution for which I had fought. The seeds were planted over a period of years; they grew and blossomed in Paris. Revolutions devour their sons; they can also betray them. Probably most Cubans sympathized with the Cuban Revolution in its initial stages; a great many turned against it when it changed course from freedom to communism and demagoguery and dictatorship.

I took part in the July 26 Revolution, but never with foreign ideologies in mind, communism, all that about proletarian internationalism. As I developed with the Revolution, I watched the revolutionary process.

While I fought in the Escambray and at Girón Beach, I was never the fanatic who did things because he was told to do them and without seeing the realities of the matter. Friends of mine, some of them not in sympathy with the Revolution, told me of arbitrary acts that had been committed within the revolutionary process, and at first I thought that these acts were the fault of extremists, extremists who had managed to get into the Revolution. But as the Revolution proceeded and these things continued, I came to realize that they were more widespread, that they were part of the process itself. There was the mistreatment of those persons who criticized the Revolution, who saw that it was changing in character, that it was betraying the principles for which it had been fought. It was said that those who were critical were 'foreign' elements, perhaps recruited by foreign intelligence. If you had opinions contrary to those held by Fidel, that was enough to label you as belonging to the CIA, as being counterrevolutionary. You then were no longer treated as a human being, but as a political enemy; you were an undesirable, a person who had to be cast off. Such a person had to be separated, he must not be dealt with, and anyone who did treat with him was viewed as a weak revolutionary, as perhaps someone who was himself suspect.

All that humbug, all those lies, all those promises that Fidel made, to elevate the level of life, to work for the social good – I remembered those promises. Whenever he would say such-and-such will be carried out in thus-and-thus time, I would remember, and when it wasn't carried out, I knew this had been a hoax. They were lies, all that about raising the standards of the peasantry to that of the cities, making the differences between field and city disappear. As I came to know and understand these demagogic plans, and saw that they were not being fulfilled, I knew that the failures were not due to counterrevolution, upon which the blame was placed. The faults were within the system itself. I was a part of the revolutionary process and I saw that the defects were inside, within itself, a sickness of the system, and not the fault of 'foreign elements'.

During 1962 – the year of the missile crisis – with the blockade in effect against Cuba, even the most basic commodities became scarce. The government mobilized thousands and thousands of workers to do 'voluntary' work in the fields in order to harvest the cane crop and other crops. Although at times this mass labor had ill results – as when amateur cutters damaged the cane – the general effect was very good, and the food level could have been raised. We were told that all that effort, that sacrifice, the product of all that work, would be used to benefit the entire people. But then we saw that it was not used to help the people, there was an unmerciful policy of exportation, ninety percent of the products were sent abroad, without heed to the fact that the Cuban people had to eat, had to have clothing. There were restrictions, rationing, and calls to more sacrifice, and there were proclamations of immense rewards to follow, great results for the people, a marvelous future. I began to understand that all this was part of the international Communist system, that this was the only way the people could be kept working. Their hopes must always be maintained.

I became disillusioned; there were disappointments and disappointments. There would be announcements of gain made by the peasants, and when I went out into the fields I saw the *campesinos*, and they were more hungry, their clothes more tattered, and there was no clear future for them. I could see the great deception that was being carried out by communism.

The reality was completely different than the reports that were given. The Cuban magazines, the publications sent abroad, told of the achievements of the Revolution as if these benefited the Cuban people. Propaganda went out to Latin America, to the entire world, aimed at presenting the Cuban Revolution as something magnificent, different than revolutionary processes that had occurred in other places.

There was that famous Agrarian Reform. The government pompously announced that the lands would be broken up and distributed, or would be used to benefit all the people. There was much propaganda about this. Books were published, and these became a catechism for revolutionaries. All the means of diffusion in Cuba told about the Agrarian Reform, this was one of the most altruistic measures of the Revolution, this was a tremendous good. But then the government took the land, the *campesino* was forced to sell; he was held by the neck, the land was seized, there was no more propaganda, nothing was said, nothing was printed.

I was part of the system, even though I saw these problems. Perhaps it was opportunism. Many of us who had fought for something different – now we were not interested in any of these questions, we had fought and won and wanted to enjoy, we wanted to rise within the system, to acquire positions of importance without concerning ourselves about the misfortunes of the people.

Did I want my children to grow up in such a society? Norma and I now had two boys (one of them born in Paris). I wanted them to respect their nation, to respect me, too.

When comes the awakening of the conscience? Friends of mine had been imprisoned, their lands arbitrarily seized. They were good people, honorable, and all their lives they had done honest labor.

I knew that I was an instrument of the system, of that monstrosity, of that deception. I was in it not because of fanaticism, but because I was carried along and did not resist, and so I could not close my eyes to what was there, to occurrences that I did not like, defects that were apparent, bad things that I saw. By the time I was preparing to go to Paris, it was probably in my subconscious that I would break with the Revolution. Then, in Paris, there were these officials who personified all the deceit, all the falsities of the Revolution, men who only wanted to keep climbing, who didn't care a fig about the calamities of the people. They were blind, or made themselves blind, to reality.

Werner Stiller

Even though I was later taught how to analyze political events critically and to understand why certain measures had to be taken, the events of 1968 left an enduring impression.

Brought up as one of three children near Leipzig, Werner Stiller joined the Young Pioneers while still at school and remained an activist when, in August 1966, aged nineteen, he started to study physics at the city's Karl Marx University.

While in his final year Stiller was approached by the Ministry of State Security and invited to undergo training as an agent in the Federal Republic. In December 1970 he was sworn into the organization and assigned the task of reporting on various acquaintances, and continued to maintain contact with the HVA's Science and Technology Directorate after his graduation and his appointment to a post in the Physics Society in Berlin.

Stiller attended the HVA's training school at Belzig and after completing the course concentrated on recruiting and running agents in the scientific community. In February 1976 he was promoted to first lieutenant and soon afterwards established contact with the West German BND. A method of communicating was agreed and continued for two years until he underwent an emotional crisis resulting from his affair with Helga, a dissident living in Oberhof.

In January 1979 Stiller engineered Helga's escape to the West with her son, and he then caught a train into West Berlin. At Tegel airport he identified himself to the police as a defector and he was passed on to the BND, to whom he exposed no less than twenty-two HVA agents in the West. Altogether he supplied the BND with 20,000 HVA documents.

Following a divorce from his wife, he married Helga and now lives in the United States, under a death sentence from the old East German state. His autobiography, which was published in Germany in 1986, contains the kind of detail which guarantees authenticity and makes his evidence so damaging to the HVA.

Beyond the Wall

In the early summer of 1976, the BND notified me of a new dead-letter drop. Once again it was located in a park, the Königsheide, which lay in the vicinity of the MfS apartment house where I lived. Concealed under a bush was a normal-looking but quite large chunk of stone. I placed it in a shopping bag as instructed and went directly to my safe house. When I pushed a needle into a tiny hole on the surface, the stone immediately split into two halves, revealing a small transistor radio inside.

Before reading the enclosed instructions, I switched on the radio and played with the dial but heard merely a hissing noise. Had an audio specialist examined the used radio, which was constructed solely from East German parts, he would have simply concluded that the expense involved did not warrant the repair. According to the instructions, only the transmissions of the BND could be received on the radio. Henceforth, after finding a secure locale, I should tune in at specified times and listen to the long lists of numbers being read aloud. The announcement of my code number meant that the following ciphers contained a message for me. To make certain that the message reached me, it would be repeated several times at stated intervals using a different code number and radio frequency.

Along with the set of code numbers and decoding strips was a letter of gratitude for the information I had conveyed about the HVA agents. Although some preliminary checks would be made, the BND assured me that my own safety had top priority and that assistance would be provided in the event of an emergency. Underscoring the dangers involved in our relationship, the BND advised me to exercise utmost caution myself, even at the expense of securing valuable information. Another set of questions, which no longer dealt with my authenticity but rather with the internal structure of the MfS and the HVA, had also been enclosed. After promptly preparing the coded response, I followed the instructions and destroyed the piece of stone and its locking mechanism.

At this stage, I felt very pleased with the direction things were going. Without having checked out my information, the BND now appeared far more trusting than before. Yet I also knew that full confidence would come only after my list had been verified. After all, no secret service organization would ever sacrifice five of its own people just to place one double agent in the enemy camp.

A week later, at the prearranged time, I was at my safe house ready to receive the initial radio transmission. First came the distinctive rise and fall of the Pullach signal – the so-called 'Wessel Anthem', named after the second man to head the BND. Then an unemotional voice stated, 'I have a message for . . .' Hearing my number, I wrote down the five groups of ciphers that followed. Once decoded, the message contained a word of congratulations on the commencement of radio contact along with some safety precautions to be observed. This first communication was designed simply to test our new linkage. To confirm receipt of this message, I sent an innocent postcard to the cover address in the FRG.

Although the radio had eliminated the need for complicated dead-letter drops, a considerable amount of time would have to be spent listening for my number, deciphering the messages, and sending coded replies. In order to get a head start on the day's workload, I now began to arrive an hour earlier at the office. Because of the number of agents I handled and my reputation as an industrious worker, no one seemed to think twice about this new routine. On the contrary, my superiors found my conspicuous dedication all the more praiseworthy. Then, too, arriving earlier in the morning – rather than staying after hours – aroused less suspicion as a general professional rule and permitted me to be at my safe house to receive the afternoon BND transmissions.

I had yet another plan in mind. Since official files could not be taken from the office, I wanted to request a small, well-disguised camera from the BND. It would allow me to photograph various documents before my colleagues arrived at work. Moreover, having acquired the recently converted bathroom as an office, I could see anyone approaching the entrance to the building from the small window.

Once Werner Heintze's departure became official, my hunch about receiving his West agent was confirmed. In making the presentation, Christian remarked, 'Unbeknownst to you, this man is working in your Karlsruhe installation.'

Unaware that I had already relayed this fact to the BND over a month ago, Christian continued enthusiastically, 'If anyone can keep us abreast of Bonn's nuclear weapons potential, then it's this person. Because he's working in the FRG's only reprocessing plant, the actual amount of radioactive material can be monitored. By profession, he's merely a tax accountant, but never underestimate the espionage value of such positions.'

Werner and I were to organize the next trip together. 'Incidentally,' Christian added, 'you'll also be inheriting the very best instructor in the division.' As I later discovered, this person's performance fully matched his reputation, and my own tasks were minimal.

As soon as Werner put the file on the desk, I saw that my reading of the name had been correct. For twelve years, Reiner Fülle had worked for the HVA. A native of the Erzgebirge like Sturm, he had gone to the FRG after completing his technical training. Quite clearly, it was a desire for adventure rather than political discontent that had prompted his decision. For the next few years, he took a series of odd jobs and evening courses until a position opened at the newly built Karlsruhe nuclear facility.

The reprocessing plant to which Fülle was assigned had special significance for the SED leadership. Viewed solely from their ideological perspective, the plant provided evidence of Bonn's imperialist aims in the nuclear field. The real explanation – that existing resources could be better utilized by recycling the burned-out fuel rods from nuclear reactors – was ignored. In addition to the periodic anti-nuclear campaigns in the FRG, the penetration of the Karlsruhe facility was given top priority. Any employee who happened to visit the GDR became an immediate target for recruitment. Ultimately, this enormous operation had little to do with ascertaining the FRG's military plans, but sought instead to aid the Soviet Union with the production of its nuclear arsenal.

Laszlo Szabo

The work between Soviet and Bloc intelligence and security services is a direct result of the co-operation between the national Communist parties and the Communist Party of the Soviet Union.

One of the very few known examples of a defector from the Hungarian AVH, Laszlo Szabo had served under diplomatic cover, with the rank of second secretary, in London until October 1965 when he sought political asylum at the American embassy in Grosvenor Square. In March the following year he gave evidence to the CIA Subcommittee of the House Committee on the Armed Services and confirmed that for the past twenty years he had been an officer of the AVH. His career had started in July 1946 when he had joined the internal security section of the AVO in Budapest. The son of a veteran communist who had worked for the Soviets as a translator, Szabo had spent the war working at a printing plant in Debrecen, where he had been born, and he had joined the Party in 1945, at the age of twenty.

For the first three years Szabo studied at the College of Foreign Languages in Budapest and served in the provinces, but in 1948 he was promoted to the counter-intelligence section of the AVO's internal security branch, and concentrated on the detection of Western agents who had been infiltrated into Hungary with wireless transmitters. He underwent a counter-intelligence course in Moscow in 1957 and later transferred to the industrial sabotage section, but in 1963, with the rank of major, he was posted to the AVO's foreign intelligence branch, known as the AVH. The following year he spent a month studying English at Oxford and in September 1965 was sent under diplomatic cover to London. Within a couple of weeks of his arrival he had defected, volunteering a detailed breakdown of the AVH's structure.

His testimony, which was also quoted in a classified CIA handbook, *Soviet Intelligence Operations Against American and US Installations Abroad: An Analysis of Soviet Doctrine and Practice*, printed in July 1968, gave an unprecedented insight into the AVH's operations. Szabo described how the American Noel Field had actively participated in several AVH disinformation schemes, and had worked as a translator on forged copies of *Newsweek* which had been distributed in Europe as part of a propaganda campaign.

Szabo also drew attention to the unusual case of Lieutenant Bela Lapusnyik, a twenty-three-year-old AVO officer who in May 1962 had made a dramatic escape across the border at Nickelsdorf to Vienna. Lapusnyik was interrogated by the Viennese authorities but died three weeks later from some mysterious bacteriological infection while in protective custody in the maximum security wing of Rossauerlande prison, just hours before he was due to be flown to the United States. The lieutenant's sudden death, apparently by poison administered while he had been under close guard either in prison or at the Federal Security Police's headquarters on the Parkring, was widely believed to have been an AVH assassination, a theory confirmed by Szabo.

Statement of Laszlo Szabo to the Eighty-Ninth Congress, Second Session

My first grave doubts about the morality of the Hungarian security service system were generated in 1948 and 1949 when I assisted in the work on a number of cases that were basically mounted by the service against certain foreigners in the country. I began to fight myself and to begin to justify this action by conceding that in the long run there might be some ultimate justice in these basically illegal actions. Thereafter, however, the AVH service began to choke out any individuality or feeling and I was always under orders. I noted in 1949 and 1950 certain AVH officers began to disappear. These men disappeared, for example one was Oscar Havas, without a trace – that was the period of the persecution of Ferenc Nagy and the period of the Rajk and other cases. But with these doubts also came my fears. What was happening in the service also began to happen in the country itself. Slogans began to repress all thinking and created widespread fear, and this was greatest within the AVH itself. I joined the AVH as a very young man. After a succession of events, I recognized it for what it was. I did not have personal bravery then to turn in any other direction and I found it impossible then to change the course of action.

During the two years that I was out of the service – 1952 to 1954 – I saw what had happened in Hungary was completely tragic, but I accepted to go back in the service. Though I hated the slogans, I felt I was probably safer in the AVH at the time and knew it better than any part of the Party organization. There was a third choice – I could have refused to go back, but I feared to do it. I knew by this time that they were ready to kill as well as pressure so I chose to go back in. It is very difficult to describe a fight that goes on inside the self. A heroic man could have refused. I was not and am not that, and I feared to do it. I talked to no one about my doubts. That would have been a mistake. I was able to leave the way I did and I am here today because I was careful.

In the period 1954 to 1956, the Hungarian security service lost in power. At the same time the country gradually was caught up in a ferment of criticism and opposition to the Communist regime. We in the AVH knew this. We were powerless to stop it in the country just as the service itself was powerless to mobilize effective counter-action.

I remember receiving in the AVH a small pamphlet printed in the west and sent into Hungary which carried the text of Khrushchev's secret speech at the Twentieth Congress. Thousands of copies of this pamphlet got into the country and were passed around secretly. Within the AVH, which had the job of picking up as many copies as it could, the document was read with great interest. It was given to me to read by a colleague. The influence on me of this little booklet was terrible and it also affected other AVH officers the same way. It was clear from Khrushchev's secret speech that Rakosi and his followers had not only followed the example of Stalin's leadership but had really carried out horrible crimes against the Hungarian people on their own. Very gradually the October 1956 Revolution developed in Hungary out of the crimes of the regime itself. First by its excesses and then by its inability to clean up its own messes. The 1956 revolt, therefore, was prepared and carried out by the Hungarians themselves, not by outsiders.

I survived the events of late October and early November because I was in the Ministry of Interior building throughout the whole time on duty. I was evacuated from the building under Soviet guard and brought back by them a week and a half later. I followed orders and kept quiet.

My transfer to the overseas part of the service was the beginning of my opportunity, finally, to decide something for myself about my life. I was able to make the change because one of my former superiors had earlier gone to the External Service as deputy chief and he picked me to follow him there. When I was in Oxford in the autumn of 1964, I thought of remaining but ultimately I decided to return. Again I was still afraid and perhaps somewhat confused, but I also knew I was sure to come back.

When I arrived in the United Kingdom, finally, on my assignment, I had decided I would not carry out any orders and soon after my arrival I made the break. I knew this was my last chance. I finally made up my mind I would not serve the AVH organization further. I have no doubts about my choice and I would do it over again if I had to. Was this a crime against my country? I am sure that it was not. It was the only thing I could do. The crime was that I was a member of a very cruel and inhuman organization. But I never did anything criminal, I never fired a gun at a man during my service, and I never initiated any cases against innocent people.

My soul is clear before God – and I hope before you.

George Mikes

*The truth is that a Communist dictatorship – or any
other dictatorship for that matter – cannot exist
without an effective organ of terror.*

Apart from his seminal work *The Hungarian Revolution*, George Mikes was best known as a humorous writer, the author of *How to be an Alien* and *Down with Everybody*. Born in Hungary and educated at university in Budapest, Mikes moved to England but returned home briefly in 1948 to witness totalitarianism at first hand. However, it was the uprising of October 1956 that ensured the full horror of Soviet repression in Hungary was realized in the West. After the ten days of turmoil Mikes became the recipient of a batch of documents looted from buildings occupied by the notorious AVH. The papers were editions of *State Security Review*, a classified publication with limited internal circulation, and two other handbooks, entitled *External Surveillance* and *Secret House Searches*, both written by named AVH officers.

Together these documents revealed the AVH to be virtually identical to the AVO, the instrument of repression that had been a hated feature of Admiral Horthy's wartime regime, and the irony is that the AVH's leadership had itself experienced imprisonment at the hands of the same organization. Gabor Peter, who in 1944 set up the AVH from the remnants of the AVO in its old headquarters building at 60 Andrassy Road, had spent years in prison, as had the Communist Party chief, Janos Kadar.

Officially the old AVO became the AVH in September 1948, but it was a mere cosmetic change, for although the name changed from State Security Department to State Security Administration, its functions and structure remained the same. In the first part of his book Mikes recorded the AVH's postwar history, and in the second reproduced the texts of the material seized from the AVH's headquarters, which acted as an eloquent indictment of their methods.

A Study in Infamy

In the early 'fifties the AVO was at the height of its arbitrary and dreaded power. Here is a description of how they treated one of their political prisoners. There is nothing extraordinary in this account: many people received much worse treatment, few got off more lightly.

'Two AVO officers questioned me in turn from 9 a.m. till 9 p.m. Then I had to type my life story till 4 a.m. The rest of the twenty-four hours I had to spend walking up and down in the cubicle because I was not permitted to sleep. This went on for three weeks. The only sleep I got was a few minutes when the guard was slack. The "hearings" soon became tortures. The AVO officers wanted us to invent crimes for ourselves because they knew we were innocent. I won't describe the tortures. There are so many ways to cause piercing pain to the human body. There were days when we were tossed about in a stormy ocean of pain. The torments alone did not make us "confess". Sleeplessness, hunger, utter degradation, filthy insults to human dignity, the knowledge that we were utterly at the mercy of the AVO – all this was not enough. Then they told us they would arrest our wives and children and torment them in front of us. We heard women and children screaming in adjacent rooms. Was this a put-up job for our benefit? I still don't know.

'After the first period of torture we were sent back to our solitary cellars for some weeks to "rot away for a while". Now we were tormented by the intense cold, by the glaring bulb and the four walls which threatened to collapse on us. We had to be awake eighteen hours a day. There were no books, no cigarettes, only thousands of empty minutes. Our fear was now insanity . . .

'After a period of "rotting" a new period of torments started. And so it went on for thirteen and a half months.'

I visited an AVO prison myself when I went to Hungary during the Revolution and described my experiences:

'I went over the AVO prisons in Györ. We had heard that there was a torture chamber in the building. The soldiers on duty there had heard it, too, but they informed me, the rumours must have been unfounded because they could not find any signs of it.

'We saw the cells – miserable little holes which had now been thrown open to let out the terrible stench of many years. The prisoners had not been allowed to sit down during the day for one minute: they had to walk up and down, up and down, all day long. Some of them were there for two years. I saw a paper-mill where secret papers no longer wanted were torn in tiny bits – a more effective and safer method than burning. I also saw a huge room which looked rather like a telephone exchange. There one could listen in to almost all the telephone conversations of Györ and its district, and forty conversations could be recorded simultaneously. There were shelves full of tapes. On top of each was the AVO man's report under separate headings such as: Name of Caller, Name of Called, Duration of Conversation, Remarks. Under this last heading were such comments as: "interesting", "suspicious", "to be followed up". An agent's signature followed. This vast apparatus cost 35 million forints (£350,000). In the same months when its building was finished the minumum wage of workers was *raised* to 650 forints (£6[.50]) a month.

'The AVO also had a large short-wave radio transmitting station in the building. During the days of my visit it was being used as the free station, Radio Györ.

'And later, in Vienna I heard from two Györ workers – both leaders of the Social Democratic Party who had seen the place with their own eyes – that the torture chamber was, in fact, there. No wonder the soldiers could not find it at once. It was a small enclosure, rather like a coffin, which a man could occupy only in a lying position. This coffin was built of bricks, with one of its walls adjacent to a large boiler. Two tubes led into it: gas could be led in through one; steam through the other. The steam was used to torture; the gas to kill.'

Janos Radvanyi

Moscow shed no crocodile tears that the long war in Vietnam had disrupted American society, had damaged the relations of the United States with a number of its allies, and had cast serious doubts on the reliability and endurance of American commitments around the world.

A career diplomat, Janos Radvanyi had studied his profession at the Academy of Foreign Affairs in Budapest between 1945 and 1947, before working as a desk officer dealing with Soviet–Hungarian reparations. One of his first tasks in the Foreign Ministry was to act as a liaison officer for President Tito of Yugoslavia, who signed a friendship treaty in Budapest in December 1947. Late in 1948 he was sent on his first overseas assignment, to Ankara as a junior attaché, and upon his return he concentrated on bilateral relations with African and Asian countries. In November 1958 he visited Hanoi on a routine inspection tour and the following year was back as a member of a Hungarian delegation which, during the week it was in Vietnam, discovered that the Democratic Republic planned to attack the south.

In April 1960 Radvanyi was appointed Chief of Protocol in Budapest, and in March two years later he was transferred to Washington DC as chargé d'affaires of the Hungarian Legation. With his knowledge of Vietnam Radvanyi became a key figure in the negotiations between the US State Department and the North Vietnamese, and he was pivotal in the secret talks that led to the temporary truce of Christmas 1965. Over the next two years he continued to act as a mediator, seeking a formula for peace, but he discovered to his dismay that the Hungarian Foreign Minister, Janos Péter, had made several proposals, suggesting a Korea-like solution, without any authority from Hanoi. Indeed, Radvanyi knew that the Vietnamese had no interest in peace, but were keen to stop the American bombing of the north. Finally, in May 1967, Radvanyi called on Dean Rusk at the State Department and revealed Péter's duplicity. He was granted immediate political asylum and moved with his family to the West Coast before taking an academic post at Mississippi State University. Following the Tet Offensive in January 1968 he wrote a long article for *Life* magazine which became the basis of his account of the Vietnamese peace talks, published in 1978, which documented the lack of sincerity on the part of the Hungarians.

Delusion and Reality

. . . on May 19, it became public that the head of the Soviet secret police, Vladimir V. Semichastny, a close subordinate of Shelepin, had been replaced by Yuri V. Andropov, a protégé of Brezhnev. Less than a month later another Shelepin man, the powerful secretary of the Moscow City Party Committee, Nikolai Yegorychev, was fired. Finally, on July 11, Shelepin himself lost his position in the inner circle of the supreme decision-making body, the Secretariat of the Central Committee. He was downgraded to a second-rate administrative post, the chairmanship of the All-Union Central Council of Trade Unions. Ustinov's role remained a mystery. Known for his ability to survive, he possibly changed sides in time. On the other hand, one can surmise that he was the one who warned

Brezhnev of Shelepin's sinister plot. In any event, Ustinov became an ardent supporter of Brezhnev. Ambassador Dobrynin returned to Washington on June 15; Major General Meshcheryakov's prophecy failed. The Kremlin 'hawks' had lost to the realists.

I had lived through the Stalinist terror of the early 1950s and was filled with apprehension that now neo-Stalinist hardliners could very well take over in the Kremlin and in Eastern Europe. I did not want any part of it. I decided not to wait for the outcome of the power struggle. I felt I simply could not delay my personal decision any longer. I crossed the Rubicon.

Late in the afternoon, on May 16, I called Secretary of State Dean Rusk and asked to see him on an urgent private matter. A few hours later we met. I was extremely agitated, wanting to tell at once everything that rankled in my mind. With a voice shaken by emotion I told him that I had been through a long soul-searching and finally had concluded that I had to quit the Hungarian foreign service. Then I said that Foreign Minister Péter had badly misled him and the United States government by stating that Hanoi would agree to peace talks if the United States would halt the bombing of North Vietnam for a few weeks. To begin with, I said, I had found out during the previous summer that Péter had no authority whatsoever to speak for Hanoi. Moreover, the messages I was passing to the secretary from Péter were false, including his proposition for direct talks between the representatives of the United States and North Vietnam during the 37-day bombing pause. Péter's sole purpose was to postpone the resumption of the American bombing. Hanoi had little concern for a negotiated settlement; therefore, Péter knew that direct talks would not take place. I went on, saying that the Hungarian foreign minister had deceived the secretary again in the fall of 1966 when he claimed that Hanoi was interested in some kind of Korea-like solution. Finally, I added that my personal involvement in Péter's machinations had become a serious personal concern and I felt myself trapped in an untenable position serving a policy with which I completely disagreed.

Rusk, who listened all the time attentively, quietly answered that he understood perfectly well that I had been used and added that I should not worry unduly since he himself had always had some reservations about the reality of what Péter had been saying and doing.

Slowly regaining my composure, I began to pour out all the resentment accumulated in me in the course of years. I started by saying that as a steadfast advocate of closer Hungarian–American ties, I did everything I could to bring back to normal the strained relations between our two countries. I had spared no effort to establish cultural exchange programs and to expand trade and tourism between the two countries. Understandably I was particularly bitter that officials in Budapest, closely following the Soviet line, had suddenly changed policy and declared that until the United States government stopped its 'aggression' in Vietnam there could be no broader East–West exchange. I also related how I was told that in reality the Johnson 'bridge-building' policy was merely a renewed attempt for loosening up the basis of the 'socialist society' and was aimed at detaching Hungary from the Soviet Union. For obvious reasons, I said to Rusk, I had to disassociate myself from this policy of hatred. Yet I was still worried that my decision might create problems for the United States, and I asked the secretary to treat my defection in as low a key as possible to prevent it from becoming a major thorn in East–West and US–Hungarian relations.

Rusk agreed with me. Here I waited for a minute or so, then asked whether my family and I could stay permanently in the United States. The secretary promised to speak with his colleagues and give me the answer as soon as possible.

Less than three hours later an aide of Rusk informed me that we were welcome in America and adequate safeguards for our security would be provided. The next day I went into seclusion and sent a simple one-paragraph letter to Péter, stating that I was resigning for personal reasons.

On May 17, 1967, State Department spokesman Robert J. McCloskey made a brief announcement in connection with my decision. He stated that I wished to become a permanent resident of the United States and would be granted asylum in accordance with the 'American tradition of extending refuge to those who seek it'.

Following the State Department announcement, I issued a statement which said in part:

> I have always tried to work for peace and better understanding in this troubled world. However, in recent months I came to realize that it was impossible for me to act in good conscience and continue to be the representative of the Hungarian Government. Therefore, I have decided to retire from all forms of public life. The reasons for this decision are very personal ones which I do not wish to explain further.

For me the diplomatic battle over Vietnam ended here.

CHAPTER IV

The Americans

*There is a difference between the act of breaking with
Communism, which is personal, and the act of breaking
with the Communist Party, which is organizational.*
Whittaker Chambers

Since the War of Independence, when Benedict Arnold attempted to betray George Washington's forces to the British, and Nathan Hale was hanged for espionage, treachery has played a significant part in American history. During the twentieth century the United States was brought into the First World War in April 1917 by the revelation that the Kaiser's Foreign Minister, Arthur Zimmermann, had offered Mexico the southern states of Texas, New Mexico and Arizona in return for a declaration of war. In the Second, Japan's surprise attack on Pearl Harbor, an act of supreme treachery while diplomatic negotiations continued between Washington and Tokyo, was dubbed by President Roosevelt as a day of infamy. In strict legal terms, however, no country can really be said to be guilty of treachery. It is individuals within a government who commit the crime, but when the original delegates drew up the American Constitution they were understandably cautious about defining treason, a concept to which the British Crown had given a wide interpretation, particularly in the colonies.

Determined to avoid the 'numerous and dangerous excrescenses' of English law, the American Constitution narrowed the crime to 'levying War' against the government, and 'adhering to their enemies, giving them Aid and Comfort', but required a minimum of two witnesses to give evidence of the same act of war. Partly due to this strict legal requirement of producing two witnesses to secure a conviction, only a dozen Americans were ever indicted on a charge of treason, seven of them radio announcers who had broadcast from Tokyo during the war in the Pacific. During the Korean War a rather larger group of Americans were persuaded to stay in the North after the ceasefire, and when some two dozen did subsequently return home they were court-martialled and in

267

most cases stripped of their citizenship. None, so far as is known, has written of his experiences.

Examples of Americans who collaborated with the Japanese are virtually non-existent, with the most significant case being the very least known. Herbert Yardley's sale of cryptographic secrets to the Japanese Cipher Bureau in 1930 was an appalling act of betrayal, but he was never held to account for it because the whole matter was judged to be far too sensitive to be aired in court. In fact, it was not until Griffin Bell was appointed Attorney-General by President Jimmy Carter that any US administration showed any determination to prosecute miscreants inside a secret agency suspected of having sold out to an enemy, a clear distinction having been drawn between them and political activists within the federal government, whose conduct and affiliations were subject to examination by a Loyalty Board created by President Truman.

Whereas a considerable number of Soviets defected to the West, the number of Americans who moved in the opposite direction is comparatively small. And in contrast to the very substantial literature generated by Soviet defectors, none of the Americans who went to live beyond the Iron Curtain is known to have released his or her story. Perhaps the only exception is Commander Lloyd Bucher of the USS *Pueblo*, the NSA signals intelligence vessel captured by the North Koreans in January 1968, but his experience, and that of his crew, had been entirely involuntary. Following their eleven months in captivity the crew was released, and Commander Bucher, having been fêted as a hero, was criticized by the US Navy's Board of Inquiry which recommended that he be 'brought to trial by general courts-martial' and charged with

> permitting his ship to be seized while he had the power to resist, failing to take immediate and aggressive protective measures . . . complying with the orders of the North Koreans to follow them into port, failing to complete the destruction of classified material . . . and permitting such material to fall into the hands of the North Koreans.

Bucher emphatically rejected all the charges in his book, *Pueblo & Bucher*, but never faced a court-martial, the Secretary for the Navy's decision being that he had suffered enough while a prisoner, and that his conduct and leadership in Korea had been an inspiration to his men. Instead Bucher was issued with a reprimand which was not rescinded until 1990, when Congress passed a law to allow medals to be issued to all the *Pueblo*'s survivors.

America's commitment to freedom of political expression has often been abused, particularly by those dissenters among prisoners of war captured in Korea who chose to remain in the North after the ceasefire, and the anti-Vietnam War campaigners like Jane Fonda who mistakenly travelled to Hanoi to demonstrate their disapproval of the Republican administration's policy in south-east Asia.

For Americans who have always lived under a democratic system, where every citizen has the regular opportunity to cast a vote to change the composition of the House of Representatives and the Senate, and to remove an incumbent president from the White House, there would appear to be few opportunities for politically motivated traitors. Yet, for a memorable period in its history, the country became preoccupied with the fear that subversives were seeking to undermine the established order and take control. Exploited to the full by Senator Joe McCarthy, it was a time of Hollywood blacklists, secret cells of fellow travellers and ideological witch-hunts. Careers were ruined, reputations blighted and potential informers encouraged to denounce their Leftist colleagues.

Certainly there was, particularly in the postwar era, a concerted effort by those who had made a commitment to communism to help Moscow, but the scale of the conspiracy remained unknown to the American authorities, which had only very limited experience of American traitors. The wholesale round-up and internment of Japanese Americans, particularly in California, in the aftermath of Pearl Harbor had proved a severe and lasting embarrassment because none was ever found to have been working secretly for the Emperor. Indeed, even in the case of Tokyo Rose, the propaganda radio broadcaster widely regarded as the most blatant example of treachery, there was never really any such single, identifiable person. The name was generic and was applied to twenty-seven women disc jockeys who had broadcast to considerable effect in the English language. Four years after the war Ivo Toguri, who had been born to a Nisei family in Los Angeles, was imprisoned on a charge of treason, but she was pardoned by President Gerald Ford in January 1977, the only American ever to have been cleared following conviction of the crime.

In the European theatre the poet Ezra Pound was considered to have committed treachery by his support for the Axis and, if he had not been judged insane, he would certainly have faced criminal charges had he returned home from Italy after the war.

The FBI's preoccupation with disloyal Americans in the postwar era had originated with a highly secret, easily compromised source, the decoded texts of dozens of intercepted Soviet messages which had revealed a massive espionage offensive and the existence of literally hundreds of intelligence assets. The challenge confronting the FBI was to eliminate the networks without jeopardizing the cryptographic nature of the information, which invariably meant the recruitment of an informant who could give evidence against other conspirators, or lengthy surveillance to catch suspects in an illegal act. The FBI recognized that if their opponents even suspected the true nature of the original tip, the Soviet cipher procedures would be changed, thereby preventing further exploitation. The requirements of public presentation in criminal prosecutions, necessitating individual witnesses to give evidence before a jury, meant that any discussion of the existence of a lapse in Soviet communications security would be bound to leak. From bitter experience the FBI knew that such a disclosure would guarantee that the Soviets would tighten up their coding systems. Accordingly, the source was given full protection and the subject still remains exceptionally sensitive, even half a century later.

The FBI successfully recruited several moles who were willing to penetrate the clandestine Soviet organizations, and among them were Marion Miller and Boris Morros. The latter was a fully fledged Soviet agent until he encountered the FBI in 1947 and agreed to operate as a double agent, a decision which the Soviets regarded as treachery. In Miller's case, however, there was a distinction. When she was originally recruited by the CPUSA, through a front organization in 1950, she approached the FBI and volunteered to infiltrate the Party but, as she said in *I Was a Spy*, 'I did not meet shadowy characters or Kremlin brass in Vienna and Moscow, in the manner of Mr Boris Morros.' Whilst she provided useful information from inside the CPUSA, she never had an opportunity, during the five years she was under cover, to qualify as a traitor to the cause, for the Soviet cause was never her own.

In addition to the infiltrators, the Bureau benefited from ideological converts who, for various reasons, opted to appear as witnesses against their former comrades. Both Hede Massing and Elizabeth Bentley have written damning accounts of how, having been approached by the FBI, they decided to give statements that amounted to long confessions which implicated other members of the spy-rings. As for the FBI, no explanation was ever given to explain exactly how the individuals concerned had been selected for interview. Into the same broad category of FBI informants falls Michael Straight, who also, belatedly, volunteered to help the FBI and thereby unexpectedly enabled MI5 to entrap Anthony Blunt, whom he had known at Cambridge as a Soviet spy.

Some of those compromised by the Soviet reliance on insecure cipher systems escaped formal prosecution for espionage. Agnes Smedley, long considered to be an important recruiter and a talent-spotter responsible for developing several networks, both in America and overseas, fled the United States and preferred to remain beyond the reach of the FBI and the House Un-American Activities Committee (HUAC). In the case of Alger Hiss, convincingly identified as a Soviet spy by his former contact Whittaker Chambers, the disclosure of all the evidence pointing to his guilt would have meant revealing what had been accomplished by the cryptanalysts who had broken the Soviet ciphers which protected the true names of dozens of the NKVD's assets in North America. Accordingly, he was never charged with espionage, despite the material against him accumulated by the code-breakers, but instead was convicted of the lesser crime of having committed perjury.

As well as those who embraced communism and remained in the United States, there are not so many examples of American citizens who travelled East to live in the Soviet Bloc. Admittedly they are few in number, with only a handful choosing to defect from positions of responsibility in which they could inflict harm on the United States from the safety of Moscow. Only three NSA officers are known to have switched sides: William H. Martin and Bernon F. Mitchell defected to Cuba in June 1960, and Victor N. Hamilton arrived in Moscow in July 1963. None has written an account of his experiences and the CIA's only defector, Edward L. Howard, who fled across the Mexican border in September 1985, is now in Moscow working on his apologia, entitled *Safe House*. Of the other CIA officers known to have betrayed the Agency's secrets to the Soviets, only one, Edward Ellis Smith, has gone into public print, with a bibliography of Soviet intelligence literature, released after his retirement from the CIA, in which he had served as Station Chief in Moscow until he had admitted to having been compromised in a classic honeytrap, and had been recalled in July 1956. Another employee suspected of having worked as the notorious double agent code-named Sasha, Igor G. Orlov, died in May 1982 before he could be charged with any offence. Altogether, only nine CIA officers have been charged with betraying the organization: David H. Barnett, a former case officer in Jakarta, was sentenced to eighteen years' imprisonment in 1980; Edwin G. Moore, a retired CIA officer, fifteen years' in 1978; William Kampiles, who sold satellite surveillance data to the Soviets, received forty years' in 1978; Sharon M. Scranage, a clerk who gave CIA secrets to her Ghanaian lover, went to prison for two years in 1985; the Chinese analyst Larry Wu-Tai Chin, committed suicide in February 1986 having been sentenced to life; and the Czech penetration agent Karel Koecher, who had worked on a CIA contract, was swapped in a Berlin exchange in February 1986. Stevan Lalas, a CIA communications officer at the Athens station, admitted supplying the Agency's secrets to the Greek Intelligence Service and Thomas Gerard, a former San Francisco policeman, was charged with selling classified data to the South Africans. The most recent case has been that of the former section head of the counter-intelligence branch in the Soviet and Eastern European Division, Aldrich H. Ames, and his Colombian wife Maria, who were arrested in February 1994.

The contrast with the very large number of Soviet escapers is startling. Numerous KGB officers have moved to the West and published books, yet there is probably only a single example of an American intelligence officer going in the opposite direction. Ericha Wallach, a self-confessed Soviet source who worked for the Office of Strategic Services at the end of the war, disappeared in Czechoslovakia while searching for her step-father, Noel Field. As she later revealed in her 1967 memoirs *Light at Midnight*, she was herself arrested by the NKVD and accused of espionage. She later returned to the United States and remained there until her death in 1993.

Apart from the agents who actively assisted the Soviet cause through their membership of underground communist cells, there are those who are judged to have acted treacherously, though not necessarily with the intention of helping an ideological enemy. Into this category fall four CIA officers who, for differing reasons, spoke out against the Agency, the most notorious among them unquestionably being Philip Agee, who may or may not have fallen under Soviet influence when he decided, four years after his resignation from the Agency, to publish his memoirs. The involvement in his project of the Cubans, who often acted as surrogates for the KGB, makes his first book more than a legitimate political protest, which is how the contributions made by Victor Marchetti, Frank Snepp and John Stockwell could be regarded.

Until Victor Marchetti broke ranks in 1974, all the books published by retired CIA personnel, such as Allen Dulles and Lyman Kirkpatrick, were broadly supportive of the Agency's objectives and none of them made any attempt to reveal classified information that might damage the organiz-ation's standing. However, *The CIA and the Cult of Intelligence* established a precedent in the field of disclosure and was the subject of prolonged litigation which confirmed the Agency's right to demand the removal of sensitive material prior to publication. But, while Marchetti and his co-author negotiated a route to legitimate publication, Philip Agee pursued a vendetta against his former employers and inflicted great damage on their operations by releasing his memoirs in England, where he had taken up temporary residence. By the time an American edition had been prepared, the book had already received wide circulation abroad, thereby giving the author the defence of prior disclosure if the Agency had chosen to restrict its contents through the US courts. By adopting this approach, Agee ensured that his conduct would be regarded as akin to treachery, whereas the other CIA renegades have never been viewed in the same light. According to Joseph Smith, who wrote *Portrait of a Cold Warrior* with only limited official approval, the news that Agee had decided to reveal operational details of his CIA career, including authentic cryptonyms, source identities and names of Agency colleagues, sent a chill through Langley and resulted in a hugely expensive damage-limitation exercise in which thousands of unnecessary man-hours were wasted in completely unproductive activity, redeploying sensitive person-nel, reviewing files and in paying off redundant assets.

> A defensive operation was started immediately and every activity, agent and officer was scrutinised to determine if Agee had already blown them or if he would write about them in his book.

Curiously, Smith's own book was not free of criticism, and he too was regarded by some of his CIA colleagues has having defied convention by his decision to publish his memoirs. According to Cleveland C. Cram, a former station chief in London who joined the CIA in 1949 and worked as a consultant on counter-intelligence matters until 1992, all four officers were guilty of 'exposing highly confidential material':

> These authors usually wrote about subjects of which they had special knowledge, and the cumulative effect was to breach the walls of confidentiality that had protected Agency operations and person-nel . . . the net effect was damaging, especially in the case of Agee, who disclosed the identities of officers serving abroad under cover.

Certainly Victor Marchetti, who fought an epic legal battle with the Agency in 1974, when Agee was still working on his manuscript, set the precedent for CIA officers breaking ranks. In more recent years several other retired officers, including David McMichael, Melvin Beck and Ralph McGehee, have been active in campaigning against their former employer, and the latter pair have released accounts of their clandestine careers. But, in contrast to Agee, all submitted their work to the CIA's Publications

Review Board and have deleted classified data in their text at the Agency's request. Two other vocal critics of the Agency, with inside knowledge, have also gone into print, with differing motives. Sylvia Press, who was compromised in Mexico by a Hungarian intelligence officer, wrote *The Care of Devils*, a fictionalized account of her own bitter experience, which led her to believe that she had been let down badly by the CIA, and David McMichael has used his journal *Unclassified* as a platform to denigrate the CIA's threat analysis of the Soviet Union. This latter theme had been the subject of *Lost Promise* by John A. Gentry, whose dissection of the Agency's policy relating to Moscow is rather more academic in tone than written with the deliberate intention of inflicting damage.

Since 1986 the Intelligence Identities Protection Act, signed into law by President Ronald Reagan on the steps of the CIA's headquarters at Langley, has proved a powerful deterrent to anyone seeking to undermine the Agency by publicly 'naming names', as advocated by Philip Agee, but to date there has not been a single prosecution of an author or journalist under this legislation. All Agency personnel who write their memoirs abide by the terms of their employment contract, which includes a secrecy clause requiring submission of all relevant material, including newspaper articles and book reviews, prior to publication. The advantage of this system, in comparison to the rather haphazard approach adopted in Britain, is that the CIA can, and does, exercise a significant degree of control over the disclosures made by its retired personnel.

The CIA's reach, through the Publications Review Board, extends only to classified information and is intended to protect from premature disclosure genuine secrets that affect national security. This power, confirmed by the US Supreme Court, acknowledges that Agency personnel waive their rights to freedom of speech under the First Amendment to the US Constitution when they sign the standard secrecy agreement upon joining the CIA.

Herbert O. Yardley

It is my aim to unfold in a simple and dispassionate
way the intimate details of a secret organisation.

The most talented cryptological brain of his generation, Herbert Yardley devoted himself to solving Japanese ciphers and gave his country a decisive advantage during the Naval Conference of 1921 which settled the 5:5:3 formula for the tonnage of British, American and Japanese battleships. By intercepting and reading Tokyo's diplomatic cables the American side were able to anticipate every one of their opponent's manoeuvres, but it was not until Yardley sold the Japanese his cryptographic system that they realized their vulnerability. His subsequent publication of *The American Black Chamber* in 1931 caused a furore in the Japanese Diet and huge embarrassment in Washington DC, so when Yardley attempted to return to the field in 1942 he was rebuffed and given an innocuous appointment in the federal Office of Price Administration.

Yardley was widely criticized for the disclosures in his book but he was driven to make them, and later to work for the Chinese government, because he was permanently short of cash. His plans for a sequel, provisionally entitled *Japanese Diplomatic Secrets 1921–22*, were abandoned when the federal authorities threatened him with dire consequences if he released further classified information, and this episode is the first occasion on which a US government is known to have intervened to ban a book. The manuscript, which bore the alternative but provocative titles of *The Listening Post, Diplomatic Eavesdropping, Embassy Keyholes, Embassy Eavesdropping* and *Diplomatic Keyholes*, and had been circulated by his literary agent, George T. Bye & Company in New York, was confiscated and has only recently been declassified and released by the National Archives.

After the outbreak of war Yardley was employed as a cryptographer in Canada by the Department of External Affairs, then headed by Lester Pearson, but his contract was terminated as soon as the British learned that a confirmed security risk had been given access to Canadian secrets. Apparently the British Security Service made the strongest objections to Yardley's presence in Canada and hinted that no further secrets would be shared with Ottawa until the obstacle to continued liaison had been removed.

He was attacked for having worked for the Chinese, and for the indiscretions in his first book, but so few were allowed to know of his deal with the Japanese that, after his death in 1958, he was buried in Arlington National Cemetery as a national hero. The only leak occurred in 1958 when the journalist Ladislas Farago alleged in *The Broken Seal* that Yardley had indeed sold out to the Japanese, but he was misinformed about the date and stated incorrectly that the sale had been made in 1928 instead of 1930. Although Yardley was to write several books, including some guides to playing poker, his most sensitive book has never been made public. In this passage he demonstrates why the US authorities reacted as they did.

Japanese Diplomatic Secrets 1921–22

PART VII CONCLUSIONS

There remains to discover what happened to the fruits of the Conference on the Limitation of Armaments and Pacific and Far East Questions, what became of the leading figures in the secret cables and to make a final guess at what might have happened if—

To prevent this from going on forever, the fate of the treaties in Japan is left for Ichihashi to tell in his previously mentioned work. Briefly, the Five Power Naval treaty was submitted to the plenary session of February 1 and signed February 6, along with the others. It passed the United States senate March 31 without much ado. The Nine Power Open Door treaty, the Chinese Tariff treaty and the resolutions on China were adopted in the plenary session of February 4. After the proverbial attack by Borah on the ground that they did not restore sovereignty to China, they were passed by the senate March 29.

The Shantung treaty, announced February 1, was signed in the Pan-American building the fourth. The Yap agreement was published in haste December 12, 1921, signed at leisure February 11, 1922, turned over to the senate committee on foreign relations two days later, reported out favorably the twentieth and passed March 1, 1922.

The mystery treaty was the one the senate concentrated its venom on. Announced hurriedly December 10, 1921 and signed three days later at the state department, it was given over to the senate February 10 and the committee on foreign relations and was approved three days later. For the text of the reservation and supplement to the Four Power Pacific treaty, see Appendices V and VI.

And what became of the chief oriental characters in Hughes' all-star production? Baron Shidehara had to be relieved from his post at Washington, because of illness, but he recovered sufficiently to serve as foreign minister from 1924–27 and again in 1929. Hanihara became ambassador to Washington 1923–24. Matsudaira was appointed vice-minister of foreign affairs 1924–25, came to America as ambassador, 1925–28 and then went on to London to serve there, where he took part in another conference on naval armament, 1929–30, the sequel to the Washington affair.

Baron Yonsuke Hayashi is now the grand master of ceremonies in the Imperial household. Ishii is a privy councillor and a member of the house of peers. Vice-admiral Kanji Kato is now a full admiral and a supreme war councillor. Vice-admiral Kichisaburo Nomura is commander-in-chief of the Kure naval station. Katsuji Debuchi, then an embassy counsellor, is now ambassador at Washington, after a period as vice-minister of foreign affairs. Toshio Shiratori and Hiroshi Saito are in the intelligence bureau, the former is a section chief there and a secretary in the foreign office, the latter is chief perhaps because of faithful service at the London naval conference.

The minister of war, Yamanashi, after governing Chosen for several seasons, retired to private life, but Uyehara is now a baron and a member of the board of marshalls and fleet admirals. Takahashi was again minister of finance in 1927 and again served temporarily as premier when Premier Inouye was assassinated in 1932 before assuming his old post as finance minister. Uchida, after a career as privy councillor, retired until he was called forth recently, 1932, to head the foreign office once more. Obata is at leisure after a session as ambassador to Turkey 1925–30. General Kunishige Tanaka, retired, is founder of the Enlightened Ethics Society, the Japanese fascist organization, composed chiefly of ex-soldiers. Eiichi Kimura is now director of the South Manchurian Railway company and Yotaro Sugimura is deputy chief of the League of Nations office at Geneva and chief of the political bureau there.

As for the other orientals, Koo, after serving as foreign minister and premier, was proscribed by his government from 1928–30. Sze became minister to Great Britain, 1914–21, 29–32, and delegate to the League of Nations; he has recently been returned to Washington where he served as ambassador 1921–29. And Wang Chung-hui in 1930 was elected a judge in the permanent court of international justice.

Picture for yourself what would have happened—

If Borah's original resolution had been acted on?

If Curzon had called the conference himself in London instead of having America call it?

If Curzon had stated his purpose to Japan and America plainly and clearly at first instead of being vague about it?

If Curzon had not insisted on a combined conference at the time he suggested to the United States to hold an armament conference?

If Harding hadn't complicated the agenda by adding land and aerial armament and putting France on the defensive?

If he hadn't complicated it further by adding the conference on the Pacific?

Agnes Smedley

I prefer death to returning to the USA.

Always a firebrand revolutionary, Agnes Smedley was from a poor family in Missouri, and committed herself to anti-colonialism when she met Laipat Rai, an Indian nationalist at Columbia University in New York in March 1917. Thereafter she was constantly in the vanguard of campaigns for radical, feminist causes and, in particular, schemes to undermine the British Empire. She was indicted on espionage charges in March 1918 after the arrest of a group of Indian nationalists who had established contact with the German government and had planned to smuggle home weapons and propaganda. She was an active member of the Socialist Party and a regular contributor to its newspaper, the *Call*. After her release from prison she moved to Berlin, where she continued her close association with Indian nationalists.

In November 1928 she travelled to China as a correspondent for the *Frankfurter Zeitung* and immersed herself in the Chinese revolutionary movement. In her absence she was tried in the marathon Meerut conspiracy trial, which began in March 1929 following the arrest of the leading members of the outlawed Indian Communist Party. Later the same year she moved to Shanghai and soon afterwards became the mistress of Richard Sorge, the famous Soviet GRU agent. She introduced Sorge to a Japanese journalist, Ozaki Hotsumi, who was translating her bestselling autobiography, *Daughter of the Earth*. Both men were arrested in Japan on espionage charges in 1941, and executed in 1944.

Between June 1933 and April 1934 Smedley was in the Soviet Union, recovering her health and working on her journalism, but by October 1934, following a brief return to the United States, she was reporting for the *Manchester Guardian* from the Sino-Japanese front. For eighteen months she lived among the communist guerrillas and became close to their leader, Mao Tse-tung. In August 1940 her health failed and she was evacuated by air to Hong Kong, where she was placed under house arrest by the British authorities. Having obtained her release she became a vocal critic of the colony's administration and in May 1941 she arrived by ship in California. Her account of the war against the Japanese, *Battle Hymn of China*, was published in 1943 and is still regarded as a masterpiece of war reporting, even if the political bias is strident. In July of that year she entered an artists' retreat, the Yaddo Foundation near Saratoga Springs, New York, but continued her political campaigning in support of the Chinese communists.

By August 1944 Smedley had attracted the attention of the FBI, although her political views had been well known for many years, not least because they had been noted in the report issued in 1938 by the House Un-American Activities Committee, chaired by Martin Dies. In March 1948 she was obliged to leave Yaddo, and early the following year she was named as a Soviet spy by General Charles Willoughby, the former director of military intelligence in Japan who had edited a report on the Sorge case, based on the interrogation of his Japanese captors. Willoughby's allegations were given additional weight by testimony of Hede Massing and Whittaker Chambers, who both identified Smedley as a Soviet agent, as well as the confession written for the Japanese by Richard Sorge. Smedley indignantly denied the charges but experienced considerable difficulty in obtaining a renewal of her American passport because the HUAC intended to subpoena her as a witness. Smedley settled for a travel document limiting her movement to

Britain, France and Italy, and in December 1949 arrived in London, where she moved in with friends she had made in Hong Kong.

In April 1950 Smedley was admitted to a hospital in Oxford for surgery on the duodenal ulcer which had been responsible for her poor health, but she died on 6 May, the day after her operation.

In this extract from her autobiography, Smedley recalls her time in Shanghai, and discusses the topic of espionage, yet curiously she never once mentioned Richard Sorge.

Battle Hymn of China

A young Chinese, Feng Da, acted as my secretary and translator. He read and clipped from the Chinese Press, translated news into English, and built up my files. My files on the Chinese Red Army alone filled many cases, but most of these were official reports. At the end of one six-month period I compiled official statistics and found that half a million Red soldiers had been reported slain, yet official releases still claimed that the Red Army consisted only of 'bandit remnants' fleeing from their pursuers. Chu Teh, Commander-in-Chief of the Red Army, and Mao Tze-tung, Secretary General of the Communist Party, had been reported killed a dozen times. A month following their 'deaths', new rewards would be placed on their heads.

I made a similar study of the execution of Communists or alleged Communists in various cities. Until 1932 the Chinese Press published details and often pictures of mass executions of the victims. One report from Chungking burned itself into my memory. The provincial Governor had offered a reward of fifty dollars for any Communist captured or killed. Immediately the schools and universities were raided by soldiers, and students were shot down in the streets. Then the murderers claimed their rewards. I once laid a summary of such reports before Eugene Chen, who had been Foreign Minister of the Chinese Government until the middle of 1927. He was a harsh critic of the Government, and he assured me that if he ever came to power again he would try to stop the Terror. When he rose to office in Canton in 1931, I went to him with a request that twelve sailors, arrested in Canton as trade-union organizers, should not be executed. He replied that the men had known what would happen to them if they engaged in such illegal activities and that he could do nothing.

Similarly, in the spring of 1931 I went to the American secretary of the foreign YMCA and asked him to help prevent the extradition to the Chinese police of two foreign trade-union officials arrested in Shanghai.

He refused, saying that I had never come to him on behalf of any Chinese. He asserted that his concern was the Chinese, and that the rights of the poorest coolie were as sacred to him as those of any foreigner. I accepted the rebuke, and a few months later went to him on behalf of five Chinese, three of them trade-union organizers, who had been arrested and would perhaps be killed. He replied:

'These men knew the law before they engaged in illegal activities. I can do nothing.'

Like other foreign correspondents, I had to build up my own news sources, and consequently maintained friendship with as many different types of Chinese and foreigners as I could. I liked the intellectual qualities of the scholar patricians and the outlook of a few newspaper men; but I particularly admired and respected the revolutionary democrats who came later to be known as the National Salvationists, and the Communists, who, it seemed to me, embodied convictions and courage such as had characterized men of the French, American, and Russian Revolutions.

For the rest, there was a barrier between most foreigners and myself, and I rarely met men of my own profession. Of these, however, John B. Powell, American editor of the *China Weekly Review*, struck me as a man of much integrity. Since he disliked the Communists and believed in the Kuomintang, we often disagreed, but he was one American democrat who always defended my right to think and write as I wished. We shared a fear and hatred of British and Japanese policies in the Far East, and after the Japanese invasion, which threw us together on a common front, he published everything I sent him.

Years later, when the Japanese began assassinating Chinese newspaper men, Mr Powell organized his colleagues to bury them decently and with honour. Only after the Japanese occupied Shanghai in December 1941 did he cease his fearless defence of China. He had been on the Japanese blacklist for years, and they soon arrested him, along with another American correspondent, Victor Keen.

Among my other acquaintances was a German pilot in the Eurasian Aviation Corporation. He was a neurotic man, inclined to mysticism, and I remained in touch with him only because he was a valuable source of news. Returning from trips to various inland cities, he would give me photographs he had taken and much information.

Again and again he declared that he saw no purpose in life. One afternoon, after a flight to Hankow, he entered my apartment and slumped into a chair. His face was pale and his lips were twitching. I poured him a glass of cognac and waited for some new outburst about the futility of existence. He tossed a package of films and prints into my lap. A few of the prints showed various stages in the beheading of a dozen Chinese Communists – that is, alleged Communists – on the square in front of the customs house in Hankow. A few showed the bodies of beheaded workers lying in the streets. One was of a very chic Chinese Army officer with a pistol in his hand; behind him towered the walls of a foreign factory, and at its base lay the bodies of a number of workers whom he had apparently just shot.

'I took all of these pictures with the exception of the one of the Army officer with the pistol,' Kurt said. 'The English factory-owner gave me that. I took the pictures of the mass beheadings from the windows of the customs house. The twelve men were naked to the waist and their hands were tied behind them. There were ropes around their necks and blood ran from the mouths of some of them. The police and soldiers were eager for the killing. They kicked the prisoners to their knees and pulled their heads forward by means of the ropes, while a fat executioner with a big sword chopped off their heads. The blood spurted out and some of it splashed on crowds of gaping Chinese, who stood with arms hanging limply at their sides.'

'Did you protest?'

He continued without heeding: 'One of the prisoners tumbled over and died before he was beheaded. A few were singing in high shrill voices. They sang the *Internationale*. When all were dead the police dipped faggot brooms in their blood and whirled them over the gawking crowd. The watchers ran like rabbits.'

He retched, rose and went to the bathroom. When he returned, his face was very white.

'Look at this modern city, Kurt,' I began excitedly. 'Suppose you or I should tell people what we have seen – show those pictures to missionaries, business men, journalists, YMCA secretaries. This city – look at it, with its paved streets, electric lights, great buildings—'

'For my part, I don't intend to get lynched for a pack of Chinese! I'm leaving this bloody country and going to Australia.'

'Chinese are a species of animal to you, aren't they?'

Later that evening he told me that he had brought back some more pictures which had been taken from the air. This was forbidden by the Government, but he took them nevertheless.

'I've earned enough money on them to live in Australia like a human being until I find work,' he explained.

I stared at him suspiciously, then asked: 'Why do your bosses want pictures of Chinese territory?'

'I don't know or care.'

'You're being used as a spy against China!'

'China? How can you have any feeling for China? Just think of those pictures I brought you!'

'Nevertheless this country belongs to the Chinese people. You are helping their enemies.'

'You're an illusionist!' he replied, and sat staring dejectedly into space.

Alger Hiss

Apparently for Chambers to be a confessed former Communist and traitor to his country did not seem to him to be a blot on his record.

A graduate of Johns Hopkins University and the Harvard Law School, in June 1929 Alger Hiss was appointed Secretary to Oliver Wendell Holmes, the Supreme Court Justice. He then practised law in Boston and New York before joining the government in May 1933 as assistant counsel to the newly created Agricultural Adjustment Administration. In August 1935, after a period of secondment to the Nye Committee, which was conducting a congressional investigation into the international arms industry, Hiss joined the Department of Justice. Six months later he transferred to the State Department where he acted as secretary to the American delegation to the Dumbarton Oaks Conference, and accompanied the Secretary of State Edward Stettinius to Yalta in February 1945. Upon his return he was appointed Secretary-General of the United Nations conference at San Francisco, and in January 1946 attended the first meeting of the UN General Assembly in London as a senior adviser to the American Delegation. In 1947 he left public service for the prestigious post of President of the Carnegie Endowment for International Peace, but in August 1948 he was named by Whittaker Chambers as a Soviet agent and one of his underground communist contacts.

Hiss denied the allegation and sued Chambers for defamation but lost the case when Chambers produced State Department cables, dated 1938, and four memoranda written in Hiss's hand, which he insisted had been given to him by the spy. Hiss was charged with perjury but the jury was unable to agree a verdict; in November 1949 a second trial was held at which Hiss was convicted and sentenced to five years' imprisonment. After his release in December 1954 Hiss wrote his autobiography, *In the Court of Public Opinion*, protesting his innocence, and in 1988 produced a second volume, *Recollections of a Life*. Since his prison sentence Hiss divorced and worked first for a manufacturer of women's hair accessories, and later as a salesman for a New York printing business. He remarried and now lives in retirement on Long Island. In this passage he recalls his visit to Yalta.

Recollections of a Life

James F. Byrnes could devote a good deal of his attention to Stalin-watching since he had no assigned areas of responsibility at the Yalta Conference. It was Byrnes's claim that his political experience (as senator and congressman) enabled him to see that Stalin was not the absolute dictator he was reputed to be. When Stalin asked for time to sound out his colleagues in Moscow about the Polish issue, for example, Byrnes speculated that this was not a pretence of an excuse for delay, but a genuine need on Stalin's part to consult those with whom, Byrnes felt, the Russian leader shared power.

Our preoccupation with Stalin was understandable. From reliable intelligence sources, we knew, as the public generally did not, of many of Stalin's monstrous crimes against his people. He was like a tyrant out of antiquity. But we also knew of his adroit skill as a negotiator and of his evident success as a war leader. He had rallied the Russian people from their near rout by the Wehrmacht to sweeping victories by massive, reconstituted armies. But none of us really knew much about his personality – not even Ambassador Harriman, who had seen Stalin only at brief fixed appointments.

Now we were to see him day after day, under varying conditions. I saw him only at formal meetings and in the moments of informality as the meetings assembled or broke up. But as participants in the ceremonial dinners, Stettinius, Admiral Leahy, Byrnes, and Harriman had additional chances to observe Stalin. At Yalta and in their memoirs, their common observation was of Stalin's calm.

Sir Alexander Cadogan, British Permanent Under Secretary for Foreign Affairs (the top-ranking civil servant in the Foreign Office), in writing to his wife in letters of February 7 and 8, 1945, was more expansive: 'Uncle Joe is in great form . . . and in quite genial mood . . . I must say I think Uncle Joe much the most impressive of the three men. He is very quiet and restrained. On the first day he sat for the first hour and a half or so without saying a word – there was no call for him to do so . . . Joe just sat taking it all in and being rather amused. When he did chip in, he never used a superfluous word, and spoke very much to the point. He's obviously got a very good sense of humour . . .'

And there were other personal characteristics he displayed at Yalta which I found at odds with my image of an imperious, anti-Western dictator. He was considerate and well mannered, but, more important, he appeared to be genuinely conciliatory in attitude, abandoning with seeming grace his position on a number of points.

He accepted, with reluctance, French participation in the control of occupied Germany, which he had vigorously opposed. Our drafts on the Declaration for a Liberated Europe and even on German reparations were finally agreed to largely without textual alteration, the Russians giving up changes they had strenuously argued for in lengthy debates. And the points abandoned did not – and on reexamination still do not – appear to be straw issues raised as bargaining chips to be surrendered in order to gain some more valuable points in exchange. On the contrary, they were always consistent with basic Soviet interests and policies. Cadogan, in a letter of February 11, dwelt on this mood of conciliation: 'I have never known the Russians so easy and accommodating. In particular Joe has been extremely good. He *is* a great man . . .'

I do not take Cadogan's reference to greatness as his considered judgment, but it does indicate what an impressive figure Stalin cut at Yalta.

After insisting on detailed explanations, Stalin accepted without change our proposal for voting procedures in the Security Council of the United Nations. This provided for the veto power of the permanent members, but narrowed it to permit discussion free of the veto. Stalin did resist tenaciously and successfully the precise Anglo-American formulas designed to liberalize the future Polish regime. But the Red Army had occupied most of Poland and was soon to occupy the rest of it, so that the Americans and British had no real bargaining power on Polish issues. We thought we had done as well as could be expected under the circumstances on the subject of Poland's new borders and even on the final form of the provisions for free elections and the composition of the government.

It is interesting to speculate as to the reason for Stalin's flexibility and agreeableness at Yalta. From all accounts, this was not his mood at the earlier Teheran Conference or the later Potsdam Conference. Only at Yalta was there a touch of graciousness in his manner. It seems to me unlikely that his mood at Yalta simply masked intransigence. After all, it was we, not Stalin, who came bearing requests.

Stalin as well as Churchill spoke frequently and emphatically of the importance of preserving Great Power unity after the war. Perhaps privately each desired such unity only if it could be obtained on his own terms without compromise. However, that was not the mood or the practice at Yalta. It was my impression that each spoke in the spirit of cooperation and accommodation. I like to think that it was later events not then foreseen that damaged genuine hopes of future unity. I like to think that at Yalta the calm dictator and his associates shared our hopes of cooperation, difficult though it obviously would be.

The Russians were remarkable hosts at Yalta. We could not help being impressed by their extraordinary efforts made for our comfort under wartime conditions of enormous difficulties. Perhaps the efforts for our comfort were due to the pride of a great power to show what it could do even *in extremis*. In any event, the setting for the conference and the physical arrangements and procedures played their parts in producing the usually relaxed mood of the meeting. There came into being for those few days a relationship among the three governments which has never since been approached – a relationship known as the 'Spirit of Yalta'.

Stalin was short and stocky, and he usually wore a freshly laundered khaki military tunic with no medals. Looking solid under the neat uniform, he reflected a strong pride of person and had a natural air of authority. Churchill, in contrast, was stooped and paunchy in his rumpled garb. Churchill's means of command was his superb eloquence, which could be sharp and wounding as the moment required. Occasionally his eloquence betrayed him, leading him into posturing declamation.

For me, Roosevelt had by far the greatest presence. His easy grace and charm were combined with serenity and inner assurance. His posture at the great round table where the participants sat at plenary sessions was one of regal composure. He radiated goodwill, purpose, leadership, and personal magnetism.

The tone of the diplomatic talks was informal, almost casual, and at the same time wary. I cannot speak for the mood of the important military talks, which I did not attend. But the informality of the political sessions came naturally from our surroundings and from how small we were in number. The total civilian personnel of the three delegations could not have been more than seventy-five or so. (The military, whose talks were quite separate, by contrast, numbered almost seven hundred.)

The diplomatic delegations and a few of the top military officers were crammed into three large country houses on the outskirts of Yalta, in peacetime a small seaside resort. The largest villa, Livadia, somewhat grandiloquently called a palace because it had been a summer residence of the czars, was assigned to our delegation. The presence of three young women – Kathleen Harriman, Sarah Churchill Oliver, and Anna Roosevelt Boettiger – who in unofficial roles accompanied their fathers to the conference, contributed to a mood that at times was almost like that of a country house party where the guests good-naturedly put up with overcrowding.

Each villa was supplied with a full complement of chefs, waiters, and housemaids. The Russians had commandeered the staffs of three Moscow hotels and brought them to Yalta together with the necessary bedding, linen, chinaware, glasses, silver, and kitchen equipment. We and the British were 'at home' in our villas and could entertain each other at meals.

The convivial mood at Livadia Palace was enhanced by a typical Rooseveltian gesture. He had brought along 'for the ride' the political boss of New York's Bronx, Ed Flynn, and his wife. They were installed in a small suite on the second floor. Flynn did not attend any of the sessions. From time to time President Roosevelt, saying Ed was 'getting very bored', would direct one of us to give the Flynns a summary of what was going on in the meetings. Among the furnishings in their suite was a huge samovar for the tea always served to the bearer of such news. As there was little else for them to do, the Flynns must have drunk more tea during their stay at Yalta than even an Irish-American could wish for.

It was, however, the exigencies of war that contributed most to the 'Spirit of Yalta'. The vastness of the war's scope in Europe and the Far East and the enormous size of the forces involved made military considerations overriding for the participants, utterly dwarfing other issues.

Whittaker Chambers

During the six years that I worked underground, nobody
ever told me what service I had been recruited into
and, as a disciplined Communist, I never asked.

Chambers, a senior editor with *Time* magazine, was one of several CPUSA supporters who had become disaffected with the Party and had abandoned the cause in April 1937, after an adherence that had lasted twelve years. Married to an active communist, he had been an editor on the *Daily Worker*, but by 1948 his ideological conversion was complete. He publicly denounced Alger Hiss as a

Soviet source, and revealed that he had first made the accusation to the State Department in 1939 but no action had been taken. Hiss denied the charge and tried to bring an action for slander against Chambers, who had given a detailed account of his work as a courier, carrying classified State Department documents between Hiss and a Soviet contact whom he later identified, with Walter Krivitsky's help, as Colonel Boris Bykov. Fortunately for Chambers, he had kept as an insurance policy a batch of State Department documents typed on Hiss's own typewriter, and annotated in his handwriting. This evidence was to prove damning for Hiss and ensure his ultimate conviction and imprisonment, albeit on the relatively minor charge of perjury, and not espionage.

Although Chambers was to become a star witness for the federal authorities, and to name dozens of members of the Soviet apparatus, including Agnes Smedley, his co-operation was gradual, and won over a period of time. When he was first interviewed by the FBI, as part of the investigation into Gerhardt Eisler, Chambers initially denied knowledge of him. Later he gave a more candid account of his clandestine activities, describing how he had handled six important sources who had operated independently in the US Treasury Department, the State Department, the Bureau of Standards and the Aberdeen Proving Ground in Maryland, where a sympathetic mathematician had betrayed the technical data of an experimental bombsight. Like Elizabeth Bentley, Chambers had been taught the technique of acquiring false US passports and at one stage it had been intended that he and his family should adopt new identities to run an illegal network in London, hidden by a convenient commercial front, a literary agency sponsored by a willing CPUSA member in New York who was anxious to expand his business into Europe. As for Hede Massing, Chambers testified that he had not actually met her but he knew of her Washington-based network by reputation.

Whittaker Chambers resigned from *Time* after his testimony and died in July 1961, but in 1984 was posthumously awarded the Medal of Freedom by President Reagan. In this passage from his memoirs he dwells upon his role as a turncoat.

Witness

To be an informer . . .

Men shrink from that word and what it stands for as from something lurking and poisonous. Spy is a different breed of word. Espionage is a function of war whether it be waged between nations, classes or parties. Like the soldier, the spy stakes his freedom or his life on the chances of action. Like the soldier, his acts are largely impersonal. He seldom knows whom he cripples or kills. Spy as an epithet is a convention of morale; the enemy's spy is always monstrous; our spy is daring and brave. It must be so since all camps use spies and must while war lasts.

The informer is different,* particularly the ex-Communist informer. He risks little. He sits in security and uses his special knowledge to destroy others. He has that special information to give because he knows those others' faces, voices and lives, because he once lived within their confidence, in a shared faith, trusted by them as one of themselves, accepting their friendship, feeling their pleasures and griefs, sitting in their houses, eating at their tables, accepting their kindness, knowing their wives and children. If he had not done those things, he would have no use as an informer.

Because he has that use, the police protect him. He is their creature. When they whistle, he fetches a soiled bone of information. He and they share a common chore, which is a common complicity in the public interest. It cannot be the action of equals, and even the kindness that seeks to mask the fact merely exasperates and cannot change it. For what is the day's work of the police is the ex-Communist's necessity. They may choose what they will or will not do. He has no choice. He has surrendered his choice. To that extent, though he be free in every other way, the informer is a slave. He is no longer a man. He is free only to the degree in which he understands what he is doing and why he must do it.

Let every ex-Communist look unblinkingly at that image. It is himself. By the logic of his position in the struggles of his age, every ex-Communist is an informer from the moment he breaks with Communism, regardless of how long it takes him to reach the police station.

For Communism fixes the consequences of its evil not only on those who serve it, but also on those, who, once having served it, seek to serve against it. It has set the pattern of the warfare it wages and that defines the pattern of the warfare its deserters must wage against it. It cannot be otherwise. Communism exists to wage war. Its existence implies, even in peace or truce, a state of war that engages every man, woman and child alive, but, above all, the ex-Communist. For no man simply deserts *from* the Communist Party. He deserts *against* it. He deserts to struggle against Communism as an evil. There would otherwise be no reason for his desertion, however long it may take him to grasp the fact. Otherwise, he should have remained within the Communist Party, and his failure to act at all against it betrays the fact that he has not broken with it. He has broken only with its organization, or certain of its forms, practices,

---

*I am not speaking of such people as the FBI and other security agencies send into the Communist Party. In the true sense of the word, they are not informers but spies, working in exposed, and sometimes hazardous positions.

discomforts of action or political necessity. And this, despite the sound human and moral reasons that may also paralyze him – his reluctance to harm old friends, his horror at using their one-time trust in him to destroy them – reasons which are honorable and valid.

But if the ex-Communist truly believes that Communism is evil, if he truly means to struggle against it as an evil, and as the price of his once having accepted it, he must decide to become an informer. In that war which Communism insists on waging, and which therefore he cannot evade, he has one specific contribution to make – his special knowledge of the enemy. That is what all have to offer first of all. Because Communism is a conspiracy, that knowledge is indispensable for the active phase of the struggle against it. That every ex-Communist has to offer, regardless of what else he may have to offer, special skills or special talents or the factors that make one character different from another.

I hold that it is better, because in general clarity is more maturing than illusion, for the ex-Communist to make the offering in the full knowledge of what he is doing, the knowledge that henceforth he is no longer a free man but an informer. That penalty those who once firmly resolved to take upon themselves the penalties for the crimes of politics and history, in the belief that only at that cost could Man be free, must assume no less firmly as the price of their mistake. For, in the end, the choice for the ex-Communist is between shielding a small number of people who still actively further what he now sees to be evil, or of helping to shield millions from that evil which threatens even their souls. Those who do not inform are still conniving at that evil. That is the crux of the moral choice which an ex-Communist must make in recognizing that the logic of his position makes him an informer. Moreover, he must always make it amidst the deafening chatter and verbal droppings of those who sit above the battle, who lack the power to act for good or evil because they lack any power to act at all, and who, in the day when heaven was falling, were, in Dante's words, neither for God nor for Satan, but were for themselves.

On that road of the informer it is always night. I who have traveled it from end to end, and know its windings, switchbacks and sheer drops – I cannot say at what point, where or when, the ex-Communist must make his decision to take it. That depends on the individual man. Nor is it simply a matter of taking his horror in his hands and making his avowals. The ex-Communist is a man dealing with other men, men of many orders of intelligence, of many motives of self-interest or malice, men sometimes infiltrated or tainted by the enemy, in an immensely complex pattern of politics and history. If he means to be effective, if he does not wish his act merely to be wasted suffering for others and himself, how, when and where the ex-Communist informs are matters calling for the shrewdest judgment.

Some ex-Communists are so stricken by the evil they have freed themselves from that they inform exultantly against it. No consideration, however humane, no tie however tender, checks them. They understand, as few others do, the immensity of the danger, and experience soon teaches them the gulf fixed between the reality they must warn against and the ability of the world to grasp their warnings. Fear makes them strident. They are like breathless men who have outrun the lava flow of a volcano and must shout down the smiles of the villagers at its base who, regardless of their own peril, remember complacently that those who now try to warn them once offered their faith and their lives to the murderous mountain.

By temperament, I cannot share such exultation or stridency, though I understand both. I cannot ever inform against anyone without feeling something die within me. I inform without pleasure because it is necessary. Each time, relief lies only in the certainty that, when enough has died in a man, at last the man himself dies, as light fails.

Sometimes, by informing, the ex-Communist can claim immunity of one kind or another for acts committed before his change of heart or sides. He is right to claim it, for if he is to be effective, his first task is to preserve himself. Sometimes, he can even enjoy such immunity, if he is able to feel what is happening to him in the simplest terms, impersonally, as an experience of history and of war in which he at last has found his bearings and which he is helping to wage. By the rules of war, common sense and self-interest, the world can scarcely lose by allowing him his immunity. It does well, provided by acts he makes amends, to help him to forget his past, if only because in the crisis of the 20th century, not all the mistakes were committed by the ex-Communists.

I never asked for immunity. Nor did anyone at any time ever offer me immunity, even by a hint or a whisper. What immunity can the world offer a man against his thoughts?

And so I went to see Adolf Berle.

Hede Massing

*By meeting with the FBI I have seen democracy at
work. It has filled me with awe and admiration.*

Austrian by birth, and married at seventeen to Gerhardt Eisler, one of the KDP's
leading figures and a friend of the legendary Soviet illegal Richard Sorge, Hede
Massing travelled to the United States in 1923 and stayed, working in an
orphanage in Pleasantville, New York, until she acquired her citizenship in
December 1927. According to the statement she made to the FBI in late 1947, she
had returned to Europe in January 1928 and, while studying in Berlin, met and
was recruited by Sorge. A year in Moscow followed, where she was indoctrinated
into the Comintern, ready for her new role as an illegal based in Berlin, and
married another NKVD agent, Paul Massing. Supervised by Ignace Reiss, Hede
Massing had worked openly for the KDP, on one occasion travelling to London to
audit the accounts of the CPGB, but also undertaking clandestine work for the
Soviets. She had operated a mail-drop for Ignace Reiss and in 1932 had been
introduced to Walter Krivitsky, who apparently rejected her as unsuitable for a
particular mission for which he had had her in mind.

In October 1933 Hede returned to New York aboard the *Deutschland* as a
correspondent for the *Weltbühne* and moved in with Helen Black, the representative of the Soviet Photo Agency. She took her orders from Valentine Markin,
whose cover was that of a director of a small cosmetics company owned by a
CPUSA member named Hart. During this period Hede acted as a courier, taking
microfilms to Paris, and as a recruiter, successfully persuading Noel and Herta
Field to join her network, but failing to acquire his State Department friend Alger
Hiss who, Hede, discovered, was already involved with a separate ring in
Washington. After a single, preliminary encounter with Hiss, Hede had been
warned to keep away from him. 'Never see him again. Stay away from him and
forget him,' she was told by her controller.

> I understood, of course. There had apparently been a reprimand and these
> were urgent, emphatic instructions. I had met a member of another appara-
> tus. I had had a conversation with him in which I had disclosed that I was
> working in a parallel apparatus. That was strictly taboo, and disliked by the
> big boss here and by the bigger bosses in Moscow.

Following the murder of Ignace Reiss, Hede expressed doubts about her own
commitment to her new controller, whom she subsequently learned was Elizaveta
Zubilin, the wife of Vassili, the *resident* in New York, and was summoned to
Moscow. Hede arrived in November 1937 and underwent months of interrogation by an officer named Peter Zubelin to confirm her continued loyalty, but she
was too disillusioned to continue. The following year she returned to New York

and broke off contact with Helen Black and the Zubilins. When the FBI approached her, after the war, in relation to its investigation of Gerhardt Eisler, she agreed to give evidence against Alger Hiss and her testimony secured his conviction on a charge of perjury, following his denial on oath of charges made by another defector, Whittaker Chambers.

Massing died in New York in March 1981, of emphysema. Her autobiography, *This Deception*, was published in 1951 and was largely a compilation of an eighteen-part story, 'I Spied for the Soviet Union', which was carried by many newspapers. Here, in a passage in which she refers to her Soviet colleagues 'Peter' and 'Fred', she recalls her first encounter with Robert Lamphere of the FBI, who was himself to publish an account of the case which broadly confirmed her version of events.

This Deception

During the four years of my operation as a Soviet agent, I was not once questioned by the American authorities. Not one of the members of the apparatus personally known to me was ever interfered with. We took elaborate precautions, but more from professional habit than fear of detection. No other country made life for spies so safe and cosy.

There was many a time when I wished that the 'authorities' had known about me and asked for my story. There was many a time when I thought that I ought to go and tell of my past. But to whom? And how does one go about it? And it was much too late, it would not help any more, I believed. The most important issue – how could you tell your story without putting the exposing finger on people who were your own responsibility? After a great deal of pro and con, I once discussed this problem with Ludwig's wife, who is living in this country, and she suggested that I speak to Raymond Murphy, a security officer of the State Department, whom she knew and who has been mentioned in the Hiss trial. We met him one evening and talked for hours with him. We told him all that concerned us and seemed essential for him to know. We felt very relieved.

It was not the end yet. After a strenuous summer on the farm, I visited friends on the West Coast during the winter of 1947. About a week after I returned to New York, R. J. Lamphere of the FBI, who had previously spoken to Paul, wanted to see me in relation to the Gerhardt Eisler affair which was making the headlines. It was my first contact with the FBI.

My conception of the Federal Bureau of Investigation had naturally been that which every European (and many an American liberal) has towards 'police', whatever name they may assume. True, I had come to know America well enough not to fear the FBI as much as I would have feared any police force in Europe, not to mention the MVD. But there were still other fears. How was I going to speak about Eisler without involving myself? Paul? What was I to do? Paul and I thought the problem out, slowly, carefully. We decided to tell our story.

I wish that it were possible to convey the great experience that this decision brought us. By meeting with the FBI I have seen democracy at work. It has filled me with awe and admiration. More than that, it has made me proud to belong to a country whose investigating arm consists of men of such integrity. All the mistrust, the fear and aversion, all the defense and rejection with which I had steeled myself that morning was gone after a few hours when, for the first time I went high up into the building on Foley Square.

Two polite efficient men asked me for some specific information regarding Gerhardt Eisler. They not only understood and respected my rights, but made it clear that my co-operation was purely voluntary. There was no coercion, no tricks; they had a job to do and they thought that I could be of help if I cared to. It was entirely up to me whether I did. They were intelligent, observant, well-informed – as I could judge by the questions asked – and pleasantly unemotional. They did not underestimate the individual under suspicion, on the contrary, they seemed to respect him and understand him in his own environment. This impressed me indeed. It was most unexpected.

The two agents, to whom I spoke the first few times, were Lamphere and a kindly, graying, middle-aged man, whose name was Finzel. It must have been the second time that I spoke with Mr Lamphere when I became aware of his extreme caution, of his desire to assure me that he was not 'prying'. I said to him, 'You don't need to be so delicate, Mr Lamphere, I am very willing to tell you my story.'

Later on, Paul and I talked separately to different agents. It was a terrific ordeal – to pour your heart out to a stranger, to face yourself, your crumbled illusions, your misconceptions – it is like a psychoanalysis without reward. In the subway afterward, tired and depressed, we would always agree on how admirably John or Bill had behaved. We got to know a few of the agents fairly well. It required many meetings until they had our full story, not only on paper, but digested. Never in all the time that I have known them has there been any pressure, any attempt to influence us. Later, when our meetings had become almost a social occasion, I learned a great deal about the organization; I learned of its function and its limitations according to law. I learned something about the men who work in the FBI. They are recruited from the very marrow of this country, they are the backbone. They are a part of the people, of all the states within the union, of all strata of all classes. They have to meet specific qualifications as to educational background (many of them have a law degree) but their training proper takes place within the FBI. To live up to the specification which the bureau requires, both morally and physically, should make any man proud. Paul once said that the amazing thing about the FBI is that they are not only a part of the people but *for* them – really for them!

This, of course, my liberal friends would deny. They see the FBI witch hunting, prying, disturbing the life of harmless citizens for their own private amusement. How carefully and cautiously the bureau proceeds, how thoroughly and fairly their investigations are conducted, dismissing gossip, evaluating information of significance; how absolutely certain they must be before their report goes out suggesting or accusing someone of guilt; this is never mentioned by such people. I refuse to believe that one cannot find justice in this country if one is willing to speak the truth!

To be 'too close to the FBI' makes you a character of suspicion in the eyes of most people, you become almost a leper. When you ask them how a traitor like Fuchs or Gold, or Communist agents within the government should be found out if not by the FBI and their method of investigating, they will merely shrug their shoulders. 'That is their job,' they will reply, 'let them find out for themselves – why must we help?'

I had decided to tell my story to the FBI as fully and honestly as I could, without bringing harm to former associates of the apparatus who lived in America and were my own responsibility, and whom I assumed to be as disaffected with the Russians as was I. When I described the setup of a specific feature, I simply said that the name of this person involved I did not want to mention, and I then explained my reasons. The response was entirely human and considerate. They trusted me and showed respect for my judgment. Only now do I understand that some of the people whom I tried to shield by omitting certain facts, were known about from other sources. The discretion of the agents was admirable.

The two most important names I did not mention in my confidential sessions with the FBI were Larry Duggan and Alger Hiss. I have already said that I was absolutely convinced that Duggan had left the organiz-ation, if, indeed, he had ever belonged to it at all. Alger Hiss had not worked with me, the relationship was a fleeting one, important only in connection with Noel Field. But more than that, he, too, I was convinced, must have broken with whatever his organization might have been. I had watched his career with great interest. I had seen him climb to prominence in the American government, by the side of President Roosevelt at Yalta, in a commanding post at the launching of the United Nations in San Francisco, as president of the Carnegie Peace Foundation. What on earth would a man with such a career still be doing in a Communist apparatus? I asked myself. Surely he had broken with them as had I, and Paul and Ludwig. How else could he have achieved such a position? I had no doubts about the accuracy of my deductions.

Yet there was probably more to all of it than I realized. I *wanted* him to have left the Communists. Though I had seen him only once, I had liked him extremely. I had thought of him often. I would have wanted him to be a 'comrade in arms' against the Communists – as he had been with me for them! He had, without knowing it, reassured me at the time that I met him. I wanted him to do the same now. Of all the people I had liked and respected in the movement, I wanted his assurance now. Every ex-Communist wants to surround himself with his former friends, wants to re-establish the niche where he is loved and feels comfortable. I had dreamed for years that Helen Black had called me and come to see me and said, 'We are together again. I, too have left them!' The wish-dreaming of the former Communist!

There was one slight flaw that occasionally would shadow my picture of Hiss. That was when I remembered the blank-faced stare that Peter had given me when I mentioned the name 'Hiss' in describing my difficulties in soliciting Noel. That stare I had seen ever so often before; with Ludwig, when I mentioned somebody of our own apparatus or a parallel one either in the Comintern or Military. Plainly, he did not want to commit himself. With Ika Sorge, the same. A 'tabu' question, or a name that was not to be mentioned, was met with that specific blank stare. It was the direct continuation of Fred's warning, 'Never mention that name! Forget it!' But this, I rationalized too successfully. The stare could be attributed to the fact that Hiss, too, was a 'traitor', out for his own; sold out to the bourgeoisie!

On the morning of August 3, 1949, when the Hiss–Chambers story broke, my worries began. Had I been all wrong in my rationalizations? No, I couldn't have been. Wait, I thought, wait. Hiss will admit his past affiliations. Why shouldn't he? It is long past, he has proved by the services he rendered his country where he stands today. At the time he was helping the Russians, many, and some of the best, did.

Boris Morros

*I have never been a traitor. If I did wrong, in the years
before I offered my services to the United States government,
I did it unthinkingly. For whatever mistakes I made I atoned
in full measure.*

The original target of what had been initiated as a surveillance operation had been Vassily Zubilin, the man believed by the FBI to be the Soviet illegal *rezident* in New York. In July 1947 Zubilin had been spotted holding a clandestine meeting with a Hollywood movie producer named Boris Morros. When interviewed, the Russian-born Morros admitted that he had been recruited by Zubilin in 1936, but at that time he had known Zubilin not as a Soviet diplomat, but as an Amtorg official named Edward J. Herbert. Morros explained that he had been persuaded to provide 'Herbert' with authentic Paramount Studios cover as a movie talent scout so he could travel freely in Nazi Germany. In return, Boris Morros's two brothers, who had been in danger of being prosecuted, were freed by the Soviet authorities and his father had been allowed to emigrate, arriving in the United States from Moscow in January 1943. It was at a rendezvous soon after this that the FBI had first latched on to Boris.

According to Morros, Zubilin had operated in the United States as an illegal for several years before his official arrival in San Francisco with diplomatic status in December 1941. After his father's release Morros had agreed to allow his independent movie production company to be used by Zubilin's organization, and it had been financed by Alfred Stern, a wealthy Soviet sympathizer. Morros was also assigned a partner, Jack Soble, who was Lithuanian by birth and had operated in Germany as a journalist until withdrawn to Moscow in 1940. Ostensibly his occupation in America, while his naturalization application was being processed, was that of manager of a grocery store in Manhattan but in reality Soble, his wife Myra and his brother Dr Robert A. Soblen were key illegals, supervising a network of other agents in Europe. Among them were George Zlatovsky, a former US Army intelligence officer, and his wife Jane Foster. A naturalized US citizen, originally from Kiev, who had come to America with his parents as a child, Zlatovsky had fought with the Abraham Lincoln Brigade during the Spanish Civil War and had served in the US Army in Austria until 1948. Jane Foster had joined OSS in December 1943 as an expert on Indonesia, having lived in Java for four years before the war. A committed communist who had become a Party member in the Dutch East Indies, she was strongly suspected of having passed OSS secrets to her future husband while based in Salzburg in 1947.

After a decade of continuous surveillance the FBI arrested the Sobles in 1957, together with Jack's successor, Jacob Albam. Morros's testimony ensured convictions for Albam and the Sobles, but the Zlatovskys resisted attempts to extradite them from France, while the others identified by Morros also remained out of reach. Alfred and Martha Stern, both wealthy Soviet sympathizers, were indicted but moved to Mexico and then used Paraguayan passports to travel to Prague. Suffering from cancer, Dr Soblen disappeared to Israel in 1962 when the Supreme Court rejected his appeal against a life sentence, and in September 1962 he committed suicide in London soon after he had been deported from Tel Aviv. His first attempt, on the plane to England, failed but a second, when his plea for political asylum had been rejected by the British authorities, was successful.

Under interrogation Jack Soble admitted his espionage and as well as providing evidence against his brother Robert, he implicated Martha Stern, née Dodd, whom he claimed had spied as a Soviet agent in her father's embassy when he had been the US ambassador in Berlin for four years before the war. Soble also identified one of his Soviet handlers in Paris as Pavel S. Kuznetsov, a KGB officer who had since been compromised in an espionage case which occurred in London in June 1952. The Sterns remained in Czechoslovakia until 1979 when, following the death of Morros, all charges against them in the United States were dropped.

In his rather luridly titled autobiography, Morros describes his relationship with Jack Soble.

My Ten Years as a Counterspy

As time went on, it seemed to me that Soble became friendlier than he had been at first. His wife was a movie fan and I think that they were coming to think of me as a Hollywood celebrity.

So things continued on that basis all through that year. And in December Jack confided something to me that gave me hope that he would be out of my future permanently very soon. He was about to be given his final American citizenship papers, which he had applied for shortly after his arrival in this country in 1940. He pointed out that this would entitle him to an American passport, which he could use on a trip he was planning soon to take to Paris. How important this American passport was to his career as a secret agent I discovered only later on.

In June 1947, when he got his papers and passport, he recklessly traveled to Europe on a Russian ship – something that would have aroused the interest of American agents if Soble had been under observation. Yes, the same punctiliously careful and cautious man who checked all hotel rooms so thoroughly, did this rash thing. 'I am traveling with a very important personage,' he added, but did not reveal who the personage was.

'In Moscow,' Jack said in our last talk before he sailed, 'I will see the bosses, the big bosses, but I'll have to talk fast when they ask me about you. In their eyes I have failed completely with you. I hope you realize that. As I've told you, I am your friend and I will do the best I can for you. However, the fact that I badly need your business as a cover may help me persuade them to forgive you.'

That, of course, crushed all hope that the Russian espionage men would tire of me, eventually, and give up the idea of using me. As I found out later, they never do tire. They have all the time in the world and they know it. They can and will wait years – just as long as they think necessary – for the right time to trap you in their net.

After that talk with Jack, I forced myself to face the fact that there was no end in sight and that there would never be one. And this was not all that was happening to keep me awake nights, half sick with fear. For some time past there had been many disturbing incidents, each unimportant in itself, that indicated the Russians might not be the only ones who had placed me under observation. On a visit I made to Chicago a short-wave radio I had just bought for my son – which was equipped to send and receive messages from abroad – had disappeared mysteriously. This happened during a press party I was giving at the Bismarck Hotel to promote *The Waltz King*. There were fifty persons at the party, including the cast. It was disquieting to learn, on making inquiries, that an unidentified, uninvited male guest had been observed walking out with the radio. Adding to my nervousness was a suspicion that Russian espionage agents had also begun to check up on me more and more carefully and with shorter intervals between the check-ups. I now also recalled that the second time I lunched with Vassily Zubilin at Perino's I had observed an alert young man in the next booth. He was apparently listening with interest to the conversation we were conducting in Russian. When he saw me watching him, he winked, as though he *intended* me to know he was there to listen. Thinking of this, along with everything else, gave me a creepy feeling.

And lately, wherever I have gone, to night clubs, restaurants, theaters, even as I arrived and left my studio offices each day, I had the uneasy feeling of being followed by one side or the other, or by both.

In addition to all this, other members of my family complained to me that they felt strangers were watching them. One morning, as my son, Dick, left the house, he noticed a car parked across the street. In it were two young men who seemed to be watching our front door. Dick had never seen them before.

Dick drove away. After going a short way, he discovered that a car – he believed it the same one – was following him. He turned, and the car behind him turned. He tried it again. The car behind him turned again. When Dick drove faster, the other driver also stepped on the gas. When Dick slowed down, the car following did, too. Worried and puzzled, he stopped off at a drugstore to telephone me. After listening to him, I said, 'It's nonsense. Forget it.' I didn't want my war-veteran son to worry. One worrier in our family was enough.

It was right after this incident that I went to the FBI. Until that day, as you can see, I had been living for years almost like a hunted creature. The worst part had been having to keep my humiliating secret from everyone – even from my wife, Katerina. We had been married in 1924, twenty-three years before. But even if I had confided in her, understanding would have been beyond her. I'm not so sure that even now she understands what happened to me, or why. For Katerina Morros's most bitter and burning memory, today as always, is of seeing several of her brothers shot by Communist rioters and looters. The pillaging Reds took one strapping brother of Katerina's after another, ordered him to stand against the wall of her father's house in Rostov, then shot him down.

She had told me the story ten thousand times. She had told it again to every Russian she met, ending it each time with the same anguished words, 'Bolsheviki! Swine! They did not even *blindfold* my brothers before shooting them down like dogs!'

It took a whole week of sessions to tell the story to the FBI men. I racked my memory to recall every detail. As I talked, each of the two men took notes independently of the other. They interrupted me occasionally, but only to ask a question or two. I think I interrupted myself just as often, always to ask the same thing: 'You boys were following me, weren't you?'

They never became angry, but always gave the same answer: 'We'll ask the questions, Boris, if you don't mind.'

They did not deny that they had followed me, but they did not admit it either. And when I had told everything, they asked me a question that I interpreted as forgiveness and evidence of their faith in me.

'Would you like to cooperate with us?'

'When do I start?'

'Now. Today. We can give you your instructions now – unless you'd like to think the whole thing over for a day or two.'

'I don't have to think anything over,' I replied.

'If you think your life was difficult and complicated before, that is nothing to how complicated it will be once you begin working with us. Because you will have to pretend to be playing ball with them all the time. You will have to remember a thousand details that you will not dare to write down, that you will be able to pass on to us only verbally.'

I shrugged.

'And it is only fair to tell you that it is dangerous,' the younger one said then. 'Very dangerous.'

I am not a brave man, and have always known it. But I felt brave at that moment and I asked, 'What are those instructions?'

The first thing impressed on me was the necessity of confiding in no one, not even members of my family, that I had become a counterspy for them.

The first thing I had to do, they said, would be to seem to yield, gradually and reluctantly, to Soble's importunities that I provide the business cover he said he so desperately needed for his ring of secret agents. 'If you quit arguing with him too abruptly,' I was told, 'he may become suspicious of your about-face, your sudden change of heart.'

I was also instructed to keep a record of every conversation, telephone call, or other message I received from the Communist secret agents.

'What about assigning an FBI man to work with me?' I asked, on hearing that. I could put him on the payroll of my film company, Federal Films, as my private secretary, I pointed out, and he would be able to keep an eye on everything that went on. They agreed, and assigned me one of their younger agents. I told my other employees that this man, whom I'll call here Bob Burton, was a nephew of Bob O'Donnell, an important film exhibitor in Texas, and that Bob had sent him to me to learn the business.

He learned the business, all right. He was so useful around the studio office that my partners complimented me on having acquired a gem of a secretary. He fully earned the $50-a-week salary I paid him. He also earned his FBI salary by listening in on every phone call I made or received, by traveling with me everywhere I went – and by protecting my life, which suddenly the FBI considered important because of the strange and perilous position I had jammed myself into.

And that Bastille Day when I went to the FBI boys I wrote in my diary, 'I don't know exactly what the two of them think of me . . . I have not hidden anything from them. I respect them thoroughly. If they respect me half as much – I'm pleased. How can I expect more? It was a day of clearing the conscience. It had to come.'

Elizabeth Bentley

*Had I any previous knowledge of the Communist Party, I would
doubtless have been more skeptical about its program, instead
of accepting it, as I did, at face value.*

The daughter of a newspaper editor, Bentley had been a scholarship student at
Vassar, and had been recruited from the CPUSA and run by Jacob Rasin, a Jewish
Ukrainian and veteran Party activist who called himself Jacob Golos and headed
World Tourists Inc., a travel agency set up by the CPUSA to supervise the
movement of volunteers to Spain during the Spanish Civil War. Golos and Bentley
had become lovers, but their relationship had been detected by the FBI, which had
placed Golos under surveillance after he had been spotted at a series of seven
clandestine meetings held with a known Soviet agent in early 1941, not long
before the latter's arrest and deportation in July. In poor health and under heavy
pressure from the Soviets and the FBI, Golos succumbed to a heart attack in
November 1943, leaving Bentley to take his place as organizer of his apparatus.
Bentley's promotion was confirmed by her new Soviet contact, Anatoli B.
Gromov, the Lithuanian case officer whose real name was Gorsky and who, until
recently, had been the Second Secretary at the Soviet embassy in London. Now he
held a similar diplomatic post in Washington DC.

Although when approached by the FBI in August 1945 Bentley could not offer
the kind of documentary evidence that Whittaker Chambers had produced, she
was able to identify more than eighty of her contacts, including several who had
wormed their way into America's secret wartime intelligence organization, the
Office of Strategic Services (OSS). For example, she named J. Julius Joseph, and
his wife Bella, as being 'of invaluable use'. He had been placed in OSS's Japanese
Section where he 'knew in advance the Americans' plans concerning Japan' while
his wife worked 'for the OSS's Movie Division, which made confidential films for
the use of the United States General Staff'. Bentley also confirmed the complicity of
an OSS translator, Leonard Mins, who was a well-known CP activist, Donald N.
Wheeler and Duncan C. Lee, a personal assistant and legal adviser to the head of
OSS, General Bill Donovan. Helen Tenney of OSS's Spanish Section was
compromised by Bentley, as was Maurice Halperin, head of the Latin America
Division of the Research and Analysis Branch. Another contact was Cedric
Belfrage, then employed by British Intelligence in New York, and of particular
interest was Fred Rose, a Canadian MP who had corresponded with Golos
through a mail-drop run by Bentley. His name was to hit the headlines in 1945, not
long after the defection of Igor Gouzenko, a GRU cipher clerk based at the Soviet
embassy, who had accumulated enough incriminating evidence to justify Rose's
arrest and prosecution.

Although the FBI's attempt to reintroduce Bentley to the Soviets as a double agent, by means of an intimate dinner held with her Soviet controller, proved a failure, she was to continue to give sworn testimony about her undercover activities for most of the decade following her initial interview with the FBI. Despite the lack of any documentary material she made a convincing witness and her recollection neatly dovetailed with the picture of Soviet illegals portrayed by Whittaker Chambers, Hede Massing and Walter Krivitsky. Furthermore, it corroborated aspects of the FBI's first penetration by a double agent, Boris Morros, of a Soviet network of illegals. Her confession confirmed many of the FBI's suspicions and provided collateral evidence from other sources. Bentley proved a credible witness. But why had she joined the communists in the first place? In her autobiography she attempted to answer that central question.

Out of Bondage

As the SS *Vulcania* sailed into New York Harbor that July day in 1934, I leaned on the deck rail and looked at the skyline wistfully. It was good to be back in my own country after a year's study in Italy, I thought, and yet what, really, was I coming back to? I had no home, no family. Nor was there much prospect of finding a teaching position. From all that I had heard abroad, the economic situation in the United States had not greatly improved. True, I still had some money left from my father's estate but that would not last too long. Somehow I must find a way to earn my living. Standing there on the deck, I felt alone and frightened.

By September, the future looked even gloomier. After days of wearing out shoe leather and nights of writing letters of application, I realized that the possibility of my getting back into the teaching field was remote. Nor did there seem to be any other positions for which I was qualified. All those years of academic study have been wasted, I thought bitterly. There doesn't seem to be any place in the world for young professionals like myself. Then I grimly determined to make the best of a bad situation. I enrolled in the Columbia University business school, took a cheap furnished room in the neighborhood, and settled down to learn shorthand and typing. After six months of this, I would be in line for a secretarial job.

Yet I was haunted by the problem of our maladjusted economic system. Although I was only in my mid-twenties, I had already seen two depressions, the second worse than the first. Each had left in its wake suffering, starvation, and broken lives. What lay ahead of us now, I wondered. Complete chaos? That was possible but not for long. Chaos would undoubtedly be succeeded by a Fascist state. I shivered at the prospect. A year of living under Mussolini's regime had left me with no great love for Fascism. There must be some other way out, I thought, some plan that would insure a just world where men could live and work like human beings. But what? I didn't know.

At this critical juncture I became friendly with a girl who had a room down the hall from me. Her name was Lee Fuhr. She was a nurse taking courses at Teachers' College of Columbia University in order to get an academic degree. Shorter than I, square and solid, with yellow hair and blue eyes that betrayed her Dutch ancestry, she gave the impression of being very sturdy and independent. I felt that Lee had a definite goal in life and was heading toward it, unswervingly.

Her life, it seemed, had not been an easy one. Coming from quite a poor family, she had spent her teens working long hours at very little pay in the cotton mills of New Jersey. That, I realized, must have been very hard and unpleasant work. I remembered vividly the time that a group of Gastonia strikers had come to solicit funds at Vassar and their horrible description of conditions then prevalent in the textile industry. Compared to her I had been very fortunate, I thought. True, my parents had never been very well off, but at least I hadn't had to work during my high school days – except, of course, to earn spending money.

Lee, it turned out, had always been determined to be a nurse. By working hard and saving her money, she had finally managed to go to nursing school and get her RN degree. She married soon after, but her husband had died while she was carrying her first child. Undismayed, she had gone back to nursing, managing not only to support herself and Mary Lee but also to put aside enough to tide her over a year at Teachers' College. It had always been the dream of her life, she said, to have a college degree. With that behind her, she could get into public health work.

Lee's glowing enthusiasm made me feel as if, in a way, I were reliving my own past. As far back as I could remember, I had passionately wanted a good college education so that I could one day become a school teacher, as my mother had been before her marriage. To that end, I had studied very hard – even given up many of my outside activities – in order to qualify for the necessary scholarship at Vassar College. Yet, in my case, had it been worth it? I hoped desperately that Lee wouldn't be disappointed, as I had been. After all her struggles it would be a pity if the prized diploma were just one more piece of paper to hang on the wall.

As I got to know Lee better, I began to realize she was one of the most unselfish people I had ever known. Her own difficult life, instead of making her callous, seemed on the contrary to have heightened her innate sympathy for other human beings. To everyone in trouble she gave unstintingly of her time, money, and understanding. She reminds me of my mother, I thought. She, too, had been uninhibitedly friendly and ready to help others in time of need. I remembered that when anyone on our block had been ill, Mother had been the first one there to cook dinner and clean the house. Our house, too, had always been cluttered up with lonely people whom she, despite our meager budget, had invited in for a 'home' meal.

I often wondered just why it was that Lee, in spite of her unhappy experiences in the textile mills, was not more cynical. Yet she would always say that although people were suffering and starving today, all this would be different in future. How this was to be done, she didn't at first tell me – indeed she gave very evasive answers to my direct questions – yet from some of her vague remarks I knew she was spending a great deal of her time working with groups that were helping to relieve poverty. Once or twice she even took me to large benefit parties given by groups whose names I have now forgotten but which at the time sounded like highly humanitarian organizations.

As time went on, I told her about my experiences in Italy and she was very much interested. My first-hand impressions had, she said, only confirmed her belief that Fascism was an ugly and dangerous thing. Moreover, she, too, seemed to be worried about the possibility of the United States becoming Fascist. Human misery was bad enough now, she agreed, but under that sort of regime it would be ten times worse. In fact, she said, she then belonged to an organization which was trying to enlighten the American people about the evils of Fascism and Nazism. The name of it was the American League Against War and Fascism. Why didn't I come over to one of their meetings at Teachers' College and listen to the proceedings? Not only would I be interested myself to learn what Americans were doing in a practical way to prevent Fascism from coming to this country, but I could contribute to the work of the group by telling them what I personally had seen over there.

I had never heard of the American League Against War and Fascism, but its title, its program, and the list of people sponsoring it were impressive. Certainly, I thought, every decent person ought to hate both these evils and be willing to do something to prevent their coming to pass. One man alone, or even a handful of them, could do nothing; an organization of this size, however, especially when it included well-known molders of public opinion, such as religious leaders, writers, and professors, could probably exert a considerable influence. I felt suddenly that Lee had given me a breath of new hope. Here, evidently, was a group of people who not only thought as I did but were willing to do something about the situation. Enthusiastically I told her I would be glad to go to a meeting.

The Teachers' College branch of the League seemed to be composed mainly of graduate students and professors, with a scattering of people from the neighborhood.

When the meeting began, I listened intently as they animatedly discussed the work they had done and their plans for the future. I was impressed by their single-mindedness of purpose and their intense energy – they look like the sort of people who would really get things accomplished, I thought. Some of my own discouragement began to ebb away as their optimism and fervor communicated itself to me. I decided suddenly that I would join the organization and do what I could to help the anti-Fascist cause.

Philip Agee

I felt very much a part of the new dawn in Latin America and of the defense of American interests against Soviet Bloc and Cuban encroachment.

The son of a wealthy businessman from Tampa, Florida, Philip Agee studied business administration and then philosophy at Notre Dame University but left the law school before graduating. In 1956 he was drafted into the US Army and while undergoing his military training he wrote and volunteered for service with the CIA. His application was accepted in 1957 and in 1960 he was sent on his first overseas assignment, under diplomatic cover to Ecuador and then Uruguay. During this time he married and had two sons. In 1966 he returned to Washington DC to join the Mexico branch of the Western Hemisphere Division but in the middle of the following year he was sent to Mexico City under Olympic attaché cover, in anticipation of the Olympic Games scheduled for 1968.

In Mexico Agee began an affair with an American divorcee with strong Leftist political sympathies, and under her influence he resigned from the CIA in the autumn of 1968 but remained in Mexico, working for a local company manufacturing mirrors. In early 1970, more than a year after he had left the Agency, Agee went to New York to interest publishers in a book project. Nothing materialized so he enrolled in a university course in Mexico, and the following year travelled, on the recommendation of the French publisher François Maspero who had released Che Guevara's diaries, to Cuba where he started work on a book that was to be published as *Inside the Company: CIA Diary*. He finished writing it in Paris, under continuous CIA surveillance, but not before he received a warning from the Agency's lawyers reminding him of his secrecy agreement, and notification of a federal court judgement against Victor Marchetti, reinforcing the CIA's right to scrutinize and censor anything written by an ex-employee.

Agee's book was published in London in January 1975, coinciding with an article Agee had contributed to *CounterSpy*, a radical magazine founded by Norman Mailer which also produced a list of what it claimed were the names of a hundred CIA station chiefs based undercover around the world. From his new home in Cornwall, Agee encouraged journalists to research embassy lists to spot the biographical entries of CIA personnel working under diplomatic cover, and in December Richard Welch, the CIA station chief in Athens, who had been mentioned by *CounterSpy* as having served in Lima, was shot dead outside his home.

Undeterred by Welch's murder, Agee planned further revelations but in November 1976, while living in Cambridge, he was served with deportation papers and in June the following year he moved to Amsterdam. Soon afterwards he was expelled from France and excluded from West Germany and Holland. In 1977 Agee launched a new periodical, the *Covert Action Information Bulletin*, at a press conference in Cuba, together with a group of supporters including two disaffected former CIA employees, Jim and Elsie Wilcott. The journal was intended to expose CIA staff and operations, and in June 1980 it named the CIA station chief in Kingston, Jamaica, as Richard Kinsman, whose house was promptly the subject of an attack.

The *Bulletin*'s objective was shared by Agee's next publishing venture, an edited compendium of articles entitled *Dirty Work: The CIA in Western Europe*, which included the biographical data of hundreds of purported CIA officers. In 1979 a sequel followed, *Dirty Work II*, concentrating on the CIA's operations in Africa. None of these publications was the subject of criminal prosecution in the United States because, as the US Justice Department confirmed, the CIA could not undergo the usual discovery proceedings associated with a trial. Instead Agee's US passport was revoked, and he was issued with a Grenadian one by Maurice Bishop, the premier of that tiny Caribbean island who was himself to be deposed and assassinated by even more extreme radicals. Later Agee acquired a Nicaraguan passport which he used to maintain his residency in Hamburg, and later to enter Canada and slip back into the United States.

In this extract from his second volume of autobiography, published in 1987, Agee describes the background to his first visit to Cuba, where his political conversion took place.

On The Run

In early 1971 I got word from Maspero that he was interested. But where could I find two things: the research facilities I needed and protection from the CIA? Paris might be a good location and so might Brussels or London. Cuba might be a possibility – Maspero had publishing connections there.

But would the Cubans, against whom I had worked before, trust me enough to let me in? And could I find there the information I needed?

If the Cubans would give me a visa I would go and see. Only one condition: I did not want to be treated as a defector, in the sense of sitting for endless debriefings on CIA operations and personnel. I wanted to write a book, but did not want to risk violation of US espionage laws.

From Maspero I received word that the Cubans would give me a visa. I didn't want to fly from Mexico City because passengers bound for Cuba in those days had to report to the airport three hours ahead of flight time, and their names were routinely checked with the CIA Station. The Agency even took photographs of all the passengers. The Mexicans would no more have let me on a flight to Havana than the CIA itself. The last thing I wanted was for the CIA to learn I intended to visit Cuba.

In April the UNAM student body went on indefinite strike. I think it was in solidarity with pay demands of administrative personnel. I would have several weeks free. Without telling anyone of my destination, I went to Montreal, got a visa at the Cuban Consulate, and took the train to St John, New Brunswick. I would have a berth on the *Bahía de Santiago de Cuba*, a Cuban freighter that was to sail in a few days for Havana.

I took a taxi to the port and almost didn't get out. My ship was a rusty old tub, a World War II Liberty Ship built to last no more than ten years. It was now over twenty-five and showing every year. The bow had no rake, neither did the smokestack. Decrepitude and corrosion were everywhere. Still, the momentum of my trip from Mexico and my strong curiosity to visit Cuba led me to pay the taxi and report on board.

As I waited to see the Captain I observed that the ship was being filled from stem to stern with sacks of powdered milk. But my vision of the moment, and the days ahead, were from my favorite books of boyhood, the sea novels of Howard Pease. It was as though I had just stepped onto one of the tramp steamers of *Shanghai Passage*, *Wind in the Rigging*, or *The Tattooed Man*. For a former CIA officer embarking for Havana in 1971 the spirit of adventure could not have been more real.

The purser assigned me to a bunk in the very stern of the ship in a small cabin with one leaky porthole. My cabinmate was Pedro, an oiler who spent most of his time in the engine room or somewhere down in the ship where I wasn't supposed to go. For the first forty-eight hours, the sea was extremely rough and each time the stern lifted out of the water the turn of the propeller threatened to shake the ship apart. A steam engine, mounted right at my cabin door, drove the tiller, and each time the helmsman altered course, which was constantly those first days, the steam engine hissed and pounded like a half-speed jack hammer.

A week or so after leaving Canada we passed Miami – so close that with binoculars I could watch people sunning on the beach. By now it was quite hot, and I spent my last days on board painting superstructure and reading in the sun. During the traditional last-night-at-sea party I couldn't help regretting it was over. I just hoped the atmosphere after arrival would be as pleasant.

It was late afternoon when we passed through the narrow entrance to Havana harbor on the west side of Morro Castle. On our right a lovely palm-fringed park fronted on the channel, and there, in large numbers were the families of the crew waving and shouting a noisy welcome home. By the time we moored it was already dark, and I went ashore with two young men who came to meet me on behalf of the Cuban Friendship Institute.

As we drove away from the port, through the oldest part of Havana, I noticed how different things looked from 1957. There was the Prado, formerly the center of town and bustling with people in the evenings. Now it was dark and almost deserted. And there was the Presidential Palace where Batista had lived, now closed and abandoned. We entered the Malecon, Havana's long seafront boulevard, for the drive out to 23rd, better known as La Rampa and now the center of Havana's night life. We turned in just as we came to the Hotel Nacional up on a bluff overlooking the sea, and a couple of minutes later we were in the Habana Libre, formerly the Hilton and easily the biggest hotel in town.

During the next few weeks I made lists of books and other background materials I needed, then visited the national library and other places where they might be found. The results were mixed, but I was determined to find everything I could there, and to write as much as possible before leaving. Nothing I was looking for involved secret information. What I needed most was information on political, economic and social conditions in countries where I had worked, along with current events from that period. I could fill in the details on our operations later, putting them into a context of local realities.

As the weeks went by my interest in Cuba and the revolution grew. I'd finished all the books I brought with me, was reading everything I could get my hands on, while battering the Cubans I met with non-stop questions. As my fascination and curiosity about Cuba grew, the importance and desirability of returning to Mexico waned. Still, I had my apartment and belongings there, together with personal affairs and other pending matters, not to mention my studies and possible future in teaching.

All the while what impressed me most was the friendliness and spontaneity of the Cubans I met – a total of perhaps fifteen from different documentation centers, from the party bureaucracy and from the Foreign Ministry. Were any of these intelligence or security officers? Considering my background some of them had to be. Yet there seemed to be no crisis of confidence. The first night in Havana I warned that for my book to be effective I must avoid any compromise that might suggest I had written it under their influence.

This meant I wanted to be treated as an author writing something of value for the people of Latin America and the United States. I did not want to go through the kind of 'processing' that an intelligence service would arrange for a 'defector'. Additionally I knew that my ability to get the book written would be jeopardized if information on specific CIA operations began filtering back to counter-intelligence analysts at Head-quarters because the finger could eventually point to me. The same might happen if the Cubans or other services began taking counter-measures against CIA operations that I knew about.

These were practical matters having nothing to do with loyalty to the CIA. I simply didn't want to get caught giving secrets on CIA operations to the Cuban intelligence service. They would come out in my book soon enough, I hoped, and in any case I was writing for another audience.

Looking back, almost fifteen years later, I admit that was a stupid and contradictory attitude: quite shallow and *petit bourgeois*. So many individuals and organizations in Latin America needed every bit of information I could have told them. But CIA officers can be so con-temptuous of defectors from the Soviet Union and other communist countries that I had an insurmountable psychological block at putting myself in the defector category. Yet defector I was – not *to* any other country but certainly *from* the CIA and American foreign policy.

After a month or perhaps six weeks I was getting nervous about returning to Mexico. I worried that people would wonder where I'd been, that my rent was overdue, that I'd miss examinations. On the other hand there seemed to be a lot more I could do in Havana. After much reflection and discussions with the Cubans who were helping me, I decided to return to Mexico only to arrange personal affairs. I would withdraw from the university and return to Havana to continue on my book. Then I would go to Paris.

My decision to leave Mexico completely, and to drop everything else to get the book done, was in large part a result of what I had seen and read of the Cuban revolution. Such a contrast with the other Latin America that I knew, where Kennedy's grandiose Alliance for Progress had been a near-total failure. In Cuba they had all but wiped out illiteracy and started enormous investments in educational programs of all kinds. Radical agrarian and urban reforms had changed forever the lot of peasants and renters. The Cubans were trying, at least, to build a new society free of corruption and exploitation. No question that they were still far from their goals, and they were quick to admit it. On balance, though, revolutionary Cuba made the rest of Latin America look like it was in a political and social stone age.

Before leaving I toured from one end of the island to the other, visiting all kinds of development projects in education, public health and the economy. With the Cubans I left lists of the materials I had located, or that I still needed to find, and they promised to bring it all together by the time I returned – at most, I figured, a month later. Yet I sensed something odd, a kind of resignation on their part that suggested they thought I wouldn't be coming back. Not that anyone thought I didn't want to, but that something, most likely the CIA, would prevent my return.

In order to avoid the controls at the Mexico City airport, I decided to return to Mexico via Europe and the US. That would be less risky and would also give me a couple of weeks with my sons. I took an Aeroflot flight to Morocco, then Air France to Paris. When I telephoned Phil and Chris I discovered that I had indeed been missed – a number of people in fact thought I was dead. Janet came on the phone to say that friends in Mexico had already turned my apartment back to the owner and divided my furniture and other belongings.

I lied that I had been in Paris all that time, from where I sent several letters that must have gone astray. I assured Philip and Christopher that I would see them in a couple of days, then called my father in Florida to relieve him. I would take the children for a couple weeks' visit with him and Nancy and forget returning to Mexico – there was no need for that now.

On the flight to Washington I thought over all the ways I could get out of the mess I'd made by staying so long in Cuba. There was really only one. I'd have to stick with the lame 'lost letters' ruse and try to make it look as if I'd been in Paris all that time. And what if the CIA had learned I was in Cuba? After all, they had computer lists of all the travelers to and from Havana, including names from flight manifests. Well, I thought, if they approached me about the Cuba trip I'd just tell them I was sight-seeing. I had as much right to visit Cuba as Canada or Mexico, and if they didn't like it, too bad. There was no visit from the Agency. They must not have known. To this day I don't know how I slipped through the controls. I was as lucky as I was reckless.

While in Washington I mended fences with Janet over the children. We agreed that they would live with her during the coming two school years but would spend Christmas and summer vacations with me. Then they would come to live with me, wherever I happened to be. I gave the details to my lawyer and asked him to draw up the papers. What a relief to have an amiable agreement after all the earlier troubles.

At the end of August I was in Madrid boarding a flight back to Havana. During the months ahead I lived in a beach house in Santa Maria, making the twenty-minute trip to Havana whenever necessary by motorcycle. The hippie look was not in style in Cuba then, never was in fact, so when people saw this guy roaring along on a motorcycle in jeans and Mexican sandals, with long hair and a Zapata moustache, they looked like they were seeing a man from Mars. Nobody told me I should 'go straight', but I got the point when a barber showed up at my house. Oh well, 'when in Rome . . .' I thought, as he cut my hair.

Gradually I accumulated a pile of books, press clippings and publications of all kinds that I needed to refresh my memory and get the facts straight. Yet all the while I had a growing feeling of uneasiness that I wasn't making progress fast enough. What I had found was valuable all right, but it wasn't enough. When Maspero visited in November we agreed that I should return to Paris and continue there.

Before leaving I decided to take two steps that for me meant joining forces with progressive and socialist movements in Latin America, in particular the Allende government in Chile that was just ending its first year in office, and the Broad Front in Uruguay, a coalition similar to Allende's Popular Unity. In Uruguay elections were due in just a few weeks, and I was certain the Agency would be much involved to prevent another socialist electoral victory, or even a good showing.

First I wrote a long memorandum for the Allende government in which I described the ways I thought the CIA would be working to undermine them. These included financing and directing opposition front organizations among workers, students, peasants and women, fomenting strikes and street violence, propaganda, rumors, sabotage and paramilitary actions. I gave examples from my own experience in all these areas, in the hope that I could contribute to the Chileans' understanding of, and defense against, Agency subversion.

Then I wrote a letter to the editor of *Marcha*, the leading left-wing political weekly in Uruguay. I used Maspero's office in Paris as a return address. In the letter I said I was a former CIA officer who had worked in American embassies in Ecuador, Uruguay and Mexico. I described some of the ways the CIA intervened in electoral campaigns to favor certain parties and defeat others, giving past examples from Chile and Brazil. I said the elections in Uruguay were a logical and traditional target for Agency intervention, and I outlined some of the visible signs that would create a pattern. At the end I said I was writing a book on my work in the CIA and that I would be glad to provide additional details that might apply to Uruguay. I signed my name.

I gave the documents to one of the Cubans who were helping me and asked him to pass them along to people who could judge their usefulness better than I could. If they were considered worth sending, fine. If not, that was okay too. He came back saying they thought it was risky, with me about to go to Paris to continue my book. The risk didn't matter to me, I said. Do with them whatever you want.

I never forgot the last words of Alejandro, the person I had come to know best in Havana, when we said farewell at the airport. 'Felipe, if you are ever able to get your book written, it will be an important work for us, for millions of other Latin Americans, and for North America too. But the CIA will never forgive. They will never leave you in peace.'

Years later in Munich, or in other public meetings, I could only give the bare outlines of how I changed. Even now I'm sure there were people whose influence I've forgotten. In many ways I was lucky to meet the right people at the right time. These were human factors, like Muriel and Veronica, who helped turn a set of intellectual conclusions into actions. But there was no sudden conversion in a religious sense. Instead I experienced a gradual, step-by-step progression, with both human and political influences constantly at work until I reached the point, when I decided to visit Cuba, that I would do whatever was required to put my knowledge and experience at the service of those who needed it to defend themselves and their ideals. I never thought I was unique in that sense – people are changing every day, and politically I was a late arrival. What made me different, of course, was my CIA background.

'And why hasn't the CIA *done something* to you?'

Aah, but they have. Through the years they've constantly used their agents and contacts in the media to plant articles discrediting me. They've tried to make me look like everything from a traitor to a drunk to a womanizer to a mental case. They, and their friends, have had me expelled from country to country like a human pinball. But these were political attacks that began after I had finished my book. By then I was a public figure, notorious to some, and it was too late for them to resort to physical violence like assassination.

Frank W. Snepp

Once I had severed my ties, CIA officials tried to discredit me with former colleagues. Memos advising everyone not to talk with me were circulated around the headquarters building, as if I were on the verge of betraying national secrets.

The son of a judge in North Carolina, and educated at Columbia University, Snepp became a news researcher for CBS in New York before joining the CIA in 1968. A junior analyst at the CIA's Saigon station for five years, during the final evacuation Snepp drove the car that took President Thieu to his plane when he left the country for the last time.

Dismayed by the loss of secret files, and the ruthless abandonment of CIA assets as the Vietcong took control, Snepp resigned from the Agency in January 1976, having been awarded the CIA's Medal of Merit. His book, *Decent Interval*, was released the following year in spite of the US Department of Justice's attempt to obtain injunctions to prevent publication. He claimed that although he had not submitted his manuscript to the CIA, as required by his secrecy agreement, he had not revealed any classified material. His main criticism of the CIA was the flawed system adopted in Saigon to assess the enemy's strength, and the Agency's refusal to accept any blame for the final defeat. The US government acknowledged that the book did not contain classified data but insisted on its right to review all disclosures made by ex-CIA employees who, it was maintained, had waived their First Amendment rights by signing the CIA's standard secrecy agreement. The case against Snepp was appealed several times and won in the Supreme Court in a controversial six–three judgement.

Snepp is highly critical of Philip Agee, whom he describes as 'a man who revels in jeopardizing the lives of CIA agents' and, of course, was allowed to retain the profits from his exposé. Now living in Arlington, Virginia, Snepp has written two novels, *Convergence of Interest* and *Irreparable Harm*, and is currently writing a screenplay. However, it was his allegations against the CIA during the last days of Saigon, including his criticisms of senior colleagues like Ted Shackley, which proved so controversial.

Decent Interval

If General Dung had chosen to attack Saigon head-on, rather than to strip away its outer defenses beforehand, the city would have become a battleground, and an airlift rendered impossible. Equally crucial was the decision of CIA officers, including Ted Shackley, in early April to cordon Saigon off from the rampaging refugee population in the countryside.

The layout of the city and the location of Tan Son Nhut itself also played a part in what transpired, and what did not. Unlike the airfield at Danang, Tan Son Nhut was some distance from the downtown area, and surrounded by military compounds that could be sealed off to limit access. Behind its fences and checkpoints General Smith was able to set up his evacuation center and move thousands out through it without the population of the city becoming fully aware.

Of all the factors that accounted for our salvation, however, perhaps the most decisive was the attitude of the Vietnamese themselves. In Danang and Nha Trang our Vietnamese friends and co-workers knew that there were still other places to escape to, and that a little initiative might get them there, even without our help. But by the time Saigon came under attack such options had disappeared, and those who wanted to save themselves had no choice but to stand back and defer to us.

The improvisatory and haphazard nature of the evacuation of course had its cost. Working under terrible pressure, without proper guidance, Moorefield, Lacy Wright, Rosenblatt and the scores of others like them were unable to screen the evacuees as Washington intended. Consequently, bar girls and maids often got seats that should have been reserved for 'high risk' individuals. Even the 'black' flights, especially arranged for 'priority' evacuees, were misused. As Colonel Legro admitted after the fall of Saigon, only twenty percent of the 2,000 Vietnamese he and his immediate staff had ushered out secretly could truly be considered 'high risk'.

Ambassador Martin tried to minimize these problems in his testimony to Congress, claiming that some 22,294 Vietnamese employed by American agencies or related to those who were had been evacuated as of 30 April 1975. On the surface, this seemed a respectable number, but in fact it was distressingly small, particularly in view of the total number of past and present employees of the Embassy and their families – over 90,000 by the final State Department estimate. To judge from Martin's figures, less than one-third of these actually benefited from the airlift. The rest were left behind, or were obliged to escape on their own.

Predictably, the Defense Attaché's Office was the only agency in the Mission that came close to evacuating all of the locals on its payroll – about 1,500 out of 3,800. The scorecard for the rest of us was far less impressive. As of the summer of 1977, the breakdown was as shown in the table below.

Agency	Total direct-hire employees, including consulate staffs*	Present in the US (evacuees & escapees)	Still in Vietnam
State Department	900	225	675
SAFFO (formerly CORDS, under George Jacobson)	1,122	218	904
USIA	167	55	112
USAID	924	362	562
Mission Wardens' Office (under Mary Garrett)	3,500	200	3,300†

* Totals do not include the thousands of Vietnamese who worked for the various agencies under contract.

† The evacuation from Can Tho, mounted independently of the Saigon airlift, yielded roughly the same kind of results. Of the 573 locals on the consulate's evacuee lists (excluding those who worked for the CIA), only 47 were among the 200 people who sailed with MacNamara down the Bassac River to the sea.

Since George Jacobson, the Ambassador's Special Assistant for Field Operations (SAFFO) was technically in charge of the latter phases of the evacuation, it is noteworthy that such a large number of his own evacuees (904) failed to get out. That in itself provides a telling commentary on the kind of leadership the Ambassador imposed on us in Saigon's final days.

Among those on Jacobson's own evacuee rolls who were left behind was a highly knowledgeable Communist defector who had provided us over the years with our most comprehensive data on COSVN and its personalities. In late April, Jacobson had offered to evacuate him, but not his two sons, since they were of draft age. The defector, needless to say, had refused to leave without them.

Jacobson also bungled the evacuation of Nay Luette, the montagnard leader, for whom he had assumed responsibility. Luette went to a designated rendezvous point on the final day of the war, but was never picked up. The Communists later jailed him.

Because of the sensitivity of their jobs, the list of CIA locals who were evacuated, or left behind, remained hidden away in agency vaults in the months following the Communist victory. Yet several of my former colleagues, who were outraged at what had taken place, saw to it that some basic statistics were made available to me. According to these tabulations, only about 537 of the Station's 1,900 'indigenous employees' were finally evacuated, together with 2,000 others – including family members – who had enjoyed privileged contacts with the agency over the years.

Victor Marchetti

The proven benefits of intelligence are not in question.
Rather, it is the illegal and unethical clandestine operations
carried out under the guise of intelligence and the dubious
purposes to which they are often put by our government that
are questionable – both on moral grounds and in terms of
practical benefit to the nation.

While serving in the US Army in Germany in 1952 Victor Marchetti attended a special course at Oberammergau to study Soviet intelligence techniques. After a brief spell on border duties he completed his military service but continued his Soviet studies at Penn University. While still a student he was recruited by the CIA, which he joined formally in September 1955.

A career CIA analyst specializing in Soviet military affairs until late in 1969 when he retired, Victor Marchetti wrote a novel, *The Rope Dancer*, in 1971. This was considered to have revealed so much about the CIA that a federal court ruled that all the author's future writing should be submitted for formal clearance. His next book, for which he teamed up with John D. Marks, an analyst attached to the State Department's Bureau of Intelligence, was *The CIA and the Cult of Intelligence*. When the CIA learned of the authors' plans from a 1974 magazine article, the manuscript was seized and a total of 339 deletions were demanded, but on appeal the number was reduced to 168 contentious passages, of which only 27 were disallowed. Significantly, the authors had the reinstated text printed in bold type in a deliberate effort to highlight the material the CIA had considered damaging to national security. In this passage, which escaped the censor unscathed, the authors describe the way the CIA handles defectors, and mentions among others, Yevgeny Runge.

The CIA and the Cult of Intelligence

Intelligence agencies, in the popular view, are organizations of glamorous master spies who, in the best tradition of James Bond, daringly uncover the evil intentions of a nation's enemies. In reality, however, the CIA has had comparatively little success in acquiring intelligence through secret agents. This classical form of espionage has for many years ranked considerably below space satellites, code-breaking, and other forms of technical collection as a source of important foreign information to the US government. Even open sources (the press and other communications media) and official channels (diplomats, military attachés, and the like) provide more valuable information than the Clandestine Services of the CIA. Against its two principal targets, the Soviet Union and Communist China, the effectiveness of CIA spies is virtually nil. With their closed societies and powerful internal-security organizations, the communist countries have proved practically impenetrable to the CIA.

To be sure, the agency has pulled off an occasional espionage coup, but these have generally involved 'walk-ins' – defectors who take the initiative in offering their services to the agency. Remember that in 1955, when Oleg Penkovsky first approached CIA operators in Ankara, Turkey, to discuss the possibility of becoming an agent, he was turned away, because it was feared that he might be a double agent. Several years later, he was recruited by bolder British intelligence officers. Nearly all of the other Soviets and Chinese who either spied for the CIA or defected to the West did so without being actively recruited by America's leading espionage agency.

Technically speaking, anyone who turns against his government is a defector. A successfully recruited agent or a walk-in who offers his services as a spy is known as a defector-in-place. He has not yet physically deserted his country, but has in fact defected politically in secret. Refugees and émigrés are also defectors, and the CIA often uses them as spies when they can be persuaded to risk return to their native lands. In general, a defector is a person who has recently bolted his country and is simply willing to trade his knowledge of his former government's activities for political asylum in another nation; that some defections are accompanied by a great deal of publicity is generally due to the CIA's desire to obtain public approbation of its work.

Escapees from the USSR and Eastern Europe are handled by the CIA's defector reception center at Camp King near Frankfurt, West Germany. There they are subjected to extensive debriefing and interrogation by agency officers who are experts at draining from them their full informational potential. Some defectors are subjected to questioning that lasts for months; a few are interrogated for a year or more.

A former CIA chief of station in Germany remembers with great amusement his role in supervising the lengthy debriefing of a Soviet lieutenant, a tank-platoon commander, who fell in love with a Czech girl and fled with her to the West after the Soviet invasion of Czechoslovakia in 1968. The ex-agency senior officer relates how he had to play marriage counselor when the couple's relationship started to sour, causing the lieutenant to lose his willingness to talk. By saving the romance, the chief of station succeeded in keeping the information flowing from the Soviet lieutenant. Although a comparatively low-level Soviet defector of this sort would seem to have small potential for providing useful intelligence, the CIA has had so little success in penetrating the Soviet military that the lieutenant underwent months of questioning. Through him, agency analysts were able to learn much about how Soviet armor units, and the ground forces in general, are organized, their training and tactical procedures, and the mechanics of their participation in the build-up that preceded the invasion of Czechoslovakia. This was hardly intelligence of strategic importance, but the CIA's Clandestine Services have no choice but to pump each low-level Soviet defector for all he is worth.

The same former chief of station also recalls with pride the defection of Yevgeny Runge, a KGB illegal (or 'deep cover' agent) in late 1967. Runge, like the more infamous Colonel Rudolf Abel from Brooklyn and Gordon Lonsdale of London, was a Soviet operator who lived for years under an assumed identity in West Germany. Unlike his colleagues, however, he was not exposed and arrested. Instead, Runge defected to the CIA when he lost interest in his clandestine work. According to the ex-agency official, Runge was of greater intelligence value to the US government than Penkovsky. This assessment, however, is highly debatable because Runge provided no information which the CIA's intelligence analysts found to be useful in determining Soviet strategic capabilities or intentions. On the other hand, the KGB defector did reveal much concerning the methods and techniques of Soviet clandestine intelligence operations in Germany. To CIA operators who have been unsuccessful in penetrating the Soviet government and who have consequently become obsessed with the actions of the opposition, the defection of an under-cover operator like Runge represents a tremendous emotional windfall, and they are inclined to publicize it as an intelligence coup.

Once the CIA is satisfied that a defector has told all that he knows, the resettlement team takes over. The team's objective is to find a place for the defector to live where he will be free from the fear of reprisal and happy enough neither to disclose his connections with the CIA nor, more important, to be tempted to return to his native country. Normally, the team works out a cover story for the defector, invents a new identity for him, and gives him enough money (often a lifetime pension) to make the transition to a new way of life. The most important defectors are brought to the United States (either before or after their briefing), but the large majority are permanently settled in Western Europe, Canada, or Latin America.*

The defector's adjustment to his new country is often quite difficult. For security reasons, he is usually cut off from any contact with his native land and, therefore, from his former friends and those members of his family who did not accompany him into exile. He may not even know the language of the country where he is living. Thus, a large percentage of defectors become psychologically depressed with their new lives once the initial excitement of resettlement wears off. A few have committed suicide. To try to keep the defector content, the CIA assigns a case officer to each one for as long as is thought necessary. The case officer stays in regular contact with the defector and helps solve any problems that may arise. With a particularly volatile defector, the agency maintains even closer surveillance, including telephone taps and mail intercepts, to guard against unwanted developments.

In some instances, case officers will watch over the defector for the rest of his life. More than anything else, the agency wants no defector to become so dissatisfied that he will be tempted to return to his native country. Of course, redefection usually results in a propaganda victory for the opposition; of greater consequence, however, is the fact that the defector probably will reveal everything he knows about the CIA in order to ease his penalty for having defected in the first place. Moreover, when a defector does return home, the agency has to contend with the nagging fear that all along it has been dealing with a double agent and that all the intelligence he revealed was part of a plot to mislead the CIA. The possibilities for deception in the defector game are endless, and the communist intelligence services have not failed to take advantage of them.

---

*On occasion, a defector will be hired as a contract employee to do specialized work as a translator, interrogator, counterintelligence analyst, or the like, for the Clandestine Services.

John R. Stockwell

The CIA's oaths and honor codes must never take precedence over allegiance to our country.

Born in Angleton, Texas, John Stockwell joined the US Marine Corps reserve in 1955, having obtained a degree from the University of Texas, and in 1964 started work with the CIA as a case officer. During two tours in Africa he worked as chief of base in Lubumbashi in Zaire, and chief of station in Burundi. In 1972 he returned to headquarters in Langley as head of the Kenya–Uganda section, and then was assigned to Vietnam where he was placed in charge of Tay Ninh province, following the suicide of a colleague.

In 1975 he was appointed head of the CIA's task force in Angola which had been set up to support two of the main anti-Soviet guerrilla movements in that country. Disillusioned with his experiences in Africa, Stockwell resigned in 1977 to write *In Search of Enemies*, a damning indictment of what Stockwell described as the Agency's waste and incompetence in Angola, and its misrepresentation to Congress of what was really a huge paramilitary intervention. The book was published without the CIA's consent, in breach of the author's employment contract, and in 1980 the federal government sued him for all profits from the book. He settled the litigation in June of that year by agreeing to surrender the book's future royalties.

A bitter critic of his former employers, he met Philip Agee in Cuba. He was divorced in 1974 and five years later married a Vietnamese secretary, Thach Xu Lit, by whom he had two children. In this extract from his first book Stockwell recalls how his confidence in the CIA was undermined.

In Search of Enemies

Where had my doubts about the CIA started? When I had realized that my intelligence reporting during six long years in Africa had made no useful contribution? When I realized that even the 'hard' target operations – the recruitment of Soviets, Chinese, and North Koreans – meant little more? In darker moments, it seemed to me that my twelve years of service had been spent in hard, sometimes nerve-racking, work that had nothing to do with the security of the United States.

But a lot of it had affected other people's lives. Many trusting individuals had been caught in our operational web. My first recruited agent was arrested. When I found him, 'Krneutron/1' was living a life of penniless indolence in a small country for which I had intelligence responsibility. His was my first recruitment, a classic, out of the training manual. He would be my eyes and ears in his country and I would solve his financial problems – we would both enjoy the camaraderie and intrigue. On my next visit I leaned on Krneutron/1 to produce intelligence: 'Are you *sure* there is no coup plotting? If anything happens and you don't tell me *in advance* headquarters will cut my money . . . What about your cousin, the ex-president's son? Mightn't he be plotting? Maybe you'd better see him . . .'

Krneutron/1 saw his cousin. He and his friends *were* dissatisfied with the regime.

On my next visit the cousin was thinking of plotting something. Over six months a coup was hatched, and Krneutron/1 sat on the inner council.

Headquarters was delighted and authorized bonuses. We all ignored that the plotters were irresponsible youths, while the incumbent president was mature, restrained, and even pro-West. Fortunately for the country, the incumbent broke up the plot, but Krneutron/1 spent seven years in jail. At that time – I was twenty-nine – I sincerely believed that I was only collecting intelligence. It never occurred to me that I had fomented the plot. If it occurred to my bosses, they didn't mention it. This was the naiveté of which Graham Greene wrote in *The Quiet American*, 'Innocence is a form of insanity.'

Or was it in Vietnam, where CIA operations were dominated by bungling and deceit? At the end in Vietnam I had participated in an evacuation in which the CIA leaders had fled in panic, abandoning people whom we had recruited and exposed in our operations. This struck at the core of my wishful conviction that the CIA was the elite of the United States government, charged with the responsibility of protecting our country in the secret wars of a hostile world. Very little about CIA activity in Vietnam was honorable. It gnawed at my conscience. I had managed other case officers and in the end I had fled like everyone else.

But conscientious officers, whom I respected, still insisted that these experiences were misleading, that there was nothing wrong with the CIA that a good housecleaning wouldn't cure. They spoke reverently of *intelligence* and *national security* and urged me to hang on to my career and use my increasing authority to help reform the agency.

I wanted to believe them. All my life I had conformed: to a boarding school in Africa, to the Marine Corps, to the CIA. I had reveled in the challenge and sheer fun of clandestine operations, the excitement of flying off on secret missions, the thrill of finding one more way to plant a bug in a Chinese embassy, and, eventually, the gratification of supervisory authority over other case officers.

After Vietnam I had spent ten good weeks with my three teenagers, all of us starved for each other's companionship. We swam, built a canoe, camped at the beach, played tennis and chess and Monopoly and Ping-Pong, and built an addition to my parent's retirement home in the hills overlooking Lake Travis on the outskirts of Austin, Texas. In the evenings we talked, often until dawn, about their lives and mine. I hadn't known whether I wanted to go back into clandestine work. After a crunch like Vietnam . . . Then the telephone had rung.

On the flight from Austin to Washington, I had only to flip through the newsmagazines to be reminded again of the notoriety of my employer. Two congressional committees were investigating CIA activities. During the past week alone, President Ford had apologized to the Olsson family for the death of Dr Olsson in CIA drug experiments some years earlier; a former CIA deputy director of plans (the clandestine services) had testified that he had approved CIA contact with the Mafia to arrange the assassination of Fidel Castro; the current director, William Colby, had admitted to a twenty-year CIA practice of opening American citizens' mail. The former secretary of defense, Clark Clifford, a drafter of the National Security Act of 1947 that permitted the creation of the CIA, had recommended that covert action to be taken away from the CIA altogether. It had not been a good year for my side.

I thought back to 1964, a better year, the year I was hired. Then, the CIA had enjoyed the highest credibility, and the nation was still 'continuing' President Kennedy's New Frontier. America was alive again, and I was young and restless. We would save the world from communism, the CIA and I. The agency was interested in me because I had grown up in the old Belgian Congo. My father had contracted to build a hydroelectric plant for the Presbyterian mission in the Kasai Province and my brother and I learned how to drive in the mission's five-ton truck. We were bilingual, speaking the local dialect, Tshiluba, with our African play-mates. After college in the States I did a tour in a Marine Corps parachute reconnaisance company, which also interested the agency. When they first contacted me, in 1963, the CIA's paramilitary program in the Congo was in full stride.

Because of my mission background, my recruiters and I discussed the CIA's 'true nature'. They had been unequivocal in reassuring me – the CIA was an intelligence-gathering institution, and a benevolent one. Coups were engineered only to alter circumstances which jeopardized national security. I would be a better person through association with the CIA. My naiveté was shared by most of my forty-two classmates in our year-long training program. Our instructors hammered the message at us: the CIA was good, its mission was to make the world a better place, to save the world from communism. In 1964, I signed the secrecy agreement without hesitation, never realizing that one day it would be interpreted to mean that I had given up my freedom of speech.

My naiveté of 1964 was also shared, literally, by hundreds of journalists, publishers, university professors and administrators who succumbed to CIA recruitment, to our collective embarrassment when the CIA's true nature began to surface in 1975.

Melvin Beck

The fact is that the KGB, the Committee of State Security,
displays ruthlessness towards its own nationals who are
considered traitors to the motherland (emigres, defectors
and the like).

Born in Minneapolis, Minnesota, Melvin Beck was a teacher in New York before becoming a Japanese translator in a cryptographic unit of the US Army during the Second World War. At the end of the war he remained in the Armed Forces Security Agency as a civilian, and in 1947 was transferred to the newly created National Security Agency. After six years as an analyst concentrating on the Soviet Union, Beck joined the Soviet Division of the CIA's Clandestine Services, and in 1959, after a year on the Latin America desk, was posted to Havana in the role of an operations officer. By the time of his arrival in February 1960 he had already undertaken two short missions to Cuba, to investigate the growing Soviet presence on the island, but this appointment was to be under the diplomatic cover of cultural attaché and lasted two years during which he worked as a counter-intelligence expert, studying local Soviet personnel. It was terminated by the arrest and imprisonment of three CIA technicians, and the expulsion of a case officer, with whom Beck had been working and sharing a house. The operation had involved inserting a listening device into the offices of the New China News Agency but Castro's security apparatus had intervened, forcing Beck to be withdrawn to Washington DC at short notice.

In December 1961 Beck was switched briefly from the Latin America desk in the Soviet Division to the position of case officer in the CIA station in Mexico City, and soon afterwards, in June 1962, received a longer posting to Mexico, lasting five years, under the cover of a freelance writer. During this period he ran double agents against the KGB and mounted technical surveillance operations on his Soviet counterparts, and towards the end of his assignment in Mexico he overlapped with Philip Agee.

Beck returned to Langley in 1967 as a desk officer, and supervised a very productive eavesdropping exercise on the Soviet ambassador to an unnamed country, in whose office a bug had been planted. However, despite the success of this particular project, Beck became increasingly disillusioned with his career and with his employer.

Beck retired in 1971 and in 1975 received clearance to publish his memoirs, subject to a limited number of deletions, and his book was eventually released nine years later, in 1984. His story is an uncritical account of his experiences in which neither Agee nor the names of any of his colleagues are mentioned. His inconoclastic approach to intelligence operations is evident in this passage in particular, in which he challenges some of the myths surrounding secret operations.

Secret Contenders: The Myth of Cold War Counterintelligence

The duel between the rival intelligence services, the CIA and the KGB, has been universally depicted as deadly, daggers bared, and no holds barred — an image perpetuated by a generation of fiction writers. That view, by my opinion formed through twenty-seven years as an intelligence officer of the National Security Agency and the CIA, is a fallacy. The truth is that, apart from covert operations, the jousting between the professionals of both services is benign and no one on either side (with the possible exception of hapless agents) gets hurt. The intrigue involved, the moves and countermoves, resemble nothing so much as an interminable chess game with no winners.

Ironically, in the classic duel of espionage and counterintelligence between the services, the fiercely contending ideologies act as a drag-weight on clandestine performance. Clandestine warriors rush to engage in sterile operations for operations' sake. And, though driven by ideological animosities, the intelligence officers of both services seldom get bloodied, few are discomfited, and all seem to enjoy their role and the perquisites that go along with it.

But the twisted mythology of deadly warfare between the services, spawned by the atmospherics of Cold War and the clash of opposing ideologies, has had serious and profound political consequences. It has fed and heightened suspicions between the United States and the Soviet Union, and has entered the propaganda of both nations to inspire fear in their own populaces. It has diverted attention from the sobering truth that it is governments, not intelligence services, that initiate covert political and paramilitary actions. And by tarring classic intelligence rivalry with the same brush as politically inspired actions, it has obscured the fact that the latter (directed at third countries) raise moral and humanitarian questions that tarnish the quest toward universal peace, freedom, and stability.

Ralph M. McGehee

Although I had been in the CIA for twenty years, I really
never had attempted to understand communism on its own terms.

Born in Illinois, Ralph McGehee joined the CIA in 1952, after graduating in business administration from Notre Dame University and trying his luck as a football coach. After training at Camp Peary he was posted to Tokyo for a tour of duty with the China Operations Group, which then moved to Subic Bay in the Philippines. In 1956 he returned to headquarters in Washington DC for a spell as chief of records for the China Operations Group, and was then assigned to Taiwan as a case officer running agents into the mainland. In 1961 he was transferred to the new headquarters building at Langley, and continued to concentrate on China. After nine months he was appointed a liaison officer with the Border Patrol Police in Thailand, and he was to deal with that country, as a desk officer at Langley and on a second tour in the north and in Bangkok, until late 1967 when he was transferred home to China Operations. In October 1968 he volunteered to go to Vietnam, where he operated in the province around Saigon, becoming increasingly disillusioned with the Agency's policies and methodology. He retired in 1976 with the Career Intelligence Medal, but remarked that he had 'lived through 25 years of illusion, the last decade of which had been filled with anger, bitterness, self-doubts, mistrust, disbelief, disgust and struggle'. Having encountered internal obstruction to his promotion, and resistance to his intelligence-reporting techniques, McGehee concluded that the Agency had lost its intelligence-gathering purpose and had become an instrument of covert action in pursuit of undeclared objectives set by successive presidents, but unreported to Congress. His solution, for which he was to campaign during his retirement, was the CIA's total abolition.

In February 1980 McGehee submitted the manuscript of his autobiography to the CIA for clearance, which was received, but only after 397 deletions had been requested on security grounds. After negotiation the excisions were reduced, with the author reproducing material from Philip Agee, John Stockwell and Victor Marchetti to circumvent the CIA's restrictions. In this uncontentious passage he considers how the CIA fell into disrepute.

Deadly Deceits

The wave of exposures of illegal Agency operations peaked in 1975 with investigations by the House of Representatives' Pike Committee and the Senate's Church Committee. The Pike Committee's final report was classified and not released to the public. Portions of it were leaked, however, and appeared in the February 16, 1976 issue of *The Village Voice*. The report recorded the Agency's intelligence performance in six major crises, and in each situation the CIA's intelligence ranged from seriously flawed to non-existent. The report noted that during Tet 1968, the CIA failed to predict the communist attack throughout all of South Vietnam. In August 1968 in Czechoslovakia the Agency 'lost' an invading Russian army for two weeks. On October 6, 1973 Egypt and Syria launched an attack on Israel that the Agency failed to predict. It concentrated all of its efforts on following the progress of the war, yet it so miscalculated subsequent events that it 'contributed to a US–Soviet confrontation . . . on October 24, 1973 . . . Poor intelligence had brought America to the brink of war.' The Pike Committee also cited flawed Agency information concerning a coup in Portugal in 1974, India's detonation of a nuclear device the same year, and the confrontation between Greece and Turkey over Cyprus in July 1974.

The Church Committee, after an exhaustive review, concluded that the Agency acted more as the covert action arm of the Presidency than as an intelligence gatherer and collator. Its final report said the CIA was heavily involved in covertly sponsoring the publication of books and that over the years until 1967 it had in some way been responsible for the publication of well over 1,000 books – a fifth of these in the English language. According to the Church Committee, the Agency was running news services, had employees working for major press organizations, and was illegally releasing and planting stories directly into the US media. Frequently these stories were false and were designed to support the Agency's covert action goals.

Pictures of CIA director William Colby testifying and holding up a poison dart gun, details of CIA failures to destroy biological warfare chemicals under direct orders, information on the Agency's illegal opening of the mail of US citizens, specifics of the Agency's years-long preoccupation with trying to overthrow the government of Chile, sordid details of Agency officers providing drugs to customers of prostitutes in order to film their reactions, and facts about numerous other illegal operations revealed during the congressional investigations all created a depressing atmosphere around Langley.

The morale of CIA employees in this period was at an all-time low. Surprisingly, few seemed particularly bothered by the activities them-selves, just upset at having them exposed. There was no remorse, just bitterness. The true believers held to the position that if the general public knew what we knew, then it would understand and support the Agency's activities.

The Church Committee's observation that the Agency was more the covert action arm of the President than an intelligence gatherer confirmed all my suspicions about the true purpose of the Agency: it existed under the name of the Central Intelligence Agency only as a cover for its covert operations. Its intelligence was not much more than one weapon in its arsenal of disinformation – a difficult concept to accept. But with these revelations I began to see where my experience in Southeast Asia had broader ramifications. The Agency refused or was unable to report the truth not only about Asian revolutions; it was doing the same wherever it operated.

To confirm this observation I began reviewing current events in Latin America, the Middle East, and Africa and saw the same patterns of Agency disinformation operations, including its intelligence supporting its covert operations. This convinced me. The Agency is not, nor was it ever meant to have been, an intelligence agency. It was created slightly after the United Nations. It was the United States' substitute for gun-boat diplomacy that was no longer feasible under the scrutiny of that world organization. The Agency was to do covertly that which was once done openly with the Army, the Navy, and the Marines. The Central Intelligence Agency, I now knew, was in truth a Central Covert Action Agency.

Michael Straight

We felt deeply indebted to the Russians for bearing the main burden of the fighting against the common enemy.

The son of a prominent American family, Michael Straight was educated in England at Dartington Hall, the London School of Economics, and at Cambridge where he had studied under John Maynard Keynes. Among his circle of friends at university were Tess Mayor, later to marry Victor Rothschild, Guy Burgess, James Klugmann and Anthony Blunt. He became a member of the Communist Party and the elite Apostles but after the death of John Cornford in the Spanish Civil War he was drawn into clandestine activity, 'a world of shadows and echoes', by Blunt, who instructed him to abandon the Party and break off contact with those on the Left.

Having graduated from Cambridge Straight returned to America and joined the State Department as an unpaid volunteer in the Office of the Economic Adviser. Soon afterwards, in April 1938, he was approached by a mysterious stranger with a European accent (whom he refers to as Michael Green), who suggested that 'when interesting documents crossed my desk, I should take them home "to study" '. In fact Straight recognized Green 'as a cog in the Soviet machine' and continued to meet him in Washington. The liaison persisted when Straight moved to a post in the Department of the Interior although nothing he had passed 'had contained any restricted material', so Green encouraged him to return to the State Department. Instead in 1940 Straight went to work for *The New Republic*, the weekly journal founded by his parents, and wrote a book, *Make This the Last War*, which was published in January 1943, two months after he had joined the US Army air reserve. Straight was trained as a bomber pilot but never flew in combat.

After the war Straight returned to politics as editor of *The New Republic*. It was not until he was offered a federal post in Kennedy's administration in 1963 that he revealed to the FBI what he knew about British communists. His statement led to an interview with MI5 and on his evidence Anthony Blunt was confronted with the charge that he had recruited Straight as a Soviet agent. The knowledge that Straight had identified him proved enough for Blunt to confess to his lifetime of espionage. Five months later the two men met again but there were no recriminations. As he recalled in his autobiography, published in 1983, Straight simply accepted his new role:

> In his autobiography *Witness*, Whittaker Chambers describes the anguish he suffered when he became an informer against the Soviet agents who had been his accomplices and friends. He found his justification in the conviction that he was acting as an instrument of The Almighty in a titanic struggle between communism and Christianity. I do not picture myself in any such grandiose role. I believed simply that the acceptance of individual responsibility is the price we must all pay for living in a free society.

In this extract Straight describes his post-war encounters with Blunt and Burgess.

After Long Silence

The House Committee on Un-American Activities played a major role in shaping political attitudes in the years after the war. Its chairmen included Martin Dies, who was known for his casual cruelties; John Rankin, a fanatical racist; and J. Parnell Thomas, a small-time crook.

A lack of serious intent marked the committee's hearings. They were hampered further by the ignorance of the members of the committee and of its staff. Thus, the role of my old teacher Harold Laski was raised by one witness and led to the following exchange between Chairman Rankin and his counsel, Ernie Adamson:

MR RANKIN: Who is Mr Laski?

MR ADAMSON: Mr Laski is, I believe, one of the leaders in England of the Communist movement.

Representative Rankin was more interested in discrediting Mrs Roosevelt than in learning the facts about the Communist party. He was alarmed, not by the growth of Soviet power but by the spread of democracy in his state of Mississippi. The Fair Employment Practices Commission promised to provide greater opportunities for black Americans. It was identified by Chairman Rankin as 'the beginning of a Communistic dictatorship the like of which America has never dreamed'.

Even when it moved to the grave issue of Soviet espionage, the committee was motivated by political considerations. Its hearings were timed, as Chairman Thomas affirmed, 'to keep the heat on Harry Truman' during the 1948 campaign.

The committee was not the first group to stumble onto the reality of Soviet espionage. In 1945, government agents had raided the offices of the magazine *Amerasia* and recovered a thousand documents stolen from the State, War, and Navy departments. In 1946, the Canadian government had arrested twenty-two officials as Soviet agents on the basis of information provided by the Soviet defector Igor Gouzenko. The impact of these events, however, was lost upon the American public. The *Amerasia* thefts were never traced to the Soviet Union; the Canadian arrests were in another country.

Unknown to the public, an American Communist, Elizabeth Bentley, went to the FBI in 1945. She stated that she had taken over the management of a Soviet spy ring following the death of her lover, a Soviet agent named Jacob Golos. She named a number of United States government officials as members of her ring. She added that two high-ranking New Dealers, Harry Dexter White and Lauchlin Currie, had knowingly cooperated in her work.

Miss Bentley was brought before a grand jury in New York. She testified in secret before it, over a period of thirteen months. Eleven officials of the State Department were dismissed or allowed to resign as a result of her revelations. But no corroborative evidence was obtained from those whom Miss Bentley named and no indictments followed the grand jury's investigation.

When legal action proved to be impracticable, publicity generated by congressional hearings seemed to be the next best thing. In eight appearances before congressional committees, Miss Bentley repeated her story for the third time. She said of her spy ring, '. . . we had a steady flow of political reports from the Treasury which included material from the Office of Strategic Services, the State Department, the Navy, the Army and even . . . the Department of Justice. We knew what was going on in the inner chambers of the United States Government up to and including the White House.'

The officials whom Miss Bentley named as members of her spy ring refused to discuss her allegations when they were brought before the House Committee on Un-American Activities. The committee turned in 1948 to a second witness: Whittaker Chambers.

Chambers made no mention of espionage in his initial testimony before the committee. In subsequent hearings, he swore that he had been a Soviet agent in the 1930s, and that seventy-five officials of the United States government had, in his opinion, been engaged to some degree in espionage on behalf of the Soviet Union. One man whom he identified as a close friend and an ardent Communist agent was a former high official of the State Department: Alger Hiss.

For six years, I had thrust all thoughts of Guy Burgess, Anthony Blunt, and Michael Green from my consciousness. From 1948 on, those memories returned like the furies to pursue me.

Foremost in my mind was a sense of fear. I had made my break in 1941. I had never heard of Elizabeth Bentley or Whittaker Chambers and had no reason to believe that they had known Green. Yet it seemed probable that my name would crop up in some context. For two years, whenever a telephone call came for me, I braced myself, wondering what I would say if a reporter who had come upon some trace of my past were on the line.

In addition to fear, I was haunted by a sense of guilt. I saw the faces of the men who had been named in the newspapers. I read the broken sentences of Julian Wadleigh who chose to confess. I shared some of his pain.

I had, as a student in Cambridge, known Herbert Norman, who killed himself after he was arrested in Canada. I knew several of the officials whom Elizabeth Bentley and Whittaker Chambers named. Frank Coe had been an inoffensive figure in the Economic Policy Club; Lauchlin Currie had given me many stories in my *New Republic* days. Donald Hiss had been a good friend of mine in the State Department. His life was shattered.

Neither in America nor in England could I escape my own past. Milton Rose and I returned to England in 1949 on family matters. We were walking down Whitehall when we passed Guy Burgess in the street.

Guy gold me that the Apostles were about to hold their annual dinner. He was the chairman for the dinner and had chosen to hold it in a private room in his club, the Royal Automobile Club. He urged me to attend the dinner, and I said that I would.

Guy sat at the head table with the speaker for the evening, the drama critic Desmond MacCarthy. Thirty members of the society took their places at two long tables; I sat by a rising historian named Eric Hobsbawm.

I remembered Hobsbawm as a member of the student Communist movement in Cambridge. He made it plain that he, at least, had not given up his beliefs.

I made some bitter comment about the Soviet occupation of Czechoslovakia. Hobsbawm countered with a comment about the Americans who had been imprisoned under the Smith Act. He said with a knowing smile, 'There are more political prisoners in the United States today than there are in Czechoslovakia.'

'That's a damned lie!' I cried. I continued to shout at Hobsbawm. I was aware that others were staring at me. I was not acting in a manner becoming to a member of the society.

Anthony was sitting at the far end of the room. I had managed to avoid him, but when the speeches were over and the dinner was breaking up, he came over to me.

'Guy and I would like to talk to you,' he said. 'We'll meet you here tomorrow morning.'

We sat in deep leather chairs in a dimly lit corner of the club. We talked about what we had been doing. I learned to my dismay that Anthony had been engaged in intelligence work throughout the war. He added that he had left the government in 1945 to devote himself to his true profession of art history. He would never return to the government, he said.

Guy, in contrast, conceded that he had moved to the Far Eastern department of the Foreign Office.

It seemed to me probable that Guy was still engaged in espionage. I reminded him that when we had last met, in 1947, he had assured me that he was about to leave the government for good.

'I was about to leave,' Guy said, 'but then this offer came along.'

He sensed my hostility. He added that he was about to go off on an extended leave and that he did not intend to return to the Foreign Office.

Where, then, did the three of us stand? We turned to the central issue of the day: the danger of a third world war. I spoke with some bitterness about the blindness of the Soviet leaders who had rejected the American proposals for the control of nuclear weapons and were attempting to disrupt the Marshall Plan. Guy's response was not to defend the Soviet government. Instead, he questioned the motivation of the United States.

Anthony listened in moody silence. I sensed that he still deferred to Guy on political issues, although his interest in politics had diminished.

The tensions between us mounted. At last, Anthony broke in.

'The question is,' he said 'are we capable of intellectual growth?'

I said, 'Exactly!'

We stood up to say goodbye. Guy looked at me intently.

'Are you still with us?' he asked.

'You know that I'm not,' I said.

'You're not totally unfriendly?'

'If I were,' I said, 'why would I be here?'

It was a weak, evasive answer; the sort of answer I habitually gave when I faced a confrontation of any kind. It reflected my continuing inability to force an issue, to resolve a conflict, to make an enemy of another individual, and, in this instance, to break completely with my own past.

I walked away, down Pall Mall, trying to sort out my feelings. I had made my own position clear and was glad of that. But I had stopped short of any clear threat to act against Anthony and Guy.

And that, of course, was what Guy wanted to hear. He had arranged the meeting in the club in order to learn if I had already turned him in to the authorities. He had satisfied himself that I had taken no action. He had sought a commitment from me that I would not act at once, although I disapproved of all that he seemed to be doing. I had failed to stand against him.

I had accepted Guy's assurance that he would soon leave the Foreign Office, setting aside the suspicion that, once again, he would break his word to me. I had determined that Anthony had moved from the world of espionage to a world in which he and I shared the same values and ends. I had not foreseen that he would continue to act as Guy's accomplice in moments of crisis.

My fear and my sense of guilt were secret, shared by no one.

CHAPTER V

The French

Using the pretense of punishing the collaborators and
those who had fraternized with the Germans, the Communists
were able to get rid of many of their adversaries.
Philippe Thyraud de Vosjoli

Ever since the conviction and imprisonment on Devil's Island of Captain Dreyfus, the French psyche has been obliged to take account of treachery in all its manifestations. French history, particularly in the twentieth century, is largely a story of betrayal and counter-betrayal, with the dominant figure of Charles de Gaulle emerging from obscurity and defeat in 1940 to lead a Free French movement, one that had no formal legitimacy, to take power in Paris in 1944. Upon their return to France after the liberation his supporters, who included the young Philippe Thyraud de Vosjoli, discovered not only the full scale of collaboration, but that virtually every Frenchman claimed to have been a *résistant*, and none had known of the fate of the 67,000 French Jews deported to German concentration camps.

De Gaulle was to attract adherents across the globe, and in French Indo-China one of his most ardent supporters was a rubber planter, Pierre Boulle, who found himself convicted of treason and sentenced to life imprisonment following his arrest in October 1942 by the Vichy authorities in Hanoi. His subsequent release, and his return to Paris, enabled him to write his famous novel, *The Bridge on the River Kwai*.

The postwar search for real traitors traumatized French society, and the revelations of misdeeds continued for more than forty years after the cessation of hostilities as one public figure after another was exposed as having helped the Nazis during the occupation. Even fifty years after the liberation the saga continues, with the trial of Paul Touvier, the leader of the notorious Vichy French *milice* in Lyons, who faced trial for murder, even though he had been pardoned by President Pompidou in 1978.

Although every imprisoned collaborator had been freed by 1964, the experience had been traumatic for French society. Pierre Laval, twice premier, was convicted of treason and executed in October 1945 after a failed suicide bid. Marshal Petain, the victor of Verdun and the head of the Vichy government, was condemned to die but was reprieved and sentenced to life imprisonment. He died of natural causes on the Île d'Yeu in 1951.

The statistics relating to the postwar trials are breathtaking: 125,000 men and women charged with collaboration, and 2,856 were sentenced to death, of whom 767 were executed. More French citizens were dispatched by the firing squad than of any other occupied country in Western Europe, but the number of those imprisoned was, in terms of the total population, a fraction of those convicted in other countries: a quarter of those in Holland and Denmark and just a sixth of those in Norway and Belgium. Quite apart from the legal proceedings, an estimated 10,000 to 30,000 died in the instant justice dispensed during *l'épuration*, the purge, in which snatch squads of outraged citizens took revenge upon neighbours whom they knew had collaborated with the hated occupation. Some put the true figure much higher, perhaps as many as half a million.

Of all the thousands who were prosecuted in France through the criminal justice system, only one person endured a trial to write an account of what had taken place. Mathilde Carré thus acquired a notoriety that reached well beyond the French capital, and for some she came to personify the lack of remorse shown by the many others who had committed greater crimes and been sentenced to long terms of imprisonment.

Philippe Thyraud de Vosjoli's crime was not one that the French state ever cared to have examined in a public forum and officially he is still at liberty to enter and leave France at will. The reality is that he knows his enemies have long memories and his decision to desert his post as SDECE's liaison officer with the CIA caused a lasting problem for his employers.

Mathilde Carré

*The Germans must have had great confidence
in me for they enlisted me in their ranks.*

Born in Châteauroux in 1910, Mathilde Belard took a law degree at the Sorbonne and at the age of twenty-three married a teacher working at a school in Oran. After six years of childless marriage Mathilde divorced her husband, who was to be killed fighting in Italy, and returned to France where, when war broke out, she enrolled as a nurse. When the army and the administration collapsed she was evacuated to Toulouse, where she met a Polish military intelligence officer, Captain Roman Garby-Czerniawski, who had acquired the authentic papers of a dead Frenchman and had stayed in France in the hope of organizing an underground network. The two became lovers and moved to Paris, where by the end of 1940 they had recruited what was to become the foundation of a *réseau* which became known as Interallié. By the time wireless contact had been established with London in early 1941 the ring had grown to more than a hundred members operating from cells right across the country.

In November 1941, following a lapse of security in Cherbourg, Garby-Czerniawski was caught at his apartment in Paris. German investigators had penetrated the network and eventually traced the organization's headquarters, where Mathilde was arrested the next day, as she approached it. From the papers recovered from the building, the Abwehr had been able to reconstruct a large part of Interallié's organization, and under skilful interrogation Mathilde Carré provided most of the missing pieces. Threatened with execution, and offered her freedom in return for her help, she led her captors to the rest of the *réseau* and was probably responsible for the betrayal of an estimated thirty-five *résistants*. Now committed to collaboration with the enemy, she became the mistress of her Abwehr interrogator, Sergeant Hugo Bleicher, and under his guidance made radio contact with London, which approved her proposal to continue the management of Interallié.

The charade lasted until February 1942 when Mathilde was collected off a beach in Brittany by a British MTB and carried across the Channel to Dartmouth. Having given a partial account of her contacts with the enemy she remained at liberty in a flat in Porchester Gate until June 1942 when she was taken into custody and interned, first at Holloway and then 'D' Wing of Aylesbury Prison. At the end of the war she was deported to France and in January 1949, after three and a half years in custody at La Sante and Rennes, was charged with collaboration. The trial lasted four days and she was sentenced to death. Upon appeal her sentence was reduced to life imprisonment and she was eventually released in 1954 to live with her mother in Paris.

In 1961, nearly blind, she published her autobiography, described by Professor M. R. D. Foot as 'frankness alternating with evasions'. In this passage she describes her first encounter with her parents following her recruitment by Bleicher.

I Was the Cat

I was fully cognisant of the greatest act of cowardice in my life committed on 19th November with Bleicher. It was a purely animal cowardice, the reaction of a body which had survived its first night in prison, had suffered cold, felt the icy breath of death and suddenly found warmth once more in a pair of arms . . . even if they were the arms of the enemy. I hated myself for my weakness and as a result of my abasement I hated the Germans even more. That morning under my cold shower I swore that one day I would make this German pay.

How could I get back into the swim? I was caught in an inexorable trap, tired and broken. It was a combination of distress on account of Interallié, the brutal physical shock to an already exhausted body, the final smashing of my pride and the shame of my cowardice of that night. Yes, that night and the fact of having abandoned my husband were the two cardinal faults of my life.

I went down to breakfast. Mme P——, one of Harry Baur's old servants, looked after the Germans. She was amiable and servile to them. Borchers, Bleicher and I breakfasted together. The two Germans treated me kindly. I was their *kätzchen*.

They went off to discuss their work in the Maison Lafitte office, leaving me by the fire with Mme P—— and two magnificent black Alsatians. Then they fetched me and we all returned to Paris.

We dropped Borchers at his headquarters behind the Bon Marché and drove to La Palette. Fortunately there was no letter. Bleicher then drove me to my parents' flat. He had promised that I should lunch there alone but he now thought it best that he should meet my parents. We owed him that since nothing had happened to me.

I arrived at the flat with Bleicher who introduced himself as a Gestapo inspector. My parents were flabbergasted but Bleicher assured them that nothing was amiss and that there was no need for them to worry. 'She deserved to be shot a dozen times over,' he said, 'but I have saved her life.' He also declared that he knew my mother had helped me and that she also deserved to be sent to prison. Violette had told him so, but that the aim of the Germans was to make us understand not to suffer. We were not enemies and must collaborate for the best, the good of Europe and the world. I had been a rather foolish young idealist, which was only natural, and he would put me on the right path!

He also said that he had a great admiration for my father and asked where he had won his decorations. Bleicher, as a volunteer of '16, had been a British POW in 1918, had stolen an enemy uniform from a dead man and crossed the enemy lines as a spy. He was arrested and sent to a camp for two years where he had been treated inhumanly by the British. At Christmas 1917 he had not only handcuffs on his wrists but manacles round his ankles. He loathed England but loved France and his little 'Lily' who was so adorably French. He repeated that he had saved my life and that I must now preach collaboration. So be it!

My father was livid and did not utter a word. Mother, my incorrigible mother, contradicted everything Bleicher said and insisted that she loved England. For her, collaboration was out of the question, and I thought she was going to slap Bleicher's face when he said 'his little Lily' but she was too well brought up. Nothing happened. As for me I was feeling too ill and I hated everyone. The luncheon was a fiasco. Bleicher advised my parents to pass on all messages to me as before for there must be no changes.

Later he uttered threats on several occasions. 'Your mother helped you, she was your accomplice, acted as a "letter box" and I can send her to Fresnes.' He also threatened to arrest Father who was on the lists the Germans kept in their files. I never mentioned these threats to my parents. I concealed the facts from a sense of shame just as I never told them the true reason why I had become a spy, or the story of my 'useful suicide' . . . One thing I had always admired above all else was my parents' conjugal felicity and I decided to protect this union. I should never have told them that I held their fate in my hands.

Pierre Boulle

Our original plan, feverishly drawn up, consisted in preparing a fifth column organisation over there, with a view to sabotaging the Japanese installations on the day war was declared against the Allies.

Originally from Avignon, Pierre Boulle was working on a rubber plantation near Kuala Lumpur when the war broke out. In November 1939 he travelled to Singapore to join the French army, and was assigned to an infantry regiment outside Saigon. He was transferred with his unit to Laos where he participated in skirmishes with the Cambodians, and in April 1941 was demobilized. By August he was back in Singapore, where he joined the Free French forces and, together with others from the same rubber company, was recruited into Special Operations Executive. After a brief period of training he was placed in a stay-behind party, but the first mission was cancelled because of Japanese activity in the target area.

In January 1942 Boulle was evacuated to Rangoon with orders to proceed to Kunming in China and act as an adviser to General Chiang Kai-shek. Equipped with false British papers he drove across Burma into Yunnan Province and reported to Kunming before starting a long trek by mule to French Indo-China, his objective being to reach Hanoi by river on a bamboo raft. In the event Boulle got only as far as the French colony of Laichau, where he was arrested as soon as he disclosed his true identity and the nature of his mission. He was charged with treason in Hanoi in October 1942 and sentenced to life imprisonment. He served his sentence first in Hanoi prison and then, from July 1943, in Saigon, and as the war swung against the Axis Boulle was transferred to Laos. However, instead of being sent to the new prison at Hue he was accommodated in a seaside villa near Vinh and he escaped to Hanoi after just three weeks and re-established contact with the Free French. He was evacuated by air and upon his arrival in Paris started work on his famous novel, *The Bridge on the River Kwai*. Following its huge success he wrote numerous other books, including *The Chinese Executioner*, *For a Noble Cause* and *The Monkey Planet*, which was filmed as *Planet of the Apes*. Despite his conviction on a treason charge he was decorated with the Légion d'Honneur, the Croix de Guerre and the Médaille de la Résistance. He died in February 1994, and in this extract from his autobiography, published in French in 1966 (in English, 1967), Boulle describes his court-martial.

The Source of the River Kwai

'Prisoner at the bar, stand up . . .'

Before the colonel had stopped speaking, the hefty gendarme behind me gave me a thump in the back with his elbow and hissed in my ear: 'That means you. Stand up.'

My behaviour in court seemed to be a matter of grave concern to the hefty gendarme who had come to fetch me that morning from the military prison of Hanoi, accompanied by a colleague. He was used to this sort of ceremony. He had spent a long time inspecting my turn-out, insisting, with his profound knowledge of humanity, on the fact that military magistrates are always susceptible to well polished shoes and a clean collar. He had harped on the same string all the way to the courtroom:

'Speak up . . . Look straight in front of you . . . Above all, don't forget to stand up each time you're spoken to.'

He wanted his prisoner to be a credit to him. Right from the start I had been conscious of him standing there behind me, restless, anxious, on tenterhooks, watching my every gesture, forever hissing in my ear: 'Now then, watch out.' His manner was beginning to annoy me even more than the farce I was witnessing.

'Prisoner at the bar, stand up . . .'

In the shuttered silence, the unsteady voice quavered and died away. Unlike the hefty gendarme, the colonel presiding over the court was not used to this sort of ceremony. He looked awkward and ill at ease, like a novice.

And indeed he was a novice, as anyone could see. Assigned by fate to this fatigue-duty, he had already made two mistakes in the prescribed ritual, which he must have mugged up yesterday from some manual. Major P, the government commissioner, who exuded professional self-assurance from every pore, had corrected him with a formality verging on sarcasm. Now there was the ghost of a smile on the major's lips, for the voice had trilled 'Stand up' in a shrill falsetto. I stood up all the same.

'Your surname and Christian names?'

This time the words resounded like a thunderclap. Humiliated and furious at his lack of self-assurance, the colonel had bellowed. All the members of the court (a major, two captains and a short-sighted subaltern, as far as I can remember) jerked upright in their seats and my advocate (a little Annamite who had been assigned to me according to regulations) was so startled that he dropped his briefcase. It was now his turn to look ill at ease, all eyes being turned on him while he picked up his scattered papers. My hefty gendarme cast a withering glance in his direction. At the end of the room a squad of a dozen soldiers under the command of a warrant officer waited in silence to present arms at the end of the hearing. I did my best to be as patient as they were. Meanwhile the colonel had recovered a little composure.

'Your surname and Christian names?'

'Boulle . . .'

Another clap of thunder, even louder than the first. This time it was I who had bellowed. Was it bravado or something to do with the acoustics? Or did I too lack experience like a novice? The hefty gendarme was desperate and cleared his throat to warn me of my incorrect behaviour. Major P himself had given a start. The short-sighted subaltern frowned sternly. The colonel looked absolutely flabbergasted.

'Age?'

'Twenty-eight.'

This wouldn't do at all. We were now both out of control, oscillating between deep theatrical tones and high-pitched warbles punctuated by senile splutters. It took us several sentences to achieve an approximately normal manner of speech. The interrogation continued by fits and starts. The hefty gendarme was almost panting for breath.

'What have you got to say in your defence?'

'Here we go,' I sadly reflected as I saw Major P spring up in his seat like a jack-in-the-box and start to wave his hands violently. 'Here we go, he's bungled things again.'

He had indeed bungled things! His papers were in a muddle and he was immersed in the notes he had carefully taken yesterday. 'The witnesses, the witnesses,' whispered Major P. The colonel flushed and looked daggers at him, but had to yield to his experience and therefore grumpily summoned the witnesses.

There were two of them. The first was an old acquaintance: the inspector of the Native Guards who had arrested me at Laichau, Lieutenant Y. I had summed him up accurately: he was without malice. He gave his evidence, then went out of his way to depict me as the most well-mannered and good-natured fellow in the world, unaware that he was annoying not only the judges and Major P but also myself, who could willingly have dispensed with this good conduct certificate. The hefty gendarme was the only one to appreciate his statement and nodded his approval.

'He was very decent about it,' Lieutenant Y kept repeating, 'he was really very decent indeed.'

The government commissioner eventually put an end to this evidence which was utterly irrelevant, then glanced enquiringly at the colonel. The colonel flushed again, looked nonplussed and fumbled with his papers. Major P thereupon decided to speak in his stead and asked me if I agreed on the facts. Yes, I agreed on the facts. 'Well done,' the hefty gendarme whispered in my ear.

A fresh silence ensued, followed by another perfidious glance of enquiry at the colonel from the major and the sound of rustling paper. The major, like a good fellow, again prompted him under his breath: 'Any questions? Any questions to put to the witness?'

'Have you any questions to put to the witness?' the colonel grumpily repeated.

My little Annamite advocate now saw fit to intervene and asked a question which had no bearing on the matter in hand. The inspector spluttered and resumed his litany:

'He was very decent about it, very decent indeed . . .'

Eventually Major P took it upon himself to make the court proceed to other matters. Exit the inspector of the Native Guards. Enter the second witness. This was the police commissioner who had conducted my initial interrogation. I can still see his flabby opium-addict's figure.

The commissioner swore to tell the truth, the whole truth and nothing but the truth, as the colonel complacently asked him to do.

He wasn't a bad fellow, the police commissioner. He was only doing his duty as a commissioner, as Major P was doing his duty as a public prosecutor, and the hefty gendarme his duty as a hefty gendarme. It was not his fault that he and some of his colleagues had had to interrogate me in relays for about fifteen days and fifteen nights, allowing me all the same an hour or two's respite from time to time. On these occasions he would tell me he hated carrying out these duties, which may have been true. He sometimes had some sandwiches and iced beer brought in and would consume the lot in front of me. He did not behave like this out of nastiness, but only to obey orders. Higher authority had given him instructions to use every means to obtain the list of my accomplices in Indo-China. The commissioner had not even used *every* means. He had not resorted to third degree methods; he had not laid a finger on me. He had merely deprived me of sleep, food and drink and relentlessly fired questions at me, always the same questions. It was not even he, I remember clearly, it was not even he but his colleagues who relieved him, who threatened me with the execution squad, who declared they would be forced to hand me over to the Japanese, while reprisals would be carried out on my mother in France. He merely indulged in vague allusions. He was a bit of a bumpkin in fact.

But this wasn't at all serious, it was just a lot of eyewash. When he had carried out his orders for fifteen days and fifteen nights and thus fulfilled his mission, he had a large meal brought in for me. And then he had looked surprised and genuinely grieved when I asked him if he was *also* going to allow me to drink: genuinely, truly grieved and shocked.

In the courtroom he seemed on the point of falling asleep. Major P stopped him as soon as he began to speak and, with a great gesture of condescension, declared that the prosecution waived the evidence of this witness since the prisoner acknowledged the facts: enlisting in a foreign army and entering Indo-China clandestinely. He turned to me:

'You do acknowledge these facts, don't you?'

As I was opening my mouth to correct the term 'foreign army', I was winded by a jab in the stomach from the hefty gendarme who chose this method of reminding me that I had to stand up whenever I was spoken to. I turned on him furiously, but he gave me such a touchingly responsive look that my anger evaporated at once. Resignedly, I rose to my feet and acknowledged that I had enlisted in the Free French forces. The colonel, who had lost control of the proceedings, tried to retrieve himself and interjected:

'Do you regret it?'

This was his bad day. The great moment had not yet arrived. Major P had to correct him once again. The colonel bridled and could be heard muttering under his breath. It was bad policy on his part to have shown his feelings; from then on the major no longer gave him a helping hand. The silence persisted, until it became almost unbearable. It was the clerk of the court who volunteered to save the situation. 'Witnesses for the defence,' he prompted in a stage whisper. I could hear him from where I was standing.

'Call the witnesses for the defence,' bellowed the colonel.

It really was his unlucky day: there were no witnesses for the defence. I took pity on him and muttered to my little advocate: 'Tell him there aren't any.' The latter told him, after shooting his cuffs as great laywers do, and in his strange accent which was full of false stresses:

'M'lud, we have no witnesses for the defence.'

By now the colonel was sweating blood but made an heroic effort to save face. He leant towards one of the members of the court and whispered in his ear, as he had seen magistrates do on the films, hoping, against all evidence, that the proceedings would follow their own course without any further action on his part. But Major P was merciless and persistently mumbled: 'Ahem! ahem!' Crimson with shame, the colonel was forced to ask him what he ought to do next. The major smiled and said out loud: 'Ask the prisoner if he has anything else to say.'

The colonel asked me if I had anything else to say. I had originally prepared a lengthy speech, then had gradually whittled it down to a single sentence which I have since forgotten. I believe I said that I refused to recognise the authority of this court in any way. But I spoke in a tone of such bland politeness that all the members seemed quite pleased. They were obviously expecting a torrent of abuse. There was a collective sigh of relief and Major P was so delighted that he stopped being unco-operative and spontaneously whispered:

'Regrets . . . regrets . . .'

This was the big moment. The colonel took his cue at once and peremptorily asked me if I regretted my behaviour. Everyone leaned forward and waited eagerly for my reply.

'No, colonel, I have no regrets.'

My 'colonel' was instinctive. I had always been impressed by senior officers' badges of rank. Once again the polite trappings outweighed the content. The court seemed to breathe more and more freely. 'Right,' said the colonel contentedly.

Then Major P took over officially and read out the charge, in which my crime was called treason and for which the prescribed penalty was capital punishment. Having read this out, he enlarged upon it.

He proved mathematically that I was fully responsible for my actions

342

and pointed out that I had expressed no regret. The hefty gendarme shook his head as though in protest. The colonel raised his, relieved at having no responsibility to take for the next ten minutes or so.

The major proceeded to sum up. Having clearly demonstrated that in my case there were no extenuating circumstances, and proved that capital punishment was therefore the only just and logical penalty, he declared with complete inconsequence, and without giving any reason, that he would not demand it all the same. Hard labour was what he suggested.

He sat down again. I believe my little advocate then took the floor, but his speech had no bearing on the subject and no one listened to him.

The court adjourned to deliberate. The hefty gendarme led me into the waiting room and lavished words of encouragement on me, followed by further instructions. I must not, above all, forget to stand no attention while the sentence was being read out, and all would be well. My little advocate came in and shook hands. Not wishing to offend him, I thanked him warmly.

I was ushered once more into the courtroom. None of the members were there except for Major P who was to read out the verdict. The sergeant-major in command of the squad gave the word of command: 'Attention.' I automatically snapped into that position. The hefty gendarme clicked his heels. The major began reading:

'In the name of the Head of State . . . declares Lieutenant Boulle guilty of treason . . . reduced to the ranks . . . deprived of French nationality . . . hard labour for life.'

Then he turned on his heels and marched out.

'Stand easy,' said the hefty gendarme, 'it's all over. It wasn't so bad now, was it?'

Philippe Thyraud de Vosjoli

Out of the blue, I was accused across the table by my colleagues of having acted without instructions in supplying French-gathered intelligence to the Americans.

A nineteen-year-old law student at the time of the French collapse in June 1940, Philippe Thyraud de Vosjoli spent the first two years of the war at his home in Romorantin, helping to smuggle refugees across the River Cher into the unoccupied zone. This brought him into contact with the resistance but, late in 1942, he was arrested in Paris while acting as a courier. In a police search an incriminating message that he had hidden was discovered and he was forced to flee to Spain. He crossed the Pyrenees in January 1943, intending to reach Madrid, but was interned by the Spanish Guardia Civil in Pamplona prison.

At the end of August 1943 de Vosjoli was released with a group of other detainees and sent under escort to Malaga, where he was put on a ship bound for Casablanca. Once in Morocco he volunteered for the Free French forces and in December was assigned to de Gaulle's intelligence organization, the Bureau Central de Renseignement et d'Action (BCRA) in Algiers. His assignment was to handle intelligence relating to the United States and Indo-China, and in July 1944 he undertook a tour of inspection across the Far East, taking in Chandernagor and Kunming. He returned to Algiers in November and then accompanied the rest of the BCRA staff to Paris, where the organization underwent a metamorphosis into the Direction Générale des Études et Recherches (DGER) and then, in 1946, the Service de Documentation Extérieure et de Contre-Espionnage (SDECE). Initially de Vosjoli worked on the investigation of war crimes, and later was responsible for liaison with the president and the prime minister, but in April 1951 he was transferred to Washington DC as SDECE's local station chief. He remained in this post until his resignation in October 1963 following a series of disagreements with headquarters.

The trouble had begun with the debriefing of a KGB defector, Anatoli Golitsyn, who alleged that SDECE and the French government had been thoroughly penetrated. De Vosjoli believed Golitsyn's charges to be true, not least because he had once participated in a secret operation in which Nikolai Khokhlov was to tempt a former KGB colleague named Volokitine into defecting. The attempt had failed because, following a tip, the KGB had bundled the hapless Soviet officer on to an aircraft and flown him back to Moscow. This incident, among others, persuaded de Vosjoli that Golitsyn's claims were genuine, and that they were being ignored deliberately in Paris. He was also anxious about an order from SDECE's chief, General Paul Jacquier, requiring him to disclose his sources in Cuba, and he decided to go into a self-imposed exile. In his absence in Mexico he heard that the French court of state security had considered his case and had imposed the death sentence, which prompted him to tell part of his story to Leon Uris, who wrote his bestselling novel *Topaz*, based on de Vosjoli's experience.

Thereafter de Vosjoli moved to Colorado, where he wrote his autobiography, using his official SDECE code-name as the title, and then to Florida, where he now lives. In this extract he describes an unexpected call from SDECE's director of security, Colonel Georges Lionnet ('X'), and the Golitsyn debriefings which led to the author's disaffection, and ultimately his resignation.

Lamia

One morning at 5 o'clock the telephone rang in my bedroom. 'Mr de Vosjoli?' a voice asked.

'Yes,' I said.

'Pardon, this is . . .' The voice went on in French giving the last name of a man well known to me as one of the senior officers of SDECE. 'I have just landed at Washington airport with five colleagues. Ask no questions, please, but I would be much obliged if you would send a car to pick us up and arrange for a convenient place for us to stay for a few days.'

I assured my colleague – I will call him 'X' – that his needs would be attended to.

'X', with five companions, descending on Washington unannounced, in the middle of the night? Something urgent must be afoot, something of the utmost gravity in Paris.

Just before noon 'X' entered my office on the second floor of the French consulate. Closing the door, he strode across the room and drove immediately to the point.

'The director general,' he began, 'has instructed me to explain to you in the fullest detail why I am here. I beg you not to take offense over the failure to give you advance notice of our arrival. The truth is that we are no longer sure of the security of our communications. We are not even sure our codes are safe. In fact, we can't be sure of who is getting our reports.'

From this ominous preface, 'X' launched into the following extra-ordinary account: Some weeks before, a special courier had arrived in Paris from Washington, bearing a personal letter from President Kennedy to President de Gaulle. The letter informed de Gaulle that a source in which Kennedy had confidence had stated that the French intelligence services, and even de Gaulle's own cabinet, had been penetrated by Soviet agents. Because of the obvious implications of such a security breakdown, the American President had chosen to employ a personal courier to transmit the warning, rather than depend upon possibly vulnerable, more formal channels. Kennedy further assured de Gaulle that he would provide his representatives with whatever means or contacts they might desire in verifying the value of this information for themselves.

To make a preliminary reconnaissance, 'X' continued, de Gaulle had picked General de Rougemont, an officer with excellent connections in Washington. De Rougemont was attached to the Prime Minister's office as director of the Second Division of the National Defense staff and had the responsibility of coordinating the various branches of the military intelligence.

About a week after Kennedy's letter reached de Gaulle's hand, de Rougemont had slipped into Washington – avoiding completely all his French friends, including me – and made contact directly with the

American authorities. The source of President Kennedy's information, he was told, was a Russian who had been a high-ranking officer in the KGB, the huge state security apparatus through which the Soviet Union conducts its foreign espionage. De Rougemont was taken to the man, to ask such questions as he wished. He was later to say that he had begun the questioning half-convinced that the whole thing was some sort of trick by which the Americans were trying to dupe de Gaulle. But after he had put the Russian through three or four days of intensive questioning, it was de Rougemont who came out shaken by the appallingly detailed information the man had on the innermost workings of the French government and its security and intelligence systems. The general flew back to Paris to make his report directly to de Gaulle's trusted assistant, Étienne Burin des Roziers, secretary-general of the Elysée Palace, and as such the aide who manages de Gaulle's staff and organizes the presidential business. Manifestly on de Gaulle's command, Burin des Roziers summoned the heads of the two main French intelligence establishments – General Paul Jacquier, Director of SDECE, and Daniel Doustin, who ran the DST (Direction de la Sécurité du Territoire), the French equivalent of the FBI. The gist of de Rougemont's report was that the KGB man was authentic, that he was indeed as important as the Americans claimed him to be, and that his assertions about the KGB's infiltration of French services demanded further and much more exhaustive questioning of the Russian by French counterintelligence experts, together with a complete checkout of the evidence which he stood ready to give. The two services – SDECE and DST – quickly assembled from their own staffs separate and expert interrogation teams, each made up of three men. These were the men with whom 'X' had arrived in Washington during the night.

After telling me all this, 'X' said, 'Our only business here is to question the source. We have a number to call and the meetings with him are to be arranged by our friends. I expect that we shall be at this for some time.'

I was not, as a matter of fact, altogether surprised to learn that such a figure as the Russian existed. The intelligence community of Washington is a freely circulating body of professional military officers and civil servants inside the diplomatic community. A certain amount of informal and more or less honest brokerage goes on among the members. In the winter of 1961–1962 I had picked up some strong clues that the Americans had recruited, or otherwise gained custody of, two and possibly three defectors from beyond the Iron Curtain, and that one of them in particular had brought very important information out with him. Naturally, I had sought out the Americans I knew who were in the business and asked about the reports. In every quarter but one I was put off with either a profession of ignorance or a bland smile. The closest I came to the truth was a guarded disclosure by an American friend that a Russian had come over who exhibited an 'amazing knowledge of the inner workings' of Western security networks, including the French, but the man was being difficult in regard to his future prospects and well-being. This meager information I passed on to SDECE in Paris and for some weeks thereafter I received daily cables pressing me to find out who the man was, where the Americans were hiding him, and what he was telling them. I met a blank wall. Then, abruptly, there arrived a jarring order from Paris: I was to cease my efforts to track down the man and to stop asking questions about him. The reason for that peremptory, almost insulting directive was now made clear by what 'X' had told me. It must have been that Kennedy's letter had reached de Gaulle, a decision had been taken to send de Rougemont secretly to Washington to assess the reliability of the source, and it was thought best to order me off the scent, lest I complicate matters.

At this juncture – before the interrogation teams had begun their work – I remained somewhat skeptical of the Russian's real value. It still seemed possible to me that he might be a clever plant – a double agent – whose mission was to disrupt relations between my country and the United States. Beyond that, I was unhappy at the way the Americans had broached the affair to my government, however urgent their concern. There were at that time any number of career intelligence officers high in the SDECE and the DST known by their American counterparts to be trustworthy beyond question. The grave implications raised by the Russian could and should have been first made known at that professional level. Instead, by being passed over everyone's head to de Gaulle, Kennedy's letter unnecessarily and unfairly impugned everyone in both services and created almost impossible tensions and suspicions everywhere.

The questioning of Martel – the code name given the Russian by 'X' and his colleagues – began forthwith. I was kept fully abreast of what he was saying.

One of his early and most disturbing assertions was that French KGB agents in NATO headquarters in Paris were so strategically placed and so facile in their methods that they could produce on two or three days' demand any NATO document Moscow asked for. A whole library of secret NATO documents, Martel insisted, was available for reference in Moscow. Indeed the KGB's familiarity with supposedly supersecret

NATO material was so intimate that its officers, in ordering fresh material from its sources in Paris, freely used the same numbering system for documents as NATO did itself. Thinking to trap the Russian, my colleagues asked him if he himself had ever seen NATO documents.

'Oh, yes' was the confident answer. 'Many.'

At a later meeting, a collection of some scores of classified NATO documents, dealing with different subjects, was presented to him. Most of the papers were authentic; a number, however, had been fabricated in Paris for the occasion. The whole lot was put down before the Russian and he was asked to pick out those he had read in Moscow. He did not identify all the papers, but every paper that he claimed to have read in Moscow was authentic, and among the papers he put aside were all the bogus ones. It was, for the French teams, an unnerving experience.

Martel gave the French interrogators another turn with an exhibition of an all but encyclopedic knowledge of the secret workings of the French intelligence services. He described, for example, in rather precise detail how a thoroughgoing reorganization of the SDECE had been carried out in the beginning of 1958. He further knew how and why specific intelligence functions and objectives had been shifted from one section to another, even the names of certain officers who were running certain intelligence operations – details of a nature that could have come only from a source or sources at or close to the heart of the French intelligence organizations.

Martel did not know everything. In some areas, he had only bits and pieces of intelligence to offer. He would tell his questioners, for instance, that in a certain city in the south of France a member of the municipal court who had made a name in the resistance was really a Soviet citizen – an 'illegal', as we say in the trade – who had acquired a false French identity and was under KGB discipline. But he did not know the man's name – only how he fitted in. Martel knew that a French scientist of Asiatic origin, who had attended a certain international meeting of scientists in London, had been recruited there by the KGB under particular circumstances. Again, no name – only a whiff of a treasonable association. He knew that an intelligence officer who had been posted to certain Iron Curtain countries during certain periods (periods which he *did* know) and who was then attached to a specific section in a certain security service had been a KGB agent for a certain number of years.

It was not in the least surprising that Martel did not know the names of these agents. He was not personally running the KGB networks for whom these people worked, and for purposes of evaluating the intelligence they supplied it was quite sufficient for him to know only in a general way where they were placed. Martel's work in Moscow had required him to sit in on many KGB staff meetings which reviewed or directed Soviet intelligence operations in a number of countries, including France, and he additionally was more directly involved in other operations. It was from his memory of these operations that he drew the links to France and supplied the leads which could be checked out there.

The French counterintelligence teams were thorough. They sat down with the Russian day after long day. They pressed him hard. Everything he said was recorded on tapes. The tapes were run back at the end of the day, the leads were separated out, and every night, a long coded summary went out to SDECE headquarters in Paris. In the interests of security the teams had brought special codes with them and did their own encoding. At the end of a fortnight the teams returned to France, taking with them all the tapes and hundreds of pages of transcript. Investigations were started on the basis of the leads Martel had supplied; and then, after further questions developed, the teams flew back to Washington to pick and test the memory of the Russian afresh. They would present a name to Martel – the name of someone who was thought to fit a certain lead he had supplied. Martel would be given certain particulars about the man's work, his position, his travels and then would come the hard question: could this man be the one who was working for the KGB inside NATO or in the political area at, say, the ministerial level? In his careful way, Martel would answer, 'He looks to be,' or 'Yes, he could be,' or 'No, there's a discrepancy.'

In the course of these interrogations, Martel would open other avenues for investigation. The Ministry of the Interior, which has responsibility for internal security, the French representation in the NATO organization, the Ministry of Defense, and the Ministry of Foreign Affairs were all penetrated in the higher echelons by KGB agents.

An official who appeared to be presently a member of the de Gaulle cabinet and who had ministerial or near-ministerial rank in 1944 in de Gaulle's first government had been identified in KGB discussions as a KGB agent.

A network with the code name Sapphire, consisting of more than half a dozen French intelligence officers, all of whom had been recruited by the KGB, was operating inside the SDECE itself.

A new section for collecting scientific intelligence had been, or was being, created inside SDECE with the specific mission of spying out US nuclear and other technological advances, eventually in the Soviet interest.

I myself had no way of assessing the accuracy of Martel's leads, but there was no mistaking the impact he had on my colleagues. His familiarity with France's supposedly most secret affairs first astonished, then depressed them, as it did me. I could no longer doubt that Martel was the genuine article, although I still was not convinced that everything he said was true. His assertion that French intelligence had a scheme for spying out American scientific secrets I found hard to accept at the outset. Yet the Russian had been most specific on this point. In July 1959, he insisted, he heard General Sakharovsky, who was in charge of the KGB's covert operations, analyze for his senior staff officers the implications of the reorganization of the French intelligence services. In the course of the lecture, Sakharovsky mentioned the plan for the proposed intelligence section, with its targets in the United States, and noted with satisfaction that the KGB expected to receive any reports within a day or two after SDECE got them. All this was supposed to have happened nearly three and a half years before. When Martel's account was related to me, in my office, one of the DST men asked his SDECE counterpart, 'Really, are you people doing this sort of thing?' None of us had ever heard of the scheme.

As the questioning of Martel went on through the summer, the procedures being used by our people to follow up Martel's leads began to create an increasingly difficult situation for me in my own work. Our teams would do some preliminary work at home and return to Washington with a number of names, any one of which might fit into the necessarily meager network of facts Martel had offered. But Martel could never answer with absolute assurance either yes or no about any of them. The problem in this for me – and, in fact, for the whole French intelligence system – lay in the fact that each session with Martel was also attended by American representatives, and each time our people dropped a name in front of Martel, that person automatically became suspect to the Americans. Small wonder, but as the list of clouded reputations lengthened, my professional contacts with the Americans (and with other Western nations) began to dry up, even on routine matters. The word seemed to be out not to take any chances with the French. I could understand this and would probably have done the same thing in their position.

CHAPTER VI

The Israelis

*The Mossad, being the intelligence body entrusted with the
responsibility of plotting the course for the leaders at the
helm of the nation, has betrayed that trust.*
Victor Ostrovsky

For a tiny underpopulated country, bounded on three sides by hostile
neighbours and on the fourth by the sea, Israel is understandably sensitive
about the prospect of any citizen committing treachery, which is regarded
as a triple sin: the betrayal of nation, race and religion. Almost permanently on a war footing, with an economy governed by the necessity to
devote huge resources to defending its fragile frontiers, Israel remains
preoccupied by its search for security. Technically a state of war continues
to exist with some of the Arab states in the region and the government
cannot erase the painful memory of the surprise attack in October 1973,
now known as the Yom Kippur War, in which Syria, Egypt and Jordan
seized advantage of an important Jewish religious holiday to launch an
invasion which took the country unawares. Despite recent talks with the
Palestine Liberation Organization to offer a measure of self-determina-
tion for Jericho and the occupied territory known as the Gaza Strip, the
Arab boycott remains a potent manifestation of Arab hostility to Israel.

In these unique circumstances, it is not surprising that very few Israelis
have been convicted of having sold out to the enemy. Of the handful of
espionage cases in Israel, the majority involve spies recruited by the KGB,
which was handicapped in its intelligence-gathering efforts because of a
lack of diplomatic representation in Tel Aviv. Without the usual embassy
cover for its intelligence personnel, Soviet operations depended upon the
use of 'illegals' and were therefore vulnerable to the efficient and
ubiquitous Shin Bet security service. In 1950 three NCOs, Uri Winter,
Gustave Gulovner and Sergeant-Major Reicher, were caught spying for the
Soviets. In February 1961 the nuclear physicist Professor Kurt Sitte was
convicted of having passed secrets from Haifa's Institute of Technology to

the Russians, and in September the following year Aharon Cohen, then a leading member of the Leftist MAPAM party, was sentenced to five years' imprisonment for the same offence. The highest level of hostile penetration was achieved by Dr Israel Beer, a senior Ministry of Defence adviser who was arrested in April 1962 and died in custody four years later.

Beer's trial was held *in camera*, a characteristic of Israeli espionage prosecutions, which are usually the subject of press bans. Only relatively recently have details of two important cases been disclosed: that of the veteran GRU officer Zeev Avni who penetrated the Israeli Ministry of Foreign Affairs and was sentenced in 1956 to fourteen years' imprisonment; and that of Colonel Shimon Levinson, a military intelligence officer assigned to the Prime Minister's office who was convicted of spying for the KGB in May 1991 and sentenced to twelve years' imprisonment. Although released in 1963, Avni's story was subjected to censorship until May 1993. Similarly, a Soviet illegal, Yuri Lenov, was swapped in 1974 having been sentenced to eighteen years' imprisonment for espionage, without any public statement whatever. His targets had been the nuclear research facilities at Dimona and in the airforce base at Nahal Sorek, just south of Tel Aviv, arguably the two most sensitive sites in Israel. Anyone visiting either establishment, or the main storage facility near the village of Tirosh on Route 302, can be guaranteed to draw the attention of Shin Bet.

When in September 1986 the nuclear technician Mordechai Vanunu was seized by Mossad agents in Rome and returned to Tel Aviv to face trial, details of his abduction were not made public either. His crime had been to reveal details of Israel's atomic weapons development programme at Dimona in a British newspaper, a disclosure that brought him a prison sentence of eighteen years in solitary confinement.

Any unauthorized revelation that is deemed to jeopardize Israel's security is treated exceptionally harshly by Western standards, but the highly disciplined climate did on one occasion prove counterproductive when in September 1990 a legal action was brought in Canada to prevent the release of Victor Ostrovsky's devastating exposé of Mossad. A former trainee, Ostrovsky wrote a detailed account of his experiences in the organization, thereby compromising the location of its current head-quarters and training facilities, and even the identities of some colleagues and their sources. The Israelis responded with undisguised rage to this unprecedented breach of security, thereby ensuring that the author's book, which had been received initially with some scepticism, was transformed into an authenticated work of non-fiction and into a bestseller. An idea of how damaging Ostrovsky's text was considered is this passage, dealing with the massacres of Palestinian refugees at Sabra and Shatila in September 1982, deleted from the Canadian first editions by the original court order, which was subsequently overturned.

> It was an unspeakable act that not only had been tolerated by Israeli occupation forces, but was facilitated by them. It prompted then US president, Ronald Reagan, Israel's strongest international ally at the time, to lament that in terms of public perception, Israel had been transformed from the David to the Goliath of the Middle East. Two days later, Reagan sent the marines back to Beirut as part of a US–French–Italian peacekeeping contingent.

Having defied his former employers Ostrovsky, who now lives in Toronto, knows only too well that he has made himself a target for retribution. When Ralph McGehee was negotiating the publication of his controversial memoirs with the CIA, his former superior, the East Asia Division chief, is reported to have remarked: 'It's too bad you didn't work for the Israeli intelligence service . . . They knew how to deal with people like you. They'd take you out and shoot you.'

Certainly it is true that Mossad and its domestic counterpart have acquired reputations for ruthless efficiency, and both organizations have received greater loyalty from their retired employees than other Western agencies have, just one measure of that loyalty being the paucity of material written by traitors. The Israeli state is, of course, the beneficiary of this exceptional level of loyalty, but there is a hidden disadvantage. In other countries local Jews, members of the Diaspora, are often perceived as having divided loyalties, in much the same way that in earlier times all Catholics were suspected of harbouring a greater allegiance to Rome. Accordingly, Mossad exercises tremendous care not to recruit members of the Diaspora in order to avoid compromising other Jewish communities who already endure a high rate of discrimination. There are exceptions, of course, such as when an American Jew, Jonathan J. Pollard, was sentenced in March 1986 to life imprisonment for having passed classified data to various Mossad personnel, including its former chief of operations, Rafael Eitan. Pollard and his wife, who was also convicted of espionage, have claimed consistently to have been motivated by religious considerations, but when they realized they had come under surveillance, and their arrest was imminent, the Israeli authorities refused to allow them refuge at the Israeli embassy in Washington DC. To have run a US citizen as an agent against that country was itself an act calculated to offend American sensibilities, but to have allowed the recruitment of a sympathizer who declared an overriding commitment to Israel was courting disaster on a wider scale and enhancing the prejudices of those suspicious of expatriate Jews.

The concept of loyalty is one that, since the beginning of the modern state of Israel, has posed problems for its inhabitants, only a small minority of whom have been born inside its borders. The law of 'The Return' allows Israeli citizenship to be granted to all those born to the Jewish faith who chose to make the *aryah* (the Hebrew for returning home to Israel), but the dual status of so many Israelis must have caused many of them to examine their consciences or led them into conflict of loyalties. Abba Eban, the South African who was to become Foreign Minister, led the Israeli delegation to the 1947 United Nations Conference in New York on the future of Palestine, and until the previous year had been Major Aubrey Eban, a Cambridge don serving in the British army. Similarly, General Ezer Weizman, who was elected President of Israel in May 1993 and had flown spitfires with the RAF during the Second World War, shot down two RAF transport aircraft over Jordan. Altogether 13,000 Palestinian Jews served in the British forces during the war, and many of them used the skills they had been taught to resist the British Mandate afterwards. Several leading Israelis fought in the Jewish Brigade and dozens were introduced to the clandestine world by SIS or SOE. The future head of Mossad, Isser Harel, had been trained by the Palestine Police (which eventually sacked him for insubordination) and General Moshe Dayan, head of the Haganah's intelligence unit, had organized a network of stay-behind radio transmitters for SIS in August 1941. None of this experience prevented the people concerned from revolting against the Mandate in the months up to the final withdrawal in May 1948.

Israel has acquired an unsurpassed reputation for not only ensuring the loyalty of its citizens but also retaining the integrity of its intelligence agencies, despite the very high proportion of the population who started life in a foreign (and often hostile) country. Although there may be others who have been motivated to make damaging disclosures of the kind that might undermine the state or its security apparatus, only Victor Ostrovsky can be said to have done so, and escaped retribution. Certainly the two retired Mossad officers who have published books, Peter Z. Malkin and Yaacov Caroz, received official permission to do so. Malkin, a veteran of twenty-six years with Mossad who participated in the abduction of Adolf Eichmann from Argentina in 1960, wrote *Eichmann in my Hands*, and Caroz, who served as Isser Harel's deputy chief, published *The Arab Secret Services*, which, far from compromising Israeli secrets, was intended to put the spotlight on Mossad's opponents. Indeed, Isser Harel has made his views known on the appropriate treatment of traitors, and confirmed that in his 'time as head of Mossad I made efforts in very difficult security questions to prevent the killing of a traitor':

> If a traitor is under the hand of the state you can give him a summons. In some cases a democratic state has no choice than to bring a traitor who threatens the existence of the state to trial or to kill him even if this causes diplomatic problems. The latter is easier and avoids the dangers to Israel at the political, security and diplomatic levels which an abduction causes. But Israel is a democratic and humanitarian country. To wipe someone out is a much more serious business.

Through authorized publications of the kind endorsed by Harel, Mossad has acquired an unsurpassed reputation for executing daring operations. The rescue of the hijacked passengers from Entebbe in July 1976, the seizure of Eichmann in May 1960, the removal of the French gunboats from Cherbourg during Christmas 1969, the air raid in June 1981 on Saddam Hussein's nuclear plant at Tuwaitha and the disappearance of the SS *Plumbat* and its cargo of 200 tons of uranium oxide in November 1968 are all regarded as brilliant coups, but according to Ostrovsky, Mossad was never so keen to take the credit for the many murders it carried out, particularly those of suspected Palestinian terrorists. Indeed, he alleged that after the Lillehammer fiasco of July 1973, when a hit-team dispatched to kill a key Black September terrorist had shot the wrong man, an innocent waiter in Norway, the team leader had remained in the organization and had involved himself with Panamanian drug deals.

Victor Ostrovsky

I was in constant conflict between my beliefs and my loyalties.

The son of a Canadian who had flown with the Royal Canadian Air Force during the Second World War, and had later moved to Israel to fight in the 1948 War of Independence, Victor Ostrovsky was brought up in Canada, where he was born, and in Israel, where he moved with his mother when he was six years old.

At the age of eighteen, and already an ardent Zionist, Ostrovsky joined the army for his compulsory three years' service and was commissioned into the military police. In November 1972 he was released and moved back to Edmonton for five years, but in May 1977 he returned to Israel and joined the navy, where he served in submarines. He left after four years to become a graphic designer, and in October 1982 underwent a preliminary interview with Mossad at their head-quarters in Tel Aviv. Two years later, in February 1984, he was accepted as a trainee and underwent two years of courses but, after his participation in an unsuccessful operation in Cyprus at the end of March 1986, he was dismissed. However, before he could be served with papers calling him back into compulsory military service as a reservist, he flew to London and then made his way to his father's home in Omaha. Later he was joined in Canada by his wife, Bella, and their two daughters, Sharon and Leeorah, and they settled in Nepean, a suburb of Ottawa.

Ostrovsky's book, co-authored with the Canadian journalist Claire Hoy, and with the title taken from Mossad's motto, contained a mass of information that the trainee, as an apprentice *katsa* (or case officer) had gleaned during his employment by the organization. As well as disclosing highly classified data, such as the two most recent locations of Mossad's headquarters in Tel Aviv, in the Hadar Dafna Building on King Saul Boulevard, and the office above the South African embassy on Ibn Gevirol Avenue, and its various training facilities, he revealed details of numerous operations, and made some startling allegations, including the claim that Mossad had withheld from the CIA advance knowledge of the car bomb attack on the US marine barracks in Beirut in October 1983; that it had trained members of both the Sri Lankan security forces and the Tamil Tigers almost simultaneously; had developed close links with the Chilean DINA and had provided facilities for the assassins of Orlando Letelier in 1976; had supplied nuclear expertise to the South Africans in return for a test site in the Indian Ocean in 1979; and had established a close relationship with the Panamanian strongman Manuel Noriega through Mike Harari, the senior Mossad officer implicated in the Lillehammer episode.

Ostrovsky's book was an unprecedented disaster for a clandestine organization that, small in size, prized itself on watertight security. As well as offering a floorplan of the *Midrasha*, the Mossad training academy on the road to Haifa, and a comprehensive structural chart of Mossad and its relationship with Israel's other intelligence agencies, including the top secret signals intelligence service, Unit 8200, it identified Mark Hessner, formerly the Mossad station chief in Paris, as head of the organization.

In a futile attempt to stop publication the Israeli government obtained temporary injunctions in Canada and New York but they served merely to enhance Ostrovsky's credibility. This one book has probably done more than any other single disclosure regarding the organization to undermine the status of Mossad and handicap its operations. The author's assertion that all Palestinian visa applications to Denmark are routinely vetted by Mossad led to a serious breach in relations, and not long afterwards indirectly resulted in the resignation of the head of the Norwegian security service, who had authorized a similar procedure.

As regards Ostrovsky's motivation, the author himself insists that 'it was the twisted ideals and self-centred pragmatism that I encountered inside the Mossad, coupled with this so-called team's greed, lust, and total lack of respect for human life, that motivated me'. Certainly he was aware of the negative impact his disclosures would have. 'The strongest curse inside the Mossad that one katsa can throw at another is the simple wish: "May I read about you in the paper." '

Ostrovsky could not have had first-hand experience of many of the events recounted in his book but his description of so many secret Israeli installations, from the special forces compound at Kfan Sirkin to the base at Petah Tikvah, gave him added weight and in 1994 encouraged him to publish a second book, *The Other Side of Deception*. In this passage from his first volume Ostrovsky describes how an illicit surveillance operation run by a Mossad cell in Washington DC caused Andrew Young to resign his post as the United States Representative at the United Nations.

By Way of Deception

By the summer of 1985, Libya's President Moamer al Kadhafi had become the devil incarnate for most of the western world. Reagan was the only one who authorized warplanes to attack him, but the Israelis held Kadhafi responsible for facilitating much of the arms supply to the Palestinians and their other Arab enemies.

It is difficult to recruit Libyans. They're not liked anywhere, which is a problem in itself. They need to be recruited in Europe, but they're not big travelers.

Libya has two main habors: at Tripoli, the capital; and at Benghazi, on the Gulf of Sidra in the northwest. The Israeli navy had been monitoring Libyan activities, largely through regular patrols around the entire length of the Mediterranean. Israel regards the corridor from Israel to Gibraltar as its 'oxygen pipe'. It's the tie to America and most of Europe for both imports and exports.

In 1985, Israel had relatively sound relations with the other countries bordering the southern Mediterranean: Egypt, Morocco, Tunisia, and Algeria, but not Libya.

They had a fairly big navy, but they had a serious problem with manpower and maintaining the navy. Their ships were falling apart. They had large Russian submarines they'd purchased, but they either didn't know how to submerge them, or they were afraid to try. At least twice, Israeli patrol boats came upon Libyan submarines. Normally, a sub would go 'ding, ding, ding, ding,' and go down. But these subs would steam back to port making their escape.

The Israelis have a listening substation on Sicily, which they enjoy through liaison with the Italians, who also have a listening station there. But it's not enough, because the Libyans, with their support of the PLO and other subversive activities, endanger the Israeli shoreline. Israel regards its shoreline as its 'soft belly', the most vulnerable border to attack, home to most of its population and industry.

A considerable amount of the arms and ammunition supplied to the PLO comes via ship from Libya, much of it passing through Cyprus on the way – or going by what is called the TNT route: from Tripoli, Libya, to Tripoli, Lebanon. The Israelis were gathering *some* information about Libyan activities at the time through the Central African Republic and Chad, which was engaged in serious border clashes with Kadhafi's forces.

The Mossad had some 'naval observers', usually civilians recruited through their stations in Europe simply to take photographs while ships were entering the harbor. There was no real danger involved, and it gave some visual indication of what was going on inside the harbors. But while they did catch arms shipments – more by luck than anything else – there was a clear need to have access to specific information about traffic coming in and out of Tripoli and Benghazi.

At a meeting involving Mossad's PLO research department and the head of the Tsomet branch dealing with France, the United Kingdom and Belgium, it was decided to try to recruit a harbor-traffic controller, or someone else working in the harbormaster's office in Tripoli who would have access to more specific information on the names and whereabouts of ships. Though the Mossad knew the names of the PLO ships, they did not know where they were at any given time.

If you want to sink or apprehend them, you have to find them. That's hard with a ship if you don't know its route or exactly when it sailed. Many of them keep close to shore – the Mossad called it 'shore scratching' – and avoid going into open waters where radar can pick them up. It's difficult for radar to locate a ship that's close to shore because the image can be swallowed by the noise of mountains, or a ship may be in one of the many harbors behind the mountains and simply not be seen. Then when it does emerge, its identity may be uncertain. There are a lot of ships on the Mediterranean. The US Sixth Fleet, the Russian fleet, all kinds of ships, including merchant ships from around the world. The Mossad is not free, then, to do anything it wants. All the countries along the Mediterranean have their own radar, so the Mossad has to be very careful what it does there.

Obtaining specific information inside Libya, however, was easier said than done. It was too dangerous to send someone in there to try recruiting, and the Mossad was by now hitting its collective head against a brick wall. At last, someone at the meeting, who had worked as a 'reporter' in Tunis and Algiers for *Afrique-Asia*, a French-language newspaper covering Arab affairs, suggested the best way to begin was simply to telephone Tripoli harbor and find out who had the sort of information they needed. That way, they could at least narrow it down to a specific target.

It was one of those simple ideas that are often overlooked when people become involved in intrigue and complicated operational details. And so, a telephone line was set aside that could be dialed from Tel Aviv but would operate through an office/apartment in Paris, should anyone trace the call. It was attached to an insurance company in France that was owned by a sayan.

Before he called, the katsa had a complete cover built for him as an insurance investigator. He had an office with a secretary. The secretary, a woman, was what is called a *bat leveyha*, which means 'escort' (not in the sexual sense). It simply refers to a local woman, not necessarily a Jew, who is recruited as an assistant agent and given a job where a woman is needed. She would be aware that she was working for Israeli intelligence through the local embassy.

The idea was based on the concept of *mikrim ve tguvot*, Hebrew for 'actions and reactions'. They already knew the action, but they had to anticipate the reaction. For every possible reaction, another action is planned. It's like a giant chess game, except that you don't plan more than two reactions ahead because it would become too complicated. It's all part of regular operational planning, and it goes into every move made.

In the room with the katsa, and listening with earphones, were Menachem Dorf, head of the Mossad's PLO department, and Gidon Naftaly, the Mossad's chief psychiatrist, whose job was to listen and try immediately to analyze the person answering the phone.

The man who answered first didn't understand French, so he passed the call to someone else. The second man came on the line, gave the name of the man in charge, said he'd be back in half an hour, and immediately hung up.

When the katsa called back, he asked for the harbormaster by name, got him on the line, and identified himself as an insurance investigator with a French underwriting company.

This was their one shot, so it had to work. Not only must the story sound credible, the storyteller must sound as if he believes it, too. And so, the katsa told his listener what business he was in, that they needed to have access to various details about certain ships in the harbors, and that they needed to know who was in charge.

'I'm in charge,' the man said. 'How can I be of assistance?'

'We know that from time to time ships put in there that their owners claim have been lost or damaged. Now, we're the underwriters, but we can't always check these claims firsthand, so we need to know more.'

'What do you need to know?'

'Well, we need to know, for example, if they are being repaired, or if they are loading or unloading. We don't have a representative there, as you know, but we would like to have someone looking after our interests. If you could recommend someone to us, we'd certainly be willing to reimburse him handsomely.'

'I think I can help you,' the man said. 'I have that kind of information, and I don't see any problem with that, as long as we're talking civilian traffic and not military ships.'

'We have no interest in your navy,' the katsa said. 'We're not underwriting its insurance.'

The conversation went on for 10 or 15 minutes, during which time the katsa asked about five or six ships. Only one of them, a PLO ship, was there being repaired. He asked for an address where he could send the payment, gave his own address and phone number to the harbormaster, and told him to call anytime he had information he thought would be useful.

Things were going so well, and the target sounded so comfortable, that the katsa felt bold enough to ask the man if he was allowed to accept another job, as an agent for the insurance company, outside his regular work at the harbor.

'I might be able to do some selling,' the harbormaster replied, 'but only on a part-time basis. At least until I see how it works out.'

'Fine. I'll send you a manual and some business cards. When you get a chance to go over that, we'll talk again.'

The conversation ended. They now had a paid agent in the harbor, although he didn't know he'd been recruited.

The next task was to summon the business department of Metsada to design the promised insurance manual so that it would make sense *and* allow them to gather the kind of information they wanted. Within a few days, the manual was on its way to Tripoli. Once you commit a telephone and address to someone in a recruitment process, it must be kept alive for at least three years even if stage one in the recruitment process was never passed – unless there had been a confrontation that could expose the katsa, in which case everything would be closed down immediately.

For the next two months or so, the new recruit reported regularly, but during one of the calls he mentioned that he'd read the manual but still wasn't too clear on what being an agent for the company would involve.

'I understand that,' the katsa said. 'I remember the first time I saw it, it didn't make a lot of sense to me, either. Listen, when do you have your holidays?'

'In three weeks.'

'Great. Rather than trying to sort this out over the phone, why don't you come to France at our expense? I'll send you the tickets. You've already worked out so well for us that we'd love to give you some time in the south of France, and we can combine a little business with pleasure. And I'll be honest with you, it's better for our tax situation for you to come here.'

The recruit was thrilled. The Mossad was paying him only about $1,000 a month, while during the time they had him on the string, he made at least three trips to France. He was useful, but he had no real connections beyond his knowledge of the ships in the harbor, so the idea was not to endanger him. After meeting him in person, it seemed the best plan would be to gently drop the attempt to have him do other things, but to continue using him for information on PLO ships.

At first, they asked only about some of the ships entering the harbor, on the pretext that they were the ones being underwritten by their company. Then they devised a plan whereby the harbormaster would provide the full lists of all ships docking. They promised to pay him accordingly. That way, they said, they could supply this information to other insurance underwriters who would be only too happy to pay for the information; they, in turn, could share the proceeds with him.

And so he went happily back to Tripoli where he continued supplying them with information on all harbor traffic. At one point, a ship owned by Abu Nidal, the hated head of the PFLP-GC faction of the PLO, was in the harbor being loaded with military equipment – including shoulder-carried anti-aircraft missiles and many other weapons the Israelis did not want to see ending up in the hands of Palestinian fighters on their borders.

They knew about Nidal's ship through their tie-in with PLO communications, thanks to a slip in Nidal's normally careful speaking habits, and all that remained was to ask their happy harbormaster exactly where the ship was and how long it would be there. He confirmed the vessel's location, along with that of another one also being loaded with equipment destined for Cyprus.

Two Israeli missile boats, SAAR-4 class, appeared to be on regular patrol one warm summer night in 1985, only this time they stopped long enough to unload six commandos in a small, electric-powered submarine with a hood on top, similar in appearance to a World War II fighter plane without the wings – or a long torpedo with a propeller on the back. It was called a wet submarine, and the commandos sat under the hood, dressed for action in their wet suits and oxygen tanks.

After disembarking from the patrol boats, they went quickly to a ship entering the harbor, latched themselves to its hull by magnetic plates, and piggybacked a ride into the harbor itself.

The hood of the submarine provided them with a life-saving protective shield, necessary because the Mossad knew from their conversations with the harbormaster that once every five hours, Libyan security cruised the harbor, tossing hand grenades into the water and creating a tremendous amount of water pressure – enough to finish off any frogmen who happened to be in the area. They had discovered this security device one time when the katsa heard explosions in the background and simply asked the harbormaster what was making the noise. It's a routine security measure in most harbors where countries are at war. Syria and Israel both do it, too.

And so, they simply waited in their wet submarine until security made its rounds, then they quietly slipped into the water, carrying their leech mines with them. After attaching them to the two loaded PLO ships, they returned to their submarine. The whole thing took only about two and a half hours. Since they also knew which ships were leaving the harbor that night, they headed for a tanker near the harbor entrance, but decided not to clamp on to it because it would be too difficult to unhook their tiny vessel once the tanker was under full steam.

Unfortunately, they ran out of oxygen in the submarine, and the battery died. There was no point in trying to carry it with them once they were in open waters, so they hooked it on to a buoy where it could be recovered later, attached themselves to one another by rope, and performed what is called a 'sunflower'. That means putting a blast of air inside their wet suits, which makes them expand like balloons, and allows the frogmen simply to float on top of the water without having to do any work at all to stay afloat. They even took turns sleeping, with one man staying awake on watch at all times. A few hours later, an Israeli patrol boat sneaked in, answering their beeper signals, picked them up, and whisked them off to safety.

At about 6 a.m. that day, there were four large explosions in the harbor, and two PLO ships went down, loaded with millions of dollars worth of military equipment and ammunition.

The katsa assumed that would be it for their harbormaster. Surely the explosions would make him suspicious. Instead, when he called in that day, the man was tremendously excited about it.

'You won't believe what happened!' he said. 'They blew up two ships right in the middle of the harbor!'

'Who did?'

'The Israelis, of course,' he said. 'I don't know how they found the ships, but they did. Fortunately, they weren't any of yours, so you don't have to worry.'

The harbormaster went on working for the Mossad for another 18 months or so. He made a lot of money until one day, he just disappeared, leaving a trail of destroyed and captured PLO arms ships in his wake.

Mordechai Vanunu

In the aftermath of the Lebanon war and the Shin Bet affair my inner soul doubted the country's leadership and their acts.

Originally an immigrant from Morocco, in November 1976 Mordechai Vanunu became a nuclear technician based at the secret research facility at Dimona, outside Beersheba in the Negev Desert. There he learned of his country's atomic weapons development programme, about which very little information had ever leaked to the West. The centre itself was surrounded by high security and only a limited number of trusted individuals were allowed access to the underground complex of buildings which accommodated the bomb production and plutonium separation area.

Disillusioned with his work, Vanunu resigned his post in October 1985 and the following year travelled to Australia, where he confided to a local journalist that he had taken fifty-seven photographs inside the Dimona plant. His story was eventually offered to the *Sunday Times* in London, which spent several months attempting to verify Vanunu's claims, that represented the first details from within the Israeli nuclear industry. His disclosures, if true, were sensational because they established Israel as a nuclear power, complete with a production line of free-fall atomic bombs and land mines, and gave the first authoritative estimate of the size of the Israeli nuclear arsenal – which amounted to enough plutonium to arm 150 devices. However, early in October 1986, a week before the *Sunday Times* was scheduled to break its scoop, the *Sunday Mirror* denounced Vanunu as a Walter Mitty character who had pulled off a fantastic hoax, and Vanunu himself disappeared without warning.

In reality Vanunu had been lured from London to Rome by a glamorous Mossad agent, where he had been drugged and returned to Israel by ship to face a secret trial in Jerusalem at which he was convicted of having compromised his country's security by disclosing details of his work at Dimona. He was convicted of treason (Section 99 of the 1977 Penal Law) and was sentenced to the longest term of imprisonment in solitary confinement handed down by an Israeli court, which he is currently serving at Ashkelon prison despite a campaign to obtain his freedom, led by his brother Meir.

Having failed to give Vanunu the protection his scoop so obviously merited, the *Sunday Times* continues to publicize his case, but was unwilling to allow the original newspaper article to be reproduced here. Instead there follows an extract from *Nuclear Ambiguity*, a study of the Vanunu affair by Yoel Cohen, an Israeli journalist who described the aftermath of Vanunu's abduction.

Nuclear Ambiguity

The British authorities were keen to dispel any notion that Vanunu was abducted from British territory. 'Israel,' Whitehall sources told the *Jerusalem Post* London reporter, 'would not have been so stupid as to abduct Vanunu from British territory, particularly since Britain has emerged, since the Hindawi trial [of an Arab backed by Syria arrested for attempting to smuggle a bomb on to an El Al plane at London airport] last month, as Israel's staunchest ally in Western Europe.' And a Foreign Office spokesman told the *Sunday Times*, that while the government would take an extremely serious view of kidnapping from British soil they could not justify intervention if UK laws were not broken.

The cover-up went a stage further when *The Economist* – which Andrew Neil had left to become editor of the *Sunday Times*, without any great love lost on either side – suggested that Vanunu had been unwittingly manipulated by the Mossad or that he was even a Mossad agent, and that the *Sunday Times* had been the victim of a gigantic public relations exercise to boost Israel's nuclear posture.

For the first three weeks after Vanunu's disappearance, Israeli officials from the prime minister's spokesman downwards claimed not to know anything about his whereabouts, even though he was in Israel and was undergoing interrogation. They broke the basic rule of spokesmanship: credibility hangs on his or her not stating an untruth. For the spokesman of the prison services, though, it was not a total lie to say that 'the Vanunu affair is not the concern of the police and we know nothing of his whereabouts', because at that time he was being held in a section of Gedera prison under the control of the Shin Bet.

There is no obligation on the Israeli authorities to confirm that somebody is under arrest. The Emergency Powers (Detention) Law, the essence of which was inherited from the British Mandate, empowers the authorities to detain a person for six months 'for reasons of state security and public security', and as long as the detention order is approved by a district court judge, it can be extended again and again. In cases of security sensitivity like Vanunu's, this process is completed behind closed doors; sometimes only the defendant's lawyer knows the full reasons for the indictment. And the appointment by Vanunu of Dr Amnon Zichroni, a veteran civil rights lawyer, was not made public. Zichroni adhered to the rules of the game. To announce that he was representing Vanunu would be tantamount to a confirmation that Vanunu was back in Israel, which in turn would raise questions regarding how he got there and how he left Britain.

Eight days after Vanunu vanished, and three days after the publication of their exposé, the *Sunday Times* reported his disappearance to the British authorities. The British police visited the room at the Mountbatten Hotel where he had last stayed, but failed to uncover any evidence that the law had been broken. Nor was there a record of his departure from any British airport or seaport. Israeli officials hoped that media curiosity would die away.

Military censorship in the Vanunu affair could be summed up in two words: damage control. When the *Sunday Mirror* came out with its hoax story about a nuclear conman, a week before the *Sunday Times* disclosures, the Israeli censor initially banned Israeli media from publishing reports from London despite both the convention that military censorship in Israel does not suppress quotes from the foreign media and the meeting of the Editors' Committee a day earlier at which Peres confirmed that foreign sources could be quoted. A few hours later on the Saturday night the censor finally passed the reports quoting the *Sunday Mirror*. Apart from his appointment by the Minister of Defence, the military censor draws his powers from the statute book, and is supposed to be free from ministerial and chief-of-staff pressures. But this is not always the case. At one point during the Vanunu Affair, the military censor had to persuade Defence Minister Itzhak Rabin of the illogicality of the censorship policy. He succeeded.

Vanunu's disappearance was a difficult story for Israeli reporters to cover. Information they gleaned came from Vanunu's family and later from his lawyer, as well as from the prison service, the Shin Bet, and the Cabinet. Israeli reporters with contacts in the intelligence establishment tend to use these sparingly. In this case, officers were tight-lipped. A key source was the Justice Ministry, which would normally have been very reticent. But the Shin Bet affair months earlier, when the Attorney General, Professor Itzhak Zamir, resisted government pressure to cover up the deaths of two Arab terrorists arrested in the 1984 Tel Aviv–Ashkelon bus hijacking, and which resulted in Zamir's dismissal, turned the press and the Justice Ministry into unlikely bedfellows. 'The Ministry of Justice had used the press in order to combat what it felt was the politicians' destruction of justice. To the extent that reporters got Justice Ministry officials to speak about Vanunu it was because they felt they owed us something,' Menachem Shalev, then the *Jerusalem Post*'s justice affairs reporter said. 'Yet it was a futile attempt to get anything past censorship which had not already appeared in the foreign media,' he added. 'The *Sunday Times* was made into the Bible,' remarked Mark Geffen, former editor of *Al Hamishmar*.

Things began to fall apart with the bizarre arrival in Israel of Reverend John McKnight of St John's rectory. He had been in London for two weeks helping the *Sunday Times* try to discover Vanunu's whereabouts. When he arrived in Israel, he turned first to the Anglican Church. While the canon of St George's Cathedral was initially sympathetic to McKnight's cause, the dean and other Anglican leaders, given the Church's sensitive position in Israel, distanced themselves from McKnight. He turned to the Prime Minister's Office, which has formal responsibility for the security services, but was given the runaround, with one official suggesting he try another, and with phone calls unreturned. 'McKnight has no standing, and we see no reason to meet him,' an official said. McKnight said, however, that he managed 'to speak to somebody who had seen somebody who had seen Vanunu and was able to confirm that Vanunu was being held in gaol' – a reference to a member of the Vanunu family who had been in touch with the lawyer representing Mordechai. In front of some one hundred foreign newsmen McKnight, speaking in the elegant surroundings of the American Colony Hotel, which is situated on the green line which once separated Israeli-controlled Western Jerusalem from Jordanian East Jerusalem, the Australian parson brought to the world the news that Vanunu was alive and well, albeit in an Israeli prison.

CHAPTER VII

The Germans

*Those who obeyed every order and every regulation of the Third
Reich destroyed, by their compliance, more spiritual values than
all the members of the resistance could manage to preserve by
their combined efforts and 'treasonable' activities.*
Fabian von Schlabrendorff

The Nazis' rise to power unquestionably placed a large number of
Germans in a deep moral dilemma. Should the loyal citizen abide by what
was, originally at least in Germany, the outcome of democratic elections,
and continue to press for change within the political system, or should one
ignore the expressed wishes of the electorate and work to undermine the
regime? And what is the honourable course to be taken when one's
country, having slipped under the control of a reviled totalitarian dictator,
opens hostilities on one's neighbours? Does one have a responsibility to
defend one's country when other nations, presented as the aggressors,
declare war?

For the overwhelming majority of Germans, including anti-Nazis, the
solution was to take the patriotic route and fight for the fatherland,
irrespective of the domestic politics involved. Certainly this had been the
position in the First World War when those opposed to the Kaiser's
determination to expand the Empire had been persuaded to take up arms
for Germany. For a few in the Second World War, like the future
Chancellor of the Federal Republic, Willy Brandt, who could not
contemplate any support for the Nazis, the preferred option was to go
abroad, and he fled to Norway in 1933, and spent the war in Sweden.

For Peter Ustinov's father, known as Klop, who had been press attaché
at the German embassy in London before the war, the obvious choice as
an anti-Nazi had been resignation from his official position, and the
acquisition of a new nationality, but for his successor in the press office,
Baron Wolfgang zu Putlitz, the issue was more complicated. His family
was still in Germany and, as a young man, he had mapped out a career for

himself as a professional diplomat. His eventual decision, based on his political commitment to communism and on his fervent opposition to Hitler, was to volunteer his services to the British Security Service as an agent. With Klop's help he became a highly valued source of information about the Foreign Ministry and about the embassy in London, and then in The Hague.

When the Gestapo eventually began to close in on zu Putlitz in 1939 he was forced to flee at very short notice from Holland to London, but other idealists who had maintained a greater degree of discretion stayed in Berlin to scheme against the Führer. Fabian von Schlabrendorff, the thoughtful Prussian aristocrat who was at the centre of the assassination plots, was careful to emphasize his loyalty to Germany when he made contact, on behalf of the resistance, with foreigners. When introduced to Churchill in 1939, shortly before the outbreak of war, he 'had no intention of letting any doubts arise about the fact that the men of the German resistance, although anti-Nazi, were unwilling to betray their country'. Clearly he was exercised by the apparent contradiction of German officers, who had sworn a personal oath of allegiance to Hitler, plotting his assassination. Could such conduct be justified as a higher form of patriotism?

> Obeying orders cannot be used as an excuse for committing or condoning a crime. This was the guiding principle of the military members of the resistance. Although technically engaged in high treason, and, with the decision to kill Hitler, in preparation for political murder, they felt that they were actually doing their duty according to the highest standards of ethics, morality, and patriotism.

Von Schlabrendorff, as one of the very few to survive Hitler's terrible vengeance, endured much hostility after the war for his opposition to the Nazis, but there were other anti-Nazis who escaped the opprobrium encountered by the German-born citizens of the Reich. His friend Gero von Gaevernitz, who acted as a link to many anti-Nazis, had the advantage of an American passport and of employment by OSS in Switzerland to protect him, and two OSS agents in particular, Fritz Molden and Fritz Kolbe, were really Austrians.

Following the *Anschluss*, of course, Austrians were considered part of the Third Reich but after the war it was entirely respectable to flaunt anti-Nazi credentials. Fritz Kolbe's story, which covered his dangerous work as OSS's master source code-named Wood, although written by him, was never published in book form, but Fritz Molden has produced a harrowing account of his numerous undercover missions into the Reich disguised as a Wehrmacht non-commissioned officer. Not surprisingly, there is a paucity of literature of this kind, for undertaking secret assignments into the Nazi heartland was not habit-forming. As for Edward Waetjen, the Abwehr agent operating under vice-consular cover in Zurich whose mother was American, the issue of divided loyalties led him to join the anti-Nazi conspirators as a courier, as he described in his never-published memoirs.

For Hans Bernd Gisevius, the anti-Nazi lawyer, the Abwehr provided a convenient billet in a consular post in Zurich which he exploited to his advantage. As a legitimate diplomat he could travel frequently, and his base in Berne provided him with a useful opportunity to establish contact with his British and American counterparts. In particular, he developed a close relationship with Allen Dulles of the OSS. However, when the attempt on Hitler's life on 20 July 1944 failed, he found it exceptionally difficult to return to Switzerland and was able to do so only with forged papers identifying him as a Gestapo official. Another conspirator implicated in the same plot, Otto John, fled to Lisbon, facilitated by his status as a senior employee of Lufthansa. His narrow evasion of the Gestapo enabled him to join the Allies, but years later many of his fellow countrymen were unwilling to forgive him for what they perceived as his treachery, even though the date of the unsuccessful assassination attempt was later declared an annual public holiday in the Federal Republic.

Some Germans who had welcomed the opportunity to take up temporary residence in neutral countries before the war could not entirely avoid becoming embroiled in the conflict. Hans Ruser, a leading German journalist based in Madrid, found himself under pressure to work for the local Abwehr organization, and reported this to his friends in the British expatriate community. Word of his predicament reached the Secret Intelligence Service, and Ruser was enrolled as a double agent with the code-name Junior. He was able to operate undetected until November 1943, when he was hastily exfiltrated from Spain, having been obliged to climb out of a window in his apartment as Gestapo officials forced their way in through the front door.

John and Ruser were among the very few Germans to defect to the Allies during the Second World War. Even Jewish refugees of German and Austrian origin who had fled persecution retained a loyalty to the Reich after their arrival in Britain. Some had agreed to work as spies as the price for their exit visas, while others could not discard an innate patriotism and were heard in their internment camps to cheer news bulletins of Axis military successes.

Naturally the opportunities for defection were rather greater for Germans stationed abroad, so only the most trusted personnel were posted to neutral countries. For the intelligence officers mixed in among the regular diplomats and the genuine businessmen, the temptation to defect must have been even greater for they possessed the professional knowledge of exactly whom to approach on the Allied side, and they were also better equipped to elude the counter-intelligence measures taken by the Nazi security apparatus to prevent such embarrassments. Nevertheless, Ruser was by no means the only Abwehr officer in a neutral country to defect, although the total number is extraordinarily low because of Allied reluctance to encourage or receive defectors. Indeed, the Abwehr was a useful refuge for opponents of the regime, protected from the unwelcome attention of the Gestapo by its enigmatic Chief, Admiral Wilhelm Canaris, and his chief of staff, General Hans Oster. Both were to be implicated in plots against Hitler and they perished on the gallows at Flossenbürg, but even in their absence some Abwehr officials, at great risk to themselves and their families, maintained a clandestine contact with their Allied counterparts, most notably in Switzerland.

In most wartime scenarios defection is a classic method of obtaining valuable intelligence. However, during the Second World War the Allies adopted a deliberate policy of discouraging potential defectors because none was judged capable of matching the depth of knowledge that had been accumulated already from the Ultra source, and from the double agents handled by MI5 and SIS. Indeed, in a memorably awkward moment in 1944 an Abwehr officer in Madrid offered to switch sides and to prove his *bona fides* by naming his organization's best spy in London. SIS knew, of course, that this individual was actually the MI5 double agent code-named Garbo, and it was obliged therefore to rebuff the putative defector. To have accepted him would have eliminated Garbo from the scene as his German controllers would have assumed him to have been compromised by the defector. Thus, far from assisting the Allied prosecution of the war, the Abwehr defectors presented a considerable hazard and were treated accordingly. Hans Ruser was an exception, and his exfiltration from Madrid became essential because if he had fallen into the hands of the Gestapo he might have revealed that he had passed information to the British over a long period, a development which would have allowed them to identify several Abwehr sources who were in fact operating as double agents. Similarly, Johann Jebsen, the Abwehr officer codenamed Artist by SIS, was accepted into the double-agent system on the same basis, with some reluctance from London. Usually to be found in the casino at Estoril, outside Lisbon, the wealthy Jebsen's plausible cover was that of a playboy and dissident German who supervised an escape line for Yugoslav evaders seeking to reach England via Portugal. This made him equally useful to both the Germans and the British but he never concealed that his true sympathies lay with the Allies. At the time of his abduction he was in a position to betray several double agents and when he was seized by the Gestapo in April 1944 the incident caused much anxiety in London because of the damage he could do. It was feared that under interrogation he might compromise several other of his acquaintances whom he must have deduced had also been double agents. As it turned out, Jebsen was incarcerated at Oranienberg concentration camp until April the following year, when he was executed, having kept silent about the duplicity of the other agents he undoubtedly suspected or knew were really under British control.

As the Allied victory became more certain, the number of Germans seeking to defect escalated proportionately, but the policy of discouragement remained intact with few exceptions. One was Dr Erich Vermehren, a devout Catholic who was stationed in Istanbul until he was persuaded to desert in December 1943. Accompanied by his wife, Vermehren was taken by SIS to Cairo for debriefing, and then flown to England via Gibraltar. For the rest of the war he worked for the Political Warfare Executive at Woburn Abbey, the propaganda unit to which Otto John was also to be attached after his arrival later the same year, in July.

The successful defections of the Vermehrens prompted more of the same kind of activity from the Abwehr at Istanbul, although those that followed found the Americans more hospitable. The Kleczkowskis, a Jewish couple operating under journalistic cover, were next, and they were followed by an Austrian, Dr Willi Hamburger, who had fallen in love with an OSS agent. All three had been recalled to Berlin to face a disciplinary inquiry, and the option of Allied captivity had looked rather more attractive than the likelihood of punishment at the hands of the Nazis, who had used the disappearance of the Vermehrens as an excuse to dissolve the Abwehr. Their defection was the catalyst for a purge of the Abwehr, which lost its chief and found its networks placed under the supervision of the Sicherheitsdienst (SD). Finally, in April 1944, Cornelia Kapp, the confidential secretary employed by the SD's representative in Ankara, defected to the Americans. She too had been persuaded to defect by her OSS lover and her information led to the exposure of an SD spy, codenamed Cicero, in the local British embassy.

An additional curiosity about zu Putlitz and Otto John is their shared distinction of having defected not once, but twice. Zu Putlitz was granted British citizenship in recognition of his invaluable work as a wartime spy but in January 1952 he disappeared without warning, only to emerge in East Berlin as a dedicated communist. Otto John's vanishing act, which took place a couple of years later, in July 1954, was not quite so simple. Mystery still surrounds Otto John but it is evident that the Nazi era and the postwar division of Germany placed many Germans in an uncomfortable moral predicament. Some of the old anti-Nazis moved abroad but the construction of the Berlin Wall restricted the path of those seeking to flee from the Soviet zone to the West. Indeed, relatively few made the perilous journey past the watch-towers and across the minefields, and of the individuals who accomplished the feat, Werner Stiller is the only senior Stasi official to have done so and to have written an account of what drove him to abandon his ideals. The paradox of his situation is that he betrayed the elite HVA and actively collaborated with the West German BND before executing his carefully planned escape. Yet the legendary head of the HVA, Markus Wolf, remained loyal to Erich Honecker's regime and, following reunification, has been convicted in Stuttgart of having conspired to subvert the West German constitution. In September 1993 he was sentenced to two years' imprisonment, which coincidentally happens to be about the period he spent in custody awaiting trial.

Soon after his retirement from the HVA Wolf wrote a history of his family, *Der Troika*, but while he described his father's devotion to Moscow, he never mentioned his own particular calling, as the Eastern Bloc's most successful spymaster, and allegedly the model for le Carré's enigmatic character of Karla. In reality Wolf did join the democracy movement in Berlin and was seen demonstrating in the streets shortly before the Berlin Wall was breached. As the HVA officer credited with recruiting and handling Gunter Guillaume, the mole who penetrated Willy Brandt's private office, Wolf is rightly regarded with some awe by his Western counterparts, and if he is considered the most accomplished agent-runner of the postwar era, then Ursula Kuczynski must be at the top of the league of successful agents.

Originally recruited by the famous Soviet spy Richard Sorge in China before the war, Ursula adopted the *nom-de-guerre* Sonya and operated undetected until 1949, when she caught a flight from London to Prague in anticipation of a visit from the British Special Branch detectives who had arrested Klaus Fuchs on a charge of betraying atomic secrets. Fuchs himself had never known the identity of his GRU case officer, the woman he met in Oxfordshire lanes around the nuclear research centre at Harwell, so he was unable to do more than give her description to his interrogators. Fearing exposure, Ursula disappeared and re-emerged in East Berlin, where she still lives, to write her extraordinary memoirs, the story of a young Jewess who dedicated her life to the Soviet cause and ended up betraying the country that had given her entire family both refuge and citizenship during the Second World War. To this day she remains devoted to the GRU, the Party, and to Len Beurton, the Briton she married to acquire a British passport.

Like the others in this chapter, Ursula would deny that she had ever been guilty of treachery, but the fact remains that if she had remained in England for very much longer she would have been arrested and at the very least charged with offences against the Official Secrets Acts. Certainly Otto John, Fritz Molden, Wolfgang zu Putlitz and Hans Bernd Gisevius were under no illusions about what would have happened to them had they been caught by the Gestapo. That Fabian von Schlabrendorff escaped with his life is remarkable.

Wolfgang zu Putlitz

It was not long before I realised that I was well and truly caught up in the web of the British Secret Service.

Upon his appointment in June 1934 to the post of press attaché in von Ribbentrop's embassy in London, Wolfgang zu Putlitz was recruited as a spy for the British SIS by his predecessor, Klop Ustinov. Having served in Washington DC and Berlin, the aristocratic and homosexual zu Putlitz, whose family came from Pots, was regarded as a key source by Ustinov and his MI5 case officer, Dick White. An active anti-Nazi, zu Putlitz was enthusiastic about helping his British friends, as he was later to confirm in his memoirs, *The Putlitz Dossier*.

In May 1938 zu Putlitz was transferred to the German embassy in The Hague, but he continued to maintain contact with SIS. However, in October 1939 the Gestapo began to accumulate evidence of a highly placed leak and their investigation concentrated on the diplomat who, alerted to their unwelcome interest, demanded to be exfiltrated. Klop Ustinov supervised the escape with Richard Stevens, the local SIS representative, flying him and his valet to England. As the first German defector of the war zu Putlitz was considered a valuable commodity and he was resettled in Jamaica with a new identity. This proved unsatisfactory and the temperamental German, loathing the Caribbean, turned up in New York where the US Office of Strategic Services hired him to compile a comprehensive *Who's Who* of prominent figures in German politics. Having completed his task zu Putlitz returned to London in January 1944, where he was befriended by Anthony Blunt of MI5, and for the remainder of the war he helped in the preparation of propaganda broadcasts to Germany.

At the end of the war zu Putlitz returned briefly to Germany but discovered that he was no longer welcome in his own country. His family estates were in ruins and there were no jobs for a man widely regarded by his contemporaries as a turncoat. Instead he returned to England to lecture German prisoners of war about democratic politics. In January 1948 Dick White helped him acquire British citizenship and later in the year he gave evidence for the prosecution at the Nuremberg war crimes trial. In January 1952, following the defection of his old friend Guy Burgess, zu Putlitz crossed into East Berlin. This was an odd move, considering that his brother had died in an East German prison in 1948, but zu Putlitz never gave a complete account of his motives, and he died in September 1975 leaving only his autobiography, which had been published in England in 1957. In it he disguises the identities of Dick White (whom he refers to as Tom Allen), Klop Ustinov ('Paul X'), his wife Nadia Benois ('Gabrielle X') and their son Peter 'Hugo X'). In this passage he recalls how the German penetration of the SIS station in The Hague compromised him and forced him to defect.

The Putlitz Dossier

Immediately the war had started the 'mystery men' attached to the Legation multiplied like rabbits. We already occupied four large houses, but now these were too small to accommodate the many new departments which were being established. A hotel with nearly a hundred rooms was taken over, lock, stock and barrel, the provide officers for the staff employed by Schultze-Bernet and Besthorn alone. The question of rent was of minor consequence, and the Dutch proprietor was only too willing to accept the terms offered, since it was unlikely that he would welcome any tourists for some time to come.

The Legation itself hummed like a beehive, and I had so much work on my hands that there were times when I scarcely knew whether I was standing on my head or my heels, for, from the moment Germany found herself at war with England and France, Holland had become Hitler's most active Intelligence centre.

Ever since diplomatic relations have existed between nations, it has always been the recognised practice on a declaration of war for the diplomatic representatives of the enemy to be treated with courtesy and afforded every facility to return home. This time-honoured custom, however, was not observed by our 'Statesman', Ribbentrop, who would not allow the British and French Ambassadors and their staffs to leave German territory until it was officially confirmed that the former occupants of the German Embassies in London and Paris were no longer on enemy soil. A formal exchange would then take place in neutral Holland.

I was informed of this novel procedure by telephone from Berlin by no less a person than Ribbentrop's tall, red-headed Chief of Protocol, Baron Dörnberg. I had instructions to see that it was carried out according to orders and 'with strict impartiality'.

The interchange with the French was accomplished fairly quickly and without incident, since the Dutch frontier is practically equidistant from Berlin and Paris and the respective trains arrived in the region of Utrecht almost simultaneously. Unforeseen difficulties, however, arose with the British. There had been some delay before a suitable ship could be chartered at Harwich for the staff of our London Embassy. Ribbentrop, therefore, kept the British Mission stranded for three days in a train somewhere just inside the German frontier. It was only when I was able to inform Dörnberg that the British ship was reported in Dutch territorial waters that the German train with its British occupants received permission to proceed.

On Dörnberg's instructions I was to go to Rotterdam to take charge of the handover, and told Willi to get ready to drive me there. Just as I was about to leave, Schultze-Bernet emerged from the Legation and handed me a sealed package.

'Here are 250,000 guilders in Dutch banknotes urgently required in Berlin to be delivered into trustworthy hands,' he said. 'Give them to my friend, Herr Z, who will arrive with the others from London. He'll know what to do with them.'

I was relieved to know that Schultze-Bernet's faith in my trustworthiness evidently remained unshaken, and with his quarter of a million guilders on my knees, I set out for Rotterdam.

During the drive Willi kept repeating: 'This is an act of Providence. Let's go aboard the British ship and hide. With that cash we could live in England for the duration of the war!'

'No, Willi,' I said frankly. 'If we get out, we'll go with clean hands, and not like thieves.'

'The swine are only going to use the dough for some dirty business anyway,' he answered fiercely.

He was certainly right, but I did not give way to his tempting suggestion, and handed the packet to the mysterious Herr Z.

Although I delivered a signed receipt from the latter to Schultze-Bernet, I was later accused by the Nazis of embezzling this money. It may, of course, have vanished when in Herr Z's possession, but certainly not while I was in charge of it.

The train from Germany had not yet arrived when the British ship docked, and our London Germans remained on board or strolled along the quay in the sunshine for nearly an hour. Everyone looked so utterly dejected that they might well have been on their way to a funeral. The Ambassador, von Dircksen, had been recalled to Berlin several weeks earlier, and Theodor Kordt had acted as Chargé d'Affaires in his absence. Kordt and his wife remained in their cabin, so I went in to see them. Both were in a state of acute distress and had tears in their eyes. Kordt told me that he had done his utmost up to the very last to prevent war between England and Germany, and even had lengthy discussions with Vansittart. But nothing would induce the British not to honour their guarantee to Poland. Hitler's foreign policy may, indeed, have been mad, but never at any time had he wanted war with England.

'It was all in vain,' Kordt added. 'Either way we are finished. If the Nazis win, Germany will become a vast madhouse; if the other side wins, we shall be wiped off the face of the map.'

'What do you intend to do?' I asked.

'I really don't know,' he said despairingly. 'It's impossible for a man with any decency to stay at the Foreign Office and share the responsibility. The right thing would be to join the Reichswehr and be killed honourably.'

I did not agree with these views, but could at least sympathise with them. I lost all respect for Kordt, however, when he emerged as Ambassador in Berne three weeks later, and was responsible for the secret Nazi news-service to England. He never once ran foul of the Nazis during the war. But he intrigued with Allan Dulles, Chief of the US Secret Service in Switzerland during the final phase of the struggle, and was subsequently regarded as one of the leading conspirators in the plot of July 20th, 1944. He was appointed Director of the Political Department on the establishment of the West German Foreign Office, and later became Adenauer's Ambassador in Athens.

When I accompanied him to the German train on this occasion at Rotterdam, I did not believe him capable of such lack of character. Followed by his mournful staff, he strode with bowed head past the assembled British from Berlin, who surveyed him with a weary, but hard and hostile expression in their eyes.

In the meantime, Willi had been talking to a waiter in the German dining-car. He told me that the latter had envied him his job in neutral Holland and showed no sign of pleasure in the prospect of returning to Germany. The unfortunate staff of the train had little chance of evading their fate, but not so the diplomats. Yet when I looked carefully through the list of their names in the hope that at least one or two would be missing, I found they were all there. All my colleagues had allowed themselves to be hustled back to the Hitlerian slaughterhouse like a flock of sheep.

When Chamberlain declared war on the Third Reich, heavy deliveries of British petrol, copper and other vital war materials were in transit to the Rhineland and the Ruhr. These were now lying in ships and railway trucks in Holland, and one of Butting's and Schultze-Bernet's main objects was to get these valuable supplies through to Germany as quickly as possible. Since the Dutch frontiers were officially closed, this would be no easy matter. Thus some form of illegal means would have to be used, which meant that Dutch collaborators would be needed.

There was no shortage of the latter. Offers of help flowed into the Legation daily and, as I was responsible for the incoming mail, these letters were submitted to me for delivery. My instructions were to forward all such correspondence immediately to Schultze-Bernet. But before doing so, I naturally read them and discovered that some employees of Shell, the Anglo-Dutch Oil Company, displayed a remarkable willingness to offer their services in supplying the needs of Hitler's war machine.

Since I was actively helping to feed the Nazi arsenals by allowing this game to continue, I felt it my duty to do something to sabotage its success. Every drop of oil, every ounce of metal to reach the German armament factories would help to prolong the war.

I therefore decided to make a list of those names which seemed to me particularly influential and dangerous, and see that it came into Paul's hands. I had not hitherto realised what intimate business relations the great international monopolies maintained, even in wartime.

I had no idea to whom Paul would pass this information, but I felt certain he would make good use of it.

It was common knowledge at The Hague that British Intelligence was directed from the Passport Office of the British Consulate at Scheveningen by a certain Captain Stevens. I had never set eyes on the latter and had always avoided meeting any of his associates.

I was completely nonplussed when three days after I had sent Willi to Paul with the list of names, Zech suddenly asked me: 'Do you think there is anyone here who is in touch with Captain Stevens?'

I asked what possible reason he could have for even suspecting such a thing.

'Schultze-Bernet has just been here,' he replied, 'and insists that Stevens is receiving highly secret information from the German Legation.'

I began to feel thoroughly alarmed, and that evening sent Willi off again to tell Paul what had occurred. But Paul merely laughed and sent back a message assuring me that my imagination was running riot. However, after luncheon the next day, I found Schultze-Bernet waiting in my ante-room with a face as black as thunder.

'What's the matter?' I asked as casually as I could. 'Is anything wrong?'

'Quite a lot,' he answered, eyeing me keenly. 'Are these names, by any chance, familiar to you?' he asked, mentioning the name of a Rotterdam banker and one or two of the Shell employees who were on the list I had sent to Paul.

'I meet a great many people, Herr Schultze-Bernet,' I fenced. 'It's quite impossible for me to remember them all. However, I may have met these fellows. What is it you want to know about them?'

'They happen to be among those working for me, and they have been denounced to Stevens,' he said, glaring at me.

'But how do you know that?' I asked. 'Did Stevens tell you? I can't for the life of me see how you could know otherwise!'

'My dear Putlitz,' he said pompously, 'I would not be Schultze-Bernet if I hadn't an agent with Stevens. I know everything that goes on in his set-up. Where could he have got hold of these names except from here? Answer me that.'

'You may, of course, be right. In any case, I can think of nothing to justify your suspicion,' I answered firmly.

'Then I must make further enquiries,' he said ominously. 'I can assure you I intend to get to the bottom of this.'

Although we shook hands as he left, he was obviously far from convinced. It was vividly clear to me that I was now in the gravest danger and would have to get out of Holland as quickly as possible.

Hans Bernd Gisevius

The more a man became outwardly involved in the system,
the more difficult it was for him to keep himself
untainted inwardly by it.

An anti-Nazi with impeccable credentials, Gisevius had used his official role as a Gestapo officer and diplomat, carrying a diplomatic bag to Berne, as a cover for his contacts with the Allies. He had been recruited as a young lawyer in July 1933 when the Gestapo was a branch of the regular police in Prussia. His career as an advocate had been cut short by his Leftist political views, which had brought him into conflict with strike-breaking employers in Düsseldorf, where he had been blacklisted. Despite this apparent handicap Gisevius joined the Gestapo and made contact with a circle of anti-Nazis. In February 1940 Gisevius was appointed a vice-consul in Zurich but his post was really a cover for a link that had been established between Canaris, as head of the Abwehr, and the Allies. Initially reporting to the British, who gave him disappointingly lukewarm support for his political testament, *To the Bitter End*, Gisevius had turned to Allen Dulles of the OSS in February 1943. His information, in the form of authentic German documents, was regarded as exceptionally valuable, and the Americans provided him with the secretarial facilities he needed to complete his manuscript.

Throughout 1943 Gisevius maintained his links with Dulles and also acted as a trusted conduit between Canaris and his Polish mistress, Halina Szymanska. In July 1944, however, he announced that he was returning to Berlin to participate in a plot to assassinate Hitler. The attempt, which took place on 20 July, failed and Gisevius went into hiding until August, when he sent a message to Dulles in Switzerland. False Gestapo papers were prepared for his use and in January 1945, and in spite of his exceptional height, 'Dr Hoffman' succeeded in crossing the German frontier unrecognized at Kreuzingen, and in being reunited with his elderly mother in Zurich.

During the Nuremberg trials in April 1946 Gisevius spent three days in the witness box giving evidence for the banker Hjalmar Schacht and against Hermann Goering and his cohorts. He later emigrated to the United States but, after a period in Texas, he remarried and moved first to Germany and then to Lake Geneva near Vevey, where he continued to write until his death in 1974. In his book, which was published in 1948, he considered the factors which led him to reject the Nazis, a path followed by so few of his countrymen.

To the Bitter End

Unfortunately, the phrase 'collective guilt' has been abused with evil intent and ill results in recent years. Generalizations are never salutary.

Often their effect is the opposite of the intended one, for after a time the pendulum swings in the other direction – and again swings too far. Then it is said that everything is relative, everything is destined; what could we 'little people' do to stop the daemonic forces? and in fact the killing, the pillaging, the cynicism, were so monstrous that we often ask whether real men were capable of these things or whether altogether inhuman forces were not behind them. Not the individual criminals but the extent of their crimes assume, to our horrified eyes, superhuman proportions. Nevertheless, at the present moment nothing would be more dangerous than to blur over the personal responsibility – and therefore the guilt – of every individual.

This is not a matter of pharasaical sitting in judgment; what we are aiming at is a vital and generally valid political lesson, and for this reason we are in duty bound not to conceal or cover up what went on in Germany during the past twelve years. Above all, we must understand the inherent logic of events; we must see why things had to happen – and to end – as they did. Today the Germans can no longer recognize themselves. The Nazi epoch seems to them a confused nightmare which they try irritably to shake off in order to clear the mind for a fresh day's work. Best of all, they would like to forget the whole diabolic business. Is it really sheer hypocrisy when they advance a thousand-and-one reasons to 'explain' all the incomprehensible facts?

We ought to consider carefully and not satisfy ourselves with the simple answer that the Germans were or are a nation of devils. The self-enslavement of sixty or eighty million people remains an historic phenomenon of tremendous importance, and in the age of the atomic bomb it is a phenomenon that must be disquieting for all non-Germans as well. It is incontrovertible that there existed in Germany a class of moral and honourable men of the highest quality. The obvious question is: How could such men permit themselves to be overrun by the Nazi usurpers without offering resistance? Is the civilization of all other nations impregnably fortified against similar outbreaks of imminent evil?

It was with this in mind that I attempted to arrange the history of 1933 to 1938 around certain psychological turning-points. I wanted to show how the Nazi catastrophe began, because the guilt that later emerged can be understood only against the background of a slow – and often initially unperceived – growth of complicity.

The Reichstag fire, June 30th, and the Fritsch crisis were plain signposts along the precipitous road to revolutionary totality. Each event provided in itself a clear, definite set of facts. To be entirely candid, however, we must admit that, in spite of the clarity of the facts, there remain elements that are mysterious, opaque and bewildering for foreign observers as well. A small group of men on top appeared guilty or responsible, and below them were millions who either were unsuspecting or without influence. In the beginning the latter did not at all perceive what responsibility they were being forced to share. Their real guilt began when they did recognize the crimes being committed in their name, and neglected to oppose them; that is to say, their duty to oppose the regime really began at a stage when effective opposition had become immeasurably more difficult.

From the middle of 1938 on, the direction in which things were heading became terrifyingly clear even to those far removed from the centres of government. From month to month the outline of things to come grew more and more distinct. It was clear that 'this man Hitler' wanted 'his' war. The history of all revolutions was being repeated: first terror raged at home; then an adventure abroad was embarked upon. By that time, however, too many people were already caught in their own trap. Is it not altogether uncanny the way these ministers, economists, scholars and bishops, and above all the hesitant generals, acted again and again against their better judgment? With open eyes they let themselves be dragged down into a general and a personal disaster.

These psychological or political considerations must not divert us from the question of guilt. Rather, they should lead us to consider that question more profoundly and more honestly. Naturally no serious-minded person can pronounce all Germans guilty in the criminal sense. We have seen how careful the Nuremberg judges were, even with so prominent a group of persons as the members of the Reich government; but when such a calamity descends upon a civilized nation, and when for twelve years that nation is incapable of throwing off the shame that burdens it, it goes against the sound ethical instinct of people to cast all the blame upon a clique of leaders, no matter whether that clique is numbered in the dozens, the hundreds or the thousands. When such a disaster takes place, there must have been something wrong with those who were led or misled.

What is that thing? One of the vital lessons that we must learn from the German disaster is the ease with which a people can be sucked down into the morass of inaction; let them as individuals fall prey to over-cleverness, opportunism or cowardliness and they are irrevocably lost. In this mass epoch it is by no means a settled thing that acts alone make for guilt. Passive acceptance, intellectual subservience, or, in religious terms, failure to pray against the evil, may constitute a kind of silent support for authoritarian rule. Once the system of terror has been installed, however, there is only one course remaining to each individual and to all individuals collectively: to fight the terrorists with the same courage and tenacity, with the same willingness to take risks, that they employ in war-time under 'orders' when they fight against the 'enemy'.

There are some Germans who mistakenly examine the history of the Nazi Revolution in search of 'daemonic forces' or other excuses. Everyone knows that terrorism and Gestapo methods existed in other places – and still exist. No one will attempt to deny that others were also guilty – and still are. In the final analysis there were millions of unteachable persons throughout the world who made a pact with the forces of Revolution and only came to their senses when the Revolution swallowed them alive. These provisos may assert many psychological or political truths; they may serve to warn the rest of the world against hasty or one-sided condemnation; but they do not excuse the Germans.

Otto John

*My permanent nightmare was that I might have to fight
for Hitler in the forthcoming war.*

A senior Abwehr officer, Otto John also worked as Lufthansa's chief lawyer, and it was in this capacity that he arrived in Lisbon in November 1942. During his stay he made contact with the British SIS and alerted his case officer to the existence of an anti-Nazi group based within his organization in Berlin. In February 1943 he returned to Lisbon to report on the progress made by his fellow conspirators but he was given a deliberately discouraging response by SIS, which was anxious not to raise Soviet suspicions by developing formal links with any German opposition movement.

Undeterred, in March 1943 John participated in an abortive attempt on Hitler's life, which collapsed when the British-made bomb placed on the Führer's aircraft failed to detonate. A further assassination bid misfired on 20 July 1944, forcing John to flee to Spain where he contacted SIS. As he later explained, 'I felt no urge to provide a lone heroic example and become a political martyr. In any case the political effect would have been nil. There was no resistance movement.'

Arrangements were made by SIS to exfiltrate John from Madrid to a safe-house in Lisbon but it was raided by the Portuguese secret police and John was imprisoned as a suspected RAF pilot. Under interrogation John acknowledged his true identity, an admission which was reported to the German embassy and caused a member of the local Abwehr, Fritz Cramer, to be assigned the task of assassinating John. Actually Cramer himself nurtured anti-Nazi sympathies and instead of carrying out the murder he tipped off SIS and allowed them to negotiate

John's release into British safe-keeping. Once freed by PIDE, John was flown to London where he was employed by the Political Warfare Executive in preparing radio propaganda broadcasts for the Soldatensender Calais station at Woburn Abbey, were he worked alongside Wolfgang zu Putlitz, a man he later described as 'an odd political crank'.

After the war John returned to Germany and acted as an interpreter during the Nuremberg trials, and in 1950 was nominated by the British as the first director of the BfV, the Commission for the Protection of the Constitution. Among his tasks was to cultivate sources in the East, and one of his contacts was Wolfgang zu Putlitz, whom he regarded as unreliable. However, it was as the head of the security agency that John disappeared in July 1954, either the victim of an abduction or a willing defector to the East. Soon after his arrival in East Germany he gave a press conference in which he announced his adherence to communism, and he left the distinct impression that his performance was a voluntary act. Later he was to insist that he had been kidnapped and, at his reappearance in the West, assert that his previous public statements had been made under duress. According to the defector Piotr Deriabin, John had been blackmailed by the Soviets, who had discovered evidence of John's secret contact and collaboration with the Nazis during the war.

After his unexpected reappearance in December 1955 he was arrested and in December 1956 sentenced to five years' imprisonment in solitary confinement for treason. He was released from Munster prison at the end of July 1958, and he now lives in retirement at Hohenburg, near Igls in the Austrian Tyrol. In his 1969 autobiography (published in English in 1972) he explains the background to his involvement in the anti-Nazi movement.

Twice Through the Lines

In the last six months of peace when the psychological build-up for war against Poland was under way, I mostly went about with people who were considering plans for the overthrow of the regime. In the spring of 1939 they had concluded that Hitler should be allowed to have his war so that, under the shock effect both on the armed forces and the people of some military defeat, they could overturn Hitler and his regime. My assistance in these plans was now counted upon, particularly by Colonel Oster. He was still impressed by the fact that I had heard of Hitler's order for the invasion of the rump of Czechoslovakia before the Head of the Abwehr.

The time of decision was drawing nearer. In the summer Gablenz made a round-the-world tour with the intention of reorganising Lufthansa's overseas representation on his return. He had picked me for South America. I still regarded the prospect of having to fight for Hitler with horror. Having no military training, I was earmarked in the Lufthansa mobilisation plan for call-up to a transport squadron. On the other hand I felt myself obligated towards the circle of men who had placed their confidence in me and I felt that to clear off just now would be a dirty trick.

I talked all this over with my brother Hans. He was at this time working as legal assistant in Leipzig University, but frequently came to Berlin to get the latest news from me. Politically he was more extreme than I and as a student had collected a circle of left-wing intellectuals around him; to my parents' consternation he had even been prominent in anti-Nazi demonstrations by various left-wing organisations. Since the Left failed to produce any real resistance to the regime, however, he lost all interest in political activity and devoted himself exclusively and intensively to his professional studies. Discussing the pros and cons of staying in Berlin with him, I came to the decision to remain.

Gablenz returned from his world tour and gave senior personnel of Lufthansa a talk on the information he had acquired about air traffic. In this he said, looking at me: 'There are many interesting jobs for us in South America. This is a field for determined young men who have the necessary spirit of enterprise to do a real pioneering job.' Hans Hickmann, a friend of Klaus Bonhoeffer and myself who ran the 'Fuel' Division, noticed this together with the fact that Gablenz had looked at me at this point and he congratulated me on my luck. Unfortunately I had to tell him that I had decided to remain in Berlin. I now had to tell Gablenz also quite frankly that I had changed my mind about going abroad. He listened to me thoughtfully – not at all his habit – and finally said: 'For God's sake don't produce another Kapp *putsch* or things will get even worse here.'

In mid-July Dietrich Bonhoeffer (brother of Klaus – five years younger) returned via London from a trip to America. I had met him and his friend Pastor Eberhard Bethge in the Bonhoeffer house but only in passing. Both later became well known as activists in the 'Confessional Church' resistance movement. Dietrich Bonhoeffer could well have dodged the war by remaining in America as many of his friends advised him to do, but he insisted on sharing such sufferings as our people might have to undergo in the war which had now become inevitable. He was martyred as a result of his battle against Hitlerian barbarity, being hanged in Flossenbürg concentration camp shortly before the end of the war. His example was often an encouragement to me. His return from America before the outbreak of war was a special source of strength to me since I had taken a similar decision myself.

Ever since the spring of 1939 we had known that Hitler had issued his orders to the Wehrmacht for the invasion of Poland. To me this meant that Poland was doomed. Thekla Hauschild, who was Polish by birth, said: 'Our people will fight to the last man,' but I was sure that dive-bomber attacks on Polish cities and communication centres would soon reduce both the country and the people to paralysis. Klaus Bonhoeffer and others had no conception of the striking power of the Luftwaffe and most of the army officers in the anti-Hitler movement thought only in terms of land warfare; they were all convinced that the Poles would hold out until the British and French came to their assistance. This seemed to me more than questionable. I saw no hope of saving Poland from invasion by the Wehrmacht until negotiations were opened between London and Moscow to encircle Hitler.

An alliance between the Western Powers and Stalin would certainly not have prevented Hitler attacking Poland because he was bent on war. If, however, he was strategically surrounded, we could count upon an early military defeat and this would have created the psychological conditions for an anti-Hitler military rising. We had no inkling, of course, that Hitler would succeed in outwitting Chamberlain once more and concluding a non-aggression pact with Stalin.

In Moscow the British and French delegations had had dust thrown in their eyes by Stalin exactly as had Theodor Kordt, the German Chargé d'Affaires, by Lord Halifax, during the 'Sudeten crisis'. Meanwhile Kordt and his brother Erich, who was head of Ribbentrop's personal staff, had made a further, somewhat peculiar, attempt to act as advisers to the British government and so save the peace. They had a friend, Philip Conwell-Evans, who had developed Nazi leanings when a lecturer in Königsberg University and who had played a not inconsiderable role on his return to England as a source of information for people close to Chamberlain. 'This silly little man,' as his British secret service watchdog described him to me after the war, was bent on maintaining peace and friendship with the Nazi Germany which he admired so much. During the Polish crisis Conwell-Evans invited the Kordt brothers, at their request, to his private apartment to meet Vansittart for a last-minute secret discussion. In a final attempt to avert war the Kordt brothers urged upon Vansittart the conclusion by the British government of a 'heterogeneous coalition' with Moscow. Once again, as during the Sudeten crisis, the British government was supposed to avert war by threatening Hitler with military measures, this time based on a British–Soviet alliance. At the time Vansittart thought that the Kordt brothers were unnecessarily anxious. The British government would definitely conclude an agreement with the Soviet Union, he said.

Vansittart was wrong. He may at the time have had the sonorous title of 'Senior Diplomatic Adviser to His Britannic Majesty's Government', but, as he said to me after the war, he had in fact been kicked upstairs by Chamberlain because from the outset he had opposed the latter's catastrophic appeasement policy. Important political dispatches were withheld from him and his advice was not listened to. Chamberlain did not want a pact with the Russians; he thought that he could come to some understanding with Hitler against the bolsheviks. Accordingly he ignored the advice of the Kordt brothers, whose secret talks – diplomatically unauthorised, of course – only became known to me after the war. Although in the post-war period much was made of this secret diplomacy as a remarkable aspect of resistance, I have never been able to see much sense in it, perhaps because I lacked the sapience conferred by diplomatic training. A British–Soviet alliance never had any prospect of restraining Hitler from war because neither Chamberlain nor Stalin wanted an alliance.

With the announcement of the Hitler–Stalin pact war became only a matter of days. Halder, the Chief of Staff, who on assuming his office had undertaken to do all in his power to avert war, waved Colonel Oster away when the latter made a last attempt to hold him to his allegiance to the plans for a *coup*. Halder said after the war: 'With the conclusion of the non-aggression pact with Russia, Germany's military situation was such that a breach of my oath could not be justified.' After the war he nevertheless presented himself as the 'foremost resistance fighter among the generals', although in a monograph he also pointed out to the German people that the war against Russia would have been won, had Hitler taken his military advice!

Until the final failure of all our efforts I was in a position to observe from the closest of quarters what resistance by this type of general meant. Frequently I was in despair. Sometimes I thought of dropping everything, getting into a Lufthansa aircraft and taking refuge in London so that I might do my best to put a quicker end to Hitler's rule of terror. I never did so, not even in the spring of 1944 when, during the final months before our *coup*, the Gestapo was hard on my heels. I was already too deeply involved in the anti-Hitler conspiracy.

Ursula Kuczynski

*What I did not like in our country was the dogmatism
within the party which increased with the years, nor
the exaggeration of our achievements and the covering
up of faults.*

Born in 1907 into a Berlin family that was to become well known for its commitment to radical socialism, Ursula's father moved to England in 1933, as the Nazis took power, to take up an academic appointment in Oxford. Her sister, Brigitte, was recruited as an agent by the Soviet GRU and her brother, Jürgen, was to lead the KDP in exile. Ursula worked in a bookshop selling 'progressive literature' and briefly visited New York to do relief work among the homeless. In 1929 she married an architect, Rolf Hamburger, and they set up home together in Shanghai, where she fell under the influence of the Soviet agents Richard Sorge and Agnes Smedley.

Already committed to the communist cause, Ursula was recruited into the GRU by Sorge, although at that early stage she was uncertain of the exact nature of the organization. 'Only two years later did I know that it operated under the intelligence department of the Red Army General Staff. It made no difference to me. I knew that my activities served the comrades of the country in which I lived.'

In February 1931 Ursula's and Rolf's son Micha was born but this event did not cement their marriage, which was under strain primarily because of political differences. 'I could not talk to him about the people who were closest to me or the work on which my life was centred.' Hamburger was excluded from Ursula's clandestine activities and had no idea that Sorge used their house to store secret information. Only later did he convert to communism, by which time Ursula had left him. In the meantime she had spent six months in Moscow undergoing a GRU training course, returning to meet Rolf in Prague and return to China via Trieste in April 1934. They settled in Nukden and in June 1935 moved to Peking where she became pregnant by Ernst, a GRU agent with whom she had trained in Moscow.

Late in 1935 Ursula returned to Moscow with Micha, and after a brief stopover continued her journey via Leningrad to London, where she was reunited with her family. She then moved with Rolf to Warsaw, where Janina was born in April 1936, but after a mission to Danzig was recalled to Moscow to receive further training, the Order of the Red Banner and a new assignment, in Switzerland. In October 1938 Ursula was living under a false passport in the village of Caux, above Montreux, with her two children, supervising a network of agents which included members of the International Labour Organization of the League of Nations in Geneva and the I. G. Farben plant in Frankfurt. In 1939 she divorced Rolf, who had been ordered back to China, and married a young English veteran of the Spanish Civil War, Len Beurton, in order to acquire British citizenship.

In December 1940 Ursula made her way to England, via Barcelona, Madrid and Lisbon, with her children and rented a house in Oxford where, in late 1942, she was joined briefly by Len before he was called up for service in the Coldstream Guards. While in England Ursula acted as a GRU case officer for Klaus Fuchs, a role that led to MI5's interest in her in August 1947. Although on the one occasion she was interviewed she denied any connection with espionage, she fled to East Germany in February 1950, the day before Fuchs appeared at the Old Bailey. She lives today in East Berlin, an unapologetic communist, devoted to Len and their son Peter, who was born in September 1943. Her biography was published in 1977, and in it she recalls her attempts to re-establish contact with her Soviet controllers, following her trek across the Continent.

Sonya's Report

We had arrived in England with the bare essentials for clothing ourselves. I possessed no furniture, had no claim to any housing and had to support two children at boarding school. I could not meet my commitments much longer. But I did not reveal these worries to my family. None of them had much to spare, and besides, moving in with any of them was out of the question. My parents were staying with friends in an overcrowded house. Weepy was herself looking for somewhere to live. Brigitte had a one-roomed flat. Sabine, wanting to marry, needed accommodation. Reni was studying in Cambridge. Jürgen's home was just large enough for his family of four. They lived modestly on an income of £250 a year.

There was no prospect of being able to pay for the children's school much longer, of finding anywhere to live, of meeting someone from Centre or of bringing Len back to England.

I was worried about Rolf, too. He had written to me from China now and again, either direct to Switzerland or via my sisters in London, and he always remembered the children's birthdays. Then he had informed me that he was going into the interior. For many months there was no news of him. Finally I heard that Rolf had been arrested by the Chinese, and I knew his life was in danger.

Later I heard the details. Ernst and Rolf had been unable to establish a basis for their work in Shanghai. Rolf had hoped to make better contact in Chongqing, the seat of government. He was arrested while he was building his transmitter or sending his first radio message. I believe he was freed through the efforts of the Soviet Union.

At last, in April 1941, I found a furnished bungalow. It was one of a row in Kidlington, two and a half miles outside Oxford. The rent was very high and I was down to the last of my savings. But I enjoyed not having a landlady and – above all – I could have my children with me.

When I went to the London meeting place in May, I had all but given up hope. A man approached me, not the first in this accursed street, but this time he was the one I wanted. He greeted me with the code words I was waiting for, and I glided down the street and along two more as if on wings to the place where we were to talk. The Soviet comrade Sergei (my cover-name for him) brought me greetings from Centre and congratulations on my arrival. He also handed me enough money to allay all my financial worries. A car accident had delayed his appearance.

With the unflappable serenity of the Russian people, he would never have understood how oppressive those months had been for me. I decided that from now on I would not let myself be shaken by things like this, but bear in mind the philosophic words of the harbour pilot on the quay at Vladivostok. I would try to think of the vast distances between the stars and the earth, and that would calm me down.

Sergei explained the significance of our work in a country that was at war with the Nazis, but where influential reactionary circles were always ready to come to an understanding with Hitler against the Soviet Union. Centre needed news. What contacts could I take up? With the military? With political circles? I was to try to establish an information network. When could my transmitter begin to function?

As always I was given plenty of time. Centre never pushed me for deadlines. I was the impatient one, and more likely to rush into something than take my time over it. I had already bought all the transmitter parts and worked on them between praying and playing cards in the Rectory. It could be in operation within 24 hours.

I hoped that Jürgen, and perhaps Father too, would help me obtain information. Father, who was very tactful, had never asked me about my work. Now it seemed right to tell him something about it, but without mentioning its military destination. He was the only member of the family who knew about my decoration. Father had no head for such things and therefore did not recognise its military character, but when I told him that Comrade Kalinin had given it to me in the Kremlin, he was moved.

I had only to let him know that I was interested in political and economic facts for my work. He nodded and that was all. It hardly had any effect on our conversations since they usually took the form of political discussions in any case. Mostly Father mixed with left-wing economists and Labour politicians; at that time many of them had some sort of job connected with the war effort, and Father told me what he heard. But as I said, there were no big secrets, but political talks we would have had anyway.

Hitler's attack on the Soviet Union in June 1941 made a powerful impact on Britain. I am sure I need not describe how shattered I felt by the event. But there wasn't much time to brood.

I listened to Churchill's speech promising full support to the Soviet Union, made notes and tried to evaluate them. As usual with Churchill, in rhetoric and style his speech was brilliant. I went to London to talk to Father, who told me that Britain's leading politicians and soldiers were counting on the Soviet Union's defeat within three months. Father had these views confirmed by Sir Stafford Cripps, a leading member of the Labour Party and Ambassador to the Soviet Union from 1940 to 1942.

'The German Wehrmacht will slice through Russia like a hot knife through butter,' Cripps added. Later this opinion became general knowledge, but at the time of my report to Centre, neither they nor anyone else in the Soviet Union appeared to have heard of it. I received a telegram of thanks from the Director. This was a rare occurrence. Perhaps that is why I can remember this particular report while I have forgotten so many others.

The governments of capitalist countries had long made the error of underestimating the Soviet Union. They simply could not get it into their heads that a workers' state with communists in power could 'hold out'. Their error began with attempts at military intervention after the October Revolution in Russia; it continued with their non-recognition of the Soviet Union over so many years and was still current, as the words of Cripps testified, at the beginning of the Second World War.

Hitler began to deploy the full might of his army and air force against the Soviet Union. This brought significant relief to England; the threat of invasion came to an end and Nazi bombing attacks also diminished.

After Hitler's invasion of the Soviet Union, several days went by without response to my call-sign, but then they came on the air again. I used the transmitter twice a week. Every fortnight I went to London. At first I only talked to Jürgen and Father. Jürgen was as always enormously productive. Apart from articles in several journals such as the British *Labour Monthly*, *Labour Research*, and pamphlets on *Labour Conditions in War and Peace* and one on *Hunger and Work*, he had embarked on his life's work on labour conditions under industrial capitalism. This was to grow to 40 volumes. Jürgen was also preparing economic analyses for the Soviet embassy. He passed on to me useful information outside the field of economics. From my conversations with Father and Jürgen I drew up four to six reports a month, but Jürgen informed me more consciously than my father did.

In accordance with the rules, I kept strictly away from the British party. Nor did I take up any contacts with the emigrant German party in England, except for Jürgen, who was at that time the group's political organiser. I talked to him about the possibility of obtaining more information, especially military, and he arranged for me to meet the German comrade Hans Kahle. As a divisional commander, Hans had been a leading light in the International Brigades in Spain, where he had been well respected for his courage and ability to make quick decisions. In England he worked, among other things, as a military correspondent of the magazines *Time* and *Fortune*, which belonged to the famous American Luce company. I do not know the background of this particular occupation, but in any case it was a fertile source of information. Centre agreed to my contact with Hans Kahle and so I began to see him, too, about twice a month. This resulted in some useful reports to Centre, who frequently asked follow-up questions which gave us some idea of what was important to them. I enjoyed working with Hans Kahle. After victory, he returned to East Germany and took over responsible work, but – sad loss for our country – he died soon after.

In London I stayed with my parents or one of my sisters. At times I would meet Hans Kahle there. My sisters were out at work and knew nothing of this. Apart from Father and Jürgen, I spoke to no one about what I was doing – neither then nor afterwards. Even my children, long after they were adults, knew nothing of my Order of the Red Banner until thirty years later, when a Soviet General located me in the GDR and awarded it to me a second time. (It was my original medal, number 944; the certificate was also there. How carefully it had been preserved through all the ravages of war!)

Apart from radio contact with the Soviet Union, I continued to meet Comrade Sergei. After I had succeeded in making some military contacts, I received material that could not be sent by radio. At one of these meetings, Sergei gave me a little parcel measuring about eight by six inches. It contained a small transmitter. Although I was still as unenthusiastic as ever about theory, I became attached to this reliable, handy and technically superior instrument. I dismantled my own transmitter, which was six times the size, and hid the parts for emergency use. Altogether I transmitted from England for five or six years. Amateur radio activities had – as in Switzerland – been strictly forbidden for the duration.

While I was in England the 'Sergeis' changed two or three times. I looked forward to our appointments which, apart from the initial failure, were always kept to the minute. The comrades were friendly, experienced and competent. We met in the street during the black-out, preferably at a time when we were unlikely to be surprised by an air-raid siren, and never for more than a quarter of an hour.

I have mentioned several times that my illegal work did not frighten me, but I must confess that in the blacked-out city, without street lamps or even a glimmer of window light, I was afraid. There was hardly a soul on the streets and anybody who did pass by was invisible. I stood in the pitch dark, expecting somebody to grab my face or throat at any minute. Whenever I heard gentle footsteps, I would hold my breath in fear and be relieved if they belonged to 'our man'.

Fabian von Schlabrendorff

Normal respect for authority is a necessary trait for any law-abiding citizen; but the average German's lack of natural poise led him to the other extreme: excessive civil and military obedience, with the inherent danger of accepting and obeying any law and any authority, whether good or bad. This trait was exploited to the hilt by Hitler.

A conservative Prussian by background, and a lawyer by training, having read law at the universities of Berlin and Halle, Fabian von Schlabrendorff had been an active anti-Nazi from the time he read *Mein Kampf*. In the summer of 1939 he called on politicians in London to persuade them to take a tough line against Hitler, but he found that only Churchill had any grasp of the Führer's aggressive intentions. During the war he joined General Henning von Tresckow as his aide-de-camp at Army Group Centre and was one of the original, key organizers of the resistance inside the top ranks of the Wehrmacht. It was created under the cover of the Wednesday Club dining association and was headed by General Ludwig Beck, who was to head the first post-Nazi government, and Carl Goerdeler, the widely respected former Lord Mayor of Leipzig who was to run the administration. As an intellectual and a lawyer, Schlabrendorff had given considerable thought to the moral basis upon which he was to act.

By itself, criminal law legislation exercises moral influence only when it coincides with the dictates of ethics and morality. Such coincidence was notably lacking in all the political laws of the Third Reich. Therefore, actions taken in accord with a higher duty were morally justified even if and when, from the point of view of the existing criminal law, they constituted high treason.

Schlabrendorff was the officer who primed and placed a bomb on Hitler's plane during a visit to Smolensk in March 1943 but on that occasion the detonator failed. A second attempt in July 1944 proved disastrous as many of the participants in the plot revealed themselves, believing Hitler to be dead. When the news of his survival reached Berlin the conspirators were rounded up, and some were executed instantly. Colonel Count von Stauffenberg was shot by firing squad the same day and hundreds of others were arrested and tortured. General Tresckow opted to commit suicide on the Russian Front in fear of naming his fellow conspirators, and this enabled Schlabrendorff to avoid arrest for a month, until mid-August, when he was taken from his unit in Poland to Berlin and interrogated by the Gestapo at their headquarters in the Prinz Albrechtstrasse.

Despite torture, solitary confinement and forged confessions identifying him as a traitor, Schlabrendorff resisted his captors and was eventually brought to trial in December 1944 accused of high treason. The first hearing was adjourned until early February 1945, and then interrupted by a daylight air raid in which the President of the People's Court, the notorious Ronald Freisler, was killed. Finally, Schlabrendorff's trial opened in March, but when evidence of his torture was produced the case was dismissed. Instead of execution, as he had been expecting, Schlabrendorff was transferred to Flossenbürg concentration camp, and as the Allies advanced into Germany he was moved to Dachau and finally Niedernhausen in Austria, south of the Brenner Pass. Here, on 4 May 1945, he was liberated by American troops and flown to Naples. Later he was interned in Capri and gave a detailed account of the resistance movement to his OSS captors, among whom was Allen Dulles's special assistant, Gero von Gaervernitz.

Schlabrendorff was returned to his wife and children in June 1945 and later travelled to Nuremberg at the request of General Bill Donovan, a deputy prosecutor at the International Military Tribunal and formerly the head of OSS. Schlabrendorff read the draft indictment and submitted a highly critical appraisal, but played no further part in the proceedings. His book, based upon a document he had prepared in Capri, was published soon after the end of the war but the complete version, which documented all the major members of the resistance, was not released until 1965. In this passage the author describes his group's first attempt to kill Hitler.

The Secret War against Hitler

The official conference with Hitler took place in Kluge's quarters, with Tresckow and the other commanders of the Army Group Center present. It would have been easy to smuggle the bomb into that room, but had we done so, we would have killed not only Hitler, but all the other army leaders, including Kluge, whom we needed for the success of the coup.

After the official meeting, lunch was served in the officers' mess. Once again the fact that the bomb would have killed everybody in the room forbade an attempt at that time.

Hitler was served a special meal, every part of which had been prepared by his personal cook. It was tasted before his eyes by his physician, Professor Morell. The entire procedure was reminiscent of an Oriental despot of a bygone age. Watching Hitler eat was a most revolting spectacle. His left hand was placed firmly on his thigh; with his right hand he shoveled his food, which consisted of various vegetables, into his mouth. He did this without lifting his right arm, which he kept flat on the table throughout the entire meal; instead, he brought his mouth down to the food. He also drank a number of non-alcoholic beverages which had been lined up beside his plate. On his orders, no smoking was allowed after the meal.

During the luncheon, Tresckow approached Colonel Heinz Brandt, a member of Hitler's entourage, and asked him casually whether he would be good enough to take along a small parcel containing two bottles of brandy for General Helmuth Stieff of the High Command at Head-quarters. Brandt readily agreed.

Now everything was arranged. Earlier that morning, I had telephoned Captain Gehre, the liaison officer whom Oster had designated in Berlin, and had given him the code word which meant that Operation Flash – Hitler's assassination – was about to be set off. We had agreed on this way of communicating, and I knew that Gehre would immediately inform Dohnanyi, who in turn was to advise General Oster of the developments. These two were then to get everything ready for the second, vital step of seizing the German capital.

After lunch Hitler started back to the airport, accompanied by both Kluge and Tresckow, while I fetched the bomb from my quarters and drove to the airport. Upon my arrival there, I waited until Hitler had dismissed the officers of the Army Group Center and was about to board his plane. Looking at Tresckow, I read in his eyes the order to go ahead. With the help of a key, I pressed down hard on the fuse, thus triggering the bomb, and handed the parcel to Colonel Brandt who boarded the plane shortly after Hitler. A few minutes later both Hitler's plane and that carrying the other members of his party, escorted by a number of fighter planes, started back to East Prussia. Fate now had to take its course.

Tresckow and I returned to our quarters, from where I again called Gehre in Berlin, and gave him the second code word, indicating that Operation Flash was actually under way.

We knew that Hitler's plane was equipped with special devices designed to increase its safety. Not only was it divided into several separate cabins, but Hitler's own cabin was heavily armor plated, and his seat was outfitted with a parachute. In spite of all this, Tresckow and I, judging from our experiments were convinced that the amount of explosive in the bomb would be sufficient to tear the entire plane apart, or at the very least to make a fatal crash inevitable.

With mounting tension we waited for news of the 'accident', which we expected shortly before the plane was to pass over Minsk. We assumed that one of the escort fighters would report the crash by radio. But nothing happened.

After waiting more than two hours, we received the shattering news that Hitler's plane had landed without incident at the airstrip at Rastenburg, in East Prussia, and that Hitler himself had safely reached Headquarters.

We could not imagine what had gone wrong. I called Gehre in Berlin immediately, and gave him the code word for failure of the assassination. Afterwards, Tresckow and I, stunned and shaken by the blow, conferred on what our next move should be. We were in a state of indescribable agitation; the failure of our attempt was bad enough, but the thought of what discovery of the bomb would mean to us and our fellow conspirators, friends, and families, was infinitely worse.

Finally, after considerable deliberation, Tresckow decided to telephone Brandt, and asked casually in the course of the conversation whether the Cointreau had been given to General Stieff. When Brandt replied that he had not yet had the chance to do so, Tresckow told him that the wrong parcel had been sent by mistake, and asked him to hold it until the following day, when it could be exchanged for the one Stieff was supposed to get. Brandt's pleasant answer made it clear that at least the bomb had not been discovered. We realized that it had to be retrieved at all costs, but as Stieff at that time was not yet a member of the conspiracy, we had to keep him out of it, and could only pray that the bomb would not go off belatedly and before we could get hold of it.

On some military pretext, I flew to Headquarters the following day in one of the regular courier planes, and immediately went to see Brandt. As I exchanged parcels with him – the one I had brought along actually *did* contain two bottles of brandy – I felt my blood running cold, for Hitler's aide, serenely unaware of what he was holding, handed me the bomb with a grin, juggling it back and forth in a way which made me fear a belated explosion. Forcing myself to display an outward calm which I most certainly did not feel, I took the bomb and immediately made my way to the nearby railroad junction at Korschen, where a special train of the High Command was scheduled to leave for Berlin that night.

As soon as I arrived in Korschen I boarded the train and went to the sleeping compartment that had been reserved for me. Locking the door behind me, I began gingerly to open the deadly package with a razor blade. After gently removing the wrapping, I could see that the condition of the explosive was unchanged. Carefully dismantling the bomb, I took out the fuse and examined it. The reason for the failure immediately became clear. Everything but one small part had worked as expected. The bottle with the corrosive fluid had been broken, the chemical had eaten through the wire, the firing pin had been released and had struck forward – but the detonator had not ignited! One of the few duds that had slipped past a British inspection was responsible for the fact that Hitler did not die on March 13, 1943.

Mingled disappointment and relief flooded through me as I looked down at the dismantled bomb. Disappointment, because our long and carefully laid plans had ended in failure through no fault of ours; and relief, because we had at least been able to prevent discovery of the plot, with all the terrible consequences such a discovery would have brought in its train.

After a night on the train, I arrived in Berlin on March 15, and immediately went to see Oster, Dohnanyi, and Gehre, to whom I gave a detailed account of the failure of our attempt. I had saved the detonator, and showed the others by what a freak of fate our plans had been frustrated. Oster remained calm, wasting no breath on recriminations or regrets.

A few days later we were given what looked like another good chance for an attempt on Hitler's life, this time during the annual ceremony for soldiers killed in battle, which was to be combined with an exhibition of captured Russian weapons in the Zeughaus in Berlin. By sheer coincidence, Baron von Gersdorff was detailed for duty at that ceremony. Tresckow took this as a sign that fate was playing into our hands. He confided in Gersdorff, and won not only his complete cooperation, but his promise to make an attempt on Hitler's life – at the cost of sacrificing his own. Tresckow told me of this offer in a code which no outsider could have understood. This information reached me late at night. Early the next morning I went to Gersdorff at the Hotel Eden and gave him the bomb. It was most difficult to find a suitable fuse on such short notice, but Gersdorff finally figured out a way to trigger the bomb and went off to the ceremony with the explosive in his coat pocket. However, he never got a chance to use it, for Hitler appeared only briefly and left after a few minutes. Gersdorff needed at least a quarter of an hour for the fuse to work in the cold hall of the Zeughaus.

How different would have been the course of the war and the fate of the world if we had succeeded in our attempt to kill Hitler that March of 1943! It would have meant an early end of the war, and an immediate end to the concentration camps and the terror in the occupied countries. We would have been spared the horrors of another two years of Nazi rule.

Fritz Molden

An oath sworn under compulsion could not entail any obligation to keep faith with the leader of a foreign country. Besides, a pledge could be binding only vis-à-vis a moral authority. Since Hitler's accession to power, however, National Socialist Germany had committed countless acts that were absolutely contrary to all moral principles, both human and divine.

The son of a prominent Viennese publisher with impeccable anti-Nazi credentials, Fritz Molden was bitterly opposed to the *Anschluss* in 1938 but followed his older brother into a Wehrmacht punishment battalion in 1942 in order to avoid facing charges of conspiracy and treason. Aged seventeen, Molden had visited his father, who had been sent to edit a newspaper in Holland, and had tried unsuccessfully to find a boat to take him to England. By the time he returned to Vienna he had been denounced to the Gestapo, and was imprisoned and threatened with prosecution.

Freed from the death penalty by the intervention of a lawyer who was a close family friend, Molden obtained his release from the Kaiersteinbruch concentration camp by volunteering for service at the front. In July 1942 he was posted to the Russian Front to participate in anti-partisan operations in the Kiev area, and was wounded in the leg. A sympathetic doctor altered his military record, to remove the reference to his political unreliability, and in November 1942 he was transferred to France to recuperate. In Paris he made contact with other anti-Nazis in the Wehrmacht and while in Berlin on leave was introduced to Colonel Erwin von Lahousen of the Abwehr. He diverted Molden from his posting to the Russian Front and instead arranged for him to be assigned to Italy.

Following the unexpected collapse of Mussolini's government in July 1943 Molden was switched from Rome to anti-partisan duties in the Tyrol, and in May 1944 he deserted, making his way to Switzerland. In Berne he established contact with Allen Dulles, who introduced him to Hans Bernd Gisevius, and under OSS sponsorship, equipped with false papers identifying him as a Wehrmacht NCO on leave, he undertook a mission to Vienna to help develop the embryonic Austrian resistance movement. In his absence a military court-martial in Bologna had convicted him of desertion but postponed the mandatory death sentence until he had been taken into custody. Between September 1944 and May 1945 Molden made seven visits to Vienna and twelve to Innsbruck, often only narrowly escaping capture, but largely thanks to his efforts the Austrian resistance, known as O-5 for 'Österreich 1945', was supported by the whole of the anti-Nazi political spectrum, from the conservatives through the social democrats to the communists.

By December 1944, when Molden reached a formal agreement with the British SIS, approved by Edge Leslie, as well as the French, the Swiss and the Americans, his organization had established relatively safe routes across the Swiss frontier and a network of clandestine radio stations reporting on German troop movements. He was instrumental in persuading the Allies to stop indiscriminate bombing of civilian targets in Austria and in May 1945 led the first OSS military mission up the Brenner Pass, which was still in enemy hands, to liberate Matrei.

After the war Molden served as the first head of security for the Tyrol before becoming secretary to Austria's Foreign Minister, and later married Allen Dulles's daughter. He returned to Vienna, where he now lives, to run his family's newspaper, the *Neue Freie Presse*, and in 1965 started a publishing business. In his autobiography he explains how the political atmosphere in Vienna changed as the Nazis exerted more influence over Austria.

Exploding Star

In the schools, teachers were somewhat at a loss as to how history should be taught, and it therefore became the custom to finish with the end of the First World War, an engaging practice which was retained until well into the time of the Second Republic. For even after 1945 teachers never knew quite what view to take of the First Republic, the Schuschnigg era, the period between the *Anschluss* and 1945, or the various phases of occupation up till 1955, nor could they decide how all this should be presented. Since the habit of cocking a snook at authority has, as everyone knows, never really caught on in Austria, where circumspection has always been the rule, they thought it best not to teach the history of the past fifty years at all. In consequence, Austrian secondary schoolchildren learned materially more about the ancient Greeks and Celts than about what went on in Austria in the twenties and thirties of this century. This all started with the Nazis and their recasting of the history of the Austrian Empire; the Habsburgs, for instance, were dismissed in extremely negative terms, while the role of the Catholic church was likewise presented in a new and derogatory light. Needless to say, it was the Protestants who were now in favour and accorded a positive evaluation, whereas the Counter-Reformation was held to be the source of all evil.

At Döbling Grammar School I was fortunate in having a very sensible history teacher, who continued to teach his subject along the old lines. On the other hand, our German teacher, Dr Müller – after the war he was pounced on in the street and killed by men newly released from Nazi gaols – was determined to convert us to the faith of good old Wotan. When he went with us on school outings to the Wienerwald, he would seek out a suitable grove of oak trees and proceed to lecture us on the old Germanic pantheon, in the hope of converting us to neo-paganism. His success in our class was small, in fact I doubt if he made a single convert, and this grieved him. As a person, Müller was quite a decent sort; thus, he never penalized me for my various inadequacies, always treated me very kindly and would even give me good marks.

The same could not be said of the headmaster; he did everything in his power to make it clear to non-Nazi or otherwise 'suspect' pupils that he was a convinced National Socialist who considered them sub-human, if nothing worse, nor did he ever cease to make life as difficult as possible for those of us who were not National Socialists. When, soon after the war, I chanced to meet this man in the street, he all but embraced me and was utterly dumbfounded by my failure to respond with equal enthusiasm to the happy reunion.

Never before had the country experienced such an outbreak of iconoclasm, and the situations to which it gave rise were often grotesque. For instance, the world of the theatre and the press in Vienna had largely been dominated by Jews. Indeed, the same could be said of medicine and the law, a fact that had materially contributed to the spread of anti-Semitism in Austria. To many non-Jews these sectors of cultural and economic life seemed difficult of access. This is not, of course, to suggest that some secret Jewish society – for example the 'Elders of Zion' so often cited by Hitler – had issued a decree whereby no one in Vienna but a Jew might become a doctor, dentist, lawyer, solicitor, theatrical producer or journalist. Rather, Jewish immigration from the east, from Poland, Roumania, Slovakia and Hungary, had given rise to a powerful concentration of gifted, ambitious and, above all, hard-working people who, since the last third of the nineteenth century, had made Vienna the goal of their professional and private dreams.

These people, coming as they did from the ghettos of Galicia and from every part of eastern Europe, were intent on one thing only – success. And in this their greatest rivals were none other than their fellow Jews, who, having been long settled in Vienna, where they had hitherto led a peaceful, undisturbed and respected existence, now saw themselves in danger, on the one hand of being placed in the same category as the newcomers from the east and, on the other, of being outstripped by them. Small wonder that the last three decades of the nineteenth century gave rise in Vienna to such figures as Schönerer and Lueger and, with them, that Viennese brand of anti-Semitism composed of commercial envy and traditional religious prejudice.

The fact remains that, at that period, the number of outstanding exponents of the creative arts who were of Jewish origin was out of all proportion to the population as a whole. In 1938, therefore, it was very difficult for the rulers of the Third Reich to persuade people that a large proportion of the writers and poets who, up till a few weeks before, had been regarded as the crème de la crème, had now, because Jewish, become bad, incompetent and repulsive, if indeed they had not always been so — Arthur Schnitzler, Hugo von Hofmannsthal, Franz Werfel, Stefan Zweig, Karl Kraus, Raoul Auernheimer, to name only a few.

In Vienna, a city in which music and literature had always played such a pre-eminent role, it was embarrassing suddenly to have to discard as the inferior products of a third-rate culture a large proportion of the works hitherto performed in the theatres, the Opera and the concert halls. A particularly amusing case was that of Johann Strauss, in whose veins there had been a drop of two of Jewish blood. Dr Goebbels and the Viennese cultural panjandrums succeeded in hushing up this defect since it was unthinkable ever to put the dear Führer in the position of learning that the King of the Waltz he so greatly revered had belonged to a group which, according to *Mein Kampf*, was incapable of true artistic achievement.

The sudden disappearance of large numbers of culturally creative people necessarily left gaps which could be filled only with the utmost difficulty, if at all, by recruiting artists able to produce a certificate of Aryanism. No one, for that matter, had a very clear idea of what Aryanism was. Aryan supermen, or so the doctrines of Alfred Rosenberg and other exponents of racism had it, were tall, fair-haired, blue-eyed and in all respects the successors of the Teutonic race of gods. But as everyone knows, neither Germans nor Austrians are in the main tall, blue-eyed, broad-shouldered, swift as a greyhound or hard as Krupps' steel, nor were these external manifestations of Aryanism discernible even in a minority of those at the top of the tree in the Greater German Reich. Neither Hitler nor Göring, neither Goebbels nor Alfred Rosenberg, and least of all Streicher, the infamous Gauleiter of Nuremberg and editor of the leading anti-Semitic organ *Der Stürmer*, bore the remotest resemblance to those Teutonic giants in whose likeness the German people was expected to evolve.

However, if these Nordic prodigies did not exist in the flesh, some attempt might at least be made to nordicize one's children by giving them Teutonic names. All of a sudden the sons of National Socialists were no longer called Karl, Leopold, Ludwig, Franz or Fritz; instead, abecedarians embarking as good little Germans on their school careers tended to have names like Hagen, Siegfried, or Rüdiger tacked on to surnames of unmistakably Czech, Hungarian or Polish origin. Nor was there any lack of similarly Teutonic names for girls, Gudrun and Siegelinde being particular favourites with which petty officials of the Nazi Party were wont to launch their daughters into life. The business also had its drawbacks, for later on, when the fortunes of war had turned, Teutonic names were something people would have gladly discarded. However, this was more easily said than done so that, several decades later, it is possible to tell from a person's Christian name whether or not his or her parents were supporters of the Third Reich.

The more foreign-sounding the surname of a Gauleiter or other leading party functionary – for instance, Globocnik or Zalesak – the greater the lengths to which he would go to prove himself a loyal German. Or, if at all possible, he would do even better and actually change his name. And, indeed, in the hope of obtaining advancement in the SA or SS, if not the upper reaches of politics, many a man who had embarked on his career in the thirties with an honest-to-goodness Czech, Hungarian or Slovene name, would suddenly turn up with a Teutonic version of it.

It was a time when political jokes proliferated as never before, something that is bound to happen under a dictatorship, where there is no other outlet for the expression of criticism or dissident opinion. Here, by way of an example, is a story about the controversy between the Catholic church and the Third Reich. Relations between the Vatican and the Reich government were going from bad to worse. Finally Hitler sent for Göring, ordered him to proceed immediately to Rome and settle matters with the Pope, cost what it might. Having taken note of the order, Göring set off. Two days later Hitler got a priority telegram from Rome which read: 'Reichsgau Vatican annexed. College of Cardinals converted. Pope shot while trying to escape. Tiara perfect fit. Heil Hitler. Hermann I, Pontifex Maximus.'

CHAPTER VIII

The Outsiders

Once you have been tried for high treason,
any other charge is hard to take seriously.
Helen Joseph

The most extraordinary treason trial in recent years was that held in Pretoria in August 1958. Originally 91 defendants were committed for trial, out of a total of 140 originally arrested in December 1956 and charged with high treason and two alternative offences under the Suppression of Communism Act. Following lengthy preliminary submissions, the main trial eventually opened in August 1959 with thirty accused of the capital crime, of whom only twenty-nine were in the dock as Nelson Mandela had disappeared to 'lead the struggle from underground'. The verdict of the three judges was not delivered until March 1961, when all were found not guilty and discharged.

Apart from the length of the trial, which lasted nearly three years, and the withdrawal of charges against 110 of the defendants, it was remarkable because of the racial mix, which consisted of twenty-four Africans, three Indians, one coloured, and two whites. Furthermore, most had been South African by birth, but Helen Joseph was the exception for she had been born in Midhurst, Sussex, and had not arrived in the country until 1931 when, as a graduate of King's College, London, she was appointed as a teacher in Durban. During the war she had served as a WAAF officer and after her demobilization in 1948 had become an anti-apartheid campaigner. Her acquittal on a charge that carried the death penalty enabled her to write *If This be Treason*, but the manuscript was removed from her home in 1963 by Special Branch detectives enforcing a banning order which restricted her to her home in Johannesburg. Undaunted by police harassment, Helen Joseph's account of the treason trial was published in London, a remarkable record of how the author and her co-defendants had endured prosecution and the possibility of being sentenced to death.

Six years after the publication of Helen Joseph's book, Gordon Winter found that the Security Police for whom he worked as an agent had been reorganized as the South African Bureau of State Security (BOSS). His employers regarded him as a loyal and reliable informant, but when news leaked of his intention to write *Inside BOSS*, he became the subject of an intense campaign of vilification. After ten years under cover he had acquired vast knowledge and his disclosures caused a sensation, particularly in London, where he had participated in some politically sensitive operations. Although the South African authorities allegedly were infuriated by Winter's indiscretions, he was never the subject of legal proceedings of the kind the British government used in 1986 to prevent another author, Peter Wright, from capitalizing upon his clandestine career in the Security Service. Winter survived the experience, and now lives in Ireland. Peter Wright, who fought the litigation against him, eventually won after a marathon battle which reached the House of Lords. Wright's behaviour persuaded Whitehall to take drastic measures to deter any recurrence, and the result was the 1989 Official Secrets Act, which created a new offence of unauthorized disclosure of any information by a member (or former member) of the security and intelligence services. This draconian law was intended to forestall another *Spycatcher*, and avoid any arguments from defence counsel about prior publication or the merits of public interest. Since the Act was placed on the statute book, however, no prosecution has been mounted against any individual, although two books have been released without permission, and in defiance of the authors' former employer.

Both Brian Crozier, whose *Free Agent* was published in July 1993, and Desmond Bristow, whose autobiography *A Game of Moles* came out three months later, were SIS officers. Both were threatened with prosecution under the terms of the 1989 Act, but the authorities chose to overlook the challenges, having obtained a few changes to the texts of both books.

The majority of books mentioned in these pages have been written by authors who have been motivated to explain why they took the action that brought them charges of treachery. Very occasionally, it is the publication of the book itself that is regarded as disloyal. An individual can have led an entirely praiseworthy life, but the release of a particular title can draw tremendous criticism. The most extreme case in recent years is that of Duff Cooper, later Viscount Norwich, a distinguished minister in Churchill's wartime cabinet, who attracted much opprobrium when in 1950 he published a novel, *Operation Heartbreak*. The cause of the threats made to him, including a promise of prosecution from the then Prime Minister, Clement Attlee, was the undisclosed fact that Cooper's story had been based on an authentic wartime intelligence operation, conducted in April 1943. Code-named Operation Mincemeat, the imaginative scheme had involved depositing a dead body, ostensibly that of a Royal Marines courier, on the shore in neutral Spain. Allegedly the casualty of an aircrash, the refrigerated cadaver had in fact been transported from Liverpool by submarine and placed in the sea off the Atlantic coast near Huelva. Attached to the corpse's wrist by the standard metal chain was a briefcase containing what purported to be important documents indicating an imminent Allied offensive in the Mediterranean. Predictably, the pliant Spanish authorities had ignored their neutrality and had shared this unexpected windfall with the German Abwehr, thereby deceiving them and giving the Allies a significant strategic advantage.

The decision made by Cooper, who by then had retired from the Commons and was serving as British Ambassador in Paris, to reveal details of a secret deception plan to which he had been privy while Chairman of the Security Executive, was considered by the British authorities to be an outrage. While Chancellor of the Duchy of Lancaster, Cooper had been appointed to the Security Executive as Lord Swinton's successor in July 1942 and therefore had been indoctrinated into Mincemeat at an early stage. Nevertheless, despite the time that had elapsed, the principle remained that Cooper was seeking to exploit classified information that he had acquired as a minister of the Crown. Undeterred by the government's hostile correspondence, Cooper proceeded with publication, assuring his family that British interests could not possibly have been harmed because such a ploy could never be used twice with any chance of success. He firmly rejected pleas from the Foreign Office to abandon publication on the grounds that his account might tip off the Russians and prevent repetition but, curiously, omitted to mention the episode at all in his autobiography, *Old Men Forget*. The fact that these exchanges had occurred was made public only by his son the second Viscount, John Julius Norwich, who contributed a foreword to a modern edition of *Operation Heartbreak* after his father's death.

Cooper was not the subject of any criminal proceedings, and in his memoirs he supposes that his unexpected departure from his post at the Paris embassy in October 1947, after only two years, was a consequence of what he alleged was 'political pressure'. Perhaps significantly, after his retirement he opted to make his home in France.

Almost in contradiction of the arguments that had been deployed against Cooper, publication of *Operation Heartbreak* prompted the Admiralty to commission Ewen Montagu, who had played a key role in Mincemeat, to write *The Man Who Never Was*, an entirely factual version of the operation, with the omission only of the identity of the dead body, and the name of MI5's liaison officer, Charles Cholmondeley. Montagu's book was released two years after Cooper's, and achieved equal success.

Duff Cooper

I need not impress upon you the importance of secrecy, but I would say to you, what I say to all those who work with me, that there is only one way to keep a secret. There are not two ways. That way is not to whisper it to a living soul — neither to the wife of your bosom nor to the man you trust most upon earth.

Having been Secretary of State for War between 1935 and 1937, then First Lord of the Admiralty and in 1940 Minister of Information in Churchill's war cabinet, Alfred Duff Cooper MP had held many of the senior positions of state in the land when he was appointed the British Ambassador in Paris. He and his wife, the legendary Lady Diana Cooper, were a huge diplomatic success at the embassy but his choice of subject for his first and only novel was to prove exceptionally controversial. Nevertheless, it did not prevent him from being elevated to the House of Lords with a viscountcy in 1952.

When word reached Whitehall that Duff Cooper intended to write about the wartime operation code-named Mincemeat, 'strong pressure was put upon him not to do so', according to his son. 'Just what form this pressure took I have not been able to establish, but it seems likely that the Prime Minister – Mr Attlee – was personally involved.' According to Charles Cholmondeley, the MI5 officer who had participated in Mincemeat, Cooper had been threatened with criminal prosecution, and had retorted that he would identify his source as Sir Winston Churchill, whom he alleged had embroidered the story somewhat for his audience at a dinner party! The book was published in November 1950, and its author died in 1954 without disclosing that his story had been based on true events, and without seeing the Twentieth Century Fox movie of the same title, which was released in March 1955 and which, incidentally, included a scene with a serving MI5 officer, Ronnie Reed, operating a transmitter.

In the meantime a *Daily Express* journalist, Ian Colvin, had been tipped off to the authentic background of the novel and had undertaken a search of cemeteries along Spain's Atlantic coast to find a British officer who had been buried at the appropriate time. His relentless research took him to Huelva where he found the grave of a Major William Martin, and to the Ministry of Defence where he was informed that the Hon. Ewen Montagu QC had been allowed access to the relevant files. Montagu had been the Naval Intelligence Division's representative on the Twenty Committee during the war and had played a key role in the execution of the plan, originally dreamed up by an MI5 officer, Charles Cholmondeley, who was then still employed by the Security Service. In 1953, as Ian Colvin uncovered the true story for publication as *The Unknown Courier*, Montagu was commissioned to write over a single weekend an official account, which was entitled *The Man Who Never Was*, and was serialized in the *Sunday Express* in February 1953.

In this passage, an unnamed Scottish brigadier in charge of deception operations briefs Colonel Osborne, a close friend of Captain William Maryington, who has recently succumbed to pneumonia in London.

Operation Heartbreak

'The purpose of this department, in which you find yourself, Colonel Osborne, is to deceive the enemy. Our methods of deception are, at certain times, extremely elaborate. The more important the military operations under contemplation the more elaborate are our preparations to ensure, not so much that the enemy shall be ignorant of what we intend to do, but rather that he shall have good reason to believe that we intend to do something quite different. I need not impress upon you the importance of secrecy, but I would say to you, what I say to all those who work with me, that there is only one way to keep a secret. There are not two ways. That way is not to whisper it to a living soul – neither to the wife of your bosom nor to the man you trust most upon earth. I know you for a loyal, trustworthy and discreet soldier, but for a million pounds I would not tell you what I am about to tell you, if I did not need your help.

'A military operation of immense magnitude is in course of preparation. That is a fact of which the enemy are probably aware. Its success must depend largely upon the enemy's ignorance of when and where it will be launched. Every security precaution has been taken to prevent that knowledge from reaching him. Those security precautions are not, I repeat, the business of this department. It is not our business to stop him getting correct information. It is our business to provide him, through sources which will carry conviction of their reliability, with information that is false.

'In a few days from now, Colonel Osborne, the dead body of a British officer will be washed ashore, on the coast of a neutral country, whose relations with the enemy are not quite so neutral as we might wish them to be. It will be found that he is carrying in a packet that is perfectly waterproof, which will be firmly strapped to his chest, under his jacket, documents of a highly confidential character – documents of such vital importance to the conduct of the war that no one will wonder that they should have been entrusted to a special mission and a special messenger. These documents, including a private letter from the Chief of the Imperial General Staff to the General Officer Commanding North Africa, although couched in the most, apparently, guarded language, will yet make perfectly plain to an intelligent reader exactly what the Allies are intending to do. You will appreciate the importance of such an operation; and you will also appreciate that its success or failure must depend entirely upon the convincing character of the evidence, that will prove the authenticity of these documents and will remove from the minds of those who are to study them any suspicion that a trick has been played upon them. The most important of all the links in that chain of evidence must be the dead body on which the documents are found.

'Now, Osborne, you are a medical man, and you must have discovered in your student days, when you were in need of material to work upon, what I have discovered only lately, the extraordinary importance that people attach to what becomes of the dead bodies of their distant relatives. People, who can ill afford it, will travel from the north of Scotland to the south of England to assure themselves that the mortal remains of a distant cousin have been decently committed to the earth. You can hardly imagine the difficulty I have experienced. The old profession of body-snatching has no longer any practitioners, or I would have employed one. I have now secured the services of a gentleman in your line of business, a civilian, and our hopes rest upon what a pauper lunatic asylum may produce. But there must be difficulties. You may have heard, Osborne, that death is the great leveller, but even after death has done his damnedest there is apt to remain a very considerable difference between a pauper lunatic deceased from natural causes and a British officer, in the prime of life, fit to be entrusted with a most important mission.'

'I see what you are getting at,' interrupted Garnet. 'You want me to agree to poor Maryngton's body being used for this purpose.'

'Bide a while, bide a while,' said the Brigadier, who had not completed his thesis. 'You will appreciate the cosmic importance of this operation, upon which the lives of thousands of men must depend, and which may affect even the final issue of the war. This morning I was wrestling desperately with the problem of the pauper lunatic for whom an identity, a name, a background had to be created. Our enemies are extremely painstaking and thorough in their work. You may be quite certain that they have copies of the last published Army List, and I am sure that they have also, easily available, a complete register of all officers who have been killed since that publication, or whose names have appeared in the obituary columns. Their first action on being informed that the body of a dead British officer has been discovered will be to ascertain whether such a British officer was ever alive. If they fail to find the name of such an officer in the Army List their suspicions will be aroused, and those suspicions, once aroused, may easily lead them to the true solution of the mystery. We should be forced to give to our unknown one of those names that are shared by hundreds, and should have to hope that, in despair of satisfying themselves as to the identity of the particular Major Smith or Brown in question, they would abandon the enquiry. But – I say again – we are dealing with a nation whose thoroughness in small matters of detail is unequalled, and it is my belief that within a few days the chief of their intelligence service would be informed that no officer of the name in question has ever served in the British Army. From that moment all the information contained in the documents, about which I told you, would be treated as information of doubtful value and of secondary importance. The result might well be that the whole operation would fail completely.

'While this grave problem is occupying my mind today, you sit yourself down before me and tell me of an officer who died this morning, whose death has not been registered, who has no relations, who was of an age and standing entirely suitable for such a mission and over the disposal of whose dead body you have control. Call it the long arm of coincidence, whatever that may mean, if you desire, but to me, Colonel Osborne,' the Brigadier's voice grew hoarse with emotion, 'it is the hand of Providence stretched out to aid His people in their dire need, and I ask you to give me your help, as God has given me His, in the fulfilment of my task.'

He ceased and both sat silent. After a while Garnet said:

'What you are asking me to do is very extraordinary, and although I perfectly understand the terrible urgency, you must allow me to reflect.' He paused – and then continued: 'In the first place I should be acting quite illegally. I have no more right to conceal Maryngton's death than I have to dispose of his body.'

'*Silent leges inter arma*,' replied the Brigadier. 'I will give you my personal guarantee, written if you wish it, that will cover you from any legal consequences.'

They sat again in silence for two or three minutes. When Garnet next spoke it was to ask:

'What should I actually have to do? And what am I going to say when Maryngton's friends, many of whom must have known that he was living with me, ask me what has become of him?'

The Brigadier was obviously relieved. He felt now that the other's mind was moving in the right direction.

'What you have to do is to lay out by the side of Maryngton's body tonight his uniform, omitting no detail of it. Don't forget his cap or his belt, and above all make sure that the identity disc is there. Put on the table his watch, his cheque-book and any small personal possessions that he always carried. At 2 a.m. some friends of mine will call upon you. There may be two of them, there may be three. You will show them which is Maryngton's room. Then you will go to bed and sleep soundly. You will, however, dream that Maryngton comes to you in the night and tells you that he is leaving England in the early morning. His mission is of a secret nature, and in case anything should go wrong he hands you his will, which you have already told me is in your possession. When you wake in the morning he will certainly have gone, and you will therefore believe your dream was a reality. It will probably be many days before you have to answer any enquiry. During those days you will repeat to yourself continually how he told you one night that he was leaving on a secret mission, how he gave you his will, and how he was gone on the following morning. You will come to believe this yourself, and it will be all that you know, all that you have to say to anyone who asks questions. One day you will read in the paper that Maryngton has died on active service. Then you will send his will to his lawyers; and that will be all.'

Gordon Winter

Yes, I was on the wrong side all right – but there was no way I was going to let that interfere with my life.

With three convictions and a twenty-one-month gaol sentence in his past, Gordon Winter was a London burglar anxious to start a new life when he arrived in South Africa in 1960. He joined the Johannesburg *Daily Express* as a crime correspondent but he was also an informant for the Security Police. For six years he cultivated a reputation as a liberal journalist sympathetic to the anti-apartheid movement whereas in reality he was a skilled penetration agent, reporting on his contacts to the Security Police.

In June 1965 Winter's activities were interrupted by a murder in which he was implicated. A business acquaintance of the notorious Richardson brothers, whom

Winter had known in London, had been shot in a gang-related killing with his pistol. Winter was detained by the police and, after he had appeared as a prosecution witness against the Richardsons' hit-man, was deported to England in December 1966.

In London Winter established himself as a freelance journalist, active in left-wing political circles and the Freelance Branch of the National Union of Journalists. He also contributed regularly to the Johannesburg *Sunday Express*, the radical black magazine *Drum*, and to Brian Crozier's Forum World Features, but he also reported regularly to his BOSS handler at the South African embassy. Among the stories he pursued were allegations made by Norman Scott, the male model who had formerly been Jeremy Thorpe's homosexual partner. In February 1974, three years after he had interviewed Scott, Winter returned to Johannesburg, his cover as a BOSS agent completely compromised, and he worked as a journalist on the *Citizen*, specializing in high-risk political scoops.

Winter's decision to defect was prompted by the arrest and torture of his maid's daughter. Winter had intervened on her behalf with his friends at BOSS headquarters, who agreed to release her, but he discovered they had continued to interrogate her using electric shock torture. Infuriated, Winter admitted to his wife his dual role and resigned from the *Citizen*, pretending he wanted to work on a reference book based on *Who's Who*. Instead he flew to Paris with his wife, Wendy, their baby son and a huge collection of files, tapes and notebooks which he used to write *Inside BOSS*, a sensational exposé of the organization's misconduct.

The book proved to be highly controversial, not least because of the record number of libel actions that followed publication. Among the successful litigants paid damages were Harold Soref MP, the photo-journalist Stanley Winer, and several African journalists. Others, including Peter Bessell MP, obtained retractions of the claims that they were CIA agents.

Following publication, BOSS was officially disbanded, but in reality it was simply renamed the Department of National Security. In this passage, which is typical of the book, the author demonstrates his ability to identify BOSS officers, their agents and their operations.

Inside BOSS

To the south-east of Pretoria there is a large farm known as Rietvlei. Access is along a small dusty track well off the main road. It looks innocent enough, but it is a secret BOSS complex where top BOSS operatives live before being posted to other areas or after they have returned from long stints overseas and have not had time to settle into a new home.

The farm has another use – training Black agents whose main target is to infiltrate the ranks of Black liberation movements in other countries. It began in 1963, and the man who first started the training there was Colonel Att Spengler, alias Mr Campbell. Later, his job was taken over by a man named Anderson.

To rule out possible betrayal by fellow agents, the Black spies are trained individually. This idea was pinched from British intelligence's tried and trusted 'monastic cell' method. The Blacks are carefully chosen and then put through some very ingenious loyalty tests. When BOSS is satisfied, the men are taught Communist theory so that they can pose as leftists. After training they are let loose and told to infiltrate liberal circles inside South Africa so that they can gain useful contacts as well as experience in the field. To give them believable cover some of them are harassed, detained and sometimes jailed for short periods on Pass Law or other minor offences. Once in jail they are slipped into the same section, often the same prison cell, as Blacks known to be politically active and well connected. This gives them more experience and those all-important contacts outside the jail.

When BOSS is satisfied that the agents have erected a good relationship in anti-government circles, they are told to flee from South Africa under their own steam and illegally. They are promised a £10,000 bonus when they eventually return to South Africa. They are also assured that if they come to any harm while spying overseas their parents or relatives will be well looked after.

Some of those Black spies did extremely well. The fake persecution they suffered while in South Africa led them to be accepted by various liberation groups, and they were sent for guerrilla training in different parts of Africa, Algeria, Russia, China and even Cuba. Eventually some of them returned to South Africa in secret along with groups of genuine guerrillas with the aim of committing acts of sabotage inside the country or setting up activist groups underground. But, being spies, they betrayed all their comrades, who were arrested by the South African security services.

When White spies return to South Africa after working overseas they get the red-carpet treatment. Like Mr Craig Williamson, the BOSS agent who infiltrated the International University Exchange Fund (IUEF), a liberal body based in Switzerland which operates humanitarian and other projects for deserving Blacks in South Africa. Agent Williamson did so well that he rose to be the deputy director, in virtual control of the IUEF's anti-apartheid contacts in South Africa. When he was exposed and fled back to Pretoria in January 1980 he was hailed by the government press as 'Our Hero'.

It's not like that when a Black spy returns to South Africa. Never in the history of that country has a Black agent been given public recognition or accolades. The reason is simple. Pretoria cannot admit that Blacks are as clever, or as brave, as Whites. It just would not fit in with the White Supremacy image.

When Blacks return they usually end up standing in the witness box as State witnesses giving evidence against the comrades they betrayed. Their story is always the same: 'I was a genuine runaway from apartheid because I thought it was a bad system. When I got overseas I fell into the clutches of White Communists who taught me to be a terrorist. I eventually realized that they were wrong and that Blacks were treated better in South Africa than in most overseas countries. That is why I am giving evidence against my friends today. They are Communist dupes but still don't realize it.'

This 'I became disenchanted with Communism' tactic is always good propaganda for the South African government and helps to cement the vote of those Whites who like and need constant reassurance that their privileged way of life is not likely to be taken away by those revolting Blacks and revolutionary Reds.

The African National Congress soon became aware of this ploy and erected security measures to stop Black spies infiltrating their ranks. These security measures in turn became known to BOSS. A returning Black spy who had been totally shunned in London and failed utterly as an information gatherer told BOSS that all politically involved people fleeing from South Africa, particularly Blacks, were being heavily vetted on their arrival in London by Mr Abdul Minty of the British Anti-Apartheid Movement.

Mr Minty, himself a South African exile, apparently did his vetting work well. Pretoria told me he had succeeded in rooting out several of our agents. BOSS retaliated by making its Black agents undergo intensive Abdul Minty-type question-and-answer interrogation sessions before they were sent overseas. But Abdul Minty and the African National Congress men in London still managed to root them out and bounce them back. It's like a never-ending ping pong game.

Brian Crozier

I was already disillusioned with Stalin and the Soviet system when the first news of the takeover in Eastern Europe started coming in.

Formerly a committed Marxist, the Australian-born journalist Brian Crozier was converted by reading Victor Kravchenko's *I Chose Freedom*, which he described as 'one of the first and, I believe, the most important of the stream of books by defectors from Soviet Communism'.

Later the editor of *The Economist Foreign Report*, and the founder of the Institute for the Study of Conflict, Crozier was also an SIS officer and his clandestine connections, with both the CIA through Forum World Features and Century House, were denounced by, among others, *The Economist*'s former Middle East stringer, Kim Philby, in a mischievous article in *Izvestia* as long ago as December 1968.

In July 1993 Crozier released an extraordinarily candid account of his activities on behalf of SIS in *Free Agent*, and his disclosures broke the convention which inhibits SIS personnel from revealing details of their intelligence work. He gave various recognizable SIS personalities rather transparent pseudonyms (Donald Lancaster becomes Ronald Lincoln and Derek Parsons is actually David Peck) but despite this subterfuge he attracted dire threats from the Cabinet Office and the Treasury Solicitor.

Crozier reveals that his principal handler, Frank Rendle (masquerading as Ronald Franks) not only studied the Sino-Soviet split, but was the catalyst for a dichotomy of similar dimensions with the Foreign Office when he chose to contribute an article under the pseudonym David A. Charles to *China Quarterly*, a journal allegedly 'sponsored by the CIA'. Predictably, the Foreign Office voiced strong disapproval of what was deemed to be the precedent set by an SIS professional expressing his opinion in a public forum, however obscure, and even if he had taken the precaution of adopting a *nom-de-guerre*.

Crozier's *Free Agent* serves as a signal that the era of heavy-handed intervention and counterproductive litigation is at an end in England. According to press reports, the book was the subject of lengthy negotiations with both the MI5 legal adviser and SIS, but only a handful of deletions were agreed by the author. It may be that the author's obvious contempt for the Security Service's very limited grasp of the threat of domestic subversion, as manifested by an incident in which Sir Michael Hanley shrugged off Crozier and disconnected him from his MI5 contact, coloured his attitude and made him less inclined to co-operate with his former masters. Whatever the tangled background to the book's release, it represents great potential for embarrassment, but no threat to security. Thus, by British standards, it is perceived as damaging.

In this passage the author hints that he was granted access by Noel Cunningham (actually Nigel Clive) to GCHQ's highly secret signals intelligence product when he was commissioned to write an analysis of Soviet influence in developing countries.

Free Agent

I was scarcely back when Ronald Franks telephoned me to suggest an urgent lunch at his club, the Athenaeum. He told me he had been authorised to take me to SIS headquarters and introduce me to some of his colleagues. 'You'll find we're still a gentlemanly outfit,' he said.

After lunch, we took a taxi to Century House, the 1960s high-rise building south of the Thames which now housed SIS. At the security checkpoint at the entrance, I was issued with a temporary pass, and Franks escorted me to an upper floor, where he introduced me to the head of his department, which dealt with Sino-Soviet questions. This was my first shock. I had met the man, Noel Cunningham (not his real name), several times. That day and on future days, I met a number of people whom I had talked to, in the Travellers or elsewhere, in the belief that they were 'Foreign Office'. One of them I had known as a colleague when he had worked for *The Economist* Intelligence Unit.

Later on, at Century House, I met a number of non-officials whom I had known for years, whose 'contact' with MI6 was similar to mine. They included academic friends of mine specialising in matters of interest to me, including Vietnam and the Soviet Union.

Ronald Franks was right in his choice of 'gentlemanly'. Friendly though enigmatic smiles were on every face. Speech was soft, and in public tended to come out of the side of the mouth: tell-tale professional quirks of the intelligence world.

From Noel Cunningham, I learned the reason for the reticence I had noted over some months in my relations with Ronald Franks. From its headquarters in Langley, Virginia, the American Central Intelligence Agency, I was told, had raised objections to further SIS contacts with me on the ground that on several occasions *Foreign Report* had carried stories that presented the CIA in a bad light. So *that* was it! I laughed, remembering the stories. They had come from a woman journalist based in India, and I had not regarded them as hostile. The real objection, it seemed, was to the fact that I had carried the stories, because they were accurate. In the end, Langley had accepted British assurances that I was in no way against the CIA, but the process of persuasion had taken the best part of a year. We were now in November 1964.

Cunningham wanted to know if I would be prepared, on occasion, to write analytical reports on themes in which I had specialised, such as international Communism and insurgencies. I readily agreed. This would involve occasional access to material not publicly available.

He told me about GCHQ (Government Communications Headquarters) at Cheltenham, the highly secret signals intelligence interception organisation. 'It's a veritable *industry*,' said Noel, adding with relish: 'That's the stuff that really gives you an intellectual erection.' It did not follow, however, that I would have access to this erectile stuff.

The fundamental rule of access to material not publicly available is 'need to know', and the rule was rigorously observed. To write this first analysis, I 'needed to know' a great deal because of the ground to be covered. I was asked to write a full report on Sino-Soviet subversion in the Third World. This was indeed the acid test of the contested genuineness of the great split. I had already dealt with this theme in an article entitled 'The Struggle for the Third World', published in the Chatham House quarterly *International Affairs* in July that year. In it, I had argued that the subversive operations of the Soviet Union and the Chinese People's Republic were in conflict everywhere in the Third World, in East Asia as in Africa and Latin America. Having identified the phenomenon, I had called it 'competitive subversion'.

The question now was to submit the thesis to the test of the material not available to the general public. Having studied the evidence, it confirmed my view, and Ronald Franks's, that the split was indeed genuine.

The ground covered was immense and the time I could spare from other commitments was limited. At last, several months into 1965, the report was finished.

At this point, I was introduced to the bureaucratic obstacle. Every specialist in every area covered had to see the draft and comment on it. The draft also had to go to the IRD specialists. In the end, Noel assembled two or three dozen of the commentators at a boardroom table, with himself in the chair, and me next to him, answering questions or dealing with queries or contestations. It was only after that gauntlet had been run that the revised report could be issued and distributed.

After the document had been 'sanitised' by the excision of secret material, I was allowed to take the scissored typescript home. The report formed the core of a further 'Background Book' with the same title as the Chatham House article, *The Struggle for the Third World* (1966). This one was yet another sequel in the series started with *The Rebels*.

Sometimes, a piece of information may not be secret, but remains classified because of its source. *The Struggle for the Third World* contained an interesting example. One day, at Century House, one of my new semi-colleagues, a large man called William, invited me to his office and showed me a Top Secret CIA report on the then current crisis in the Dominican Republic.

At the end of April 1965, President Lyndon B. Johnson, acting on his own executive authority (that is, without consulting Congress), ordered the US Marines to land in the Republic to protect American lives in the civil war that had broken out there. This was his stated pretext, but the true reason for his decision was implicit in the report William showed me, the contents of which he encouraged me to note.

For months, Dominican Communists trained in various countries, including Cuba and Czechoslovakia, had been smuggled back into their half of the island of Hispaniola (the other half of which was the wretchedly poor Haiti). The training the Communists had been given covered sabotage, terrorism and guerrilla warfare. A military revolt by followers of an ex-President was their signal. The Communists used their own military contacts to gain access to the arsenals, and within hours distributed arms to hundreds of well-prepared citizens.

If Johnson had not intervened, it is safe to say that the Dominican Republic would have joined Cuba as an outpost of the Soviet empire (as indeed happened many years later with Nicaragua and the island of Grenada). The intervention, however, caused an outcry from the Left, from American liberals and from well-meaning others who were unaware of the true circumstances. There was much talk of blows to America's peace-loving image and to Dominica's budding democracy, and of a return to Theodore Roosevelt's 'Big Stick' behaviour.

Had President Johnson stated the true reason for the intervention, he would have at least disarmed some of the critics, although he would not have appeased the leftists. He weathered this little storm better than the much deeper one in Vietnam, and a presidential election in Dominica on 1 June appeared to vindicate his action and enabled him to pull the Marines out.

The CIA had actually compiled a list of fifty-five Communist ring-leaders of the projected takeover, though without giving the necessary background. The correspondents who flocked to the island to cover the crisis were surprised and indignant not to trace any of them. I was astonished at their naivety. Did they really suppose the Communists would stay on to be exposed?

At that time, I had become a regular contributor to the *Spectator* which, as a stop-gap, was being edited by the Tory MP Iain Macleod, who had declined to serve in the Douglas-Home Cabinet. I wrote the story (minus the attribution) which duly appeared; and duly attracted indignation from my critics.

Ronald Franks shared an office with a tall, reserved colleague, whom I shall call Derek Parsons. More controlled than Franks, better organised, he was on the same high level intellectually. He had served in Moscow and was, in the view of some leading experts, the best Sovietician in the country, although the least known by the nature of his career. I shared that view.

In general, I found the level of intellectual attainment and rigour of analysis higher in SIS than in any other institution with which I had dealings. In those days, MI6 was required not only to obtain secret intelligence by whatever means was judged necessary, but also to produce analyses for the benefit of the Joint Intelligence Committee, and of course of that committee's Foreign Office component. In later years, I understand, the analytical requirement was considerably reduced; mistakenly, in my opinion.

To recognise the intellectual level of the SIS analysts is not to disparage the attainments of the Foreign Office personnel, in comparison. The factor that gave the edge to SIS was corporate. Foreign ministries are constrained by the nature of diplomacy to seek accommodations or agreements, often with hostile powers or groups. This imperative, which I call 'pactitis', inevitably involves compromise, whether territorial or thematic. In the end, more often than not, *any* agreement is held to be better than none. This constraint is a powerful disincentive to objectivity in analysis. In contrast, intelligence analysts have a constraint of another kind. Their requirement is the objective truth, even if it is hurtful or obstructs the negotiating of a possible pact.

Desmond Bristow

Of course, Philby was allowed to escape. Perhaps he was even encouraged. To have brought him back to England and convicted him as a traitor would have been even more embarrassing.

One consideration which may have influenced the authorities seeking to dissuade Crozier from publishing must have been the imminent prospect of Desmond

Bristow's *A Game of Moles*, which followed in October 1993. A wartime SIS officer who stayed on at Broadway until 1954, Bristow exercised no restraint whatever in naming his former colleagues, but concealed John Caswell and Al Ulmer, who had been senior CIA officers in London and Madrid respectively. In addition, Bristow explains the significance of the wartime MI5 agent and Swiss diplomat code-named Orange, who had been run by Guy Burgess. Although he does not identify Eric Kessler by name, he does note that the envoy had allowed SIS to use the Swiss diplomatic pouch for its messages to Berne. More significantly, although he conceals the true name of Junior, the Abwehr officer who defected in November 1943, he discloses enough information for the German journalist, who was exfiltrated from Lisbon just as the Gestapo had closed in on him, to be identified.

Fluent in Spanish, Bristow had joined SIS in 1941 to serve in its Iberian section at headquarters under Kim Philby, and then in Gibraltar. In January 1943 he was transferred to Algiers and a year later he moved on to Lisbon for a few months before returning to North Africa. Soon after D-Day he was recalled to London before being posted to liaison duties in Paris.

At the end of the war Bristow took over responsibility for the Iberian desk at SIS in London and in September 1947 he was posted to Madrid as head of station. He remained in Spain until April 1953, when he was appointed to SIS's strategic materials section. This lasted a year, and instead of accepting an assignment in Buenos Aires he retired to work for the de Beers diamond combine. He now lives in the south of Spain, near Malaga, and his book was originally released in a Spanish edition in September 1993, with the English version following soon afterwards. Although he submitted the manuscript to the Ministry of Defence for scrutiny, and agreed after lengthy negotiations to several deletions on security grounds, the legal action threatened by the Treasury Solicitor never materialized. In this passage the author recalls discussing the Philby affair with his CIA counterpart, Al Wallace (who was actually Al Ulmer).

A Game of Moles

At the end of May, my life as a Secret Service man fell prey to doubt and misconceptions, as the news of Burgess's and Maclean's flight to the Soviet Union spread through the world. I became especially disturbed when I heard about the inefficiency of Dick White (MI5's director of counter-espionage) from internal sources. As soon as he heard about the flight of Burgess and Maclean, White had gone to Newhaven to follow their trail. On presenting his passport to immigration he was informed it was six months out of date; and they did not care who he was, he could not leave the country with an out-of-date passport. I was beginning to wonder about SIS.

My friend Kim Philby was then withdrawn from Washington due to demands from the CIA. Kim was suspected of informing Burgess and Maclean about the up-and-coming investigation of Maclean. I was stunned and shaken by what I was hearing through the service grapevine, and by what I was reading in the newspapers. Kim was politely forced to resign by Sir Stewart Menzies.

Trying to avoid thinking about Kim's possible treachery was virtually impossible. Joe Presley (FBI), Al Wallace (CIA), Bill Milton, Tommy Harris and all of us could not help speculating. In the autumn Kim was cross-questioned and found not guilty, despite the amount of circumstantial evidence found . . . Where was the flower with the petals; not to ask about being loved or not, but was he? Or wasn't he?

I wrote privately to head office saying the uncertainty was intolerable, and suggesting, 'Why not lock him up in a flat with two bottles of whisky and see if he confesses?' Needless to say I had no response. But I did receive a visit from a member of the London office, Mary Neigh. This was the first official visit in three years by a head office representative.

At first Mary Neigh was very guarded and asked a lot of questions. I remember being irritated by the officialness of her visit, in light of the fact that head office had hitherto left us alone in the Iberian section.

Perhaps I was under suspicion as well?

After she left I met with Al Wallace who informed me that the CIA had been trying to warn Britain about a 'mole'. Al could not believe we had blundered so badly over Burgess and Maclean.

'Do you mean to say they escaped – or were allowed to escape?' Al asked. 'When you tell me that Dick White arrived with an out-of-date passport I have to think it was deliberate.'

'I don't know,' I replied rather despondently.

'Do you mean to say that it is possible for your lot, having orchestrated the D Day deception, suddenly to turn into an outfit not worthy of the Keystone Cops? Oh no! There must be more in it than that! And what about the guy who is being interrogated, or has just been interrogated – Philby? Is he in it too?'

'I hope not. Kim Philby is someone I consider quite a close friend . . . I just don't know,' I replied. 'I find it very hard to think about let alone believe. Burgess, well, the couple of times I have run across him I have, I can honestly say, despised him. He must have got to know that Maclean was a Soviet spy. Perhaps he saw some communication in Philby's office. After all he was living with Philby in Washington, much to poor Aileen Philby's horror.'

Accepting the drink Al offered, I continued. 'Listen, Al! Here I am in Madrid; all I can do is surmise what happened or why. All I can say is that no one seems to be saying anything definitive to anyone. I have been on the best of terms with Philby, and the office well knows that, but that does not mean to say I would be kept informed of any developments. In fact with him being interrogated and now thrown out I would say the opposite. It is all very confusing and I just do not know what to think. I simply hope head office knows what's going on and what it is doing.' We talked back and forth for a long time. Fortunately Joe Presley did not press me on the subject, and just left Al to quiz me.

I did trust head office to sort the mess out, so that things would settle down. Unfortunately this was not to be. The internal bush telegraph, the press and others continued to ask the same questions. It turned into a perennial cloud of doubt hanging over the present, the past and the future. I lived up to my Gemini birth sign. I did not want to believe that Philby was the Third Man, as MP Marcus Lipton had called him, yet I could not clear my head of nagging doubts, not least of which was his friendship with Burgess, which I never understood.

In early 1952 I received a message from head office advising me, 'Philby is due to arrive in Madrid on a contract for the *Observer*, and has been briefed not to have anything to do with you! We strongly advise you not to have any contact with him.' I did not know whether to laugh or cry. Philby and I were, as I thought, good friends; we had worked together during the war. He had been my boss and in many ways my teacher in the ways of espionage. For him to come to Madrid, and for me to pretend that I did not want to see him would have been ridiculous and could possibly have raised his suspicions. I telegraphed London saying that I was well aware of the circumstances, but if the situation arose I would see Philby.

It was a Tuesday at 2.30 p.m.; a tremendous thunderstorm was raging when the phone rang. 'Desmond.' I immediately recognised the voice.

'Hello, Kim. Where are you?'

'I'm at the Iberian bus t-t-terminal in the m-m-middle of M-madrid and I'm stuck. I was wondering if you might know of a small hotel.'

'Oh, don't worry, I'll come and fetch you and we'll see what we can sort out.' Confronted by him directly like that I could not bring myself to think of him as a Soviet agent.

I telephoned Bill Milton who lived near the city centre and organised to meet him after I had picked up Kim. In the event, Bill offered to put Kim up for that night, taking him next day to a small hotel in Calle Miguel Angel.

I warned Joe Presley and Al Wallace of Kim Philby's presence. We agreed to play the game with him as though nothing had happened. 'He might make a false move,' suggested Al.

Well, Kim was looking for journalistic leads so I introduced him to Sam Brewer of United Press and Bobby Papworth of Reuters. Through them Kim was able to meet all the Anglo-American journalists in Madrid, and become a member of the Journalists' Club.

Kim's friend Lady Frances Lindsay-Hogg arrived during his stay. They joined us on one of our picnics. Kim and I spoke very little about the Burgess and Maclean affair. He once reminded me of how I had never liked Burgess. 'How on earth do you remember that?' I asked. 'Oh, just one of those things.' Somehow we never discussed politics, or the weight of suspicion he was carrying on his shoulders.

He seemed to enjoy his months in Spain, and being a journalist. We gave a party for him when he left.

Bibliography

Agabekov, Georges, *OGPU: The Russian Terror* (Brentano's, 1931)
Agee, Philip, *Inside the Company: CIA Diary* (Penguin Books, 1975)
– *Dirty Work: The CIA in Western Europe* (Lyle Stuart, 1978)
– *Dirty Work II: The CIA in Africa* (Lyle Stuart, 1980)
– *On the Run* (Lyle Stuart, 1987)
Akhmedov, Ismail, *In and Out of Stalin's GRU* (UPA, 1983)
August, Frantisek, *Red Star Over Prague* (Sherwood Press, 1984)
Baillie-Stewart, Norman, *The Officer in the Tower* (Leslie Frewin, 1967)
Bakhlanov, Boris, *see* Romanov
Barmine, Alexander, *Memoirs of a Soviet Diplomat: Twenty Years in the Service of the USSR* (Dickson, 1938)
– *One Who Survived* (G. P. Putnam's, 1945)
Beck, Melvin, *Secret Contenders* (Sheridan Square Publications, 1984)
Belfrage, Cedric, *Seeds of Destruction* (Cameron & Kahn, 1954)
– *The Frightened Giant* (Secker & Warburg, 1957)
– *Something to Guard* (Columbia University Press, 1978)
Bentley, Elizabeth, *Out of Bondage* (Ivy Books, 1988)
Bessedovsky, G. Z., *Revelations of a Soviet Diplomat* (Williams & Norgate, 1931)
Bittman, Ladislav, *The Deception Game* (Syracuse University Press, 1972)
– *The KGB and Soviet Disinformation* (Pergamon, 1985)
Borodin, Nikolai, *One Man in his Time* (Macmillan, 1955)
Boulle, Pierre, *The Bridge on the River Kwai*
– *The Source of the River Kwai* (Secker & Warburg, 1967)
– *The Chinese Executioner*
– *For a Noble Cause*
– *The Monkey Planet*
– *Time out of Mind*
Bristow, Desmond, *A Game of Moles* (Little, Brown & Co., 1993)
Carré, Mathilde, *I Was the Cat* (Four Square, 1961)
Chambers, Whittaker, *Witness* (Random House, 1952)
Cohen, Yoel, *Nuclear Ambiguity* (Sinclair-Stevenson, 1992)
Cooper, Duff, *Operation Heartbreak* (Hart-Davis, 1950)
– *Old Men Forget* (Hart-Davis, 1953)

Cram, Cleveland, *A Monograph on Counterintelligence* (CIA, 1993)
Crozier, Brian, *The Struggle for the Third World* (Bodley Head, 1966)
– *Free Agent* (Harper Collins, 1993)
Deriabin, Piotr, *The Secret World* (Doubleday, 1959)
Dzhirkvelov, Ilya, *Secret Servant* (Harper & Row, 1987)
Foote, Alexander, *Handbook for Spies* (Museum Press, 1964)
Frischauer, Willi, *The Man Who Came Back* (Frederick Muller, 1958)
Frolik, Josef, *The Frolik Defection* (Leo Cooper, 1975)
Gentry, John A., *Lost Promise* (University Publications of America, 1993)
Gisevius, Hans Bernd, *To the Bitter End* (Cape, 1948)
Golitsyn, Anatoli, *New Lies for Old* (Bodley Head, 1984)
Gordievsky, Oleg, *KGB: The Inside Story* (Hodder & Stoughton, 1990)
– *Instructions from the Centre* (Hodder & Stoughton, 1991)
– *More Instructions from the Centre* (Frank Cass, 1992)
Gouzenko, Igor, *This Was My Choice* (Eyre & Spottiswoode, 1948)
– *The Iron Curtain* (Dutton, 1948)
Granovsky, Anatoli, *I Was an NKVD Agent* (Devon-Adair, 1962)
Harel, Isser, *The House on Garibaldi Street* (Viking Press, 1975)
Heissler, Joseph, *see* Hutton, J. Bernard
Hidalgo, Orlando Castro, *A Spy for Fidel* (E. A. Seamann, 1971)
Hiss, Alger, *In the Court of Public Opinion* (Alfred A. Knopf, 1957)
– *Recollections of a Life* (Seaver, 1988)
Houghton, Harry, *Operation Portland* (Hart-Davis, 1972)
Hutton, J. Bernard, *Frogman Extraordinary* (Neville Spearman, 1960)
– *Danger from Moscow* (Neville Spearman, 1960)
– *School for Spies* (Neville Spearman, 1961)
– *Stalin: The Miraculous Georgian* (Neville Spearman, 1961)
– *The Private Life of Josif Stalin* (W. H. Allen, 1962)
– *The Traitor Trade* (Obolensky, 1963)
– *Out of this World* (Psychic Press, 1965)
– *Healing Hands* (W. H. Allen, 1966)
– *Commander Crabb is Alive* (Award Books, 1968)
– *Struggle in the Dark* (Harrap, 1969)
– *The Fake Defector* (Howard Baker, 1970)
– *The Great Illusion* (Bruce & Watson, 1970)
– *Hess: The Man and his Mission* (Macmillan, 1971)
– *Women Spies* (W. H. Allen, 1971)
– *The Subverters of Liberty* (W. H. Allen, 1972)
– *Lost Freedom* (Bruce & Watson, 1973)
Hyde, Douglas, *I Believed* (Heinemann, 1950)
– *The Peaceful Assault* (Bodley Head, 1963)
– *Dedication and Leadership* (Sands, 1966)
– *The Roots of Guerrilla Warfare* (Dufour, 1968)

– *Communism Today* (Gill & Macmillan, 1972)

John, Otto, *Twice Through the Lines* (Harper & Row, 1972)

Joseph, Helen, *If This be Treason* (André Deutsch, 1963)

Kaznacheev, Alexandre, *Inside a Soviet Embassy* (Lippincott, 1962)

Khokhlov, Nikolai, *In the Name of Conscience* (David McKay, 1959)

Kostov, Vladimir, *The Bulgarian Umbrella* (St Martin, 1988)

Kourdakov, Sergei, *The Persecutor* (Fleming H. Revell Co., Old Tappan, NJ, 1973)

Kravchenko, Victor, *I Chose Freedom* (Robert Hale, 1947)

– *I Chose Justice* (Scribner's, 1950)

– *Kravchenko versus Moscow* (Wingate, 1950)

Krivitsky, Walter, *In Stalin's Secret Service* (Harper, NY, 1939)

– *I Was Stalin's Agent* (Hamish Hamilton, 1940)

Krotkov, Yuri, *The Angry Exile* (Heinemann, 1967)

– *The Red Monarch* (Norton, 1979)

Kuczynski, Ursula, *see* Werner

Kuzichkin, Vladimir, *Inside the KGB: Myth and Reality* (André Deutsch, 1990)

Levchenko, Stanislav, *On the Wrong Side* (Pergamon-Brassey, 1987)

Lincoln, I. Trebitsch, *Revelations of an International Spy* (McBride & Co., 1916)

– *The Autobiography of an Adventurer* (Henry Holt & Co., 1932)

Litvinov, Maxim, *Notes for a Journal* (Deutsch, 1955)

McGehee, Ralph, *Deadly Deceits* (Sheridan Square Publications, 1983)

MacKinnon, Janice, *Agnes Smedley* (University of California Press, 1988)

Maclean, Fitzroy, *A Person from England* (Cape, 1958)

Marchetti, Victor, *The CIA and the Cult of Intelligence* (Cape, 1974)

Markov, Georgi, *The Truth that Killed* (Ticknor & Fields, 1984)

Massing, Hede, *This Deception* (Duell, Sloan & Pearce, 1951)

Mikes, George, *A Study in Infamy* (André Deutsch, 1959)

Miller, Marion, *I Was a Spy* (Bobbs-Merrill, 1960)

Molden, Fritz, *Exploding Star* (Weidenfeld & Nicolson, 1978)

Monat, Pawel, with Dille, John, *Spy in the US* (Harper & Row, 1961)

Montagu, Ewen, *The Man Who Never Was* (Evans, 1953)

Moravec, Frantisek, *Master of Spies* (Bodley Head, 1975)

Morros, Boris, *My Ten Years as a Counterspy* (Viking Press, 1959)

Myagkov, Aleksei, *Inside the KGB* (Foreign Affairs Publishing Co., 1976)

Orlov, Alexander, *The Secret History of Stalin's Crimes* (Random House, 1953)

Ostrovsky, Victor, *By Way of Deception* (St Martin's Press, 1990)

– *The Other Side of Deception* (Harper Collins, 1994)

Pacepa, Ion, *Red Horizons* (Regnery, 1987)

Penkovsky, Oleg, *The Penkovsky Papers* (Avon, 1966)

Petrov, Vladimir, *Empire of Fear* (Praeger, 1956)

Philby, Kim, *My Silent War* (McGibbon & Kee, 1968)

Poretsky, Elisabeth, *Our Own People* (University of Michigan Press, 1969)

Putlitz, Wolfgang zu, *The Putlitz Dossier* (Allan Wingate, 1957)

Radvanyi, Janos, *Delusion and Reality* (Gateway Publications, 1978)

Romanov, A. I., *Nights are Longest There* (Hutchinson, 1972)

Rurarz, Zdzdislaw, *An Ambassador Speaks*

Sakharov, Vladimir, *High Treason* (Putnam's, 1980)

Schlabrendorff, Fabian von, *The Secret War against Hitler* (Hodder & Stoughton, 1966)

Sejna, Jan, *We Will Bury You* (Sidgwick & Jackson, 1982)

Seth, Roland, *A Spy has no Friends* (Deutsch, 1952)

– *Forty Years of Soviet Spying* (Cassell, 1965)

– *The Executioners* (Cassell, 1967)

Shainberg, Maurice, *Breaking from the KGB* (Shapolsky, 1986)

Shevchenko, Arkadi, *Breaking with Moscow* (Ballantine, 1985)

Sheymov, Victor, *Tower of Secrets* (Naval Institute Press, 1993)

Sigl, Rupert, *In the Claws of the KGB* (Dorrance, 1978)

Singleton-Gates, Peter, *The Black Diaries of Roger Casement* (Grove Press, 1959; custody of the original diaries held by Public Record Office, London, Document Reference HO: 161/3)

Smedley, Agnes, *Battle Hymn of China* (Alfred A. Knopf, 1943)

Smith, Edward Ellis, *The Okhrana* (Hoover Institution, 1967)

Smith, Joseph, *Portrait of a Cold Warrior* (G. P. Putnam's, 1976)

Snepp, Frank, *Decent Interval* (Random House, 1977)

Spasowski, Romuald, *The Liberation of One* (Harcourt Brace, 1986)

Sproat, Iain, *Wodehouse at War* (Milner & Co., 1981)

Stiller, Werner, *Beyond the Wall* (Brassey's, 1992)

Stockwell, John, *In Search of Enemies* (W. W. Norton & Co., 1978)

Straight, Michael, *After Long Silence* (Norton, 1983)

Suvorov, Victor, *The Liberators* (Norton, 1983)

– *Aquarium* (Macmillan, 1984)

– *Spetsnaz* (Hamish Hamilton, 1987)

Svanidze, Budu, *My Uncle Joe* (Heinemann, 1952)

Svredlev, Stefan, 'Who Killed Georgi Markov?' by Maurice Cockerell (*The Listener*, 12 April 1979)

Szasz, Bela, *Volunteers for the Gallows* (W. W. Norton, 1971)

Thyraud de Vosjoli, Philippe, *Lamia* (Little, Brown, 1970)

Tokaev, Grigori, *Betrayal of an Ideal* (Indiana University Press, 1955)

– *Comrade X* (Harville, 1956)

Tokaty, Grigori, *Rocketdynamics* (1961)

– *The History of Rocket Technology* (1964)

– *A History and Philosophy of Fluid Mechanics* (1971)

– *Cosmonautics-Aeronautics* (1976)

– *The Anatomy and Inculcation of Higher Education* (1982)

Tumanov, Oleg A., *Tumanov: Confessions of a KGB Spy* (Edition Q, 1993)

BIBLIOGRAPHY

Ushakov, Alexander A., *In the Gunsight of the KGB* (Alfred A. Knopf, 1989)

Vassall, John, *Vassall: The Autobiography of a Spy* (Sidgwick & Jackson, 1975)

Werner, Ruth, *Sonya's Report* (Chatto & Windus, 1991)

Winter, Gordon, *Inside BOSS* (Allen Lane, 1981)

Wolfe, Bertram D., *Strange Communists I Have Known* (Allen & Unwin, 1966)

X, Mr, *Double Eagle* (Bobbs-Merrill, 1979)

Yardley, Herbert O., *The American Black Chamber* (Bobbs-Merrill, 1931)

– *Yardleygrams* (Bobbs-Merrill, 1932)

– *The Education of a Poker Player* (Simon & Schuster, 1957)

– *The Chinese Black Chamber* (Houghton Mifflin, 1983)

Acknowledgements

For permission to reprint copyright material the publishers gratefully acknowledge the following:

PHILIP AGEE: to Carol Publishing Group for *On the Run* (Lyle Stuart, 1987).

ISMAIL AKHMEDOV: to Greenwood Publishing Group, Inc for *In and Out of Stalin's G.R.U.* (UPA, 1983).

ALEXANDER BARMINE: to Putnam Publishing Group for *One Who Survived* (Putnam's, 1945), © 1945 by Alexander Barmine.

MELVIN BECK: to Sheridan Square Press, Inc for *Secret Contenders*, © 1984 by Melvin Beck.

CEDRIC BELFRAGE: to Reed Consumer Books for *The Frightened Giant* (Martin Secker & Warburg, 1957)

LADISLAV BITTMAN: to Syracuse University Press for *The Deception Game* (1972).

PIERRE BOULLE: to Editions Julliard for *The Source of the River Kwai* (Martin Secker & Warburg, 1967).

DESMOND BRISTOW: to Little, Brown UK for *A Game of Moles* (1993).

YOEL COHEN: to Reed Consumer Books and Vernon Futurman Associates on behalf of the author for *Nuclear Ambiguity* (Sinclair-Stevenson, 1992).

BRIAN CROZIER: to HarperCollins Publishers Ltd for *Free Agent* (1993).

ALEXANDER FOOTE: to Pitman Publishing for *Handbook of Spies* (Museum Press, 1964).

JOSEF FROLIK: to Leo Cooper Ltd for *The Frolik Defection* (1975).

HANS BERND GISEVIUS: to Random House UK Ltd for *To the Bitter End* (Cape, 1948).

ANATOLI GOLITSYN: to Random House UK Ltd for *New Lies for Old* (The Bodley Head, 1984).

ALEXANDER GRANOVSKY: to Devin-Adair, Publishers, Inc., Old Greenwich, Connecticut, 06870 for *I Was an N.K.V.D. Agent* (1962), all rights reserved.

ALGER HISS: to Seaver Books for *Recollections of a Life* (1988), © 1988 by Alger Hiss.

HARRY HOUGHTON: to David Higham Associates Ltd for *Operation Portland* (Hart-Davis, 1972).

ACKNOWLEDGEMENTS

J. BERNARD HUTTON: to C. W. Daniel Company Ltd for *School for Spies* (Neville Spearman, 1961).

ALEXANDER KAZNACHEEV: to HarperCollins Publishers, Inc for *Inside a Soviet Embassy*, copyright © 1962 by J. B. Lippincott Company.

VICTOR KRAVCHENKO: to Robert Hale Ltd for *I Chose Freedom* (1947).

YURI KROTKOV: to Reed Consumer Books and A. M. Heath & Co on behalf of the author for *The Angry Exile* (Heinemann, 1967).

URSULA KUCZYNSKI: to Random House UK Ltd for *Sonya's Report* (Chatto & Windus, 1991).

VLADIMIR KUZICHKIN: to Andre Deutsch Ltd for *Inside the KGB* (Deutsch, 1990).

STANISLAV LEVCHENKO: to Pergamon Press/Brassey's, Inc for *On the Wrong Side* (Pergamon/Brassey, 1987).

RALPH MCGEHEE: to Sheridan Square Press, Inc for *Deadly Deceits* (1983), © 1983 by Ralph McGehee.

VICTOR MARCHETTI and JOHN MARKS: to Random House UK Ltd and Alfred A. Knopf, Inc for *The CIA and the Cult of Intelligence* (Cape, 1974), © 1974 by Victor L. Marchetti and John D. Marks.

GEORGI MARKOV: to A. M. Heath & Company Ltd for *The Truth that Killed* (Ticknor & Fields, 1984).

GEORGE MIKES: to the Estate of George Mikes for *A Study in Infamy* (Deutsch, 1959).

FRITZ MOLDEN: to George Weidenfeld & Nicolson Ltd for *Exploding Star* (1978).

PAWEL MONAT and JOHN DILLE: to HarperCollins Publishers, Inc for *Spy in the U.S.* (Harper & Row, 1961), © 1961, 1962 by Pawel Monat and John Dille.

BORIS MORROS and C. SAMUELS: to Viking Penguin, a division of Penguin Books USA Inc for *My Ten Years as a Counterspy* (Viking Press, 1959), © 1959 by Boris Morros, 1987 renewal by Cathrine Morros.

VLADIMIR PETROV: to André Deutsch Ltd for *Empire of Fear* (Praeger, 1956).

ELISABETH PORETSKY: to Oxford University Press for *Our Own People* (1969).

A. I. ROMANOV: to Random House UK Ltd for *The Nights are Longest There* (Hutchinson, 1972).

VLADIMIR SAKHAROV and UMBERTO TOSI: to Putnam Publishing Group for *High Treason* (Putnam's, 1980), © 1980 by Vladimir Sakharov and Umberto Tosi.

RONALD SETH: to David Higham Associates Ltd for *A Spy Has No Friends* (Deutsch, 1952).

ARKADY SHEVCHENKO: to Alfred A. Knopf, Inc for *Breaking with Moscow* (Ballantine Books, 1985), © 1985 by Arkady Shevchenko.

VICTOR SHEYMOV: to Naval Institute Press for *Tower of Secrets* (1993).

AGNES SMEDLEY: to Alfred A. Knopf, Inc for *Battle Hymn of China* (1943), copyright 1943 and renewed 1971.

FRANK SNEPP: to Random House, Inc for *Decent Interval* (1977), © 1977 by Frank W. Snepp.

ACKNOWLEDGEMENTS

JOHN STOCKWELL: to W. W. Norton & Company, Inc for *In Search of Enemies* (1978), © 1978 by John Stockwell.

MICHAEL STRAIGHT: to Robert I. Ducas and W. W. Norton & Company, Inc for *After Long Silence* (1983), © 1983 by Michael Straight.

VICTOR SUVOROV: to A. M. Heath & Co on behalf of the author for *Aquarium* (Macmillan, 1984).

PHILIPPE THYRAUD DE VOSJOLI: to Little, Brown & Company for *Code Name: Lamia* (1970), © 1970 by Little, Brown & Company.

GRIGORI TOKAEV: to Indiana University Press and Harvill Publishers for *Death of an Ideal* (1955), English translation © The Harvill Press, 1954.

Every effort has been made to trace or contact copyright holders. Faber and Faber will be glad to rectify, in the next edition or reprint of this volume, any omissions brought to their notice.

INDEX

Bessell, Peter, 410
Betrayal of an Ideal (Tokaev), 8, 131–3
Beurton, Leon, 373, 387
Beyond the Wall (Stiller), 13, 205, 256–8
BfV, *see* Federal German Security Service
Bialoguski, Michael, 142
Bishop, Maurice, 306
Bitov, Oleg, 78
Bittman, Ladislas, 12, 200, 203, 224–6
Black, Helen, 291, 292
Black, Mervyn, 117
Black September, 355
Blake, George, 27, 151
Bleicher, Hugo, 335–7
BLIZZARD, 76
Blunt, Anthony, 1, 2, 15, 23, 28, 151,
  270, 327, 328, 330–2
Blunt, Christopher, 2
BND, *see* Federal German Intelligence
  Service
Boehm, Gerhard, 225
Bonhoeffer, Dietrich, 384
Borodin, Nikolai N., 8, 81
BOSS, *see* Bureau of State Security
Bossard, Frank, 28
Boulle, Pierre, 15, 16, 333, 337–43
Brandt, Willy, 367, 372
Breaking from the KGB (Shainberg), 20
Breaking with Moscow (Shevchenko), 10,
  181–8
Brewer, Sam, 421
Brezhnev, Leonid, 208, 217, 264
Bridge on the River Kwai, The (Boulle),
  16, 333
Bristow, Desmond, 19, 403, 417–21
British Intelligence, *see* British Secret
  Intelligence Service, British Security
  Service
British Naval Intelligence, *see* Naval
  Intelligence Division
British Secret Intelligence Service (SIS), 2,
  8, 10, 17, 28, 42, 84, 105, 131, 152,
  190, 221, 229–31, 370, 371, 377, 382,
  403, 413, 417–9
British Security Coordination (BSC), 5, 57
British Security Service (MI5), 2, 4–6, 28,
  42, 54, 57, 62, 65–8, 96, 157, 202, 218,
  328, 368, 370, 374, 405, 406, 418;
  Director-General of, *see* Hanley
British Union of Fascists (BUF), 27
Britten, Douglas, 28
Britts, Lawrence, *see* Bittman
Broken Seal, The (Farago), 275
Brooke, Gerald, 127
BSC, *see* British Security Coordination
Bucher, Cmdr Lloyd, 268
Bulganin, Marshal, 66
Bulgarian Intelligence Service (DS), 12,

201, 206–10; Director of, *see* Stoyanov;
  defectors from, *see* Kostov, Svredlev,
  Tipanudt
Bulgarian Umbrella, The (Kostov), 12,
  208–11
Bulik, Joe, 152
Bundespolizei, 54
Bureau Central de Renseignement et
  d'Action (BCRA), 344
Bureau of State Security (BOSS), 410–12;
  defector from, *see* Gordon Winter
Burgess, Guy, 1, 2, 15, 27, 143, 327, 330–
  2, 374, 418–21
Burgess, Nigel, 2
Burundi, 320
Butkov, Mikhail V., 80
By Way of Deception (Ostrovsky), 16,
  357–63
Bykov, Boris, 287
Byrnes, James F., 283

Cabinet Office, 413
Cadogan, Sir Alexander, 283
Cairncross, John, 28
Call (newspaper), 278
Callaghan, James, 233
Cambridge Conversazione Society, *see* The
  Apostles
Camp King, 317
Camp Peary, 325
Canaris, Adm. Wilhelm, 370
Care of Devils, The (Press), 274
Carnegie Endowment for International
  Peace, 282
Caroz, Yaacov, 354
Carr, E. H., 85, 86
Carre, Mathilde, 16, 334–7
Carter, President Jimmy, 268
Casement, Sir Roger, 3, 23, 32–6
Cassandra, *see* Connor
Castro, Fidel, 12, 252
Caswell, John, 418
Catholic Herald, 25
Ceauçescu, Nicolai, 13, 201, 202, 206,
  215–17
Cech, Jan, *see* Heissler
Central Intelligence Agency (CIA), 8–14,
  16, 62, 65, 82, 134, 138, 149, 150, 152,
  162, 190, 204, 205, 216, 231, 235, 248,
  252, 271–4, 305–27, 353, 356, 419;
  Director of, *see* Dulles, Colby;
  Counterintelligence Staff, 78; Eastern
  Europe/Russia Division, 76; stations of,
  see Burundi, Saigon, Subic Bay
Central Office of Information (COI), 28
Chamberlain, Neville, 385
Chambers, Whittaker, 15, 271, 278, 282,
  286–90, 295, 302, 328, 330